STREETLIGHTS
PENGUIN BOOKS

DORISJEAN AUSTIN was a journalist, critic, former newswriter for NBC radio, and a novelist. Her first novel, *After the Garden*, was named "New and Noteworthy" by the *New York Times Book Review*. Her work has appeared in fiction and essay collections in the United States, Europe, and Japan. She instructed advanced fiction workshops at Columbia University's School of Writing from 1989 to 1994. She was a member of the world-renowned Harlem Writers' Guild, and executive director of New Renaissance Writers' Guild, which she co-founded. Austin lived and worked in New York City, until her death in 1994.

MARTIN SIMMONS has taught fiction and nonfiction writing and literature classes at a number of schools and art organizations, including Bronx Community College, NYU, the College of New Rochelle, and the Frederick Douglass Creative Arts Center. He is a former member of the Harlem Writers' Guild and a co-founder of New Renaissance Writers' Guild, and has been published in *Blacks on Paper*, *Blackstage*, *Essence* magazine, *MBM* magazine, *New York Newsday*, and numerous other publications. Mr. Simmons lives in New York with his wife and two children. He is working on a novel, *Blood at the Root*, and a screenplay.

PENGUIN BOOKS

STREETLIGHTS

*Illuminating Tales of the
Urban Black Experience*

Edited by

DorisJean Austin and Martin Simmons

PENGUIN BOOKS
Published by the Penguin Group
Penguin Books USA Inc., 375 Hudson Street,
New York, New York 10014, U.S.A.
Penguin Books Ltd, 27 Wrights Lane,
London W8 5TZ, England
Penguin Books Australia Ltd, Ringwood,
Victoria, Australia
Penguin Books Canada Ltd, 10 Alcorn Avenue,
Toronto, Ontario, Canada M4V 3B2
Penguin Books (N.Z.) Ltd, 182–190 Wairau Road,
Auckland 10, New Zealand

Penguin Books Ltd, Registered Offices:
Harmondsworth, Middlesex, England

First published in Penguin Books 1996

1   3   5   7   9   10   8   6   4   2

PUBLISHER'S NOTE
These selections are works of fiction. Names, characters, places, and incidents either are the product of the authors' imagination or are used fictitiously, and any resemblance to actual persons, living or dead, events or locales is purely coincidental.

LIBRARY OF CONGRESS CATALOGING IN PUBLICATION DATA
Streetlights : illuminating tales of the urban Black experience / edited by DorisJean Austin and Martin Simmons.
p.   cm.
ISBN 0 14 01.7471 0 (alk. paper)
1. City and town life—United States—Fiction.   2. Afro-Americans—Fiction.   I. Austin, DorisJean.   II. Simmons, Martin, 1947– .
PS648.C5S77   1995
813'.0108321732—dc20   94–24868

Printed in the United States of America
Set in Sabon
Designed by Cheryl Cipriani

2

For John Oliver Killens,
for the New Renaissance Writers,
and for all the writers in all the Harlems in America.
But, especially, for our mothers,
Tommie Letitia Austin
and
Evelyn Marie Simmons

Preface

This is where we, as the editors of *Streetlights: Illuminating Tales of the Urban Black Experience*, are expected to present lofty ideological, scholarly, or literary truths about the deep purposes and meanings of this collection of stories. We will not do so.

Like most of you, we come to this anthology as readers, as lovers of a good story. And as readers we are not anxious to read (or write) a long pedantic preface. When we pick up anthologies, we want to get to the good stuff.

Be assured that this volume is full of good stuff.

There is probably some law of publishing, however, that dictates that we write *something* here, so we will tell you why we decided to put this collection together.

Both of us were born and raised in the city. As people and as writers we were nurtured by the city. We fell in love with the city, and if we love America, we love it because of its cities. We are not blind to urban problems—in fact, our daily lives are affected by the grimmer aspects of city life—but we are equally aware of the vitality and passion of America's cities and the people who populate them. So this volume is meant to celebrate, as well as document, contemporary urban life in the United States.

Think of this book as a vehicle, a guide that has been put together to take you into the heart and underbelly of America, one that reveals the human mechanism of the city and of the nation. These are stories of and by people who live in the cities: people who were brought to America "by the people who came here on the *Mayflower*" and people who have more recently and voluntarily arrived. Listen to them: they truly know America, they truly understand the cities. Cities, after all, must be defined by those who live within them—repeat, *within* them—not those who commute to work from the exurbs or those who live on America's gold coasts.

Speak, on the other hand, to the encoders and buzzword artists, and they will tell you that the title of this volume, *Streetlights: Illuminating Tales of the Urban Black Experience*, is very nearly redundant.

In the boardrooms, newsrooms, and cloakrooms (the order is correct) of this nation, where policy is enacted and dispensed, the word "urban" *means* black, or, at the least, black and brown. In addition, to them, the word "urban," like the term "inner city," means crime, drugs, degradation, and despair.

We do not agree.

The writers of these forty-nine stories do not agree. Black America does not agree. Crime, yes. Drugs, yes. Degradation, yes. Despair, yes (though a discernment that takes into account the economic, political, and social disparities of this country must be held). But these things do not define the city, and they certainly do not define us or our humanity. We Blacks are a community, we are a nation, we are a diversity of individuals; and though we are some forty million strong, it is doubtful that any one of us wakes in the morning wondering what he or she did to be so black and blue.

Thus, when we set out to compile and present this volume, we knew what we did not want: we wanted no stories that whined or begged, we wanted no stories that venerated our oppression. In short, we wanted no plantation stories.

What we did want, we got in trumps: forty-nine stories that speak to our specific humanities; forty-nine stories about love and lust, joy and hopelessness. In all of them the contemporary city, with its positives and negatives, is there, sometimes in the foreground but usually playing more of a bit role in developing plot and determining character.

Richard Wright said that the Negro is the metaphor for America. By simple extrapolation, we therefore understand that these stories are America's stories. For make no mistake about it, the United States is defined by its cities. Verification of this can be found in the art and popular culture born in the cities and diffusing into the towns and farmlands coast to coast.

We are proud to introduce this collection of American stories. The majority are printed here for the first time. Tales of the city; tales of black and brown and tan and sand-colored people as we approach the twenty-first century.

We particularly want to thank Donna Brogdon-Simmons for her loving help and support, and our editor, Beena Kamlani, for her hard work and sharp eye.

Here is the good stuff.

—DorisJean Austin,
Martin Simmons

DorisJean Austin
[1944–1994]

DorisJean . . .
Not enough words to evoke her spirit
incandescent
Not enough poetry to describe her beauty
immutable
Not enough tears to define our grief
insufficient

Contents

Introduction

JOHN A. WILLIAMS

No one captured the city like the great Langston Hughes, but writers have never stopped trying. Hughes loved New York's Harlem obviously and completely. Ann Petry may have been ambivalent about New York. Richard Wright, whose most powerful stories are set in the South, may not have loved Chicago or its South Side completely, but Gwendolyn Brooks does. Ernest Gaines shuns the cities in his southern-set works.

Black writers clearly have a love-hate relationship with cities. Yet African Americans have been residents of the American city ever since it was formed out of evolving villages, towns, and clusters of people with like-minded purposes and habits. Cities were where the action was—the jobs, the bright lights, the dangling ladder to the get-rich floor; cities were, though we did not so name them then, the power centers. Black people were always as much of the land as of the city.

More than two hundred years before Horace R. Cayton and St. Clair Drake published their monumental *Black Metropolis* (a study of Chicago, which was founded by black trader Jean Baptiste Point du Sable in 1772), African Americans, in bondage or free, lived in all the major cities of the colonies that stretched north to south along the eastern seaboard.

Streetlights: Illuminating Tales of the Urban Black Experience extends the history of African American urban literature up to the present; what we discover is that the black American who today most defines the city (and also is defined by it) is still America's metaphor.

In this volume the interiorized language of the streets is pitched so piercingly true that the stories often seem to conceal other stories within themselves. The characters seem so utterly familiar because we have seen them on the streets and on television and therefore believe we "know" them and the conflicts upon which these fictions are structured.

But to presume that we know the characters and all about their lives is the arrogance of the ignorant; the present volume examines new dimensions of street characters we think we know. To conclude that the folk in these fictions have little or nothing to do with the rest of us would be, as it has been, an error of infinite magnitude.

Since fiction can often teach us more than academically or politically gathered fact or dollar-driven filmic portraits or twenty-two-minute TV sitcoms, we look to these stories of urban life streets for lessons on how the folk in them really live. And how their lives affect ours.

The teachers here are a mix of generations of African American writers who in this collection number forty-nine. They hold no illusions about the future.

Their themes are both universal and particularly American. Characters hurtle down these illuminated streets—from one another to one another, from themselves into themselves, from darkly outlined destinies to illuminating revelations.

Love is a gritty shadow, more often than not pantomimed because its disappointments are not unexpected, as we see in Richelle A. McClain's "Yellow Rooms," Martin Simmons's powerful excerpt from *Blood at the Root*, Kalamu ya Salaam's "Raoul's Silver Song," and Lolis Eric Elie's "Scotch and Curry," among other pieces.

The sensibilities and sensitivities of the homeless, a socioeconomic indicator of the unraveling of America, are viewed through new lenses in Devorah Major's "Nzinga's Treasure," who wrings from this theme new truths: there is something worse. Carolyn Ferrell's highly stylized story "Can You Say My Name?" explores the motivations of a teenage girl in a loveless world who wants to receive love and give it to the only being she believes will accept it: her baby.

DorisJean Austin's "Room 1023" explores the lives of several women, particularly that of Lelah (Lee) Vanessa Frederick (Alexander), who is threatened with homelessness in New York on a day when the temperature is close to 100 degrees. No job, no check from her nearly ex-husband, the women's hotel where she lives about to evict her, Lee wonders what life on the street will be like. She knows that the help the women can give each other is miserably minuscule. Tough, but splattered with tenderness, "Room 1023" leaves a strong, resounding echo.

In a stinging, menacing stream-of-consciousness mode (like Ferrell's "Can You Say My Name?"), Nan Saville's "Four and Twenty" theme of retribution leaves a lingering echo, one of many to be found when the lights fall on the relationships between men and women. Ferrell's story and Garrett McDowell's "In Sight of the Killing" weave a mix of present and past tense in which to set their work. McDowell's is another raw stare at the mean streets, the confrontations, the near-death misses, the crowds, the constant urban menace, the unimportance of dying violently anytime, anywhere, for anything. His characters pass and meet again and fade from beneath the streetlights. Death is as constant as the shadow his protagonist makes beneath the lights.

Ronald Strothers's story "You Can't Have Greens Without a Neck Bone," framed mostly around the macho dialogue between garage mechanics, at its end quietly underlines the power of women who control the money. Indeed, among the sensibilities reflected in this collection, it is the proud reassertion of womanhood and the determination to make men understand that power.

Told from the viewpoint of an immigrant from India, Jacqueline Joan Johnson's "West Wind" successfully tackles the newest problem of the African American urban dwellers: the immigrants who take up space and jobs that might have gone to Americans. Johnson gives us the clamor, tension, and intrigues of the street in broad daylight.

Steven Corbin explores the intricacies of the gay life of African American men with his "My Father's Son," which is both poignant and powerful. The protagonist's desire for the love of his father, and the father's awkward though loving response, reflects the understanding that African American parents must arrive at if the black community is to survive the streets or anywhere else.

There is impressive evidence of "good ears" throughout this collection, as well as a different angle of vision and an often caustic interpretation of the life these authors find under the streetlights. They understand the truth of the American city: It is both a destroyer and a progenitor of life.

Streetlights: Illuminating Tales of the Urban Black Experience is, collectively, a new and powerful perspective on American literature.

STREETLIGHTS

Room 1023

DorisJean Austin

*Blah . . . blah . . . blah . . . blah*, on and on he drones, his words reminding me of one of those fire&brimstone Baptist sermons on the eternal damnation of the slothful, which I'm not, or the jobless, which I am—at the moment. (God! The look on his face when I told him I didn't have a credit card. . . . "You have no credit at all?"—he'd asked with such disdain that I hung my head to hide my contempt. He knew perfectly well I never paid with a credit card.)

His voice has drifted so far away that I can barely hear him. I lean forward to stay in contact.

"I've decided"—he pauses in the distance, adjusts his glasses, and waggles my check above his receding hairline—"I say . . . I've decided to give you until Monday to make this good"—he leans forward and sails my offending check across his desk—"with cash this time, eh?"

DorisJean Austin was a journalist, critic, former newswriter for NBC radio, and a novelist. Her first novel, *After the Garden*, was named "New and Noteworthy" by the *New York Times Book Review*. Her work has appeared in fiction and essay collections in the United States, Europe, and Japan. She instructed advanced fiction workshops at Columbia University's School of Writing from 1989 to 1994. She was a member of the world-renowned Harlem Writers' Guild, and executive director of New Renaissance Writers' Guild, which she co-founded. Austin lived and worked in New York City, and her death in 1994 was a profound loss to many.

His smile is as counterfeit as my check as it floats to the edge of his desk, wavers briefly on his desk calendar, then falls in a graceful loop at my feet, a pale green rectangle that lands face down on the burgundy carpet so I can see the black computer symbols that let the bank and the hotel know I'm a zero balance, about to get ousted, banished, ejected, cast out by the manager of a women's residential hotel, from a five-by-twelve room with bath.

I bend over and pick up the check. I half stand and place it on a corner of his desk beside the manila folder with my full name (married name in parentheses) in large block type on a white label with a red border: LELAH VANESSA FREDERICK (ALEXANDER). Under that, ROOM 1023. He picks up my check, he sighs, a patient white man who's done all he can, dealing with another incomprehensible female tenant. He waits; I recognize my cue; it's my turn. The silent offense I swallow is familiar.

"You can leave your key out at the front desk"—he continues—"I'll have to consider what steps to take next if you don't make this good by Monday." He waves my check some more. He's making me dizzy. He's assumed a quasi-British accent so I'm having trouble understanding. He clears up my confusion.

"I say"—he says—"just leave the key to your room at the front desk. . . . *Please*"—he adds elaborately.

"So you just intend to put me out in the street?" I wait, poised and patient, while he glares down at me, silent, myopic. I'm out of ideas. Except . . .

> . . . *the homeless guy begging outside the subway this morning with his paper cup lifted up to me. He sat at the top of the stairs at the 12th Street and 7th Avenue IRT exit, right across the street from the emergency room of St. Vincent's Hospital. His filthy cotton shirt was open, exposing a skeletal rib cage that reminded me of an old-fashioned scrub board. His long, dirty arms were the wooden frame tenuously holding his rippled ribs in place. Once, in a New Orleans nightclub, I saw a musician playing a board like his ribs. I stood over him for some time—stunned, unable to move on—before I recognized the "ragged tagged scarecrow" we used to sing about in kindergarten. I didn't know back then that he was a Black man. Around twenty-five. My age. Unshaven. Unwashed. Totally believable.*

"So"—I repeat briskly, without the question mark, in the wise tone of the newly enlightened—"you just intend to put me out into the street."

No comment.

It's twenty minutes to one on a Thursday afternoon in August by my watch. It's 95 degrees outside but it's cold in the office without windows where I sit, making a conscientious effort to listen to the harangue of the manager of the women's residential hotel that is my home, where I sit wincing at the acrid aftertaste of too many cups of black coffee that repeat and repeat while my stomach makes audible rumblings that resemble the metal wheels on the tracks of an approaching A train.

"I'd like to explain"—I interrupt the silence, rising from the chair I sit in, but he waves me back into my seat before I can stand. His chair—I note—must be elevated somehow because behind his desk he sits taller than I am sitting.

"No." He lifts the slender hand that holds my bounced check higher. "No more"—he forbids. "I say . . . no more, Lee." He quotes himself so sadly you'd think it was himself he was threatening to put out into the streets of New York.

My mouth has gone too dry for me to swallow so I gaze at my hands folded in my lap. I can feel my breath shorten. I need oxygen as I tend to hyperventilate under stress. Also, I faint. I breathe deeply and console myself with the knowledge that the money is on the way, even while I sit here: *The check is in the mail.*

Actually, I've been too lenient when John's been late with my checks before. He doesn't want this divorce and insists I stop acting foolish, return to our air-conditioned home in New Jersey that has a machine in each room to remove impurities from the air. This is for my allergies. "Let's call this thing off before it's too late"—he demands every month. But it's already too late, and his demands are only about the money he must send me every month until the court decides the final dollar value of our marriage and grants us the separate but equal spoils of our union.

I examine the top of Roger Crowell's desk, the framed picture of his wife and daughter with their perfect teeth. I fold my full lips in to camouflage my overbite, and explore the soft black leather of his desk set, the black pens jutting from mahogany. Breathe in: Contemplate the paintings on the dark paneled wall behind Roger. Breathe out: Behold the huge American flag in its ornate metal floor stand in the corner directly behind me. I grope for words to reverse this fantastic situation: *The check is in the mail.*

"So, you just intend to put me out into the street?"

"You leave me no choice"—Roger lies confidentially—"I'll give you until Monday afternoon to make this good. If you haven't paid by Monday"—his words float to me luminously, from far away—"I'll have your belongings removed from your room and put in storage so I can rent to a paying tenant."

I give myself a firm push farther away from Roger's censure, trying to remember the words to an old 78 rpm record, a favorite of my mother's that she used to play over and over. It's been haunting me all day.

—

It is rumored Roger Crowell has worse habits than verbal contempt for his female tenants. Rumor has it the young model in Room 1208 who works around the hotel as a masseuse pays her bill with weekly massage appointments in Roger's office. Just one big happy family here at Martha's Inn! We would make a ridiculous couple—I think—Roger and I. He is as white as I am black, as tall as I am short. He sits in his raised seat behind his desk, reducing me and loving it. I've begun to sweat around my hairline. Even though the air conditioner is on frigid, my forehead is wet with perspiration. My scalp itches, I ignore it.

Presently he calls my name in a tone of conclusion: "Lee"—he says.

Ahh.

Actually, Roger knows quite well that each month I receive a check around the first. His signature is required for me to cash the check here at the hotel. He also knows that, for reasons unknown, my check sometimes arrives late. Anyway, *he's* the one who insisted I pay all the back rent before my check arrived. So he deserves whatever he gets.

The scarecrow said, "I'm hungry. Can you spare some change?" His chapped lips continued to move but an ambulance siren drowned out his words. I faltered, caught the iron handrail at the top of the subway stairs. A gaunt teenager excused himself past me while I gathered the change in my pocket and dropped it all into the proffered cup, accidentally including my subway token.

"Lee . . ."

"Yes, Roger."

Roger's mouth falls open comically. His eyes narrow. "You must realize"—his thin lips barely move—"how much I hate to do this."

Sure, Roger.

Blah . . . blah . . . blah . . . blah . . . blah. . . .

My call will be very stern. "John"—I'll say—"if you don't wire me that money right away, I swear . . ."

John is a corporate tax lawyer who moonlights as an accountant. He is arrogant about his ability to balance his life (and mine) down to the penny. It's his inheritance that has revealed the irreparable decline in our marriage. John is no longer able to resist the violence in his nature. His blows are casual responses to the mildest frustration, always catching me off guard. When his father died, John inherited the family business, a funeral parlor, a large and thriving corporation. John is unwilling to give up his chosen profession, but he is unable to let go of the business of death inherited. So he continues the legacy of John, Sr. He walks in two worlds: the business of death inherited, and his chosen professions. Afraid to leave either, satisfied with none. When I left last year, John's scowl had become constant. He had lost or forgotten the possibility of modest pleasure. He seemed to consider laughter synonymous with frivolity. It was after John received his inheritance and insisted I quit my job at the day care center that he dubbed me *"ungrateful black bitch"* because I refused to quit my job until he guaranteed me an allowance. And when I got the allowance, I refused to work in the funeral home. I'd've had no money at all if my aunt hadn't died kindly and left me several thousand already taxed dollars. John is terribly frugal since his inheritance.

Yes—I think—I will call John: at home, at the funeral parlor, and at the law firm. I'll leave a message at his office that he can't possibly misunderstand. His reputation at the company is as sacred to him as his possession of the funeral parlor. He'll be shocked that I dare threaten him at the office. I'll have to be firm. It is safe to be firm with John over the telephone. *When you're low woman on the totem pole, you have to stand en garde as if you're in a chess game with a master player: Knight takes Queen. Checkmate. I am aware that today I am playing two experts: John, my almost-ex-husband who sends checks late for spite, and Roger Crowell.*

Actually, I'd like nothing more than to leap across the desk and kick Roger Crowell's narrow pink butt, to relieve—with direct action—the anxiety he is causing me. I need a cigarette. But there's no smoking almost anywhere anymore—especially not in Crowell's office. So instead of lighting up, like a broken record, I repeat, this time without tremor or question in my voice, "So, you would put me out in the street."

"After Monday you'll also have to pay for each day's storage of your belongings . . ."

The fog clears, the song returns to me and I smile with satisfaction at the snatch of lyric. . . . *wake up to reality. But each time I do just the thought of you—*

". . . can avoid further action in this matter"—Roger sums up—"if . . . *I say, are you listening to me?*"

He's startled me with his shouting. I cannot speak or I may cry. Then I'll have to kill him. I seriously consider this solution. Kill Roger Crowell. Kill him. Just kill him. It begins to sound reasonable. I am—I remind myself—after all, a Leo. If I'm not allowed to purr, I feel the need to roar. Yes. I've decided. If I cry, I console myself, I will kill him. I hold my eyes wide and dry to show that I hear, to spare his life.

As if sensing his reprieve he lowers his voice, calls me back to his authority. "I say, you must realize the rules of the hotel cannot apply to everyone except you, Lee. I'm sorry"—he lies.

Ah, Roger.

"I'm hungry"—the black scarecrow whined again. "Can you spare some change so I can get something to eat?" While he spoke, he jiggled his cup with my change in his right hand while his left hand disappeared down between his legs. I barely moved my feet in time to miss the stream he guided up into the August sunlight. I stepped quickly down two subway stairs while he peed straight up in a shower that splashed back down on the sidewalk and splattered his grime-encrusted bare feet before it poured in a black stream across the sidewalk to the curb. I looked for more change in my bag. There was none. I added a dollar bill to his cup while he finished peeing. He smiled at me from his terrible lostness. I found it hard to stand, some gravitational thing wanted to pull me down to sitting position on the stairs.

"I'll have to have the key to your room by five o'clock today. Understand? But I'll give you until five o'clock Monday to make this check good. Until then, just take whatever you need from your room and lock it. Anything you leave will be perfectly safe until Monday. Geeta's on the desk now.

Give her your key before five o'clock. I say, before five"—he says. "We'll have to double-lock your door until—"

"I found a job today"—I lie, each word sticking to the roof of my mouth. "I start on M—"

"Monday"—he concludes, interrupting my lie with his deadline. "Don't say anything more. Please. We've been through this already. You still owe twenty-six dollars on your July phone bill. Your August bill, as of today, is eleven. And this makes five weeks' rent you owe."

"I paid—"

"I know"—he waves me quiet. "I know you paid." He flips through the stack of bills and receipts in the folder on his desk. "Let's see. You paid a forty-dollar phone bill in June—which is also the last time you paid your rent. You paid a nine-dollar phone bill on July third. Then nothing. I didn't refuse you phone service until this week. I just can't let your bill get any higher. For your own sake. You owe the hotel over five hundred dollars. This check is a crime. A felony. I could press charges against you for grand larceny, theft of services. Do you realize—?" He stops to stare at me as I'd stared this morning at the homeless man pissing in the street across from St. Vincent's Hospital.

I forced myself upright and walked down the subway stairs carefully, slowly, looking back. The scarecrow gazed blankly into my eyes, shook his paper cup. "Have a good day"—he urged sincerely. I listened as I continued downstairs to my train. "I'm hungry. Can you spare some change so I can get something to eat?"

Roger has stopped talking for some unguessable time before I hurl myself into the silence. "I beg your pardon"—I say brightly and immediately regret it. He already thinks I'm the worst kind of fool—the kind with no money. But I really didn't hear him. I should have been listening. But my hearing has got all tangled up in the hum of the air conditioner, the dream of an ex-husband, a black scarecrow. I go back and reel in his last words: *For your own sake . . . grand larceny . . . felony. I say . . .*

I lean forward in my chair once more. "I lost my wallet on the subway"—I lie recklessly, and am immediately ashamed. "Yesterday, after my job interview—"

"Five o'clock." He glares. "Today!"

He waves my check at me. "Monday!"
Ahhh.

I have become brand-new here, younger than when I arrived thirteen
months ago with a cast on my arm. Since then I have acquired the habit
of surviving. I think I will never lose this habit. It makes me arrogant at
times. Implacable . . .

Ah, yes, the cast.

Last summer—it was June twenty-fifth, our anniversary—John took me
to a restaurant at the top of the World Trade Center. Our third anniversary.
We were the most splendid looking Black couple in the restaurant. We were
the only Black couple there. (John thoroughly disapproved of the cleavage
my new dress displayed.) Our table by a window looked down on the
engineering miracle of mini-Manhattan Island. I watched the lights of elfin
vehicles travel their perfect north/south, east/west corridors below us while
John drank straight scotch and muttered about cost, about how far we
were from home, about how long the drive back to Jersey would be. He
scowled when I smiled and laid my hand on his knee under the table. So
I turned from him and was gay with the waiter, letting him guide my order,
never glancing at or considering the empty right side of the menu where
prices usually were but weren't. I was determined—with or without my
husband—to have a memorable evening. John . . . *we* could more than
afford it. And it *was* our anniversary. So hard to believe I was having dinner
with the same man who used to call me his Black satin doll.

So John just ordered soup. Although lobster bisque isn't *just* soup. Said,
after the waiter left, that he lost his appetite while I ordered, while he
guessed at the prices. He ordered and drank a split of champagne by himself
while I ate and pretended we were having a good time.

The real problem came when we were leaving. I saw our bill and
watched Mr. Cash&Carry count out a miserly tip. I sneaked an additional
ten dollars on the tray and of course John caught me at it. He snatched up
my ten and half dragged me to the elevator. The tense drive home felt
death-impending—like a high-tech crypt speeding through silent night.
Wordless Lincoln Deluxe. Silent air-conditioning. Moving too fast. Faster.
All the way home.

And when we got home, John broke my arm. Accidentally, to be sure.
Another bruising accident. He only slapped my face—not hard, just shock-

ing. Then he pushed me, intending to knock me down to the couch, I suppose. Instead, I fell on the stone in front of the fireplace. John refused to believe me when I said later that I believed my arm was broken. I could feel it swelling. I couldn't get to the emergency room until after he'd gone to sleep. I drove to the hospital with a compound fracture of my left wrist and a hairline fracture of the long bone from left shoulder to elbow. The next morning, when John left for his office, I moved here—to Martha's Inn—the cast still on my arm. I began the process of becoming my own self again.

Crowell and I both know that I cannot stand and leave his office until I'm dismissed. Although he hasn't had anything to add to our situation for what feels like hours, he keeps finding new ways to convict me. I'm numb. The low temperature of the room is raising chill bumps under my short-sleeved linen suit from the Ralph Lauren collection. I sneeze and startle myself alert. The desk lamp catches his glasses at an angle that throws splintered light and keeps his eyes a secret. As if he can read my mind, he snatches off his glasses so I may see what he thinks of me. Alarmed, I yearn for my sunglasses, which are in the bottom of my bag. His eyes are a disconcerting albino gray. His suit is a darker shade than his eyes. His shirt is blue with a gray tie. I look straight at him, wanting but not daring to get my sunglasses from my bag and put them on. An excessive move will, I'm sure, reveal my distress and reduce me to the mute hysteria at the back of my throat.

I open my mouth for one more effort at conciliation, but Roger cuts me off at the pass. "For God's sake, Lee"—Roger implores—"how far do you expect me to go?"

I desperately want to tell him. Instead, I reach into my handbag and remove my sunglasses.

Nobody looks up when I come out of the office. Women are scattered in muffled clusters around the lobby, dwarfed under the high domed ceiling, mocked by the indiscriminate mix of eighteenth- and nineteenth-century reproductions of European art on the walls—hunt scenes with dogs leading the chase after the red fox racing toward the viewer at the bottom left of the canvas; costume balls, dances and feasts in French palaces, powdered wigs on men and women; a somber white man in a golden helmet—all utterly depressing and perfectly suited to the occupants of this huge chamber. As variously as cactus in the Arizona desert, the women in the lobby sit. Some rest here at the hotel—refueling before they move back out into the sexual fray "at the behest of the Absolute Genital." Some are relieved to spend their remaining years, months, days, right here, sitting out the war that originated in Eden, in Europe, America, Australia, China, Japan, Africa. Here they read, doze, murmur to themselves, to each other; audio and visual hallucinations confine a few whose whispers echo under the dome of the fourteen-foot ceiling. Some merely sit in regal unspeaking dignity. Many work nights, although most have nine-to-fives and are seldom in the lobby on Thursday afternoons in August. The working women won't add their stability to the daytime dirge until after five. Then life in the lobby will accelerate, will become New-York-with-a-purpose once again. Although there are a few of us throughout the hotel, I am the only Black in the lobby today, the only woman of color on my floor, except for Mei Ling. Chang Mei Ling in the formal Chinese way, Mei Ling Chang in the American. She is my friend, a tall aristocratic Eurasian who looks like a high-fashion model. Always smiles and speaks when we meet on the 10th floor, at the elevator, in the laundry room. This is a compliment, as Mei Ling does not speak to everyone. Today I prefer my isolation.

I take off my sunglasses and check myself in the wall of mirror to my right. I smile at my image, reminding her that I love her. She looks responsible, I think. Still dressed for this morning's two fruitless job interviews, at a temp agency and a law firm: brand-new designer suit, kelly green linen, three-inch heels that bring her all the way up to five-foot-six. I should look as if I have a job. This outfit cost enough. Although my suit looks as if I slept in it, I assure myself that linen and Ralph Lauren have always been forgiven their wrinkles. God, I never would have bought the suit if I'd known John was going to screw around with my money this month. I examine my evicted image in the mirror. My hair shines in black lace filigree four inches above my head. Actually, I look like a little black puppet dangling from all that hair. One day I'll take a fit and cut it all off. Actually, I hope it adds statuesque inches to my height. I hope the cut of the jacket minimizes my full D-cup breasts that John learned to hate so. They wouldn't draw so much attention—I think—if the rest of me wasn't so small. (That's what John always said.) Both interviewers this morning were women so I wasn't as self-conscious as yesterday, down on Wall Street, when the interviewer kept looking from my breasts to my eyes with a question on his silly face.

My second interview was at a law firm down on Perry Street in Greenwich Village. The woman who tested me was all business but so emaciated—a tubercular blonde with dangerously sharpened elbows and knees that I suspected were linked to her vocal style: cocaine aftermath. She kept blowing her postnasal drip into endless yellow tissues from the box on her desk while I tried not to betray my craven need for the job. When I fell two paragraphs behind the dictating machine I stopped trying to bluff my way through the test. The truth is, I haven't typed or taken dictation since college, except for practicing alone in my room for the past six months, after my cast came off, taking down radio dialogue, unable to transcribe my notes five minutes later.

Truth is, this summer I've applied for as many jobs that I haven't gotten as there are apartments I can't afford in the daily classified.

I cross the lobby to the newsstand concession and buy two bags of potato chips and a pack of cigarettes. *I only started smoking again when I left John and New Jersey.* Mei Ling enters the lobby from the stairwell wearing her off-duty summer uniform: shorts and halter. She smiles and waves on her way out. I wave. She's always walking down those long double flights of stairs, sometimes even walking up. I recross the lobby and enter the empty elevator under one of the NO MALES ALLOWED BEYOND THE LOBBY signs. I push the button for the 12th floor. From 12 I can walk up to the roof garden. I need air. I need time to think. Just before the doors close, the old woman from 8 gets on, talking to herself; she runs a constant conversation with an invisible taller person to her left. Two more from my floor get on: Room 1007—Erin, I think—the Irish fashion designer, somewhere in her forties, doesn't look a day over thirty, shares the double bedroom/sitting room and kitchenette with her invalid sister; and at the very last minute Room 1025 lurches past me and stops herself at the waist-high bar on the back wall. She propels herself forward and punches 12 as the car begins its slow ascent and the air turns to stale alcohol and unwashed woman. I make my breathing shallow and change my mind about going to the roof. I know that 1025 lost her two kids in a custody battle with her banker husband. She's twenty-seven years old. Only her black hair saves her from the anonymity of her pale skin. She was here when I moved in. She's from . . . Budapest—I think—a shy, gentle girl, mostly, who sometimes drinks too much in order to scream her rage through the lobby before falling asleep on the roof. Like me, she waits for checks.

I watch the lights change as the elevator climbs to 8, discharges the old woman still chatting to her invisible companion. Room 1025—Haviva, I think—asks me for a cigarette (we have been sharing my cigarettes since the day I moved in), so I open the pack and shake four or five into her hand, without breathing. When the doors open again, Erin and I smile a distant lie to each other as we exit. I make a sharp left and I'm home: Room 1023, right next to the elevator shaft.

I walk into the narrow corridor of my single room. I note that it has never felt so much like home. I sit on the bed where every night I dream that I can fly, and wake to taste the dregs of flight, but now I feel totally earthbound, alone in the pit of my room. I haven't locked the door. Few of us do unless we're actually leaving the hotel for the day or the evening. I eat my potato chips, drink a large glass of icewater from my tiny refrigerator, whose top doubles as a stand for my black&white television. Meal settled, I light a cigarette. The key to my room is on the dresser by the clock-radio. Two-twenty-five, the clock reads. I sit in the chair by the open window, rest my face on the back of my hands on the windowsill, and blow smoke rings outside to distract myself from the subject of myself. At the juncture of four-way traffic below, tiny pre-rush-hour yellow cabs outnumber pedestrians, whose numbers will soon double, triple, to hundreds per hour, rushing, competing with waving arms for the scuttling livery. Personally, I prefer the subway. I could write ads, do voice-overs for TV and radio commercials praising the New York City subway system: "The fastest, most affordable way to travel," I'd say. (Although you can't deny the convenience of New York taxicabs.) My ads would provoke an influx of New Jerseyites. They'd move to New York in droves just to ride the subway. Never again would they need to call a taxi from home like they do in Jersey. Just go out, stand on a corner, and wave your arm. Except rush hour, of course. During rush hour—so many arms waving that they look like snakes from up here—arguments break out as to whose cab it is, waiting for its single occupant. They should all take the subway.

From my window I can just make out Mei Ling in her red shorts and halter, leaving Gristedes with a large grocery bag. Hard to miss, she's so tall. She has the small sitting room/kitchenette near the stairs, Room 1005. Mei Ling is a nurse on a locked ward at Bellevue Psychiatric Hospital over on First Avenue. She seldom leaves the hotel when she's off duty. Several times she has invited me to her room for tea when her boyfriend visits. With his clean shaven cheeks, his ponytail and slouched denim hat, jeans and sneakers, Mei Ling's boyfriend passes quite easily through the lobby, right under the NO MALES ALLOWED sign. Suspicious five-o'clock shadows are blue on the cheeks of many of the ladies' evening visitors. Mei Ling introduced me to Ah Lum in her room most casually. Translated his Cantonese greeting to me, my "Hello, pleased to meet you" to him.

"The tyranny in your country"—Mei Ling assured me once in the laundry room—"is not so unique. It did not move so far from Europe as your history proposes. I believe everyone here strives to perfect the singular acceptable caricature of themselves in order not to expose their difference. Maybe"—Mei Ling further provoked—"you could never have become a proper American wife. It seems to me a perfectly impossible thing to become." She has been in this country so long that she doesn't realize she is no longer a proper Cantonese girl. I detected Ah Lum's subtle disapproval several times during tea. They spoke an occasional dialect that Mei Ling did not translate. I believe Ah Lum was anxious for me to leave.

I watch Mei Ling's sensuous gait as she defies the red light, ignoring the swerving traffic around her. I can hear the angry shouts of the drivers even from this high up but I can't distinguish words. Mei Ling never glances their way. Her panache fills my lungs, makes me smile. When she disappears around the corner coming toward the hotel, I'm reluctantly free of external focus and the subject of myself reintrudes forcibly.

I flick the long ash from my cigarette, take one last drag, and crush its fire to black ashes on the cement ledge. I strip quickly, tossing my suit on the foot of the bed, removing bra, pantyhose, and panties to the hamper. I take a cool shower. Even though my scalp still itches and I'd love a shampoo, I deny myself the luxury and use my shower cap since I haven't the time or patience to dry my hair. I brush my teeth. All the while I avoid looking in the mirror of the medicine cabinet or in the full-length mirror behind the bathroom door. By now I'm too embarrassed to face myself. My ablutions complete, I dry myself thoroughly, turn on the tiny wall fan over the bed, and lie down. I kick my suit aside and place the ashtray on my naked stomach, to smoke one last cigarette. I tell myself I feel calmer, more equal to the situation. It comes to me that shelter is one of life's necessaries. I only have to make it until September. Then I'll be tutoring and teaching English Composition 101. In my new life. That's less than a month to kill time—or John.

I wait until three-thirty by the clock, then force myself up, hang my suit in the closet, and take my gray paisley overnight case from under the bed. I pack a few things in less than fifteen minutes. I take fresh underwear from my top bureau drawer, put on a light cotton T-shirt and jeans, slip my feet into sandals. I'm ready. There is still nowhere to go that would be less painful to me than living in the street. I'm so ashamed of John for his part in this humiliation. My shame is sapping my energy. Even if I want to call John, I can't use the phone until I pay my bill. Oh, they'd ring me if someone called—say, like Roger Crowell just called me to his office.

I take my watch from the dresser and put it on. I put my rings in the pocket of my jeans, close my suitcase, grab my address book from the telephone table and stick it in my pocketbook as I leave, slamming the door behind me without locking it. I go back to the lobby to the front desk to hand in my key. There is indignity in my cotton mouth, in my paper dry hands as I ring for the elevator in a state that bears for me the earmarks of a high-wire act at the World Trade Center. No net.

I admire my performance as I stride to the desk. "Hi, Geeta." I hand her my key. "Anything for me?"

"Only this note." Geeta replies in a subtle tone that embarrasses me because, of course, she knows. She hands me a hotel envelope with my name written, not typed. She takes my key. That's all. Silently, I thank her. No scenes for the other clerks, the switchboard operator. "Nothing else today. Maybe tomorrow"—she suggests and smiles. She's positively beautiful when she smiles, white teeth exciting her ruddy complexion.

"So long, Geeta." I wave her envelope, turn, and walk toward the first set of double glass doors to nowhere in particular. I stop at the newspaper stand and buy a bar of candy for energy—chocolate with peanut butter. I also buy a newspaper that I already have. But it's upstairs, about to be double-locked in Room 1023. I have plenty of change but I pay for the candy and the paper with my last twenty-dollar bill, wondering why these delay tactics. Sooner or later, I have to go outside to nowhere. I take the paper, stuff the change into my jeans pocket with my rings, keep the candy bar handy, and put my sunglasses back on. Just then some noisy young women enter the lobby and turn right, into the EXIT stairway against the far wall. Without thinking I turn left and duck into the stairwell behind them. I follow them—summer school, college students—to the second floor, where they swing the door open and leave me alone in the stairwell. Newspaper and suitcase clutched to my chest, my sunglasses casting further gloom on each landing, I climb the remaining double flights to the tenth floor. I walk slowly and finish my candy bar before I reach my floor and enter the hallway. I lick the chocolate from my right thumb and index fingers as I walk the tunnel of closed doors on each side of the carpeted hall from the stairs to my room. I enter and lock the door behind me, dump the candy wrapper and the newspaper in the trash. I still have no plan. Only these heightened instincts.

I sit on the side of the bed and open the envelope Geeta gave me at the desk. One sheet of white paper folded around a crisp twenty-dollar bill. The note is written in the same tiny script as the envelope and perfectly centered. I read,

My Dear Lelah Vanessa Frederick,

It is not so bad as it seems to go through many trials, dear friend, when you are a first-class citizen. I am sending you this $20 to help some. I am here only until I too am a first-class citizen. Roger Crowell and his wife are sponsoring me. I am sincerely wishing you good fortune. And I am hoping that your check is in the mail tomorrow.

The note is signed *Geeta Kumar*. I am amused by Geeta's ceremonious reassurance, her simple faith in the security of first-class citizens. Perhaps —I think—she knows something I do not. Her charity makes me smile, and momentarily I am unimpressed by my present danger.

I put Geeta's letter aside and rise from the bed. I take my suitcase deep into the closet and set it on the floor against the back wall. I make the necessary trip to the toilet and empty my bladder. I take a flowered silk scarf from my top drawer and tie my huge Afro smoothly to my head, granny-style. Then, as if I'd always known I would, I slide under the bed with my letter and my pocketbook. The bed isn't high enough off the floor for me to lie on my side so I lie on my stomach, my breasts crushed against the prickly carpet, my shoulder snug against the wall, my face turned toward the room outside. The carpet seems free of grit and dust. I thank the maid that I probably will not have an asthma attack. I stick my arm from under the bed into the sunlight on the carpet to check the time. It's twenty minutes after four. I settle down to wait for the double-locking ceremony with my rings in my jeans pocket digging into my thigh. The only thought that comes to my mind while I wait is Miss Sinclair, an old tenant of my mother's whom I haven't thought of in thirteen years nor seen since I was in high school. I am thinking of things so long secret that they appear to be lies.

My mother put Miss Sinclair out of our three-family house. Funny, I think she said the same thing to Miss Sinclair that Roger Crowell said to me. I almost remember Mother's patient voice: "But Miss Sinclair, you simply leave me no choice"—Mother said. I was shocked at Mother's heartlessness. (Wasn't I?) She was gone—Miss Sinclair—when I got home from school. I never saw her again. How long had my mother given Miss

Sinclair to find somewhere she could stay with no money? I wonder where Miss Sinclair went. She couldn't hide under the bed, Mother always escorted those who left to the door. Did Miss Sinclair sneak back in when my mother wasn't looking and live in the basement for a while? What did she do? Where did she go?

And me? I can't just hide under the bed, can I?

The telephone rings and startles me so badly I jerk up toward the box springs, smashing the back of my head against an unyielding strip of metal. I am grateful for the cushion of scarf and hair. The phone keeps ringing, long demanding rings that only a switchboard operator can effect. My heart beats irregularly. I feel as if I may die. I don't mean a hysterical premonition. I literally feel a deathlike swoon. If I have a heart attack, I wonder curiously, when will the maid find my body? Maybe not until the next tenant complains about the smell. God, I want a cigarette. Someone is on the way up to double-lock my room—just in case I've somehow had an illegal duplicate made of the key before turning it in. My cigarettes are in my bag on the floor to my right. I wish for just a couple of quick drags before the turnkey arrives. I picture the desk clerk's surprise when smoke comes from under the bed through the strands of fringe on the white chenille bedspread. If it's dear Geeta, she might be a good Samaritan and ignore the evidence. I don't know how long I lay waiting, wanting a cigarette—ten minutes? thirty?—before I hear the elevator stop and the rare phenomenon of a muffled male voice right outside my door, then loud knocking.

The first thing I notice is that they do not lock the door—and there are two of them. The sun is shining on the faded red cabbage-rose design of the carpet and I can see their shoes quite clearly. Crowell's are a navy/black color that shows blue only when the sun hits them at certain angles. His socks are gray. Geeta's shoes are burgundy, the color of the hotel's uniforms. I listen with mild interest to their voices overhead. They speak softly, the way people speak at funerals. Crowell, himself, has come. He's brought Geeta. Does he need a witness?

"Check the bathroom, Geeta, they steal anything not welded to the wall."

What, I wonder, could I possibly steal from the bathroom?

"Shower curtains, toilet paper . . . anything. I say . . . once this Irish kid who looked just like Peter Pan stole all the light bulbs from 801. She left owing me over four hundred dollars. Never saw her again."

I watch their shoes.

"Clothes still in the closet"—Crowell notes above my head.

Geeta responds near my feet—I am surrounded. "The bathroom is intact, sir." Geeta speaks in the formal way of the British-educated Indian. I think I hear disapproval in her voice.

"I say, smells like a dirty ashtray in here, doesn't it, Geeta?" His shoes are out of sight. I can tell he's over by the open window, maybe sticking his head out for some fresh air, frowning at the cigarette butt on the ledge. The refrigerator opens. Closes. Then in a stronger voice that suggests pleasure, "Well, I see she's left her TV. Ummm, and typewriter. Good. This is her refrigerator too. Looks like she'll come back. If she doesn't . . ."

I hear the TV come on.

"Good. It works. I say, check the radio, Geeta."

I note that he seems to love to say her name. For a moment the TV and the radio change stations, complementing and competing with each other. I try to recognize channels and stations switched too fast for identification. I give up. I hear a drawer open. Crowell's hoarse whisper is amused. "Good God, look at this. It's big enough for a cow. Udders!" He stands facing Geeta's shoes. With shock, I envision him holding up one of my brassieres. I hope it's one of the black or white lace numbers and not my running bras, whose sturdiness implies a medical prescription. "Udders!" His awed distaste is that of the healthy judging the deformed.

"I do not think this is a respectful thing, sir." Geeta speaks softly. And I thank my little friend, who is as short as I, and I remember that she insisted on taking me to lunch in another late-check month.

Crowell is silent. He's still opening drawers. There is less air under the bed. I'm suffocating. I want to surrender before he looks under the bed and I have the heart attack that's moving up my left arm. At least that way I'll be in control of my own death. I've read or heard somewhere that an irresistible urge to surrender, or to stand and fight, strikes all prey at some point in the hunt. I understand the seduction. But it would take great courage, I think. I am not crying; therefore I am surprised that there are tears rolling left over the bridge of my nose to the rug. It is just that I am so tired. I hold my purse closer to my side and clench my fists in an effort at control. *John told me that I'm still covered by his life insurance.*

"Hey, I guess we're all done here, Geeta." Crowell's phony accent slips. Until now, he has been doing a sly imitation of Geeta's cultured speech. I am intrigued by a subtle softening in the tone of his voice. His shoes move from my line of vision. I hear the door lock. Then I see his shoes again straight ahead. I can see Geeta's burgundy pumps over by the bathroom. Crowell sits on the bed, blocking a good portion of light. His heels are a few feet from my face. He's moving about on the bed. I hear him unzipping. The thin air under the bed disappears audibly. I hear it go with my own intake of breath.

"Geeta?"

"Please, sir, let's get back to—"

"Oh, Geeta, don't be like that, a little indulgence, eh?"

I could slide over a bit on my stomach and bite his ankle thoroughly, but would it improve my position? Or Geeta's? There's a struggle above. I have actually begun to slide out from under the bed when I hear the shot. *Crack!*

Oh, my God! She's shot him and I'm a witness to murder. I've just tensed my muscles for my move when I hear . . .

"Oh, Geeta." His voice suggests disappointment, a joke misunderstood.

I slide back quickly. I realize what has happened. I've heard a slap that sounded that loud once before. My father had come to visit and, after a few drinks from the bottle he brought with him for courage, he followed Mother into the kitchen. Mother slapped him so loudly that my brother and I thought she'd shot him.

Geeta's voice is trembling. With rage, I think.

"I am most ashamed of you at this moment, sir. I am most ashamed. I have never struck another human being in my life, sir."

Of their own accord, my tears fall more freely, as if I am weeping when I know I am only mad and growing madder.

"It's all right, dear." Crowell's voice is fatherly. Understanding. "We'll put this entirely behind us. The heat . . ." He stands, zips up, and sits back down rather heavily on the bed.

I press my face harder against the dampened rug to avoid the bouncing of the metal above me.

Geeta walks over and unlocks the door. Her voice still trembles—with ice. "You will lock up, sir?"

The door closes.

Crowell stands again and opens the door. "Geeta"—he calls into the hall; then, softer, "I say, Geeta, if my wife calls, put her through up here. Okay? I think I'll take a nap. Miss the rush-hour traffic going home. Be a good girl and ring me in an hour or so. Okay?"

I don't hear Geeta's response, but the door closes and locks. I watch Crowell's navy shoes pass by the length of chenille fringe. He chuckles softly as he sits in the chair by the window to remove his shoes, his pants. "Feisty little bitch"—he murmurs.

The radio comes on, changing stations until it comes to strings and piano, soft music, the kind I've always believed helps plants to grow. A moment, and I hear the whirring of the little fan over my bed. As he stretches out above me he sighs deeply. Then he is still.

Although I envy him the fan, I welcome the sounds of radio and fan that together let me breathe less cautiously. I wonder if John would be impressed by my cunning handling of this situation he's created. Softly, I cross my hands on the floor for a pillow and rest my cheek so gently where my fingers meet. I hope I don't nod off. I might snore. Once, I actually whisper—or perhaps I only mouth the words—to myself, to John, to Roger Crowell: *The check's in the mail.*

The Rejected Buppie

History & Science are outlawed
    persons guilty of possession
    of these
    are brought before
    a council
    of cannibals
    verdicts
    of red
        Slobber

 L moved out to Elklock, a suburb of Chocolate City, an all-white upper-middle-class neighborhood close to the big city but encircled and all but hidden by a circle of giant oaks. Halfway up a mountain. But then I saw him a few days ago, in White Castle. He looked a hundred years old and fixed all who passed near him with a maniac stare that seemed almost electric yet dull, blank.

As I approached him, he turned suddenly, "Amiri . . . yeh, I'm back and I don't look good. I know."

He was sad and tired, but he pierced me with this magnetic knife his eyes pushed. He put out his hand to shake and at the same time took a frayed clipping out of his pocket and shoved it at me.

"See?"

The clipping was from the *Elklock Call*. It showed L on the front page: his mouth open and crude fangs drawn in his mouth and a tail curled over his shoulder. He seemed to have on a red and black plastic space suit. A

AMIRI BARAKA is a poet, political activist, and teacher. He is the author of *Transbluescency: The Selected Poetry of Amiri Baraka*, another collection of poetry entitled *Wise, Why's, Y's: The Griot's Song, Jesse Jackson & Black People*, essays collected since 1972 about Jackson and his politics, and *Eulogies*. He has taught at the State University of New York at Stonybrook since 1979.

STREETLIGHTS

20

bloody hatchet hung from his hand casually. The picture's caption read FIEND AT LARGE!

I didn't know whether to laugh or back up. But it was funny. L was not a fiend last time I saw him. And he looked even less fiendlike now, sheepishly peeping at the newspaper in my hand.

"Fiend?"

"Yes. They say I used spells to remain Black in spite of their kindness. They say I was observed dancing a black ritual and trying to evoke the evil James Brown spirit. And conspired with the forces of darkness to remain emotional.

"They say I chanted madness and was transformed into a huge black genital of flame. And that I terrorized the citizens by appearing just anywhere suddenly, reeking of nigger spy rhythm.

"That I had tried to preach the evil cynicism of history and science. That I acted lewdly and illegally in doing this and exhibited all the characteristics of a serial coon resister. That I chewed the heads off white fetish symbols and spat blood like a judge in a black pointed hat and mask. That I hated what they loved and loved what they hated."

"What?" I didn't think it was a joke. Just stretched out past clock or calendar. "Is this real? It's some . . . nut shit?"

"No. They formed a lynch mob. It was legal. The sheriff headed it. He had a writ, a subpoena, a machine gun, a rope. A head full of drooping tissue, wet with spider shit."

"What? What shit is this? What happened, really?"

"They ran me out of my new house. They set the gingerbread on fire. They tore up the treaties that made us tolerated vomit.

"A little ol' lady shit in the middle of the floor, in intriguing patterns. Some of the mob took pictures and scooped up the shit, sucking their fingers as they destroyed the house.

"They arrived in garbage cans with wheels made of Indian skulls."

The brother was running it like some kind of priest or preacher, like destroyed history could erupt as a slanted colored structure, flowing hot beneath an arctic veil; experience sounds deadly.

"But it's not the mob-crazy white people rushing into your house. I could accept all that, like a statue given to someone as a reward."

Now, you can dig what all this sounded like to me, Knowing some portion of what all this really is and really be coming from. You dig? But when strange happen, it be strange to you too!

"But, you see, I don't know how much you understand about bullshit."

"I know what I understand." Where he had taken this story was out anyway. The form, and you know in the store, like that—an anonymous fullness.

"People like you, Baraka, said all that garbage about brainwash. I could dismiss that when it gave me pleasure. I could aspire to be in my world, where I was what I wanted anyway."

"People like me?" He was looking at the television set of my expression and the narrative of my random acknowledgments. Grunts and blowing short breaths.

"But you see, the dumb shit is completely inside it, unexpressed by anything outside it."

"Yeh." What the fuck?

"Yeh." He paid the cashier. "You see, if you really understood America, you would disappear into it and be calm and holy."

"I know." He was television's future.

"But its lie is all the way always in all ways. A lie. I love lies and it lied to me. The truth is what hurts."

When you find people talking to you like this it makes you want to help them, in a way that would've made the discussion never happen. Like bullshit about heart wrenching or being heart wrenching about bullshit. I know. But then I knew he was something already alien. That he lived in a space between what he thought and the actual. I couldn't understand him totally at first, it was a definition that scrambled his speech. Drifted his face into clichés.

"You see, even now I am not rejecting the experience. . . ."

"Experience?" It was like therapy; even racism was useful as a measure for these guys. These guys . . . ?

"The lie was they did not hate me. The lie was they were ignorant. Bullshit. I saw them behind closed doors, dressed in white sheets, feeding on skinned children, Negro children."

What can you say. "What?" I caught a hacked snicker my throat would've sounded like a laugh. He had flowed out of his own skin, calm, a yellow and brown puddle smoking. The skin kept talking without eyes, empty as a pocketbook.

"I knew then that we were excluded. That they felt we couldn't hang. Couldn't understand their huffy ritual."

"Is this shit for real?" Came half thrown away. . . .

"That's why they attacked us in the press. Because we saw the lie."

"Yeh." This was actually a "guy."

"And you see, some of them knew we could fit. That we could eat the nasty nigger anytime, anyplace, anywhere."

The eyeless skin bent and picked up the yellow spotted bleeding mess of his insides and slapped it on the scale there at the checkout counter.

The manager had come out and checked the scale. Then gestured to a gray bow-and-arrow negro with a white jacket, who sliced it neatly so the flesh and guts would fold, then dumped it in a plastic sack and carried it away.

"I'm going to sue." He was getting a stack of dollars pushed through his empty eyeholes.

"Yeh," was all I said, turning to leave.

Red Lipstick

YOLANDA BARNES

 Lettie's coming.

She's coming. On her way.

That was her calling on the telephone. Telling me she'll be here soon.

Lettie.

Jesus Lord. So much to do.

"Who is this?" I said. "Who?" My voice harsh, not like me at all. That ringing phone had pulled me from my bed, that's how early it was, and I'm up by seven every morning. It's been that way for years. "Who?"

"Albee?" she said. I didn't know her voice. Imagine that. She spoke again, this time adding a weight to her words, leveling her tone with authority, calm. "Albertine."

"Lettie."

Lettie Lettie Lettie. Her name rolls along in my mind like a prayer, a curse. Like the singsong of a children's nursery rhyme, a chant to jump rope by: Here comes Lettie. Here she comes. Lettie. Lettie. My best-best friend. Lettie. Lettie. The one I loved. *Oh, but that was a long time ago.*

On her way back to me at last. I stood in the hallway after we hung

YOLANDA BARNES is a writer living in Los Angeles. Her novella and short stories have appeared in various publications. "Red Lipstick" was first published in *Tri-Quarterly 81*, Spring/Summer 1991.

up, wearing just a nightgown, my feet bare against the hallway floor, bumps on my arms and the back of my neck, a chill I was feeling and at the same time not feeling. I was bound to get sick, I was thinking, in spite of the flu shots. Nothing would save me. Such strange thoughts. About my heart, leaping so against my chest. It would jump out, I was certain, and I crossed my arms, trying to hold it back. All these bits jumbled inside me. Until I couldn't think at all, like the times now I am driving and suddenly people honk their horns at me, an ugly, rude chorus, when I have no idea what wrong I have done, making me stop in my tracks, same as the little brown rabbit startled in the woods, black eyes bright and body stiff, stopped in the middle of the intersection and so nobody can go until I'm able to breathe again.

I have to reach for breath after Lettie calls. The weight of my crossed arms squeezed against my breasts: What a sight I would make for the woman doctor who worries about my blood pressure. Until I begin to rub my arms, my cheeks, the still rabbit coming back to life. Lettie's on her way and I have to prepare.

First move I make is to pull on my old housedress with the green and brown and yellow checkered squares, torn and stitched with safety pins beneath the right arm. Tie a kerchief around my head on the way to the front yard, the first sight that will greet Lettie. I carry the broom for sweeping the curb where dirt and slips of paper and soda cans have collected. But first the lawn. Down on hands and knees, my eyes narrowed and searching the grass for weeds, I crawl about, snatching at dandelions and crabgrass until green streaks stain my palms. When the walk catches my sight. My new walk that Mr. James in the green house on the corner just finished building without taking a penny. Mr. James with his pretty wife who nudges him to help the old widow down the street. He laid the walk just the way I asked, with bricks of different colors—pink, of course, but also coral and burgundy, yellow and green and gray. Like a crazy quilt, that's what I told him. Like Joseph's coat.

I squeeze my eyes tight and see Lettie strolling along that new walk. The way she was years ago, wearing one of her dresses, bright-colored and the skirt swinging, brushing the back of her knees. Her plump cheeks and skin the shade of black plums. Her hats—the straw one with the scarves tied around the brim, the tails drifting down her back and that man's hat tilted on her head, shadowing one eye. I see her hair dyed yellow. (How my Harald talked her down for that! "A woman with skin that black," he said, like it was some crime. "She's got no *business*.") I see tripled strands of fake pearls slapping against her breasts as she stepped, and her lips, slick and shiny red, open and stretched across laughing teeth.

"Miz Clark?" I hear, and open my eyes. Sonya from across the street stands on my lawn. "Miz Clark?" she says. They all call me that. "How you doing today, Miz Clark?" they say; "You getting along all right, Miz Clark?" No longer Albertine. Nobody remembers Albertine but me. "Miz Clark?" Sonya is saying. "You doing okay, Miz Clark?" Her little boy and girl dressed in blue uniforms, on their way to the Christian school. They hold Sonya's hands and stare at me with dark brown eyes, the girl's hair all in braids and fastened with blue-and-white barrettes.

"You've been working hard," Sonya says. "I saw you." Her voice is weak, surprising because Sonya's a big woman. A big yellow woman. The way she fusses at me is how I imagine a daughter would. I know I should be thankful for neighbors like her. "Maybe you should rest," she says, but I just grin and pat her fleshy arm. Tell her to stop worrying. That's all I say. She wouldn't understand the rest, that I haven't felt so good in a long, long time.

Lettie never said what she wanted when she called. But I know. The same as how I know almost everything about Lettie. More, probably, than in those days we talked all the time. I know about that new house of hers and how each of her daughters turned out, about each wedding, each birth of a grandchild, each baptism, communion, graduation. I know about her boy, her baby. How his motorbike skidded on an oil-slicked road. He was nearly killed and I know that nearly killed her. There are people who tell me these things, Essie in particular, but sometimes I wonder if I need them. I feel I would know no matter what. I would just know.

"Can I come over today, Albee?" she said. "I've got something to ask you." What answer possible, except "Of course, Lettie." All this time her words swirling in my mind until, finally, while working in the yard their meaning comes to me, makes me sit back on my heels although this causes great pain in my legs. Already my palms sting, my back hurts from all the pulling and stooping, but I have taken certain pleasure in all these aches, accepted any sufferings stemming from Lettie's visit as natural and ex-pected. Now, at this moment, I don't feel a thing. "So that's what she wants," I say, then snap my mouth shut, in case Sonya's back across the street, watching.

There's a sickness eating through Lettie, Essie told me. She says it can't be fought. "They put her in the hospital time after time," Essie said. "But she always comes out." I could picture Essie on the other end of the telephone, shaking her head, black curls trembling. But I know better. Lettie is a cat. What else Essie tells me, that Lettie's alone. "Alonso's left her." She lowered her voice when she told me this, and on my end of the phone I nodded my head. My whole body nodding, my shoulders rocking back and forth, my toes in it too, tapping the floor. Ah, Alonso. Couldn't take any more. Lettie's carryings-on and her lies. Her arrogance. See there. I'm not the only one. "And the children," Essie said. "All gone too." That boy turned out no better than her. Traipsing around the country. Living with one woman after another. The twins, Claire and Carla. "They won't have nothing to do with her." Essie's tone hushed. Gleeful. "Won't even let her in their homes."

"It's payment due," I said. "Fortune's wheel turning round. All Lettie's deeds coming back to her. All the evil, all the lies, all that boozing, all her selfishness. All the suffering she's caused." I had to catch myself, listen to Essie's silence. It made me press my lips tight. Nobody wants to hear me talk that way.

Alone. That's why Lettie's coming back. She needs my help.

She'll be here soon, and so I move inside to the living room. She'll only pass through here, Lettie and I were never living-room friends. Still I take my old dust rags and wipe the Beethoven bust on the piano. I grip the bench and lower myself one knee at a time to clean the instrument's feet, pushing my fingernail through the cloth to get at the dust in the carved ridges. I pour lemon oil on the coffee table and knead it into the wood. The centerpiece is an arrangement of silk-screen flowers. It would be nice to replace it with a token from Lettie, but there is nothing. A punch bowl that Harald dropped years ago. When we were children I'd give Lettie presents. Little bracelets with dangling charms and necklaces with mustard seeds captured in glass balls. I stole from my mother's jewelry box a pin shaped like a bird with rhinestones in its breast. Lettie and I believed they were diamonds. How Mama whipped me when she found out! I gave Lettie the toy circus animals my daddy bought me when I was sick with chicken pox. Tiny, tiny things. When I shut my eyes now I can see them still: a lion, a monkey, a capped bear holding a little red ball. Lettie won't remember.

In the kitchen I fill a bucket with ammonia and hot water, sink my bare hands in, and swirl the rag about. My fingers look strange, puffy, bloated, plain except for the wedding band I still wear though Harald's been gone, what?, almost ten years. In the moment it takes to squeeze the rag my hands have turned a raw red. I was the fair-skinned one with the pretty hair. Lettie standing in the schoolyard behind me, playing with my pony-tail, saying "This is good stuff." Combing it with her fingers, plaiting it, dressing it with ribbons. She chose me, I remind myself as I clean. "Me." Wiping down the windowsill above the sink where I keep my pot of violets, the ceramic swan with the white curved neck, the goldfish bowl. Harald's glasses. The last pair he owned, cracked in the brown frame. Oh, Harald never liked Lettie. He saw before I did. The way his face turned mean at the sight of her children here. But I didn't mind taking care of them, I tried to tell him, since we couldn't have any of our own. "Fool," he said. He knew what Lettie was doing, how she got those fancy hats and bottles of perfume cluttering her glass-topped vanity. "Fool," he said, and I thought he meant Alonso.

I want Lettie to see those glasses. And the drawings held by magnets to the refrigerator. Sonya's children colored those and signed them with love and kisses. I want Lettie to take note of the cabinets beneath the sink; Mr. James built those, yes, the same one who did the walk. And the large bowl on the table, let her see that too, filled with figs and oranges and lemons and tomatoes and yellow squash. My neighbors pick these from their trees and gardens and carry them over in grease-stained paper bags. All this will show Lettie. "See, I have friends. See what my friends do for me, Lettie? Do you hear? I have a good life. I keep busy. I substitute-teach and lunch twice a month with Essie. I attend all the meetings of the neighborhood block club, elected secretary two years in a row."

I shake my head. Standing in the middle of my kitchen, hands on hips, the rag dripping ammonia water on the floor. I have no time for this, there is much more to do. A new, fresh tablecloth and the good curtains, yellow ones that match my kitchen, I need to get them down from the hall cabinet. I will fix tuna sandwiches, cut in triangles and trimmed of crusts, just how she likes, and put the rest of the coconut cake on the party platter with the red and yellow tulips decorating the border. When Lettie comes I will put on a pot of coffee. We used to sit at this very table and drink cup after cup, Lettie making me laugh. If I had more time I would get on hands and knees and scrub the floor. I would wipe down the cabinet doors, the wood-work, the walls till free of fingerprints and grime and grease. Sort through the cupboards, throw out the clutter, the excesses, and reline the shelves with fresh, new paper. I would clean this house to its bones, its soul. I would cook Lettie her favorite meal, gumbo with sausage and crab and shrimp. All that and more if I had the time. But a million years would not be enough to prepare for Lettie.

It's remarkable to me that I didn't know her voice. Of course it's been several years since we spoke on the telephone or anywhere else. But that doesn't mean I had stopped hearing Lettie. No. I've heard her voice often. Still it follows me around, sits on my shoulder and whispers in my ear, pops up at the strangest times. Once when I was slicing eggplant and something about it, its deep black purpleness, I think, like Lettie's color, made me think of her and I swear I heard her laughing. Another time I was humming some nonsense tune I made up as I leaned over the back-porch sink washing my clothes, and her voice rose up over mine, singing one of those common, nasty songs she used to know. I must hear her in my sleep too, because sometimes I wake in the night answering her.

Something to ask me, that's what she said, and that is just like Lettie. Seems like she was always wanting something from me. Never the other way around. Didn't Harald say that? And Essie? Oh, I was a good friend to her, everybody knows that. But I've learned my lesson now. I'm stronger than before. "Where are my little toy animals now?" My voice bounces against the tile walls of the bathroom. I hear in it the frantic pain of the old crazy woman filthily dressed who stands at the bus stop and shouts all her business. With trembling fingers I unbutton my old plaid dress and soap a washcloth to rub against the back of my neck, my ears, beneath my arms. Fill the basin with water and bring my face down.

People wondered after I let Lettie go. Prying, nudging questions. Essie tried to find out, oh, how she tried. She was so certain it was some one huge thing. She questioned me about Lettie and my Harald; she knew how Lettie was. But I never answered. Let Essie think whatever she wants, tell her tales. But this is how Lettie and I came to end.

The Christmas party at Essie's house and me still in my widow's black although Harald had been gone more than two years. That's how deeply I felt, Lettie should have known that. At this party I was sitting on Essie's flowered couch, a paper plate on my lap, listening to Chloe. I was eating one of those big black olives, nodding my head to whatever talk she was talking, when I heard Lettie's voice coming from the kitchen (who did not hear?) saying, "No, I don't think it's time Albertine stopped wearing black. Black suits Albertine." And then she laughed. I heard her laugh.

I went home after that and took off that black dress. I sat on my bed dressed only in my slip, my arms folded against the chilled night air, and began to think about Lettie and me. I combed through our history together.

Pulling memories like loose threads. One for the time after my third miscarriage when Lettie said to me, "Obviously the Lord doesn't intend for you to have babies, Albertine. Not every woman is meant to be a mother." A thread for the time creditors were after me, when I could have lost this home Harald and I worked so hard for (and I'll let you all know I never asked for a dime) and Lettie's answer: "Every tub must stand on its own bottom." Another for those two days Harald stayed in the hospital, those terrible last days, and she never came. Every insult, every hurt, every slight since childhood. All thought forgotten or excused or forgiven. All that I had chosen not to see. I sat there in the dark with goose bumps on my bare arms, pulling them from a place deep within me, weaving these threads together. Lettie had never been my friend. She had never loved me as I loved her.

The face I wash is old and full, skin loose and drooping beneath the chin, at the neck. Never have I been one of those women to worry about vanity and I do not try to hide my age now. I pat on a little bit of powder and line my mouth with lipstick, pale pink, not red like Lettie. Once, foolishly, I asked Essie, "Does she ever mention me?" Anything would have pleased me, even spiteful words. "Does she?" And Essie waited, I could hear her thoughts weighing whether to spare me, before answering what I knew to be true. "No," she said. "Not once." I hold my brush with tight, curled fingers. My knuckles hurt. Twist my hair and pin it in two tightly wound coils.

At the closet I fumble through my hanging dresses. Which one? The black dress with the white polka dots? No. Eh-eh. Nothing black today. The green one? The striped one? None of them seems right. Lettie will show up here in something red, hem swinging, slapping. She'll wear a hat with a feather sprouting out, or the brim trimmed with fur. Strutting up my walk without shame.

I could say no. That would serve her right. Laugh at Lettie when she asks for my help. Like she would do me. Leave her deserted. Yes. Exactly what I should do.

Such unchristian thoughts ruling my mind as I stand before the closet.

Finally, I shake my head and get back to business. It's the striped dress I finally choose.

Getting time now. She'll be here. Here. I rush over to press my dress, scorching my arm below the wrist. A bad burn, but the hurt will come later. For now I am free. Standing next to the ironing board, it takes long minutes to button up that dress. Lettie.

Sometime past two o'clock I wrap the sandwiches in wax paper and push the plate far back in the refrigerator. Cover the cake and set it back on the counter. She should have been here two hours ago. Just like Lettie. To keep me waiting. And then I realize, such a horrible thought it makes me sink into one of the kitchen chairs. I brace my elbows against the table. She's not coming.

Has nothing changed?

I hear her first. Jump up and run to the window with loud thudding steps that shake the floor, stand behind the sheer yellow curtains. Lettie's here. That's her car. The gold Cadillac. I remember how she fussed and nagged until Alonso bought it though they barely had money enough for a house to live in. I step back from the window, clap my hands, lift my feet, and turn in a circle. I have to do something with all this feeling bouncing inside me. "Lettie," I sing.

Does she ever think of the time she took me to the beach? I watched through the window that day too when she drove up in the Cadillac, new and gleaming then. "Let's go somewhere," she said, and I tugged the kerchief from my head. We drove, little Alonso not even born yet and the twins mere toddlers, fussing in the back seat, nearly two hours along the coast to a mission town. Lettie wearing her straw hat that time with a yellow scarf tied around the brim, the tail fluttering out the window. We came to a beach with the prettiest, clearest water I've ever seen, white pebbles that hurt my stockinged feet.

Lettie left us behind, her two babies and me, to climb the rocks. She found herself a place to settle, her straight black skirt pulled up, showing her thighs, and a bottle of orange pop in one hand. Her hair still colored yellow then. Harald was right: a common-looking false blond. I remember the babies crawling over my stomach, their reaching, slapping hands in my face struggling for attention, when all I wanted was to stare at Lettie sitting so bold on her rock. Not seeing us at all. And I was thinking, We ought to take these babies, Harald and me. Away from her. Raise them right. Treacherous thoughts, not like me at all, and I tried to shrug them off, a burdensome cloak around my shoulders, heavy, anchoring me. "We could run into the ocean," I whispered to those babies, gathered in my arms. "Disappear. Drown. She'd never know." And though it was hard I waited and waited until it seemed enough time had passed so I could stand and call to her, wave her back to us, shouting, "Lettie. Lettie. Let's go home."

All the times I have remembered that day and what warning I should have taken. But I've learned. I won't be a fool again.

I hurry back to the window. It's her. Lettie. Starting up my new walk. "What will she say about that?" I whisper. "My walk of different colors? About my dress? What cruel things?"

And then I see her. I see Lettie.

She's got skinny. Too skinny. Oh, that's a bad skinny.

A step closer to the window, my face pressed into the curtains. Where is her hat? She wears a wig, a cheap one, too obvious; it is brown with strands thick and straight as a horse's mane. She wears a black dress.

Black!

Lettie is dying.

Essie was right, I can see that now. This sickness has defeated her and now me too. Robbed me of my Lettie. Left me empty-handed. What business have I got against this woman here? I leave the window, don't want to see any more. Betrayed again.

Racing all around my kitchen, the nervous little brown rabbit. All the things that should give me comfort. I reach up and take Harald's glasses from the windowsill, hold them to my lips. But from them get nothing. No power. Compared to Lettie it's worthless. Everything in my pretty yellow kitchen, worthless.

So I walk back to the window and push the curtains aside. A ghost stands on my front porch, and inside myself I feel something falling. Falling.

"Lettie." Her name leaves my mouth in a wail. It carries through the glass pane and causes her to look my way. Through the window our eyes meet. Startled eyes, wondering, watchful. And then I see, what I have been searching for all along. Her red lips. Red. Red. Nothing but red. Oh, Lettie's always worn the brightest red lipstick, ever since she was a girl and her mother couldn't slap her into stopping. *See there.*

At once I am laughing. *Lettie's here. Still. She hasn't left me. Not yet. Why, I'd bet anything, beneath that wig, she still dyes her hair blond. Scarce, nappy, yellow hairs. I'd bet my life.*

She stares at me. And then, slowly, smiles.

I let go the curtain, fall back, and lean myself against the wall. Breathless.

She will ask me for this favor. I know it, and without hesitation I will answer. Yes. Always yes. Anything to keep Lettie near.

And I begin to imagine the caring of Lettie. Shopping in the market, picking out the finest okra, the best green beans. For her. Plaiting Lettie's hair, pinning it up at night so she can sleep in comfort. Peeling potatoes to simmer in a stew to feed her. Washing her soiled underclothes. Bathing her, soaping and scrubbing her pathetic, racked limbs. Sitting by her bedside, squeezing her hand when she cries out in pain.

All these visions bring me joy. My victory.

Now I stand in the middle of my kitchen, alone on the checkered tile floor, and listen to the doorbell ring. Twice more I hear it, dainty and distant, but still I have trouble moving. Finally, after what seems an instant, what feels my lifetime, I take my first step. On my way toward greeting Lettie.

Polo

CARLYLE BROWN

 Fat Polo wandered round the green felt tables, stumbling along as he always did. Unthinking, unaware. Deaf even to the *knock-clack* of the rolling billiard balls. He shuffled silently over the soft wood floor, squinting hopefully through the din and the gloom for a familiar face. He could see, in the spotlight of the hanging lamp, two players. Scratching, smoking, shifting. Their shadows looming large and distorted across the room's walls. The short one was Brooklyn Davey and the other, bright under the light of the lamp, was the albino, Amboy. Amboy's eyes glared beneath their bushy white brows, watching Davey stalk and prowl about the pool table. Little Davey was hot, and the hundred dollars in bills of fives and tens and ones that lay on the near bench were almost surely his.

Polo lifted his eyes and smiled. He recognized Duffy Eaton over in the corner. He had played a game of eight ball with Duffy just the other day. Duffy noticed Polo's glance and put a finger to his lips. But Polo meant no

CARLYLE BROWN is the author of the stage plays *The African Company Presents "Richard III," The Little Tommy Parker Celebrated Colored Minstrel Show, The Big Blue Nail, Buffalo Hair, Yellow Moon Rising, The Pool Room,* and *The Negro of Peter the Great.* He is a two-time winner of Penumbra Theatre Company's National Black Playwrighting Award, and has twice been a national PlayLabs participant. He is a core member at the Playwrights' Center in Minneapolis, and a member of New Dramatist.

harm. He only wished to watch the game in the company of a friend. He moved toward Duffy as Davey was leaning at the rail. The leather-tipped stick drew back to strike the cue ball, when Polo bumped his arm and Little Davey scratched. There was no sound except for the hollow falling of the little white ball, disappearing, deep into a corner pocket. When it stopped, the silence was enormous. Every eye was without expression. Apologetically, Polo lifted his eyes and smiled. Brooklyn Davey cocked his fist.

"Don't hit 'im, Davey!" Duffy yelled.

But it was too late. Polo had already been cut. The long thin line from the corner of his eye to the edge of his lip had already parted. Pale white tissue pouted out against his tight black skin and thick blood oozed from his face.

"Oh, shit, Davey popped him," somebody said.

"Y'll better get that dude outta here," said another.

Duffy took Polo by the arm. "C'mon, man," he said. "Let's go, Davey."

But Davey wouldn't move. He stood in the edge of the light, his arm raised and the razor wet and cradled in his fingers. Amboy wrinkled his brow and stared at the blood on the floor.

"You scratched, Davey," he said. "That bread ain't yours."

Davey turned at Amboy and cocked his fist again.

"Easy, Davey," came a low and mellow voice. "A half a hundred is cool."

Diamond Studs stepped from the shadows: his hat broke down, his sheepskin coat heaped high about his shoulders, his pinky ring gleaming in the lamplight. He picked up the money from the near bench in a hasty, full-fisted counting. Leaving fifty dollars, he slid the rest in his pocket. Boldly he stared about the room. He smiled and backed away. It was all a blur to Polo. He was there, locked inside himself, shocked and isolated even from his own pain. He moved along at Duffy Eaton's insistence, with Brooklyn Davey and Diamond Studs stepping silently behind. Together they vanished through the door, without protest or resistance. Amboy shaded his eyes as he watched them leave the edges of the hanging light of the lamp. They led Polo down the hallway and up the long narrow stairs to the roof. The rumpled tar strips bumped and buckled beneath their feet as they tiptoed near to the roof ledge above the iron fire escape below. They sat Polo down on the cold grilled steps. Diamond Studs spoke slowly, stabbing a finger in his face.

"Them face cuts is always worse than they look. It's a lucky thing you wasn't hit any lower. There was a lotta money out there ridin', man. People don't like to just give their bread away. You was wrong, my man, whether you meant to be or not. So if you got a beef with Davey, then you got a beef with me and Duffy too."

Duffy handed Polo his red bandanna, and Davey rocked with a nervous roll as if he'd strike again.

"That's all I got to say to you," Diamond Studs went on, and then he turned and walked away.

Davey stood there glaring and wouldn't move until Duffy tugged on his arm to come and go away. Polo watched them feed the shadows, walking calmly and detached into the darkness across the roof. He saw their shapes and felt their manner. Sensed their security and relief, stirring envy in his hate. He looked up into the black, lifeless sky and blood fell in his ear. It made a noise like water dripping on porcelain from a leaky tap, and he sat there quietly, listening to its sound.

Goodbye Washington

WAYNE BROWN

Okay, so there's this girl on the bus. Smallish, thirty, thirty-five, hard to tell—these women age faster than our women—with dark-blond careless hair and a face you'd like. It's a face that's lived, that says things haven't always been easy, that it's known its fair share of men and grief but that it's come up each time smiling.

It's a nice face and its owner is sitting there, in corduroy jeans and a black corduroy jacket and a silk scarf, and I'm thinking she's hard to place. Brazilian, maybe, but not typical, or French, but not typical French. But then we get to talking and it turns out she's Italian and her name is Cinzia. She has a gaze that attaches to you while you're talking, and her voice is like that, friendly, steady, and she talks with an accent, only not so's you'd notice it; not unless you were attentive to such things.

I'm in Washington for a week en route to a convocation of writers in, of all places, Iowa. She is a student of film, or so I gather, here for some seminar on the art of moviemaking. Cinzia. Cinzia something. She told me her last name but I forget it.

WAYNE BROWN, a native of Trinidad and Tobago, is the author of *The Child of the Sea* (stories and essays), *Voyages* (poems), *On the Coast* (poems), and *Edna Manley: The Private Years* (biography). He has also edited two books of poetry: *Derek Walcott: Selected Poetry* and *Twenty-One Years of "Poetry and Audience."*

Anyway, we hit it off, and soon we're laughing and joshing the driver, all the way in from the airport, because the bus is nearly empty and because there's a fine spaciousness and serenity about Washington—which isn't strictly speaking a city, but the administrative capital of the Greatest Nation on Earth—and because we're both here on vacation from our lives and feeling already ten years younger, or at least I am.

We're driving north toward Constitution, past the pristine white phallus of the Washington Monument, standing by itself in a faultless blue sky, with, on the right, past the Smithsonian, the grassy slopes rolling up Capitol Hill, wide open, as if this could be country, the wind banging on the panes of the bus; and there's something quite ingenuous yet truly impressive about the Federal architecture. Graeco-Colonial, I'd call it, if that made any sense, because behind it you can feel this phenomenal placid self-confidence, yet also this little air of surprise; and it's all splendidly proportionate yet somehow lighthearted; self-confident, whimsical, and fine. There are places in this country where, if it ever reached them, the idea of America has been lost; in its daily doings, Washington may be one of them; but the men who built Washington never doubted for one moment the grandeur and insouciance of that idea.

Something French here: a feeling of *boulevardes*. The wind smells of the sea. Up close the White House looks less formidable, looks like somewhere you could conceivably live. I do not see Mr. Reagan. Neither, reports Cinzia, does she. 'What a shame,' I say, and 'What a shame!' she echoes, and the driver chuckles: 'You guys'll jes' have t'cum beck!' For her benefit mainly, I bet him he doesn't remember Brando's great line in *On the Waterfront*. He glances at me amusedly. 'You mean—' and he says it in a wry drawl: 'Charlie, Charlie, Charlie! Ah coulda bin a cun*tenda*h! Ah coulda bin sambaady!' I say, 'Aw-*riiight!*' and slap him on the shoulder, and Cinzia is looking out the window, smiling—she knows the line too, you can tell—as we hang a right on Pennsylvania and then another right, and now the city closes in a little.

I disembark at the Du Pont; she's going on. We shake hands, and I wish her a happy life and a great career and a dozen Italianate babies, and mostly that she should behave herself while in Washington, which is the administrative capital of Quote Unquote; and I leave it at that and follow the porter inside, because sometimes you have to leave it at that, sometimes you have to take what the moment gives and not get greedy and push—and half a minute later, I'm checking in, this guy I'd hardly noticed on the bus comes in and says Chinzy says to tell me she's staying at Hotel X; and he goes back out to the bus.

This is nice, but so strange (I mean, who's that guy?) that I neglect to write down the name of her hotel, and up in my room I discover I've forgotten it. I try hard, but it's gone. I think, Fool!, knowing now I'll never see her again—and two days later, whaddaya know, me and Cinzia, we run into each other in a stand-up eatery in a mall.

So we're talking, standing there, not eating, till it's nearly time to go; and then she says they're showing her film at the Kennedy Center tomorrow night, and would I come to it and to the party afterwards. I say 'Sure,' and she turns to this guy, who materialises out of nowhere once again, and tells him (*who* is this guy?) that Mr. Brown will be coming to her showing, and he pulls out a notebook and obediently writes this down.

But the funny thing was, I wasn't going! I said 'Sure,' but I just wasn't—don't ask me why. And even if I'd been maybe going when I said it, by the next day I definitely wasn't, because by then I'd come down with the airport flu and was feeling self-cherishing and petulant; and how I ended up going was: I had this *other* engagement I couldn't duck out of. It was a formal do hosted by the Institute of International Education, and I felt I had to go, flu or no; so I suited up and went over to the place.

And it was one of those horrible, glitzy, dead affairs, where five hundred people each talk to you for seventeen seconds exactly and you end up feeling lonely as hell; and to cap it all somebody wrote out a name tag and said smilingly that I should wear it. WAYNE BROWN, TRINIDAD, it said.

Now, I have to tell you: you ever want to get rid of me in a hurry, give me a name tag to wear. I don't know why, but wearing a name tag makes me feel the way a racehorse looks that definitely doesn't want to race, stutter-stepping down to the starting gates with its neck lathered, its head swung sideways, and the whites of its eyes showing. I mean, it's that bad. Name tags blow my mind, like the promise of immortality suddenly rescinded. I hid it under an hors d'oeuvre but it was no use, everybody else was wearing theirs, and the lady who'd written mine out caught up with me and said, 'Naughty boy, you've lost it,' and wrote me out another one.

So I had to get out of there. I remembered Chinzy and thought, An appointment at the Kennedy Center might sound like a grand enough excuse; and so I made the rounds of my hosts, making it. My hosts shook their heads and made clicking noises which sounded like disapproval feigning disappointment, but I was out. I dropped my second name tag in a plant pot, lit a cigarette, and took a cab back to the hotel; and then got bogged down in the idea of going to the Kennedy Center after all. Because Chinzy was *nice,* and we'd gotten on so well, and she probably wanted moral support while her little documentary ran before the critical eyes of two dozen fellow seminarians, who would pick it to shreds, artistically speaking, at their next seminar, and besides—yeah—who could say what the ensuing party might bring?

The evening had gotten cool, and by now I was sick, *sick*; so I changed and put on a sweatshirt and a jacket over that and then I hailed a cab and went over to the Kennedy Center—and got lost. I got lost in the Kennedy Center, and couldn't find Chinzy's theater, and not one but two extremely unpleasant middle-aged ladies asked me at different times, with extreme nastiness, kindly to put out that cigarette, smoking having become the newest apparition of evil to American Puritanism, and smokers being pursued here nowadays every bit as humorlessly as the flower children once stoned with petals returning Vietnam vets. And I was about to give up and go back to the hotel and take a dozen aspirins and get into bed, when the elevator doors opened—not by my hand—and I looked full face into the reception of Chinzy's film.

And it was a big thing.

I mean, the place was full, the guys all had on tuxedos, the ladies all had on, like, gowns, there were chandeliers . . . there was even a reception line! I looked at the reception line and thought: Cinzia? I looked at the reception line and thought: I am the only sweatshirt-wearing person in a roomful of tuxedo-wearing persons. I looked at the reception line and thought: I am too damn sick to even *think* about all this, and anyway they said this was America; and like that I went down the reception line, being introduced as a writer from Jamaica—and, when I corrected this, as a writer from Treeneedad, Jamaica—and a friend of Cinzia's; and met the Deputy Chairman of, I think, MGM, guy called Rosenthal, who graciously offered me a ride to the party afterwards in his limousine (he said that: limousine); and I mean, these people had class! Not one of them glanced at my sweatshirt. Not one of them betrayed anything other than cordial welcome. Can you imagine if this had been, say, the Royal Albert Hall?

And so I came out at the other end of the reception line for the premiere of this full-length feature film *Hotel Colonial*—starring John Savage and Robert Duvall and directed by my little Cinzia—and stood around dazed and discovering to my dismay that when I said my name in this country, Wayne, everybody replied uncertainly, William? Wyn? ('Say Waaayne!' said a friend, weeks later, 'You have to draw it out,' but I never could bring myself to do that, not to my own name, for chrissakes, and so it must be goodbye America, because how do you abide in a country where they can't even pronounce your name?) and in due course was introduced to John Savage.

He looked a nice enough kid, manly, clean, no foppery, none of that; but 'Chinzy's friend' is a phrase, the more it's said, the more meaningful it starts to sound; and it wasn't long before I registered that his conversation had the not-so-covert goal of discovering how well—how well, *exactly*—I happened to know his director. Which is the wrong tack to take with a Treeneedadian Jamaican who's feeling sick and sorry for himself, and who's already had about as much drama as he's willing to take in one night. I essayed what felt at least like an evil smile, and then looked around and said I hadn't seen his co-star, and learned from him that Duvall was off in France filming; and then an admirer pounced and led him away, and someone else was standing in front of me saying, 'Hi, I'm X. I gather you're a friend of Cinzia's?'

And Cinzia was late. Cinzia was so late that everybody gave up standing around and went and sat down in the theatre; and the ol' Savage was just taking one last shot at me, twisting around to inquire across several intervening rows of seats whether I had Chinzy's hotel room number on me, when she arrived, with—bless her cheerful heart—the dark-blond careless hair still so, and dressed in the corduroy jacket and jeans and the scarf, but looking distinctly unfocussed as she glided in, gently propelled by a tuxedoed gentleman. Everybody clapped and clapped, and Savage rose and went over to sit with her in the front row, and the guy Rosenthal made a short speech in which he talked about 'the privilege' of having Cinzia present in person for the premiere; and then they killed the lights and the movie began.

And, O my people, *Hotel Colonial* was bad! That movie was so bad!

Savage had a strong face, good bones, strong lines, and every time he appeared on screen the camera made love to it ('Ah-ha!' I thought, suddenly thinking I understood), but for the rest she had overreached herself, had tried to make a humdrum thriller about the Colombian cocaine trade into some kind of Statement and failed; failed in that awful overreaching way that mashes up everything: the timing gone wrong, the pace of the movie shot to hell, the dialogue sounding portentous-absurd, the plot not artfully staccato, just incomprehensible; and I sat in the dark shivering with fever —because American public buildings, the grander they're supposed to be, the higher they turn up the air-conditioning—and thought with pain for her, *Oh, Jesus, Cinzia,* because at the end the lights would come on and she'd be there, helpless before five hundred pairs of eyes, with her frank, level gaze, and the careless hair, and the corduroy outfit with the scarf.

And then, I don't know, but somehow the fever and the shivering and the pain for her got mixed up with the glitz of the occasion, but also with the true civility of it, and then with the badness of what we were watching—and all of it swirled together and started draining away like water through the black hole of a sink when you pull the plug, and I knew I was losing Washington, which I'd only just found, and all I could think was: I want to go home.

And then it's over, and the lights come on. There's a moment's silence, then everybody starts clapping, and I'm watching Savage sitting there, slowly shaking his head, the *bastard*, with Cinzia sitting unmoving next to him and looking straight ahead.

The guy Rosenthal makes a short speech thanking everybody and reminding them of the party at his place, and we all rise, talking, and start filing out. I know by now I'm not going to any party, I'm going *home*, but it occurs to me I may be the only person there who can tell her what she needs to hear, which is, 'Okay, so you blew it. Forget it. It happens to everybody sometime. Go back to Italy and start again.' And I'm thinking I'll tell her that, and maybe after all this is over and done she'll be okay; or at least she and I, we'll have been okay.

But I must be either sicker or a bigger heel than I thought, because I come up to her and I say—nothing. Not a word. She is standing there, stoned with pain, and as I come up she glances at me, but without hope; and what I do is, I kiss her, gravely, precisely, on the cheek. She murmurs, 'You're going?' and I look at her and nod, doing everything now with a somnambulist's glide and not saying anything to anybody, and get into the elevator.

In the elevator there's this young guy and this bejewelled matron, and they're strangers to each other but they're talking. She's connected with a Washington newspaper. Going down, she asks him what he thought of *Hotel Colonial*, and, 'I thought it was terrible,' he tells her flatly. There is a silence while she considers him expressionlessly; and then she asks him his name. He gives it, and I think to myself, This kid's editor had better stand by him, because in her voice and look now is a certain steel that says, There's a billion dollars behind me that's going to string you up like a scarecrow, young man. And then I'm out of the Kennedy Center and crossing over to the bus stop, feeling the Washington night less cold than her theatre had been, and fumbling for a cigarette.

Okay. So in the bus stop, waiting, there's this girl. Angular, high yella, amused eyes, bony hands. We get to talking and turns out she's Jamaican, over from California, where she lives, to vacation with a girlfriend in Washington. 'I used to live in Jamaica,' I tell her, and as I say it it sounds to my ears like a phenomenally portentous piece of information. She asks, and I say I'm a writer, but she thinks, I think, I'm giving her a line and in that lovely Jamaica woman's drawl, centuries of bored amusement and disbelief behind it, inquires the name of a book I've written: any book.

I look at her and want to smile, despite everything—despite how sick I'm feeling, and the pain of Cinzia and *her* pain, and despite how bad I'd let her down, and how bad her film had been; despite, even, how I'd gone and lost Washington, which I'd only just found—and I'm smiling, I can't help it, because in her gaze, and in the skeptical dry amusement of her voice, is a place that feels to me like home. I say, 'A biography—*Edna Manley: The Private Years*,' and, '*Rah-tid!*' she says.

Playing the Game

BEBE MOORE CAMPBELL

Way before the three husbands and three divorces, Hannah had figured out that all men are saps, without sense enough to eat three squares a day unless some woman handed them the food; they were ruled by their lower heads. You don't question that, she learned so very long ago, you work it. That way, you're not calling them; they're begging you. Hannah hadn't loved any of them. Not even in the beginning. She'd made sure enough of that.

Of course, her father's walking out on the family when she was six had something to do with her hostility, she acknowledged to the counselor they went to after Ted, the third one, pleaded with her to try to "save our marriage." Sitting in that cool gray office, a kind of inchoate rage began to grip her by the throat. She sputtered the words.

"No, I didn't grow up with my father, Dr. Bergman." What passed through her mind like a dark, drifting cloud, what made her shiver as she sat in the Naugahyde chair, was the memory of that frigid day in February when she was twelve, the last time she ever waited for her father. She stood

BEBE MOORE CAMPBELL is the author of the memoir *Sweet Summer: Growing Up With and Without My Dad* and of the novels *Your Blues Ain't Like Mine* and *Brothers and Sisters*. Her work has appeared in *The New York Times, The Washington Post, Los Angeles Times, MS., Essence, Black Enterprise, Ebony, Working Mother,* and *Adweek,* among many others. She is a regular contributor to National Public Radio.

at the corner of Broad and Susquehanna, because her father had told her to be there, said he would come and take her to buy a dress. The snow began dancing in the air around her, flakes swirling in such a thick haze that she could barely make out the marquee on the Uptown Theater, bringing Philly's finest in black entertainment. NOW APPEARING: DINAH WASHINGTON, QUEEN OF THE BLUES. Hannah waited, bareheaded and gloveless —in her rush to meet her father, she'd left her hat and gloves at home— searching through the crowd for his jovial face. Where was he? Where? He had promised to come. And even though he'd broken his word before, she remained steadfast, like a little soldier, watching every breath she took turn into frosty jets that slowly disappeared. Her trancelike endurance was broken abruptly when a tiny boy in a red snowsuit slid and then slipped on the icy sidewalk, landing just at her feet. His head made a cracking noise against the sidewalk, like a doll-house door being slammed shut. Instant screams cut through the frozen air, jolting Hannah from her reverie. When she looked down, the boy's tiny mouth was gaping open, his eyes were clenched shut; blood dripped in small circles onto the ice. A man's hands —strong, dark hands, she recalled, with scars across the knuckles— snatched the child from the ground and lifted him away, leaving behind only the drops of blood, small indentations in the snow.

Streetlamps flashed on and the crowd on the street thinned out. An old woman hobbling on a cane asked her, "Little girl, you waiting for someone? You lost?" Yes, she wanted to scream, a gradual near-hysteria enveloping her. The snow was falling furiously, getting into her mouth and eyes. She was trembling. When she tried to speak, to nod, no words came out. It was as though her voice and everything inside her had frozen into something hard and impenetrable. She stood on the corner for nearly two hours, then finally trudged home alone in the dark.

Her mother greeted her silently at the front door and led her upstairs, where she ran a hot bath for her. Later, she massaged Hannah's feet, which were stiff and aching. She was a dark, heavy woman, her beauty lost in the hard set of her mouth, the frigidity of her glance, and as her fingers stopped kneading Hannah's toes and ankles, she suddenly clamped her daughter's chin in between her thumb and pointing finger. Hannah felt her mother's eyes boring into hers. Her mother spoke in a clear, level voice; she didn't sound upset.

Days later, when her father called with excuses and more promises, Hannah held the phone away from her still numb ears; anything that touched them hurt. So she barely heard her father, wasn't even sure he'd finished speaking to her when she gently hung up the telephone. Her mother was in the room with her, and she said very quietly, "You don't waste your time waiting for any of them. Not ever."

"We had no relationship, Dr. Bergman," Hannah affirmed, her back straight and rigid, her hands in two tight fists, so that her long red fingernails cut into her palms. Ted, sitting near her, didn't dare touch or hold those tense fingers.

"And how do you feel about that, Hannah?"

"I don't feel anything about that."

Asshole, she said to herself, staring at the therapist's placid white face, his pale throat, thin lips moving erratically as she uncrossed her long lovely legs. Her high heels cracked sharply against the oak floor. The clicks reverberated as she strode to the door, scarcely noticing the two astonished faces she was leaving behind. Asshole, she mentally repeated, looking straight into Ted's wide, anxious eyes. Assholeassholeasshole.

"Hannah? Hannah?"

She thought, as the door slammed closed, For 75 dollars an hour, ask me something that matters.

"Baby," she called to Ted later that night. She had emerged from the bathtub and walked into their bedroom, her nude body glistening from the lotion she was rubbing across her breasts, her thick dark hair skimming her golden shoulders. "We're just dragging this thing out." He walked toward her, hearing nothing but his own desire. He was wearing that goony, mesmerized look that she despised. Absolutely despised.

"You sure are a beautiful woman, Hannah," Ted mumbled, staring at her. "Still look like a young girl, you know that. God, you're fine." He was whining now. She continued rubbing herself as she watched him, concentrating on her nipples, but at the same time she tilted her head slightly and with just a flicker of her eyes the tiny bit of amusement faded from her face and when Ted looked again, there was no kindness there. Ted stopped and stood absolutely still, as though he were straining to understand the last lyrics of a fading song. He yelled suddenly, his voice rippling with shock and pain, "This is just a game to you, isn't it?"

Hannah didn't answer. She was staring at her nipple, fingering it carefully, her lips parted sweetly, her eyes now half-closed slits. The laughter she heard was completely in her head, as was the answer to his question: Yeah. Monday night football.

By the time Ted was scheduled to move out, he was, of course, given to unpredictable fits of rage and violence. One night he snatched a crystal clock off a shelf and smashed it to bits. Another day he hurled a pan through the kitchen window. He grabbed Hannah by the throat and pushed her into a wall; the veins and blood in his eyes blinded her. The hot spurts of his jagged whiskey breath on her cheeks and eyelids, her mouth, made her gasp. "Bitch," he said dully. She didn't scream, just stared at him the whole time.

"Are you satisfied?" she asked him quietly when he released her.

"Are you?" he rejoined, his breath still in her nostrils.

"Always."

"The usual he-man bullshit," Hannah told her friend Terri, who had come as soon as she called. She was laughing when she said this, her shoulders hunched, her head thrown back so her heavy hair tumbled halfway down her silk shirt. "You're my protection."

"You're crazy to be here with him," Terri admonished sternly. She ran short, stubby fingers through her cropped hair, which was wild and uncombed. There were paint stains on her jeans and sneakers. "Go to my house. I'll stay here and lock up. Give me your keys."

Hannah handed her the keys, the tips of her long, lacquered nails clicking against the metal.

"A lot of women would be dead doing what you do, Hannah. He's a nice man. He loves you."

"What do I do?" Hannah's tone was mocking and proud.

"You dog men. Just because you can."

"No. I don't love them, that's all. I never love them."

"I worry about you, girl."

"I should be worrying about you. You're the one always falling in love and getting hurt. Didn't you lend the last one five hundred dollars? Have you seen the dude? Or your money?"

"So I'm a sucker," Terri said evenly, looking into her friend's eyes.

"So I'm not," Hannah quipped.

"All right, all right," Terri said wearily. "Just go to my house. Where is he?"

"In the bedroom."

After Hannah left, Terri took a long, hard breath before knocking on the bedroom door. When she spoke, it was in the cajoling tone of a mother to a three-year-old. "It's Terri, Ted. Sweetheart, open the door. I know you're upset, dear. I just want to talk with you."

In the end Ted gave Hannah the house without a fight and kept calling her until she changed her number. A year after the divorce she ran into him at a party. He was drunk and with a woman that Hannah would later describe to Terri as "a child." "But the funniest part," Hannah said, giggling helplessly, her hands gripping Terri's wrists, as her friend solemnly shook her head, "when I started to introduce him to Andrew, I couldn't remember his name. I forgot his name!" She howled, dropping her head and butting Terri gently in her chest. Still laughing, she put her arm around Terri and drew her close.

Andrew didn't last long either. In the seven years since Hannah's third divorce there had been a steady progression of dates and boyfriends. Now she was about to drop Michael, her latest lover. "He's getting too close," she told Terri one Friday evening when the two of them were stretched out on her living room floor watching videos and painting their nails.

"Maybe he's in love with you."

"He's not giving up enough cash to be in love with me."

"You're really amazing, you know that? Most women are complaining that they can't find anybody decent, and you're constantly discarding men because they want to get too close."

"That's because most women want a commitment. I don't."

"Well, what *do* you want?"

Hannah angled her head so that the large diamonds in her ears shimmered. "I want to call the shots."

"You'd better think about what you're doing, Hannah. You're getting too old to throw over every nice man who comes your way."

Hannah snorted. "A true hot mama never gets old. She just goes up in flames, baby."

Too old! None of her lovers ever guessed that she wasn't young, Hannah told herself. Some of her boyfriends were in their early thirties! All of them were attentive. She had a mink coat to show for one affair, a trip to Paris from another, and several cruises. The trips, especially the cruises, were not all that pleasant actually. She had only recently sailed the Caribbean with Michael. Cramped into the airless cabin, she felt claustrophobic, forever bumping into a man she didn't want to touch her. The good part was dinner at the captain's table, walking around the promenade, her gown barely brushing her escort's shoes. She could manage Michael's hand resting lightly on the small of her back, an imperceptible touch, easy to wriggle away from. Under the table her hand meandered up the curve of his thigh, squeezing, squeezing, squeezing, until his eyes glazed over with the abject weakness that was her triumph. On the dance floor she stared at him, opened her mouth a little, made tiny circles with her tongue, and then, when she could see desire outlining every movement in his body, danced away. Dancing away, that's what she liked best.

She certainly didn't want to be like Terri, all strung out over some middle-aged lothario, sitting by the phone waiting for it to ring and being ridiculously happy when it did. Enraptured over some man who wasn't even hers. At her age *that* was ridiculous. She looked over at her friend and decided that Terri could stand to lose a good fifteen pounds and definitely needed a haircut and another dye job; the gray was beginning to show. A frown creased Hannah's brows as she watched Terri apply a second coat of polish to her fingernails. So stupid, falling for some asshole! Being so damn happy about it. "How's your friend?" Hannah snapped.

Terri's face got soft, her eyes dreamy; she didn't even notice Hannah's tone. She held the tiny nail polish brush still in midair. "He's wonderful."

"Didn't you tell me he was married?"

"He's in the process of getting a divorce."

"Process, huh? Where do you find them? In other words, the man is still living with his wife and kids."

"The kids are grown and gone. And Hannah, the wife's been playing on him for years."

"Oh, she's been cheating," Hannah said sarcastically. She sighed. "Baby, you need to learn how to play the game. A man like that: You let him buy you things, take you places. You don't get close. You don't risk your heart. You never risk anything. Learn how to play the game."

Terri stiffened. "Don't lecture me, okay? I'm a big girl. Anyway," she said, her tone warming, "Randy's taking us out for Mother's Day." Her face brightened when she spoke of her son. "Did I tell you he's already lined up interviews with law firms?"

"Coming out of Penn with a JD and an MBA? What do you expect? The boy is probably the most educated black man on the planet."

"And he's in love."

"Oh, Lord."

"He's bringing her with him. We're all going to dinner."

"But I'm not his mother."

"You know Randy's crazy about you. Besides, you're his godmother."

Which had been poor judgment on Terri's part. Hannah had told Terri that from the get-go, more than twenty years ago, when she bestowed the dubious honor upon her friend. "I'm not godmother material, and I don't baby-sit" was the first thing out of Hannah's mouth. She wasn't going to have any children of her own; she'd already decided that. She'd wanted to tell Terri that if she had had any kids, they wouldn't have been boys. Her body never would have committed such a betrayal.

"You'll grow into the job," Terri told her.

But she hadn't. She gave Randy lavish birthday and Christmas presents, and when Terri's ex-husband balked at paying for private school and later for college tuition, she helped out with a more than occasional check. But Hannah had never been at ease with children, and as for hands-on god-mothering, she'd come up short. During all the years Randy was growing up, Hannah had taken him to three movies and to the circus once. Although, of course, he was always with Terri whenever the two women visited, which was often. Hannah marveled at how her friend could listen to the child's whining and crying without murdering him. How could she stand being interrupted a million times with *Mommy! Mommy!* But he was a cute little boy. One year he gave her a homemade birthday card, brought it to her house and stood in front of her grinning, two blank spaces where his two front teeth should have been.

"Hold out your hand, Aunt Hannah," he commanded. He slapped the card down in her palm of her hand. "Happy Birthday!" Then he kissed her. His lips felt like soft suede; his breath smelled like bubble gum. She put her arms around him and squeezed him tight. The card was still in the bottom of her desk drawer.

But really, through all the years of Randy's childhood, Hannah was better at hearing about his exploits, being Terri's sounding board for all the boy's growing pains, than ministering to him herself: the nightmares and bed-wetting when he was five and six; the allergies when he was seven and eight. She remembered an occasion when Randy was eleven and she dropped by, and when he opened the door she saw that the skin beneath his eye was as black and shiny as licorice. "Do you think I should put him in another school?" Terri had asked worriedly.

And Hannah told her, "Listen, there are bullies everydamnwhere you go. Don't make a little sissy out of him. Send his butt to karate school. Toughen him up."

But Terri sent him to private school anyway. Went into debt paying for the tuition and lessons, the designer this and that the boy never even asked for. Brand-new car for high school graduation. Hannah couldn't quite figure out how Randy had turned out to be as quiet, smart, and decent as he had. Always remembering his mother at holidays. Even remembering Aunt Hannah. A fluke, she thought.

Mother's Day was cool, the wind crisp as it brushed Hannah's face. The restaurant was out-of-doors. Miriam, Randy's girl, was pretty, like an exotic wild bird, with a graceful body and tinted hair that kept blowing around her face. Hannah watched as she pushed her hair out of her eyes and then looked up at Randy with a glance so penetrating that he stammered in mid-sentence. Hannah observed this gaze and stammering all during dinner, and by dessert she realized that it occurred at regular intervals. The thought intrigued her. Under the table Hannah sensed movement between Miriam and Randy, a faint rustling, back and forth, back and forth. While the waiter poured the water she perceived the faint metallic rip of a zipper. She told herself this was only her imagination, and to reassure herself she looked steadily at Miriam, whose hands were hidden. The girl was chatting about their future plans, hers and Randy's, in a soft, self-assured voice, a monotone really, nodding toward Terri, who smiled at her every now and then, only looking at Randy occasionally. His eyes, Hannah noticed at once, were glazed over and unfocused. Before she could stop herself, Hannah kicked him. She met his startled gaze with her own unflinching eyes. "You with us, baby?" she asked mildly.

Terri called her the next day. "They want to get married." She paused; Hannah waited. "I don't know. I want him to be happy. She's nice. No. She's not nice. I shouldn't say that. Something tells me she's wrong for him. You always read people so well. What do you think?"

"She'll eat him alive."

"Talk to him, Hannah."

"Me?"

"Please. I can't be . . . detached."

When Hannah opened the door the next evening, Randy and Miriam were kissing, the girl's arms wrapped tightly around his neck. They were taut arms, Hannah noted, firm. Jane Fonda arms. Randy put his hands around Miriam's waist and pulled away from her. She continued to stare into his eyes with a look that could pass for intensity, except Hannah knew better. Watching her, Hannah thought, The kid's good.

Miriam giggled. "Sorry, Mrs. Kinsey. We got carried away." She pressed herself against Randy until he looked at her. "I guess I'm just weak for him," she said, slowly and softly.

"Call me Hannah, baby."

There was only so much she could say to Randy while Miriam went to the bathroom. The trouble was, Hannah didn't really know what was propelling her. He wasn't her kid; he wasn't her man. She felt unsettled, confused. "Randy. You know your mother and I talk a lot."

He looked at her with bright, alert eyes, and for a second she smelled bubble gum and felt the velvet of his dark face against hers.

"You don't want to—uh, rush into anything. You're a young man, with a whole lot going for you. Take your time, sweetie." She touched his arm with her fingertips.

He smiled and reached out for Hannah's hand. "I've found what I want. I'm in love."

Hannah leaned forward. Searching Randy's face, she was amazed to still see that gap-toothed kid. Her words spilled out. "Look. You're grown. I know that. But I also know that everything that's good *to* you ain't good *for* you."

"You don't even know her—"

"Live with her. Don't get married."

"She's pregnant," he blurted.

Oldest trick in the book, she thought. Randy read the look on her face and it was awkward between them after that. Miriam walked in and seemed to sense discord. Hannah offered them another glass of wine, but they declined and left quickly. When they had gone, Hannah sat on her sofa for a while. Then she went to the mirror, rolled up her sleeves, and stared at her upper arms.

The baby boy was born five months after the small, somber wedding. Hannah sent Randy a check for $500 and scribbled *Send me a picture* at the bottom of the card. According to Terri, the problems started immediately. Miriam wanted Randy to do everything: Take care of the baby. Keep the house clean. Work. "She doesn't even pay attention to her own child, let alone Randy," Terri fumed. "I don't even think she's giving him any, or maybe just enough to keep him hanging on." Then Terri laughed. "But my grandson, honey, that boy is something. You know, he's trying to sit up."

Hannah mumbled, "I'll bet he is," and hung up as quickly as possible. She poured herself a glass of Chablis and sat down at her kitchen table, the newspaper spread before her. Hardly paying attention, she glanced down at the page. Obituaries. Death didn't interest her. When she thought about it later, she'd recall that the name John Kinsey, her father's name, didn't leap out at her at all. Rather, she saw the words at first and continued to read with only a vague sense of familiarity: *74 years old . . . of cancer. . . . Survived by his wife, Elizabeth Bennett; a daughter, Hannah Kinsey; a stepson, John . . . services have been held.* The words began to blur. She held the newspaper in front of her, seeing nothing, wondering vaguely why the pages were moving when she couldn't feel the wind.

She drove the few blocks to Terri's like something frightening was chasing her. "What's wrong?" Terri said after Hannah had come in. She was wearing an apron. Her hair was wild, the gray at least an inch thick at the roots.

"My father died. Ten days ago. I just read it in the paper."

They both looked up when they heard the heavy footsteps.

"Oh," Hannah said.

"Hannah, you remember Rick?" The man stood between the two women. He put his hand on Terri's shoulder. She reached up and held his fingers.

"Sure. How are you? Listen, I'd better be going."

"You don't have to go. Stay. I'm cooking dinner now."

"She can really cook," Rick said happily. He smiled at Terri.

"No. No. I'll—uh, I'll call you later."

Hannah sat in her car in front of Terri's and listened to three rap songs on the radio before she even looked at the clock and remembered she had a dinner date. She had to go home and get dolled up. That would fill her night.

Mike bought a bottle of champagne at the restaurant. The best. After three glasses, Hannah was seized with a sense of giddy delight at the way the flame in the candles on their table frolicked before them. She leaned toward Mike and whispered softly, so as not to disturb the light, "My daddy died. He was seventy-four."

Mike carefully placed his glass on the table. "I'm sorry to hear that, baby. He die recently?"

Hannah nodded, observing how sad the light was, how sad, really, everything was.

Mike looked at her, his gaze openly curious and with a lack of desire that Hannah found alarming. "Seventy-four? So how old does that make you, baby?"

Randy brought his son to see Hannah when he was three months old. It was a spontaneous visit, and Hannah was still in her robe and rollers. Her hand flew to her face as she unlocked the door. He carried the infant in a car seat that became a kind of portable rocker when he set it on Hannah's kitchen floor. They drank coffee, and later she scrambled some eggs and made toast. They ate and talked while the baby gurgled softly, and when the child did start to cry, Randy reached in a soft bag and pulled out a bottle of milk. Holding the boy close to his chest, he put the bottle in his mouth, staring as he sucked. "Yeah, man, that's good, huh?" he whispered to the baby. Hannah moved closer to them.

"You were right, Hannah," he told her after the baby drifted off to sleep.

"About what?"

"Miriam and me. It's not working." His face sort of crumpled, like a sugary pink bubble going flat.

"Well . . ." she said, patting his hand, then holding it. "Well."

She began calling him once in a while, always beginning the conversation with a light "Just checking in," which was, of course, all she was doing. Sometimes they talked for just a few minutes. Sometimes for an hour.

"Remember that time you picked me up from school when my mother's car broke down?" he said once.

"Yes." Truly, she'd forgotten.

"Boy, I was so proud."

"Of what?"

"You had on a cape. Red. I remember that. And you ran toward me and the wind lifted up your cape and your hair was blowing all around your face. You looked like a queen. Really. All the kids asked me the next day, 'Who was the beautiful lady that came to get you?' "

"Well, honey, the beautiful lady is fading fast."

"No, you're not. You look great. You don't look much older than I."

"I don't think I'm talking about the way I look."

He called one night after eleven o'clock. His voice penetrated her somnolent haze. "Hannah, Miriam left today. She took the baby. I didn't want to call Mom. She can't handle this kind of stuff." He began to mumble something. She thought he was crying. Hannah could see his shoulders shaking, his face contorted. She held the phone away from her for a moment, then put it close to her ear.

She didn't sleep that night.

He came to her house one Friday evening three weeks later. She opened the door and saw that his eyes were so wild, his expression so strange and disconnected that for a moment he looked like a different man, a man who could break things, hurt people. This man was familiar to her. In that brief space as he stood in her doorway she could see his future drifting away from him, right out of his hands. The baby was behind him in a backpack.

"I have to go to class. Bar review. Can you keep him for me?" His eyes were pleading with her.

"Is this kidnapping?" Hannah asked, her voice unsteady.

"He's *my* son too, goddammit. She doesn't give a damn about the baby. She just wants to punish me. She's been punishing me ever since we met. What did I do, besides love her? What?" He looked at her.

She shook her head.

"Look, I don't want to complicate your life, but I just need a favor.

Rick moved in with Mom. They're getting married. He's an okay guy. I don't want to impose on them. She's sacrificed a lot for me, you know. She's not getting any younger. I don't want to mess things up for her."

"I didn't know that."

"What?"

"That they were together." She clutched her arms to her chest as though she were embracing herself.

"You've always been so . . . so, I don't know . . . cool. I always thought you could handle everything."

Hannah laughed and clenched her fists.

"So, what do you say? Can you do this for me once a week for the next three months?"

"Baby-sit."

They stood in the doorway silently for a moment, and then the baby began to whimper. Hannah hesitated. Her Fridays were for expensive dinners, champagne, for dancing away. Away. There was wariness in her eyes, but her hands were already on the child, pulling the boy in to her chest. The heat from his small body was so sudden, so penetrating, that she almost cried aloud at the joy of it. She had never known there was baby talk hidden deep inside her.

"Come here, little man. Come to Hannah."

The Drill

BREENA CLARKE

 "Take the bus out Forty-second Street—the cross-town bus, the M42—and get off at Seventh Avenue. Then take the Number One train. Get off at 157th Street. Don't get off at 168th Street. Okay? When you're riding the Number One and you get off at 168th Street, you have to ride the elevator and the elevator is nasty. Also, there are too many homeless people on the platform at 168th Street. Anything can happen in that station. Don't get off at 168th Street. Take the Number One at Times Square and get off at 157th Street. Okay? I'll wait in the station at 157th Street. But if you don't see me, don't wait for me. Start walking up on the east side of the street, and I'll walk down on the east side and I'll see you. So walk on the east side of the street."

She starts off a good ten minutes earlier than the earliest time he could have gotten to the station at 157th Street unless they got let out early. It's the middle of winter and has been dark for hours. She turns over in her mind the color of the cap he wore that morning and recalls what color the

---

BREENA CLARKE, a native of Washington, D.C., is an actress, writer and journalist. She is co-author with Glenda Dickerson of *Re/Membering Aunt Jemima, A Menstrual Show*. Her work has been published in *Time*, *Black Masks*, *Heresies*, *Conditions*, *Quarto*, and *Women and Performance*. Ms. Clarke is currently working at a novel on black life and experience in Washington, D.C.

coat was. As if she needed clues to recognize him! She is absolutely certain that blindfolded and unable to hear or touch him, she'd be able to distinguish her son in a stadium full of fourteen-year-olds. She knows him in every cell of her body. But when you love someone, you memorize their clothes.

It's ten P.M. and she wishes she were reclining in front of the TV. She is playing and replaying in her head the tape of his itinerary from the deck of the docked aircraft carrier *Intrepid*, through the midtown streets, north on the subway, to the subway station where she'll meet him. "He can do it. I mean, there's no reason to think he'll get lost or anything."

They'd struck a bargain. He wanted so badly to be independent and out after dark that he agreed to all her prerequisites. If she would agree not to go over there with him—after the first time—and stand around waiting for him to be finished and walk him home, he promised to follow the one and only agreed-upon itinerary and not make any unauthorized stops. She agreed he should have money for a slice and a Coke or a hot dog and a Coke and some candy probably. He agreed to travel quickly and prudently in the company of his new friend, Derrick. He would sit in the subway car with the conductor in it—only.

His smile when she was finally won over was triumphant. He exchanged a victory glance with his stepfather over her head as if they'd been together on a strategy against her. They thought she didn't catch it, but she could smell the testosterone in the air. She detected a difference in the house lately. Those two sharing a certain odor of complicity. Their hormones lined up against hers.

She is letting the kite out a little farther every day. She's giving it more string, exposing it to the wind, but holding her end tighter and tighter. The city closes in around kids nowadays, and walking through the streets is like passing through a gauntlet. Her husband thinks it's queer the way she leaps into the gutter to put her arms out like a crossing guard when the three of them approach a street corner. "Look at all these people," he says sarcastically. "Most of them born and raised in New York City, and somehow they've survived as pedestrians without your help." This is not amusing to someone who regularly tests her own reflexes to be sure she's alert enough to charge in front of a raging bull of a car, driven by Lucifer's own taxi driver, careening directly toward her child.

Her letting him go by himself to the cadet practice way across town, his walking in a part of the city that's dark, his having to move through the gaudy neon swirl of Times Square, his traveling by himself on the subway at a dicey hour—this is all new.

He's had to memorize four different combinations for four different locks this year: his locker for coat and books, his locker for gym stuff, his swimming locker at the Y, and the lock for the chain on his bike. She bought him a bicycle, but they both know he better not take his hand off it unless he puts on the fifty-dollar lock with the money-back guarantee. When he had to replace a defective part on the bicycle, she put on jeans and a sweatshirt and rode with him and the bike on the subway. They're both glad he prefers his skateboard. It's easier to defend and cheaper to replace.

He's not a street child, but he's got pluck. He's not a fighter, but he's scrappy. He's tall, brown, with a sweet face, and she ruminates about what the cops will think if he reaches into his pocket for his gloves.

His wanting to join the cadet drill team is all tied up with the new friend, Derrick. They want to solidify their friendship with uniforms and syncopated walking. She disapproves of mumbling, but likes this boy who mumbles shyly and respectfully. He's got home training.

"Better to exit up this stairway than that because you'll be facing the right direction. Best to stand directly under the streetlamp so the bus driver will see you. Remember how we decided that standing well back from the edge of the platform is the best protection against an insane person pushing you onto the tracks in front of an arriving train? Keep your eyes and ears open, your mouth shut. Don't spend the transportation money on junk snacks and then try to get away with using your school pass after seven P.M. Don't jump the turnstile no matter what except in a case of being utterly stranded and having exhausted all other alternatives, including pleading with the token clerk."

Per the agreement, on the first night of the cadet program she went with him. She traced the route and discussed the idiosyncrasies in detail. She rolled her head from left to right and back again, surveying the street ahead—a walking defense mechanism picked up in the city. You let your eyes sweep the street broadly as far in front of you as possible. This way, you see certain crazies and drunks and friends you're not in the mood for before they see you. Leaving the *Intrepid,* standing with the two boys in the full bloom of a streetlamp, she was quietly annoyed with Derrick's people for not sending someone to accompany him. "He lives in the Bronx, for chrissake!" Suddenly she was not sure if she wasn't overreacting to the perceived dangers. "Don't smother the boy." Even her father chimed in. Acutely sensitive to the Daniel Patrick Moynihan school of thought on pathological black female emasculators, she checks herself. "No, they should've come. These boys are still too young to scrabble around New York at ten o'clock at night."

They mounted the bus finally and the driver was cheerful. She fought the impulse to ask him if he always drove this route and if it always rounded the corner at exactly this time. When the bus crossed 42nd between Eighth Avenue and Seventh, the boys stared out the window into the nine-hundred-watt sex and sadism marquees. She saw some woman's tits and name lying across her son's cheek and *Terminator* and *Friday the Thirteenth* flickering across his blinking eyes. She really wanted to tell him not to look out the window, but realized how stupid it would sound.

Most often she believes forewarned is forearmed, but once or twice she has surrendered to an overwhelming desire to pretend that some things don't happen if you don't ever see them happening. One time she surveyed the street ahead of them as they walked together and caught sight of a man pulling down his disgusting pants and bending over and tooting his ass over a pile of garbage right on the corner of 50th Street and Eighth Avenue. She reached around and put her hand over the boy's eyes. It was a simple reflex, but he pouted a long while because he knew he'd missed seeing something interesting.

Tonight she walks down the east side of the street but sweeps the whole thoroughfare with her eyes, in case he didn't do what he was supposed to do. One of the pillars of maternal wisdom: after you've drilled into the child's head what he must do, you try to imagine what will happen if he does exactly the opposite. You've got to be prepared.

She waits at the turnstiles. She can see the platform. There is only one way to exit the station. If he's sitting in the car with the conductor, he'll be in the middle of the train. As each train enters the station, she looks at the middle first, then fans out to scout the front and back. Three trains come through and he doesn't arrive. She is sick of looking at the token clerk and annoyed that he is looking at her. She walks back toward the stairs. He's the kind of bullet-headed clerk who thinks the Transit Authority is paying him to scout fashion models rather than sell tokens. Out of his line of vision, she reads the subway map, traces grimy tiles with an index finger, and wipes her finger with a tissue.

He is not on the next train. She's getting angry and mutters to herself. She's getting scared. "Walk to the bus stop, ride across Forty-second Street, get off at Seventh Avenue, catch the uptown Number One, sit in the car with the conductor, get off at 157th Street. Simple."

Her stomach is not quiet. One hundred and thirty-eight pounds. The last time he went to the doctor's that's what he weighed, one hundred and thirty-eight pounds. I think that's accurate. Five feet eight inches tall. Half an inch taller than she. She can feel the brush of the bird's wing—the bird who brushes his wing against the mountaintop and in an eternity will have worn it to a pebble. This tiny bird of worry who brushes his wing against the soul of a mother and thus shortens her life by minutes, hours, days.

A throng of people come out of the next train and he is not among them. She sits disconsolately on the crummy station steps next to a plaque about the Jumel Mansion and silently begs whoever is listening to give her a break. "Let him be on the next train. Please!" All the while knowing that personal prayers don't alter events already in motion.

A train pulls in. She leaps to attention at the turnstile, leans over, looks anxious. She searches the windows. He bounds out of the middle of the train, poised for fussing but begging with his eyes for her to be calm. "They let us out late and the bus took forever." His voice is trembling. Words dam up behind her front teeth. She takes his hand silently and climbs the stairs behind the exiting crowd. At street level, he tactfully disengages his hand to show her the badges that have to be sewn on the sleeve of a white shirt. She stands looking at the knit cap he wears fashionably above his naked ears. Worried about the cold, she pulls it down. They walk home.

My Father's Son

STEVEN CORBIN

When I pick up my father and his girlfriend at Los Angeles International Airport he stops short before embracing me, blinks repeatedly in disbelief, smiles or smirks crookedly and tentatively, judging me, sizing me up through his trademark horn-rimmed glasses and ultraconservative mud-brown eyes, which cut immediately to the wiry dreadlocks bouncing around my forehead, and his glare that screams *What the hell kinda weird thing you gone and done to yourself this time?* disturbingly familiar yet intimidating and benevolent at the same time, reduces me, as it most often does despite my thirtysomething years, to the little tyke in tattered dungarees and dirty high-top sneakers I once was, in dire need of my father's love and approval. For weeks I was preoccupied with and vexed myself over what my father and I would possibly talk about for seven days and seven nights, constantly being together and sharing each meal, sleeping in the same house day in, day out, after our years of estrangement sealed by an impromptu reconciliation. We hadn't slept in the same house since I was ten or eleven, and I wondered, when he mentioned he would be bringing his girlfriend to Los Angeles, if

STEVEN CORBIN was the author of the novels *No Easy Place to Be*, *Fragments That Remain*, which was nominated for the Lambda Literary Award; and *A Hundred Days from Now*. His short fiction has been published in *Breaking Ice*, *More Like Minds* and *Frontiers*. He taught fiction writing at UCLA, and lived in New York City until his death in 1995.

he was using her as a buffer. But now that he's here and we move toward one another, weaving in and out of the advancing, rushing labyrinth of motley commuters, I suddenly acknowledge that seven days might not be sufficient time to encompass all that we have to say to each other.

His girlfriend Delores scoops me up in her arms, delighted to see me again, even more ecstatic to be sharing some semblance of a vacation with my father, their first together in a twelve-year relationship, where she can play dutiful wife to him and doting mother to me. After tattooing a wet lipstick-print kiss to my cheek, Delores pushes away from me, holding me at length with both hands fastened around my elbows and gathers me in with her eyes as if assessing how much bigger I've grown, although I was a full-fledged adult when she last saw me. My father stands off to the side, nervously awaiting his turn, large, rugged, callused hands thrust deep inside his pants pockets, head submissive with an *Aw shucks!* bent, as he silently psyches himself up for a fleeting, ephemeral moment of intimacy with another adult male. Surprising me, he locks me in an embrace that is both macho and compassionate and he doesn't let go first, which is foreign to me since I can count, on one hand, the paucity of occasions when my father has embraced me; and in his touch I can feel, almost palpably, his gratification in seeing his firstborn for the first time since two Christmases ago. Before leaving the terminal, Delores insists upon taking a photo of us, father and son, day one of the arrival, my arm wrapped around him and the rigidity of his pose, the tightening of his muscles and the tautness of his spine, that won't be captured by the aperture and recorded on the celluloid. As the lightbulb flashes and momentarily blinds us, I speculate about his current wife, conveniently left behind in cloudy and cold New Jersey, and what she would think if she could see us, the three of us, my father, his girlfriend, and me, on vacation and posing for snapshots in sunny and warm Los Angeles. Poetic justice, I think, considering how this wife surreptitiously secured my father from my own mother, his first wife, keeping up a mocking charade and talking and laughing with my mother on those rare public occasions when they were forced to share the same room and air, while sneaking around and sleeping with her husband behind her back. And at the same time, I cannot in any way justify or condone what appears to be my father's chronic, terminal, self-absorbed need to juggle a wife and mistress, both of whom, though tentatively, precariously airborne, are subject to inevitable misjuggles and alternate crashes to the floor, an arrangement both women abhor yet tolerate.

As I leave the airport terminal and pull into Century Boulevard, they exchange gut-level reactions and first impressions of Los Angeles, my father in the front seat, Delores in the back, snapping away with the camera at any and everything, her eye squinched behind the viewfinder, head rotating back and forth to either side of the street, as if she were at a tennis match. I like Delores. Always have. The childlike enthusiasm about the most mundane things. The earthiness of a deeply southern woman and the down-home manner with which she deals with people. The no-nonsense way in which she treats and handles my father. Pushover, she isn't. Neither was my mother. But there are things Delores does and says to my father that my mother wouldn't have been "allowed" to do or say as his wife and the mother of his three sons. And when my mother did and said things that angered or offended him, he beat her up. The second wife, far more representative and reflective of her generation of subservient, emotionally deprived women who don't deem themselves whole and complete without a man in their bed, would never regard him the way Delores does—as an equal. I surmise that Delores is perhaps the first woman in my father's life who can go the veritable distance with him. She's as passionate, if not more, about professional football and boxing and straightforward jazz as he is. She can match him drink for drink when they get drunk together. Though my father's a former navy man, it's his girlfriend who cusses like a sailor.

My father leans over and switches on the radio, predictably, frantically searching the dial for the local jazz station. His horrified expression freezes as I explain, in the apologetic tone of a parent informing the child that the ice-cream man won't be coming today, that Los Angeles' only jazz station, KKGO, is now defunct, preempted by another classical station. But I believe, I say quickly, in an effort to smooth out the wrinkles in his face, that there's another noncommercial broadcast from one of the local universities. His radar ever intact, he finds the local broadcast from the campus of Cal State, Long Beach. His fingers stop moving only when the dial slides into Miles Davis's muted horn blaring out at us. The disc jockey is spinning a recent composition. My father and I inhale deeply, both of us immediately recognizing the signature horn, pretending we don't, my foot and fingers tapping to the rhythm of genius, as we consciously sidestep the potential argument we engage in from time to time regarding the merit of Miles's contemporary contributions. My father, jazz elitist and purist, firmly and unequivocally and inexorably theorizes that the legendary horn blower has done absolutely nothing musically worthwhile since what my father terms his electronically smothered, nonacoustic, funk-thumping milestone of *Bitches Brew*. After that, says the gospel according to my father, Miles has never been the same. He sold out, my father upholds. He's growing, I contradict. Did you know, my father said to me in a past debate, playing his trump card, his tone chock full of confidence that what he was about to say next would convince me of his reasoning and force me to abandon my position once and for all, that Miles Davis has so burned out his brains on drugs and alcohol and God knows what that he actually likes and endorses people like Sting and Prince? Why shouldn't he? I argued. It takes a visionary to recognize one—or two. We can't and shouldn't expect him to repeat what he did in the fifties and sixties.

Studying my father at red lights and through intermittent glances that punctuate our conversation, I realize, understand, and accept, as I never have before, that he is indeed aging. Still remarkably handsome, even dashing for his middle age, his once taut, pretty-boy beauty has thrown itself on the mercy of gravity, puffy darkness encircling his eyes, jowls I've never seen before pulling at his face. His silky hair, short and black and wavy and parted at the side as it was the day he married my mother at age twenty, is his sole physical attribute that remains timeless. He has become overweight, especially after bouts with cancer, first losing pounds, then gaining them back double, stomach spilling over his pants, flabby around his once firm upper body, resembling his own octogenarian father more and more, the futuristic, genealogical mirror of what I could possibly become in a couple of decades, though I exercise and pamper and take care of myself in a way he never did. When I became a teenager, then segued into young adulthood, the maturation of my growth having kicked in, shaping and molding the adult face through which I would see the world, a face that would pretty much stay the same forever and always, people began physically comparing me to my father, a comparison it took me awhile to get used to. Because of my father's perennial youthfulness up to the time of his illness, people claimed that we looked more like brothers than father and son. Except his hair was wavy, mine nappy. His complexion cornbread yellow, mine coffee-with-milk brown. Even my mother would look at me, shake her head in a way that only a black woman can, smile almost embarrassingly as she *hmm-hmmed* to herself at the alleged stark resemblance I could never see. You are your father's son all right, she'd say, chuckling to herself, privy to the punch line of her own implicit inside joke.

My father mentions that he wants to see my brother, as we unlock and walk through the front door of my home, which he's never seen before, our arms weighted down with luggage, and my father's eyes dart erratically around the large living room and adjoining dining room, visibly surprised yet pleased that I live in such a large, spacious, sparsely furnished house. Despite the cancer and his overall failing health, my father sucks on one consecutive Marlboro after another, as he's always done, teeth and fingers yellowing, constantly clearing his throat and hawking up phlegm, and I, a nonsmoker barely tolerant of tobacco smoke, consciously brace myself for an entire week of playing host to, and sharing my space with, two heavy smokers, a reality I've failed to consider until now, and although I uphold an ironclad no-smoking rule in my home, I wouldn't dream of denying either of my guests the privilege of their nasty habits.

Heading downtown along Sunset Boulevard, smog so thick the skyline appears as a choking apparition holding its breath, I am relieved that my father is decidedly not a tourist and couldn't care less about staring at meaningless, pointless footprints in cement, or meandering down Hollywood Boulevard, or shaking hands with Mickey Mouse. He came to see nothing and no one but me, his son, and my brother, his other son, this thrice-round-the-world traveler who has been everywhere and seen everything, northern Africa being his favorite. Though he's never been to Los Angeles, he appears to be minimally interested in the sights and sounds of the basin metropolis, while Delores, a study in contrast, refuses to miss anything with her eyes or the camera, unable to sit still, bouncing around in the back seat like a child entering the gates of Disneyland, and admittedly, unapologetically, she intends to visit the footprints in cement and the pink and gold stars lining Hollywood Boulevard's pavement and to shake hands with Mickey Mouse.

As we head east through downtown where monolithic skyscrapers cast ominous shadows on the corporate financial district and the stampede of bustling office workers and pedestrians, the surroundings transform before our very eyes as we cross Hill Street, as does my father's sudden appalled expression when he eyes throngs of the homeless hauling their belongings on their backs and waves of impoverished gold-toothed Latinos and tawdry prostitutes and loud drag queens and street hustlers and thugs and indigent, stumbling winos and jabbering derelicts. I park the car in front of the Union Rescue Mission where the denizens of destitution stand around or scatter back and forth, suspiciously regarding the automobile that has just pulled up to the curb, like weathered and tarnished wind-blown statues, eyes bloodshot, hands and feet black and crusted, searching for handouts and bumming cigarettes. My father swallows, glances quickly over his shoulders before unlocking the door and pushing it open. Delores clings to my father's arm and mine, having wondered aloud in the car before we disembarked whether it was a good idea to leave the camera behind, wrapped up and stashed under the seat, or to take it with us.

At the main window, we ask to see my brother. A messenger is sent to inform him that he has visitors, his family has arrived. We're shown to the main waiting room, a large gymnasiumlike assembly with high ceilings and loud, blasting overhead televisions people appear to be watching, which makes me wonder who can possibly hear them, given all the deafening white noise in the background, and we sit, the three of us, Delores sandwiched between us, carefully, gingerly, making certain we don't sit in something wet or disgusting, the sights squalid, the eclectic stench clashing, ranging from urine to vomit to defecation to bodily filth, and our stomachs execute a collective turn. We all exhale when my brother enters the room, handsome, well groomed, well dressed, face full of teeth. My father stands and the two of them heartily embrace each other, standing there holding each other for what seems like several minutes, as Delores and I, off to the side, admire them, expecting one or both of them to cry, sharing a vicarious thrill that my father and his second son are blessed with this opportunity to see each other after who knows how many years.

Proudly, my brother proceeds to introduce the junkies and transients to us, his father from New Jersey, his brother the writer he'd been telling them so much about, and Delores, his . . . his stepmother, he says, finding the explanation quickly enough without offending or hurting her feelings, to which Delores winks her approval, now more than ever reveling in her self-imposed role of third wife. My brother escorts us outside, at Delores's request, where we can all resume breathing freely. My brother looks well. Always does. Best-looking and best-groomed bum we know, my mother and I are known to tease him. Because my parents' marriage had crumbled and my father had chosen subsequently to be negligent and absent from our lives, the lives of his three growing boys, my brother had decided to retaliate and pay them back for shaking and toppling his familial foundation by filling his veins with, and devoting his life to, heroin. He'd started shooting up early in high school, a kid of thirteen, fourteen, who purportedly turned away from the big fat empty nothing in his life to the recreational outlet of quinine-cut heroin, crawling deeper, abysmally so, to the lower depths and clutches of insidious chemical slavery, the chains from which he has never since been free. He has been in and out of an assortment of rehabilitation centers and programs from Jersey to Texas to California, none of them having any real, lasting effect in keeping him drug free. I think my father is beginning to assume partial responsibility for my brother's drug addiction, which is a novel, refreshing approach for the man who historically buried himself in deeply rooted denial and who wouldn't accept any of the blame despite the fact that he'd never ever been there for us as we approached our prepubescent, adolescent, teenage, and young adult years: this from the man who, during his marriage to my mother, took interest in our lives whether we played on a Pop Warner football team or sang with the school choir; the man who taught us to shine our own shoes but never to shine anyone else's and who taught us how to swim in the Hudson River and how to address our elders in Sunday school with Yes, ma'am, and No, sir; the man who obsessively monitored our report cards and disciplined us when our grades displeased him; the man who taught us manners and social etiquette and instructed us to groom and present ourselves as well-behaved, starch-collared proper Negro children; the man who disallowed profanity in our presence and who vehemently clicked off the television one Saturday morning as we sat unsuspectingly, engrossed in what my father considered a particularly racist episode of *The Little Rascals* where Buckwheat had been mysteriously turned into a monkey.

Studying my drug-free-as-we-speak rehabilitated brother in the outdoor patio where residents not unlike my father, my brother, and Delores stand and smoke, I wonder if this is the magical rehabilitation that will stick, recalling how many times he's been through this and the years he lived with me and I took care of him when he had no one else. I crave so desperately to see him get on with his life, for him to know what it's like to pay rent, to juggle bills and responsibilities, to have steady, gainful employment. For years, more than I care to count, I was his provider and enabler and security blanket, weakening and retarding his fragile survival skills, giving a lot, asking for little, requiring even less his contribution to the household, all under the auspices of allowing him to pull it all together at his own unpressured pace, step by step: getting a job, saving money, finding an apartment. As he smiles animatedly, the sparkle of his grin reflecting off the midafternoon sun, I flash on an old color photograph of us as children, ages six and four, sitting on the hood of my father's brand-spanking-new shamrock-green Buick, the chrome so shiny my mother could apply her dark red lipstick in it, and there's me, erect, smiling, confident, staring almost confrontationally into the camera's eye, and there's my younger brother, tentative and visibly uncomfortable, looking as if he's about to burst into tears, his focus not on the camera but on me, his grubby little fingers holding on to my pant leg. Pictures never lie, my mother used to say. The camera takes what it sees.

I buried my lover nearly three weeks ago.

When my father and I were planning his trip to Los Angeles, it wasn't clear to me then, any more than it is now, whether the timing of his visit would be beneficial or taxing. My father knows about my lover having died from AIDS and he seems willing—perhaps eager is the word—to be there for me so that I could have family close to me during this turbulent period of my life. Worse, Thanksgiving is days away, which is the day I first met my deceased lover, and all I can contemplate about the upcoming eerie anniversary is whether or not it will be a traditional family holiday which I don't have the luxury of enjoying much anymore, living three thousand miles away from my family, or if it will be a day of profound mourning when all I'll want to do is visit his grave site or stay locked up in my bedroom all day, refusing to surface. I am leaning toward the former since, if for no other reason, I can't recall the last Thanksgiving dinner I had with my father and I don't want to isolate him and Delores or cause them to feel awkward as I plow and scratch and claw my way through God knows how many months and years of grieving and healing. They're both incredibly supportive, which is encouraging, and I sometimes can't believe that the same macho, homophobic father who raised me can feel any modicum of sympathy over a homosexual relationship that has been shattered by a virus. When we spoke on the telephone before his arrival, my father assured me that he wanted to be in Los Angeles to figuratively, spiritually, perhaps literally hold my hand, insisting that I shouldn't be alone and it would be advantageous to be with family, but, he added, if I felt I wanted to be alone . . . ? But he was right, because I didn't care to be alone. Since they've been here, Delores has delicately brought up my lover's name on occasion, curious about him and the relationship we had and how I'm faring since his death. She can't believe, she says, that I'm holding up as well as I am, though she can see, now that she's looked a bit closer, the controlled grief dormant in my sometimes forced expressions; there's no way in hell, she further assures me, that she would be able to entertain out-of-town guests during such a crucial period. When I speak to my father about my lover, as we sit on the sofa and face one another before the coziness of the fireplace in my living room, more often than not he averts his eyes, sometimes looking at the floor, or away at a distant object in the room, unable to meet my gaze, and I can't tell if his inability to do so is rooted in the refusal to see suffering and loss mirrored in his son's eyes or if it's sheer denial and repulsion of a homosexual relationship or the fear that the plague could possibly be killing me too. In either case, it pleases me that my father has grown and evolved from his dislike and misunderstanding of homosexuals, and it has to be some kind of litmus test of his growth since I can be so honest with him about my life and he be so supportive.

Even as a kid, I knew, on some intuitive level, that my father wasn't too pleased when I displayed what he considered to be sissy behavior, which is not to say that I was effeminate. It was a lot more subtle when, for instance, I had requested a bat and ball. I can still remember my father's eyes lighting up almost incandescently when I approached him and voiced the request, one of the few occasions he would react that way when I was asking for money. Two days later, to my utter disappointment, my father marched into the house after work, calling and looking for me in every room, and he proudly presented to me a baseball and bat, which I took hesitantly, perplexed. With a child's innocence, I informed him that he'd gotten me the wrong thing, that the bat and ball I was speaking of was the foot-long wooden paddle with a rubber ball and elastic string stapled to it, which at the time was the neighborhood craze and everybody on the block and at school had one. Disillusioned and crestfallen, his mirthful expression collapsed upon realization that the bat and ball he thought his son wanted so badly, like any other red-blooded American boy would have wanted, turned out to be the latest recreational fad my father associated with girls. Another time, my family and I were leaving my aunt's house late one night and I was tired and grumpy and eager to go to sleep, the late hour way past my bedtime, and after having consumed more than a few drinks, my mother was exhausting herself trying to coax my father to leave, he being oblivious, taking his sweet time, throwing just one more shot glass to the back of his throat, while I, working in conjunction with my pleading mother, locked my arm inside my father's and implored him to take us home, when he glared at my arm wrapped securely around his and seemed to sober up momentarily before he peeled my fingers from his arm and asked if I thought he and I were getting married. These incidents and others like them led me to believe that I was unloved by my father during the years of my parents' painful and petty separation and that he had consciously chosen to be negligent and absent from my life because I had become something he no longer claimed or associated himself with, something perverse and unseemly, something that even I couldn't identify or understand, all the while assuming that my brothers, too, were suffering on my account.

MY FATHER'S SON

Before my parents' bitter separation and the subsequent pleas for delinquent child support and the constant ongoing court appearances and my father's no-shows and the poisonous warnings about my father that my brothers and I were subjected to from my maternal grandmother and my mother's sisters and brothers and my own mother, although she swore sideways that she never once attempted to taint us with her feelings about our father—and I think she actually believed it—I remember always feeling safe at night when we slept simply because my father also slept in the same house. No harm could befall us. No monsters could attack or eat us up. No slimy web-footed creatures could ever crawl from under my bed or my brother's so long as my father was there, the patriarch, the protector, the invincible. And many times I had trouble falling asleep, a contrast to my brother, who snored the moment his head hit the pillow, and I would listen through the closed door to the muffled theme music of *Perry Mason* or *The Untouchables* seeping from the Motorola black-and-white television that kept my mother company until my father got home from wherever he was, doing whatever he was doing, and I would not feel safe and relaxed enough to fall asleep until I heard his key turn the lock and the door open and his work boots boom like explosions across the linoleum floor, and the smack of his perfunctory kiss to my mother's lips and her whispered voice reminding him that his dinner was being kept warm on the stove, and then, and only then, would I be able to rest in the assurance that my father was home and nothing bad could happen to us now.

This feeling of security returns to me, wraps its brawny arms around me, nearly twenty-five years later, as I toss and turn and snuggle with a wet pillow I've learned to cradle in my arms to fill an emptiness that continues to rock me, enveloped in an inky darkness where I cannot see my hand in front of my face, and I recall the curves and textures and scents of my dead lover's body now decaying and decomposing in a cold ground, and somehow I am at peace, despite my emotional unrest, because my father is sleeping in a bedroom down the hall and somehow I know that no harm will come to me and nothing or no one can hurt me anymore, physically, psychologically, emotionally, so long as he is here, and after arriving at this stark and unusual realization, I effortlessly fall asleep.

My father and I hadn't been speaking for a number of years until I ran into him at my grandparents' house one Christmas Day and made my rounds, kissing cheeks and embracing bodies and shaking hands, attempting to promote yuletide cheer, keeping a stiff upper lip and a smile on my face, though my father's unexpected, ill-timed presence nearly diminished my spirit, and when I approached him for a hug, despite the fact that we hadn't seen each other for several years since I had gone away to college and had barely spoken ten words to each other since that time and I had convinced myself that I irrevocably despised him as I had assumed he despised me in kind, he gave me the look of a Mississippi redneck coming face to face with a civil rights activist and turned away, mumbling something *sotto voce,* as he uncrossed and then recrossed his legs. It was all the rejection I could take from him and I couldn't abort my reaction, which was one of sauntering almost absentmindedly toward the sofa, where I sat down and sobbed uncontrollably in a roomful of relatives, my aunt, my father's only sister, watching me, disdain for her brother's behavior distorting her face, her sympathy spreading its fingers and reaching out to me across the room, and my grandparents, my father's parents, sliding into traditional, familiar roles of pretending that none of it had actually happened, which caused me to momentarily despise them since they had spoiled their first son ragged and had never reprimanded, at least not to my knowledge, his flagrant shortcomings, such as what a poor excuse of a father he had been to my brothers and me; and in a matter of seconds, like clockwork, my grandmother pierced the tense silence and changed the subject, as she had always done, rather than take control of a family crisis for which her darling never-does-anything-wrong son was clearly, singularly responsible.

Next day, my father telephoned me at a friend's house in Manhattan where I was staying and asked me to meet him for a drink at his watering hole, the C.I.O. Club in Jersey City, where he spent more time than he should have, waterlogging his troubles and woes with alcohol. When I arrived and my father ordered two Heinekens after introducing me and showing me off around the tavern to any and everybody who was genuinely or disingenuously interested, we embarked upon what would probably be our first honest conversation, with a no-holds-barred approach that had been lacking in all of our adult exchanges, and he confessed, first time ever, his dire shortcomings as husband and father: that he didn't know what possessed him to batter my mother, his wife, especially when he hadn't come from a tradition of wife battery, his own father and mother having never called each other anything outside their proper names, and the subsequent punishment he inflicted on his three sons, my brothers and me, because he was devastated and outraged by the separation, underscored by the fact that my mother had left him, and not he her, a surprise that tripped him up severely when he returned home from work that day and found an empty house reeking of evidence that his wife and three sons were gone; and that somehow through the twisted, perverted rationalization of it all, he used his children as pawns of retaliation against my mother, knowing precisely how to get to her through manipulation. I sat stunned, transfixed, unable to finish my beer, bearing witness to his profuse apologies as he assumed whole, absolute blame and responsibility for everything that had gone wrong between him and my mother and my brothers and me, listening to and savoring and freezing in time my father's first admission of his immense love for me, his fierce, unexpressed pride in my accomplishments, and, more importantly, his aching desire to reconcile with me and his sons and get on with our lives from this point on and not to forget the past but to use it as a springboard, a launching pad into healthier, happier remaining years, if only I could find it within my heart and conscience to forgive him. I had often worried about the prospect of one of us dying, my father or I, before we could arrive at reconciliatory terms, to patch up the holes that the winds of discontent and unresolved anger and bitterness were blowing through. This was the day I first met Delores, who joined us later, once my father and I had smoothed out enough wrinkles, in our dark, private corner of the bar, and it was safe to enter and penetrate the space. When my father went to the men's room, Delores explained to me, in his absence, how the day before, during the afternoon of Christmas Day, my father had walked into the bar, sat on a stool, and drunk one scotch after another for six hours straight until he was no longer coherent but, instead, weepy and self-pitying and remorseful for what he'd done the last few years and the incident that had just taken place at my grandparents' house. Delores had convinced him to appeal to me, to strip away the façade of pride that was no longer effective, his displaced anger, and his cloak of self-righteousness, and to talk to me, directly and honestly, man to man, humbly and meekly, with no pretense of father and son, right or wrong.

My first short story has been published in a highly visible, much celebrated anthology, a story that blossomed from deep autobiographical roots, which is uncharacteristic of my work, and although my father, my number one fan, exerts a concerted effort to acquire any and everything I write and, more aptly, any and everything that is written about me, insisting that I forward him copies of it all, he is not privy to the publication of this story, though he is aware of the anthology. Among the story's fifteen pages there is roughly one page, three or four paragraphs, where I detail his failings as a father and the estranged relationship we once had, not meaning to publicly bash him or shame him before my readership, but in an effort to tell the truth as I experienced it, keeping it undisguised, unadorned, close to the bone, healing myself, licking my wounds, exorcising my demons from the past on a printed page; and in doing so I inevitably unearth unflattering verities that I am certain, beyond a doubt, will cause my father to cringe, perhaps withdraw or seep deeper into major denial, even though my drug-free-as-we-speak brother has read it and agrees wholeheartedly that I wrote the truth and nothing but the truth. And despite my efforts to hide this published story from my father since I don't believe his first trip to visit me in Los Angeles is the proper time and place to air it, my efforts are undermined, unbeknownst to the good friend who, over a Sunday brunch, innocently asks my father what he thinks of my recent publication, at which point my father turns to me, mouth shaped in an O, eyes wrinkled, and inquires as to why he hasn't been informed about it. Shrinkingly, I shrug my shoulders, exchange a knowing glance with my friend, who certainly means well, and immediately she realizes she's just committed a *faux pas*.

In the early evening after my father has watched his Sunday afternoon football game and I prepare to go out with a friend, I walk from my bedroom into the living room, where my father is sprawled on the sofa before the fireplace, head nestled into a pillow, stockinged feet crossed, the anthology open on his chest, and I retrace my steps and retreat to my bedroom, where I sit and wait until I hear the doorbell ring. Delores, who has already read the story some days before but keeps it a secret, knocks on my door and enters with a conspiratorial expression on her face. She whispers to me that my father is reading the story, and as we both await his reaction, she reiterates to me, as she had told me some days before, immediately after she read it, that she is astounded and appalled by his treatment of three growing boys who had absolutely nothing to do with his breakup from my mother, something he's never told her in the twelve years she's known him, and, further, she admits that it frightens her to be with a man who would do such a thing, that if one word of it is true, my father is lucky *and* blessed, though he doesn't deserve to have a son like me who has forgiven him, that God is punishing him with a firstborn son who's grown up to be a writer, that if he had it in him to treat his children this way, she wonders what hope there is for her. By the time Delores leaves and returns to her bedroom to watch television, the doorbell rings, which I jump up to answer, and as I reenter the living room I notice that my father is now sitting on the sofa and he has removed his trademark horn-rimmed glasses and is rubbing his mud-brown eyes of tears, the shocking sight of which nearly halts me in my tracks.

It is the first and only time I've ever seen my father cry.

When I return later in the evening, my father is not at home, but rather down the street at the Drawing Room, the neighborhood tavern that I pass thousands of times but have never entered, and Delores, who is on her way to meet him, informs me that they had a little time to discuss what he had read and, predictably, he denied every word, sentence, and punctuation mark, claiming that I had it all wrong, that all of it was lies and none of what I had written had ever happened, and when Delores asked why then was he crying and he couldn't answer, she said, When the stone was thrown, how'd you know it was aimed at your window?

Nowadays, my father and I regularly stay in touch by exchanging letters on cassettes, keeping each other apprised of the ups and downs and the agonies and ecstasies of our lives, although since my father is now retired, the drama of his life has sizzled down tremendously and the high point of his otherwise uneventful days and mundane nights is going out in his boat to fish, a hobby he lives for. A professional fisherman, he has made several trips to exotic corners of the world, including Cuba and Costa Rica, where he has caught marlin, swordfish, even sharks, and one of his prizewinning catches was photographed and written about on the pages of a national fishermen's sports magazine, my father standing beside a conquest nearly twice his size. The frequent appearances of his cassettes in my mailbox and the almost immediate turnaround response to my cassettes tell me he has more than enough idle time on his hands and that he's attempting to cram many of the lost years into sixty-minute Memorex tapes. And whenever I make one of my rare once-a-year sojourns back home to visit my family, he makes a point of trying to capitalize all or most of my free time, requesting that I visit him nearly every day, to sit and listen to vintage Miles or Ellington or Bird or Robeson, to discuss politics or any number of books we're reading; and while I appreciate it, getting the attention I craved from a man who ignored me for the better part of a decade, I also feel resentful that he makes such demands to which he expects me to comply, unquestioningly, despite my intention to rest while I'm home visiting, not to mention all the other family members and friends I have to visit and the gallivanting around New York I tend to do with my cousin. And yet I feel an intense pressure to be there for him, the only son he has left who willingly, consistently, keeps in touch with him. Neither of my brothers do. My father has virtually no relationship with my youngest brother, who was not quite two years old when my parents separated, and who resents my father for so much, he can't find it within himself to strike up any relationship with him at this stage of the game, and who has vowed never ever to abandon or neglect either of his own two children, regardless of his marital status. The middle son, the drug-free-as-we-speak brother, tolerates my father, though he too harbors plenty of rancor and unresolved bitterness.

I was my father's twenty-first birthday gift, born two days after him: same date, though decades later, that Gore Vidal was born in New York and Edgar Allan Poe died in Baltimore, same year of the publication of James Baldwin's first novel, and the year before the *Brown v. Board of Education* Supreme Court decision. And though I'm not a die-hard astrology buff, I have to admit there's something to be said for being born two days apart, given the almost carbon-copy personalities my father and I share, to the extent that we are exactly alike in virtually every imaginable way, except who we sleep with. Growing up, I was constantly reminded by my mother how similar I was to my father, especially when she was angry with me, and she wasted no time in paralleling our identical negative personality traits, which I vehemently fought against because the last thing I wanted to be at that point of my life was him, or anything remotely like him.

Watching my father consume an endless succession of beers, since his doctor has forbidden him from drinking anything else harsher and more detrimental to his health, I'm reminded of the heavy drinkers both my parents were throughout my entire life, which undoubtedly contributed to the disintegration of their marriage, realizing now in adulthood and accepting wholeheartedly that they were both functioning alcoholics who didn't miss a beat going about their daily responsibilities; and I am saddened by my father's obvious addiction and I wonder how loudly the voice of anguish whispers inside him that he's trying so desperately to silence.

My fondest memory of my father is of the two of us alone in a fishing boat on a tranquil lake on an idyllic Father's Day. The recollection sticks with me especially because it's nearly impossible to recall any other occasion in our lives, up until the impromptu reconciliation, when it was just he and I. Since my father took his fishing expeditions seriously, my brother and I were almost never allowed to accompany him, unless his fishing spot that day was particularly close to home, and I can't for the life of me remember why I got to go along with him or, for that matter, why we left my brother behind. After my father taught me how to cast my line and reel in the catch and I took great sadistic pleasure in impaling live earthworms as bait, we sat silently in the boat, a flock of honking geese flying overhead, the calming lap of the lake against the hull, our hooks probing the depths several fathoms below, at least in my imagination, my father appearing to me as the old man and the sea, a story we had recently read in class, his still profile etched and rocking against the cloud-filled sky, just he and I and the elements; and for the first time ever, I felt at one with him.

Fortuitously, I continue to feel more and more at one with him, especially during his trip to Los Angeles, where, like two former college roommates, we persist in our bonding and compensation for lost years we strive to recover and reclaim, and I am pleased and feel perhaps fortunate, given the ill-fated relationships some of my closest friends share with their fathers, that I am his firstborn, even proud that we have overcome our collective demons and excess emotional baggage and have established a table of compromise where we both can sit and cross our legs and fold our arms and break bread and be comfortable with each other and genuinely like one another; and as I see my face reflected in his, hear my voice in his throat, perceive, analyze, and judge the world through his mud-brown eyes, I realize, more than ever, as my mother has for years, that I am, indeed, my father's son.

The Ethical Vegetarian

ALEXIS DE VEAUX

 The kitchen stank to me. Maybe it was the smoking dismembered smell of them in the Styrofoam take-out box. Heaven only knows why but I clucked like a chicken as Grett sucked clean a spicy pile of buffalo wings. She looked up at me, her face contorted. The lips I loved greasy with carnivorous pleasure.

That ain't funny, Sahara.

You are what you eat, darlin.

I tossed another stump of broccoli in my mouth for emphasis. Savored the delicate taste of sesame oil and sautéed garlic seasoning. Strictly vegetarian since college, I hadn't eaten meat in ten years. It hadn't been easy to change. Over time I'd lost my taste for it though. Chicken like my momma made was hard to give up. eating other animals was a matter of ethics to me now.

Several nights later I bolted up in bed wet with sweat. In the blink between sleep and not, I struggled between shadowy worlds.

ALEXIS DE VEAUX is a poet, short story writer, playwright, and essayist whose work is nationally and internationally known. Born and raised in New York City, she is the author of several works, including *Na-ni* (Harper & Row, 1973); *Spirits in the Street* (Doubleday, 1973); *Don't Explain: A Song of Billie Holiday* (Harper & Row, 1980); *Blue Heat: Poems* (Diva Publishing Enterprises, 1985); and *An Enchanted Hair Tale* (Harper & Row, 1987). She holds a doctorate in American Studies from the State University of New York at Buffalo, where she is currently on faculty.

You okay? Grett mumbled.

The chicken woman took my baby.

What?

In the supermarket. I took her basket of eggs. Then she took mine. The baby was in it.

You been dreamin, sugah. You don't have no babies.

Grett sighed turning over. I snuggled against her back wanting to feel safe. Drifted back to sleep restlessly.

Hovering above the sleeping characters the hand of the cartoonist drew a square box meticulously around the bedroom scene. Her freshly sharpened pencil shaded in dawn.

The smell of coffee brewing automatically awoke me early the next morning. I showered and dressed, groggy from too little sleep. In the kitchen I poured myself a cup of the piping hot stimulant black which burned my throat going down. I sank into one of the chairs at the table. Awake; but for some reason, out of sorts. When Grett came into the kitchen I was throwing eggs from the carton one by one into the garbage can.

Something wrong with the eggs? she asked.

No.

So why'd you throw them away?

People shouldn't breed animals just to eat their parts, I said, closing the can's lid.

And what am I supposed to eat for breakfast?

I opened the pantry closet and took out a box of Quaker Oats. Grett looked at me like I was crazy.

You know I don't eat that shit, she said. And fumed out of the kitchen back to the bedroom. Down the hall I stood in the doorway watching her. Dressed for work in a red wool sweater sheath strands of black and white African beads red and green rectangular earrings Grett was good-looking. All urban Masai. At WBFM she was the only female disc jockey. Her daily talk show was number one in the city.

We'd met through mutual friends one night at Three Steps Forward. A favorite hangout of Black Brooklyn's artsy crowd. Everybody in the restaurant's bar was talking about M'Boyd Thomas's death. The well-kept secret of his AIDS. A loss to the Black dance world. Grett knew him. Laughing and crying she told us all story after story about their freshman days at Howard. There was a tough tenderness to her I found seductive.

Grett put on some deep-berry lipstick. Then splashed her neck with a few drops of Egyptian Musk. Checked herself out in the mirror. Watched me watching her. I blurted out something I'd overheard at the clinic.

Did you know that embryo transfers for women were first developed by experimenting on cows?

I really don't wanna hear it, Sahara, was all she said before she snatched her coat and bag from a hook in the hallway closet, stormed out without goodbye.

The left hand of the cartoonist poised above its storyboard. Flexed short fingers. Tired from drawing all night, it swept away lint from its overused eraser. With its first finger traced the scratched-out revised dialogue above the characters' heads. The hand signed the cartoonist's code name "1619" in the lower right-hand corner, then reached for a new storyboard. Drew an outline of the brownstones jammed between stores along Nostrand Avenue. Drew the sidewalks' slippery ice traps. Stale snow frozen in dingy piles against the buildings. Gave the street a look of winter hung over not even the cold bright of blustery morning could blot out. Drew Sahara. Bundled up and bent over in a bitter wind. Maneuvering the blocks to the subway to the other side of Brooklyn. Then drew the four-story edifice which was the Frankel Clinic. Nestled amid the commercial establishments on Orchard Avenue. Rows of naked trees out front of it stiff as skeletons on duty. Stopped. Started again drawing. The interior of the first floor inside. The registration and reception area. Stark and sterile-looking. A streamlined counter which partially hid from view Sahara. Awash in a headful of kente-wrapped short thick dreadlocks, frighteningly wild to the child-needy clients who stared at them. While waiting to start the process that would end in their in vitro fertilization.

Five o'clock came and I was glad to go home. But at the end of the day the streets were an obstacle course of grouchy holiday shoppers. Overburdened with bags of expensive family expectations. Suckered into the *fala lalala*. Whether they could afford it or not. People carried home the biggest Christmas trees they could find. With no care for the shrinking forests.

What it might feel like to be uprooted and sold. Indignant and distressed by the whole scene I walked along the outskirts of the sidewalks.

The hand of the cartoonist paused. Drummed an impatient rhythm on the unfinished storyboard. Doodled. Waited for the downbeat of inspiration. Slid its fingers over the pout of her mouth. The hand folded into the fingers of its mate for comfort.

The day after Christmas we went to Trazana and Roy's Kwanzaa party. The three floors of their DeKalb Avenue brownstone were packed solid as usual wall to wall. The bass blasted. Grett and I squeezed past clumps of dancers slinking to the steamy lyrics. Roy descended the spiral stairs gracefully lean. A Romare Bearden collage dressed in kente silk. His trim mustache tinseled with perspiration. Roy lit up when he spotted us.

Bout time y'all got here.

Wouldn't miss this for nothin, baby, Grett said, eyeballing the crowd.

Otis died, Roy said. This morning.

Oh no, we both said.

Yes.

How are Carmen and the kids? I asked.

Takin it hard.

This is so fuckin unfair, I said.

"And another one bites the dust," Grett said, sucking her teeth.

He was a comet, Roy said. A beautiful poet comet.

A loud crash erupted from the dining room. Trazana's scream propelled Roy through the pause of dancers. Grett gathered my hand in hers. We moved toward the parlor room. And the buffet table. When she hungrily downed several deviled eggs I bit my tongue. Just to keep the family peace. Pretended not to feel suddenly disgusted.

Hours later we got home danced out and giddy. Our lovemaking sweetened by the supple mauve of velvet couch our half-dressed bodies red candles burning in the living room a wee morning apartment chill the smell of want you.

Satisfied and sleepy the cartoonist cut out the lamplight on her drawing board.

I became a regular nuisance. To Grett my sermons on Black people's eating habits and good health and what if humans were bred for food were irritating. Rude. One evening while munching some cold quiche for dinner in bed she'd begged me to please leave her food the fuck alone.

But I was out of control now. Driven to monologues on the virtues of vegetables and comparisons between the meat industry and slavery. I talked about food incessantly. Ran my mouth. Ran Grett out the bedroom to sleep on the couch.

Late one Friday night while shopping downtown Brooklyn I stopped in a Dalton's Bookstore to browse. Spotted copies of *The Enchanted Broccoli Forest Cookbook*. Decided to buy one just for the hell of it. Took it home. About a week later I noticed that my taste for broccoli was now a craving. I had to have it. Day and night. Whenever Grett was late getting home from the station I experimented with broccoli recipes from the cookbook secretly. Made broccoli shakes. Fried broccoli patties. Broccoli pancakes. Broccoli soup. Broiled broccoli over stuffed steamed broccoli stalks. I was a broccoli junkie.

The cartoonist drew a box around that last frame. Of the previous night's work she particularly liked the desperate confusion executed with fine simplicity of line on the main character's face. It was the mark of an artist to do so much with so little. Was what she learned at Pratt her four years. Admired and well liked by the faculty there, she was envied by other students who found her design projects too original to copy. Already a gifted architect by her junior year she'd published her first cartoons in a neighborhood weekly City Lines. *After graduation she'd turned down a handsome offer in a Manhattan company and took a job with the New City Restoration Project, a group of local business people who bought up abandoned houses in Brooklyn and restored and sold them way below cost to deserving families. It was a job she was proud of. But it was the cartoons she could spend all weekend drawing—the smell of ink and paper the sun the solitude in her Washington Avenue loft above Naomi's Beauty World and Ling's Chinese Take-Out that propelled her forward. She reached for another clean board.*

But that wasn't the half of it. One morning I woke up and went to the bathroom. Turned on the light. Saw myself in the mirror. And screamed in shock. Grett came running into the bathroom.

What the hell happened to your hair?

She circled around me as the two of us bucked our eyes in utter amazement. I had become what I had eaten. The broccoli crop of dreadlocks sprouted up like a petrified forest all the fuck over my head.

Believe

CARLA R. DU PREE

 Rising above a situation was unspoken gospel in the Fauntroy household. So when Gaby peered out of the cab window at her family, who sat on the porch awaiting her arrival, she held strong to that belief. She pushed the door open and stepped onto the pavement. The South Bend heat pressed against her. The driver placed her bag near her feet, barely waiting for his tip as she shoved a bill into his hand. As she nudged the bag away from her swollen stomach, her family rose in unison like brown birds on the verge of flight.

It was Duchess, the mother, who descended the steps first, eyes wide with disbelief. Duchess made no effort to embrace her but exclaimed in horror, "Gabrielle, is that you?" Her sister, Dorcas, pushed past her mother, caressed Gaby's belly, then gently pulled her close. Her brother remained on the porch, looking in wonder at the dark-hued women assembled in a circle before him.

It took a moment for things to settle. Room was made on the porch for Gaby to sit. She sank into the cushioned rocker, travel-weary, and tried in

---

CARLA R. DU PREE is a founding fiction editor of *Shooting Star Review*. She has a Master of Arts degree in writing from The Writing Seminars at The Johns Hopkins University. She writes about families and the pain and pleasure of memory. She lives with her husband and children in Columbia, Maryland.

vain to think of what had made her believe it'd be easier to tell them in person rather than over the telephone.

Their eyes rested on and then shifted away from Gaby's fullness. Fingers tapped against the banister. Arms folded, then unfolded. Each one of them retreated to a place on the porch to watch her from a distance. And as if they couldn't take her in all at once, they regarded her in pieces, first the full face, then the auburn hair that hung to her shoulders in a limp curl, from the wattle of her thin upper arms to the lights in her maple-colored skin. Gaby sat across from them with her eyes cast down, a hat atop her head, a rayon dress fit for travel but too warm for the southern heat, and her legs held apart to cradle her protruding stomach.

The duchess squared her shoulders and walked away from Gaby. Everett eyed her with suspicion and wondered if her luck had run out. A smirk on his face weighed the idea of a boyfriend who'd left her holding the bag.

In the quiet afternoon the sun raged above them while they sat with discontent creasing their faces, their postures as telling as the walls they erected around them. To a stranger passing by, they were picture perfect. Pretty people, mysterious and regal.

The duchess walked the length of the porch, then stood across from Gaby and waited. Her fingers knotted and eased beside her. The air was close, but she wore her usual starched blouse and black skirt. "So you've found your way home," she said.

"I figured it was time," Gaby said, fanning herself with her hat.

"That boy John Jacob has been asking after you, but I guess you won't be needing his attention."

Gaby couldn't answer that and didn't. She was unsure of the duchess's stance and looked around at her siblings for a small measure of hope. They wore their father's shape, tall and angular, but bore their mother's fortitude. While their silence carried its own weight, the heat roped around the porch like a noose. A pearl of sweat traveled the length of her back, along with an uneasiness with what the weekend would bring.

When it seemed as if Gaby could no longer bear the silence, she excused herself. She lifted her bag, tottering as she walked, and opened the door. And though Dorcas rose to help her, Duchess caught her by the arm, warning her with her eyes to be still.

The screen door slammed on Gaby's back and placed her in the center of the front hall. She took the stairs, struggling each step with the weight of her load. When she reached the landing, something drew her eyes downward, where Duchess stood at the foot of the stairway. Duchess looked up and into Gaby's eyes. Neither woman spoke, and one didn't join the other.

The duchess spun on her heels and disappeared onto the porch, headed back from where she had come.

Gaby smoothed the wrinkles in her red swing dress that she pulled from the suitcase. The brass buttons and the above-knee length were too much for Sunday service, but she could get away with the linen dress that gave her ample room to move. She rustled through her bag, pulling out clothing that needed to be hung. She had packed more than she needed, figuring if things went right she'd make it a longer stay.

Her room was small, and were it not for the chenille bedspread on the twin-sized bed it would be anchored in the past. The wallpaper that had taken hours to choose had bleached from the sun. The red flowers had faded to a somber pink, the blue background now gray.

As she draped the dresses over the crook of her arm, she looked up and found Duchess reflected in the bureau mirror. The moment she turned around, Duchess stepped into the room.

"I brought something for you, Duchess," Gaby said as she began to fish through the suitcase.

Duchess stood back and watched Gaby fumble through the disheveled arrangement of clothing. After a moment the duchess drew in a deep breath, waiting longer as Gaby searched farther into the bag.

Sweat formed on Gaby's brow and she lifted a limp wrist to her forehead to wipe it.

"Get it later," Duchess said, starting for the door.

"No, wait; I'm sure it's right here," Gaby said, looking inside the pockets and under a shelf of lingerie. Each time she came up empty.

At the point when she was convinced she had forgotten it, Duchess said again, "Get it later when you're a little more settled."

"Settled" came out hard, without warning, jolting Gaby in a way that made her catch her breath sharply. And Duchess left, cutting the warmth right out of the giving. As Gaby heard the duchess's footsteps hurrying away, she spotted a pinch of cranberry tissue in the back of her bag. She raised the small offering out of a nest of clothing. She turned it over in her hands and wondered if it would be enough, if anything would ever be enough.

It was Dorcas who pressed life into the air. She snatched Gaby by the hand and pulled her into the kitchen. "Want some sweet milk?" she said.

"Mama hasn't changed none," Gaby said behind her.

"Why are you surprised?" Dorcas said. And then, "You don't see it, do you?"

"See what?"

"Gaby, Duchess hung her faith on you."

"Don't go there, Dorcas."

Silence fell between them. Dorcas poured canned milk into a pot on the stove and added water. They were raised on warmed sweet milk. Even when the humidity was thick enough to lay on, they drank warm milk. Papa had insisted that milk protected a soul from harsh words. Dorcas handed her sister a mug filled to the brim. As she sipped from her own, she eyed Gaby carefully, enchanted with her sister's roundness and the way she held herself, like her future was a sure thing.

Growing up, Gaby had been the one who got into scrapes with the neighborhood kids. She was the one who twisted Silly Sally's arm for calling her a "wannabe," for Gaby talked proper and wore socks right below her knees.

Gaby and Duchess were clothed from the same patch. In Gaby's elementary years they fought in a fashion that left Duchess ready to lay claim that their father wouldn't have raised them at all, had she been the one who died, but would have shipped them off to their Aunt Suzie, who had raised a bunch of Fauntroy hellions. Duchess's own mother had warned her "not to worry about your young babies around near your feet, but to consider your adult children who will have you around your heart."

And so it was that long-ago summer when Gaby turned sixteen and changed the way she would live her life. They had argued over a simple thing, so simple that to this day the retelling of their story left out details of why it happened, just that it did.

On an afternoon in the early days of summer, the sun had become so unbearable that the sun-scorched grass cracked beneath their feet. The heat drove them indoors, leaving them to pace the house with little to do. Gaby and Duchess found themselves on the brink of flaring. They stood erect, their bodies clenched, in cotton dresses damp against their skin. When Dorcas found them, Duchess had her palm open, ready to knock sense into her elder daughter's face. But when she raised her hand to strike, Gaby snatched her by the wrist. In a small voice, Gaby had said, "Enough."

She left the room with a sense that she had won, and she knew her mother watched her stride out with a Fauntroy back and the duchess's raised chin. The next day Gaby packed her bags and left.

The memory of that moment outlived the reason for it. And now today in the kitchen, with Duchess on the porch wondering where Gaby went wrong, with paint peeling from the ceiling and windowsills cluttered with ivy, Gaby and Dorcas sat with more thoughts than words crowding the room.

Gaby sipped her milk and wished her thoughts could drown out the voices she heard on the porch, "That fool girl," she heard Duchess say. "I've tried to keep you kids from that 'nigger mess.' "

"You shouldn't worry," Dorcas said, reaching across the counter to pat Gaby's hand.

"Oh, no?"

"She'll get over it. You were the one child who left and made something of yourself, who did right by her," Dorcas said, her voice trailing off. "You know, once the baby is born, she'll be singing a different tune." And then Dorcas looked square into Gaby's face. "You could've said something to me."

"There was never the right moment, Dorcas. Each time I thought I could, the words wouldn't come."

"But aren't you afraid—to do it alone, I mean? You know what Duchess went through after Papa died. It was hard for her."

"It's not the same. I don't have to survive widowhood. Duchess had means but she had to pull her life together first," Gaby said.

"And Duchess will say, 'A woman and child leaves no room for a husband.' "

"Not necessarily. I just chose my baby first."

"She may need time with this one, Gaby."

"Well, baby sister, she's got three months."

Duchess prided herself on how she reared her children carefully. Every chance she got she supplied the local *Tribune* with Gaby's success: when she was promoted to middle management with her company, when she got preengaged to Payson Sheets (who later broke things off after steeping his presence into their lives), when she bought a brownstone in the city. Gaby's misstep unnerved her. Single mothers existed in the Fauntroys, products of divorce or relinquished loves, but not under the duchess's roof and not in her immediate family.

She carried her widowhood like armor. It became a symbol of her strength—outliving Papa—a badge of honor that required weekly visits to his grave. She wore it like a cast-iron bracelet linking her to the past, giving her reason to call up the dead any time she saw fit.

Tonight she had prepared dinner alone. She had held the potatoes under a flush of cold water, so tight her fingers cramped. The baked brisket of beef sat like a lump of worn leather in the center of her table and was horrible to cut. Once the napkins were placed and the candles lit, in celebration of Gaby's homecoming, the family bowed their heads and formed a ring with their hands. It was the closest Gaby and Duchess had come to touching that day.

Everett said grace. "Lord, make us true and thankful, indeed, for the food—um, and baby, we're about to receive. . . ."

As he blessed their dinner, Gaby glanced across the table at her mother, whose eyes narrowed and then embraced her with scorn. The evening sun would set on Duchess working a way to steal the words from her neighbors' lips which she knew were bound to fall.

Quietly Gaby shifted in her seat as the baby stirred within her. Never before in her life had she so worn her mother's shame.

On the edge of morning Gaby stood in the kitchen, pushing her gift from home toward the duchess's hands, which were covered with flour. Gaby had taken much effort to find a dove-shaped crystal.

Duchess held the gift in her palm, then slowly disengaged the wrapping. For a moment Gaby thought the sight of the lone bird in cast cranberry would soften Duchess's face. But the duchess gave it a once-over glance and placed it on the counter beside the canister of flour.

She had been kneading a mound of dough when Gaby first entered and continued to do so as Gaby stood at her back. The set of her erect shoulders motioned forward as the duchess leaned into the spongy heap. "Cynthia Early got engaged this past week and expects a spring wedding next year. You remember her, don't you?"

Yes, Gaby remembered Cynthia Early. Cynthia managed to do everything before Gaby. She was early to graduate from college, early to land a job, to get a promotion, to lay herself down to the first man asking, and equally as early to claim otherwise. But the duchess heard the good.

"Oh, is she?" Gaby said. "Well, good for her."

"And do you know *who* she's going to marry?"

"No, I don't, Duchess." And to herself, But I'm sure you'll tell me.

"Why, Payson Sheets. He owns several stores now since you two were last together. Doing quite fine for himself these days. Yes, indeed. And to think he could've been my son-in-law."

Gaby pulled out an apple from a bowl on the table. She bit down hard and savored the sweet white flesh that crunched inside her mouth. She ate it down to its core without saying another word. She tore off a paper towel from its spool and wiped her hands.

"You hadn't planned on going to church, had you?" Duchess said, her back still turned, leaning the heels of her hands farther into the dough.

"As a matter of fact, I had," Gaby said.

"I would prefer if you stayed home."

"Duchess."

"Your papa would want you to stay put," Duchess said, turning to face Gaby, and as she did her floured hand swung out, pushing the glass bird over the edge.

They both looked down at the fallen bird, which landed at the duchess's feet. Duchess's hands fluttered to her face, then dropped, white and soiled, to her thighs. She stepped over the bird toward Gaby. Instead of the comfort Gaby expected, Duchess brushed past her with hands that whitened her skirt, pushing the black near a muted gray.

Gaby lifted her nightgown as a dry wind lurched through her open window. Unlike anything she'd ever felt, the heat took to South Bend with a passion. With it came a heaviness that weighted her skin. With a child on the way it seemed even more brutal. She drifted in and out of sleep, shifting her body to reach the right valley in the mattress. It was old—everything about this house was old and noted for an unclaimed past, from the winter green awning along the southern porch to the furniture cluttering all three floors. Most of the furniture was purchased from secondhand shops. Old things were reliable, Duchess had said. Old things dragged their history with them, Gaby thought.

Despite the clutter, as a child Gaby learned to move through darkness, making a game of seeing how far she could go without turning on the lights. Duchess frequently scolded her but Gaby had taken to the night, had learned the feeling of closed space and the lightness of an open room. Her brother and sister would never see to a banging shutter in the middle of the night. Gaby didn't mind, though; the darkness made things bigger than they were, so daylight brought convenience.

She rose to lift the window farther on its hinge, then peeled her gown away from her body. She crept downstairs to the kitchen for water, opened the back door, and stepped onto the porch. She looked up at the maidenhair ferns and spider plants that hung from the ceiling and swayed in the breeze. A floral scent wafted from the garden and reached Gaby's nose in gentle bursts. Weeping willows combed their branches along the awning, and the night blooms of moon plants stood stark white against the blanket darkness.

She thrust her weight to and fro on the glider. As she did, the kitchen light came on. Duchess pushed herself onto the porch. A heaviness came with her entry. "I figured it was you out here stirring up the night," she said, pulling the air away.

"It's this heat."

"A little thing like the heat shouldn't bother you none. Thirty South Bend summers can make you get used to anything. Seems like the only way I can tell it's here is by looking at my flowers. My dragon lilies start to wilt. Water can't help them, and the shade is the devil in disguise."

"Well, I'm going to head back to bed. Get you some rest," she said, moving toward the door.

Gaby called out after her, "Mama, we should talk," but the words were lost as the screen door slammed into place.

In the doorway Duchess paused. Gaby held her breath, hoping she had heard after all. She wished her mother would come sit beside her like they used to sit, with their hands touching in the dark.

Gaby heard Duchess turn to switch off the light and start for the stairs. The farther her mother stepped away, the easier it became to breathe. The lightness of air surrounded her.

But the duchess hadn't stepped away. She emerged from the darkness of the house to the porch, careful not to misstep. She swept across the landing to the railing, where she stood with her chin lifted to the moon, whose blue light splintered through the shaded trees and marked her face gray.

Gaby waited until her eyes adjusted to the shadow of her mother before she said, "It'll be your first grandchild, Duchess." There, the words escaped before she could breathe them in again.

"I would have preferred a first son-in-law."

"The baby's due this fall."

"That's just what you need, a temperamental child."

"I keep craving boiled peanuts."

"*Hmh*, peanuts will make you fat for sure. I remember when I was pregnant with you I couldn't get enough of raisins. I swore I'd never so much as eat a grape after I had you."

"Did you like being pregnant, Mama?"

Duchess paused before she said, "I guess I did. My skin stayed clear.

My hair was so thick I had to wear it in a French braid, and my nails—my nails were splendid." Her voice trailed off as she looked down at her splayed hands, remembering. "But that was years ago and times were different. Your daddy took good care of me. I didn't so much as want for a glass of water, he was right there tending to my every need.

"I keep wanting to ask you what is it, this thing you've done?"

Gaby watched Duchess clench her hands.

"I've got it all worked out, Duchess," she said. Then, after a moment, "You don't understand, do you? I planned this pregnancy. It wasn't a mistake."

"Then you're a bigger fool than I imagined. What smart girl throws away her life on an idea that she can handle another? What if your baby is sickly or you can't find someone to care for him?"

"My friends will help."

"Friends aren't family," Duchess said, snapping back the air.

She bristled, and the starchiness of her night clothes sounded out her movement from the porch steps to the door. As she reached for the handle, Gaby said, "I think it's a girl, Duchess."

"You're carrying too high. Your hips are as wide as a Hottentot's and your back is too broad. It's a boy."

The door opened, yawning until it reached its frame, and the words hung in the air, weighted like magnets to the evening sky. And in the stillness of the night, Gaby sat measuring what she had heard. A thin smile spread across her lips. The willow's leaves rustled, and a breeze blew in that stayed with her till morning.

The next day Gaby rose from sleep and made her way to the third floor porch. Peeking through the trees' foliage had been a childhood treat—watching neighbors leave and return home from work with no wear on their minds at all of who could see them make public their private acts. On occasion she caught Julie Birk's boyfriend slipping out of her house. Gaby knew when Mr. Stokes pulled into the drive across the way, Mrs. Stokes appeared on the lawn.

But today as Gaby breathed in the faint scent of morning, she spotted a woman in black striding purposefully along the sidewalk, a spectacle of grace. It was the duchess returning home from Sunday service. Her gait was unusually spry. She touched the ribboned heads of youngsters playing on the sidewalk as she hurried past them. Now and then she reached up to press the flat of her sprawling hat down on her head. Her Bible remained tucked beneath one arm as she waved to a neighbor, who sat on his porch reading the morning paper.

Gaby imagined the duchess at her usual station at Mt. Zion, the aisle seat in the front left pew, with her hymnbook open in the cradle of her hand. With the first note sung, Duchess stole away from life's circumstances. And when Reverend Lee's words struck a chord that mirrored her life, she raised a gloved hand, a testament that she understood what life had wrought her. Gaby imagined her reading scripture with parted lips, wiping dry her watering eyes, while she looked around, making sure no one saw them.

A yard from home, Duchess stepped down from the curb, and rather than look for oncoming traffic she leaned back toward the open sky. As she did, a solid wind caught her full face, lifting her hat off her head before sailing it toward the street. Before it flew completely out of reach, she lunged forward and caught it like a bird between gloved hands.

But what threw Gaby the most was the way Duchess's face broke into a smile, not broad and wondrous, but a giving smile that's born from a stirring in the heart. Gaby pulled her robe tighter and hurried downstairs to the back of the house. She wanted to greet Duchess with flowers, so she stumbled through the brush in her bare feet, looking for roses that didn't bow at the stem but looked toward the sun, like Gaby, pressing their faith against the very thing that could harm them.

The Insiders

LOUIS EDWARDS

When he dreamed, he never dreamed of people. He was never chasing anyone, and no one was ever chasing him. He was never kissing anyone or being kissed. No one was calling his name. There was never a plot or the weird kind of unpredictable story line usually associated with dreams. No—when he dreamed, he dreamed of geometric shapes and silently mutating figures. Passive rectangles and squares. Aggressive triangles and parallelograms. Rolling, thunderless clouds and the shadows of trees, shifting with the wind, cast upon a plane that, though utterly abstract, might have been the side of a neighbor's house. The only actions were those of the shapes moving here and there, in and out of one another, forming patterns that, upon repeated appearance, might come to have specific meanings. Even the individual shapes could have meaning. For instance, a simple square, drawn in the center of his mind's canvas, represented the scientific aspects of the universe. If it rotated once, clockwise or counterclockwise, it became the mystical. If it was off-center, it was a window; if it was blue, the season was winter. And, yes, a circle, regardless of color or placement, was joy and perfect peace.

LOUIS EDWARDS is the author of the novel *Ten Seconds*. He lives in New Orleans, where he writes other novels and works for the New Orleans Jazz & Heritage Festival. He also works for Festival Productions, Inc., in New York. He was a 1993–94 Guggenheim Fellow.

However, Paul rarely dreamed of simple figures. There were usually more complex forms and patterns interacting with one another, as had just been the case. He was awaking now with a fright from his imagination, having witnessed in a dream a large red oblong figure being bombarded by a series of bluish-black triangle shapes; sweating, he was, and screaming, "Go away! Go away! This ain't no party! This ain't no disco!"

He had been napping, something he did a lot of lately. Sitting up in bed, he opened his eyes and listened as his breathing slowed. His eyes closed again softly, and the silence of the house broke upon him, only the echoes of his shout masquerading as sound. He didn't feel the least bit groggy; the jolt of the nightmare splashed like ice water over his sensitive spots: his ankles, genitals, navel, nipples, earlobes, the corners of his eyes. And since he'd only recently reached the age of eighteen, he was, indeed, quite sensitive. His left nipple in particular—the more excitable one, the one that had always been the recipient of the majority of his lovers' attention (due mainly to Paul's suggestion)—would tingle well into the evening.

His eyes opened themselves now, and when he saw his digital clock glow 7:47 at him he jumped out of bed, remembering his date to meet Faith in Armstrong Park at eight o'clock. Faith was his best friend, a shy, brilliant girl, the valedictorian of his recently graduated class at McMain Magnet. Right after graduation, Paul and Faith had decided that because they would be attending different colleges, miles and miles apart—she out of deep loyalty to her father and respect for his opinion about her going to a predominantly black school, Howard University; he out of respect for Faith's father's opinion and out of an infatuation with his hometown, Xavier—they would spend the entire summer saying goodbye to each other. They had already met to say goodbye at most of their favorite spots in the city: on the corner of Canal and Basin streets in front of Krauss Department Store; at the bus stop at Canal and Broad streets, where they caught the bus going down toward the river; at the central library on Loyola Avenue; in the Greyhound Bus Terminal on Loyola; aboard the Algiers ferry; at Two Sisters' Soul Food Restaurant on North Derbigny; at Gallatoire's; on the St. Charles streetcar; at Record Ron's on Decatur; and at the amazing (they believed) Schwegmann's Supermarket on Broad at Bienville. Upon parting after each meeting they would make a point of telling each other goodbye, of actually saying it.

"Goodbye," Paul would say.

"Goodbye," Faith would respond.

Or vice versa.

Tonight's rendezvous in the park was to be their last goodbye. Faith had relatives in Washington, D.C., and they had invited her up a few weeks early to help her get settled before the fall semester began. Paul was not expecting this final meeting to be sad; none of the others had been. They had all been short and sweet, simple. The theory behind them (with him and Faith there was a theory behind everything) was that to say goodbye was a necessity. You could be laughing or crying as you said it, pretending to be carefree or indifferent, but the important thing was to say it. Tying the laces of his sneakers, Paul tried to remember which of them had formulated the Goodbye Theory, but he could not recall. Though his mind was sharp at present, his memory was still in a free-form mode, the mode of dreams and artistic creation. He knew this because his quick search for the Goodbye Theory had uncovered the name of a character from a short story he once wrote about a young boy, Iris; the line from an obscure poem he'd never gotten around to writing: "And everyone was running around saying 'mauve' when what he really meant was 'purple' "; and the last two bluish-black triangle figures dashing off into blinding white light after the fleeing red blob—the latter giving him a chill even as he rested in the safety net of consciousness. He would have to ask Faith about the origins of the Goodbye Theory. Paul went into the bathroom, used it, grabbed a hand cloth to wipe the sweat from his face, and hurried out the front door.

Armstrong Park was just up the street. It was one of the best things about living in Treme, one of the oldest parts of New Orleans. Paul didn't care what the politicians and media alarmists had to say about the park, and he hated the arguments of the neighborhood organization demanding power to decide the park's future. He knew something needed to be done (the park and its facilities were wasting away), but he almost wished they'd just leave it alone to rot slowly without actually crumbling, matching the city's own state of perpetual decay. Armstrong Park had given him hour after hour of pleasure. He had read countless books there; written volumes of diaries and journals; been to concerts, both inside and outside the halls; graduated (in Municipal Auditorium); admired green; met lovers; had sex; and once, as hot puffs of masculine breath stung the back tip of an earlobe, wondered, Is an orgasm the moment sex ceases to be an act and becomes an emotion? All his passions had been pleasantly incited in the park, whose physical beauty he saw as a microcosm for the world's beauty and a macrocosm for his own. The rounded top of that young oak there, for example, in its perfection (he was about to turn right and enter the gate on the St. Philip Street side of the park), might be a huge, majestic, arboreal cloud hanging for miles over the Carolinian coastline, or perhaps the flawlessly bitten nail of his left thumb (left, for he was walking toward the river, making this side of the park the left from his perspective); Carolinian, for what he felt without certainty was a similar geographic reason and for the vagueness of its implication—North, South, or both—and because he simply liked the word "Carolinian").

He walked into the park and headed for the Congo Square area, where he and Faith had agreed to meet. Meeting there seemed corny to him now, but it had been easy just to say, "Okay, let's meet at Congo Square." One of them had said that.

He saw only a few people still about, and they seemed to be milling around near the exits. He'd never been sure what time the park officially closed, because it seemed that no matter how late he found himself hanging around the vicinity, he had always managed to find ways in and out. The lights weren't very bright, and some areas were not lit at all. He decided he'd better jog over to meet Faith, just in case she was starting to get a little frightened; she could be timid under much less threatening circumstances. There was no doubt in Paul's mind that she would be there waiting for him to arrive. She was always at the meeting places first, waiting for him. There was something in her that made her feel comfortable sitting still and waiting. Maybe her stomach was tied in knots while she waited or maybe she actually enjoyed it. He didn't know. But if she actually did enjoy it (and Paul was inclined to think she did, mainly because she waited so consistently), then her pleasure was a sensation he would never understand. The pleasure of waiting. Something to do with anticipation, heightened desire, a concomitant sense of increased fulfillment, ketchup commercials, Carly Simon. He was guessing, without much sympathy. He couldn't see how anyone wouldn't much prefer to throw open the French doors and stun the gallery of guests; or suddenly appear at the top of the stairs to the sound of gasps, or; as he was now doing, come thumping along on the paved carpet, part poet, part jester, with one hundred percent of the spirit of one who arrives, and without saying anything, not even the faintest "I'm here," witness the risen light in her eyes.

She was a wait-er; he was an arriver. Only in his last slow stride toward her did he admit to himself that either one without the other amounted to humiliation.

"You made it," Faith said, glancing at her watch. "Right on time."

"Sup, girlie?" he asked.

"Sup, homey?" she answered.

It was their imitation—coated with a deep affection and longing—of late-eighties black teen hip, of a million things they could never be, their struggle to glimpse all the proms, house parties, and rap concerts they had never attended, would never attend. Outsiders, together they had built walls around themselves, and they could sit inside these walls and feel the great perfection of being normal. Only they. Paul sat down beside her.

"You been here long?" he asked.

"Not really. I got a couple of funny looks from some guys passing, though. I was hoping you would hurry. One of them I know you would have been crazy about. The lips."

"You know me and lips."

"Yeah. You know," she said in her near-whispering voice, "I don't think we should stay here too long. I don't know if we're supposed to be here at all. The whole park is empty. And now look how fast it's getting dark. Where are the damn lights in this place? Can you see anything?"

"So it's a little dark," Paul said. "I don't mind the dark."

"I know."

Paul took her hand. "Oh, look, wow." He touched the lapel of her blouse. "This is new. Did you make it?"

"Of course." A talented seamstress, Faith made all her own clothes.

"This is great. Is it black or blue?"

"Navy."

"That's really nice. What is it, linen?"

"Yeah."

"How clever."

"You really like it?"

"Girlie, girlie, girlie . . ."

"Really?"

"Leave that here with me." They laughed. Faith stopped first.

"I think I forgot to tell you on the phone last night—guess who I saw yesterday?"

"Who?" Paul asked.

"Denise. Did I tell you that?"

"No."

"She told me she's not going to go to Harvard after all."

"Why not?"

"Money, she says. But I don't believe her. She has all the scholarship money anybody could ever need. As much as I have. And I think they offered her even more. I think she's just scared."

"So, what's she going to do?"

"Go to LSU, I think."

"Really?"

"Yeah." She paused. "You know, sometimes I think we should all be going to Ivy League schools."

"Do you think we're not because we're all scared?"

"Possibly. Provincialism breeds fear."

"But I thought we were so *worldly*," Paul said, forcing a whine on "worldly."

"Worldly, like everything else, is relative. We're worldly compared to the average New Orleans eighteen-year-old, whoever that is. But compared to the average New York eighteen-year-old, we're probably just barely on a par when it comes to the worldliness quotient. And the problem with that, of course, is that we're not average."

"Speak for yourself."

"No, seriously," she said. "I hate being afraid—but it's one of the few things I can be certain that I am. I'm terrific with a needle and thread, I'm very bright, and I have irrational fears. Of these three things I'm certain. Howard is my daddy's alma mater and all. But if my Aunt Rose wasn't there in D.C. begging me to come, I probably wouldn't even be taking that little leap. I'd probably be staying home too. No offense. You know what I mean."

"Hey, I wouldn't leave New Orleans on any account, for anybody. Not for a dozen Aunt Roses. Not for a bouquet of them."

Faith chuckled. "I'll miss the wit."

She leaned against his shoulder and said, in the voice of a little girl, "Tell me a dream."

With boyish excitement, Paul began, "Oh, just before I came over here I had this one about—"

"No." She interrupted him. "Once-upon-a-time it."

"Okay," he said, restraining himself. "Once upon a time"—he started slowly in a mock adult tone—"there was nothing. Then one day there appeared, in the center of the nothing, something red. The red thing was uncertain about what its purpose was, where to go, what to do, what to be." Faith hummed a little laugh. "It finally settled on being an elongated thing, resembling, remotely, a fish standing on its tail fins, an hourglass, a woman. Then one day, above the red thing, the sudden appearance of dark blue things. Shaped kind of like Doritos. Then the blue Doritos immediately began to drop themselves upon the red thing, hitting it with solid blows, each blow temporarily disfiguring the red thing."

"But why were they hitting her?"

"I don't know. But maybe because they thought she was going to dance."

"What?" Faith asked more loudly than usual.

"Yeah, because that's when I woke up shouting something about 'This ain't no party, this ain't no disco.' "

"Talking Heads? You woke up with—I mean, doing a David Byrne impersonation?"

"I think so."

"That's pretty weird, Paul." She was laughing. So was he. "You should see somebody about all that. Tell me one with circles in it. I want to hear one of those. They're the best ones. Don't you have one of those?"

"Not tonight. Sorry."

"What was that?" she asked.

"What?"

"That noise."

"I didn't hear anything. Us laughing."

"It was a rustling sound. Like bushes."

He looked up at the large trees surrounding them. "The ghosts of strange fruit," he said.

They sat there in silence for a while. Then Faith put her arm around him. "I don't think coming here at night was such a good idea, Paul. It's not so safe, you know. I really don't think we're supposed to be here at all. Don't get mad at me. I know you like it here. But I think maybe we should go now."

Paul looked at her and smiled. "If you want to," he said.

"I do. There's no light in here."

"Well, come on, girlie."

They stood up. Faith turned to him and said, "Ho-mey . . . ," softly lowering the second syllable. She was waiting for him to look directly at her again, Paul knew, and she was about to say it. He didn't know why, but he wasn't ready to say it yet. He would stall her by asking her which of them had come up with the Goodbye Theory.

"Say, Faith—" He stopped. A couple of seconds ticked away, but it was as if time stood still. Then these two fragments, barely audible, passed together through his lips: "Oh, God . . . people." Standing in the darkness of the park, he suddenly knew that the Goodbye Theory was his own. (This recognition was part of the "Oh, God," but only a small part.) He had invented the theory out of a brief memory of a man named Malcolm, a lost friend from his childhood. As he had glanced away to avoid Faith's eyes—just as the impression of Malcolm had entered his conscious mind —he had seen a couple parting in the distance beneath a streetlight on Rampart Street, the man heading toward Canal Street, the woman going in the opposite direction, downtown. (This vision was part of the "people." And just before he said "people," he had thought he was going to cry. But no, he blinked and he was all right.) The "Oh, God" of *Oh, God . . . people* had even come out sounding a little bit like Malcolm's voice—or at least that voice as Paul remembered it. Paul had met Malcolm during the summer he lived in the city of South End, just before he came back to New Orleans to live with his grandmother. It had been the most difficult period of his young life—only eleven years old at the time. He and his sister Grace had been placed temporarily with foster parents, a minister and his wife. Paul met Malcolm at Lancaster Park, and Malcolm befriended him, like a big brother. Paul confided in him the most private of his precocious thoughts. It was obvious to Paul that Malcolm, a man in his midtwenties, was amazed by him, and he developed, he admitted in retrospect, something of a crush on Malcolm. When Paul found out he was going to be coming back to New Orleans, they planned a special last meeting. Malcolm was going to buy him a going-away present. But something had happened to move up Paul's planned date of departure, and he had missed that last meeting. He had never seen Malcolm again. A kind, observant man who seemed to be in search of something. Where was he now? And what was the gift Paul would never receive?

In the moment of *Oh, God . . . people,* he missed Malcolm intensely ("Oh, God, he was the only person ever to call me Paulie!"), and in a flash he lamented hundreds of hellos and goodbyes, some spoken, some un-, and here the utterance of the sigh of "Oh, God . . . ," and during this same breath he saw the couple parting on Rampart Street and faces from the past (Malcolm; his mother; his dead brother, Frank), the teeth of their laughter, grimaces, the eyes of joy and feigned naïveté—(we'll meet again, of course, we'll meet again)—and beneath the teeth and the eyes, a flowing caption: "The people who come in and out of your life, who kiss you or hold your hand even briefly, and who never say goodbye, I love you, or anything; and, oh, my, how you miss them now, oh, my"—all of which came out limp and defeated, most of it wiped away by a tear-clearing blink, the denouement of a gasp: "people."

Oh, God . . . people.

"Hmm?" asked Faith.

"I was just about to ask you who came up with the Goodbye Theory."

"Well, you did."

"Yeah, I know. I just remembered. But now I think I was wrong."

"What do you mean?"

"Well, when I came up with it I was thinking that you actually have to *say* goodbye. But that's not right. The important thing is to know a goodbye is taking place, to know you're in the middle of one, to acknowledge it and not be afraid of it. You know?"

"Hmm. Maybe you're right."

"I think I am. The actual acknowledgment of the goodbye is everything. The goodbye itself can be silent. It can be spoken, but it's okay if it is not."

They started walking toward the St. Philip Street gate.

"Which leads me to the notion," Paul said—he was rolling—"that Paradise will be a place where everyone will have the capacity of perfect and wordless articulation of the truth. Where everyone can explain his or her actions without fake rationalizations or, rather, by using some greater system of rationalization common to all universes."

Faith chimed in. "And that common system of rationalization might in itself be all the truth we need?"

"Yes!"

"I see," she said. And he knew that, indeed, she did.

"And the souls of all saints are circles," he said.

"And everyone is a saint?" They had agreed on this some time ago.

"Circle after circle after circle."

"I see." He knew she did.

As they walked along St. Philip Street, Faith asked, "You have the address I gave you?"

"Yeah."

"And you'll write to me?"

"Every day."

"Good."

"Even if my pen never touches paper again, I'll write to you every day."

"I see," she said.

And he was certain that she did.

Scotch and Curry

LOLIS ERIC ELIE

Wandalyn wears glances like a shawl. And if in the beer and smoke of this place a pair of eyes should slip from her neck and off her shoulders and away from her, she gathers it back, if she wishes, and puts it in place. Hers is a beauty which, even now that it has been made important, I cannot explain.

Curry saw it and in a flash asked who she was. He wasn't the first to ask, for Alvin's response was pat. "Seventeen," Alvin said to him, "she'd as soon cut you as look at you." And it began.

Curry, at seventeen, felt he had mastered childhood.

Children—sixteen, seventeen, eighteen—sometimes steal into these places. In this city who would stop them? Their eyes, wide for a foretaste of life, see adventure in the darkness of bars. But Curry worked here. Looked down on them from the elevation of the bandstand.

He had mastered the guitar and so played with us. Men fifteen or twenty years older than he, but men who could tell him very little about playing

LOLIS ERIC ELIE is the author of *Smokestack Lightning: The Art and Culture of Barbecue*, published by Farrar, Straus & Giroux. His varied career has included stints as a business reporter for *The Atlanta Journal-Constitution* and road manager for the Wynton Marsalis Band. His work has appeared in *The Seattle Review*, *African-American Review*, *Callaloo* and *Double Dealer Redux*. He now resides in his native New Orleans.

music. Off the bandstand he couldn't help but wonder, Who was he to play with?

Wandalyn—if a place like the Lion's Den can be said to have a queen —is that woman. Hers is the stool at the corner of the bar closest to the entrance. Upon entering, you see her first. And no matter where else your eyes may wander, they never really leave her.

Curry, looking at her, thought little of Alvin's advice. He walked over to Wandalyn after the second set. I saw them from a table near the bandstand: she laughing (I thought politely), he cocking his head and making gestures with his hands like an older man in this place would make. I expected the conversation to be over quickly. Wandalyn did little more than flirt even with men her age. How much time would she have for Curry, who, even in the light of the bandstand, even with his athlete's frame, looked so obviously seventeen? But they talked and laughed until the break was over.

As I plugged my bass into the amplifier, I saw Curry approaching. He was trying hard not to blush, his face begging for comment from one of us. I refused. Skeet didn't.

"Ah, the sweet bird of youth," Skeet said.

"The sweetest bird there is," Curry said.

"So you're going to give it a try."

"No try in it." Curry smiled. "No try about it."

The sound of this place—the sound of drinks being poured and jokes being told and lustful courtships being danced to life—is the sound of Alvin "The Boss of the Blues" Jackson. And his sound, electric blues songs of men and women in desperate search of one another, is part of what makes so much so imaginable and even so possible in the darkness of this place and in the lateness of these hours. These songs awaken fantasies. And in no one is that more true than in Alvin himself.

Alvin changes suits after each set. It's an old habit. Years ago, in small country towns where people didn't have many clothes, the idea of having three suits to change into was itself a fantasy. The fantastic life of the traveling blues bard. But in New Orleans, so close to the twenty-first century, cheap suits, even in great numbers, are not impressive. But these old suits help to explain Alvin. For he sincerely hopes the train of history will return to a previous stop, where he still waits, and pick him up and take his life somewhere else.

Twenty years ago, Alvin had a few minor hits. On the posters that advertise our engagement at the Lion's Den there are photographs of him from that period. Then he opened at larger clubs for big names, and at smaller, less prestigious places he headlined.

There is hope in that. This is what he tries to express to the young white reporters from the newspapers. That with a few words from them he could be discovered. This great diamond could be unearthed.

And he will tell you this: One lucky break and so much could have been different.

He will tell you this at 4 A.M., when the gig is over and he has had a couple of drinks: his small eyes, sunken deeply, his meaty right hand melting the ice in a highball glass.

And he seems vulnerable then. For you know that a sixty-year-old blues singer who has not had his break is not going to get it. And you know these are no longer the days when the sight and sound of a sweating man pounding out blues at smoky, crowded dances is going to entice some sultry young brownskin to bring herself to him, naked under her dress and ready to reward him with herself. And you know that sometimes Alvin sings off key and that his jokes are old.

Which is not to say he is without talent.

Which is not to say these things are determined by talent.

But you know, as he does not, that his voice is not sufficient to defrost and bring to life his particular fantasies.

But you also know this voice is oh so fitting a soundtrack to the fantastic ruminations of this place.

The Lion's Den does not have a dressing room. Alvin dresses in the men's room and sits at a reserved table in the front row before he is called to the stage. The band plays the first tune alone, a funky blues. Then into "Alvin's Theme." From behind his drum set, Skeet begins the introduction.

"Ladies and gentlemen, put your hands together and welcome to the stage the Boss of the Blues, former Del-Ray recording artist, the singer of such hits as [*drumroll*] 'One Trick Pony' [*cymbal crash, drumroll*], 'It's Even Raining Inside' [*cymbal crash, drumroll*], 'Wonder Who's Knocking on My Baby's Door' [*cymbal crash, drumroll*]. Ladies and gentlemen, help me welcome to the stage the Boss of the Blues and the king of this here thing, Alvin Jackson!" (*cymbal crash!*)

Some people applaud when we begin a song they know. It is more than recognition. There is catharsis there. We are playing exactly what they would play if they could play and were on the bandstand. The songs break down, lend credence to, that which they have felt most privately.

But what does Wandalyn feel?

Often she doesn't even look at us. Her eyes scan the room, selecting other eyes to play with. When she is in the mood, she may snap her fingers to the music—even dance!—hips still planted firmly on her stool. Or, if she is in a very good mood, she may even dance with one of the men here.

Knowing that it is possible for Wandalyn to snap or dance to our music makes the band play harder. Bands hope too. But Wandalyn doesn't share herself with us even through the music.

When Wandalyn's friends are here they call her Cheeky Red. It fits her. She has a thin, sharp face framed by a mane of hair that's been dyed auburn. Her nose is small and broad and her eyes are a temperature of tan that can burn. When she smiles the light catches the star-shaped cap on her front tooth so consistently it seems practiced. How to practice catching light on a gold tooth I cannot say. But she never misses, and this is certainly part of what Curry saw.

Alvin didn't let Curry drink between sets. The bartenders knew this. But after the gigs, before everyone packed up to leave, Curry was allowed a beer or two. That night, sitting on the stool, Wandalyn's tooth flashing, he ordered a premium scotch, her drink. And since the musicians don't pay, the bartender served him the bar brand.

Their conversation was quieter this time. I sat with Skeet at a table near Wandalyn's stool. Our conversation was kept sparse so we could hear theirs. But Curry, still cocking his head and gesturing with his hands, spoke in the low, late-night whispers of the men here. From time to time he would put his hand on her hand or on her shoulder as if to make a point. She listened (without seriousness, I thought) to this young boy. When Curry's second scotch came, he put his hand on her knee as he reached to take a sip and she just looked at him, not moving, watching him take a smooth, long swallow. I shuddered.

Curry finished his drink and quickly got up. We expected that he would come over to our table then but he didn't. He picked up his guitar and walked along the bar back to Wandalyn's stool. With her cigarette still in her mouth she got up and they walked out together.

Looking blankly around the room, I pretended it was nothing.

It is a different world inside the Lion's Den. A world far from the world where the mayor is who is the mayor and the stage is held by whichever municipal or international crisis is current. Those things exist in here and are even discussed. But while these patrons know that politicians and events affect much of what happens on the streets and sidewalks outside this place and even affect their lives outside these walls, this place doesn't feel as if it itself is impacted.

This is a neighborhood lounge. Almost everyone here grew up together, and they have known this place and each other through dozens of administrations and crises. The world has changed, but really this place has not.

What mostly happens here is men and women have a good time, make flirtatious remarks, tell lies, sometimes act out on the dance floor what they hope to act out later in the damp warmth of each other's arms.

Thelma Sargeant has known Lamar Morton since high school. He didn't want her then and doesn't now. But she will still take his hand and put it—laughing all the time—into her bra. There are stories of men and women who have fallen in love after hours or even years of flirting here. Men and women like Thelma know this. Know that even the familiar can be discovered.

Wandalyn has hips like a Yoruba fertility doll. Large and round and firm. Her dresses—and she always wears dresses or skirts—are not tight, but they caress her hips, gliding with them. She entered during the first set that next Saturday and Curry lost it. Alvin had hired him, the young guitar wizard, as an added attraction. He was to play fills behind Alvin. But he was also given a feature in each set in which he could really play and show just how good he was.

When Wandalyn walked over to her stool, the slit in her skirt showing enough thigh to make the mounting of the chair an event in itself, Curry began playing fills that took up more musical space than Alvin's melodies. It was as if he were the leader and we were accompanying him. Sometimes this happens with young musicians who are good. It takes time to learn that being good is demonstrated as much by what you don't play as by what you do play. He played like that on every tune until Alvin glared at him and finally walked over and said something to him during a piano solo.

During the break I wanted to speak to Curry. I moved near his side of the stage so we could talk as we put our instruments in their cases.

"You need to check out some of the older guys," I said to him. "A lot of times they don't play a note and it's the sweetest note you never heard."

"Right," he said.

"Be careful," I told him. "You don't want to step all over what Alvin's singing."

"If he sounded better I wouldn't."

"That's not the point," I said.

"I'll tell you what the point is," he said. "Wandalyn is the point."

"What does Wandalyn have to do with what happens on the bandstand?"

"Alvin's just pissed because I'm doing what he isn't man enough to do."

"What can't he do?"

"Wandalyn," he said, "Wandalyn."

And he told me how it felt to kiss her and watch her kick off her shoes. The way she looked as her bra was unsnapped and how it felt to run your hands up her legs and to palm her ass and to smell the slick wetness between her thighs. And he almost lost it, he said. Sitting on that big brass bed, she standing, the window and the moon behind her, her hips writhing as he pulled down those panties, over those same hips and down those legs, he almost lost it.

She's kind of quiet, he said; when she's just sitting over there at the bar, she starts off quiet. But when you start working and plunging and grabbing that ass, she will first lick your ear and then put her whole mouth on it, plunging her tongue into your skull. Then talk to you. Telling you how it is to be done. Exactly how this is to be accomplished.

And it's so sweet, he said. She talking so much shit, you working so much harder, he said, working, grabbing the bedposts and digging your feet into the sheets like they were hind paws in search of traction.

And when it is right, he said, when it is truly right and can get no better, she screams. Screams and claws you and thrusts as if she were moving inside of you and not you inside her. As if she was in control of the whole thing.

"Bruh," he whispered, beaming, "I never had it like that!"

And at least that much I believed.

And I tried to imagine this scene, and to see Curry acting in it. But I couldn't. As if to prove my suspicions wrong he walked over to her. Approaching her from behind, he kissed the back of her neck and seemed to be groping for her breasts. She stopped him firmly, I thought, but then she smiled and he sat down on the stool next to her. She ordered another scotch and he drank the one she already had. She ordered two more. Then two more.

Putting his glass down, Curry's hand moved to her knee. She moved it off and went to the ladies' room. Without a word she left him sitting there, trying to act natural. She didn't return until we had started the second set.

Curry didn't know Larry Wilkes. While we were playing "As the Years Go Passing By," a slow, grinding minor blues that Albert King used to play, Larry walked up to Wandalyn's stool.

Larry is a lot of fun. He will sometimes get into the middle of the dance floor, pushing everyone back with large gestures, and put on a show. He knows the movements of other dancers and parodies them with finesse. Li'l Brother, who hurt his leg, so he says, in some war, dances with a limp. And Larry will dance over to Li'l Brother doing what he calls the Li'l Brother One-legged Two-Step.

Then somebody like Thelma Sargeant will start laughing loud and say something like "Ooh, Li'l Brother, he got you good." And Larry will stick his hips out in one direction and his chest way out in the other and start dancing like Thelma. Perhaps too much like Thelma, for many suspect that Larry is not all man. But regardless, it is understood that this is Larry and it is fun.

Larry danced over to Wandalyn and grabbed her hand as if deciding for her that she wanted to dance. When she didn't move he put his left arm in the air and his right to his breast as if embracing an imaginary partner. Dipping and grinding. Then he motioned to her again to join him. When she didn't he repeated his gyrations with more force and suggestion, then grabbed Wandalyn off of her stool, pulled her close to him, and began doing with her that which he had done with his imaginary partner.

No one else would have mistaken this gesture. But Curry, seeing this, all but slammed his guitar down. Loudly, the strings sounded wrong notes, terribly wrong notes. I walked over to the other side of the stage to silence this noise and salvage the song, but as I looked up I realized that the song was the smallest of problems.

Curry had grabbed a beer bottle from the bar, its contents running down his sleeve as he turned it bottom up. Curry, large for his age and powerfully built, pulled Wandalyn roughly from Larry's arms. I saw him raise his arm to hit Larry with the beer bottle.

We kept playing. You learn from experience that if the band keeps playing, fights sometimes can be curtailed. Onlookers can convince combatants to rejoin the party. In a flash he had brought the bottle down, but someone had grabbed his arm and stopped him.

Larry, effeminate but no less proud, struggled to free himself from the men who had grabbed him. I could not hear his voice, but I could see his mouth moving rapidly, angrily.

Curry struggled as well, trying to get to Larry. They were kept apart, and finally some of Larry's friends took him outside. Curry rejoined us on the bandstand, all the time looking around the room for Wandalyn. Before we started the next tune he called to me, "Where's Wandalyn?" But I had seen her leaving.

Long before the fight had been settled, I had seen her leave.

By the end of the night little was said of the incident. Just Alvin, really. "Man," he said, looking at Curry's torn band jacket, "that comes out of your money."

And how did I come into the beer and smoke of this place? To know characters like Alvin and Wandalyn and Curry?

Well, their lives are as the stuff of my dreams. And if Freud is right, if we are ourselves each of the actors in our dreams, the pursuers and the pursued, the virtuous and the blemished, then I am each of these men and women. In fact, in speaking so freely of them I may be ascribing to them some of the motivations and frailties of my own character. For that I would ask to be indulged.

But when I speak of Alvin waiting for a train long gone to make him a star, I know that wait. I have been playing with bands like Alvin's, some bigger and better, some smaller and lesser, for almost twenty years. I'm not stupid. Of course, the odds are against success and I, unlike so many of these musicians, never take the prospect of success too seriously. Playing this music is fun for me, even with all that goes wrong here. It is true that I never expect nights of playing in clubs like this to ever be more than nights like this. Yet I would be lying if I said I have not hoped that they would be transformed into something else. I have imagined myself on the road in distant places seeing in life what I now see only in books.

And I know, to whatever extent anyone can know, what it is like to be Wandalyn. If she went to New York to model, or to Los Angeles to be a movie star, hers would be another pretty face. Perhaps not even a very pretty face when entered in competition in those places. But here, in this place, she is truly a queen.

I teach English to high school students. And I teach English because I like books and because I need the money and because I think it is a good thing to do. But I also teach to feel the excitement of being at the center of the stage. To have an audience to control. Those young faces are my audience as these old faces are Wandalyn's.

And I know the stirrings and ambitions within men of which women like Wandalyn are the authors.

There is an immaturity to each of these people. An unreality. You can't by clenching the corpses of hollow fantasies bring them to life. You can't look into the faces of a small and adoring crowd and multiply them with your inner ear to create the roaring adoration you wish to hear. And you can't by living life faster and among those who are older gain maturity more quickly.

Skeet did not necessarily see all of what I saw in this place, but he could see the danger with which Curry was flirting. And since I teach school and am therefore assumed to be able to explain such things to teenagers, Skeet suggested that I speak to Curry. I knew it would be useless, but what could I do?

We talked, but it was a strange conversation. Knowing it was futile before I opened my mouth meant there was a halfheartedness with which I approached it, and that was probably inappropriate. But there was a halfheartedness with which Curry approached the listening as well. I explained to him that he should be careful. That the incident with Larry could have been worse, and not just worse for Larry. I explained to him that his future lay not with women like Wandalyn but with his music. A second before the abrupt end of the conversation, he said, "Sounds to me like you have a crush on her too."

I have seen Mack Taylor many times since, but that third Saturday was the first time I saw him. We were playing, but as he walked in people paid more attention to him than to the music. He went from table to table shaking hands and kissing cheeks. People yelled out "Mack! Mack!" but he himself, wearing a wide-brim hat and smoking a black cigarette, was quiet. He waved at Alvin, and from the stage, Alvin nodded back.

Wandalyn did not look up when he walked in. She stared at her drink and at the stage as if she didn't notice that something had changed. Mack sat down at two or three tables for a few minutes each. The waitress brought him a drink and pointed to the man who had sent it. Mack stood up as if at attention and saluted the man. He sat down again at the table. When he had finished his drink he got up and went to the bar.

He seemed surprised to see Wandalyn there, sitting on her stool. As he waited for his drink, he said something to her. She looked up with apparent indifference and responded. When the bartender returned, Mack pointed to Wandalyn's glass. Pulling out a money clip, he paid for both drinks and sat down on the stool next to Wandalyn's.

From the bandstand I could not hear their words, but it seemed to me they were making a dance of conversation. Each giving the shortest possible responses. I still don't know whether they knew each other before, or if they met only that night.

Shortly before the band took its break, Mack walked outside. So when Curry walked over to the stool next to Wandalyn's it was empty. He sat and they talked. She ordered two scotches and he drank one. Mack returned before the break was over but walked straight to the men's room. By the time he came out we had started playing again. Mack sat next to Wandalyn again and ordered two more drinks. They talked and even laughed a little during the set.

When we finished for the night, Mack was still on the stool next to Wandalyn's. Curry slowly put his guitar in the case. Then he walked over to Skeet and they talked about nothing for a few minutes. Then he walked over to me and asked how he had sounded. I told him he sounded much better, that as long as he didn't overplay he always sounded good. We talked, but our eyes never met. The whole time, he was looking behind me.

Finally, he walked over to Mack and said to him, "You're in my seat." It sounded like something a kid would say in a high school lunchroom, and I'm sure Mack was surprised by it.

He turned around slowly and said in the tone of voice with which he would shoo fly, "No names on the seats."

"No names on the women either, but that one's mine."

Mack looked at Wandalyn as if telling a joke. "You know him?" Wandalyn didn't say anything.

Curry put his hand on Mack's shoulder to bring his attention back to their conversation. Mack slapped it off and warned Curry to leave him alone. I got up from my seat to calm Curry down, but even then it was too late. He said something to Mack and Mack replied. I clasped Curry's shoulders and told him to calm down.

Mack stood up. He was about three inches shorter than Curry and so had to look up to talk to him. But it wasn't like he was shorter. It was like a sergeant in the army talking to a private that's taller than him. It's the rank, not the height, that is important.

They were talking loudly by that point. Mack telling Curry that he was getting himself into something that children should be kept out of. Curry telling Mack that if he saw a child, then he should kick that child's ass.

Skeet had joined me at Curry's side by that time. He was also trying to calm Curry down, telling him there was nothing to get excited about. That really, he should not get upset. But Curry wouldn't listen. He turned around and faced both of us and told us he didn't need our help. Then he turned to Mack and said he was getting tired of talking. And Mack told him to shut up. But Curry was determined. He told Mack this thing should be settled like men and started to walk outside.

Somebody said, "Mack, you wanna to leave your hat, man. You wan' leave your hat?"

But Mack, steady walking, said no. "I don't take off my hat," he said. "I don't take off my hat."

I would have stopped him. Curry was foolish and arrogant, but I would have stopped him. But so much was happening so quickly. Curry and Mack yelling at each other, the jukebox playing, and all the time Alvin in the background saying Curry was going to have to learn, it was about time Curry learned. I know Skeet would have stopped him too, but Mack was following Curry outside, all the time talking to him, and it seemed already too late then, like it was over and had already happened. For a moment, we heard them outside the door, threatening each other. Apparently they moved from in front of the door, because after a moment no one heard them talking anymore and there was silence. Silence except for Alvin, talking vaguely to everyone and no one and to himself, saying, "That boy's got to learn."

Even now, it is difficult to look at Wandalyn. Knowing that, whatever else she is, she is dangerous makes it hard to even glance her way.

We sat there like we were paralyzed, waiting for whatever was going to happen to just be over with. Everybody went back to their conversations and to their drinks, because to not act natural was to be reminded that we should have acted differently. It was quiet above the sound of words and drinks and the jukebox. Wandalyn, who had said nothing through the whole thing, just sat, smoking a cigarette.

Skeet couldn't take it. He was standing between me and Wandalyn, and he started fidgeting nervously. His eyes grew wide and he glared at her. "What the d-d-d-damn hell are you going to do?" he stuttered. "What the hell are you going to do? That boy is about to be killed and you're just sitting there!" And he grabbed the cigarette out of her mouth and threw it at her. I stopped him from doing worse. But as I heard Alvin in the background saying, "It ain't her fault; that boy's got to learn," I wished I hadn't stopped him. Skeet calmed down and Wandalyn, not saying a word, lit another cigarette.

It wasn't long then. The door opened slightly. The whole room stared to see who was coming back in. Mack, his hat still on, didn't even come in all the way. With one foot in the door he beckoned to Wandalyn.

Coolly, she put out her cigarette and finished her drink. Opening her purse, she took out a mirror and some lipstick and watched herself put it on. Then one by one she put the lipstick, the mirror, the cigarettes, and the lighter back into her purse and walked toward the door obediently. Not even looking at us.

After she left, we walked out to find Curry, me and Skeet and the piano player. The air was wet and thick. And cars passed by and blew and I was surprised by these sounds and the feeling of being out of the air-conditioning and onto the street.

There is an empty lot on the corner from the Lion's Den. In the darkness of that lot, one of us saw a mound. We walked over to it. Moving closer, we heard crying. Still closer, we saw Curry on his side, quietly sobbing. I bent down to help him. The fingers of both his hands were spread over his face. Between them there was blood. I pried the fingers away. The piano player gave me the silk handkerchief from the pocket of his band jacket, and I wiped the blood from Curry's face.

In each cheek there were two gashes, almost like Mandinka tribal markings. To Mack's credit, though, he could have done more harm. There were no cuts anywhere else. We kept wiping Curry's face and his hands, but the blood kept flowing. Skeet said we should take him to the hospital, that he would probably need stitches or surgery. But the piano player disagreed, saying they were only minor cuts.

And I kept expecting Curry to say something, to ask to be taken to a hospital or to go home or something. He looked up at us, saying nothing. Then, quietly, he spoke. He just kept repeating, as if it was really all that mattered, "Wandalyn where's Wandalyn where's . . ."

CAROLYN FERRELL

 We have two facts in front of us—one: babies, once they're here, stay (and can do our work for us); two: men love love. Bri threw up in homeroom almost every day and it seemed like a awful commotion. But whenever she turned around and saw Roc two rows back, and felt his blue eyes reciprocating love and understanding, it was like it was *his* hands that were wiping up her mouth, all the baby throw-up, and not the teacher's, who is scared shitless, and so Bri didn't have anything to fear. Me, I'm still waiting. I'm trying to reciprocate, but I'm doing it alone. Boy Commerce bops past me in the hall on his way to practice and sometimes has a stone frown, or sometimes he laughs all in my face when he catches me rubbing my belly. He don't talk to me anymore. He pretends to dis me any chance he gets. Like when he knows I'm following him down the hall, he'll put his hand up some other girl's ass and say, "Did I do that? Sorry," like it's supposed to really make the girl laugh, like I'm supposed to get jealous and shit.

He pretends to dis me. But it ain't no real disrespect, 'cause it's strange, but you know that one day your waiting will come to an end. I don't have

CAROLYN FERRELL has lived in Manhattan, the South Bronx, and West Berlin. Her work has appeared in *Callaloo*, *The Literary Review*, *Ploughshares*, and *The Best American Short Stories 1994*. She is currently at work on a collection of short stories, to be published by Houghton Mifflin.

anything to fear. My plan is gold. I can even go so far to say this: whenever I look at Boy Commerce, I see him as the black ship sailing out to the wide free sea, and me as one of the slaves in the hold. Like we learn about in school and are supposed to feel proud of. The waves are crashing against the side of the boat and the dolphins are trying to catch the sun rays in their open mouths with their tiny rows of teeth and I am licking the toes of the other slaves lying around me. Maybe there is something else out there, but I am the one who dies in the hold, on the trip to the New World, the new life. I will never leave. There is not a damn thing to fear.

Do you like tongue-kissing a dog? No, I ain't tried that shit. Would you try it for me? Hell, are you crazy? No, I ain't, it's real simple, all you do is pretend you got someone in your arms that is ready for you to do just about anything, and you're hot tonight. Shit, that's some sick shit; I will never put my mouth on a dog's. Then you won't ever put your mouth on mine. Don't say that. I just did. Why you treat me like this, don't you know my loving is all for you, you my number one, ain't nothing gonna come between us? Look, I'm not asking for too much, just something little and crazy, you want to prove you will do anything I say, that's what I call love! But that dog been licking his ass. The dog's mouth is clean, and I just want to see you do it, please baby. I only want your kisses. I just want to see. Will you promise to never leave me, I'm doing this crazy shit only for you and you better not fucking go nowhere. I just want to see. Look I'm the boss now, and I want you to promise you will never leave, because you can't imagine how much I love you. Please. Please. Please.

Bri and me decided in ninth grade that we were going to be wives in school. The cheerleaders turned up their noses and shook their asses at us. One of them, Sam, said to me, "You got to lose that shit, girl! There *are* ways to get out, and the one you doing is crack open for a dick and get a public assistance check shoved up there instead. Don't get it too wet or they won't cash it." Another one, Mandy with the imported box braids, said, "Become a cheerleader! This way you can save yourself all by yourself, and *then* the shit that gets served up to you is choice shit!" Teeny, cornrow cheerleader, said, "Geez Christ, *mens do pain me!*" The last time any one of them said anything, it was Marge, real name Margarita Floretta Inez Santamaria, who really could've had any boy in the whole damn school: "You will go through all that work but you ain't gonna have the reward. You gonna be two women, sitting alone in the laundromat, contemplating making easy love with a tube of toothpaste when you get home."

Me and Bri laughed them off. Homegirl logic: you know things better than anyone else and their mama and their mama's mama.

The teachers didn't think we were so crazy. One of them, the old science lady, puckered up: You folks are all the same. Laying up under men like that. It's a god-honest shame. Don't you ever wonder where you'll be?

Mrs. Mary, the Irish teacher who used to be in Catholic school, chimed in: No, they sure as hell don't. We show them the history of the world, and they are doomed to repeat all the mistakes. They just want to spend the rest of their born days *here!*

Mrs. Faulkner, Elizabeth Taylor lookalike, homeroom: Here? But they'll just wind up statistics! Heavens! Don't you think we should perhaps guide them at least a little into the light?

Blond sissy Mr. Hancock, the math teacher: You mean *our* way! Are you kidding, Althea? We don't want them *our* way! Let them stay the fuck where they are. They ain't got a clue. And I ain't gonna be the one to give it to them.

Wrong, of course, because that dumb false-English-accent ass was the one who didn't have the clue! Still, all this talk tended to make Bri get all nervy, and she would start asking, "Toya, do we know what we're act-chully gone do? I mean, should we have babies or become junior year cheerleaders?" Bri was always the unsteady one. I started to get sick of that shit, but then again, I didn't want to do it all alone. So I calmed her down, because she couldn't figure a damn thing out. The only thing she seemed to get together was this Africa thing. Wearing African-looking clothes, bamboo earrings, a map of Africa on her jacket. She was really into that before-slavery shit. She called me her sister under the skin. She even wants us to give each other African names like Tashima and Chaka and things. Like that is going to solve some shit! Sometimes she made me sicker than the baby throw-up.

Bri was always freaking about the baby, but I managed to talk her out of her commotion and even got her to make a compromise: she relaxed her hair like the cheerleaders but wore T-shirts that said BABY = 1 + 1 and SOMEBODY DOWN THERE LOVES ME.

There was no question for me. I was going to be a wife in school. Boy Commerce was planning on a basketball scholarship (I think he still is), so I'll have me an educated man. I *do* have a clue. It's just that people have clouded-up, fucked-up minds, and they refuse to see the truth and they live like snails underground in a garden, slimy. Blind. Dark. Like that hold.

Why you being so good to me all of a sudden, I thought you was mad at me, baby. Me, hell no, I just think I'm finally ready to give you all my loving. What's that supposed to mean, what I ain't already got? Me, the whole me, my heart. Well then, hurry up and give it. It's yours for the taking. *I like that shit, lemme feel your lovin.*

My uncle Marion busted his best pair of glasses upside my head. "You what?" He rammed me into the refrigerator, so hard the door popped open and the milk crashed on the floor. *Big-time dis!* "Hoe, hoe, you been hoeing in my house!" He had the wooden spoon, the one that used to belong to my mother and me on Mott Street, and he was drumming out a funeral march on my ears. (I admit, it was hard not to bust out crying, but I kept my plan in mind, and that was like my light at the end of the tunnel.) "Hoe! You got what you deserve! Grinding up 'neath that boy! You worse than a African! Is that how I raised you? Is that how I done?" Uncle Marion grabbed one of my cheeks and tugged till his nails left his permanent mark of love on me. "Hoe! What was you thinking?"

Don't say nothing till it's too late to have an abortion.

It took a lot out of me to try and learn this scared-ass Bri the basics. I told her to keep on going to gym class, keep on doing the fifty warm-up push-ups, the hundred sit-ups. Volunteer to be the kickball team captain, not just a regular player. Keep on wearing Wah Wah lipstick and doing your hair up like, if someone better came along, you'd go for him and leave that other sorry-ass—the one who was going to be your husband—behind. Don't put your head down on the desk because you say you're tired, or another kind of baby-related shit. Be like you were in the old days and get the right answers and say them in front of the rest of the class: *you are still a genius like before.* Just don't zip your pants, just wear a big sweater over so nobody sees you can't bend over no more. Don't let anybody know until it's too late. I could just laugh myself to death! We are so fucking smart! That's how you become a wife in time for Homecoming and Thanksgiving break.

I have been in love since the seventh grade. One day I sat in Reading with my enlarged-print version of *Tale of Two Cities* propped up on my lap and dreamed of what I am doing now: being big with somebody's love. My destiny was as clear to me then as it is now. You might say that since I was a child then, I was illing because I was hoping I would be Boy Commerce's wife in tenth grade. But not so. You're only illing when you dream of things that can't possibly come true.

Bri took it upon herself to fall in love with Roc, and at first the cheerleaders said they wouldn't even consider looking at me or Bri because of this move of hers. Sam had said that Bri was taking some white girl's boy away, and they didn't go for that man-snatching the cheerleaders. The only way the girls could be sure you wasn't playing dirty was if you had some homeboy or some Puerto Rican dude as yours. What do a white boy want with one of us? What do Roc want with Bri, who's dark and not the prettiest girl you ever seen? That's some fucked-up shit. Men like that only see the girl as a dark-skinned beauty, like some Pam Grier in the action movies, and they want to experience some bad pussy. Bri ought to have known that shit. And if it ain't that, then some white girl is crying her eyes out because her boy has left her for some dark ass. And that ain't right, because it's the same thing as man-stealing, and that goes against all cheerleader rules of order. We *are* all sisters when you get down to it.

Bri said love never happened like it was planned. She said love was a flower with no name in the garden of mankind. A flower like the kind that grew in the Motherland, Africa. She said, "You are *illing*. This man wants me for me!" So she said she was going to prove it. Roc followed her around like a puppy. Once I caught them in the science lab, and it was like Roc's hands was straightening Bri's whole body like a relaxing comb. Smooth, unbroken, knotting-out movements. I laughed out loud. Bri flushed and was ashamed, and Roc said, "So now you know!" He looked scared like a true white boy, but he did put his arms around big Bri to try and cover her up. I think that was the real reason Bri said she was going to be with Roc as his wife in school. Maybe if I hadn'ta caught them planting the seed, maybe she would have left him afterwards. I had wanted to apologize, but they ran off dragging their clothes down the hall.

Bri blushed and was ashamed, and Roc said, "You can't stop me!" So I made it my job to convince her to stay with him because, first: I knew she would never get a man like him (who loved love) again in this world, and, two: I didn't want to be alone.

You know, I feel like I want to open up to you, ain't that weird? Why, I feel the same way. Nah, really, I'm not used to that kind of shit, and now I'm feeling like: hey, I want this girl to know a part of the real me. I'm all ears, forever. You know my father, he ain't raised me to be a sissy, he raised me to be a real man, and so it's hard, it's hard. You want to lay your head on my shoulder? I got things to do, I got places to see—but don't talk to me about any of that when I'm lying next to you making some good love. What do you mean, places to go? Baby, I got feelings; sometimes I just look at all the people in the street lying around, or sometimes I see my father dealing out a deck of cards and kissing my mother's cheek, and I start feeling so low. Don't worry, you always got me. Do you know I feel like killing my fucking self, getting on the track and touching the third rail? Baby, don't say that shit, don't! Word. Don't. That's how it gets to me sometimes, and I wonder: am I going to get a chance to kill myself, or will I just be buried alive? *But where you talking about going, am I gonna be with you, how do I fit in, baby?* There you go talking all that shit, you don't listen to a word I say, do you? Sure I do, baby, it's just I don't know where you thinking about going, that's all, and I always want to be there with you, understand? I ain't talking about you, I'm talking about staying the fuck alive! Don't worry, baby, with me you will always be alive, now go on.

I used to be five foot six with pretty box braids, skin the same color as the singer in that movie *Mahogany,* and a nice voice. I could sing me some beautiful songs, like "Reveal Him To My Soul" and "Precious Is The Son." I used to be skinny and used to could dance to music. I used to go to parties with my mother's permission, then with Uncle Marion's. My nose came out in a perfect point, and I used to have dimples. Cute, you could've called me, or even a fox.

Then there is this time where everything disappears, everything. I make up my mind, I look in the mirror and make up my mind. Tired of all this being alone and shit. They all think they can book whenever they like.

Therefore, now I am five foot three with relaxed hair in a runt ponytail. I travel with a belly now. My face is spread out like a ocean, with rocks and seaweed in every wave. I always have throw-up in my mouth, sometimes I carry a little cup with me in the train. Now I don't dance at parties to the record player no more. I dance underneath a boy who says, "Put your butt this way, I am almost *there*."

I look into the mirror and still see a fox. Hell, I will go so far as to say: I am badder than bad.

I took Bri to the new STOP-BY Supermarket and to Tinytown. She had to learn the good sides that were to come. This was part of the gold plan. It's like we learned about in school: this was a "science."

Look, I'ma show you what you *don't* learn in Home Economics. This here is the most important aisle: Borax, Mr. Clean, 2000 Flushes, Fantastik. You got to know how to keep your husband happy, and this is gold. This is the surefire way. This is the way so that when his boys come over to check out the crib and hang and smoke some herb, you earn a A+.

This aisle is of utmost importance to the new wife and mother: Alpo, KittyKat Delight, Friskers, Yum Pup. Now, you can bet your bottom dollar that once you're in, the husband is going to want to get you a pet so you have some hobby to take your mind off the kid sometimes, because you don't want to go having a nervous breakdown on me, right? If it's a cat, then you also got to think about kitty litter, and somehow boys don't like cats too much, all that rubbing up on you and shit. Boys get jealous when they see the cat laying up with you in the bed, and then they act like, It's them or me, and you about ready to fall out laughing because they sure as hell don't seem like grown husbands but like spoiled kids. But you don't laugh, you take the cat to a shelter. Let 'em get you a dog. Boys like to be around dogs because it makes them into husbands faster. It's the kind of thing where they can go out on a Sunday morning to the park and jog and run and play catch and think in the back of their minds: Hey, this shit is *down*, I'm feeling good. Husbands need to feel good. And that's when they thank their lucky stars they got us back at home. Dogs' breath sure do smell like shit, but just think of *him* in the park. You take the dog out for a walk in the weekday morning and let it protect the baby.

Here's my favorite aisle, because it always changes: DIET FOODS and ETHNIC. They got all these Slim Control foods, like Slim Control Salad Dressing, Slim Control Apple Snack'ems, Slim Control Malted Milkshake. Slim Control is what's going to keep us going, girl! And they keep on getting more: Slim Control Ketchup, Slim Control Jelly. You can eat all this shit, then take one or two of their Slim Control Diet Pills and you aren't hungry for three days. Get it? You lose weight that's really not weight at all. And you can laugh at the men getting their beer bellies in front of the TV, because you ain't going to be in the same boat. Then the homies that come by the crib start checking *you* out. Wouldn't you love to stay skinny forever? Not blow up the way all those mothers do? We got to hold on to our world, honey, and this is the way we going to do it. I want to look beautiful like a cheerleader forever. I love Slim Control Cheddar Cheese Popcorn.

Bri, like I had figured, loved Tinytown. She kept saying, "Oooh, I'ma get me this for the baby, oooh, I like this toy machine gun if it's a boy." Bri held the black baby dolls like they were her own and kissed their cheeks. She said they looked like African goddesses! I was thinking, This store is too goddamn expensive, how these kids nowadays get all their toys from, selling drugs? My child will do like me in the old days: play in the bathtub with the spatula, the wooden spoon, the rice pot, the strainer. Man, I had me some good times once.

Bri asked the Tinytown saleslady how much the black baby doll was that said, "Can you say my name?" The saleslady said eighty-nine fifty. And do you believe Bri was thinking about asking her mother for the money for that thing? *Typical.* Ugly-ass doll. *Can you say my name!* But at least I got Bri to look for a moment at the positive side of motherhood and being a wife in school. Yeah, we know what we are doing.

Listen up I'm only gonna say this once, I know I done some fucked-up things in life but it's never too late to make things change for the better. You ain't done anything that fucked-up and listen we got more important things to talk about like what's gonna be the name and when you coming over to spend the night with me again. Shit Toya you ain't gonna let me get a word in is you, sorry, sorry my ass, sorry.

Listen up we can still be together but don't you want to go to college like me or you was talking about that business school where you could learn something useful; man, all that stuff's in the future we got other things to think about; no *this is what we need to think about;* no, this is what we need to think about: are you always gonna be there for me, in other words are you always gonna be faithful?

I want you to be happy even if I been doing some fucked-up shit; you mean with them other girls; yeah, I mean like that; shoot, I know you don't really care about them; yeah, you right I don't; so why you bring them up?

Because I want the chance to maybe care about them.

Listen up, you: I ain't going to college or business school or nothing, when it comes you are gonna give it a name or else!

Else what?

Don't do like that because I know that what you really want deep inside is love love love and that's what I got to give, let me show you again.

Listen to me, *listen to me,* listen to me, listen to me.

In seventh grade, my mother was still alive. The house on Mott Street was cold indoors because the bricks were falling off. When I came home from school, I used to have to feed her applesauce and overcooked vegetables from a spoon. Uncle Marion called from his house on the other side of the city, Washington Heights, where Margarita Santamaria lived. He used to check on us and ask how my mother's breasts were doing. I used to have to hold Mother's head in my arms like a warm ball and smooth out her hair with my hands, she couldn't take no brush. She would ask me to sing "Unforgettable You" and "Breakaway" to her so she could sleep better. My voice was high in those days. I was in the after-school gospel singers. I used to love to sing, but songs like "In Times Like These" and "Send a Message"—songs that gave you a good feeling, like you are in seventh grade and your whole life *is* spread out in front of you like a red carpet—but I hated it when her head dozed off in my arms. It made me too old.

Her favorite animals were fishes, that much I remember. She dug them all: angelfish, blue whales, sharks, dolphins. She liked the free way they swam the ocean. They moved without breathing, it seemed. They traveled light and determined. They never thought about getting caught, about being on a dinner plate, about swimming in a tank before hundreds of fascinated eyes. They let the currents brush them along, and they tasted ocean water the way we tasted the air in the room with the air conditioner on. Mother had the kind of yearning remembering that cut deep when she talked and when I held her head in my arms.

It was going okay, I thought. I did get tired of holding her head, but I did it—*for her.* But then one day, sure as shit, Mother announced like she was a loudspeaker in a subway station: I am going to kill myself. She said, I won't be here for you when I do that, but you will have Uncle Marion. You can hold on to him.

I said, under the water of tears, "Don't you think you could change your mind? Don't you think you could think again and decide to stay with me till I am a grown-up? I want to hold on to you."

She said, You just don't understand the pain, Toya. It has to give way. I have to make it give way.

So she sent me off to Uncle Marion's house and she drowned herself in poison air with her head laying in the gas oven. Uncle Marion said that was because her breasts were on fire on the inside, that's how he explained that shit to me then.

She couldn't stay for me. Damn, she couldn't even do it in the water, take her life where I knew she'd like to do it the most.

Mandy with the imported box braids said, "You *gots* to be crazy, baby! I ain't giving up being a cheerleader for nothing! And I don't want to have stretched-out legs!" Mandy had seven brothers and sisters and you could understand that she need to spend all that time at cheerleader practice to get the hell away from them.

Margarita Santamaria said, "Bri, you aren't stupid. Do like I did."

Sam, head cheerleader, told us, "Naw, I see things different now. You girls is *on!* Lemme be the godmother, okay? I can give it a god name, right?"

Boy Commerce got cheerleader Sam's boyfriend, Big Daddy Dave, to let us into the biology lab. He had some big secret for me, Boy, he even held my hand on the way there from the boys' locker room. Big Daddy unlocked the door, and Boy held it open as I walked on through. He was like a real gentleman when he said to Big Daddy, "Catch you in a sec, bro."

I made sure to keeps my hands off my belly. I didn't complain one time about my big swelled-up feet. I wore my old raincoat so Boy wouldn't have to notice my shape if he didn't want to. One time I even linked my arm in his and pressed a little and said, "Are we really here?" Boy lit up a cigar in the lab and just let the smoke out his mouth like a chimney. In the dark I could see the outline of his pick sticking out the front of his Afro.

So I asked him, "Do you want my loving now, baby?"

So he waited a moment and pulled me by the hand over to a table with glass jars and beakers on it. There was a row of fat glass cylinders. When he went to turn on the light, I saw little baby bodies in the cylinders. They were just little babies floating in gray water. They were holding their hands in prayer.

Boy Commerce said, "If you have this kid, it might come out all twisted and small like this, Toya. Why you want to do some nasty shit like that?"

In my heart, I felt like Boy was really breaking down. If he woulda just taken one long hard look at one of those cylinders and maybe had held it, he mighta known what a pretty future with me he would have in store for him. I didn't want to talk to him. I wanted to let it all sink in. I let him do all the talking, just like me and Bri had agreed to do beforehand in our gold plan.

He said, "Toya, you think you gonna trap me like this baby here? You gonna tie my hands up? Well, *think again*. That's some stupid-ass shit. And you're a stupid-ass girl." It looked for a second like he was going to put his hand on one of the cylinders, the one where the baby looked like a bad dream.

Boy's eyes were red-lined. By accident, the basketball under his arm slipped out and fell on another table and knocked a beaker to the floor. "You see what you made me do, asshole?" He swept the broken pieces under the table with his foot. The smell of ammonia hit my nose, but it wouldn't make me say anything or do something stupid like cry. That was the way to lose them. Wives in school didn't cry. They just carried their load and thought their thoughts, just like old women. I didn't say a word. I would keep him better by silence.

Boy switched off the light and opened the door. "Toya, get this fact through your head: I won't let you end my fucking life. You want to end yours, fine. I always thought you were smart. But tell me: how many black men age of eighteen you see out here raising families? How fucking many? And you want to know why? 'Cause they don't feel like ending life just when it's beginning."

Silence.

"So forget it, bitch. You ain't nothing but a skeezuh." He left.

But he never said he wouldn't change once the baby got here. He had turned off the lights and I was alone in the dark lab. I slipped off my shoes and put my hands just like the praying babies and thought: God, I do love him. Let him recognize my love for what it is. Let him follow Roc's example of loving love.

Then I let my own damn self out.

Boy is the ship, I am in the hold. Mrs. Mary taught us in history that that was how the slaves traveled. They couldn't see the outside, they were in chains. (They could maybe hear it, though. Maybe it was a dolphin flying through the air, telling them their iron buckles would be off in about four hundred years, and maybe they were grateful for that dream from the fish.

They might've even got so happy, they woulda wanted to kiss each other, but the chains wouldn't reach, so the one who was able to slip the chains went around kissing the others for joy. She kissed their feet. That made them more together.)

Mrs. Mary told us that the slaves had been a primitive people. That's why they didn't rebel—they were too primitive. And sure, they had the hardships of slavery to endure before them, but that would be only a short chapter in their history, and then they would be free! Mrs. Mary said that Negro people in our country had it so much better than the Africans that were still in Africa. Some of them still didn't even live in houses. The Negro has definitely come a long way in America. The Negro has become—*sophisticated*.

All I knew was that Bri was wrong. I couldn't have no African name. I had me my slave name, and I wasn't going away from it never.

Bri called me up all hysterical and shit, and I wanted to say, Like I don't have enough of my own problems. But I didn't say that. She cried so hard I thought the phone would melt.

"Toya," she whimpered, "what if I wake up one day and realize I don't love Roc?" Her crying was impossible. We had agreed not to do it. Why couldn't Bri get her fucking act together? I knew I would have to take her to Tinytown again. She was due.

I said, "Bri, calm the hell down. You haven't come to that point. Wait till you get married before you start in with all the soap-opera shit. By that time you will need to have an affair; maybe we can fix you up with Big Daddy Dave." I was still grateful to him for that night in the lab.

She screamed, "But I don't love Roc *now*! The day in the future was this morning, and the baby throw-up almost choked me out! Fuck!"

I told her to calm the hell down, but secretly I was afraid. Bri had heard about a place that would get rid of it almost at the same time it could be born, and she was going around school trying to get the information. She didn't have to become a school *wife*, I had told her before, because she could just *be* with him and be his woman. But she had to go through with the kid. How the hell could she know she was wanted if she didn't have the kid? How the hell could she have her anchor if she backed out now? And Roc was a white boy, an ugly one by white-girl standards, flat nose and a caved-in chest, only he had this thing for Bri's hair when it wasn't relaxed, just natty Afro and shit, and he had this thing for her African ass, and logically we all knew that meant he would be easier to keep. Even the cheerleaders knew it, even if they were too stuck up to admit it. That white boy *wasn't* going back.

"Bri, just think about it for a moment. He won't ever make you work a day in your life. All he will want is children. Baby, most people would say you got it made."

She musta fallen out her seat because the phone hit the floor and I could hear her sniffling close by. "Toya, he told me that he got me pregnant on purpose, that I didn't have a damn thing to do with it! He wanted to have me forever! That's some sick shit! I don't want his fucking hands to touch me again. I'm going to throw me down the bleachers at school."

I said, "It doesn't matter who got who. Point of the matter is, you got the prize at the end of the rainbow. You got your whole life ahead of you."

Bri whispered, "I don't want his fucking hands to touch me again."

Dear baby, I want a rock. I want a long root in the ground. Baby, you will come into my life and I know I will always have you. You ain't leaving me. With you I won't know what it's like to be scared—ever. Baby, I want solid dirt underneath my feet. I want us to be in a house where all the bricks are tight. The rain can come down and hit us, little baby of mine, but we are watertight. I'm not asking for life around me. I'm just asking for something hard that won't ever budge. Dear baby.

I ain't your goddamn vacation home! You think you can come and go if you like? *You think I'ma always be here?* Look me in the eye! I got feelings too. You think you can come and go and it ain't gonna make me break inside? No, don't be looking at me like that! I got pride, damn you, and I got me; yeah, that's right, *me!* And it's about time I took care of me! Yeah, I know you been fucking with Margarita Santamaria, and I know she told you she came *after the first time!* Well, that's bullshit! It's hard for girls to come; they only say that to make you feel like a man! Yeah, I'd like to see you try and make me come! Try it! Just remember: when you're done, you ain't gonna have me to push around no more.

That's not how my mama raised me! She raised me with good loving!

What you talking about: *good loving?* Is that what you been wanting all this time? Good loving from a good woman? Well, baby, that's what I been offering you all this time, you just been too blind to see. Let me love you. Let me show you what loving is all about. It's all in here, just for you.

Just relax on me. Let's you and me reciprocate. Let me be sure. Let's reciprocate. You don't have to make me come, neither.

Boy Commerce wrote a poem for the school newspaper. That is about the craziest shit I ever heard! He don't even know how to spell, and he hates English class! He hates books and he hates using your hands and your head to do what you can do with your mouth in two seconds flat.

He wrote a poem, and he had all the cheerleaders sighing in the hallway. Bet they wished they was in my shoes.

FOR YOU

I want to say
but then I stop and think
Did you think I
could keep this song
in the bottom of my heart
with my everlasting love
I'm just an ordinary man
doing all I can.
Wandering around
till it's true love I found.
Where's my future
Is it you?
I'm a bird
but you want to be sea
So let me spread my wings, you done yours
Better let's stay that way
And I'll never forget you down there
If you ever learn to forget me.

Mother, Mother, Mother, Mother. Mother, Mother, Mother, Mother. Mother, Mother, Mother, Mother. Mother, Mother, Mother, Mother.

(I want you.
I need you.)

(This was the beginning of my own poem. I would never show it to anybody 'cause there ain't anybody.)

I don't want a African name. I know we should be proud. Bri calls herself Assata, and when she isn't thinking about the future, she is feeling proud like there is something else to live for. I know we should be proud.

But face it, why don't you? Here Mr. Hancock is telling me that I could get a vocational diploma and go on to do work in food service like he used to say I could do when I was back in his class reading *Tale of Two Cities* and not paying attention really. Here he is. He said, "Toya, you still have a chance for a brilliant future, you don't have to throw it all away." *Right?* Only a primitive person would turn their nose like I did. *Right?* Fuck Mr. Hancock. Shit, I knew damn straight I wanted a better future than in food service.

Slave of a slave. I don't want a African name. I'll keep my slave name.

Boy was voted Most Valuable Player. Margarita Santamaria was voted Homecoming Queen. Bri went and had the secret abortion but promised me she would always be my friend. Big Daddy Dave asked her to check out a private party at his crib and she said yes she would sneak out her mother's house at 4 A.M. in the morning. Mr. Hancock asked me if I would want Boy's newspaper poem dedicated to me in the yearbook, as someone had anonymously requested. Roc called me up late one night at Uncle Marion's and asked me if he could start coming over and shit, and I said, Why the hell not? There is nothing to fear. Sam the cheerleader still wants to be the godmother. She and I are going over to Tinytown to check out what's new and happening.

ARTHUR FLOWERS

Tucept got off the dusty silver Greyhound at NYC's crowded Port Authority Terminal and looked around for Willie D. He spotted him almost immediately, a tall brother in a faded army field jacket, standing still in the milling crowd. Willie D saw him, raised a hand, and pumped twice. Tucept put his bag on his shoulder and walked over. They embraced, Willie D bear-hugging him.

I was afraid I would miss you, said Willie D, shorn of the North Carolina accent Tucept remembered. Do you have more bags?

This is it.

Willie D's hair was dreaded; thick snaky locks peeped from under a blue baseball cap. He smiled from the depths of a thick beard.

How you get your hair to do that, man? said Tucept, touching a shoulder-length strand lightly.

Just don't comb it, said Willie D.

Don't it get dirty?

ARTHUR FLOWERS, writer and delta griot, author of *De Mojo Blues* and *Another Good Loving Blues*, is co-founder of New Renaissance Writers Guild, in New York, and The Griot Shop, in Memphis, Tennessee. He was John O. Killens Visiting Writer at Medger Evers College. In 1991, he received an award from the National Endowment for the Arts for Literature. He teaches at Medger Evers College in Brooklyn, New York.

I said I don't comb it brother, not don't wash it.

Just don't comb it and it does that?

You got it.

Willie D reached for Tucept's bag. Well come on, man, the family is waiting to see you. My lady don't believe half the stories I tell her about the Ghetto. Whatever she asks you about you just agree, whether you remember it or not.

He laughed, head back, dreads bobbing.

Tucept shouldered his bag. I got it, which way?

Infected by Willie D's bubbling camaraderie Tucept stepped sprightly as he followed Willie D through the crowded bus terminal and onto a racketing subway car. With both of them standing at the door in their field jackets they looked like matching bookends. Head steady swiveling, Tucept was fascinated with the press of people and the spastic pace.

Mighty public town you got here, he said.

Totally lost, Tucept blindly followed Willie D as they got off this train, on this one, switched to that one. At Willie D's signal they got off and went aboveground. Finally.

The Bronx, said Willie D, weaving surely through bright streets paved with both English and Spanish, through densely populated urban canyons bracketed with tall brick buildings.

Soon they moved into no-man's-land, burnt-out hulks and deserted streets violated by an occasional purposeful pedestrian.

They turned up an alley and followed it halfway down a block of deserted buildings. Tucept felt hedged in by the empty-windowed buildings towering on both sides of the alley. Here and there a dark window had a flowerpot in the shadows of the alley and he wondered if the sun ever reached down to the ground.

They turned into the back door of one of the buildings. The lobby was a shambles, the front door hanging off its hinges, huge pieces of the wall missing and grass growing from the cracks of a buckled-in floor.

Fire and water damage, said Willie D, in response to Tucept's stares. Pipes have been gone and we had a fire here recently.

They started climbing broken stairs, dark and cluttered with debris. It was a huge building and the floors disappeared into imposing darkness. Tucept was spooked. Willie D can't live here can he?

You live here man?

Yeah.

Yeah?

Some other people too, two new families last week.

Willie D laughed at him, the sound carrying hollow echoes in the deserted building.

Heavy huh? We're reclaiming it, rebuilding it and negotiating with the city for it. Willie D shrugged. But we have to live here to do it.

On the 5th floor they went down a lit hall. At a door about halfway down the hall Willie D worked open three sets of locks.

A spindly little brown babygirl waddled at them and into Willie D's arms. Hey Daddy, Daddy.

Willie D lifted her up and she squealed. This is my little girl, aint you little girl?

Daddy, Daddy.

Abeki, say hello to Tucept HighJohn.

She turned shy. Who is he?

He's a friend of daddy's. Now get it girl, don't you keep daddy waiting for you to be polite.

Hello daddy's friend, she said, laughing quickly at her play on words.

Willie D laughed and swung her into the air. Tucept, girl, he said, Tucept HighJohn. From Memphis Tennessee.

She giggled wildly. He put her down, locked the locks, dropped the deadman's bar. Tucept went through the foyer into the apartment. The space was large but crowded, a big sound system against the wall, African art and sculptures scattered haphazardly amid books, plants and records. A shotgun and bat leaned against the wall beside the door. The walls were covered with political posters, some framed: *One People, One Struggle. If There Is No Struggle There Will Be No Progress. People's War. Forward Ever, Backwards Never. Martin, Malcolm, Marcus and Maurice.*

Linda came into the room in jeans and a white blouse, dreaded hair tied back with a blue leather ribbon. A fine woman with a vibrant spirit that made Tucept smile immediately.

Linda, this is Tucept HighJohn, my old buddy from the Nam.

They shook. Nice to meet you, she said. Willie's told me a lot about you. Just put your bags down anywhere.

I asked Willie D how you get your hair like that, said Tucept. All he told me was by not combing it.

That's it, she laughed, running her hand over her dreads and smoothing stray strands.

That's all? I figured he just didn't want to tell me the secret.

He told you.

excerpt from DE MOJO BLUES

Tucept stone cold enjoyed the evening. They made him feel right at home, fed him a real good dinner and left him full. He and Willie D told every tale they had about Vietnam.

So there we were at the party with these blowouts on our heads, said Willie D, we looked like clowns.

Tucept howled. It was those Hong Kong special suits that did it Willie D. We were a year behind.

What do you call him, asked Abeki, you keep calling him, what, Williedee?

Huh? said Tucept.

Willie D, laughed Willie D. Everybody around here just call me Willie man.

Oh, we used to call him Willie D in the war.

Oh, that's too cute. Linda laughed. Willie D? What else about him do I not know? Like Hong Kong for instance.

Willie D and Linda laughed a long-drawn-out old-friends laugh. Tucept laughed with them, greedily sharing their pleasure. He felt a pang of loneliness and wished he had somebody that he knew like they knew each other.

A sudden knocking on the door cut their laughter abruptly short. Willie went to the door and asked who it was.

From behind the door, a muffled murmur. Me, man.

Willie threw the door open. A tall excited brother stood there. Hey, man, Mrs. Murphy heard noises in the apartment below hers.

A thick stocky dude stood in the door of the apartment across the hall. He darted in his apartment and back out with a pistol. Willie grabbed the shotgun and a heavy flashlight from beside the door. He stuck the flashlight in the tall brother's hand, Here, man!

The three of them took off down the hall.

Damn, muttered Tucept the Cowardly Lion. He darted after them, thought about it, went back for the bat, and ran to the dark mouth of the stairs. He heard them running down the steps below and went barreling down the stairs trying to catch them, moving so fast he would've run past the floor if not for their voices and a sudden commotion.

He ran down the hall and into a room lit by the big flashlight. With the pistol and the shotgun, Willie and the other two tenants covered two black dudes with their hands up in the air. Between them sat a can of kerosene.

As Tucept walked in, Willie jammed the shotgun into one man's stomach. As he fell, Willie D went upside his head with the stock.

We caught this motherfucker here once before. He grunted as the man went down. We warned him then.

Hey, man, I didn't know, his partner whined, I didn't know.

Shut up, motherfucker, you didn't have to know, the tall brother with the flashlight growled, you knew people were living here.

I—

The tall brother kicked him in his balls. He doubled over and spouted vomit as he fell.

Bring him over here, said Willie, dragging the repeat offender over to a water-warped stool.

They arranged his legs on the stool and Willie asked Tucept for the bat. Tucept's eyes went wide but he kept his mouth shut. He didn't live here. The bat arched. *Craaaaacck!*

Bones cracked and splintered through the dark flesh.

The man woke up screaming, a thin wail that pierced Tucept's every nerve.

The man whimpered and begged as they put the other leg up. He struggled and they held him down. Willie D raised the bat and it came down a blur in the light of the flashlight.

Craaaack!

The man passed out. His buddy was whimpering and begging. Please let me go, please, I won't come back, I swear.

The dark room stank with fear and hostility.

You take him out of here, said the brother from across the hall, and you tell him that next time we see him on the block we'll assume he's hunting.

The man looked at his moaning buddy. How I'm gon get him out? I can't carry him.

I don't give a shit what you do with him, snarled Willie. I know you better get him the fuck out of here.

The tall brother kicked the broke-leg man again, bringing a new whimper of pain.

Lowlife mothafucker, a kid died the last time we got torched. Here, mothafucker, take this back to the sucker that hired you.

He kicked the screaming man again. And again. Again. Agai—Willie grabbed him. That's enough, man.

Get him out of here, he said to the other.

But how—

Get him the fuck out of here!

excerpt from DE MOJO BLUES

The man scurried over and after a moment of trying to figure out how best to do it, he put the whimpering man around his shoulders. They escorted him out without helping him with his load.

Tucept was sober for the rest of the evening. Willie didn't bring it up, like it happened all the time, like picking up his mail. After the dinner Tucept stood at the window looking out at the darkening street. A moody bombed-out landscape. The empty row of buildings across the street were burnt-out hollow shells, some nuke movie, silent, brooding sentinels of a dead civilization. Tucept was impressed with Willie's heart, he couldn't hang.

Willie D came up beside him. Rough huh?

Yeah man, this is heavy, how long you been here?

Not long, we may not stay, we have a chance to get a place in Harlem. We'll probably take it. We hate to leave after we've put so much into it. Check this out.

Willie showed him where they had plastered the walls, replaced the plumbing and wiring, showed him a gaping hole half fixed in the wood floors.

Linda's doing this one, she should be through with it in another week.

Ha, more like a month, Linda said from a thick chair in front of the TV. Since we've moved here we've become competent carpenters, plasterers, and handyjacks, and we thought we were activists before. Workers.

They laughed. That old friends laugh.

Linda and Abeki went to bed. Tucept and Willie sat around drinking wine, smoking herb, swapping memories. In the quiet of the wee early hours the street outside looked softer, easier, slower. Willie enjoyed himself immensely, talking about Sin Loi, the Ghetto, their courtmartial. Ole Willie D still a believer, realized Tucept, serious about being a vet. He knew how Willie felt. He still wore his field jacket too, thought of himself as a vet, nostalgic for the time when they had felt strong, powerful, brotherme, brotherblood, brotherblack.

Say man, Jethro ever say anything to you about a Lost Book of Hoodoo?

Naw, said Willie.

He thought on it some more, face frowned up in thought, the old fine-line grenade scars accented. Naw, he said finally. I don't remember no book to speak on. Lost Book of Hoodoo? Sounds interesting. What is it?

I don't know, Tucept shrugged, It's this hoodoo book that Jethro spoke on a couple of times. Black secrets of power or something like that.

All this in a book. Willie started laughing, expecting Tucept to join in.

Tucept's chuckle was forced. He was half-ass defensive about the whole thing.

Yeah well if you find it, get me a copy, said Willie. I could use some power.

You don't remember him saying nothing about no books of no sort, asked Tucept, never heard of it?

Naw man, sorry.

It's okay man, no problem.

In the morning over waffles, Linda asked him if he would like to go see the Nigerian art exhibit at the Met. They had tickets but they had already seen it once. He could have hers, he and Willie could go.

Tucept wasn't that thrilled about it, but he had a little time before his train left. He told her yes and thank you, he appreciated the offer.

He and Willie stopped by the museum on the way to Penn Station. Tucept checked his bag and they strolled through the place. Tucept was fascinated. The stuff was heavy, intricacies and techs that astounded him and filled him with a new appreciation for the African genius.

He felt a strange sensation as he moved through the room, a vague uneasiness that he couldn't identify, a sense of unseen activity. As he walked through looking at the work, the sensation grew, drenching him. A charge. He started sensing it as strength. He defined it. Power. Force. The room seethed with power. The mojo was strong. The pieces themselves became insubstantial, merely focal points of the power throbbing through the huge cavernous museum. Willie D and the milling crowds faded into the background as Tucept bathed himself in waves and eddies of power. As if led, he found himself eventually in front of a little piece sculpted of stone. Two hands broken off at the wrist held a small creature. He stood and stared, greedily drinking the power emanating from it and exalted with the intensity of the charge.

He noticed the nails on the stone hands and looked closer. Blunt triangular nails. Riveted, he looked at the information plaque. An African sorcerer making a sacrifice, nails delta cut in the tradition of some African sorcerers since before recorded history. Hoodoo men.

excerpt from DE MOJO BLUES

The Quality of Silence

MARITA GOLDEN

 "Public morality is a requirement, private morality an
option, don't you think?" Joseph Llwelyn said.

They were discussing a Capitol Hill sex scandal
involving a homosexual congressman, his prostitute
lover, and large sums of cash. Buoyed by a new twist
on a very old story, the two couples had dissected the
tale over appetizers, drinks, and the main course. The friends were the kind
of people who always knew what to say. Over dinner they had celebrated
the reconciliation of one couple, the impending marriage of the other.

"Oh, God, here come the late-day profundities, and he's not even drunk
yet," Peter said.

"And the worst part is, he's convinced it's all unique, every word,"
Meredith said, tossing her burnished red hair as she gave her husband a
light peck on the cheek. "Don't you, Aristotle?"

"Surrounded by barbarians on all sides." Joseph sighed. "Come on,
Deidre, you're the psychologist. Surely you agree?"

MARITA GOLDEN is the author of the classic memoir *Migrations of the Heart* and the
novels *A Woman's Place, Long Distance Life,* and *Do Remember Me.* She is editor of the
anthology *Wild Women Don't Wear No Blues: Black Women Writers on Love, Men, and
Sex.* In 1995 Doubleday published *Saving Our Sons: Raising Black Children in a Turbulent
World* and *Skin Deep,* an anthology of fiction and nonfiction on the subject of race by black
and white women writers, edited by Marita Golden and Susan Shreve.

"You're the lawyer, Joseph. You have a talent for revealing the self-evident. Who at this table would disagree with you? Not because you're right, but we're your friends."

"Maybe I should just leave now." Joseph faked a rise from the table.

"How'd we get on politics anyway?" Peter asked.

"We're always on politics when we sit for longer than two seconds with Joseph." Deidre smiled.

"Hey, I work on the Hill."

"That'd be a great insanity defense if you ever need one," Peter said, handing Joseph a lighter across the table.

Finished with dinner, they sat companionably on the roof of an Italian restaurant near the Capitol. The surprise of a 70-degree evening in early March had brought out the aides, secretaries, and assistants who made Alfredo's a Hill hangout. The feverish gossip about pending legislation, office politics, press leaks, and committee hearings was a verbal rite of passage, a way to slough off the remains of the day.

As Peter's girlfriend, Deidre Stockton had met Meredith and Joseph two years ago. Now, as Deidre sat leaning against her fiancé's arm, Peter squeezed her shoulder repeatedly, as if to assure himself that she was there. Her hand rested beneath the table, on his thigh.

"You know, now I think of it, I get relatively few patients whose problems are rooted in issues of morality, either public or private," Deidre mused. "Mostly, what brings clients to me are broken promises, violated trusts, emotional burdens thrust upon them when they were too young to handle them."

"Politicians inflict much the same things on unsuspecting voters," Peter said.

"Voters don't have the luxury of being unsuspecting anymore," Joseph told him.

"But definitions are terribly important here," Deidre continued. "I think you're right, Joseph. Just about everything springs from our sense of what's moral and what isn't. Incest, wife beating: in the confines of one's home these aren't considered moral issues by the people who are doing it."

"Until they're discovered," Meredith added.

Looking closely at each of them, Deidre asked, "When was the last time you even used the word 'morality' without a sneer or a sense of embarrassment?"

Washington, D.C.–born and Yale-educated, Deidre Stockton sat at the table wearing cornrows and an Anne Klein suit. What a package, Meredith thought. Only a black woman could wear such a contradiction as though born to master it. Meredith studied Deidre's face, as she often did, for some sign of uncertainty that would inspire relief. Deidre's eyes were large as small moons. Her face, subtly made up to enhance those eyes, was a declaration. But of what, Meredith did not quite know.

At the moment, Deidre was using her hands, as she often did, for sophisticated, fine-tuned emphasis. When she spoke, pressing her palms together or letting her perfectly manicured nails form a triangle or resting her hands flat before her on the table, her elegantly cut engagement ring sparkled.

Once, Meredith had teased Deidre about the way she used her hands when she spoke. Deidre had stared at Meredith quizzically and then said, "I've worked hard all my life to be listened to. To be understood. I guess that has something to do with it. Maybe I don't trust words alone. They're almost all we have, and they're so easily distorted."

"I still say this whole thing is about the congressman having sex with men instead of women," Joseph said.

"That's a neat summation." Peter motioned for the waiter.

"We start out talking about politics and then end up on morality. Isn't a quiet little dinner safe from the onslaught of the monumental?" Meredith was clearly annoyed. "I thought tonight was to celebrate."

"Yes, I've been back home two hundred and sixty hours and thirty-five minutes and six seconds," Joseph announced, squinting at his watch. "Home to stay," he added uncertainly, as he gazed at the head of foam on his beer.

"Let's order dessert," Meredith said, her cheeriness as hard and transparent as glass. Her false cheer and Joseph's grim mood rubbed together like dry twigs.

Meredith had wrested her husband of twenty-five years from the competent but less experienced grip of a young Senate aide from New Jersey. Joseph had begun the affair with the woman and then moved in with her, after informing Meredith that he wanted a divorce. Meredith had met this demand with single-minded patience. She lost weight, displayed no rancor or bitterness, and every week invited Joseph to their house for dinner to discuss "a purely business matter" or to lunch "so we can at least still be friends." When it was over Meredith informed Peter, "All that little bitch had to offer was a size twenty-four waist and potentially great sex. I know the man inside out. There was no way she could keep him."

With her thick dark-red hair highlighted by strands of gray, her drill sergeant's gaze, and determined mouth, Meredith was a woman who would simply never allow her husband to leave her.

"And how would you analyze this moment?" Meredith asked Deidre.

"I wouldn't."

Joseph, stocky and rumpled, even in expensive suits, was a lobbyist for an international trade association. For a story, Peter had spent a week watching Joseph work the Hill. Joseph was exceptionally effective, Peter had told Deidre, combining reasonableness with enough crucial information to make a congressman feel informed but not deluged. Joseph practiced law part time and loved to say that the difference between being a lobbyist and a lawyer was purely in the eye of the beholder.

And yet there were moments, in the middle of conversations at dinners, at parties, when he lapsed into lingering, solemn silences. And when Meredith roused him, Joseph looked at those around him with disappointment, as though preferring what he had left behind.

The first silence of the evening arrived. And to their surprise, they were all relieved by this unexpected break. Joseph ordered another drink, switching from beer to scotch. Meredith took tiny cautious bites of her chocolate cake.

Twenty-five years. The thought horrified and intrigued Deidre. She and Peter were to marry in June. Twenty-five years. How many affairs would it take to survive? How soon would they become bored with one another and become publicly abusive, like friends she had seen who reached a point where even a facade was too much effort.

They had already gone through several weeks of premarital counseling. Peter had resisted the idea at first, arguing that years of counseling had not saved his sister's marriage. Deidre had countered that they would get help before they needed it, and that there was the racial matter to consider. During the first session, she admitted to doubts about whether they could survive other people's prejudices.

"There are issues of credibility in my own community. The bonds of racial loyalty," she'd begun. "Also, there's the fact that Peter's parents are opposed to our marrying. My parents have gradually come to accept Peter. But Peter's father wrote him a letter telling him that it was all right us to be involved, but that in the end men like him just didn't marry women like me."

"We go to parties with Peter's friends and I'm virtually the only black person there, and no one would dare talk about what that means. I love Peter and I know he loves me. But I'm surprised by how much resentment I feel sometimes."

The revelation shattered Deidre's cherished composure. She felt Peter stiffen with anger beside her. They had gone through almost four difficult months of counseling. She wanted everything out. All the secrets. All the weaknesses that could foil them later. Peter had blown up one evening after a particularly traumatic session. "You treat our relationship like it's one of your clients, to be analyzed, repaired, and then added to your list of success stories," he raged. "Well, damn it, I'm not a client! I want to marry you. I'm not perfect. I never will be. And I don't necessarily want you or some damned shrink pawing over my emotions like this."

They first met when Peter covered a convention of black psychologists for his newspaper. Over coffee at the Washington Hilton, he interviewed Deidre about a paper she delivered on the emotional adjustment of black students to white college campuses. After discussing her methodology and the significance of her findings, Peter asked where she had gone to school. Deidre described her years at Wayne State in Detroit, where she had graduated a year early, and the rigors of Yale, where the need to prove herself had given her a drive that everyone thought came from popping pills. She even found herself sharing with Peter the mixed feelings of family and friends about her academic success. Her mother, though proud, urged her not to get "too smart." "I think she just wanted me to remember my place as a woman, the way she'd had to," Deidre said. "I think she was afraid that the more I knew, the more discontent I would feel, and the greater risk I would be for a man to love." And she told him of her minister uncle who, because of her proper-sounding speech and her passion for discussing psychology, had tossed down his fork in disgust during one Thanksgiving dinner, glared at her across the table, his eyes narrowed in suspicion, and said, "Girl, you been around those white folks too long."

"And what hurt the most, I think," she told Peter, "is that nobody else defended me. Nobody said a word. So in a sense I was condemned by them all." Embarrassed suddenly, Deidre grew brisk and businesslike. "And black students still face the same attitudes. They want the dream. But they're afraid it will feast on them rather than save them."

Peter Caldwell was tall, nearly six feet, and looked Mediterranean. And at this moment, his face was transparent, lit by an unapologetic desire for her. The presumptuousness of white males, Deidre thought, suddenly unable to bear his glance. She finished her coffee and excused herself. She had another symposium to attend. She could hardly breathe when she left him in the booth.

Peter had never dated a black woman. And the black women he knew navigated through his world clutching a profound sense of who they were and where they wanted to go. Their schools and colleges were like the ones he had attended. These women had mastered, he thought, the geography of his universe. He never wondered how much that mastery had cost them, or why a similar fluency in their world was not required of him.

His parents were professors at the University of Virginia, his father a noted biologist, his mother a professor of French. They practiced a form of genteel, aristocratic southern racism, so mannered and fused with paternalism as to inspire in them bouts of self-congratulation whenever they had to state an opinion on "that issue." They were both considering early retirement in order to work on projects they had not found time for in recent years. But Peter knew that "unrest" on the university campus was a part of his parents' decision as well.

In the world of Archibald and Jessica Caldwell, "unrest" took in everything from the increasing numbers of black and Asian students in their classes to the recently formed Nazi student union, to what they deemed the unseemly debates about the canon. The university, they liked to remind Peter, was to be a pure citadel of learning, untainted by political fads and cultural fashions. "Some ideas are universal and endure," his mother had informed him sweetly. "And we all know in our hearts what those ideas are."

Peter rebelled by attending U. Mass Boston, a school whose atmosphere was so unlike the numbing homogeneity of 1970s Charlottesville that he had gorged himself on the strangeness of everyone and everything around him, as well as on his parents' considerable disapproval.

After graduating, he joined the Peace Corps and served in Liberia for two years, digging wells and teaching illiterate adults to read. In those years he had concluded that most of the world was a mess. And that, despite the Peace Corps ads, one person rarely made much of a difference.

When he chose journalism as a career, his parents' regret was deeply felt and entrenched. They had wanted him to be a scholar and he had chosen, in their words, to be a "journeyman" instead. And yet he loved them. They were his blood.

When Peter called Deidre at her office to check the quotes he used in the story, he knew he would ask her out. He never allowed himself to consider the possibility that she would say no. She didn't.

A year later he was in love with her. She bristled with the will to be significant, to live her life as legacy rather than mere experience. He found her hunger irresistible.

Dessert revived them. Conversation picked up again. Over coffee, they talked of movies, books, the dramatic shifts in the weather. Joseph was blustering and defensive, his voice rimmed with a jagged edge. He and Meredith had sparred when he ordered another drink. As the two men settled the bill, Meredith methodically stroked Joseph's shoulder, as though trying to tame something within him.

Leaving the restaurant, they walked down the well-lit gentrified streets around Capitol Hill. The houses, once the property of blacks, now gleamed with a studied showiness. As Deidre walked beside Peter, holding his hand, their footsteps echoing in the dark, she watched Meredith and Joseph walking up ahead, their voices occasionally erupting, Joseph insisting, in a hoarse whisper, "Just give me some time, just give me some time."

They passed the Library of Congress and the other Federal buildings, the ornate dome of the Capitol lit dramatically, looking like nothing so much as a huge white marble wedding cake in the middle of the road. The buildings claimed the night as naturally as the stars overhead. As they neared Union Station, Meredith turned and said, "Let's window-shop a bit."

"Oh, no." Joseph groaned.

"I'd like that," Deidre said.

Union Station was majestic after an extensive renovation. The great hall, with its marble floor and fountain, was ringed with stores and shops and looked like an upscale bazaar. They stood for a few seconds, taking in the cacophony of good times, a pianist near the fountain accompanying the relentless pursuit of happiness in the restaurants and bars.

The store windows overflowed with objects needed and unnecessary, playful, optional, catering to vanity. There were stores that sold only fragrant soaps, stores devoted to paper and cards, accessory shops, stores that sold only socks. They gazed longest in the window of a store that specialized in model trains. Joseph and Peter traded childhood memories, and Meredith and Deidre recalled their worst train trips.

As they stood before a store that sold art deco ceramics and sculptures, Joseph, eager to leave, turned abruptly and collided with a young black teenager. "Watch it, man," the youth said, his tone sharp but jocular. Joseph turned away as though the young man's presence was more inconsequential than harmful and said, with a shake of his head, "Niggers."

Fists clenched, a shallow pool of grief forming in his eyes, the young man stood watching Joseph walk away. Spotting Deidre, he lanced her with a contemptuous gaze as he said, "That bastard's crazy." His lips curled in disgust as he looked at each one of them, then dismissed them with a swift brutal hunch of his shoulders. He strode away, stopping to look back twice at Deidre, who felt herself melting beneath his stare, guilty of a crime greater than Joseph's.

"Let's get out of here," Peter said. They hurried to the parking lot, silent, breathless, walking fast, like refugees from a specific, very horrible terror. When they reached their cars, parked side by side, Meredith hugged Peter and Deidre, whispering as she did, "I don't know what's wrong. I think he had too much to drink." Joseph sat in their car on the passenger side, his face shrouded in shadow.

The drive to Deidre's apartment was a long one. Peter tried to pull her close to him but Deidre struggled out of his hold. When he attempted to talk, Deidre turned on the radio to drown out his words. Twisting the dial off, Peter yelled, "What do you want from me? Just tell me what you want."

Deidre stared out her window in silence. Once in her apartment she turned to Peter in fury. "Why didn't you say something?"

"What was I supposed to do? He had too much to drink."

"That's no excuse. Why didn't either of you say something to him?"

"Say what?"

"That boy was abused. So was I."

"What could we say?"

"Why couldn't you just acknowledge what happened?"

"Oh, please, don't turn psychologist on me. I can't take it tonight."

"I should have let you know, each one of you, right there, how awful what happened was."

"Don't you think we could imagine that?"

"No, I don't think you can."

"That's not fair, Deidre, and you know it's not true." Peter stood up. "Look, I've got to go. You know I leave for San Francisco in the morning. We'll talk again when I get back. And Deidre, I don't want you confronting Joseph and Meredith about this."

"Why not?"

"I'll talk to them."

"I thought they were my friends too."

"They are. They're good people," Peter insisted.

"The world is full of good people like them," Deidre said bitterly.

"Look, I'm sorry about what happened. We all are."

"It must be nice to be white, Peter, to never have to imagine any other reality than your own."

"You're upset," he said. "We'll deal with this when I come back."

"If you had any guts you'd be upset too."

"You want to argue. Not tonight. Not with me." Peter kissed Deidre and said, "I'll call you from California."

Sitting on the edge of her bed wrapped in a silk kimono Peter had given her, her head still throbbing, Deidre realized that she had never been called nigger in her life. In the black neighborhoods of her childhood, the word was remarkably flexible and resilient. It could be used to deride slovenly, unacceptable behavior and people. And sometimes, when properly decoded, it was a term of affection. But tonight there had been only one meaning.

In the white circles that had shaped her academic and professional life there were other ways to express the word's intent. There had been visible, sometimes audible, discomfort when she entered meetings during her internship at New Haven. There were the frequent questions from colleagues about "life in the ghetto." For it was assumed that her blackness made her streetwise and tough, despite her polish.

As they had rushed to their cars, words had clogged her throat so she feared she would be sick. Now, stretched out on her bed, Deidre again felt words rise in a rush that caught in her throat. She began to sweat and thought that if she did not speak soon, she would choke on her own words. If she embraced this silence, she could not marry Peter. If she broke it, she wasn't sure what he would do.

Deidre looked at the clock beside her bed as she dialed the phone. It was midnight. The phone rang three times. "Hello." Meredith's voice was sharp and clear. Deidre's palm was slick with perspiration. The phone nearly slipped from her hand.

"Hello, Meredith. It's Deidre."

She had wanted to talk to Joseph but Meredith told her he was asleep.

"Deidre, dear, we're both so sorry about what happened tonight. Joseph feels just awful. You know him, what happened is totally out of character. He didn't mean it."

"What *did* he mean, Meredith? Tell me that!" Deidre shouted.

When she hung up the phone ten minutes later, Deidre turned off the light, removed the kimono, and slipped naked into bed. In the dark, she saw again the face of the young boy. She could not forget how he had looked at her or how she had stood mutely in the shadow Peter and Meredith cast, gazing at the youth as brother and stranger. She imagined searching the city to find him, yet standing before him still bereft of words. Deidre removed her engagement ring and laid it beside the clock. She had no idea what she would say to Peter when he returned. She only knew, this time she would not be silent.

HOWARD GORDON

FOR MAC

 His audition at the Mills Repertory Theatre has ended, and Virgil is happy to head uptown. He can already taste the cold soda he will buy to satisfy his thirst. The caffeine may help calm his nerves. More than anything else, he looks forward to the rows of tall buildings, which will provide sanctuary from the early autumn sun.

Virgil pulls one shoulder strap across his back, heaving the cumbersome tote bag against his right side. Fitting the bag completely across his back is uncomfortable. The weight makes his chest protrude and gives him the impression of an arrogant bodybuilder eager to show off his muscles. The bag also gives him the giddy feeling that he is forever falling backward. But, he carries it nonetheless, for it houses what he proudly refers to as his work clothes: an assortment of pants and shirts, sweaters, leotards, neckties, and a variety of footwear and, his most valued possession, a makeup kit. The kit is a gift (secondhand, but still a gift) from his grandfather, who

HOWARD GORDON is the author of *The African in Me* (George Braziller, 1993), a collection of short fiction. His stories have appeared in *Imagining America: Stories from the Promised Land, Rites of Passage: Stories About Growing Up by Black Writers*, and *The Best Short Stories by Black Writers*. At work on a novel, *Missed the Revolution*, Gordon is Assistant Professor for Academic Affairs at SUNY College at Oswego. He lives in Syracuse, New York.

believes, despite recrimination from Virgil's parents about wasted opportunities elsewhere, that indeed there is an acting career in the boy's future.

"Old Poppa Josh," Virgil whispers. "I really need to get by and see him one of these days."

Virgil swings the tote bag to his left side and pushes through the theatre's thick cedar door. As he exits, an old man steps into his path. He startles Virgil, but not only because they nearly knocked each other over. The old man grins at him. Across his face, he opens a horribly wide, yawning chasm and suddenly exposed is loose pink flesh hanging like udders from the roof of his mouth. Not a single tooth is evident. Before Virgil can excuse himself, the man speaks.

"Don't come back," he says.

"What?"

Unconsciously, he takes a half step sideways, but the old man moves with him and blocks his path.

"You heard me," he says, and he still grins at Virgil. His face looks soft but bruised, like a browning apple. When he speaks, his mouth makes suckling noises at the end of each sentence.

"I said don't come back. You have no history."

The man steps around Virgil but bumps his shoulder, nearly knocking the tote bag from his grip. Virgil turns as the man walks quickly but unsteadily into the theatre without looking back.

Virgil shakes his head incredulously. Someone else walks past him, and Virgil rolls his eyes.

"Probably just an old drunk," he says aloud.

Twenty minutes later, he has completely forgotten about the incident. He sits in the food gallery atop the mall, eating a cheeseburger and sucking listlessly at a cola through a straw. From his seat in the atrium, he is able to observe all of the activity on the streets below. He stares at the hundreds of shoppers who stroll in and out of department stores and restaurants as hundreds more line up at intersections to await city buses. Red lights change and a procession of automobiles crawl through the intersection, and crowds of people—puppet in size from where Virgil sits—float and stroll into the crossing lanes as if time lacks purpose. Two or three people attempt to cross just as the lights turn red again, and a few others jaywalk leisurely into traffic, causing vehicles to swing wide or brake abruptly.

If Virgil believes the odds his parents give him of getting steady paying work as an actor, his chances of getting hit by a car in the middle of downtown are much greater. He turns away from the window. No one seems to ever get hit. Try as he might to avoid them, he also realizes that his thoughts eventually wander back to acting. These are thoughts about the audition earlier that morning that he tries to blot out. The second and final tryout is scheduled for the next morning. Old questions resurface. Will he get the part? How good is he? Can the director see past the color of his skin?

He tosses the cola into the trash. He decides it makes little sense to speculate over one audition. Everything cannot possibly depend upon a single opportunity; there will be hundreds of others if this one fails. And that, Virgil assures himself, is the *business*. With this decision behind him, he boards the escalator and descends to the mall's main level.

Virgil enjoys the festive energy of downtown life. He loves crowds. They create a theatrical atmosphere of their own, a street stage for their bustle of loud conversation, for their posturing, and for their animated gestures. He also admires those individuals who separate themselves from crowds, those who walk with a sense of private urgency, as well as those who saunter about with a fashion-show leisure. To him, all this is theatre.

As he walks, Virgil seeks the pleasing afternoon aromas of fresh popcorn and roasted peanuts, and he anticipates the sizzle of grilled concession-stand hot dogs. He smiles at the endless clothing-store promotions, the shops outside of shops, and the fly-by-night one-person businesses that promote hocked jewelry and other useless wares. Equally amusing is the often silly elevator music spewed through invisible speakers in clothing stores. He delights in taking long elevator rides, which allow him time to study the faces of strangers, mimicking their diverse expressions and logging them for future reference.

At the dinner table everyone in Virgil's family, except his youngest sister, Belinda, fidgets as if they themselves have auditioned for the role he seeks in *A Remembered Future*. Belinda stuffs her mouth with spoonfuls of butter-whipped potatoes and sweet corn. She eats quickly and asks Virgil whether he has secured a job before running off to telephone a girlfriend. Her older sister, Cary, makes faces at her but says nothing. She often does this when she feels Belinda is being a pain.

Virgil's parents, normally talkative during family meals, also say little. Cary stares at Virgil. His father, Josh, once lean and fit during his mid-forties, is at fifty still lean but now owner of a protruding belly, the girth of which requires that he loosen his belt after eating. He looks tired most days. And, although he eats well, his face seems famished. His copper skin is stretched over a sunken jowl. His hands shake. He is getting old.

Virgil's mother, Zelie Amelda, enters her fifty-first year without showing a single thread of gray hair. She refuses to wear makeup, not even a light rouge, yet she could easily pose for a magazine cover. Her eyes carry a hazel brilliance, her skin the color of marinated liver.

Tall and thin and top-heavy, Zelie runs her own hair and beauty boutique. After helping finance a college education for her two sons—Artemus, Virgil's brother, graduated from the university three years ago and now struggles to support his wife and two children on an assistant bank officer's salary—and with Cary entering the military in September, profits from Zelie's shop can finally be invested in an early retirement fund for Zelie and her husband.

Zelie winks at Josh, and Virgil catches it. The incredible love they have for each other frightens Virgil. The stealing of kisses when one or the other is preoccupied—he playing with her hair as she watches television and she nibbling at his neck like a lustful adolescent and inventing intimate names for him like "milk cheeks"—to Virgil, all of it is somehow superficial and disturbing.

He often wonders if it is simply fate or acting or perhaps children that keeps couples harmonious. What will happen when he has a wife and when fate does not see fit to grant the two of them harmony? As an actor himself, might he fake it—perhaps for the sake of their children—or could he just pick up and leave? On his bedroom wall, Virgil keeps a poem he has written:

how would you react in a fire
would you panic
would you run
would you scream help help
would you just fall down and die?
would you run run run next door
save the kitty or your wife
could you pull your child from
a burning bed or
would you just fall down and die?

Virgil wrote the poem, but he has never answered the questions it raises.

Zelie is also the money manager in the family. She takes care of all financial matters, and she is also the one person who constantly reminds Virgil how hard work will lead to success later in life.

"Sure, I want success, Ma," Virgil has told her. "But first I need to find out how to make my own life."

"Hard work is life. Makes the man," his father will add as if on cue.

And Virgil will never argue. Even at twenty-two and with a college degree in hand, he feels his parents are more educated than he can ever become. Though they understand his artistic aspirations, they also dismiss them. Any argument he has with his parents about his future is certain to culminate with Virgil feeling less self-worthy than he did when he started. And he was always made to promise that if his acting career did not work out he would get a "real job," like the ones his father happily points out from the middle of the evening newspapers.

Cary breaks the dinner-table silence. She announces that her date is expected to arrive in less than thirty minutes. Her father stands at attention and salutes her.

"Then you're dismissed, young lady—I mean, sir," he says.

"Aw, Daddy." She giggles. She kisses him on the forehead and he whispers something that sounds to Virgil like: "It'll be all right."

"Curfew at twelve," he adds as Cary leaves the room.

Virgil moves to help his mother clear the table. She waves him off.

"Why don't you just sit awhile? Talk with your father."

Virgil eyes her suspiciously. He looks at his father, who is seating himself again and staring blankly at the tablecloth.

"Okay," Virgil says, his eyebrows arching and his mouth open. "What's up? Something's up, isn't it?"

He watches his mother carry an armload of plates into the kitchen. His father runs his hand across his brow. He looks at his fingers as if examining them for perspiration that belongs to someone else. Finally, he looks directly at Virgil. Then he stands suddenly, causing the chair to squeak against the floor when he pushes away from the table. He loosens his belt and walks around his end of the table toward Virgil.

"My father's dying, Virgil," he says.

"Poppa Josh?"

"Hospital people don't believe he can last more than a few more days. And you know he won't stay in bed."

Virgil knows his grandfather has been ill for some time. Two years ago, he was diagnosed as having terminal cancer, but the doctors had given up on a prognosis. Poppa Josh refuses any medical treatment and forswears confinement to a hospital bed despite obvious pain. At eighty-four, he lives alone in a government-subsidized apartment building for the elderly, though half the time a visitor will not find him at home. Having lost his wife nine years earlier to heart disease, Poppa Josh spends most of his time roaming the city streets, answering to no one and available only when he sees fit to be so.

Virgil shies away from his father's eyes. He has not seen his grandfather in eighteen months. Poppa Josh did not attend Virgil's graduation, and so eager was Virgil to begin auditioning for roles he forgot to stop by and thank his grandfather for the makeup kit.

"He's in bad shape. I saw him before dinner. Bad shape, but he knows it's his time."

"I'm sorry, Dad," Virgil says. He stands, and his father touches his shoulder.

"I've got it too, son."

At first his father's statement does not seem to register clearly. Virgil steps back and gazes at the floor as if he has accidentally urinated there. He looks at his father, who is quietly crying.

"I don't understand. You mean you've—"

"Cancer. It's in my stomach, in my bowels. There'll be treatment, but they've already told me."

"Dad." He doesn't know what else to say.

"I won't last long, Virgil. Your mother and I have talked about this. She's been through a lot, but I'm trying not to worry too much about her. She's strong; she'll make it. And our Cary was always independent."

"Belinda?" Virgil says. His eyes are glazed, but no tears fall.

"Uh-huh. Belinda's a baby. Eighth grade, but it'll be years before she can stand on her own. I'm afraid for her, Virgil. We had her so late. I guess I was always worried about something like this happening."

"I'll take care of her, Dad."

"I know, Virgil. That I know. It's just that we can't expect Zelie to shoulder all the financial burden. If you can help out there—well, I think you understand."

Virgil stares at the oak china cabinet that stands in the corner of the room. He can see his father's reflection in the glass doors. He has turned away from Virgil, but his shoulders lift and drop as he weeps. The light falling on the cabinet distorts the picture and creates slivers of shadow, as if Virgil is peering into stained glass. He cannot see himself.

"Yes," he says. "I'll need to get a job. A real one, as you always say."

"I don't want you to be upset with your mother. We both know how strongly you feel about your acting career."

He holds out his arms. They hang awkwardly in front of him because Virgil is slow to embrace him. When he finally does, Virgil pats his father's back. He sighs heavily. In their semi-embrace, they stand in the middle of the room saying nothing, and Virgil looks to the ceiling as though praying for strength to hold up his arms.

Forty minutes before auditions are to begin, Virgil arrives at the theatre. He has contemplated seeking out the director and withdrawing his name from consideration. But he decides that he has prepared for too many hours to simply give up. He will have to find a job; this, he knows. And, if offered a part in the play, he will respectfully decline and begin his search for employment in earnest.

Most important, Virgil convinces himself, is to be offered the part. He has to know. In the afternoon he will telephone home to learn the director's selection. All actors are to learn of the decisions by midafternoon.

He enters the theatre and heads toward the dressing rooms below stage.

"Boy!" someone shouts.

Virgil looks up and sees the old man who confronted him the day before. He stands on the stairwell leading to the mezzanine. No one else is in the hallway.

"Didn't listen to me, did you?" the man says.

"Look. I don't have time," Virgil says.

He starts to walk away, but the man shouts to him again.

"I *will* be heard."

Perturbed, Virgil nearly shouts back. He checks himself because of the one value that his parents insisted he adopt: unequivocal respect for older people. From childhood on, his mother enforced this code of conduct. Occasionally, she found reason to emphasize its importance by adding an open backhand to his mouth.

"Never sass or otherwise disrespect your elders," Zelie has always warned. "And if those elders are black folks, don't even *think* about disrespecting them."

"Okay, mister," Virgil says. "What do you want?"

He stops walking and reaches into one of his pockets to probe for coins.

"Come up here," the man says. "I must talk with you."

"Sir, I really don't have the time."

"I have your history," the man tells him.

As he speaks, he wobbles against the railing, then sinks to his knees.

Virgil runs up the stairs, jumping three steps at a time in hopes of catching the man before he can injure himself in a fall. When he reaches him, the man is still.

"You could break a leg or something up here," Virgil says. The man says nothing. "Mister, you haven't been drinking, have you?"

"Been drinking all my life. It's how I got this way."

The man's stertorous breathing does not provide any hint of liquor consumption. He points toward the balcony.

"Up there. Please," he tells Virgil.

Reluctantly, Virgil unhooks his tote bag. He lifts the man's arm over his shoulder and helps him to his feet. He has to be at least seventy years old, even though from afar his voice, loud but deep and sullen like bass chords, made him sound youthful and energetic.

Virgil lifts him easily. The man possesses a small frame. His well-worn suit dwarfs his body, giving him the appearance of a child wearing his father's clothes.

"Here?" Virgil asks. He stops and indicates the seats closest to the balcony entrance.

"A little farther up," the man says.

Virgil walks him up the stairs near the top and middle of the last row. He seats him and notes that he has been wrong about the man's age. Close up, his time-ravaged face betrays him. Without his toothless grin, the face is a mask of deep lines that circle his eyes and bony cheeks, much like the worn wrappings of a mummy. His hair, brittle and uneven strands of dust-gray antennae, wavers slightly when he moves his head. And his skin is a dull yellow color. It wrinkles and folds under his neck and along the inner forearms like chicken flesh.

"Just like the *Phantom of the Opera*, huh?" the man says.

"I don't understand," Virgil says.

"Me. Up here sneaking a peek at all you young shoes."

"You mean, you sneak into the theatre?"

"Whenever I can. I love the theatre. Try to see every play that comes here. And I usually don't have any problems getting in. 'Course, no one checks the house during rehearsals."

Virgil smiles. Despite the sucking noises the old man makes, his voice is serene. His placid, whispered sentences appeal to Virgil, as an artist. Standing next to the man, he senses that actors imitate older people not only because the elderly are cranky or forgetful or eccentric—or even because they are old. From older folks actors hope to capture a voice, a true authenticity in measured but natural tones, which can only come from experience.

"Okay. Why did you tell me not to come back?" Virgil says.

"I was acting," the old man says. He grins and his sagging cheeks lift. "I really *wanted* you to come back."

"Why?"

"Humph. Because you don't even know who you are. You have no history."

"You keep saying that. What do you mean?"

"Sit," the old man says. He grunts again. "You heard me; sit your ass down."

Virgil sits next to him. The man leans forward and stares down at the empty stage.

"We don't have much time," he says. He pulls himself back into his seat.

"You know that before they built this theatre there was another one in the same spot? The Palisades. Beautiful theatre. Torn down after a fire thirty-seven years ago come December. And you know something else? I really was an actor. Yep. Played vaudeville right here fifty years ago. Much more talent back then, I do believe. We could act; we could sing and dance; we told jokes—even did magic. Boy, I'm telling you we were colored actors with a chance to make the world."

"Go on," Virgil says. "What happened?"

The old man laughs, but he looks at Virgil solemnly.

"Do you know what vaudeville was?"

"Not much more than what you've said."

"That's what I mean, son. You gotta know your history or you ain't got none. *We* were vaudeville. We were a big part of it. Thousands of colored breaking into the business. So what happened? White folks happened. They decided we weren't gonna make that world. At least not on equal footing. Took it away before you could say Jack Robinson."

The old man tries to snap his fingers but his hand falls weakly to his lap. He grins again.

"Hope you don't ask me who he was."

Virgil does not say anything right away. He waits to see whether the old man has finished before venturing another question.

"How'd they stop it?" he asks.

"They had their ways. Here at the Palisades, a lot of us came to work one day and found out we didn't have jobs anymore. The theatre and the property it was on was all bought up. Even the show we'd been doing was taken. I remember seeing a sign on the stage door. Said COLORED HELP NO LONGER NEEDED.

"But I didn't believe it until I walked into the dressing room. Never will forget that scene. It wasn't bad enough that they were turning us away. But, Lord, what a mess. White actors putting on nappy-headed wigs, and some greasing down their own hair so it looked close-cropped. Paint all over their faces. And this one bald-head little man running around the room shouting, serious as he could be, 'I can't find my blackface. Anyone seen my blackface?' I felt like dying right there, but they ran me out."

The old man is quiet. He looks toward the stage again, then at the house lights. Virgil checks his watch. He stands.

"Sir." He holds out his hand, but the old man ignores it. "I wish I could stay longer. It's just that I'd better get dressed for—"

"Still don't understand, huh?"

He grabs Virgil's wrist. Although his grip is soft, the suddenness of his move causes Virgil to fall forward.

"Hey, look. I do understand. If I want to know anything about real acting, I should learn a lot more about my own people. Good advice. And I appreciate it."

"Acting?" the old man says. He spits involuntarily. "I'm your history, boy. Your blood."

He pulls Virgil to his face. But he is not angry. His grin returns.

"Whatsamatter?" he says. "Afraid they gonna run you out the way they did us? I could see it in your eyes, boy. Eyes can be like the soul; expose whether you got it or whether you weak-kneed. Yesterday, you looked weak-kneed, like you scared of your own self."

"You don't understand. There's a lot of pressure."

Virgil looks him over from his ragged clothes to his recently polished shoes. He smiles at Virgil as if smiling is the only gesture his muscles can manage.

"I can tell you about a little bit of pressure," the man says. "Pressure is when people try to get you to do things you ain't ready to do. Like the way they tried to run us out."

"But they did run you out. You told me—"

"Yeah, they ran us out, all right. But I wasn't ready. It's why I'm still here."

"I still don't understand."

"That's what I've been trying to tell you. How you gonna have any history unless you're around to make it? Me, I decided to stay here forever."

"You mean you've been actually living here?"

"Been right here since the whole thing happened. Been here when the Palisades burned down and when they put up this new theatre. Helped build it, matter of fact. Reach up under that seat you're sitting on. Go on. Put your hand under it."

Virgil slowly moves his hand under the seat.

"Uh-huh. Feel that? It's a sort of switch. Now, stand up and turn it to the left."

When Virgil does this the entire seat moves backward, and attached to it is a section of the floor.

"It's a door, a trap door."

"I wouldn't go down if I was you. Hard to see the steps without a flashlight. And I don't use one except when I'm staying down there, since I know how to get in and out so well."

On his knees, Virgil examines the entrance but can see only the dark outline of a narrow room. He looks at the old man, his mouth open.

"Like I said, I decided to stay here forever. Built that little room myself when they needed cheap labor to put this old building up. I installed most of these here seats and just never told nobody what else I was doing. It's the closest thing to back pay I could get after all those lost years."

Virgil pushes the seat back down and sits.

"You started that fire, didn't you?" he says.

"Ain't no matter now."

"But you started it."

"Most people run away from fire. Let's just say I saw it as an opportunity and used it."

"But how could you stay here without someone knowing?"

"Oh, it's pretty easy. The building's so big nobody likes to sit way up here. Ushers usually stay out 'cause they're scared of the rats. Once every year or so, seems I have to duck down into my room when a pair of young lovers decide this is as good a place as any to be young lovers."

"You mean, guys bring girls up here?"

"Mostly girls. But I seen it all."

"You're something else, old man," Virgil says.

"Know why I was really never caught?"

"Tell me."

" 'Cause this ain't no damn opera house." The old man giggles, and Virgil laughs with him. "Yep. I might look like a phantom, but nowadays people like me are what you call homeless. And when I get locked out, I go down to the Y to put in my occasional appearance. That way no one will report me missing. I'm a good actor, you know."

"What about your family?"

"You're my family. You and any other colored actor trying to make a little history. So this here is my house, and you're welcome to it as long as you stay in the family."

"But you are sort of taking a chance, showing me all of this."

"Naw. You won't say nothing. Besides, I'm more scared of you running out than anything else. It would kind of be like running away from home."

"I don't think I will," Virgil says. "Not now, anyway."

"Then you'd better get down there. They'll be starting soon."

Four of the cast have come onto the stage. Virgil picks up his bag and stands over the old man. He is not sure whether to shake the man's hand or hug him.

"I don't even know your name."

"That don't matter now, either. I've been watching you a long time and I think you might be ready now." He pushes an open hand into Virgil's chest. But he also reaches up and squeezes Virgil's neck.

"You've gotta go act. Go take off that mask you been wearing inside your head and show them what you've really got."

"You know, you sort of remind me of my grandfather."

The old man pokes Virgil in the chest before leaning back into his chair. Then he waves his hand at Virgil as if dismissing him. Virgil walks quietly toward the stairs. "Don't let 'em run you out," the old man says, showing another grin.

"Hey. Thanks for the history lesson," Virgil whispers.

Late in the afternoon, Virgil decides against calling home. He no longer worries about the results of his audition. He knows he can act, that he *is* an actor. He feels it. After searching the theatre for nearly an hour and not finding the old man, he somehow also knows that his parents are waiting at home to tell him that Poppa Josh is dead.

Horses on a Rooftop

CLYMENZA HAWKINS

Helen lay down across the sidewalk like an animal with an open wound. People looked at her as they walked by, wondering what was the matter but not bothering to ask her. Traffic moved swiftly down the avenue. A late-September sun shined weakly as leaves scattered against roots of trees, sidewalk curbs, and battered trash cans. Helen thought about her daughter, Angela, who would be waiting for her after school.

Three weeks had passed since their apartment had been burned out. Ben left her shortly afterward. Then, four days ago, she had been fired from her job at a clothing store over some missing cash from the register. They said it was happening too many times, not bothering to question the other cashier, who was a junkie.

What money Helen had left wasn't much. The few pieces of furniture they'd saved from the fire had been moved into the basement of a used furniture store. She paid $200 for two months' storage; after that, if she didn't claim the furniture it would be brought to the main floor to be sold.

For two weeks after the fire they had lived in a room in the YWCA.

CLYMENZA HAWKINS, a native of New Britain, Connecticut, has performed texts she has written on the subject of AIDS. She has produced and hosted *Artline*, an art magazine for Hartford Community Television. Currently, she is writing a trilogy of novels on an African American woman's life in the Southwest.

Helen told Angela it was temporary until she could find a better place. Angela smiled and said, "Oh, Ma, I'm eleven years old. I can handle it. I still get to practice my school dance." She gave her mother a kiss for confidence.

Apartment first, Helen thought, then I'll find another job. But when she started looking for apartments, she quickly found that the most affordable should have been condemned. The money was slowly running out from eating in restaurants, doing laundry, taking the bus, buying canned fruit and food to eat in the room. Otherwise, when she found a place, she wouldn't have enough left for a deposit.

Helen's thoughts went back to Angela. It was lucky she had been able to use the Y's dance studio to practice when there weren't classes. The staff was so charmed by her that they invited Angela to be included in the classes for the advanced. However, Angela's school harvest program and her performance in it was only two weeks away.

At the end of the second week at the Y, the crisis counselor finally suggested an emergency shelter and an application for state assistance. Helen and Angela moved into a shelter in the neighborhood community center's gym. They had to leave by seven every morning and return for dinner at five. The doors were locked by eight.

Helen and Angela held hands for courage as they lived their lives out in the open. They saw so many others who lived in the streets for months, between church basements, shelters, and hotels. Many of the children looked underfed, wore the same clothing for days, and often missed school.

Angela continued to do her homework in McDonald's, Kentucky Fried Chicken, and Chinese restaurants. She helped handwash their underclothes every night and kept most of her personal things in her knapsack along with her schoolbooks.

Helen thought about how Angela must miss being home. Angela's favorite place to be was the rooftop. It was where she played in her solitude, where she did her dancing, where she could see the colors of the sky and the flight of the birds closer, much closer.

But there was no kind of solitude to go to when a woman in the shelter couldn't keep her screams to herself anymore. They were long, painful screams that left her soul in tight knots as she tried to pull her hair out. Her children clung to her, crying and screaming out her name, as the security guards and counselors tried to hold her down. She kept screaming until the sound echoed into rings of sorrow around the other women, who knew she had given up wondering how long it would be before it would happen again to one of them.

Helen tried not to look but there was no way of avoiding it. Angela watched wide-eyed and trembling. She heard the staff making calls for the children to be taken away to another center, which she knew was some kind of orphanage. Helen grabbed her daughter, who was quietly crying, and held her tight. "Don't worry, you'll never lose me, Angela," she said. "You'll never lose me. I promise."

Helen spent most of her time during the day applying for assistance from the state. She had to explain three separate times to arrogant professionals that she didn't have a place to live and why. It took several trips to find extra identification, certificates, and receipts to prove their living situation before the paperwork was settled and approved.

She was given a small check to live on, till she began to receive the full amount monthly, and continued looking for apartments every day before meeting Angela after school. To rest her feet from so much walking, she would stop and try to collect her thoughts in a park, a library, or a movie. In the movies, though, she didn't know what she was watching and couldn't remember later on. She would sit and sink into the darkness, questioning herself as a woman and as a mother.

She remembered the pastel-colored pages of her high school autograph book, filled with schoolmates' good wishes for her life. Under her yearbook picture was a prediction—she would become a successful fashion model/entrepreneur. Helen laughed bitterly at herself. If she hadn't been so lazy and had tried to do something better with her life a lot sooner, she wouldn't have her child living with her in a shelter now.

If she didn't have Angela, how different would her life be? It seemed like Angela was a true blessing. Helen believed that without her daughter life could have been worse; that Angela's innocence spared her from prostitution, drugs, and prison.

During one movie intermission, Helen went to the ladies' room. She saw her face in the mirror. She was too ashamed to attend Angela's rehearsals, didn't want to embarrass her daughter. Her hair was sloppy, pulled back in a bun with a nappy hairline. Dark circles sagged under her eyes, and she could smell her body's odor from not washing thoroughly. The water from the showers sometimes came out so thin and lukewarm that the soap didn't rinse off too well. So she smelled like soap, sweat, and yesterday's clothes.

Her scent wasn't far from that of the other women in the shelter—old dirt, stale smoke, medicated cough drops, perfumed deodorant, and urinated underclothes. Some of them gave her smiles with looks that said she really wasn't any different. In time, she would be sharing a cup of cold coffee with them.

Helen saw the days ahead, looking at the same sidewalk, wondering where their new place would be, what it would look like, while she sat on the shelter's stairs waiting for the doors to open, keeping an eye on their bags, ignoring obscene remarks from men and scolding frowns from women. She felt the endless length of an hour, even of fifteen minutes. She thought about the screaming woman and saw herself instead. The crying spiraled around her soul until it tightened into a knot of pain, into numbness.

So Helen lay down on the sidewalk three weeks after the fire. Eyes half closed, she saw the sunlight fading slowly away. Chilly breezes blew leaves against her face while she listened absently to talk of the night's fight between Muhammad Ali and Ken Norton.

"So, uh, what you wearin' to the fight?"

"Well, I gotta get to the cleaners to pick up Leroy's suit, then get my hair done."

Whispers followed.

"Yankee Stadium is gonna be packed! I gotta get the kids and get them fed first before I can get started on myself. See ya lata."

"Yeah, uh, lata."

Suddenly, Helen's body went stiff in panic as Angela's face flashed in her mind. She was supposed to pick her up at school. As she stood, heavy soreness tingled her feet while her knees became weak from fear. She chanted, "I'm coming, Angela, I'm coming!" while she hoped the teacher, the principal, hadn't called Youth Services, the police, or the social worker. Just the thought of Angela, scared, crying and waiting, frightened Helen so much that the usual way she went to school seemed to take forever. Each block that brought her closer to her daughter became longer to cover. Her heart felt like it was choking in her throat, while burning tears spilled from her eyes.

When Helen reached the schoolyard, she recognized the other parents she usually saw waiting for their children and let out a sigh of relief, realizing she was on time. Wiping her face, her heartbeat slowing down, Helen stood tall and regally still as she waited.

Just the sight of Angela gave Helen a new kind of strength. She greeted her daughter in a tight embrace as Angela told how well she did in rehearsal. As they walked away hand in hand, Helen was filled with blind determination. In the restaurant, she waited patiently for Angela to finish dinner and her homework. They repacked their things into new plastic bags in the restroom.

That night, Helen knew they would never return to the shelter. She didn't know where she was taking them but she kept walking. Twilight was rising fast, the air filled with excitement over the fight. As they walked, her feet and legs felt like iron and her shoulders like stone from carrying the things that gained weight with their problems. Angela bravely claimed she wasn't tired and continued to carry the knapsack and a plastic bag. Cold breezes blew. Helen looked straight ahead because she didn't want to see the lighted windows of homes where it was warm, where there were beds to sleep in, a roof and four walls. It was too late to go back to the shelter.

"Excuse me, miss, but would you want another bag?" asked a voice.

Helen turned to see an older woman, wearing a magenta sequined hat, poking her head out the window of a brownstone.

"I can give you another bag if you want it." She pointed at Angela. "That bag the chile is carryin' got a big hole from scrapin' the ground. Only so much plastic, y' know."

Helen looked at Angela, who tried to pull the bag up from the sidewalk, but parts of clothes were already coming through. Helen nodded her head to say yes because she was about to cry.

"Well, then, come on up here in the hallway," said the woman. She ducked inside and reappeared at the stoop.

Slowly they went up stairs that looked to Helen like a curved bridge leading to an urban castle. They followed the woman through tall lace-curtained doors and stood in a dark warm hallway. A grand fireplace practically covered a wall, its mantelpiece a few inches higher than the women's heads.

"Oh, thank you so much!" said Helen as they put the bags down.

"Sure nuff welcome. Gotta have some kind of privacy to repack your clothes," the woman said as she gave Helen new bags. "I don't mind. The chile can sit in my kitchen to rest a bit while you take care of them bags."

"She can stay with me till—"

"She'll be fine. Don't worry, ain't nobody else in my place. I'm by myself."

"Well, thank you."

"Aw, ya done thanked me enough already. We'll be right back." She put an arm around Angela.

"I'll be done in a few minutes," said Helen.

"Take your time."

Helen knelt on the floor to rest while taking the clothes out of the bag. The warmth of the hallway settled around her. She smelled cooking spices and incense.

"Your daughter's got a pretty name," said the woman as she stood before Helen again, opening another plastic bag and holding it out toward her. "She tole me you're Helen. If you don't mind me callin you Helen, you can call me Flo."

"I don't mind," said Helen, smiling as she put the clothes into an open bag. She hoped Angela had told Flo just their names. She got up, tying the bag into a knot, and was about to call Angela when Flo raised her finger and motioned with her hand for Helen to follow.

Helen looked over her shoulder toward the kitchen.

"She'll be fine," Flo said. "C'mon."

Helen followed Flo to a door at the end of the hallway. Flo pulled out some keys and used one to open it.

"There ain't no electricity or gas on in this place, but you can see it's decent," said Flo as they stepped into an empty apartment. "Nobody can never say I don't take care of what I got! This here is a one bedroom. It's all that's available."

"But Miss Flo, I didn't say—I wasn't—"

"Somethin' can be worked out—if you're willin', that is. Now unless I'm bein' nosy and assumin' wrong, I'll let y'all go on 'bout your business and I'll get back to mine."

"No, Miss Flo," Helen said quietly, as she looked in the woman's eyes. "You assumed right."

"Well, then, somethin' can be worked out and I can sure say it's so because I own this place! Now! There's somethin' else we gotta settle on."

"What's that, Miss Flo?"

"Girl, you betta call me Flo!"

For the first time in weeks, Helen laughed.

"Go on and take a look," Flo urged. "I believe there's a couch in one of the rooms. Back at my place, I got a cot you can use and some blankets."

"Oh, Miss—I mean Flo, thank you, thank—"

"Oh, hush!" said Flo as she left.

The apartment had high ceilings, windows tall and wide, and wooden floors. The view from the windows was of a tiny backyard enclosed by other brownstones, but with enough space to sit and even have a barbecue. Helen thanked God over and over with every living beat of her heart for Flo and for this blessing. She saw it as a chance to do something better with her life and for her daughter.

Helen walked back into Flo's living room, which was filled with antique furniture and knickknacks and curtained with dark floral drapes. On the coffee table was a Bible and a green glass bowl of peppermint candy. Angela was sitting in a wingback chair watching a TV program featuring highlights of the fight. People were coming into the stadium in tuxedos and furs, the lines of limousines and bleachers filled with people. Seeing her mother staring at the highlights, Angela smiled.

"I already know, ma," said Angela. "Miss Flo told me."

"Miss Flo?" asked Helen, lifting an eyebrow.

"Miss Flo," said Flo as she nodded her head in a definite conclusion.

"Now as I was sayin' to Angela, me and Freddy—that's my husband who died of cancer ten years ago—me and Freddy used to have such good times back then. We used the basement as a neighborhood cabaret. It was a way to pay the mortgage.

"He used to greet our customers, sayin' 'Hey there, hi there, ho there!' That's how he'd do it. He played the sax and I sang. Our performers and customers were the neighborhood. We had ourselves a jumpin' after-hours joint that could give the Cotton Club a run for its money!

"But we lost the neighborhood to changin' times," she continued, more slowly. "Some moved, some died, some are in jail. Freddy closed the place and played just for me. We used to watch *Dragnet* together. That's how we used to do it," Flo said quietly, sadly.

"Ma?" Angela asked, "could I go see our new apartment, please? Then we could watch *Dragnet* together."

"All right, you can."

"Keep that back door locked, y'hear?" said Flo.

"Yes. And Miss Flo, I want you to know my momma don't take no drugs or got a drinking problem. We won't give you no trouble."

"Sweet of you to say. Me and Freddy never had any children, so it's nice of you to say you'll watch *Dragnet* later on with me. Some of these young folks today got no time to be with us older folks no more. Now you run along and remember what I say about the door."

As Angela left, she overheard Miss Flo reminding herself to find some candles while her mother made a phone call. For a moment, the girl stood in the hallway. It held a peaceful silence that made her feel secure. She started to the apartment, but then she looked up the stairs where arched balconies led to each floor. Swiftly she ran all the way up and opened an unlocked door to the rooftop.

The sky was streaked dark twilight blue with an apricot-colored horizon. She walked over to the black iron fence surrounding the roof and looked down at her new neighborhood. Across the street was the Wash n' Jam Laundromat, Harold's Cleaners, Regina's Beauty Salon, Candyland Cornerstore, and a newspaper stand. To her right were several brownstones that led to an open fish and vegetable market where vendors sold incense and oils. Beyond was a grocery store and the subway. Angela smiled and did a few pliés, singing, "Hey there! Hi there! Ho there!" She twirled and started a leap when suddenly she stopped. There was a man on the rooftop across from her, standing at an easel, painting horses running across multicolored landscapes. He looked at Angela with slow, graceful eyes and a beautiful smile. Narrow locks of hair reached his shoulders.

"Hi there!" said he.

"Hello." She looked at the painting.

"Never seen you around here before."

"I live here now with my mother. Those are pretty horses."

"Thank you. Are you a dancer?"

"Yes, I am. I was practicing for a performance in school next Thursday."

"My name is Byron. And you?"

"Angela."

"Very pretty."

"That's what everybody says."

They smiled at each other as a cool breeze soared around Angela's arms. The twilight turned darker, the white of his shirt brighter. She watched him paint another horse, amazed at what he could create with just a few strokes. After what she had been through with her mother, living in several places off the streets, watching this man painting horses was the most peaceful moment she'd remembered in weeks. The only other good thing was sleeping with her mother, holding her, their arms entwined as they breathed together as they dreamed.

"What you're doing doesn't hurt anybody," said Angela quietly.

He looked at her curiously. "That's the best compliment I ever heard about my work. Thank you, Angela."

"You're welcome. It's just that my mother was seeing this guy for a while and he left her. She got hurt real bad." Angela caught herself and covered her mouth in fear. She was silent for a few seconds. "Oh, please don't tell her what I said. I didn't mean—"

"Angela." He stopped painting and looked at her. "He hurt you too," he said.

She stared at the horses until the threat of tears was gone.

"I promise I won't tell," said Byron as he returned to painting.

"Thank you." Angela smiled weakly, as she watched him paint another horse, and swallowed again.

"I gotta go now," she said, moving back. "Can I watch you paint next time? I won't botha you with all that talkin'."

"I can talk and paint at the same time. I'd like that." He smiled and saluted her with a paintbrush of yellow. She reminded him of a favorite niece in South Carolina who used to talk to him about art and recordings of her day while she watched him paint. Sometimes she would paint pictures to show to his sister.

Angela waved and ran down the stairs. She decided to keep Byron a secret for a while. Because they were neighbors, she knew her mother would get to meet him. Angela giggled at the thought of her mother getting to see how funny his hair looked.

When she entered the apartment it was almost dark. Quickly she looked around. Her mother was calling for her to help bring the candles. Angela took another look at home, twirled a few times, and leapt out the door.

Helen and Angela settled into the first night in the apartment. Angela's breathing warmed Helen's arm. Stroking her daughter's hair, Helen thought about the shelter, the screaming woman, and of lying on the ground giving up only a few hours ago. Of Flo's kindness, which sparkled like her sequined hat. She began to make plans for the next day, what she'd have to get done, following into the next one and the next one and the next.

In the meantime, sounds of celebration filled the streets. Cars honked, people whistled and shouted "Champ! Champ!" Helen settled deeper in her daughter's breathing and wondered who had won the fight.

Sixty Years After Hiroshima Thirteen Years After Rodney King

SAFIYA HENDERSON-HOLMES

once upon a question:
"can't we all just get along?"

aug. 5th 2005

everything's still warm. her dance magazine's on her thighs.
the latest issue opened to page twenty-five, showing her high on her left
foot. she looks at picture, closes her eyes, places magazine on floor.
warm floor.

how many days? a week? no less. it can't be more.
she takes a deep breath. opens her eyes. counts her fingers: ten
fingers. counts her toes: one toe. she closes her eyes.

she tells herself to be funny: she says, she looks like burnt beef with
too much ketchup.

mark hates ketchup. hates sauce and oozing things on his food.
tomorrow she'll become a strict veggie. these are great times for
veggies, many healthy green things to choose from. hahahehe.
her mouth does something which feels like a smile.

The poet SAFIYA HENDERSON-HOLMES is also a mother and a physiotherapist. She is an Assistant Professor in the Creative Writing Program of Syracuse University. Her first book of poems, *Madness and a Bit of Hope*, won The Poetry Society of America's William Carlos Williams Award. Her second book is *Daily Bread*.

yes, c'mon keep it loose. keep them doggies rollin through the rawhide. yep, keep it glib. it's the only way, her way, her attitude of choice. even here. even now.

mark hates her way. "zane," he says, "your humor at inappropriate times pisses me completely off." she tells him that being completely pissed off can lead to renal retention, which could lead to renal failure, which could lead to death, which could lead to a very cheap funeral since she's a poor underpaid dancer loving her work even while things are falling apart. yep, she's a scream but doesn't scream. closes her eyes again.

she lost her left foot on the morning of the second day. she should've stayed inside, but she thought she heard him: mark. she thought she heard him calling to her from across the street. she ran out. it's another one of her ways. to dash. head on. it's the bull in her, the bitch. mark says it's too much red meat and hot sauce. but she ran out on the second day. she wasn't the only one. there were others. she saw them. she sees them now. a piece here, a piece there.

she lost four toes on her right foot during the night of the first day. she was standing by the window watching a sneaker fly through the air with the greatest of ease.

mark wears sandals. in winter. in summer. damn near to bed. mark and his sandals. he has long toes. grab-hold toes. she is sure he was some kind of climbing animal in his other life. she's sure of that. on his more human days, after lovemaking, she'd play patty-cake with his toes, or paint faces on them, have a glee club. sing-alongs with stink feet.

but mark wore sneakers on his patrol the first night. helping the wounded and injured, he's such a boy scout. mark wore his running shoes. his marathon elites. he was going to be the first african american to win the new york city marathon. he was fast. she waited for him by the window, in their living room, on the first night. yes of course she was prepped not to stand by the windows. mark prepped her. mark prepped everyone on the block. even the druggies.

but this window and their house were safe, built to take the shaking and baking. she and mark had bought the house from a woman whose husband had died in an earlier war. the woman had bought the house because of its thick stone and deep basement.

so she stood there, watching a sneaker fly through the red air. no, yellow air. high noon at ten p.m. everything bright as christmas. everything hot as hell. a circle of brilliant blue raced toward her. she ducked, fell quickly to her knees, arms curved over her head as mark had instructed: the fetal position for the twenty-first century. tucked tight enough to nearly kiss your sweetass goodbye.

well hell, that brilliant blue broke the window, landed on her right foot, and ate four of her toes. yep, a nuclearized baseball got her at home base. she's out.

shucks. sometimes, during mark's block meetings, in the middle of all his grand seriousness about the coming bomb, she'd make a smartass remark, maybe something about fallout and farts. she did it to keep life in the room. she did it to keep her life in the room. but mark was dead on her. he'd cut, then hold her with his eyes, keep his lips moving for the other people, but say with his eyes to her: baby this is too real and too serious for foolishness. black people got to know what to do in this situation. this ain't just bullets and cops, baby, or some crazed racist action. this is bombs, baby. big ones. everybody dies and goes straight to hell.

then he'd close his eyes, take a deep breath, smile, and keep talking.

she opens her eyes, sees mark upstairs in the shower. he's trying to relax, stay focused, calm, collected. he had two meetings at the house three days ago: people wanted to know about bombs and shelters and radiation disease and the possibility of surviving if they live. and living where? black people, brown people, beige and white people, all there, banging on the door, ringing the bell, looking for mark. but a year ago there were only the hungry armageddon types, the curious, the fearful, and a few who remembered other marks, other bombs. most people didn't have the time of day for mark and his nuclear age hoodoo voodoo. there were other ends to meet, dollars to stretch, tables to set, beds to make, housework, homework, extra work, then no work, homeless, or less, or nothing. yeah, yeah, even the have-nothing people came to hear mark. what could be less than having nothing?

mister mark had studied too much, had been to nevada and stood on the land of nuclear test sites, looked at the glaring mushroom photographs and the wings of lethal lights. he had gone to those test-site

subcommittee meetings, heard testimony from women dying of cancer or giving birth to dead children. mark had read the books on love canal and three mile island, talked to some
russian man who was over there when a nuclear plant melted like a glacier and flooded nearby cities and towns like an angry ocean. mark was the original headset man, listened to world watch as if it was his own heart beating, snuck into government press conferences as if they were the birth of christ. he was too personally involved. why, mark? why?

"like i told you, because they been killing us for a long time, zane, and i'm tired of dying and i ain't into drugs." his mother, grandmother, and ten-year-old sister had died of cancer. what kind? mark says the nuclear kind.

one of mark's skeptical friends kept trying to get mark to stop worrying about white man madness. he'd say, "man, i told you that i read too, and i read somewhere that when you got the darker pigment, you're safe, you know, like we don't absorb all that radiation shit. god like did us a cute number. we nuclear free, my man."

mark didn't even laugh.

she watches mark wash. he's six feet four inches tall. two hundred and fifty pounds, dark as the space between her legs before she opens for him and after she closes around him. that black. that private. a secret. hers.

she pinches his left thigh, takes a deep breath, goes head on into funny. "a fine time to be clean," she says. "i reckon your funk is a lethal weapon, people may mistake you for the bomb. i know, i've smelled your explosions, and i do fallout." she pretends death.

mark splashes water on her face.

she sits up on the toilet. there's a slight tremble in her lower lip. she tries steadying it with a smile, but mark sees it, he sees everything on her. she does her louie armstrong grin: all her eyes, all her teeth on him. through him.

their doorbell rings. she thinks, what are the sounds of bombs?

"that's everson," mark says. "the caribbean cat. the shit just became real for him. he's going to go around with me to some houses. talk to the folks, give out masks, see if people need and know how to get to the armory, check the food supplies in stores, you know, baby, shit like that." why, mark, why? "he's an ex-army man: gulf, cuba, yugoslavia. he knows a lot about this whole business, said he's finally come face to face with the enemy, and he says he's been calling him captain too damn long."

she leaves the bathroom, opens the front door for everson, walks him to the basement. he thumbs through a pamphlet on the minuteman missile. she folds her arms across her chest. they wait for mark.

she closes her eyes. mark hasn't been in the shower for three days. she closes the dance magazine, holds her one toe, "and this little piggy wee-weed all the way home."

behind her eyes: her block brilliant blueblack and quiet.

aug. 9th 2015
once upon a question:
"can't we all just get along?"

days after

i eight. i eight fingers. i eight toes. i boy. i smart. i spell many once-living things. i spell cat: c-a-h-t. i spell dog: d-a-w-g. i spell bird: b-e-r-y-d. i spell sun: s-u-n-g. i spell flower: f-l-a-h-o-u-r. i collect eyeballs. see? this dog eye. this old black lady eye. it best eye. you can't touch it. only me.

i many eyeballs. i blue eyeballs: many. i green eyeballs: many. i gray eyeballs: no many. i brown eyeballs: many.

i keep eyeballs in small earth hole. i keep watery stuff in earth hole. we living no to drink watery stuff. earth no to drink watery stuff. we living drink water of masters. we living drink once in gray.

earth drink when gold rain fall. we living no stay in gold rain. we living stay in earth hole. my eyeballs float in small earth hole, in watery stuff. some eyeballs float good. some eyeballs float bad. some turn to glow and sink. glow bad. glow in earth. earth much glow.

once in gray, eyeballs in earth hole glow bright. i think moon fall and crush eyeballs. older living say moon once fell from gray and crushed living. i run to eyeballs. see eyeballs glowing and sinking. oh, i many pretty eyes: newborn baby eyes, rabbit eyes, deer eyes, cow eyes.

in that gray i lost my eyes. earth hole glowed for one full gray. but i go in next gray and go around and around in gray, longer than living stay in gray, i get more eyeballs. many, much, more.

i no tell you how many, much, more. but i tell you, i put them in two small earth holes. and i and girl living watch my eyeballs every gray. and there many, much, more eyeballs on earth. many, much, more.

aug. 9th 2015
once upon a question:
"can't we all just get along?"

another part of town

he enjoys the memory classes on sun and seasons: how summer magnified cities, filled oceans with people and fish, filled skies with birds and funny toys he doesn't quite understand: balloons. and the incredible power of winter: hiding the living in sheets of ice only penetrable by something called spring. unbelievable! it makes him laugh.

yesterday he remembered how to laugh.

he equally enjoys the memory classes on war. sometimes, as it was on tuesday, he feels completely at one with the viewing screen: he is a soldier in a hole in a ground, a weapon in his hand, other men, other soldiers, other weapons around him. or he is a wounded soldier: legless, armless. blood like water in his mouth.

tuesday he remembered how to cry.

but he enjoys body memory classes the most: to sit in front of a mirror nude, alone: admire, remember, and talk quietly with his body. all the limbs are there, are his. his legs and arms are well formed. his chest and shoulders: full, wide. his hands lift heavy objects, hold on tightly. his nose smells. his tongue tastes. his ears hear. his eyes see. his toes wiggle. his legs walk.

he stares longest at his penis: asleep without memory between his legs.

he has ten minutes per week in front of the mirror. he has organized the time in this manner: two minutes on mondays for hand and eye memories, two minutes on wednesdays for memories with legs and arms, one minute on thursdays for feet work.

today, friday, he has five minutes for his penis.
it is very slow memory work.
he is careful, gentle. he cups the organ with his right hand: a soft caress, as important to him as learning about sun and war.

he opens his right hand. with his left he assiduously stretches the organ across his right palm.

he doesn't move, scarcely breathes, concentrates every point of memory through his right arm, right hand, his penis.

four minutes.

an attendant stands behind him, the attendant's fingerless hands on his shoulders. "it'll come up again, doc. but it takes a fortune of memory." the attendant covers his lap with a yellow robe, rolls him from mirror.

another man is placed in the mirror's view.
this gentleman has arranged his body time differently: his entire ten minutes for his organ.

the other men watch: fearful, hopeful, trying to remember.

The Birthday Present

LINDA SUSAN JACKSON

I do not want much of a present, anyway, this year.
After all I am alive only by accident.

—Sylvia Plath, *A Birthday Present*

 I hate them. It's June 5, 1965, and I hate both of them. They think just because I'm in high school, I'm old enough to deal with all this stuff. They forget I'm just turning fourteen today. That's one reason I'm not going to school; I want to celebrate my birthday alone. The other reason I'm not going to school is because my parents' divorce becomes final today. I don't want to see anyone. After today, I won't have to wake up to the sound of breaking glass, angry voices, or slamming doors ever again. This is the first year I didn't get a birthday card from my father, and I'm sure I won't have a birthday cake because he's the one who always brings home the birthday cakes.

Last year, four months after my thirteenth birthday, my mother called me and my brother, Charles, upstairs. She said she had something to tell us. Charles, who is two years older than me, went up first. When I got upstairs, Charles was sitting on the cedar chest at the foot of my parents' bed. I had to sit in the black leather chair in the corner of the room facing

LINDA SUSAN JACKSON is living her second life as a writer of fiction and poetry. This is her first fiction publication. She lives in Brooklyn, New York, with her husband and son. She writes, "I would like to give special thanks to my husband, Rod, for his unequivocal support, my son, Rodney, who helped me grow up all over again, and Frederick Douglass Creative Arts Center, where I was guided by the genius of DorisJean Austin and B.J. Ashanti."

the window because it was the only place left to sit besides the bed and Mom always said, "The bed is not a couch."

Mom was standing at the window with her back to me. I was staring at her long black hair, wondering why she didn't give me her hair, why my hair had to be straightened. Everyone says Mom looks like a cross between Dorothy Dandridge and an Indian princess (we are part Cherokee). Whenever we go out together people walk up to her and start speaking Spanish or some other language I never heard before, but not English. I guess they don't know what she is.

I keep trying to figure out if she's really my mother because we look so different. Her eyes are dark; mine are amber colored, almost see-through. Her hair is jet black and grows to the middle of her back; mine is sandy brown and only shoulder length. She wears a size 6½ shoe and already I wear a size 8. She has slim fingers with long tapered nails; I bite mine. Her voice is soft and sounds like a song most of the time (she does yell if all the chores aren't done by the time she gets home from work); I sing with the altos in the school chorus.

"Athena, are you listening to me?"

"Huh? What'd you say?"

"I said your father won't be coming home anymore."

"What?" I asked, not believing what I heard.

"We're getting a divorce."

My breathing stopped. The room heated up. My face was about to explode. I searched the room for Charles. He was staring at something on the ceiling. Everything was blurred. "What about us? What's gonna happen to us?" I blurted out.

Mom turned her head away from the window and said very sharply, "Watch yourself, *miss*. I'm *still* your mother. What I said was, your father and I are getting divorced."

I slumped back into the chair, not sure what she wanted us to do now. Charles shot a glance at me but I looked away. Just as he was about to get up from the cedar chest, I yelled, "Why are you doing this?"

"That's between your father and me."

"But where's he going?"

"I really don't know and could care less."

"I wanna go with him."

"I should let you. You're more his daughter than mine. He named you." (She didn't let me go, but whenever he didn't do something he was supposed to, like send money, she'd get mad and say to me, "You're just like your damn father.")

"No, I'm not."

"You are. You're just like him. You look at me with that same 'I'm better than you' look."

"No, I don't."

"That high forehead, those same light brown eyes, the same short fingers—"

"Mom, please, please stop. I'm not like him. I'm not." I would force myself not to cry every time she said those things, because she was right. I do look like him. But if I'm so much like him, how could he leave me? At night, I would lie awake and threaten Mom in my mind that Dad would come to get me. Tomorrow.

What makes me so mad is that everyone on our block knows everybody else's business. The houses are all the same, all attached to each other, and you can hear everything that goes on in the house next door. I know because I hear how when Mr. Portis comes home drunk he threatens to beat up his whole family. He never actually hits anyone. He just threatens. But the kids scream and cry anyway. And on the other side of us are the sisters, Miss Rose and Miss Frances. I know when they're in a good mood. They play those old records over and over again and sometimes they even sing along with the records. I know all the words to every Dinah Washington record they have. Dad says they have the best collection of 78s in Brooklyn. I wouldn't mind it so much if they played some of today's music, something like "Shop Around" by Smokey Robinson and the Miracles or "My Girl" by The Temptations or even "Rainbow '65" by Gene Chandler. I wonder why they never had husbands and why they live in that big old house all by themselves. I hear everything, loud and clear.

I hate going to school sometimes because I know all the other girls are looking at me. They're all talking about me and the fact that my parents are getting divorced. Charles said I shouldn't worry about it, but I can't help it.

I love my brother so much. He says no matter what happens we'll always have each other. He lets me go with him and his friends because he knows I hate being with girls. Who wants to play their old silly games anyway? They don't do anything that's fun. At least when I'm with Charles and his friends, we do things. We play all kinds of ball games. We always have lots of fun. The only thing girls do that I like is jumping double Dutch. But they only do that once in a while. Charles doesn't care that I'm a girl.

I remember when I was eight, I was fighting the twins, Paulie and Jamesy. Johnny yelled to Charles, who was sitting on our stoop, "Hey, Charlie, aren't you gonna help your sister?"

"Nope. She can take care of herself." I felt so good when he said it that I beat the mess out of the twins. I don't have to fight much now because the other kids know I can take care of myself.

I try to remember if there was ever a time when my parents didn't fight, when maybe they were happy. I can't.

Their fights would start out of nowhere.

"Who was that man you were smiling at?" my father would ask.

"What man?"

"I saw you. Don't deny it."

Arguing and fussing. Over and over again she'd just keep asking, What man? and he'd keep insisting he saw her smiling at some man. Sometimes he'd try to help her remember by pushing her a little, but he never hit her. She hit him. With her hands, fists, a dish, a glass, anything within reach. Until she got tired or he was out cold. Then she'd go upstairs and lock herself in the bathroom with the lights out and smoke her one cigarette for the day. My brother and I would be so scared, we'd just lie in our beds hoping that the quiet would last, and sometimes he'd say, "Athena, let's go see what happened."

Charles would knock lightly on the bathroom door, waiting for Mom to make a sound. He would plead for her to open the door. But she wouldn't. He told me it was like Mom would disappear when she went in the bathroom. We wouldn't hear anything in there. The only sign she was there was we could smell the cigarette smoke. I couldn't stand to hear Charles begging her to come out of the bathroom, since he knew she wouldn't. I'd go downstairs to look for Dad, just to make sure he was somewhere still breathing. Although she only knocked him out with a soda bottle that one time when I was in sixth grade, I can still remember to this day what he looked like lying on the kitchen floor with all that blood pouring out of his head. Blood isn't really red like people think. In fact, it's like brown, purple, and red all mixed up together. As I looked at that puddle of blood that Dad's head lay in, I remember thinking that Mom was gonna be upset because she said bloodstains are hard to get out.

Once when I fell and cut my hand open, I wrapped my hand in my shirt, hoping it would stop bleeding. It didn't. I ended up getting thirty stitches in my hand, and when we were on our way back home from the hospital, the only thing Mom said was she'd never be able to get the bloodstains out of my shirt.

As I stood there, in the kitchen, I kept wondering how I was going to clean Dad's blood off the linoleum.

Charles came running downstairs yelling, "Athena! Athena! Mom *still* won't come out of the bathroom. We've got to do something."

"Go get Miss Portis."

Charles went next door to get Mrs. Portis. She was the one who called the ambulance. Dad stayed in the hospital for two days. Mom wouldn't even take us to see him. I wasn't old enough, but Charles was over twelve.

Sometimes when we were really scared, we'd wait until morning to look for signs from the night before, but there'd be nothing, no broken glass, not one chair out of place, no black eyes, no bruises. Everything would be normal. Dad would be gone already, and Mom would be in the kitchen stirring oatmeal or farina for me and Charles. Unless it was the weekend. On weekends we got scrambled eggs, sausage and toast or salmon cakes, spoon biscuits, and fried potatoes. Mom believed you needed something home-cooked in your stomach to start the day off right.

Once when I was eleven and Charles was thirteen, we were sitting on the couch in the front parlor watching *The Donna Reed Show* on television, and I asked him, "Do you think he loves her?"

"That's just on TV."

"You think they all act like that?"

"Not in real life."

My grandmother and my mother's sisters would come over mostly when my father wasn't there and they'd be in the kitchen, cooking, eating, drinking, and talking. We were never allowed near the kitchen when they were having their talks. In fact we used to get chased upstairs. They would whisper or speak pig Latin until they were sure we were out of hearing range. I taught Charles how to speak and understand pig Latin by the time he was eight and I was just six. Only Mom and them didn't know it. We would lie on the parquet floor at the top of the stairs and listen. On that floor, we learned how our family came up here from North Carolina during the 1920s looking for work, how hard it was on my grandma when my grandpop left her with six children to care for by herself soon after they came to New York, how she scrubbed floors and cleaned other people's houses to make ends meet, " 'cause the worst thing you could do was to go on relief," and how what she wanted most was for her daughters to get high school diplomas so they could get decent jobs and not have to depend on no man to eat. She told them that story about scrubbing white folks' floors every time one of the daughters wouldn't do what she wanted. I wondered why my grandma never laughed or even smiled.

I only saw Mom cry one time. It was after one of Grandma's visits. I don't know what they talked about, but when Grandma left, Mom lay on her bed crying for about an hour and then went into the bathroom to smoke her cigarette. I was still awake when she came out. I tried to wake Charles up without Mom hearing, and although our twin beds are right across from each other, he wouldn't budge. Mom went into her bedroom and called up her sister Barbara and I overheard her ask Barbara, "Why does she have to say things to hurt me? She knows how hard I tried to stay with a man I never really loved." I strained to hear more, but I couldn't make anything else out between the crying and her blowing her nose. I wanted to know what could anyone say to make her cry, but most of all I wanted to know why she married my father if she didn't love him.

Later that night after the house was quiet and I was tired of looking at the ceiling, I whispered, "Charles, are you sleeping?"

"Nope."

"What's gonna happen to us now?"

"Things are gonna be different without Dad here."

"I don't understand how they could let this happen."

"You heard what Dad said tonight. He said he has proof."

"Proof? Proof of what?"

"That's all he said. He's got proof. That's all he kept saying."

"They make me sick."

"Don't worry, Athena, you still got me."

I closed my eyes, hoping this was all a dream. I never did get to sleep so I was awake to hear their bedroom door open and the bathroom door close. I wondered if it was Mom or Dad. I wanted to see Dad before he left, if he really was leaving. I decided to take a chance. I peeked into their bedroom. The bed was already made. The top of my lip began to sweat, and my heart was beating so hard I was sure Mom would hear it.

I crept downstairs. I could smell the coffee percolating, and as I got closer to the kitchen I could smell buttered biscuits. I pushed open the swinging door. Dad was sitting at the kitchen table with his head in his hands. I ran over to the stove because the coffee was beginning to spill over and burn on the stove and Dad did not move.

"Do you want coffee?"

"Huh?" he muttered without moving.

"Dad, do you want a cup of coffee?"

"Throw it out," he yelled, scaring me to death. "Throw it all out."

"Dad, don't say that!" I screamed back at him. I was screaming and crying. "Dad, please. Don't leave us. Please!"

Dad got up and started hugging me and said, "I'm not leaving you, I'm—"

"You are. Mom said you're leaving us."

"Athena, please, honey, please stop crying," Dad said, but because he was crying now too I couldn't make out anything else. I think he mumbled something about having to leave now, having no other choice.

The next thing I knew, Charles burst into the kitchen yelling at the top of his lungs. "Let go of my sister. Let go of her! If you're going, go. Just leave us alone."

"Charles, now—"

"You wanna leave? Go ahead, get out."

"No, Daddy, please don't. Take me with you. Don't leave me here," I pleaded. I couldn't hear anything else because we were all yelling and Charles was trying to pull me away from Dad.

"No, Athena. Let him go. He wants to go, then—"

"Charles, listen to me," Dad said in a low but firm voice while he was still hugging me. "I know you're angry. You kids have to know I love you both. You're all I have in this world that belongs to me, but—"

"Shut up, shut up! I don't want to hear any more," I screeched, covering my ears. I pulled away from Dad and Charles and ran back upstairs past the closed bathroom door and fell on my bed.

A few minutes later, Charles came upstairs and sat on the foot of my bed. After a little while he said, "Hey, we still have each other."

We heard the front door slam and the bathroom door open. "You kids better get yourselves ready for school."

"Everything's back to normal," Charles whispered as Mom went downstairs to finish breakfast.

A couple of days later, I asked Charles, "Why do they have to get divorced? People don't get divorced, they just leave. Grandpop left Grandma. Uncle Chilly left Aunt Odessa. Aunt Minnie left Uncle Sol—"

"Athena, you know what Dad said to me yesterday when he came to get his clothes?"

"No, what?"

"He said, 'Son, don't ever trust a woman.' "

"Why'd he tell you that?"

"Guess it's something he wanted me to know."

"You think he means me too?"

"Nope. You're just a girl."

"If Mom wasn't so pretty, maybe Dad'd still be here."

"I don't know."

"Since I look like Dad, I'll never have to worry."

"I'm *never* getting married," Charles promised.

It seems like all this just happened yesterday, but it's been about a year since I've seen my father, and now I have a four-month-old baby sister (she's the real reason Dad left).

As I said, today I turn fourteen. This is the first year Dad didn't give me a birthday card and a present. All I got today was a cupcake with one candle on it from Charles. When I blew out the candle, I wished my baby sister would go away so my father could come back.

I hate them. I still hate both of them.

Jumping Ship

KELVIN CHRISTOPHER JAMES

Bountin sat on the foredeck grinding teeth into his frustration. His eyes were fixed on the steamer's tie ropes as they sagged and tautened with the rhythm of the swells. They swayed a patient beat of tide rising, of sun going down. Of time moving as it would. Moving and leaving Bountin stranded. The long summer day was moving on, and he wasn't. Binding him on this steamer's deck was his partner, him sitting over-shoulder behind on a bale of rope: Ruinsey, his friend, a man treating Opportunity like a slave.

Bountin, for one, never took on this last three weeks of stevedoring up the Gulf Stream to end it sitting on deck taking in orange-colored sunrays. That was never the why he had ridden this sea-sickening steel bridge across the ocean. He, for one, had come here to get in onto the solid land of plenty.

Yet, for more than an hour now, he had been watching other ship workers filing down the gangplank, all just walking off and up the pier. Among them were some he suspected of having travel arrangements just

KELVIN CHRISTOPHER JAMES is a Trinidadian-born writer living in Harlem. He holds a B.Sc. from the University of West Indies, and an Ed.D. in Science Education from Columbia University. In 1989, he won a New York Foundation for the Arts fellowship in fiction. He has published *Jumping Ship & Other Stories*, and *Secrets*, a novel, short-listed for the 1994 Commonwealth Writers Prize.

like his. And none of his suspects had returned. So it seemed the gate into the place was working. And all Bountin wanted to know was why they, too, weren't trying it.

Bountin's generous resolve to bear up in silence slackened under this assault of reasonableness. He heaved a deep sigh, and his independent head twisted toward where Ruinsey was comfortable. Before he could complete his glance, though, Ruinsey hawked and spat a pellet between them; cleanly clearing the ship's rail six feet away, it seemed to banner rebuke in its comet's tail, making Bountin wrench his guilty attention back to the ropes. Although now the grind of his teeth could've crunched diamonds and the response in his mind was, Why y'don't spit up your stagnant backside?

For the nth time, Bountin's eyes, restless as the seagulls gliding above him, roved to midships where the gangplank joined ship to shore—his gangway into the American port city. A swift tension ballooned within him. To stifle it he forced a deep draught of the damp sea air, and at the back of his nose the tension found a taste: a foreign tang suggesting machined air. The sort of taste action would have.

Still, he refused to ask the question eating him, shy to because, in truth, the whole venture—the scheming, arranging, all and else—did belong to Ruinsey: Bountin himself being along for company and to seek his own luck. With this thought, he shy-eyed his partner with fresh indulgence and tried harder to deal with the creeping time. For here he was, at the end of that master of a move: he country-wild and Caribbeano, jumping ship into America.

That they were so close! A thrill seized him, shivering across his back and chest, crawling like ants about his balls. He almost jumped to his feet, but caught himself. Instead, he tensed and stretched—his legs, his arms, his back—then yawned extra wide like a wakeful lion.

A hailing voice provided a distraction. "Yow, Coconut! Ain'tcha goin' t'town? Afraid to lose yer monkey ass, huh?" The taunt ended with its owner's laughter, like a jackass braying after it had farted.

It came from a chubby brown-skinned fellow Ruinsey called Flabber. He was an American, the ship's cook. He had decided that, of all the Caribbeanos in the crew, Ruinsey was to be jape's stock on the menu for the three-week freight run. So, at chow time in the galley, it was Ruinsey he pestered with "Coconut" and "Monkey" nicknames. Other bloods wore hair in braids or natural locks, yet it was Ruinsey's tresses that suggested "golliwog" and "snakehead" to Flabber. Every time they went to eat, Flabber became the pesky mosquito: bites and buzzings and all.

And what had Ruinsey done about all this? Nothing but play the statue.

As if he didn't see, or hear, or feel. He just sat and listened. Still, on good sea days, when they were eating topside, he would calm down Bountin's yearning to revenge him. "Man, I have a plan," he'd say. "Every fatted hog got his Saturday, and Flabber day is coming."

Now Flabber swaggered down the gangplank and, not satisfied with his joke, turned at the bottom and made an ugly face at them. Then he shouted something else. But the distance and the gulls' cries and the breeze took it.

"Fuck you, Fat Lips!" Bountin screamed back, maybe in vain, as Flabber began striding away up the long pier into America.

When Bountin turned around, though, Ruinsey had stood up. His beat-up leather bag was swung ready over his shoulder. And in a flash the answer snapped into Bountin's head. That was why they had been waiting! Grinning with his insight, he gleamed a look in Flabber's direction. But the target was already gone, lost in the eight-o'clock waning of the long and tired day.

Eyes full on him, Ruinsey cocked his head and asked, "You understanding now?"

Bountin nearly answered with the lie that he had divined the plan years ago. Instead, being easy, he said, "Yeah, yeah, yeah."

And not wanting the lesson that might follow, he looked away—toward the narrow, sloping gangplank inviting them down. "So . . . we going now, right?" he said.

"Unless y'don't want catchup to catch him!" Ruinsey answered.

For Bountin the gangplank was no real necessity. His anticipation alone could've shot him across the space from rail to pier; he could've sprung up and glided over, like those after-hours gulls. But he was with Ruinsey, on his mission. So Bountin merely slapped at whatever might've stuck to his pants seat. Then he bounced off.

All the walk up the long pier Bountin stoppered his excitement and refrained from asking Ruinsey his intent for Flabber. He was still trying to determine it by himself when a chain-link fence surprised up out of the evening. He looked it over: where the lock was, the clearance at the bottom, the barbed overhang at the top. A sudden banging interrupted from his left. They turned and saw the window half of the sentry-hut door opening. A head with a guard's cap poked out and sounded a bleat in nasal pitch, like a goat inquiring after grass. There was a pause.

Bountin looked sharply at Ruinsey, fishing for a clue or a signal. Ruinsey was staring at the man from eyes edged with blankness. Then his eyes turned to the gate, as if it could offer help or translation. Bountin fixed on the gate also, now measuring its height, the size of the links, the number of steps it'd take to climb over.

The guard broke the silence. With the same accent, but slower, he said all in one, "Say, y'all—speak—English—or—what? *Habla—say—español?* Eh! *Qué—bota?*"

Ruinsey cleared his throat, said, "Cargo vessel, *Flying Jenny*. Shore leave. . . ."

His voice, sounding a little higher than usual, stopped short, interrupted by a purposeful buzzing, which continued long enough, as the guard pulled his head back in like a turtle. The window slid shut, *thumptt!*

Nothing else happened. Checking Ruinsey for understanding, Bountin found Ruinsey checking him.

Vluuppt! The window slid open again. The guard's head popped back out. Glaring, grimacing, it jerked at the fence. "Get—da—gawddamn—gate!" it snarled.

The fed-up head disappeared. And the buzzing began again. It sounded more riled-up.

This time they both started fast for the gate, which, as it was pushed upon, clicked open and let them, easy so, into the paradise America.

Their first scene was a long, wide, empty highway disappearing streetlight by streetlight into the darkness.

Bountin took it all in, looking about for some signs of life: people, a car, anything. He needed more—community? He had this zest to shout at somebody. Or throw a stick. Or say "Hiya!" Yankee-style.

Ruinsey caught his arm roughly. "First thing is, we have to make Flabber remember. Right?"

Bountin came down to earth. He nodded, looked along both ends of the disappearing street, and asked, "Y'know which way he went?"

Ruinsey pointed to the left, a bit up beyond the streetlights. "That glow over there is the shining city. That's where he gone. And no car passing here this hour. So he gone walking."

It was such common sense, Bountin knew he could've figured it out also. He just hadn't known how high to look or how to read what he saw. And all that was the stuff Ruinsey taught him. Every day, past and now.

On impulse he grabbed Ruinsey's arm and stopped him soft eye to hard. Then he had so much thanks to say, he told him only, "Ruinsey, mi'man, this place ent so hard."

Ruinsey looked at him queerly and broke out his full smile, which disappeared his eyes into wrinkles.

"I knew you'd like it, man. From the 'f' in first, I knew it."

All their backslapping dislodged the bag from Ruinsey's shoulder. And, as if that had knifed his mood, his grin turned down grim. "But I don't want to feel good yet, man," he said, then looked up the road to the city lights where Flabber was heading.

Bountin said eagerly, "Ay! man, I'm ready like Freddy." He recalled all the times Flabber had played the nettle for his man, and raked and stirred these angers into the working rage that'd drive him now to sting back. For yes! prickle-cutting-down time was come.

Ruinsey adjusted his bag so it hung on his back. Then, muttering, "Now for his ass," he set off at a brisk lope, Bountin easy at his side.

At first sight of Flabber, they crossed from the far side of the over-wide double street. Directly behind him then, they closed in with silence more than speed until, with a pouncing spurt, they were upon him. Bountin kicked him behind the knees into a crouch, while Ruinsey caught him in a choke hold and wrestled him down to the edge of the sidewalk, crushing his face into the scrawny grass. So the first idea Flabber had of something happening was when he tried to scream.

But his voice caught on too high and failed, and by then he had lost his wind to a gargle. For with a pull, a rip, and a tug-over, Ruinsey'd covered Flabber's head with his own denim jacket, leaving him well trussed up. Just for something more to do, Bountin kneed Flabber in the ribs, making him squeal and choke out, "Oh, God! Oh, God! Don't kill me."

Meantime, Ruinsey drew his gilpin, it with an edge like a new tooth-ache, he eyeing Bountin with silent strategy as he pulled it out. Bountin caught his design in an instant, and they changed holding positions slightly, allowing easier breathing for Flabber.

Thus he was begging for mercy more plainly when Ruinsey made his strike. As the blade sliced across his seat, a spitty wheezing joined with Flabber's cry, blending into an indrawn whimper, softer than the whisper of his splitting seating layers: the jeans blue one, the white shorts one, then the skin itself—a lighter brown than expected and, innermost, a pale pink flesh springing tiny drops of blood which quickly flooded down the new-cut crevasse.

Henceforth, Flabber'd know stretching pains each time he stooped to shit. Good vengeance, since it was relieving his other hole that had brought this on. Bountin grinned at the logic of it as Ruinsey spat finally on his cringing victim. Then they walked off to the city, leaving him huddled and blabbering there.

They took a few false turns around long wasteland blocks before they got near the source of the glowing. Then they could see headlamps flashing by cross streets not far in front of them. Here they paused to set themselves: to resettle the clothes on the body, to gather an easy pose for walking, to ready their eyes in their faces. Then, when they felt right, they walked up to the next intersection and turned into the flow of the actual, living American street.

"This must be a main avenue . . ." Ruinsey kept repeating softly, mostly to himself.

Bountin had no contention with that or anything else. He was taking in the lights. There were so many lights everywhere he turned bedazzled eyes. Not only sizes, but every shape and color. Blinking and flashing. Action lights. Sliding along picture advertisements. Popping on, emptying off. Pairing up in beams on shining cars, going and coming, red and brilliant. Shimmering the streets into golden streams, and rippled silver, and weird glitters, and hanging-tree shadows from the looming gooded-necked lamp poles, lamp poles tall and aloof as royal palms.

Several times Bountin stared himself into collisions: with people, poles, poodly dogs, and potholes. After enduring some verbal abuse and vague pain, he marshaled his attention to immediate focus on the people flowing beside and about him like river sands eddying. They passed in multitudes of vital, plain, and regular sorts. Many carried a flair. Regardless of how it came out, they tried for a difference, in clothes or makeup or walking stride. No one seemed to care when the gimmick didn't work. No jibes, no embarrassment, even if frogface wearing silks was escorting pussycats in satin. Everybody was full of themselves, going along intent, overlooking any disturbance that'd vary their own destinations. Bountin marveled. This was all right!

A girl coming past him was wearing cutoffs that never stopped. Just loudly enough he hailed her. "Hey, Sugar-Juice!"

She caught the pass, together with his bold eye. Bold right back, she smiled full and close at him, then mouthed him a kiss as they passed each other forever, indulging him with a lasting moment of honey. Hers was the city's welcoming kiss. It said he was among his kind of people. He was in his native place.

Ruinsey's voice nudged into his attention, insistent about transport they needed to find: some "subway" train to get them to his contact in the city, to some woman expecting them.

Bountin waved an arm at his bothering, indicating the scene about them. "Which city? This isn't the city?" he asked.

Ruinsey let the question rise into the night. He only muttered, "Well . . ." and turned to searching through his bag, from which he took a notebook page and read it with many puzzled looks, as if the words were making strange signs at him.

"This could be any part of it. Look, man! I never been here, y'know. . . ." Ruinsey stopped, "Hmmm'd" like a lawyer, then went on. "Listen! These directions say we *have* to get a subway . . . whatever it is."

Bountin couldn't figure why Ruinsey sounded so concerned. Finding the train couldn't be that difficult. It was a public vehicle. They just had to ask somebody, and he, for one, wasn't shy. And even if they missed the train, he was sure they could walk to Ruinsey's contact. It was one city, after all. They had all night, and he wasn't tired.

"You want me to find out from that papers-man over there?" Bountin asked.

Ruinsey shrugged okay and handed over the directions. Then he added, "But don't make show of yourself too much, eh? We've got to be inconspicuous. You understand?" His forehead was all frowned up in anxious ditches as he spoke, his eyes red with trouble lines.

All his show of dread was only firing up Bountin's temper. Why all this advice and concern? How come suddenly he was a cross to Ruinsey's shoulder?

"Since when you so worried about me?" he demanded, unable to keep the sarcasm and heat out his voice. "You don't think your partner could handle, eh? Tell me!"

But he didn't wait for Ruinsey's answer. Didn't want one. The question was his point. He just stalked off to the newspaper stand.

With his partner's misgivings policing his mind, Bountin was strict on his politeness. He waited until the man was free, then said, "Good night, mister."

When nothing happened, he repeated it louder, twice.

Finally the man looked at him and said, "Yeah, what?"

"Can you direct me to the train? Please."

"Which 'un?"

"The subway one."

"Yeah, yeah. Which 'un?"

Bountin looked him over and saw the man was serious. So he tried, "Any one going in the city."

"Better y'take the bus," the man said. "Stops one block over."

Bountin leaned his elbows on the counter and struck a pondering pose. He shook his head. "No, I want to catch the train."

"Same token," the man answered.

Bountin couldn't follow this meaning. So he remained thoughtful: began turning about the note he held and looking at it as if *it* had failed to satisfy.

The man took the hint. "Here, let's see that!" he said, and reached over his counter and plucked the note away. He waved it to arm's length and squint-focused to read. Then he returned it to Bountin.

"You'd be better off with th' bus," he said. "Your train's way 'cross town."

Bountin kept his pose, added a this-is-great-news smile. "Yes? Which direction?"

He spoke with much marveling in his tones. The man pointed. Bountin nodded as if heady with privilege. Then, as if after thinking, he asked, "So, how far is 'cross town?"

The man looked at him curiously, grimaced a clown mouth, fingering down the ends while he considered. "Thirty, maybe forty blocks," he said.

Bountin smiled at him, straightened up, and put the directions in his pocket. Before he walked away, he said, "Thank you for your kindness, mister."

The man called after him, "Y'should take th' bus . . . same token."

Bountin, feeling champion, dashed into the street, noticed the red DON'T WALK while lithely skipping through some braking traffic toward the other side of the road. His satisfaction would've been really complete if Ruinsey had witnessed his handling the man. That certainly would've finished all the anxious nonsense in his mind: that the Bountin had lost his touch.

The man had pointed back along the way they had come. So they crossed a broad, busy, one-way street and went. Right away Bountin became spellbound by the lights again, all so close around from lamp pole to ground level, while straight up above was opaque blackness. It was all upside-down: as if the sky had upended its contents all around them, transforming the people, the stores, even the plain concrete he walked. The scattering star-fall had drenched the street with sparkle and changed the place into bustle of glaze and glitter.

A glance at his partner striding alongside made Bountin realize that

Ruinsey hadn't been sparking at all. Much more than his fashion, he had gone silent. Bountin began worrying for explanation. About Flabber? Not likely. They had done a good revenge—not even the victim was witness. In any case, Ruinsey never took on that sort of problem. His motto was "Make life simple, take it as it comes."

It occurred to him that Ruinsey might be tired. Or hungry. That just might be it. He himself, on thinking, was middling peckish.

"You slowing down or what? How you so quiet?" he asked.

Ruinsey acknowledged him only a distracted, no-comment look.

They were coming up to a one-door store whose neatly laden stalls encroached halfway across the sidewalk. Pyramids of citrus, apples, bananas, mangoes, and other fruits competed colorfully for attention. Inspired, Bountin approached quickly, as he said to Ruinsey, "Man, what you need is some vitamins."

And with that, he had crouched over the banana stall and swiftly slipped a yellow-ripe hand into his shirt's bosom. Then, with a big grin, he sped off surging through the sidewalk's throng, casting backward looks.

It was a few moments before he realized there was no pursuit. No one had come out of the store to throw even a look at him. So he slowed down to the pace of the crowd, which had just so calmly accepted all his shoving and rushing through. Finally, he stepped off the curb between two parked cars and waited for Ruinsey to catch up. The incurious crowd went by as if he weren't there. So he broke out a banana to munch while his partner arrived. And when he did, fell into step beside him and offered him some food.

As if taking example from Ruinsey, the street was becoming quieter. The several past blocks carried less and less traffic: people, business, and otherwise. Bountin commented on this.

"It must be getting late," was all Ruinsey said.

Being patient with the man's mood, Bountin let that comment remain where it dropped. He himself hadn't been thinking of time, but of how the quiet streets seemed relieved and freer in the more space they now had. And about how the air even had a lighter smell. And how the soft slap of the tossed banana peelings carried truer. And how he felt betting certain it was easier now to jump higher or explode a lungful in a shout. But Bountin didn't bother bringing up all this. Not to a Ruinsey seeing the night only as a clock face.

It was a dimly lit, vertical sign placed abruptly next to some stairs leading underground. Involved with the rhythm of walking blocks and crossing streets, they nearly missed it. Seeing the stairs, right away, Bountin realized that "subway" meant underground railway system and, with more excitement, that the trains ran through tunnels in the earth. That idea made him laugh out loud. He clapped Ruinsey's shoulder. "Y'see that, Ruinsey? And I was looking for a railway station, y'know, the water tanks, a platform, a signalman. Y'following me?"

Ruinsey nodded understanding but didn't talk. Although, from the way his front foot was groping for the first tread, Bountin decided Ruinsey, too, had to be getting impressed right past his popping eyeballs.

Halfway down, at the zig in the zigzag staircase, Ruinsey took a packet of slugs from his bag. They were ten tokens, he said. Bought from his contact man on the cargo ship, they were part of the stowaway job package. He handed five to Bountin.

"I hope these tokens working for this train, y'know," Ruinsey said, worried.

Bountin considered this. "Well that ent the worst," he said. "If they don't work, we could just jump over. That turnstile ent a good three feet."

Ruinsey looked him over a long one. Then he said, "Bountin, you must stop thinking that way now. Okay? You not home. This is America. We can't be drawing attention so, or they will catch we. You have to calm down, man."

Ruinsey was being so solemn, Bountin made a checkup grin at him. "But how you so serious, Ruinsey? You sermonizing in paradise, man. I was only making joke. I know we not jumping."

Ruinsey didn't acknowledge him. Instead, back stiffened, token in hand, he led off for the turnstile. They put their tokens in the slots, and they worked just fine.

The underworld train ride was the final gate through which the city stormed to possess Bountin. Its assault began immediately, as, with hurricane roaring, a one-eyed dragon monster filled the tunnel, rushing up to them. Then, with a great shrieking, it turned out to be their grumbling train, restrained and shuddering but, unnaturally, blowing steam nowhere. No sooner it had stopped than side panels scraped open and people tumbled out like finished batches. Doing as others who had waited, Ruinsey and he pushed into the carriage against the outflow. Then, inside, propped on hard plastic seats, they watched the doors guillotine shut, and with a jolt they were fast off, shrieking like a cross dragon again. But now inside it.

Under mountains? Under rivers? From what Bountin could make out of their passage, it could've been anywhere. Outside the row windows, the carriage's lights reflected off whizzing walls and sudden poles, where the checkered patterns of light strung into speeding bullets that disappeared for dark moments before returning to dazzle. All this was close to hypnotizing him when another charging rumble *vroomphed* by, going the other way, and shattered his trance with a fist of sound-force.

Bountin palmed away a slack feeling from his face. The dripping sweat was one thing; the bigger bother was a glazed view he tried squinting away. Yet it still seemed they were inside a bolt of lava, hurtling through the earth, aiming for eruption at some volcano, somewhere, and soon. And very powerful they were; very dangerous, too. He had this sense that, although his feet were standing still, they were really flying, skimming over ground. One supporting proof was the wheel-whirring in his soles, which was also vibrating through his seat and setting an annoying edge to his teeth. He stood up abruptly to change the pressures, and the annoying thrilling stopped; but on standing, he was unbalanced and almost fell. He only saved himself by an instinctive snatch overhead, where his hand found a securing hook. It was so exactly in the right place that Bountin realized it must have been put there for just that convenience. To him, it was such a practical forethought that he hung his head down close to Ruinsey's to speak his admiration for the designers.

"Isn't this something else again?" he began, and couldn't hear himself above the train's roar. So he cleared his throat for the challenge and shouted, "Ruinsey, isn't this something?"

As if Bountin's shout had caught him in a mean dream, Ruinsey jerked up, aggressive with alarm, asking, "What! What!"

This startled, fighting readiness put Bountin off his cheery mood. He was about to scream, *Forget it!* But right then his throat broke into a coughing fit from strain. And he could only hang there from the handhold and rack his belly bones narrow with spasm after weakening spasm.

Meanwhile, Ruinsey kept repeating, "Calm down, man, you have to take it easy," as if it were mischief Bountin was making. As the seizure passed, Bountin felt the train slowing down. So he sat down to compose himself.

The door panels crashed open. Some people got up and hustled out. One or two rushed in as if under catchup pressures. Then, through the door right in front of him, three guys dressed up female sauntered into the carriage ever so coolly, as if they never noticed how the gates just missed smashing their shitting ends into skinny streaks. With lots of chichi and wiggling, they teetered their high heels to the metal bench and sat primly, as if cautious of their hard ends testing against the plastic hardness.

Bountin was never so astonished. They were so weird, and so comfortable at it, he couldn't believe their boldness. He wondered at them, amazed. Did they never pass mirrors? Had they no family or caring friends to advise them of their appearance? Of their makeup caking between sprouting moustache hairs, of those muscled hairy calves, of those high-coloured, pointed-heel size fifteens? How could these guys stand up anywhere in public? Had they hidden in the toilet to wait for this train? Suddenly amused, Bountin decided these guys truly deserved a "Big-Balls Boldness" trophy. For with their display of gumption, they had to be carrying at least three sets of the daringest miracles ever.

The Perspiration Moustache one stared back at Bountin. "What's your problem?" he asked in girlish tones.

Bountin could hold it in no more. He burst out laughing, weakening himself so, he leaned on Ruinsey for support.

"How quaint," commented the Eyeshadowed one with scarlet lips, then closed heads with the others for a giggle chorus.

Ruinsey eased Bountin off as if he didn't know him. "Take it easy, man," he muttered.

Right away a part of Bountin's mind raged, *Take what easy?* But he was still laughing in part also. Only now there was nothing funny to his mirth. He just continued with the noisy grimacing from spite.

The Plucked Eyebrows one was now staring him down. Then he proceeded to japing with flirting blinks, and moues, and tossing head. Bountin sprung up and stood over him. "You like me, Horse-mouth?" he challenged, "You want mih cock? Y'want it crowing in your face, eh?"

He hefted his crotch in Plucked Eyebrows' face, who pulled back and ladyed, "What is your problem, sir?"

"I don't have none, you no-cunt monster," Bountin said threateningly, "But look yuh eyes on me again, and I'd fix your problems for you."

Bountin's hand was hot and damp on the blade handle stuck in his waistband. He was ready for anything. But before he could move, Ruinsey had armlocked his neck and was dragging him away to sit close with him, holding him there.

"Don't let them vex you, Bountey. Y'have to take it easy. Forget them. Just take it easy," he repeated urgently.

As he spoke, the he-shes got up and sashayed downrange to the far end of the carriage.

Ruinsey had led them off the train onto a major interconnecting platform. But for the many pillars, so large it was, it could've made a full-sized concrete soccer field. They were standing now against a passage wall. Ruinsey held the directions crumpled in his hand. "Man, I can't see how we go make it, y'know," he said.

"How y'mean?" Bountin asked. "She didn't write down what to do next?"

"Is not that . . ."

"Well, is what?"

Ruinsey looked away, slow eyes roving all around the big space. Shaking his head, he regarded the giant girders lying close over them. Finally, he said, "If those things break, I wouldn't even know where I die. Not if is east or west. Or day or night. And if is a crowd here when it come down, I'd die just like a common ant mashed up in a melee."

"But, Ruinsey man, they have all those signs about," Bountin said reasonably. "Look around. Look at all those arrows and numbers and colours and lines you could follow. They could—"

Ruinsey cut him off. "Bountin, you can't see? You don't realize they only crowding you, steering people like cows, like tame animals. Y'think you could stand that? Y'could live so?" He stopped and nodded in a final manner. Then he said, "Yes, man, we have to take that other track. I can't manage it here. We can't make it."

At Ruinsey's conclusion, a quaking notion zinged into Bountin's mind. Stubbornly he pushed it away. Instead, he pointed up to the subway signs. "But Ruinsey, that is the outtown track y'looking at. We going intown."

Ruinsey shot him an odd look. And Bountin saw his partner's face in a new mask: one sharp and anxious, shining with greasy sweat; one with straining eyes that stared at everything too long. Then he acknowledged what was past working out. His partner really didn't want to go on anymore. For Ruinsey had turned and headed for the back-out track.

Bountin stared after him. He felt as if betrayed by some foolishness. As if his necklace charm had cut his head off, his whole spirit wilted. Vacant-minded, he stood there for minutes, until in the distance he heard the first urgent rushing, which before had roared into a train. That giving him life again, he sprinted off after Ruinsey.

Bountin found him before the angry dragon thundered past. On an inner track, it was skating farther into town. There was plenty of time for Ruinsey's train.

Their eyes made four and all was said. They reached for and embraced each other. In the hug, Bountin thought, they were close as blood to skin, and now they must bleed apart. Then they stepped back and, shy with each other for the moment, gazed together up the dark train tracks.

"I'll 'company you back to the gate, okay?" Bountin said. "I mean, if that's all right with you?"

Ruinsey worked his vanishing-eyes smile. He said, "Well, you settle your mind already, right Boldman? So how I could ever stop you? Sure, make it back halfway with me."

He handed Bountin the crumpled directions.

HERSCHEL LEE JOHNSON

Paul Strayhorn hurried down the subway steps. When he reached the landing, the train was already in the station. Almost late for work, he dashed through the turnstile and leapt aboard the train.

Paul edged his way through the crowd and grabbed one of the hanging steel support straps. A white cop standing in the middle of the car stared at him. He returned the cop's gaze. He realized that despite his suit all the cop probably saw was the "young black male average build about six feet tall" they always seemed to be looking for. Ironically, while everyone lived in terror of this black male, it was actually he who was the most endangered species in the city. The cop moved to another car.

Paul looked at the other passengers. There was a middle-aged West Indian woman with a shopping bag on her lap and her legs open. Farther down were several tight-lipped businessmen, and, farther still, a young white couple dressed identically in down jackets, khaki pants, and boating moccasins. Their faces had a fresh, unused look. Nearby, three Hispanic women chattered away in Spanish and occasionally punctuated the air

HERSCHEL LEE JOHNSON was born in Birmingham, Alabama. He was educated at Dartmouth College and Columbia School of Journalism. He has worked as a journalist, public relations writer and bartender.

with sharp, quick gestures. They seemed oblivious of the other passengers.

At the opposite end of the car a bagman leaned against one of the exits. All his belongings were in an overstuffed shopping cart. His foul smell drifted through the car and clung to everything it touched.

The New York City subway system teemed with crazies and derelicts geniuses and saints murderers whores ministers and messiahs, graffiti filled with anger and weirdness and sometimes love, fake cowboys and genuine Japanese tourists Guardian Angels and the raucous screech of steel wheels against steel rails as ancient rocking cars hurtled through dark labyrinthian tunnels at fifty miles per hour and sometimes jumped the tracks, shit and piss and vomit bitter cold in winter and torturous heat in summer chronic delays and eerie abandoned stations, ubiquitous books and newspapers and magazines being read in a panoply of languages hurt and fear and ambition and determination all packed together as tightly as the two black teenage lovers who now stood at the front of the car watching the hypnotic shimmering yellow tunnel lights as the train zoomed toward its ever-receding destination.

The train stopped. A young white woman got on and found a seat. She was quietly weeping. The tears welled in her eyes, then streamed down her cheeks and fell onto her coat. Nobody inquired about her pain or offered her any consolation. Paul wanted to help but wondered what would happen if the woman misinterpreted his actions. And what if the cop returned and found a distraught white woman in his presence? He let her cry.

The train was barely under way again when Paul heard a blaring saxophone. Through an adjoining car walked a young black man wearing dark wraparound shades, long beaded braids, and a skin-tight silver jumpsuit covered with shiny spangles. He sent blazing avant-garde jazz riffs bouncing throughout the subway car. Then he stopped his performance abruptly and said, "Good morning, ladies and gentlemen. I am an interplanetary traveler who is temporarily stranded here on earth. My spaceship is broken down and I am trying to raise funds to get it repaired. As you know, everything on earth costs money, and since I don't have any of your currency I am asking that you give a small donation toward my quest. Thank you for your kindness."

The crowd loved the pitch, and when the man extended a small tattered paper bag, dollar bills got stuffed into it.

"I am now going to leave you," the spaceman announced after making his collection. "People of earth, I thank you for your generosity. Peace! Peace! Peace!"

excerpt from KINGDOM OF NIGHT

He began to play an anarchic version of the theme from *The Twilight Zone* as he headed for an adjoining car.

Paul got off at the next stop. When he walked onto the platform he saw several cops standing around a body covered with a dirty blanket. A black hand extended from underneath the blanket, which was edged with blood. A train pulled out of the station. Scrawled across several of its cars in giant pink Day-Glo lettering was the graffiti message JUST A SILLY PHASE I'M GOING THROUGH.

Paul exited onto 57th Street and Broadway. Diana Ross walked past him in a long fur coat. She didn't speak.

He grew up in the deep South on the edge of poverty, but he was bright and during his high school years in the late sixties he became one of those blacks who were anxiously recruited by white colleges that had suddenly become socially conscious. He chose a prominent school in the Northeast. While there, his interest in literature deepened and broadened. He realized that he had to write stories. He felt himself especially drawn to Wright and Baldwin and Ellison and Baraka. He knew, too, that his vision would encompass Beckett and Celine and Nathanael West. He also knew that his vision would be filled with terror.

After college, he got a job with a black magazine in New York City. He started as a researcher, but the magazine was chronically short-staffed and within a year he was writing features for it.

He was excited by the opportunity at first but soon realized the limitations of the job. Although the magazine was the only national black general-interest magazine in the country, it resolutely ignored vast stretches of black life—namely, the ugly and the desolate. It was relentlessly upbeat. Its focus on successful entertainers and athletes and bureaucrats was almost surreal in its intensity. Meanwhile, he felt, the country was steadily pushing itself toward a racial explosion.

Paul had been in the office for about an hour when his telephone rang. It was Betty, the receptionist. She said that Jesus Christ wanted to see him and that he refused to leave without an interview.

"It's too early to be talking shit, Betty," he said. They were good friends. Betty was real. He liked her.

"This ain't no shit," she said. Her voice was calm, but there was a nervous edge in it. He knew she wasn't kidding.

"I'll be right out," he said.

When Paul entered the lobby Betty motioned her head toward a tall, extremely thin young black man sitting quietly in a corner. He was dressed in a white robelike garment. His eyes were aflame.

Paul introduced himself.

"I am Jesus Christ," the man said with great authority. "Are you in charge here?"

"I'm one of the editors," said Paul.

"Good. I'd like to talk with you."

Paul began to tell the man that he couldn't talk to him at that time but the man interrupted him.

"You don't believe me, do you?" the man said accusingly. He stared at Paul. "You don't believe that I am Jesus Christ."

Paul assured the man that he did believe him but the man was agitated now.

"No," the man said intensely, "you are not a believer. But I can prove it to you."

Paul tried to ease the man out of the door but he couldn't budge him.

"I can prove it to you," the man insisted. His voice was higher than before, and this time it trembled. "Let me show you the wound in my side."

Before the man could open his robe, Paul said, "What about your hands?"

"My hands?" said the man.

"Where are the wounds in your hands?" asked Paul.

The man held his hands up to his face. He looked closely at one, then the other. He turned them slowly from side to side. He ran one hand over the other gently.

"And your feet," said Paul. "Where are the wounds in your feet?"

The man inspected his feet, which were bare despite the winter cold.

"There are no wounds in my hands or my feet," said the man with hushed amazement. "There are no wounds in my hands or my feet."

He stood there dumbfounded for a minute, then walked slowly out of the office.

"Boy, you sure get all kinds coming in here," said Betty. There was great relief in her voice, and Paul realized she must have been holding her breath. She was happy now, and she smiled.

"Yeah," said Paul. He felt uneasy. To wake a dreamer is a dangerous thing.

Paul went back to his office. He wondered about the man who claimed to be Jesus. Then he heard a light tapping on his door. He looked up and saw Sherrell McTear.

"Mind if I disturb you for a minute?" she asked coyly.

excerpt from KINGDOM OF NIGHT

"Not at all," said Paul. "Come on in."

Sherrell was chocolate brown and easy to look at. She had big hazel eyes and a full mouth that stayed puckered. She sometimes tried to form her mouth into a seductive smile but the result always looked too obvious. She was only twenty and needed practice.

The women in the office called Sherrell Little Miss Hollywood. They called her that because her goal in life was to become a top model and star actress. It was an old ambition but one that was never too worn for new recruits. In that pursuit, Sherrell was sometimes given to "Hollywoodish" mannerisms, especially that of the vamp. Most of these mannerisms came from television soap operas, which she watched relentlessly, and they therefore had a kind of third-hand grotesqueness about them. Many of the women also resented Sherrell's youth and brashness and the upward tilt of her breasts, which she never failed to emphasize, and they sometimes called her things other than Little Miss Hollywood.

Sherrell was always dressed and made up as if she expected to be discovered any minute. She believed that possibility was real, and who knows but that on a miraculous day it might have been.

When Sherrell spoke she struggled to put sophistication and worldliness into her voice, but she had barely finished high school and words sometimes tripped her. When this happened she would try her seductive smile. It sometimes worked. She sat in a chair facing Paul's desk and crossed her legs.

"I brought my portfolio with me today," she said, uncrossing her legs. Her legs were long and expressive. They were good legs. "Would you like to see it?"

"Sure," said Paul. He had seen a lot of portfolios. He had seen too many portfolios. "Why don't you bring it by this afternoon?"

"Well, I was thinking that after work might be better," said Sherrell, crossing her legs again. "I'm real busy today."

One of the legs bounced up and down on the other.

"I'm supposed to go to a reception for Sarah Del Rio tonight," said Paul. "Why don't we have a drink after work and then go there together?"

"That sounds wonderful," said Sherrell, and she meant it.

Sarah Del Rio ran the top black modeling agency in the country. Once, she held near dictatorial power over which black models did and did not make it. That power had faded as white agencies realized they could make money with black models and grudgingly began to handle a few. But Del Rio still held considerable sway in the business.

Sherrell fidgeted in the chair for a minute, then said, "Well, I guess I'll let you get back to work."

She got up and walked toward the door. Her hip movements were slightly exaggerated. They were good hips. When Sherrell reached the door she turned and smiled.

"See you later," she cooed.

For a moment, Paul thought she was going to blow him a kiss.

The rest of the day passed slowly. At the end of it Paul stood at the window of his thirtieth-floor office and looked at the tiny people scurrying along the streets below.

He enjoyed the feverish energy of the city, even relished it, although he was from a small southern town where people believed there was no real need for speed unless you were engaged in some illegal activity.

There was the usual traffic jam. The blasts of car horns floated up to him. They were angry and unrelenting. He could imagine the curses that accompanied them. He smiled. What an ugly, mesmerizing, effulgently beautiful city! he thought. Then he heard a voice barking almost in his ear.

"Strayhorn, are you going to finish that story today or are you going to spend your time daydreaming?"

Paul stared out the window a few seconds longer. Then he turned to face Willie Straeger, his editor, whom he had nicknamed Bobo.

"It's finished," he said, handing the manuscript to Straeger.

The short, pudgy man skimmed through the pages and grunted. Paul knew the grunt meant the story was okay, that it had the requisite mix of the sentimental and the sordid.

"It's about time to knock off now," said Straeger. "Stop by my office in the morning. We've got another assignment we want you to get on right away."

"What's the story?" asked Paul.

"Carol Hendricks just landed a part in a big picture. We want you to do a profile. You know, the usual sort of thing."

Paul felt his eyes start to glaze over. He had been writing for the black monthly tabloid for three years now, and the constant stream of stories about stars and their cars and their homes and their diets and their money and their sexual preferences had become an unbearable ordeal. At first, he had looked upon the job as an apprenticeship. Dues. There was also a practical side. It was a job at a time when jobs were scarce.

But as the months dragged on he had found it harder and harder to put words together on the magazine's recurrent themes. Now the tolerably absurd had become fully grotesque. While the overwhelming majority of black people continued to scramble for their lives, their one major national publication chose to focus cheerily on the few of them who had made it.

excerpt from KINGDOM OF NIGHT

"Strayhorn, did you hear what I said?" Straeger shouted.

Straeger always shouted. He had a grating, grinding voice that always seemed to be ten or twelve decibels above the necessary level. It wasn't that he was hard of hearing. He could hear perfectly well. But it was as if he felt that his words gained a force and conviction when shouted that they could never hold in normal conversation.

Straeger's bluster, however, always contained the scent of fear. Paul believed this fear emanated from Straeger's constant apprehension about what turn the big boss's whims might take. The big boss made the final decision on everything, including the smallest stories. He ruled through terror. Straeger knew his decisions as editor could be arbitrarily overruled at any time or, worse, crushed humiliatingly in front of the entire staff. Even after twenty years on the job, he still referred to the big boss as Mr. Nelson. The mention of the big boss's name seemed to make Straeger want to genuflect. His shouting, it seemed, was his ritual way of warding off the foot that seemed to stay aimed at his butt.

"Yes," said Paul.

"And, oh, yeah, don't forget that reception tonight," said Straeger.

"I'll be there."

"Good. Just go and show your face and shake a few hands. You know the deal. And be sure to pat Del Rio on the butt. She likes handsome young men. Who knows, maybe she'll buy an ad."

Straeger left. Paul returned to the window. It was after five and thousands of office workers were on the streets now, hurrying home or other places. The traffic was more heavily snarled. Pedestrians darted between the cars. The cars didn't brake for them, and they had to run for their lives. In the approaching darkness, the lights of the buildings began to sparkle. The lights were pretty and they were deceptive.

While they had drinks, Paul leafed through Sherrell's portfolio. The pictures in it were almost caricatures of glamour and sensuality. There were shots of her in a cheap gown in embarrassingly studied poses. There were outdoor shots of her in a swimsuit. She was well-proportioned, and in the swimsuit shots she seemed comfortable and natural.

"Well, what do you think?" she asked.

"I think you'll be a star," said Paul. He knew this was a lie. Such chances were slim for anybody but they were a thousand times slimmer for blacks. Still, this was America and every once in a while a runaway slave managed to slip through the net.

She lowered her eyes and said, "Do you really think so?"

Paul had planned to try to get Sherrell to come back to his apartment but now he realized that there were already too many people lined up to try to take advantage of her and he couldn't do it.

"Yes," he said.

The reception was in honor of Sarah Del Rio's twentieth anniversary as founder and head of the country's first black modeling agency. It was a big event. Practically every prominent black in the city was there.

Everyone was dressed in a way meant to radiate success. The men's suits ranged in tailoring from conservative to designer cut, but all the colors were somber or neutral. The women were more adventurous. Their outfits all seemed to sparkle and cling and show great stretches of leg or back or breast. They wore dazzling smiles and their eyes were vivid and direct.

The models all looked nineteen. They wore the trendiest clothes. They looked sexy but not sensual. Theirs was a vacant, store-bought eroticism. Their own heat couldn't be felt at all. They managed to look alternately excited and bored. When they were excited their mannerisms had a frantic intensity about them. When they saw someone they knew they squealed with delight and engaged in cacophonous chatter. Their hands fluttered about like frightened birds.

Paul introduced Sherrell to one of the models. They became instant friends. He went to get a drink and they went off to become famous.

There was a hum of conversation throughout the room. Occasionally there was laughter, which erupted suddenly but then quickly died away. Everyone drank cheap white wine which they referred to as "Chablis" but which was simply jug wine from California.

Most of the people knew each other. It seemed that the same blacks kept coming to these events. They were the elite. They were the blacks who appeared in print or on television speaking for less-well-off blacks whom they studiously avoided in their daily lives. Unlike the deep spirituality of their heritage, ambition had become their religion. Whenever there was a small crack in the dam of discrimination, they hurried to dash through it. There was nothing inherently wrong in this, except that most of the blacks who did it seemed to wind up as empty and troubled as their white coun-terparts. They had nothing to hold on to, and since their progress could be shut down at any moment by a change in the country's economy and therefore its sentiments about racial progress, they lived in perpetual fear of having their ambitions suddenly thwarted. At the reception there were

excerpt from KINGDOM OF NIGHT

many hand slaps and cordial greetings, but they were stiff and artificial and full of lies. They were almost a parody. They were ugly and they were sad.

Paul returned to the bar. He took one of the plastic cups and asked the bartender to fill it with bourbon.

A man shouted for quiet, and when the noise dropped off he introduced Del Rio. She was tall and light-skinned with jet black hair that cascaded down her back. She was at least sixty and she had gained weight, but she was still stunning. She carried herself with the black version of old-money haughtiness, and when she swept her way to the microphone you felt that perhaps everyone should drop to one knee.

"Darlings," she began in a way reminiscent of Tallulah Bankhead, "I want to thank you all sincerely for coming out tonight. You're all so beautiful and so kind."

She paused for dramatic effect.

"You know, it's been a tough time in a tough business, but I've managed to hang in there."

Del Rio talked about her early pioneering days. She had been the first black model to crack the major white magazines. Her face was seen around the world. It was a step up for black people. She smiled throughout her delivery, and she made sure her smile reached every corner of the room. There was a brief burst of applause, and Del Rio lowered her head in feigned humility.

In the middle of the speech Paul realized that he was not going to pat Del Rio on the butt. He was not even going to speak to her. He was going to leave the magazine. He had found the story he had to write. He found Sherrell, but she wasn't ready to leave. She said she was about to meet Del Rio.

Paul left the reception. It was a cool spring night. The streets on the East Side of Manhattan were fairly crowded with well-dressed people. Most of these people were white, though there were a few blacks here and there.

Every once in a while some black teenagers drifted by. These groups seemed incongruous with the rest of the crowd. The boys were dressed in loose-fitting jeans and expensive sneakers, which were laced in varied and elaborate fashions, or they contained no laces at all. They wore down jackets and high-peaked ski caps. The girls, too, wore loose-fitting jeans. They favored black, thick-soled, clog-type shoes. Some of them had elaborate beaded braids; others had straightened hair that had been pulled into fierce designs.

Many of these teenagers were barely literate. Hardly any of them were employed, and each day their chances of employment declined. Many of the boys became dangerous and many of the girls became pregnant. Forever confronted by their limitations, many of them lived in perpetual anger and frustration. Even in childhood their faces were old and hard and defiant. Each day their numbers grew. Each day their chances of survival through conventional means decreased. Paul felt they might be the match that would ignite the upheaval. They were a part of the story he had to write.

Paul had thought of leaving the magazine many times before, but he had always found an excuse to avoid taking the leap. Now he understood that taking the leap was the only path to freedom. Perhaps then his tumbling mind could rest.

When Paul reached 72nd Street he decided to walk through the park to the West Side. He liked to walk. It invigorated him and cleared his thinking.

On the West Side the streets were not as clean or as well kept as those on the East Side. Here, too, there was a far greater mixing and brewing of the races. Walking up Broadway, Paul saw Koreans with their sparkling fruit stands and fish markets, Chinese with their ubiquitous restaurants, Arabs with their cigarette shops and newsstands, Jews with their delicatessens and real estate, the bodegas and discount cosmetics shops of the Hispanics, East Indian spice shops, and slick boutiques and bars owned by young whites. But he saw hardly anything along this stretch that was owned by blacks, though many black professionals lived in the area.

A lot of the blacks here didn't own anything. They lived in dilapidated single-room-occupancy hotels or on the streets. Many of them simply shuffled from one corner to the next and back again, asking passersby for change. They were often filthy and they sometimes stank. Many of them had been released from state mental institutions. They talked to ghosts in long, loud, convoluted conversations. They recorded old hurts and worldly homilies. They screamed.

People tried to ignore these derelicts, even when they were stretched out across the middle of the sidewalk, even when they came stumbling out of doorways with outstretched hands and saliva running from their mouths. But they couldn't be ignored. They never went away. And their numbers grew. As Paul passed two of them, he heard one of the men say to the other, "The bitch had the nerve to call me a bum, then she come back and ask me to loan her two dollars."

There was anger and hatred and vindictiveness in the man's voice. He spat the words. He wasn't wearing an expensive suit. He wore a rumpled shirt and a dirty pair of pants, which were both his business wear and his pajamas. The wine he drank was a sweet, wretched, purple brew that turned the mind to jelly. When he slapped his partner's palm, the action was solid and direct and serious. His grandest ambition was to live through the day. In his rich and varied years of travel throughout the city he had never heard of Sarah Del Rio, and if he had he wouldn't have given a shit anyway.

JACQUELINE JOAN JOHNSON

West wind blow ye gentle,
all the souls of yesterday . . .

—*South African Prayer*

 It had happened accidentally several months ago. Hafiz had never planned to have a woman living in his place, practically married to him, but he did. Who would have thought, after so many years alone, he would find such happiness. Hafiz could never have predicted that a casual response to a woman in need would change his life as he had known it for the past eight years. Even now, the awareness of how all this had happened still quickened his heart and surprised him. That spring day had been like so many others.

Hafiz had rolled up the accordion steel gates that surrounded his newsstand. He looked both ways on the uptown side of the street before he walked to the back and began to move the bundles of old papers to the side of the newsstand. Every morning, it was the same thing. Rise at 5 A.M., catch the Number 2 bus to 72nd Street and Broadway, and cross over to Eden's coffee shop for his morning tea. By 6 A.M. his magazines and newspapers were usually delivered.

Hafiz always started the day by checking the street before he set up.

JACQUELINE JOAN JOHNSON is a native of Philadelphia, Pennsylvania. She is the author of *Stokely Carmichael: The Story of Black Power*, published by Simon & Schuster. She has been a contributor to *UpSouth: African American Migrations in the Twentieth Century*, *Obsidian Literary Quarterly*, *Upscale* magazine and *Catalyst* magazine. She is a founding member of New Renaissance Literary Guild. Current works include a book for children, *In Pursuit of Art*, and a poetry collection, *A Gathering of Mother Tongues*.

Years ago, he had been mugged at the close of an evening's business. Ever since that night, he was on the lookout for would-be robbers. Hafiz was prepared. He kept an old machete hidden between the layers of wood inside the newsstand. At a moment's notice, he could whip it out and whirl it around, threatening to put out any fucker's lights, just as easy as chopping back a stalk of unruly raffia. Shit, he always had to keep an eye out for these damn Americans. How long had they been here and *still* didn't have their act together.

Sometimes he questioned why he left his village in India to come to a city like New York. The answer, which he pretended eluded him, always rushed to the back of his eyes. On some levels, New York had turned out to be no different from India: the same congested streets, a peddler's paradise, and the gentle clash of extravagance and poverty. The squalor of the people and New York City were one and the same; it merely spoke to Hafiz in varying degrees of cadence, hue, and accent.

Hafiz thought he saw something protruding from the side of the Dumpster but excused it as garbage. He looked closer and realized it was a dead bird. Hafiz quickly covered it with some old papers. He continued to stack newspapers. This early in the hot belly of this city, one saw many things half sane, disoriented and disembodied people. Sometimes at the end of a week, he too felt half sane. At times, there were whole colonies of people living on one avenue or another, camped around a fire or living in vast numbers of cardboard boxes. On occasion, these makeshift villages of the homeless were a welcome sight in comparison to some of the other things Hafiz saw.

Broadway and 72nd Street was a densely populated strip of stores and street vendors. So it was common to see small inconsequential scraps of paper, old clothing, one boot here, an earring over there, but a dead baby or a dead animal were against Hafiz's sensibilities. What kind of people did these things? Just who was supposed to clean up behind them? Of course, nobody took responsibility as others tripped or spent a few minutes cursing, rubbing dog shit off the bottom of their shoes. In his little newsstand, seventy hours a week, Hafiz had time to consider such issues. Sometimes his friends called him "Professor Hafiz," because of his constant questioning of everything and his quiet passion for learning.

Hafiz let out a low sigh, as his brown, slender hands reached inside the waist pocket of his brocaded vest. He took out a worn used-to-be-black wallet, lifted several bills from the wad, and placed them inside his pants pocket. The wad wasn't as big as it looked because Hafiz had put all his business cards and identification on the inside layer and wrapped his money around that. Secretly, Hafiz kept most of his money in a little pouch that hung around his neck, inside his shirt. Hafiz hoisted a stack of papers onto the stand. He placed the rumpled ones on the bottom. Some motherfuckers would not buy a rumpled newspaper, so Hafiz always mixed them into the bottom or the middle of the stack. Those crazy ones who rushed everywhere with their leather briefcases would be in too much of a hurry to dig for a better paper. Of course, there were those people who never took the top one. They would always mess up the order of the stack, forcing him, later, to lean over half the length of his body to fix it.

Damn Americans. He would be glad when he made it, so he could go back to his little town. The possibility and the impossibility of that was a thread he hung onto, never letting himself sway for too long in either direction. Longing was all it was, and Hafiz kept it cultivated with three 4-by-6 photos of his family back home. The pictures were over ten years old, yellowed practically beyond recognition and taped to the bulletproof glass of his newsstand. It had only been fifteen—no, seventeen—years since he had been home.

He glanced down at his watch, a cheap Taiwanese make. It read 6:41 A.M. There were a couple of people on the streets now. One came over to the stand. Gray-suited, he read the headlines of several papers before he decided on the *Wall Street Journal*. Hafiz remained outside the stand and gave the man change from his outside pocket. Hafiz had money everywhere. It wasn't anyone's business, though. Hafiz worked hard for what he had.

In a couple of hours, several Malian and Senegalese men had set up shop, with their prayer rugs and TV tables. They sold rain gear, cheap pocketbooks, belts, and scarves that were usually all the same, bought in bulk from the same jobber. It didn't make any difference to Hafiz. They were all black, lean, and far away from home.

Most of the day, Hafiz could overhear their conversations, peppered with Islamic phrases, French, and pidgin English. They were so black their skin shone with a brilliance all its own, even on the dreariest of days. Over three or four months, they had set up shop next to his newsstand every day. Hafiz had made friends with several of them.

All day long, these men re-created their African village. On rainy days the sounds of "ombrella, ombrella, ombrella," rolled off their tongues and filled the air as they sold in groups of six or seven. Every day they set up shop together; they sold their wares, ate, and left together. Each man had his own designated space, which changed daily. Their wares were set out in an orderly fashion and dusted once a day, better than any department store.

For these Africans, everything depended on the moment. Each day was different. Depending on sales, they either ate or braved the day without food, standing motionless like statues over their tables. Their fate depended on chance, luck, and the blessings of their gods. They might be in the New World but Hafiz knew them as Old World souls. At times, they would have big fantastic fights. Today was one of those fight days.

"No, you can't pay me seventy-five cents for this magazine. It cost two dollars. Put the magazine back, man. Pay the right price, that's what I ask."

"It's good money, it's good money." Chaba motioned, pushing a handful of silver toward Hafiz. "I'll give you the rest later. Let me make a sale, I'll get it back to you."

Chaba was an occasional customer at Hafiz's newsstand. He never paid the full price and had a credit bill that was growing. Hafiz had broken the rules of the newspaper selling trade and had a small number of people who he let have credit. Though Hafiz was tired and fed up with Chaba's delinquent ways. "Chaba, man, I ain't going with it today. Put the magazine back or give me the rest of the money. You know the deal, this is America. In America you pay."

Chaba smiled at Hafiz. "I ain't got it all today, but I swear to you, in the name of—"

Before he got the words out his mouth, Hafiz began to yell, throwing Chaba's money back on the counter. The last thing Hafiz wanted to hear was some African calling on his god. "Man, pay up!"

At that, several of the men jumped up, screaming Islamic and Malian phrases and gesturing wildly at Hafiz. Hafiz held his ground. With all the noise these Africans were making, he knew not a one would touch him. They would just embarrass him to no end and frighten off his business until he finally relented on the $1.25 that Chaba owed him. All this trouble for a damn magazine.

"You know, you should go back to your country," Hafiz yelled, frustrated and angry at the whole lot of them. "You should pack your black asses up and go back to your country!"

One of them, a little more sophisticated than the rest, yelled back, "No man, you go back to *your* country!"

Hafiz countered, standing to his full height and leaning across the papers. "No, you go back to your country, I'm *in* my country."

"Go back to your country," they all said, making it sound like the worst curse.

Hafiz began to yell, sweating as his neck muscles began to bulge. "You! Chaba! Get the rest of my money and stop trying to rip people like me off.

You should go back to your own country and rip your own people off," he added.

Chaba started to curse, detailing explicitly what he intended to do with Hafiz, never letting go of the magazine. "Fuck you! If I go back to my country, I'm gonna take a piece of your Brahman ass with me!"

Hafiz was one step from pulling out his machete and really giving Chaba something to deal with.

Suddenly, all the men turned away and ran back to their rugs. The police were coming. The men hurriedly rolled up their rugs and shoved them into black and brown duffel bags and bunched together in a circle, becoming at once allies and a village of young African men. The two policemen approached the men with victory already smirked across their faces and began to nudge the Africans' bags and even their shoulders with nightsticks. These New World Africans were like trees, rugged, yet able to bend in the strongest of winds. None of them spoke or moved. Hafiz stared at the money, still strewn on the counter, and over at the lean tall men with their life on their shoulders, who were, at once, more vulnerable than he ever would be. Hafiz stared at the scene, angry about his money but really more concerned than he dared let them know. They had become his friends, his lookouts. He shook his head while trying to look indifferent. These poor suckers, with their prayer rugs and life's possessions on top of them. Underneath he knew, much as they knew, there was no going back home, either to his country or theirs. The streets of their country were already overfilled with hundreds of men just like them.

"Eh, officers!" Hafiz yelled, as he tried to looked indignant and officious. He hoped his position at the newsstand would give him some legitimacy and authority he otherwise lacked and that the Africans did not seemingly possess. Hafiz hoped his flimsy airs would allow him to act as negotiator. "They haven't done anything, they just stopped to get a magazine," he said.

As if on cue, Chaba, who had beat him out of the full price, fanned the pages of *Ebony* in front of the policemen. The men stood for a while, scrutinizing Hafiz, Chaba, and the rest. Hafiz, wondered if his ruse would work. The policemen moved closer to the circle of men, pointing to their duffel bags.

"What's in there?"

"Officers, we are just visiting this country. We don't want any trouble," one of the Africans said, gesturing to heaven and hell with his hands. "We don't want any trouble."

The policemen looked at each other, then at Hafiz and back at the

Africans. The lie was so blatant it was sickening. The policemen went to the side for a moment, whispering together; then they returned. "Any of you fellas live around here?" The Africans remained quiet. "Okay, let's see what you got there in those bags."

All at once, the Africans began to talk in French among themselves, going from one to the other but never once addressing the policemen.

"I'll lock you all up," said the shorter of the two policemen as he put his hands on his holster and the other on his nightstick, looking like he was in some Western. "Don't let me see you around here with those rugs on the ground or I'll lock you up, you hear? I'll lock you up." The policemen turned away, walking slowly and every now and again looking back. The men stayed in their circle. Hafiz by then had put the silver in his money pouch.

When the police were out of sight, the men relaxed and withdrew their prayer rugs from the bags, pulling their merchandise out again. They laughed and talked. The sounds of buses and cabs rode by them, like so much of life in the city.

Hafiz leaned out the window of his stand. "Can't one of you motherfuckers say thank you?" he yelled at them, cutting the air with his words.

The one with the sharp clothes yelled back, "Thank you, motherfucker. *Merci beaucoup,* motherfucker!" They all laughed.

Hafiz joined them. More than he was willing to say, Hafiz was no more safe than they were. All their lives were tenuous strings caught in a funky western wind. He sighed and turned back to his papers. Better them than me, he thought. I could never live here risking the police and the possibility of arrest all the time. They had heart, those men. They had heart.

It had been a long day, full of drama, but Hafiz had sold most of his papers. It was nine-thirty. Hafiz began to count up his money and stash it in his secret places. The wad in the pouch around his neck, hidden underneath his shirt, was thicker than the one that was inside his sock. He wanted to get to the bank and deposit all his money. Tomorrow. He would do it tomorrow. For now, he was too busy making money. Hafiz secretly enjoyed the feel of his wealth. An hour later, he closed his newsstand and put on the eight locks and said goodbye to the Africans, who would remain out there for several hours more. Hafiz didn't know where they lived or if they had someplace to go. He only knew he left them there at night and saw them again about midday. Where they went at night, he didn't know.

He decided to stroll up Broadway before getting on the bus to go home. It was spring, the one time he really enjoyed the city. He decided to stop at a Jamaican restaurant and get some curry rice and chicken to take home.

They made it real hot there, and the meat was fresh. A little while later, Hafiz came out with two packages in hand.

Hafiz saw her before he had a chance to reach the corner. She was gorgeous, from half a block away. Hafiz decided to wait for her. She was dressed in a lace see-through top. My God, these American women! Hafiz swallowed, peering at the impression of her nipples through her blouse. Hafiz thought she was a hooker, but after another glance he thought better of it. The closer she got to Hafiz the more he realized something was wrong. Her eyes were glazed over and she mumbled to herself incoherently. Men along the street stared at her lustfully; women looked quickly and got out of her way. She seemed no more than twenty or twenty-five.

When she got up to where Hafiz was, he could see she was a little older and had been crying. There was a slackness in her face and arms that suggested she was barely holding on, barely in control. She seemed oblivious to her beauty and her effect upon people. She walked like one whose mind was no longer connected to her body. Hafiz trembled inwardly. Everything in him told him this woman was in trouble. He always tried to stay out of the affairs of Americans; it was better that way. If he didn't get involved, he couldn't get hurt. You never could tell when a person might, all of a sudden, turn around and kill you. Still, something in her face called out to him. Hafiz couldn't shake the feeling. He watched the young woman pass by and decided to follow her. In her state, anything might happen to her. For now, she was safe; people walked around her, avoiding her. Hafiz walked behind her, keeping up with her. He hoped he wasn't getting in over his head.

"Miss, are you all right? Can I help you with anything?" he finally asked, two blocks later. Again, something in her face haunted him, called him. Was it her eyes, her mouth, the set of her shoulders? Part of him wanted to run to the bus stop and get on his bus and pretend this wasn't happening, but he could not leave her on the street like this.

She muttered, "I been . . ." The rest was lost in her throat and trailed in the wind. Hafiz looked at her intensely, understanding all too quickly what had happened to her.

"Miss, are you all right?" he repeated. "Would you like me to call an ambulance so you can go to the hospital?"

That question seemed to awaken fear in her, and she shook her head violently. She tried to walk away.

"Wait. Wait, miss, I mean you no harm." Again, against his better thinking, Hafiz coaxed the woman to stay. He didn't know what made her trust him this far, but he was thankful for it.

The woman remained quiet for what seemed to Hafiz like an eternity. Hafiz studied her. Up close, he could see her blouse had been torn in several places. Even with puffiness under her eyes and streaks of makeup on her face, her beauty shone through. Hafiz ended up giving her his jacket to cover herself. He doubled his bags in one hand and reached for her hand with the other. She refused. It was a while before Hafiz could convince her to go with him to the hospital. He waved for a cab. She got in reluctantly, her eyes full of questions. Under her breath, she muttered, "Mister, you don't have to do anything for me. Really, it's all right, I'll get home on my own." Fear was all over her face. Despite what she said, Hafiz stayed with her.

He stared into her face and realized what called him. She looked like his Yasmine. The woman was beautiful. Her complexion was a honey brown and clear and the same color as her hair and her eyes. Her eyes were so striking, Hafiz found himself falling into them. "What's your name, miss?" he said, trying to find an anchor by which to save himself. She didn't answer. She barely seemed aware of her surroundings. Hafiz leaned his head back on the seat for a moment; then he turned and stared at her, letting out a slow, deliberate sigh. He dreaded what the rest of the evening would reveal.

She began to talk, her words like the ebb and flow of a river. "You know, I—" She stuttered, clasping her hands across her stomach looking, into the smoky scratched glass of the cab. "I didn't think I would get away alive. I lost my pocketbook, all my money, and some of my clothes. He took them when he—"

She began to shake and cry in deep, quick breaths. Hafiz rested his hand lightly on her shoulder. For a second, he was aroused by touching her, but he willed himself to listen with his mind and not his body. Her name was Amina. It suited her. To him it immediately spoke of her beauty, not only on the surface but in the soul.

Amina had gone out earlier in the evening on a boat ride with a new acquaintance. On the way back, this acquaintance both raped and robbed her. "I feel so violated." Her face contorted into a mask of misery. She seemed to be searching the very air for answers. He had pushed her out of his car onto Riverside Drive. "You know, I prayed to die, but I got up and started to walk. That is how I came to be here. I was too afraid . . ." Amina's whole body seemed to shake as the memory flowed through her. "I feel dirty, like I caused this to happen. Did I cause this to happen?" she said angrily, waving her fists in the air.

Hafiz dared not answer her, feeling more of her sadness than he wanted to. He shook his head from side to side, barely able to take in the enormity of what she had gone through. "Ms. Amina, you should go to the police and file charges. Come, I'll go with you."

She refused. She looked at him and gently moved his hands from her shoulder. "You can understand, I don't want to be touched right now." Hafiz stared at her awkwardly, hoping he had not made things worse for her. He wanted to do the right thing, call the police as soon as they got to the hospital. She refused again. "I don't want this out. I don't want people to know."

Who was to know? Hafiz was amazed at how much power people's opinions could have over one's common sense. He realized that she did not know, could not know, how much her life might change. Back home, a woman such as this would be stoned to death, as the cause of bad luck on the village. Her rape, her robbery, would be her own fault. For a moment Amina stared at him, with narrowed eyes. Something in her face had changed. Hafiz felt her closing to him. He took her hands in his, and said, "It is all right, you are safe here. I'll stay with you until your people come. Or when you're ready, I'll put you in a cab and send you home; I mean— that is, if you want me to." Her lips were tight with tension, though her eyes remained still and unreadable.

Hafiz realized he was going to have to get more involved than he planned. He listened to himself as he extended promises to do more. What was it about this woman that he was agreeing to help her? She really was a stranger to him. Why? Why was he investing even this much time? He argued with himself silently. Why not let her own people take care of her? Yasmine's face flickered in his mind's eye. Hafiz realized he was helping Amina not only because he wanted to but also to keep back the fear that something like this might happen to his daughter. This black woman with all her beauty, being treated and used in a less than human way, angered him. It was a sacrilege. Hafiz felt an enormous anger welling up in him. Here was this woman who looked so much like his Yasmine, young and almost gone. Hafiz hoped she would recover. He sat staring out the window, seeking a wisdom that evaded him. He realized he never would understand what motivated some people to harm others.

It was clear that it was going to be a long wait at the hospital emergency room. Amina was number 23 on the list of people waiting to see a doctor. The waiting area was painted a bright orange with the top half of the wall painted white. There were chairs lining three walls and a small table that held magazines in the middle of the room. There were no windows and no food. Several of the people present could be heard quietly moaning, while others talked. Amina sat holding herself in the chair.

Over the next three hours Amina and Hafiz exchanged life stories. Hafiz was a middle child, with fourteen sisters and brothers. He and two others had made it to the States. The rest floundered and prospered off and on back home. His children were grown and still lived in India. He had left his wife and children in the haven of his family.

As long as he could remember, Hafiz knew his life was destined for a different and better road than that of his brothers and sisters, although he had never counted on getting as far as America. One winter, Hafiz had taken a job on a British cruise line and all too quickly sailed for Britain and then America. When the ship got to New York, Hafiz was paid one thousand dollars and informed that the cruise line had gone bankrupt. Hafiz literally had gotten off the boat in New York City. Luckily enough, he soon found shelter and work. Later, two of his brothers moved to America, each making his home only a couple of blocks from Hafiz.

In comparison, Amina was the fourth daughter of well-to-do parents. She had lived most of her life in Virginia but came to New York on a college scholarship. She now worked as a research assistant in a lab. She had almost married but had decided to stay a free agent and keep dating. She had grown up privileged and protected. She lived alone in a three-room apartment in the West Eighties, where there was still an enclave of affordable housing. She had just started to date again and, as fate would have it, she had dated a nut case.

For a while, they both sat quietly, absorbed in their own thoughts and each other's story.

Hafiz, at fifty-three, was more western than Indian. However, he still held true to the old ways and believed in protecting women and children. He thought again of Yasmine. It had been almost ten years since he had seen her. She would be in her early twenties by now. She would probably not recognize him. His hair was almost white, though he was still lean and attractive for his years. His face was angular, with a sprinkle of freckles over his nose. Hafiz had deep, penetrating eyes that seemed to pull everything in. He loved women, and he was proud of his daughter.

His Yasmine probably had children by now. Hafiz sighed. The possibility of having grandchildren he had never seen depressed him. No ties to the past, no ties to the future. Such was the fate of aging men like himself. He belonged neither to India nor the United States. Deep down, Hafiz knew he served no country except himself. He fingered the pouch underneath his shirt. For a moment he relaxed, enjoying Amina's beauty and the feel of the money just below his heart. The security of money and all it could buy reminded Hafiz that he had indeed risen above his caste and the poverty of his birth.

Amina suddenly got up and went to the ladies' room. When she returned, she said, "I should try to get home and forget this emergency room mess." She stood in front of her chair, nearly swallowed up in Hafiz's bulky jacket. She had wiped the makeup off her face. Her hair was now in a single braid that came to the center of her back. Amina looked both drawn and strained, though she seemed to be more alert. "We'll be here all night. I know everyone is looking for me." Somehow, when she said that, Hafiz did not believe her. Everyone who? If others cared so much, why did she not call them? No, Hafiz decided, she was the everyone for herself. Amina caught a shiver and sat back down in the seat, looking even more forlorn.

Hafiz decided to get some coffee and Danish for both of them. He needed to push back the tiredness and so did Amina. He didn't know if he could sit through much more of this. He had never handled personal tragedy well. Over the years, he had developed a finely tuned sense of people, reading them quickly for wealth, position, and class first, for their attachments and obsessions second. If they had problems, he avoided the hell out of them. Was all this true? Why didn't she call her people? Did her "everyone" include another man? Hafiz decided Amina would tell him when she was ready. For now, he was content to be her sentry, her guard and her door back to reality.

Despite all that had occurred, Hafiz felt something larger than pain or pity growing between them. He realized that he surprised her by staying, by being there with her in the first place. In a way, he wanted to thank this young woman. She was the first person in a long time to remind Hafiz that he had a past. For too long now he had blocked out the reality that he had children and possibly grandchildren. She was the first to tear at the closed door of his heart and remind him that, indeed, he would have to return home. Hafiz always knew he had never really escaped; he had just changed geographies.

Amina's number came up and she went in. "I'll be here when you come out," Hafiz assured her. Two hours later, she emerged from the doctor's office. She was angry and just wanted to get out of there. The doctor had wanted to admit her but she refused. Most of her tests had come back negative, though she would have to return to the hospital for follow-up. She had one prescription for her nerves and another to ward off infection. Hafiz convinced her to see the police first thing in the morning. She agreed it would be the best thing to do. Her eyes were dark with anger. "I know his telephone number, and when I see the police I'll make sure he gets his. I know that sucker didn't expect me to live. But I am alive, and what goes around comes around. It's not fair, it's not fair," she said.

For a moment she seemed to have become another person. Hafiz wanted to put his arms around her and comfort her but he didn't know how to do that without upsetting her, so he put his hands on her shoulders and just stood there with her. She was crying, yet no sound came from her, just dry heaves. After what seemed an eternity, she came back to herself.

Outside, Amina became quiet and neutral, almost wary with being in the world of the streets again. They hailed a cab, and a short while later Hafiz walked her to the curb in front of her building. They stood and looked at each other for a while. Hafiz allowed himself to fall into her eyes one more time.

"Thanks for caring, Hafiz. If it were not for you, I think I would have lost my humanity and done something really crazy. Thank you for your help, and for what I cannot thank you for." She smiled for the first time and squeezed his hand. "Good night—I mean, good day, Hafiz."

He watched as she went to her door. He didn't know what made him do it—was it a combination of guilt, lust, and fear for her?—but Hafiz reached into his shirt and pulled out the pouch. He silently emptied the contents into his hand and fingered his money. He studied the young woman. Feeling helpless yet victorious, he ran over to her and wordlessly pressed the money into her hand.

"Oh, no, I can't take your money. You've been too kind already. I'm sorry, but I really could not do that."

"Please take it. It would make me feel better about tonight."

"I can't."

"Please take it and use it however you need to." They went back and forth like that several times. Amina finally gave in, promising to return it. He didn't care whether she returned the money or not. Hafiz knew deep down he had made more than a friend of Amina. Time would show him just who she really was.

Amina and Hafiz were survivors amid the tall gray buildings that could pass for a giant mausoleum. Their meeting was a New World bas-relief in a city long dead from apathy. Hafiz shivered in the light spring wind as he watched Amina's door close. He looked to the sky. The soft mauve of a new day told him he barely had time to get coffee and get to the newsstand. For some reason he was not tired. He would sleep later. The city rose up around him as he got back in the cab. As usual, it neither embraced nor rejected him.

The Girl Who Raised Pigeons

Edward P. Jones

 Her father would say years later that she had dreamed that part of it, that she had never gone out through the kitchen window at two or three in the morning to visit the birds. By that time in his life he would have many notions about himself set in concrete. And having always believed that he slept lightly, he would not want to think that a girl of nine or ten could walk by him at such an hour in the night without his waking and asking of the dark, Who is it? What's the matter?

But the night visits were not dreams, and they remained forever as vivid to her as the memory of the way the pigeons' iridescent necklaces flirted with light. The visits would begin not with any compulsion in her sleeping mind to visit, but with the simple need to pee or to get a drink of water. In the dark, she went barefoot out of her room, past her father in the front room conversing in his sleep, across the kitchen, and through the kitchen window, out over the roof a few steps to the coop. It could be winter, it could be summer, but the most she ever got was something she called pigeon silence. Sometimes she had the urge to unlatch the door and go into

---

EDWARD P. JONES was born and raised in Washington, D.C. He was educated at Holy Cross College and the University of Virginia. His work appears in several collections, including his first book, *Lost in the City.* He lives in Arlington, Virginia.

the coop or, at the very least, try to reach through the wire and the wooden slats to stroke a wing or a breast, to share whatever it was the silence seemed to conceal. But she always kept her hands to herself, and after a few minutes, as if relieved, she would go back to her bed and visit the birds again in sleep.

What Betsy Ann Morgan and her father Robert did agree on was that the pigeons began with the barber Miles Patterson. Her father had known Miles long before the girl was born, before the thought to marry her mother had even crossed his mind. The barber lived in a gingerbread brown house with his old parents only a few doors down from the barbershop he owned on the corner of 3rd and L streets, Northwest. On some Sundays, after Betsy Ann had come back from church with Miss Jenny, Robert, as he believed his wife would have done, would take his daughter out to visit with relatives and friends in the neighborhoods just beyond Myrtle Street, Northeast, where father and daughter lived.

One Sunday, when Betsy Ann was eight years old, the barber asked her again if she wanted to see his pigeons, "my children." He had first asked her some three years before. The girl had been eager to see them then, imagining she would see the same frightened creatures who waddled and flew away whenever she chased them on sidewalks and in parks. The men and the girl had gone into the backyard, and the pigeons, in a furious greeting, had flown up and about the barber. "Oh, my babies," he said, making kissing sounds. "Daddy's here." In an instant, Miles's head was surrounded by a colorful flutter of pigeon life. The birds settled on his head and his shoulders and along his thick, extended arms, and some of the birds looked down meanly at her. Betsy Ann screamed, sending the birds back into a flutter, which made her scream even louder. And still screaming, she ran back into the house. The men found her in the kitchen, her head buried in the lap of Miles's mother, her arms tight around the waist of the old woman, who had been sitting at the table having Sunday lunch with her husband.

"Buster," Miles's mother said to him, "you shouldn't scare your company like this. This child's bout to have a heart attack."

Three years later Betsy Ann said yes again to seeing the birds. In the backyard, there was again the same fluttering chaos, but this time the sight of the wings and bodies settling about Miles intrigued her and she drew closer until she was a foot or so away, looking up at them and stretching out her arm as she saw Miles doing. "Oh, my babies," the barber said.

"Your daddy's here." One of the birds landed on Betsy Ann's shoulder and another in the palm of her hand. The gray one in her hand looked dead at Betsy Ann, blinked, then swiveled his head and gave the girl a different view of a radiant black necklace. "They tickle," she said to her father, who stood back.

For weeks and weeks after that Sunday, Betsy Ann pestered her father about getting pigeons for her. And the more he told her no, that it was impossible, the more she wanted them. He warned her that he would not do anything to help her care for them, he warned her that all the bird work meant she would not ever again have time to play with her friends, he warned her about all the do-do the pigeons would let loose. But she remained a bulldog about it, and he knew she was not often a bulldog about anything. In the end he retreated to the fact that they were only renters in Jenny and Walter Creed's house.

"Miss Jenny likes birds," the girl said. "Mr. Creed likes birds, too."

"People may like birds, but nobody in the world likes pigeons."

"Cept Mr. Miles," she said.

"Don't make judgments bout things with what you know bout Miles." Miles Patterson, a bachelor and, some women said, a virgin, was fifty-six years old and for the most part knew no more about the world than what he could experience in newspapers or on the radio and in his own neighborhood, beyond which he rarely ventured. "There's ain't nothing out there in the great beyond for me," Miles would say to people who talked with excitement about visiting such and such a place.

It was not difficult for the girl to convince Miss Jenny, though the old woman made it known that "pigeons carry all them diseases, child." But there were few things Jenny Creed would deny Betsy Ann. The girl was known by all the world to be a good and obedient child. And in Miss Jenny's eyes, a child's good reputation amounted to an assent from God on most things.

For years after he relented, Robert Morgan would rise every morning before his daughter, go out onto the roof, and peer into the coop he had constructed for her, looking for dead pigeons. At such a time in the morning, there would be only fragments of first light, falling in long, hopeful slivers over the birds and their house. Sometimes he would stare absently into the coop for a long time, because, being half asleep, his mind would forget why he was there. The murmuring pigeons, as they did with most of the world, would stare back, with looks more of curiosity than of fear or anticipation or welcome. He thought that by getting there in the morning before his daughter, he could spare her the sight and pain of any dead birds. His plan had always been to put any dead birds he found into a burlap sack, take them down to his taxicab, and dispose of them on his way to work. He never intended to tell her about such birds, and it never occurred to him that she would know every pigeon in the coop and would wonder, perhaps even worry, about a missing bird.

They lived in the apartment Jenny and Walter Creed had made out of the upstairs in their Myrtle Street house. Miss Jenny had known Clara, Robert's wife, practically all of Clara's life. But their relationship had become little more than hellos and goodbyes as they passed in the street before Miss Jenny came upon Clara and Robert one rainy Saturday in the library park at Mt. Vernon Square. Miss Jenny had come out of Hahn's shoe store, crossed New York Avenue, and was going up 7th Street. At first, Miss Jenny thought the young man and woman, soaked through to the skin, sitting on the park bench under a blue umbrella, were feebleminded or straight-out crazy. As she came closer, she could hear them laughing, and the young man was swinging the umbrella back and forth over their heads, so that the rain would fall first upon her and then upon himself.

"Ain't you William and Alice Hobson's baby girl?" Miss Jenny asked Clara.

"Yes, ma'am." She stood and Robert stood as well, now holding the umbrella fully over Clara's head.

"Is everything all right, child?" Miss Jenny's glasses were spotted with mist, and she took them off and stepped closer, keeping safely to the side where Clara was.

"Yes, ma'am. He—" She pushed Robert and began to laugh. "We came out of People's and he wouldn't let me have none a the umbrella. He let me get wet, so I took the umbrella and let him have some of his own medicine."

Robert said nothing. He was standing out of range of the umbrella, and he was getting soaked all over again.

"We gonna get married, Miss Jenny," she said, as if that explained everything, and she stuck out her hand with her ring. "From Castleberg's," she said. Miss Jenny took Clara's hand and held it close to her face.

"Oh, oh," she said again and again, pulling Clara's hand still closer.

"This Robert," Clara said. "My"—and she turned to look at him—"fiancé." She uttered the word with a certain crispness; it was clear that before Robert Morgan, *fiancé* was a word she had perhaps never uttered in her life.

Robert and Miss Jenny shook hands. "You gonna give her double pneumonia even before she take your name," she said.

The couple learned the next week that the place above Miss Jenny was vacant, and the following Sunday, Clara and Robert, dressed as if they had just come from church, were at her front door, inquiring about the apartment.

That was one of the last days in the park for them. Robert came to believe later that the tumor that would consume his wife's brain had been growing even on that rainy day. And it was there all those times he made love to her, and the thought that it was there, perhaps at first no bigger than a grain of salt, made him feel that he had somehow used her, taken from her even as she was moving toward death. He would not remember until much, much later the times she told him he gave her pleasure, when she whispered into his ear that she was glad she had found him, raised her head in that bed as she lay under him. And when he did remember, he would have to take out her photograph from the small box of valuables he kept in the dresser's top drawer, for he could not remember her face any other way.

Clara spent most of the first months of her pregnancy in bed, propped up, reading movie magazines and listening to the radio, waiting for Robert to come home from work. Her once pretty face slowly began to collapse in on itself like fruit too long in the sun, eaten away by the rot that despoiled from the inside out. The last month or so she spent in the bed on the third floor at Gallinger Hospital. One morning, toward four o'clock, they cut open her stomach and pulled out the child only moments after Clara died, mother and daughter passing each other as if along a corridor, one into death, the other into life.

The weeks right after her death, Robert and the infant were attended to by family and friends. They catered to him and to the baby to such an extent that sometimes in those weeks, when he heard her cry, he would look about at the people in a room, momentarily confused about what was making the sound. But as all the people returned to their lives in other parts of Washington or in other cities, he was left with the ever-increasing vastness of the small apartment and with a being who hadn't the power to ask, yet seemed to demand everything.

"I don't think I can do this," he confessed to Miss Jenny one Friday evening when the baby was about a month old. "I know I can't do this." Robert's father had been the last to leave him, and Robert had just returned from taking the old man to Union Station a few blocks away. "If my daddy had just said the word, I'da been on that train with him." He and Miss Jenny were sitting at his kitchen table, and the child, sleeping, was in her cradle beside Miss Jenny. Miss Jenny watched him and said not a word. "Woulda followed him all the way back home. . . . I never looked down the line and saw bein by myself like this."

"It's all right," Miss Jenny said finally. "I know how it is. You a young man. You got a whole life in front a you," and the stone on his heart grew lighter. "The city people can help out with this."

"The city?" He looked through the fluttering curtain onto the roof, at the oak tree, at the backs of houses on K Street.

"Yes, yes." She turned around in her chair to face him fully. "My niece works for the city, and she say they can take care of chirren like this who don't have parents. They have homes, good homes, for chirren like her. Bring em up real good. Feed em, clothe em, give em good schoolin. Give em everything they need." She stood, as if the matter were settled. "The city people care. Call my niece tomorra and find out what you need to do. A young man like you shouldn't have to worry yourself like this." She was at the door, and he stood up too, not wanting her to go. "Try to put all the worries out your mind." Before he could say anything, she closed the door quietly behind her.

She did not come back up, as he had hoped, and he spent his first night alone with the child. Each time he managed to get the baby back to sleep after he fed her or changed her diaper, he would place her in the crib in the front room and sit without light at the kitchen table listening to the trains coming and going just beyond his window. He was nineteen years old. There was a song about trains that kept rumbling in his head as the night wore on, a song his mother would sing when he was a boy.

The next morning, Saturday, he shaved and washed up while Betsy Ann was still sleeping, and after she woke and he had fed her again, he clothed her with a yellow outfit and its yellow bonnet that Wilma Ellis, the schoolteacher next door, had given her. He carried the carriage downstairs first, leaving the baby on a pallet of blankets. On the sidewalk he covered her with a light green blanket that Dr. Oscar Jackson and his family up the street had given the baby. The shades were down at Miss Jenny's windows, and he heard no sound, not even the dog's barking, as he came and went. At the child's kicking feet in the carriage he placed enough diapers and powdered formula to last an expedition to Baltimore. Beside her, he placed a blue rattle from the janitor Jake Horton across the street.

He was the only moving object within her sight and she watched him intently, which made him uncomfortable. She seemed the most helpless thing he had ever known. It occurred to him perversely, as he settled her in, that if he decided to walk away forever from her and the carriage and all her stuff, to walk but a few yards and make his way up or down 1st Street for no place in particular, there was not a damn thing in the world she could do about it. The carriage was facing 1st Street, Northeast, and with some effort—because one of the wheels refused to turn with the others—he maneuvered it around, pointing toward North Capitol Street.

In those days, before the community was obliterated, a warm Myrtle Street Saturday morning filled both sidewalks and the narrow street itself with playing children oblivious to everything but their own merriment. A grown-up's course was generally not an easy one, but that morning, as he made his way with the soundless wheels of the carriage, the children made way for Robert Morgan, for he was the man whose wife had passed away. At her wake, some of them had been held up by grown-ups so they could look down on Clara laid out in her pink casket in Miss Jenny's parlor. And though death and its rituals did not mean much beyond the wavering understanding that they would never see someone again, they knew from what their parents said and did that a clear path to the corner was perhaps the very least a widow man deserved.

Some of the children called to parents still in their houses and apartments that Robert was passing with Clara's baby. The few grown-ups on porches came down to the sidewalk and made a fuss over Betsy Ann. More than midway down the block, Janet Gordon, who had been one of Clara's best friends, came out and picked up the baby. It was too nice a day to have that blanket over her, she told Robert. You expectin to go all the way to Baltimore with all them diapers? she said. It would be Janet who would teach him—practicing on string and a discarded blond-haired doll—how to part and plait a girl's hair.

He did not linger on Myrtle Street; he planned to make the visits there on his way back that evening. Janet's boys, Carlos and Carleton, walked on either side of him up Myrtle to North Capitol, then to the corner of K Street. There they knew to turn back. Carlos, seven years old, told him to take it easy. Carleton, younger by two years, did not want to repeat what his brother had said, so he repeated one of the things his grandfather, who was losing his mind, always told him: "Don't get lost in the city."

Robert nodded as if he understood and the boys turned back. He took off his tie and put it in his pocket and unbuttoned his suit coat and the top two buttons of his shirt. Then he adjusted his hat and placed the rattle nearer the baby, who paid it no mind. And when the light changed, he maneuvered the carriage down off the sidewalk and crossed North Capitol into Northwest.

Miles the barber gave Betsy Ann two pigeons, yearlings, a dull-white female with black spots and a sparkling red male. For several weeks, in the morning, soon after she had dutifully gone in to fill the feed dish and replace the water, and after they had fortified themselves, the pigeons took to the air and returned to Miles. The forlorn sound of their flapping wings echoed in her head as she stood watching them disappear into the colors of the morning, often still holding the old broom she used to sweep out their coop.

So in those first weeks, she went first to Miles's after school to retrieve the pigeons, usually bringing along Ralph Holley, her cousin. Miles would put the birds in the two pigeon baskets Robert would bring over each morning before he took to the street in his taxicab.

"They don't like me," Betsy Ann said to Miles one day in the second week. "They just gonna keep on flyin away. They hate me."

Miles laughed, the same way he laughed when she asked him the first day how he knew one was a girl pigeon and the other was a boy pigeon.

"I don't think that they even got to the place of likin or not likin you," Miles said. She handed her books to Ralph, and Miles gave her the two baskets.

"Well, they keep runnin away."

"Thas all they know to do." It was what he had told her the week before. "Right now, this is all the home they know for sure. It ain't got nothin to do with you, child. They just know to fly back here."

His explanations about everything, when he could manage an explanation, rarely satisfied her. He had been raising pigeons all his life, and whatever knowledge he had accumulated in those years was now such an inseparable part of his being that he could no more explain the birds than he could explain what went into the act of walking. He only knew that they did all that birds did and not something else, as he only knew that he walked and did not fall.

"You might try lockin em in for while," he said. "Maybe two, three days, however long it take em to get use to the new home. Let em know you the boss and you ain't gonna stand for none a this runnin-away stuff."

She considered a moment, then shook her head. She watched her cousin peering into Miles's coop, his face hard against the wire. "I guess if I gotta lock em up there ain't no use havin em."

"Why you wanna mess with gotdamn pigeons anyway?" Ralph said as they walked to her home that day.

"Because," she said.

"Because what?" he said.

"Because, thas all," she said. "Just because."

"You oughta get a puppy like I'm gonna get," Ralph said. "A puppy never run away."

"A puppy never fly either. So what?" she said. "You been talking bout gettin a gotdamn puppy for a million years, but I never see you gettin one." Though Ralph was a year older and a head taller than his cousin, she often bullied him.

"You wait. You wait. You'll see," Ralph said.

"I ain't waitin. You the one waitin. When you get it, just let me know and I'll throw you a big party."

At her place, he handed over her books and went home. She considered following her cousin back to his house after she took the pigeons up to the coop, for the idea of being on the roof with birds who wanted to fly away to be with someone else pained her. At Ralph's L Street house, there were cookies almost as big as her face and Aunt Thelma, Clara's oldest sister, who was, in fact, the very image of Clara. The girl had never had an overwhelming curiosity about her mother, but it fascinated her to see the face of the lady in all the pictures on a woman who moved and laughed and did mother things.

She put the pigeons back in the coop and put fresh water in the bath bowls. Then she stood back, outside the coop, its door open. At such moments they often seemed contented, hopping in and out of cubicles, inspecting the feed and water, all of which riled her. She would have preferred—and understood—agitation, some sign that they were unhappy and ready to fly to Miles again. But they merely pecked about and strutted, heads bobbing happily, oblivious of her. Pretending everything was all right.

"You shitheads!" she hissed, aware that Miss Jenny was downstairs within earshot. "You gotdamn stupid shitheads!"

That was the fall of 1957.

Myrtle Street was only one long block, running east to west. To the east, preventing the street from going any farther, was a high medieval-like wall of stone across 1st Street, Northeast, and beyond the wall were the railroad tracks. To the west, across North Capitol, preventing Myrtle Street from going any farther in that direction, was the high school Gonzaga, where white boys were taught by white priests. When the colored people and their homes were gone, the wall and the tracks remained, and so did the high school, with the same boys being taught by the same priests.

It was late spring when Betsy Ann first noticed the nest, some two feet up from the coop's floor in one of the twelve cubicles that made up the entire structure. The nest was nothing special, a crude, ill-formed thing of straw and dead leaves and other uncertain material she later figured only her hapless birds could manage to find. They had not flown back to Miles in a long time, but she had never stopped thinking that it was on their minds each time they took to the air. So the nest was the first solid indication that the pigeons would stay forever, would go but would always return.

About three weeks later, on an afternoon when she was about to begin the weekly job of thoroughly cleaning the entire coop, she saw the two eggs. She thought them a trick of the light at first—two small and perfect wonders alone in that wonderless nest without any hallelujahs from the world. She put off the cleaning and stood watching the male bird—who had moved off the nest for only a few seconds—rearrange himself on the eggs and look at her from time to time in that bored way he had. The female bird was atop the coop, dozing. Betsy Ann got a chair from the kitchen and continued watching the male bird and the nest through the wire. "Tell me bout this," she said to them.

As it happened, Robert discovered the newly hatched squabs when he went to look for dead birds before going to work. About six that morning he peered into the coop and shivered to find two hideous, bug-eyed balls of movement. They were a dirty orange and looked like baby vultures. He looked about as if there might be someone responsible for it all. This was, he knew now, a point of no return for his child. He went back in to have his first cup of coffee of the day.

He drank without enjoyment and listened to the chirping, unsettling, demanding. He would not wake his daughter just to let her know about the hatchlings. Two little monsters had changed the predictable world he was trying to create for his child and he was suddenly afraid for her. He turned on the radio and played it real low, but he soon shut it off, because the man on WOOK was telling him to go in and kill the hatchlings.

It turned out that the first pigeon to die was a stranger, and Robert never knew anything about it. The bird appeared out of nowhere and was dead less than a week later. By then, a year or so after Miles gave her the year-lings, she had eight birds of various ages, resulting from hatches in her coop and from trades with the barber ("for variety's sake," he told her) and with a family in Anacostia. One morning before going to school, she noticed the stranger perched in one of the lower cubicles, a few inches up from the floor, and though he seemed submissive enough, she sensed that he would peck with all he had if she tried to move him out. His entire body, what little there was left of it, was a witness to misery. One ragged cream-colored tail feather stuck straight up, as if with resignation. His bill was pitted as if it had been sprayed with minute pellets, and his left eye was covered with a patch of dried blood and dirt and decaying flesh.

She placed additional straw to either side of him in the cubicle and small bowls of water and feed in front of the cubicle. Then she began to worry that he had brought in some disease that would ultimately devastate her flock.

Days later, home for lunch with Ralph, she found the pigeon dead near the water tray, his wings spread out full as if he had been preparing for flight.

"Whatcha gonna do with him?" Ralph asked, kneeling down beside Betsy Ann and poking the dead bird with a pencil.

"Bury him. What else, stupid?" She snatched the pencil from him. "You don't think any a them gonna do it, do you?" and she pointed to the few stay-at-home pigeons who were not out flying about the city. The birds looked down uninterestedly at them from various places around the coop. She dumped the dead bird in a pillowcase and took it across 1st Street to a grassy spot of ground near the Esso filling station in front of the medieval wall. With a large tablespoon, she dug two feet or so into the earth and dropped the sack in.

"Beaver would say something over his grave," Ralph said.

"What?"

"Beaver. The boy on TV."

She gave him a cut-eye look and stood up. "You do it, preacher man," she said. "I gotta get back to school."

After school she said to Miss Jenny, "Don't tell Daddy bout that dead pigeon. You know how he is: He'll think it's the end of the world or somethin."

The two were in Miss Jenny's kitchen, and Miss Jenny was preparing supper while Betsy Ann did her homework.

"You know what he do in the mornin?" Betsy Ann said. "He go out and look at them pigeons."

"Oh?" Miss Jenny, who knew what Robert had been doing, did not turn around from the stove. "Wants to say good mornin to em, hunh?"

"I don't think so. I ain't figured out what he doin," the girl said. She was sitting at Miss Jenny's kitchen table. The dog, Bosco, was beside her and one of her shoes was off and her foot was rubbing the dog's back. "I was sleepin one time and this cold air hit me and I woke up. I couldn't get back to sleep cause I was cold, so I got up to see what window was open. Daddy wasn't in the bed and he wasn't in the kitchen or the bathroom. I thought he was downstairs warmin up the cab or somethin, but when I went to close the kitchen window, I could see him, peekin in the coop from the side with a flashlight. He scared me cause I didn't know who he was at first."

"You ask him what he was doin?"

"No. He wouldn'a told me anyway, Miss Jenny. I just went back to my room and closed the door. If I'da asked him straight out, he would just make up something or say maybe I was dreamin. So now when I feel that cold air, I just look out to see if he in bed and then I shut my door."

Sometimes, when the weather allowed, the girl would sit on the roof plaiting her hair or reading the funny papers before school, or sit doing her homework in the late afternoon before going down to Miss Jenny's or out to play. She got pleasure just from the mere presence of the pigeons, a pleasure that was akin to what she felt when she followed her Aunt Thelma about her house, or when she jumped double Dutch for so long she had to drop to the ground to catch her breath. In the morning, the new sun rising higher, she would place her chair at the roof's edge. She could look down at tail-wagging Bosco looking up at her, down through the thick rope fence around the roof that Robert had put up when she was a year old. She would hum or sing some nonsense song she'd made up, as the birds strutted and pecked and preened and flapped about in the bathwater. And in the evening she watched the pigeons return home, first landing in the oak tree, then over to the coop's landing board. A few of them, generally the males, would settle on her book or on her head and shoulders. Stroking the breast of one, she would be rewarded with a cooing that was as pleasurable as music, and when the bird edged nearer so that it was less than an inch away, she smelled what seemed a mixture of dirt and rainy air and heard a heart that seemed to be hurling itself against the wall of the bird's breast.

She turned ten. She turned eleven.

In the early summer of 1960, there began a rumor among the children of Betsy Ann's age that the railroad people were planning to take all the land around Myrtle Street, perhaps up to L Street and down to H Street. This rumor—unlike the summer rumor among Washington's Negro children that Richard Nixon, if he were elected president, would make all the children go to school on Saturday from nine to twelve and cut their summer vacations in half—this rumor had a long life. And as the boys scraped their knuckles on the ground playing Poison, as the girls jumped rope until their bouncing plaits came loose, as the boys filled the neighborhood with the sounds of amateur hammering as they built skating trucks, as the girls made up talk for dolls with names they would one day bestow on their children, their conversations were flavored with lighthearted speculation about how far the railroad would go. When one child fell out with another, it became standard to try to hurt the other with the "true fact" that the railroad was going to take his or her home. "It's a true fact, they called my daddy at his work and told him we could stay, but yall gotta go. Yall gotta." And then the tormentor would stick out his or her tongue as far as it would go.

There were only two other girls on Myrtle Street who were comfortable around pigeons, and both of them moved away within a month of each other. One, LaDeidre Gordon, was a cousin of the brothers Carlos and Carleton. LaDeidre believed that the pigeons spoke a secret language among themselves, and that if she listened long enough and hard enough she could understand what they were saying and, ultimately, communicate with them. For this, the world lovingly nicknamed her "Coo-Coo." After LaDeidre and the second girl moved, Betsy Ann would take the long way around to avoid passing where they had lived. And in those weeks she found a comfort of sorts at Thelma and Ralph's, for their house and everything else on the other side of North Capitol Street, the rumor went, would be spared by the railroad people.

Thelma Holley, her husband, and Ralph lived in a small house on L Street, Northwest, two doors from Mt. Airy Baptist Church, just across North Capitol Street. Thelma had suffered six miscarriages before God, as she put it, "took pity on my womb" and she had Ralph. But even then, she felt God had given with one hand and taken with the other, for the boy suffered with asthma. Thelma had waited until the seventh month of her pregnancy before she felt secure enough to begin loving him. And from then on, having given her heart, she thought nothing of giving him the world after he was born.

Ralph was the first colored child anyone knew to have his own television. In his house there had been three bedrooms, but Thelma persuaded her husband that an asthmatic child needed more space. Her husband knocked down the walls between the two back bedrooms, and Ralph then had a bedroom that was nearly twice as large as that of his parents. And in that enormous room, she put as much of the world as she and her husband could afford.

Aside from watching Thelma, what Betsy Ann enjoyed most in that house was the electric train set, which dominated the center of Ralph's room. Over an area of more than four square feet, running on three levels, the trains moved through a marvelous and complete world Ralph's father had constructed. In that world, there were no simple plastic figures waving beside the tracks. Rather, it was populated with such people as a hand-carved woman of wood, in a floppy hat and gardener's outfit of real cloth, a woman who had nearly microscopic beads of sweat on her brow as she knelt down with concentration in her flower garden; several inches away, hand-carved schoolchildren romped about in the playground. One group of children was playing tag, and on one boy's face was absolute surprise as he was being tagged by a girl whose cheek was lightly smudged with dirt. A foot or so away, in a small field, two hand-carved farmers of wood were arguing, one with his finger in the other's face and the other with his fist heading toward the chest of the first. The world also included a goat-populated mountain, with a tunnel large enough for the trains to go through, and a stream made of light blue glass. The stream covered several tiny fish of many colors which had almost invisible pins holding them suspended from the bottom up to give the impression that the fish were swimming.

What Thelma would not put in her son's enormous room, despite years of pleading from him, was a dog, for she had learned in childhood that all animals had the power to suck the life out of asthmatics. "What you need with some ole puppy?" she would tease sometimes when he asked. "You'll be my little puppy dog forever and forever." And then she would grab and hug him until he wiggled out of her arms.

By the time he was six, the boy had learned that he could sometimes stay all day in the room and have Thelma minister to him by pretending he could barely breathe. He hoped that over time he could get out of her a promise for a dog. But his pretending to be at death's door only made her worry more, and by the middle of 1961 she had quit her part-time GS-4 clerk-typist position at the Interior Department, because by then he was home two or three times a week.

Gradually, as more people moved out of Myrtle Street, the room became less attractive for Betsy Ann to visit, for Ralph grew difficult and would be mean and impatient with her and other visiting children. "You stupid, thas all! You just the stupidest person in the whole wide world," he would say to anyone who did not do what he wanted as fast as he wanted. Some children cried when he lit into them, and others wanted to fight him.

In time, the boy Betsy Ann once bullied disappeared altogether, and so when she took him assignments from school, she tried to stay only the amount of time necessary to show politeness. Then, too, the girl sensed that Thelma, with her increasing coldness, felt her son's problem was partly the result of visits from children who weren't altogether clean and from a niece who lived her life in what Thelma called "pigeon air" and "pigeon dust."

When he found out, the details of it did not matter to Robert Morgan: He only knew that his daughter had been somewhere doing bad while he was out doing the best he could. It didn't matter that it was Darlene Greenley who got Betsy Ann to go far away to 7th and Massachusetts and steal candy bars from People's Drug, candy she didn't even like, to go away the farthest she had ever been without her father or Miss Jenny or some other adult.

She knew Darlene, fast Darlene, from going to Ralph's ("You watch and see," Darlene would whisper to her, "I'm gonna make him my boy-friend"), but they had never gone off together before the Saturday that Thelma, for the last time, expelled all the children from her house. "Got any money?" Darlene said on the sidewalk after Thelma had thrown them out. She was stretching her bubble gum between her teeth and fingers and twirling the stuff the way she would a jump rope. When Betsy Ann shook her head, Darlene said she knew this People's that kinda like y'know gave children candy just for stopping by, and Betsy Ann believed her.

The assistant manager caught the girls before they were out of the candy and toy aisle, and right away Darlene started to cry. "That didn't work the last time I told you to stay outa here," the woman said, taking the candy out of their dress pockets, "and it ain't gonna work now." Darlene handed her candy over, and Betsy Ann did the same. Darlene continued to cry. "Oh, just shut up, you little hussy, before I give you somethin to really cry about."

The assistant manager handed the candy to a clerk and was about to drag the girls into a back room when Etta O'Connell came up the aisle. "Yo daddy know you this far from home, Betsy Ann?" Miss Etta said, tapping Betsy Ann in the chest with her walking stick. She was, at ninety-two, the oldest person on Myrtle Street. It surprised Betsy Ann that she even knew her name, because the old woman, as far as Betsy Ann could remember, had never once spoken a word to her.

"You know these criminals?" the assistant manager said.

"Knowed this one since the day she born," Miss Etta said. The top of her stick had the head of an animal that no one had been able to identify, and the animal, perched a foot or so higher than Miss Etta's head, looked down at Betsy Ann with a better-you-than-me look. The old woman uncurled the fingers of the assistant manager's hand from around Betsy Ann's arm. "Child, whatcha done in this lady's sto?"

In the end, the assistant manager accepted Miss Etta's word that Betsy Ann would never again step foot in the store, that her father would know what she had done the minute he got home. Outside, standing at the corner, Miss Etta raised her stick and pointed to K Street. "You don't go straight home with no stoppin, I'll know," she said to Betsy Ann, and the girl sprinted off, never once looking back. Miss Etta and Darlene continued standing at the corner. "I think that old lady gave me the evil eye," Darlene told Betsy Ann the next time they met. "She done took all my good luck away. Yall got ghosties and shit on yo street." And thereafter, she avoided Betsy Ann.

Robert tanned her hide, as Miss Jenny called it, and then withheld her fifty-cents-a-week allowance for two months. For some three weeks he said very little to her, and when he did it was almost always the same words: "You should be here, takin care a them damn birds! That's where you should be, not out there robbin somebody's grocery store!" She stopped correcting him about what kind of store it was after the first few times, because each time she did he would say, "Who the grown-up here? You startin to sound like you runnin the show."

The candy episode killed something between them, and more and more he began checking up on her. He would show up at the house when she thought he was out working. She would come out of the coop with a bag of feed or the broom in her hand and a bird sitting on her head and she would find him standing at the kitchen window watching her. And several times a day he would call Miss Jenny. "Yo daddy wanna know if you up there," Miss Jenny would holler out her back window. Robert called the school so much that the principal herself wrote a letter telling him to stop.

He had been seeing Janet Gordon for two years, and about three or four times a month, they would take in a movie or a show at the Howard and then spend the night at a tourist home. But after the incident at People's, he saw Janet only once or twice a month. Then he began taking his daughter with him in the cab on most Saturdays. He tried to make it seem as if it were a good way to see the city.

Despite his reasons for taking her along, she enjoyed riding with him at first. She asked him for one of his old maps, and, with a blue crayon, she would chart the streets of Washington she had been on. Her father spent most of his time in Southeast and in Anacostia, but sometimes he went as far away as Virginia and Maryland, and she charted streets in those places as well. She also enjoyed watching him at work, seeing a part of him she had never known: The way he made deliberate notations in his log. Patted his thigh in time to music in his head until he noticed her looking at him. Raised his hat any time a woman entered or left the cab.

But the more she realized that being with him was just his way of keeping his eye on her, the more the travels began losing something for her. When she used the bathroom at some filling station during her travels, she found him waiting for her outside the bathroom door, his nail-bitten hands down at his sides, his hat sitting perfectly on his head, and a look on his face that said Nothin. Nothin's wrong. Before the autumn of 1961 had settled in, she only wanted to be left at home, and because the incident at People's was far behind them, he allowed it. But he went back to the old ways of checking up on her. "Tell him yes," she would say when Miss Jenny called out her back window. "Tell him a million times yes, I'm home."

Little by little that spring and summer of 1961, Myrtle Street emptied of people, of families who had known no other place in their lives. Robert dreaded coming home each evening and seeing the signs of still another abandoned house free to be picked clean by rogues coming in from other neighborhoods: old curtains flapping out of screenless windows, the street with every kind of litter, windows so naked he could see clean through to the backyard. For the first time since he had been knowing her, Miss Jenny did not plant her garden that year, and that small patch of ground, with alien growth tall as a man, reverted to the wild.

He vowed that until he could find a good place for himself and his child, he would try to make life as normal as possible for her. He had never stopped rising each morning before Betsy Ann and going out to the coop to see what pigeons might have died in the night. And that was what he did that last morning in mid-autumn. He touched down onto the roof and discovered it had snowed during the night. A light nuisance powder, not thick enough to cover the world completely and make things beautiful the way he liked. Though there was enough sunlight, he did not at first notice the tiny tracks, with even tinier intermittent spots of blood, leading from the coop, across his roof, and over to the roof of the house next door, the schoolteacher's house that had been empty for more than four months. He did, however, hear the birds squawking before he reached the coop, but this meant nothing to him, because one pigeon sound was more or less like another to him.

The night before there had been sixteen pigeons of various ages, but when he reached the coop, five were already dead and three were in their last moments, dragging themselves crazily about the floor or from side to side in the lower cubicles. Six of them he would kill with his own hands. Though there were bodies with holes so deep he saw white flesh, essence, it was the sight of dozens of detached feathers that caused his body to shake, because the scattered feathers, more than the wrecked bodies, spoke to him of helplessness. He closed his eyes as tight as he could and began to pray, and when he opened them, the morning was even brighter.

He looked back at the window, for something had whispered that Betsy Ann was watching. But he was alone and he went into the coop. He took up one dead bird whose left wing and legs had been chewed off; he shook the bird gently, and gently he blew into its face. He prayed once more. The pigeons that were able had moved to the farthest corner of the coop and they watched him, quivering. He knew now that the squawking was the sound of pain and it drove him out of their house.

When he saw the tracks, he realized immediately that they had been made by rats. He bent down, and some logical piece of his mind was surprised that there was a kind of orderliness to the trail, even with its ragged bits of pigeon life, a fragment of feather here, a spot of blood there.

He did not knock at Walter and Miss Jenny's door and wait to go in, as he had done each morning for some thirteen years. He found them at the breakfast table, and because they had been used to thirteen years of knocking, they looked up at him, amazed. Most of his words were garbled, but they followed him back upstairs. Betsy Ann had heard the noise of her father coming through the kitchen window and bounding down the stairs. She stood barefoot in the doorway leading from the front room to the kitchen, blinking herself awake.

"Go back to bed!" Robert shouted at her.

When she asked what was the matter, the three only told her to go back to bed. From the kitchen closet, Robert took two burlap sacks. Walter followed him out onto the roof and Betsy Ann made her way around Miss Jenny to the window.

Her father shouted at her to go to her room and Miss Jenny tried to grab her, but she managed to get onto the roof, where Walter held her. From inside, she had heard the squawking, a brand new sound for her. Even with Walter holding her, she got a few feet from the coop. And when Robert told her to go back inside, she gave him the only no of their lives. He looked but once at her and then began to wring the necks of the birds injured beyond all hope. Strangely, when he reached for them, the pigeons did not peck, did not resist. He placed all the bodies in the sacks, and when he was done and stood covered in blood and viscera and feathers, he began to cry.

Betsy Ann and her father noticed almost simultaneously that there were two birds completely unharmed, huddled in an upper corner of the coop. After he tied the mouths of the sacks, the two birds, as if of one mind, flew together to the landing board and from there to the oak tree in Miss Jenny's yard. Then they were gone. The girl buried her face in Walter's side, and when the old man saw that she was barefoot, he picked her up.

She missed them more than she ever thought she would. In school, her mind would wander and she would doodle so many pigeons on the backs of her hands and along her arms that teachers called her Nasty, nasty girl. In the bathtub at night, she would cry to have to wash them off. And as she slept, missing them would take shape and lean down over her bed and wake her just enough to get her to understand a whisper that told her all over again how much she missed them. And when she raged in her sleep, Robert would come in and hold her until she returned to peace. He would sit in a chair beside her bed for the rest of the night, for her rages usually came about four in the morning, and with the night so near morning, he saw no use in going back to bed.

She roamed the city at will, and Robert said nothing. She came to know the city so well that had she been blindfolded and taken to practically any place in Washington, even as far away as Anacostia or Georgetown, she could have taken off the blindfold and walked home without a moment's trouble. Her favorite place became the library park at Mount Vernon Square, the same park where Miss Jenny had first seen Robert and Clara together, across the street from the People's where Betsy Ann had been caught stealing. And there on some warm days Robert would find her, sitting on a bench or lying on the grass, eyes to the sky.

For many weeks, well into winter, one of the birds that had not been harmed would come to the ledge of a back window of an abandoned house that faced K Street. The bird, a typical gray, would stand on the ledge and appear to look across the backyards in the direction of Betsy Ann's roof, now an empty space because the coop had been dismantled for use as firewood in Miss Jenny's kitchen stove. When the girl first noticed him and realized who he was, she said nothing, but after a few days, she began to call to him, beseech him to come to her. She came to the very edge of the roof, for now the rope fence was gone and nothing held her back. When the bird would not come to her, she cursed him. After as much as an hour it would fly away and return the next morning.

On what turned out to be the last day, a very cold morning in February, she stepped out onto the roof to drink the last of her cocoa. At first she sipped, then she took one final swallow, and in the time it took her to raise the cup to her lips and lower it, the pigeon had taken a step and dropped from the ledge. He caught an upwind that took him nearly as high as the tops of the empty K Street houses. He flew farther into Northeast, into the colors and sounds of the city's morning. She did nothing, aside from following him, with her eyes, with her heart, as far as she could.

Savannah

WENDY JONES

 "Hello. . . . What? . . . No! . . . I'll be right there."
I was out of the bed, face washed, clothes on, almost
before I put down the phone.

"Jess, Jess." I pushed on her curled form. "Honey,
Mama has to go out. Go and get in my bed so you
can hear the phone. Don't let anybody in and don't
try to use the stove." I guided her by the shoulders and repeated my instructions as, her plaits sticking up at odd angles from the night's sleep,
the pink bunny feet stumbled down the long hall to my bedroom. When I
placed the white bedspread over her, she huddled into the same question
mark she'd been in when I'd gotten her up.

I didn't want to wake her up completely, there would be too many
questions I couldn't answer just then, but I had to get behind her wall of
sleep enough to make sure she *got* me.

"What did Mama say, honey?"

"Don't let anybody in, don't use the stove. Mama, where you goin'?"
Her doe eyes opened as if she were fully awake.

Although she is primarily a short story writer and novelist, WENDY JONES's first play, *In
Pursuit of Justice*, was recently produced in Harlem by The H.A.D.L.E.Y. Players. Wendy is
co-creating her mother's biography while teaching composition and literature at the County
College of Morris. A member of The Dramatists Guild, Inc., and The National Writers Union,
this Harlem-born-and-raised writer lives in New Jersey with her life partner, David Mitchell.

"I'll be back. I have to go out for a little while, honey, don't worry." Why did I say that? She didn't know there was anything to worry about; she had closed her eyes and started back to sleep. She'd be all right. She was seven this year and a little lady. I kissed her flat forehead and grabbed my purse from the dining room doorknob.

Once out on the street, walking to Bannah's feeling that bright, early September sun, I was thinking that it couldn't be true—not on a day like this. It couldn't be true. I reached down in myself for that calm I could always find when I needed it. I had to be steady when I got there, not tearful or hysterical. Like soap in the bathtub, first it eluded me completely; I almost had it; then, it was mine. I would be all right. I would make it there in one piece.

It was too early for the churchgoers. Night people were still holding court on Seventh Avenue. They were wearing Saturday night's loud clothes and gazing out of Sunday morning's hung-over eyes.

Looking around at the wide sidewalks asplash with the early morning sun, I remembered another September more honest about winter coming. I remembered when I'd first come to New York, when I'd first met Savannah.

"Hello, Frankie." A stout cinnamon woman with one gold tooth in the middle of white, gold-hammered triangles hanging from her ears, had greeted me. Her face: a carefully applied mask of powder and lipstick. Her hair: in a pompadour. It was a combination of black and Indian hair: an improvement on the stubborn kinks of the African and the boring strings of the Indian, a wavy black slickness unaided by hot comb or hair grease.

"Come in, chile, you look just like your mama. I'd know you anywhere, those same beautiful eyes. Let me help you with that. You so thin, turn sideways, think you was a broom."

She took my bag as I followed her up a flight of back stairs to the bedrooms. I hadn't thought an apartment would have stairs inside it like a house and told her so. It was a duplex: one apartment, two floors. On the lower floor: two bedrooms and the living room. On the upper floor: two bedrooms, kitchen, dining room and the smokehouse. A smokehouse! In New York City! Cu'dn Savannah showed me two fine Virginia hams hanging from the beams before she took me to my room, which was the bedroom next to it. My room was right off the head of the stairs.

She left me alone to take off my travelin' clothes and get comfortable while she finished making supper. As I took off my black gabardine suit and white blouse and hung them in the oak closet, the sweet-hot smell of biscuits came under the door. I changed into a blue cotton long-sleeved shirtwaist. All my clothes had long sleeves. My arms were too thin and reedy to go bare.

"What did your pa say about you leavin' home?"

"He didn't say much, ma'am. I was at the creek down near the bottom fields when I turned to him and said, 'Pa, don't make a way for me next year 'cause I ain't hoein' no more cotton nor ironin' no more white folks clothes.' "

" 'Frankie gal, what you mean to do?' " I mocked Pa's low growl.

" 'I'm going to *New York City*,' I said, throwing my sack in the creek.

"After a while he said, 'That's a long ways off. Buy you a round-trip ticket so no matter what happens, you can always come home.'

"I didn't know he'd take it so easy, but he *did* ask me to write to you and see if I couldn't live with you. He said you and Mama bein' kin and so close growin' up it'd be just like Mama had come down from heaven to watch over me."

"Well, I'm glad to have you. Sometimes it gets lonesome here with just me and Vernon. Now, Frankie, this is your home, eat as much as you want, that's what it's for," she said, putting a plate piled high with pot roast and brown gravy, greens, biscuits, mashed potatoes, and a large pitcher of iced tea in front of me.

Savannah's kitchen was long and narrow. As you entered, on your left was the door. It was permanently open with a wedge under its foot. Hanging on the door was an assortment of swordlike knives and sharpeners complete with hilts. On the left was a Kelvinator only a little stouter than Cu'dn Savannah herself. Continuing down this wall was the sink on its heavy white legs. It was a combination sink with a deep basin for washing clothes and a shallow one for dishes. At the end of the room, right next to the sink, was a low window. Cu'dn Savannah stood about five four. When she was at the low sink cleaning the greens, the bottom of the window hit her at the knee.

Coming back up the right side of the kitchen was a black and white four-burner stove with dainty legs and a little hood. The brown-gold chairs gathered around the brown-gold kitchen table were made of shiny-backed stuff that was washable like porcelain but not breakable. The deep chocolate of the table was a fine background for the golden-brown fruit-basket design with its curlicue frame. The table was clothed only on Sundays.

Only Cu'dn Savannah and I ate. Vernon was "working" late that night. Both of them had been retired for years but Vernon took what Cu'dn

Savannah had explained to me was single action for a friend of his. It seemed that up north here they bet on the last three numbers in the horse race. Single action was just one number. You didn't bet as much as you would on the whole number, and what they called the banker didn't have to pay as much when you won. Vernon picked up these "numbers" and got 10 percent of the winnings plus tips from grateful customers.

Cu'dn Savannah sat down and we talked about when she and Ma were growin' up double first cousins in Cross Hill and what had happened to her since: the move north for a better-paying job, meeting Vernon at church, the marriage, setting up housekeeping, and how she and Vernon had started a restaurant because people always talked about how well she cooked.

"People came to our place from all over. Some of the best Negro entertainers, the Ink Spots, Ruby and the Romantics—Brook Benton even came in one time."

"Ma'am, where was this restaurant?"

"Right downstairs."

"On this road, ma'am?"

"No, Frankie, not on this 'road,' as you say, right downstairs." She caught my puzzled look and shook her head. "Chile, didn't you see that hole in the wall, I can't call it a restaurant, on your left as you came in the house, before you came up the stairs?"

"Yes, ma'am, yes, I did and there's a dress store on the other side."

"Well, that used to be *our* restaurant. After six months, Vernon put in the billiard parlor. It used to say right there on that plate-glass window with a curve and dip on the top and a curve and dip on the bottom coming together like two sides of an egg: *Savannah's Home Cooking* in gold with white edging and *Vernon's Billiard Parlor* in black with white edging. I used to clean that window every day till it shone like the sun."

"Sounds real nice. What happened?"

"Somebody reported Vernon for operating a billiard parlor and letting in people under age. How was he supposed to know? He couldn't ask everybody come in there for their birth certificate. Found out it was Sylvia up the street. Her place had had all the business until ours opened up, so she sicked the cops on us. After they took away our license, she just moved right in. I look in there sometimes. No *quality* folks eat there like they did when *we* had the place. . . . Well, that was yesterday," she said, as she hoisted herself out of the chair and over to the Kelvinator.

She took out a bread pudding that looked like it had a dozen eggs in it from the yellow floating in the little dish she gave me. She had forced seconds of pot roast and gravy on me, to get some "meat on my bones," she said, and now there wasn't a crack or crevice in my ninety-pound frame to pour that bread pudding in, but I was tired of arguing with her so I talked to her some more about the restaurant, hoping she wouldn't notice I was just rearranging the pudding in the bowl, not eating it.

Vernon, a lanky high yaller with a mustached smile and a gold tooth to match his debonair air, always wore a suit and hat. He carried a black cane, gold-tipped like his tooth. I wondered if he got the cane and the tooth at the same time. I also wondered if he and Savannah had gotten their gold teeth at the same time, but I never asked so I never found out. When he wasn't working late, he was right there at the table: thin as his cane and I didn't see how he did it. But I noticed Savannah didn't press him for second helpings. It was just, "Vernon, you want somethin' else?" "No, honey. That was right good. I think it'll do me for now, but I might get a piece of cake after a while."

There was always dessert at Savannah's.

Vernon and Savannah together were hard to place; they didn't seem to love each other or hate each other. And could they *fight*! Cussin' and fussin', my Lord, about everything and nothing! I can hear Savannah now: "I wouldn't marry you if you was the last man on earth." I always said to myself, but you *did* marry him. Why? I never had the nerve to come straight out and ask her, and I never figured it out. They couldn't sit down for two minutes and talk without getting into an argument about something. Whether Ching Chow had his hand up or down, whether that meant the first figure was going to be a two or the second figure was going to be a one, what insult Vernon's sister had hurled at Savannah in 1934 at camp meetin' in Beauford.

How they got on it I don't know, but one night they started talkin' about dyin':

"And don't think you gon' get another woman and bring her back here to live in this house after I die."

"You bein' dead, what could you do about it?"

"If I die first, I'm comin' back to get your ass, that's what, nigger, and don't you forget it."

There wasn't a thing they couldn't find to argue about.

One day I came in to find Savannah watching the sunset from the dining room window. There were no tall buildings in Harlem then except for the Theresa Hotel, and it was too far away to make a difference. You could see a whole stretch of sky, the tops of the trees of Central Park, and the roofs of six-story buildings, their clotheslines draped with clean clothes.

The purple, pink, red, and gold of the sky, the green of the trees, and the white dish towels and underclothes flapping like flags: it was beautiful, but Savannah wasn't looking at it. She was resting her eyes on it and looking inside herself.

"I went to see Marly-Ann today." She spoke without turning around.

"How was she?" I pulled up a high-backed dining room chair and sat down beside her. She was quiet so long, I didn't think she'd heard me.

She finally shook her head in answer. "The doctors say she's just given up. Somebody has to feed her, too. It's so hard now. Before she could write down what she wanted to say; now all she can do is point at the alphabet on the pad." She started to cry.

Patting her shoulders as she cried, I held her. *Me* holding Savannah, trying to comfort *her*. Kind of strange, but kind of nice, too.

"My poor baby sister!" She leaned away from me, drying her eyes with the white handkerchief she kept in her dress pocket. "She can't talk; she can't feel. She can't feed herself. She can't even walk. That's not living; it's dying slow. I couldn't take it, I know I couldn't."

I had never seen her so sad. Even though I didn't understand till later all she meant, her words scared me. *I couldn't take it, I know I couldn't.*

I settled into the rhythm of life in New York City. I still said it in my mind the way I had said it to Pa at the creek, with an eternity of space between each word, enough space for wealth and dreams and romance of infinite amount. But when I said it out loud I said it normal. I didn't want people to think I was a hick from the sticks. I was a city girl now. My first job was way downtown on Hudson Street in a book factory. I never thought I'd find a job in New York City that was so much worse than picking cotton. After two weeks of going deaf from the binders and wheezing the cardboard dust from the trimmers, I left without picking up my check. They could have it. I was never going back there again.

I sat at the kitchen table reading the job listings. I had been ordered there by Savannah when I offered to help her with dinner. That was one thing I missed: cooking. I'd never weighed much over ninety since I'd been grown. I still weighed that despite a month and a half of Savannah's good but heavy cooking. Down-home food, fine for working in the fields but not for what little I was doing, especially those last five days when I was looking for work.

"You got to eat to help you keep up your strength when you out there looking for a job. You got to do a lot of walkin' in this man's town to find a job."

"Yes, Savannah," I said, smiling to myself, but I'd have to walk from here to Greenville, South Carolina, and back to need all that food, and that's two thousand miles all told.

The second-helping ritual had by now been well rehearsed.

"Frankie, don't you want some more?"

"No, thank you, ma'am. That was real good but I've had enough."

"I don't want your pa to think I ain't feeding you. You better have some more to eat, put some meat on your bones."

"Ma'am, I can't eat another drop. I eat any more, I'll bust."

"You'll just have to bust then," she said, dolloping two snowballs of mashed potatoes on my plate.

The best way with Savannah was to just let her put the food on the plate and not eat it. Arguing didn't do any good.

I was sitting there missing cooking for Pa, cooking *what* I wanted to eat *when* I wanted to eat it, when it jumped out at me: FINE AND DANDY. This was a concern that hired maids, butlers, bartenders, and cooks to work for different people on a free-lance basis. They got a certain percentage of what you made. Sounded good to me. I didn't want to work for a family because they always wanted you to sleep in. Once you slept in, all your time was theirs. Lazy as some white folks were, you'd end up being cook, maid, and governess all for a cook's pay. This sounded good. You were in and out.

I went down to see the man and he hired me on two weeks' probation, since I didn't have any work experience in cooking. He was short on good cooks and he said he'd try me out. I did fine. I went into most of the places and nobody was there. Just a note about where things were and what was to be made for the party. That was all right with me. I never did like to work with people breathing down my back. After those two weeks, things went smooth as glass. It got so certain people would plan their parties around my time. If I wasn't available, they'd postpone the party until I was.

Then I met Leroy. I'd been working at Fine and Dandy for six months when I was called to do a party in Connecticut. It was one of my regulars, the Holsteins. I'd been to their house on 72nd Street but I'd never been to the one in Connecticut, though I'd heard about it. Me and the bartender were leaving from 125th Street on the 8:10 and we'd be met at the station. Leroy was a dark, thin man with his Indian coming out in that wavy slick hair and cheekbones so sharp they could cut. We talked all the way up on the train, me doing most of the talking out of nervousness. Telling him all about the Holsteins and Mama dyin' when I was four and me and Papa livin' alone, talking so much that by the time we got off to meet the Holsteins he knew all about me and I knew nothing about him.

I learnt in time though. He was a fine dancer. When we went out it embarrassed me that I was such a bad partner, but I felt good that he would dance with me at all. Secretly, I started taking dancing lessons from one of those books with the footprints in it, humming to myself in place of the phonograph I didn't have.

Savannah and I fell out about Leroy. From the first time I asked him over for dinner, she seemed to hate him. I was hurt. I was sure she'd like him as much as I did. After that night, I couldn't mention his name without us exchanging sharp words. Nothing he had said or done that one time she had seen him could have made her hate him so.

When we danced, he always wore white gloves that set off the mahogany of his face. He was cool, dark, and elegant. I liked the way he looked, I liked the way he acted. There was nothing about him I *didn't* like.

I don't know whether she'd forgotten how it was to be young or what, but she should have known that opposition is the worst weapon you can use against a young girl in love. Maybe I would have thought more about it if I'd given myself time to let my feet touch earth again. Between my young fierce love and her doomsayings, when he asked me to marry him within three months of meeting him, I said yes.

When I told Savannah, she went through the smokehouse roof.

"Listen, Frankie, you grown, you do what you want, but that black nigger don't mean you a *bit* of good."

I wanted to say that if he *is* a "nigger," black is a good color for him. Was that it? Was she color-struck? Even though I'd dropped the ma'ams from my speech and the Cu'dn from Savannah's name, I couldn't argue with her like I could if she'd been my own age. I'd learnt that old downhome respect for older people from Pa.

"I know how you feel, Savannah, and I'm sorry for it. But I wanted you to know that you and Vernon are invited to the wedding if you change your mind."

Except for Jess, I wish I had changed *my* mind. Leroy, I found out, had many talents: bartender, auto mechanic, baker, construction worker. He worked at all those things in the year we were married, but of all the talents he had, he didn't have the most important one of being able to keep a job.

I'd gotten pregnant with Jess almost immediately. I worked for Fine and Dandy until the uniform two sizes too big didn't fit anymore; then I went to work for the Holsteins until my time came. They had taken a liking to me and agreed to let me work as long as I could. I didn't want to keep working so late in my time but I never knew when Leroy would have a job and when he wouldn't, so I thought I'd better depend on myself. Leroy stayed long enough to take me to the hospital for the delivery and cause a scene the next day when he insisted on wanting to name the baby Marietta after the town he came from. All along we'd said that if was a boy, he'd name him. If it was a girl, I'd name her. Finally, I put down Girl Williams so we could leave the hospital in peace. A month later, he had danced out of my life for good. Savannah forged his signature so Girl Williams could become Jessica Anne Williams.

Savannah was a big help to me during that time. I'd had to go back to work when Jess was only three months old. Savannah kept her until I came home. She was good with children, I guess because she was one of the oldest in a big family and had to help take care of the little ones. Although she *could* have, she never said "I told you so," and I was glad for that.

Jess had her father's deep, dark skin and my eyes. Even though I hated her father for using me and then leaving me, I loved Jess with all I had. I was glad she was a girl. I don't think I could have raised a boy who might have grown up to look and act exactly like the father he had never known. Savannah got me through my hatred. Savannah told me Leroy was yesterday and Jess was today, and I had to live for today, not for yesterday.

Sundays after church, Jess and I would walk down Seventh Avenue, my long thin legs trying to slow their pace to Jess's short toddle. She looked so sweet in her pink organdy dress starched and pressed, her little black patent leather Mary Janes with buttons on the side, the pink anklet socks with the frilly lace at the top, and the little white hat with the pink bow tied in the back, just like the bow tied at what would someday be her waist. I felt her tiny hand curled around my index and middle fingers, damp in the late May warmth.

"We goin' to Aunt Bannah's, Mama?"

"Yes, honey. But don't say 'we going,' say 'are we going?'"

"Are we *going*? Are *we* going? *Are* we going?"

She was making my correction into a song, putting the beat on a different word each time. I'd given up trying to get her to say Aunt Savannah. It always came out Sabannah, which she later shortened to Bannah, so I just let it stand. Bannah and Jess got on like white on rice.

Pease porridge hot
Pease porridge cold
Pease porridge in the pot
Nine days old

Some like it hot
Some like it cold
Some like it in the pot
Nine days old

Without missing a beat, Bannah and Jess clapping into the next rhyme. Bannah's ham hands stopping just before patting Jess's miniature ones so the force wouldn't push her tininess across the dining room.

Miss Mary Mack, Mack, Mack
With silver buttons, buttons, buttons
All down her back, back, back
All dressed in black, black, black
Went to the store, store, store
To buy a sack, sack, sack
And never came back, back, back
All dressed in black, black, black
Miss Mary Mack, Mack, Mack

Jess dissolved into giggles in Bannah's lap. Giggling because she'd one-handed the last "Mack" instead of two-handing it. She'd made me clap it out every evening this week so she'd do it right.

"Well, Miss Jessie, you almost did it that time. *Al*-most," said Bannah, as her gold rings rubbed the back of Jess's dress.

"Next time." Jess took her giggles out of Bannah's lap and floated them toward her face, the sunlight from the dining room window sparking the hoops at Bannah's ears with golden fire. "Next time, I'll get it *right!*"

"I bet you will, Miss Jessie, I bet you will." Bannah picked Jess up and sat her on her lap. Jess put her head on Bannah's cushion bosom and smiled. When she was no more than two she'd embarrassed me by saying that when she grew up she wanted "bumps" just like Aunt Bannah. Bannah had nearly fallen off her chair laughing.

"Careful with your shoes, honey, you'll dirty up Aunt Bannah's pretty white dress." Bannah always wore white on special occasions. Sunday was a special occasion.

"She's all right, Frankie. Yes, Miss Jessie's all *right* with *me*."

We always stayed for dinner. Bannah would congratulate Jess if she succeeded in finishing her meal without spilling anything on her white tablecloth and tell her to try to do better next time if she *did* spill. Jess always had to have a bag to take home with her. A piece of fruit, the second piece of cake or pie that she couldn't eat and Bannah insisted she have: always something in a little paper bag. Sunday after Sunday, year after year, that's what Sunday meant to me and Jess.

Right after Jess was born, I went to work in the cafeteria at Woolworth's, which meant less money than Fine and Dandy but better hours and benefits. The Holsteins had told their friends about me so I still did parties on the side, which helped me with the tuition for Jess's school. Jess was going to have a good education, which she'd never get in the public school up the street from where we lived. Like Pa always said, "Get an education, can't nobody take that away from you." He'd died the year I got married.

Most of the time I worked parties, Jess went with me. She did her homework in the maid's room in back of the kitchen. When Jess didn't go with me, she stayed with Bannah. I changed jobs, Jess started going to school, but we still went to Bannah's every Sunday after church.

It was the beginning of this year that Bannah started losing so much weight. Her sister, Marly-Ann, had died the summer before. She hadn't grieved much then. Maybe this was her way of grieving now. From January to March, she lost nearly fifty pounds. I was in her room in July about a week before she and Vernon went down to Beauford for camp meeting. She was getting the clothes together that she was taking with her.

"I had to buy all new clothes. Nothing fits me anymore."

"Bannah, I know you needed to lose some weight, but you're going to have to take it a little slower. You have to keep some meat on those bones."

She laughed at my feeble joke. I joked because I knew something was wrong. Nobody lost weight that fast unless something was wrong. Bannah had to be sick.

"Have you been to see Dr. Anderson?"

Bannah stopped on one of her trips from the cedar wardrobe to the big canopied bed she was spreading the clothes out on and sat down on the bed. One of her old big dresses swallowed up her body, hanging off her like unneeded skin.

"Frankie, sit down." She patted the blue embroidered spread, and I sat down in the middle of the peacock's tail alongside her. "I don't need no doctor. I'm telling you all this, Frankie, because I know you'll do what I want done." She stopped and looked off past the dressing table and through the wall of the apartment. I didn't know where she was, but it was too far for me to reach her. Then, slowly, like climbing up a flight of stairs, she came back. Patting her hand on the bed we were sitting on, she said, "They have coffins that have springs in them just like the mattress on this bed. That's the kind of coffin I want to be buried in."

"Bannah, what are you talking about dyin' for? You've got many more years ahead of you. Who would Vernon have to fight with?" Again that look that was too far away for me to reach; then she came back.

"Everybody has to die sometime."

"Yes. Yes, I know, but why—"

"Frankie, just listen. No matter *when* I die I want you to be in charge of everything, so just listen. I've got fifteen thousand dollars altogether, that's cash and policies both. I want it all in the ground with me. Vernon has his pension. I don't want him spending my money on some other woman."

So I stopped protesting and listened. Bannah had it planned down to the underwear she wanted. In fact, some of the new clothes were clothes she had selected for her funeral. She wanted to be buried in a white dress with a white collar, which she showed me. She wanted to wear her hoop earrings and all her rings. She wanted a steel deep-rose casket with springs like she'd said.

While I was walking home that night, I thought that Marly-Ann's death had made Bannah worry about dying. She had no close kin left, just me and Vernon. But something kept nagging at me. This was more than grief. Bannah was sick and seemed to *know* when she was going to die.

When I got there, Mr. Brown, the neighbor who had seen Bannah go out the window, was there with the police and Vernon. He told me he'd been watering his plants in the back room and had seen a person fall out the window. He called the police, who came immediately. He'd directed them through Sylvia's restaurant to get "the unfortunate lady," as he kept calling Bannah, out of the courtyard. But all he could give me was the facts, nothing but the facts. I wanted more.

After Vernon came back from the morgue, back from identifying the person who used to be Bannah but now was "the body," he told me more about how Bannah went to her death. I could see it just as clear as if I'd been there myself.

"Vernon, if you don't get off that phone, I'm going to make you eat breakfast alone!" Bannah yelled to Vernon that morning from the kitchen.

Vernon had been on the phone talking to his sister for the last half hour. For the last half hour the salt fish had been sitting in their grease, the grits had been growing a cold skin, the toast had been ready to be pushed down in the toaster, and the buttermilk sitting on the table had been heating to the temperature of the sun hitting it from the kitchen window. After the first ten minutes, Bannah had gone to the door of the bedroom next to the kitchen and stood in the doorway, hands on hips, elbows sticking daggers in the air. She stared at Vernon for a full two minutes while he motioned with his hands that he was getting off soon and laughed at something his sister said, or maybe he was laughing at Bannah. He acted like he wouldn't get off the phone until he was good and ready.

Going back into the kitchen, she decided to make some biscuits. She had to move, had to keep busy to keep from going in there and jerking the phone out of his hand. While she was making the biscuits she'd stop every once in a while to take a drink from the mayonnaise jar or to refill it from the corn liquor jug under the sink, liquor she and Vernon had brought back from Beauford.

Suitcases so full of liquor, they had to buy *more* suitcases to put their clothes in. A cousin of Vernon's down there ran a 'splo house and made some good stuff. Liquor had always been reserved for special occasions with Bannah. In the past month there had been many special occasions a day requiring that she have just *one* drink or two; then she'd stopped counting.

She and Vernon were fighting now even more than ever. Stopping halfway through the dough, the rolling pin pulled halfway down, she looked out the window at the girdle hanging on the line, the girdle she had hung there last night.

Why not now? She had to do it sometime. She wasn't going to let this eatin' cancer kill her bit by bit; she'd do it herself all at once. She looked around the kitchen. She had swept the floor after she'd finished making breakfast, but she swept it again. She looked at the table with its white tablecloth, shining silver, sparkling dishes. Butter, salt, pepper, sugar, hot sauce, homemade apple jelly all in order on the table. Soldiers lined up for inspection, and the commander approved.

And Vernon. She decided she'd give him one more chance. She was a betting woman. If he came by the time she finished this last drink, she wouldn't do it now; she'd wait and do it some other time. But if he didn't come by the time this drink was gone, she'd be gone too. Then she yelled to him from the kitchen, "Vernon, if you don't get off that phone, I'm going to make you eat breakfast alone!"

"Comin', honey!"

Maybe she didn't believe him, or maybe she was just ready to go. She finished the drink, drinkin' slow, and he still hadn't come. She opened the window, smoothed her dress down, held her hands next to her so her dress wouldn't fly up, then jumped out the window.

Vernon was still on the phone talking to his sister when the police rang the bell to say they'd come to investigate. A neighbor had reported that someone had fallen out of a window in this apartment.

The official report said she had "fallen out of the window while hanging out a girdle while under the influence of an inordinate amount of liquor."

I knew better. Bannah was too particular a woman to take her hands out of biscuit dough to wash a girdle and hang it out. Besides, she never washed anything on a Sunday.

I got there no more than an hour after she was supposed to have hung out that girdle, and it was dry as dirt.

The only time I'd ever thought about it was when they were going to garnishee my salary to pay for my delivery after Leroy left. I was paying them ten dollars a week. They didn't want that; they wanted it all at once. I'd just got the job at Woolworth's and thought they'd fire me if they had to garnishee my salary. I didn't want them in my personal business anyway, but I was going to take Jess with me. We were going to go just like Bannah did: right out the window. But before I had to think about it twice, a lawyer in the neighborhood wrote a letter for me saying I was doing the best I could and if they garnisheed my salary I might lose my job and they'd never get their money. I'd thought about it and laid it aside. Bannah had thought about it and done it.

I did what Bannah asked. I put all but two hundred of that fifteen thousand dollars in the ground with her. Vernon shook off his grief enough to start worrying about the money I was spending on Bannah's funeral. He kept trying to suggest cheaper coffins, "more reasonable," he called it. But I told him no, Bannah had told me what to do and I was going to do it.

MINA KUMAR

I read a few chapters of Dany Laferrière. You might think I already knew how to make love to a Negro, but I was tired, so very tired, so obviously there was something I was not getting right. My stomach turned and turned.

The first time I read Laferrière was when I was sixteen or so. I found the book at a Queens Street bookstore, with Moira. I was still a virgin. My experiences consisted of two white boys and a Sikh who ate my pussy badly. I loved the book. What *profondeur*, what glamour it had, what wisdom about interracial sex. Having spent my early adolescence in the very white suburbs of Toronto, I saw my dark self easily in Laferrière. I forgot my other selves: my eleven-year-old self in Scarborough, being beaten up by white-trash Angel and enormous West Indian Jasmine; my sweet-pussy self of labyrinthine crimson and cocoa folds so easily crushed; my woman self who would one day be so miserable because I had inveighed against Driss for having a white wife, and then he left her six and a half months pregnant for a Brazilian from Bahia. I loved the book because our hero satirizes the white women he sleeps with. They simply

MINA KUMAR was born in Madras and lives in New York City. Her work has appeared in *Christopher Street*, *13th Moon*, *Hanging Loose*, *Premonitions* (Kaya), and other publications.

wanted the experience of the exotic, so he punishes them with ridicule. I knew what it was like to be desired for my difference. I was everyone's first Indian girl. One man in Florence while kissing me in a hotel stairwell wanted to discuss his passion for Sanskrit philosophy. Someone else pulled away from my mouth to ask me why Indian women wear dots on their foreheads. These things happened afterward, but they are the best examples of what always happened. Except with the Sikh, I guess, but that was just too lousy to matter, and he liked me with too much hysteria.

By the time I read the book, I was almost wondering if I was subconsciously racist because there were few black men I was attracted to. There had been one Nigerian with incredibly good bone structure, who had said, not two feet away from me, that as a rule he didn't like black girls. And even though there were plenty of Indian-black couples in the school I was attending at the time, the girls were either impossibly fair like Sukhinder or mixed beauties from the West Indies like Anne Mohan, and I knew that for the Nigerian I was one of the black girls. So you see Laferrière's charm.

Claude, too, called me black. When I protested, he accused me of wanting to be white, so there was nothing left to say. He was the kind of black man whom white women fawned on, so I was puzzled by his interest in me. He was very "downtown" and hip, had spent half his life in clubs, and whatever I looked like, or however I had lived, I was still a gauche and pudgy middle-class Indian girl awed by the chic I did not have. I was amazed he wanted me, so glamorous did he seem. Okay, also dissolute, but I wasn't going to marry him.

Claude called me black because I wasn't white or yellow, but he differentiated me from the dark-dark-skinned girls. "If I am with a girl that dark," he said, "it is only fucking." I fidgeted uncomfortably. I wasn't used to this side of the bridge. "It's not prejudice," he said. "I like black women. I just don't need to lie down next to a jet-black girl who will scare me when I wake up in the morning." I nodded, but absently. But when I told him I didn't like flat noses, he turned his flattish-nosed face away from me; he said I had been brainwashed by white people.

I had met Claude with Joyce at a Japanese bar in the Village that was populated mainly by Haitians. It turned out that said bar was famed as a den of iniquity, and everyone we ever mentioned it to knew it was a hangout for drug dealers. A friend of Joyce's had moved out of a nearby apartment because of the preponderance of dealers. It was common knowledge, only we didn't know it when we went there. Claude was the bartender. I had never seen anyone quite like him. I had seen dreads on Rastas (and on sants) but his were different: thick, neat locks that fell to his jaw. I don't think he had his beard then, and I wasn't sure how attractive I found him. He spent a long time talking in a low voice to Joyce, who was quite drunk. I sat making an airplane out of the napkin of Joyce's drink and listening to a male crooner sing about how he wanted to have fun while he was young.

I said, What are we going to do, because you are an illiterate, unemployed drug-dealing bastard, and I am young, and while I'm young, I want to have some fun.

I was surprised when he wanted me to write my number on the airplane, and Joyce slurringly told me he liked me. Neither of us thought he would call. Whenever I blame Joyce for taking me to the bar, she reminds me that she told me not to go out with him. He was too ornery and too horny, she said. But he was an adventure I was determined to embark upon.

Meeting him for our first date, I eyed another man, and the hurt look in his round brown eyes peeking through his dreads seduced me. He is vulnerable, I thought, and I blanched only slightly when his friend, a pale, feline man, talked openly about selling drugs as I sat beside him in his red jeep. How exotic it was, not the dreads but the clubs and the drugs, like a story I had read in *Christopher Street*, like Henry Miller, like the girls I had despised and admired in high school who wore leopard coats and short-shorts to go dancing all night with strangers, and with eyes half-closed like *gai Paris* with absinthe and debauchees. Within a certain circumference, I wanted to be debauched.

It's amazing to me that I got pregnant. First of all, I was nearly religious in my use of condoms; I wasn't promiscuous, and I didn't like babies. I always said my womb would reject the idea. But soon I discovered my womb held six millimeters of risk, stupidity, hunger, and lust, six millimeters of us. My days were spent in bed, staring at the ceiling and contemplating nausea and hunger. My stomach turned and turned. Pregnancy heightens the senses. The salsa played by people in the building opposite mine seemed to come from speakers built into my pillow. The fire engines seemed to scream up my legs. In the distance, I could hear what simply could not have been—a man saying *Allahu akbar*, over and over. And smell! Paint varnish and chicken soup and my own juices skewered me with their odor. I was nauseated and dizzy from the smell of toothpaste and orange soda and exhaust fumes. Almost any food made my stomach turn, but I dreamt helplessly of garlic *rasam* and *porichche kute*, helplessly and hopelessly. I lay in bed and tried to read.

I remembered Barbara Pym as innocuous, but *Quartet in Autumn* was depressing. It hardly distracted me from my anxiety about death. Before I was certain of my pregnancy, I thought I was going insane. I was obsessed with death, the snuffing out of my bright, beautiful consciousness, the uncertainty of every day. I took a taxi to the Japanese bar he still hung out at, though he had long since stopped working there. I clutched the seat belt, sure the car would veer off the road, sure I would die, sure the headlights of cars passing in the opposite direction were turning toward me and coming closer and closer. My heart raced and I wanted to tell the driver to slow down, but that was so out of character I simply couldn't. When I arrived at the bar, he wasn't there. The next day, at a loss as to what to do, I stumbled from a useless visit to a psychologist to an uncomfortable dinner in the Village, where I nibbled at jerk chicken and wondered about a chicken's consciousness, trying to read Ama Ata Aidoo. The book was just too depressing, or maybe it was me. I lurched out into the rain, walking and walking in my treadless shoes to the bar to tell him what was growing inside me.

I had known Claude for slightly over a year. He had left me in March, a week before he was supposed to return the $300 he had borrowed from me in January to pay off his suspended driver's license, and a month and a half after he had punched me with my own fists until my lips and nose were bloody. Truth be told, months earlier I had kicked him in the face in a fit of rage, and a few days after he hit me, he was mugged and those thick lips of his were bloodier than he had made mine. I took him back when he called me at 6 A.M. after the mugging, mostly to see how badly off he was. "You don't care, do you?" he said, sinking into my bed. I sat on the futon, laughing. "I care about as much as you cared when you hit me," I said, which of course was far from the truth.

When he tried to come home in the fall, it was easy to forgive the beating, which was not foreshadowed or repeated, and which was punished by karma in seemly haste. I could turn a blind eye to the unpaid debt because he so often said he would repay it—"I wouldn't talk to you if I didn't mean to repay it," he would say—I could dismiss it as merely irresponsible. I could think around anything that I didn't like because I wanted him to cuddle me. The man had a PhD in cuddling and the equipment to match: broad shoulders, strong arms, a hard, flat chest with tiny little nipples like brown dots. I loved sleeping next to him, my arm tightly wound around his waist, head on his chest, leg over his leg, rubbing my mound against his thigh for comfort or raking my hand through his dreads.

It wasn't just the cuddling, there were memories I could summon up that teased me with their remembered warmth. The ginger ale and Fisherman's Friend cough drops he bought me when I was sick. The times he watched over my grades and what I was eating. The time I told him about someone else's lovely eyes, and he said in a butterscotch voice, "You have nice eyes." The time I was drunk and bawling that I knew he would rather be with a white girl, and I apologized through drunken sobs for not being white, and he said, drawing me to him, that the girl he wanted was a beautiful Indian. Claude said plainly what could have been the lines in a song. "You make me feel hurt," he once said, "and you know I love you." And artlessly, he uttered clichés that were fresh in his mouth. When I asked him why he came to my house only to sink wordlessly into slumber—or, rather, I screamed, "You don't want to talk to me or make love to me. All you want to do is go to sleep. So why are you in my house?"—he said simply, "You do something to me." Sometimes, he said things that made me feel like he had cut to my very quick. He gave me that precious feeling of being understood. Once, when I was helplessly hungry, he cooked rice and garden vegetables, saying, "I'm your daddy, and I'm going to take care of you." I remembered the times he talked to me about his family beating him, about his childhood and Haiti. The time after we broke up, when Michelle and I ran into him in a coffeeshop: we said hello and he left, only to return, only to leave, only to return. He did this dance five times, before he finally asked if he could come home with me.

Yes, eventually, in the fall, he tried to come home again. He claimed he had never left. For the seven months we had talked and he had laughed at my hunger, I frustrated him for seven weeks. I would turn his lines onto him, this Laferrière hero, his skinny black dick his access to the world, who said to me when I asked why I should wash his clothes or buy him presents or why he never took me out, "I fuck you, don't I?" So for weeks I told him I couldn't afford his sex and turned my back as he lay hard and telling me I was his girl. I refused to be his girlfriend. I told him about every handsome man I knew until he clasped his hand over my mouth. But finally he said, "I'm lonely, I miss you," and kissed the top of my head and I opened myself. He came hurtling in, telling me how tight I was and how he knew I was faithful to him—which I had been, somewhat accidentally —and he told me he wouldn't come inside me and he called out my name. Over and over again. And then he came.

It was the first time anyone had come inside me, and not being in love I was revulsed by his semen, but I felt too languorous for a fight, and besides it was all over. Of course, it had also just begun.

After a few weeks of cuddling, there was a dark and stormy night when I raged and raged, hungry for him to caress and comfort me. My mood swings had begun—how quickly the body changes—and I was convinced

I was failing school, and my crazy mother seemed about to appear at the fringes of my life, and all I wanted was for him to pull me to that chest, but instead he left.

For weeks I heard nothing from him. I was sure he would call, but he didn't. That accouterment of drug dealers, his beeper, was no longer in service even before that night. I didn't know how to reach him when the time came, except to stand out in front of the bar in the pouring rain like in a hokey country song.

He stood under the awning, waiting for me to start and finish what I had to say. He didn't have the beard, which made him look as old-fashioned and kindly as his name. "I think I'm pregnant," I said. He shook his head. It's not possible because he used a condom. It's not possible because he no longer wanted me and I was using it as a ruse to win him back. He drove me home and I abased myself because of this new reason and all the old reasons, but he wouldn't stop and really talk and wouldn't stay the night. That was it, I thought, but what was it?

Often, I missed him, like when I watched a video with Bobby Brown entwined with a lovely girl on a beach. "If it's not good enough, I can work harder," he sang. It's not good enough, and he's not working at all. I watched the video enviously, yearning for that embrace, flesh against flesh, the warmth and womblike comfort of Claude lying between my thighs, and suddenly I remembered the jab of the needle inside me. Was it some kind of metaphor that receiving the anesthetic was the most painful part of the operation?

I rose, restless. I had called just about everyone I knew to engage them in a conversation about death. "It could strike so suddenly and the spark of life is extinguished," I said. Sometimes, I was afraid to go to sleep. When my stomach turned, I didn't know whether it was my fear or some physical problem. My fear became a physical problem. "I don't want to die," I would say. I calmed the panic partially by realizing that I wouldn't know, that it would be like fainting or being knocked unconscious. I was anxious, waiting for the blow to be struck.

Other times, I talked about Claude. He had called me eventually. He wanted me to have a child and give it to his grandmother. When I had elicited his comment before, he had snarled, "What should I say? Let's go buy a ring?" When I tried again, he said, "Are you going to have an abortion? You are a child and not ready to have a child, and I'm not ready to take care of a woman and a child." By the time he called me with his third take on the situation, I was no longer interested in what he had to say. The call, which he had made from a pay phone, was about to get cut off.

"I'll call you back," he said. He did. The next night. I hung up on him. He called some more, but I had already left for New Haven to try to put an end to the problem we had caused. By the time I finally talked to him, there was something else to discuss.

Days later, after a day spent in the emergency room with a temperature of 102 degrees, after a second abortion on the same pregnancy, days bridged by doses of doxycycline for the chlamydia, I mulled over our last conversation. "After hitting me, taking my money, making me pregnant, and giving me chlamydia, what is next?" I had raged.

He had paused. "You couldn't wait to yell at me, could you?"

"I don't ever need to hear from you again," I replied, banging the phone down. My friends cheered at this point in the story. Then they discovered that I had left my number in New Haven on my answering machine message and asked him to call. Michelle was quite displeased at all the calls I got. But none of them were from him.

"Forget him!" she cried, worn from the demands I was making on our friendship: the complications of the abortion that made me stay with her longer, the wretched conversations about my fears of dying, the lyrical descriptions of cuddling with Claude, the neediness I felt. I fell silent. I didn't explain why I talked because she knew why, and she didn't explain why she was fatigued with listening, because I knew why.

My body, that instrument of pleasure, that violin we had played, Claude and I, was now a fragile, crumbling, mortal case for a queasy stomach and liquid shit and a heavy head. I could not read or watch television for fear of coming across death, and so I stuck to romantic videos and felt my buzzing anxiety compounded by dull aches. All I wanted to assuage my fears of death was to have love, as illogical as that may seem.

I hadn't seen him since that night he drove me home, and he hadn't slept next to me since the night we had fought. It had been five weeks. I wanted him in that desperate, ashamed way that a starving person wants someone else's leftovers in a garbage can. I wanted him the way a baby wants to feel strong loving arms. Only thinking of him and the sadness it brought to the back of my throat stopped me from thinking about dying.

I thought of Dany Laferrière. I had found Claude exotic. I had bought him a mustard shirt and made countless pots of spaghetti and bought bottles of wine. I had sucked his cock well, and he wouldn't even kiss my breasts unless I whimpered and begged. I had been impressed by certain of his pronouncements and I had asked him if I was disturbing him when I clanked his dirty dishes as I washed them. I liked his dreads.

The first time I went out with him, we sat in a diner, eating hot bagels with melting salty butter, and I, for the first time, touched his hair. I raked my fingers through the woolly locks and massaged his head. He was uncomfortable at first, because he was used to women liking his locks. I understood how he felt, because I was glad he wasn't particularly impressed with my (long, straight) hair. Soon, he shifted his legs, because the way I was touching his hair was making him hard.

Sometimes he would say I was using him for sex. "Sex we have, where you come and I don't?" I would respond. But other times, he would say that he wouldn't go out with white women because they couldn't love him. But he treated me much the way Laferrière's hero treated his white girls. And reading the book again, I wonder which of the white women were listening attentively because they were impressed a black man could speak intelligently and which were genuinely interested, which didn't want to disturb him because the sight of a black man reading was the sacred goal of colonialists and "civilizers" and which didn't want to disturb him because they were polite, which were using him for the sexual skill they presumed him to have and which loved him? I think of Laferrière's McGill girls and Claude's Barnard girl.

It's all very to well to tell us *comment faire l'amour avec un nègre sans se fatiguer*, but that is only half the story. I took a long time to come to this, but I am no longer sixteen, and I need more than to know how to make love to a Negro. How do you make a Negro make love to you back?

Lilly's Hunger

BRIDGETTE A. LACY

I've been washing and ironing clothes for Miz Lilly for the past two years. It look like she just lost her strength after Mr. Jones died. He was her husband.

They had been my neighbors for most of my life. When I was about ten years old, they moved into the old Stamps house, right next to my mama's.

That was thirty years ago. They stood by me as I buried my mama and a drunken husband. So I didn't mind helping Miz Lilly.

Mr. Jones always called me EmmaJane. He would say it real fast, as if Emma and Jane were one name instead of my first and middle names. But I didn't mind.

I was upstairs picking up clothes from Miz Lilly's bedroom floor when I heard her downstairs on the front hall telephone.

"Olivia, I'm hungry. I ain't got nothing to eat. Bring me some food," said Miz Lilly and then slammed the phone down on her sister.

Miz Olivia was used to that call. She received it almost every day around noon for the past two years.

BRIDGETTE A. LACY is an award-winning feature writer at *The News & Observer* in Raleigh, North Carolina. She was awarded a three-month residency at La Napoule Art Foundation in the south of France in 1994. She also received a feature writing award from the National Association of Black Journalists for a profile of author Dori Sanders. She is working on her first novel.

I guess Miz Olivia thought she was too old and crippled to be waiting on her younger sister, who was a month shy of seventy.

Miz Lilly had been hungry ever since Mr. Jones took his own life. I guess he got tired of that woman nagging him to death.

I remember the day the poor man went outside, sat under his peach tree, and pulled the trigger. That man had survived Pearl Harbor and the Great Depression but I guess he was just tired of that woman meddling with him.

Mr. Jones had put up with her nagging during the years, but it seem as she got older the nagging got worse. During the youth of their marriage, Mr. Jones could escape her complaining about money or something he hadn't done. But when his diabetes threatened his eyesight, I guess he decided he didn't want to depend on her for nothing.

I had been out in the backyard feeding my dog, Fluffo. And I spoke to Mr. Jones and he just tilted his hat. That was a bit peculiar for Mr. Jones. He would normally mention something about the weather or his garden.

Several hours later, I saw his daughter, Zelma. She told me that Mr. Jones had gulped down a pint of homemade dandelion wine and sat against the trunk of his tree and pulled the trigger.

I hated to even look over at his yard after that. I couldn't understand how a man who worked so good with his hands could take his own life. In the summer, his melons were so sweet, they tasted as if he poured sugar in the ground.

That Mr. Jones was a mighty fine man. He would always say, Here, EmmaJane, take some of these pears and peaches for your girls. His trees were so heavy with fruit, they look like they would split down the middle sometimes.

Oh, and he could cook. Mr. Jones was always baking blackberry cobblers and coconut pies. When his hands started hurting with arthritis, I would stir the fruit and nuts in his cakes.

He would send each of his daughters a fruit cake for Christmas. Zelma lived in Washington and Althea, the oldest girl, lived up in New York City.

Here comes Miz Olivia now. She always blows her horn as she approaches Ivy Street. She parks her Plymouth on the wrong side of the road. She throws out her walking cane and clutches two plastic bags of groceries and starts up the cement steps.

Miz Lilly peeks through the screen at her.

"Hi, Olivia, I ain't doing worth a damn," Miz Lilly says. Miz Olivia brushes pass Miz Lilly and takes a seat in the dining room.

"I don't want to hear it," Miz Olivia says. "You done let that tater-mater man drag you down even from his grave. You look like skin pulled over bones," she says, as she pulls out four golden delicious apples.

"Now, Lilly, if I leave these four apples, are you going to eat them?" Miz Olivia asks.

"I think I will," Miz Lilly replies.

Miz Olivia must have grabbed the apples from the table because I heard her say, "Well, I'm taking them home with me because I know I will."

By this time, I had come down the back stairs and started washing clothes on the back porch, next to the kitchen.

I heard Miz Olivia clear her throat as she stood up and walked to the kitchen and got a knife from the drawer. She cut a roasted chicken in half and placed it on a paper plate for Miz Lilly.

Miz Lilly asked Miz Olivia how much was that going to cost her.

Miz Olivia then threw the remainder of the bag toward Miz Lilly and told her don't call anymore this week. "Call that damn country man that left you like this," she said.

Miz Olivia always hated Mr. Jones. He was a tall, handsome man with wavy hair and a perfectly molded head. He smiled with his eyes.

My mama told me they called Mr. Jones Mr. Do-It-Good. The women gave him that name. And it wan't for his cookin either. He came from a family of sweet-talking men. They called his younger brother Bandit. They say Bandit stole other men's women. But he was a lover, not a thief.

Yeah, Miz Olivia hated Mr. Do-It-Good because she said he wasn't an educated man. But shit, he had plenty of common sense. And he knew the worth of a good woman without having to peek at the price tag.

You see, Miz Olivia failed to realize it don't take no education to love a woman. But she was always telling her sister that man was beneath her because he came from the country and didn't have no college degree.

When I would be hanging clothes on the line in the backyard, I would hear Miz Olivia telling Miz Lilly, "You let that man belittle and berate you and then you turn around and act like that man's lapdog."

I'd never heard them proper sisters talk like that in school. You see, both Miz Lilly and Miz Olivia were schoolteachers. And Glimmerburg, Virginia, was such a small place I had both of them, Miz Lilly in sixth grade and Miz Olivia in eighth.

Miz Olivia always dressed nice but she didn't have her sister's height or beauty. Miz Lilly was tall and willowy. And she was so poised and charming.

She only had one good suit then. It was tomato red. And when she wore it she would sweep her hair to the side like Billie Holiday. I could see why Mr. Jones fell in love with her.

They say she and Mr. Jones met on a riverbank. Miz Lilly was walking down the bank from that one-room schoolhouse up in Bedford, and Mr. Jones spotted her. His people were from the country. They had plenty of land, large fields full of potatoes, squash, corn, and tomatoes.

In class, Miz Lilly would tell stories about how poor her family was. She said they would often eat sugar on a biscuit and onion and mustard sandwiches. But after she married Mr. Jones, she never had to want for any type of food again.

Sometimes, I would overhear Miz Lilly telling younger teachers, who weren't married, "Once you find yourself a good man, never eat crumpets without jelly or biscuits without jam." And then she would laugh softly.

I liked that saying. I tucked it away in my memory.

But back to Miz Lilly and Mr. Jones. Now, Mr. Jones didn't like thin women around him. He said a skinny woman looked like a poor racehorse. He fed everything and everybody he loved.

They were always having large Sunday suppers. Bowls of butter beans, fried chicken, corn on the cob, homemade rolls, and iced tea complete with mint.

And Miz Lilly was getting plump off that good food and lovin. But she kept throwing Mr. Jones's lack of formal education in his face. I think it was because her sister kept throwing it in *her* face.

That drove a wedge in their marriage. You know love can cover a multitude of sins and fault, but you can't keep bashing your man and expect to keep him.

I know because I did the same thing. I would find fault with every man who tried to court me after my Nathaniel died. And now my girls are all grown, I'm here by myself.

In a way Miz Lilly and Mr. Jones were my family. In the evening time, I could sit on my porch and they would tell me how Zelma and Althea were doing or mention one of the grandchildren.

You see, I think Miz Olivia was jealous of Miz Lilly. Miz Olivia was married to a cheap man from Maddox County. They didn't have no children.

Her husband had an associate's degree in something but he was nothing but a janitor at the hotel downtown. Mr. Jones would tell me how he would ask him for his stale bread. I use to hate to eat around Miz Olivia's husband.

He use to have the shakes. That man shook like a spoon in a teacup. I believe he had palsy. The old folks called it Saint Vitus' Dance or something like that. He choked on a piece of toast a few years ago.

But back to Miz Lilly. The last big meal I saw her eat was at the funeral. And they did have lots of food. Mr. Jones's sister Glady baked a pound cake. You could taste the butter in it. And Miss Irene, who was married to Miz Lilly's brother, came with her coconut cake.

They had so much food, they could have packed Mr. Jones a lunch for his journey.

But it looked like after the funeral, when the daughters left, Miz Lilly just got into a funk. She kept drinking prune juice and eating grapefruits all the time.

I guess her appetite just left her. She done almost melted down to nothing. Well, I'm getting ready to go to the store, let me see if Miz Lilly needs something.

Annette Estimé

MARIE HELENE LaFOREST

When the money arrived Annette danced in the yard, embracing her children, all jumping and laughing. She was going to New York! And buy all the things people in New York bought. No more *kenedis*, no more of those hand-me-downs for her. High-heeled shoes, red Cutex on her nails like the women in the two-story houses on the Grande rue of Gonaïves. No outhouses in New York either. All those who'd gone abroad wrote saying, "Only WC, *wi*, for everybody."

"You'll have to take the iron pot with you. How you gonna cook rice over there?" her mother shouted from under the grapevine that had wound its way up a beam and spread out to shade and cool the house.

Annette stopped her dance to look at her mother and sucked her teeth.

"With the children, the boxes, the papers you think I can take the iron pot too?"

"How is she gonna cook rice for the children?" Man Lolo muttered as she made to rise, helping herself with both hands against the chair's straw seat.

MARIE HELENE LaFOREST was born in Haiti. She currently makes her home in Italy, where she teaches post-colonial literature at the Istituto Universitario Orientale in Naples. She grew up in New York and Puerto Rico, has an M.A. in creative writing and was a 1992 recipient of a James Michener Fellowship.

Annette's house stood behind the church, the last shingle home before the dirt roads, before the huts that had risen back-to-back and the wattled walls that kept pigs safe at night after they'd oinked all day in search of mango peels and banana skins. Annette watched her mother's heavy legs take her slowly to the coal fire where the *tchaka* for her last meal was simmering. A latticed wall nailed to the trunk of the sandbox tree protected the stove, three kegs of water, and a pile of enamel plates from the dust the sea wind blew some afternoons. Man Lolo stooped over the pot.

"The *tchaka* is almost done." She pointed the large wooden spoon at her daughter after licking it.

"Yes," Annette replied, raising dust as she slapped her way across the courtyard filled with the smell of corn, beans, and pork.

"As soon as I have the money, I'll send for you and the children," Toussaint had said when he went away. The day has come, but she has to leave the three youngest with her mother. The money has not stretched to buy a suitcase or a handbag. She sends Loulouse, her seventeen-year-old, to ask her godmother if she can spare a purse. Loulouse comes back with a square patent-leather bag, beige with a large gold clip. Annette will put the papers in it, will carry it on her right arm, hold it tight until the airplane lands and she shows them to the authorities. She has already spoken to the bus driver, told him to save her four seats for tomorrow because she has an airplane to catch. She said the word "airplane" with a fall in her voice, with a tightness in her stomach, her heart beating faster. She was embarrassed as she could not believe it was true.

On the doorstep of the house her two youngest squatted, waiting for her to tie the boxes. She'd promised she'd give them a piece of string to play with. She crouched before the boxes, pulled the string, longer than she needed, so the ends could go to the boys. Man Lolo arrived and sat on the step where the children had been, pushing the orange leaves under her head tie. Annette had picked them from the bitter-orange tree this morning for Man Lolo to put near her temples to soothe that *thump-thump* like a drum in her head she complained about when she woke up. Annette made the last knot on the last box, went and sat near her mother on the porch.

"*Bon*, I'm ready," she said.

"Ay, ay . . . so, you're leaving." Man Lolo put her hand on her daughter's and left it there. "Ay . . . ay . . . ay," she repeated, swaying her body.

Annette knew what was on her mother's mind, knew the words she was not saying. Man Lolo thought it was in part her own fault, that she had not wished hard enough for her daughter to stay, for her six grandchildren to crowd in bed with her when rain came with thunder and lightning, for them to argue over who would scrape the bottom of the iron pot for the crust of cornmeal or rice. Annette was right to want to make a better life for the children, to become a better someone. There was no other way out.

She had sat too many years in that front room with the large round jars of candies half empty and the tray of *douce-lait* she made. Man Lolo was happy for her child. But if she had imagined her stomach turning on itself like a snake, she sitting on the doorstep, her daughter's hand in hers, without finding the words to speak, she would have gone to a *hougan* who could have kept Annette here.

Annette too sat silent. She closed her eyes and saw the yard: the grapevine, the chickens pecking earthworms, the *cachiman*, which had grown into a large tree since Toussaint's departure, the outhouse by the fence. "No outhouses in New York," Ti-Michel, her neighbor, had said when he came back for a visit after five years. Her two small boys continued to pierce bottle caps with a rock and a nail; Toto had strung three already. Jojo, her twelve-year-old, was killing a colony of ants under the almond tree. She knew Jojo resented being left behind; as if she could take a child who could not work! The whole yard was in her head, to take with her.

The bus would leave at four o'clock, before the rooster's crow. At seven they would be at the airport in Port-au-Prince. She didn't want to think whether Toussaint had aged in those six years. Now that she was seeing him again, she was no longer afraid to remember the good things about him. How he opened his mouth wide and said a long "Aah" each time he drank a large glass of ice water. How he clapped his hands when a story made him laugh. How he cropped up behind her in the yard and circled her waist tight. How he'd felt for her body in the dark as if his hands had eyes. Now she could remember all these things because he'd sent her the money to come join him.

An airport is nothing like a bus station, Annette thought. She did not see the plane until she went through the checkpoints and walked out onto the runway, her head high, hand in hand with Loulouse, Roro and Parice close behind. The children did not speak during the flight, not a single word. They giggled and laughed, touching the small bags of sugar, the tiny salt and pepper packets, the plastic forks and knives. They turned to look at her, put their hands over their mouths, and sneaked them in their pockets.

She saw a garden of fireflies below and knew it was New York. People who had been abroad had told her about the many voices making all sorts of announcements. She should give them no heed. All she had to do when the airplane landed was follow the crowd. Once in a room where they were checking people, she should show the green cards. Then she would really be in New York.

But they hadn't told her they would cut the strings of her boxes—strangers would examine her clothes—and she would have to carry them open like that. She didn't know the doors would open by themselves into rooms that were like avenues and she would not know what to do.

The crowd shoved and waved, and she and the three children could not find a quiet spot to stand. They kept pushing them forward and all of a sudden Toussaint was there.

He laughed, his face full of creases.

"*Mezanmi! Mezanmi!* Annette! Oh, Loulouse, Roro, look at you! Parice, oh!"

He wore a checkered pair of trousers and a checkered shirt.

"You look like an American!" she exclaimed.

Ti-Michel was with him, taking the boxes, telling Parice and Roro to follow him. Annette felt her head spin and could not speak.

Toussaint and Ti-Michel passed through the crowd like Moses through water, Toussaint glancing over his shoulder at her. They arrived outside. Cars, thousands of cars, lines of yellow cars and men in uniforms and caps. Toussaint laughed when she asked if they were police guards.

Ti-Michel, too, had a car. Roads went up and down and turned into tunnels. Everything disappeared too fast. Lights flashed and blinked. The constructions were tall like schools, police stations, or churches. She knew they were places where people made money, but she said it anyway, "It's a city of churches."

"That's New York!" Toussaint beamed. He pointed to the Williamsburg Savings Bank, off Atlantic Avenue.

An older church, Annette thought.

Toussaint sat in front with Ti-Michel, his head toward them, his hand reaching out to pat Loulouse's and Parice's knees.

"How's Man Lolo?" he asked.

"Fine, fine," they answered at once.

"And the three little ones?"

"They've grown, Toussaint, like you wouldn't believe," Annette said.

"I can't believe you're here," he said. His eyes searched Annette's. She looked at him, her gaze shifting to the frail trees and reddish buildings, coming back to Toussaint. She closed her eyes for a second. *Papa bon Die, merci,* she said to herself.

The car stopped before a house.

"Two-story houses!" Annette exclaimed. "Things are good here!"

"People here don't live in a whole house. It's bits of houses people live in." Toussaint pushed a low gate against black iron poles. He stepped aside for her to go in. Before Annette stood steep wooden stairs. She'd put her foot on the first step when Toussaint touched her arm and nodded to a side door. She stepped down.

Her bit of house was a basement with a table and four chairs as soon as the door opened and a real cooker in front. There was a square plastic sack with a long zipper that partitioned the rest of the room.

Toussaint hurried to pull the zipper open for her.

"You can put your clothes in it."

"It's so pretty," she said, running her hand along the pink and black dotted plastic.

"I bought it this morning."

He pushed a door open to the bathroom, WC, and shower, flushed the toilet. They looked at each other and hugged right there, Toussaint delighted with her delight. "You need to rest now," he said. "I'm going to work."

"What have you become, some *lougawou* who works in the dark?"

"What are you saying? Lights are on at night too. What do you think? It's just like daytime. I can't be late. Lock the door well. Come, I'll show you."

Annette pushed the table and chairs against the door, just to make sure. She lay on her back, shaking her head, smiling to herself. Her heart pounded like when she took the airplane, like when the money arrived, like the day she went for the papers. That was two years ago. She took the bus to Port-au-Prince, always wearing her good dress, the green *kenedi* Madame Luce, a Grande rue woman had given her, the only wealthy woman whose clothes did not constrain her shoulders and did not need letting down.

Maître Duperval's *Agence Amérique*. She'd rather not recall. Four birth certificates, X rays, the man with the bushy eyebrows scribbling on those long sheets of paper. The Virgin of Altagrace came to her help when he asked her to sign. She drew a chair close to his desk, rested her left arm on it, then cocked her head. As by a miracle her hand began to write, one letter at a time, as it had learned to do those three years at school so long ago.

"You've come at a good time; many visas are being given to people like you these days." The man nodded.

She looked up and dried her forehead with the back of her arm, thinking she would have shortened her name if it had been even one letter longer. But she had made it. She had signed her name in full.

"People like me?" she questioned, thinking, "People who can write."

"The embassy wants people who won't cause trouble over there, people like you," he repeated.

Later, she would find out that he meant people who could hardly read and write and would accept any job.

"A year, two years," he replied, when she asked how long she would have to wait. But now here she was. Annette Estimé, you're in New York, she assured herself before closing her eyes.

Annette listened to the still night, to an occasional car passing, to the humming of something electrical in the background. These were the sounds of New York that would lull her to sleep from now on. No dog barked, no nocturnal bird sang. She didn't mind; those things were behind her. She shifted to her side, the bed creaked, and she rose. Her skirt dressed the back of a chair. She picked it up, turned it inside out, and found the piece of cloth she had pinned there. Tied inside were three *maldjok* beads, two blue, one red against the evil eye, the same ones she had strung around each child's wrist at birth. She pinned the cloth to her nightshirt and whispered her prayer about the house. "Not next month, not next year, in due time. Not with as many rooms as Madame Luce's, but a house that wouldn't disfigure on an asphalted street. With a porch where two rocking chairs can fit, the larger kind with armrests. But one favor: it must be on two floors, a real two-story house. I must be high up so I too can start to look at people from above."

Annette and the children woke up breathing an unfamiliar air. New York smelled of things foreign, unnatural, of plastic and air-conditioning. She did not touch the stove in case she turned the wrong knob. She allowed the children to open and close the Frigidaire, to zip and unzip her plastic closet. They took turns in the bathroom, each flushing twice to hear the water gurgle down. They put on the Sunday finery they had traveled in and sat around the table to wait for Toussaint. Annette looked out the window and felt dizzy seeing the street above her. Summer was drawing to a close. Leaves swirled yellow past her window.

Toussaint opened the door. The cold air made them shiver.

"It's cold," she said.

"Cold, you haven't seen cold yet," Toussaint answered. He gave them each a sweater from his closet.

He took a roundabout way to a small park. He did not want them to walk on their first day among toilet bowls, gaping TV sets, and mattresses with their guts out. The park had five swings, all metal. The children ran to them, sat cautiously at first. The drinking fountain was a sight. Water sprouted instead of running downward. Annette and Toussaint sat on a bench.

"I'm gonna leave one of the jobs when the children start working."

"Why, you've got two jobs?" she asked.

He nodded.

She didn't like it when his face turned serious. He looked old.

"I've been getting these pains in my back. You don't know what I have to do not to scream. It's good that you and the children are here."

"If I had the *palmaschriti* oil Man Lolo wanted me to bring I could rub your back."

"Annette . . . sometimes I thought I was going to die. There were days when my head was heavy like a cannonball and I was here alone, no one to boil me up a few leaves for the pain. Now I take these pills the doctor gave me. The first time I went I don't know what he treated me for. I gave him all the wrong answers. I wanted to tell him my eyelids fell heavy and I said my eyes hurt. Of all the English I had, none of the words were right in that doctor's office. It's been hard."

They looked at Loulouse, Roro, and Parice; they still called them the children.

"They'll become their own bosses when they'll start work," Toussaint said. "Parice can work at Burger King."

"Where?"

"Burger King. The place we passed before. He has to learn English first. He'll look good with a cap on his big head."

"What about me?"

"There are plenty of jobs where I will take you tomorrow: cleaning jobs, factory jobs, everywhere you turn there are jobs."

"Factory," she said curtly. "Didn't come all the way here to clean for other people!"

"We'll go where Rose works. That's a good factory."

"Rose? The Rose in that little house near the cemetery?" Annette thought she'd moved to Port-au-Prince. She used to take in sewing, didn't send her children to school.

"Rose her very self and her whole family!"

Annette fell silent. She had not considered that those six years Toussaint had met people, had a life away from her.

Annette told Toussaint, This will do for the time now, as she and Loulouse took the job at Poultry Inc.

The machine plopped a chicken before Annette for her to scoop out the clots of blood in between the thigh bones. Sweat ran along her arms in the cold room. She turned the chicken around to where the neck had been; the small fatty lumps on either side made chicken bitter. Before she could rip them off another fowl dropped before her. "If they eat them with their teats . . ." she mumbled, letting the first one slide away on the conveyor belt.

The same paleness she'd noticed outside in the early morning light hit her when she and Loulouse waited for Toussaint at four. The whitish sky had lowered itself to cover the top of the buildings, sucked up the colors. Toussaint waved from the other side of the street, signaled them to wait for the light to change. He took his wife and his daughter by the waist.

"Are you sure they will pay me Friday?" Annette asked. "Who will actually pay me?"

"They will, Annette. That's the law." Toussaint walked with them to the subway station.

She and Loulouse settled in a seat, eyes half closed in anticipation of the thrilling speed. The train zoomed into tunnels; their bodies swayed with the clanking of the car. In Annette's mind it headed toward a tall blue house with a slanted roof.

Once outside, her eyes searched for the empty lot across from their apartment like a missing tooth between the row of three-story brownstones. She recognized the uneven sidewalk, the fire hydrant that dripped, evenly spaced trees—the one before her apartment spread over the tarred road. Before pushing the iron gate open, she paused in its shade. She was home.

While Annette and Loulouse cleaned chickens, Roro and Parice scraped a pool at a YMCA. The first Friday they added up the five paychecks in that basement apartment. Annette danced; she'd never counted so many dollars.

"A little rum I would drink now," she said.

"Here, have some of this beer," Toussaint answered.

She made a face.

They would buy coats and shoes, used coats for now, but new shoes since they were in New York.

ANNETTE ESTIMÉ

273

Numbers continued to twirl in Annette's head as she lay in bed that evening: money to put aside, money to send Man Lolo. The refrigerator hummed. Five pairs of shoes. She felt Toussaint's hand on her breast—so much for the coats—his hand slid down, went in circles on her belly. She remained still, felt her petals closing themselves off as if they were *wont* leaves.

The first Christmas came. At the factory the workers spoke in all languages, likes talking to likes. Lunch hour became shopping time, but only two women ever came back with anything. Annette bought each child a present, no wrapping paper. The few dollars she saved would go toward the house.

Saturday evening Ti-Michel drove them across the bridge to Union Square. "This is Manhattan." He opened both arms to the lights, to the glittering trees, tinsels, garlands, painted balls, and people hurrying, white people.

"Now you're talking," Annette exclaimed. "This is beginning to look like *peyiblan*. We kept calling New York the white man's country, and I didn't know where they were all hiding." Annette rolled down the window and the children leaned forward, their three heads around hers. "You gotta find me a church for midnight mass, Ti-Michel."

"I'll find you a church, Annette, but there won't be any '*Minuit Chrétiens*.'" Ti-Michel knew she would be disappointed.

Each year the town had stayed awake for mass, for the moment when the priest held baby Jesus in his arms and intoned, "Midnight is the solemn hour." Their voices exploded in his wake, loud, fervid. "Fall on your knees, beg God for your deliverance."

God had at last delivered them from hunger and from barefootedness.

"I'll do without '*Minuit Chrétiens*,'" Annette said.

"Let's celebrate," Toussaint said, forgetting his back pains, the festive, brisk New York air contaminating him. "Let's visit Rose, let's go for ice cream."

The note of admiration she detected in his voice when he said "Rose" made Annette uneasy.

Toussaint was glad to pay when they stopped at a Carvel shop for sundaes topped with cream and nuts. Still licking their lips, they reached Rose's.

A screen door opened on brown-and-black striped furniture wrapped in plastic as if in a store, plastic runners on the carpeting. Annette could not link this impressive house to the petite woman who had lived near the cemetery.

"Coke for everybody?" Rose asked, the sodas popping as she pulled the rings one after another. "Ah, ah, Toussaint, that's why I haven't seen you these past months."

"Yes, they're here." Toussaint looked at his family around the room.

"We have three more back home," Annette said.

"Think about leaving one home with Man Lolo"—Rose turned to Toussaint—"because next thing you know she will want to come here too. Even mountain people are coming here."

Annette thought of her three children, of the dust blowing in their faces on a street corner in Gonaïves.

"One day I said to myself," Rose continued, "my family ends here. I don't care who's left behind, what happens back there, I'm gonna think of myself. Children, why don't you go watch TV in the kitchen? Your heart hardens, you know. Where do you work, Annette?"

"I'd like to change job."

"If your English is good, come to my factory. We make trees and flowers and label them." Rose pointed to a large vase of purple and blue irises in a corner of the living room.

"Rose's English is good," Toussaint said.

"You could also try the belt factory by Utica; the more you make the more they pay you."

Ti-Michel and Toussaint had said, "You'll learn English at work." But with all the noises the machines made. . . . Annette stood up to leave.

"Did you see, did you see the size of her TV set?" Loulouse said in the car.

"How does one's heart harden?" Annette asked.

"Actually, she's brought a cousin over too," Toussaint said.

Even mountain people are coming to New York, Annette thought. She could rent out rooms to pay the mortgage on her house. That way she could have the three little ones join them. If Toussaint hadn't quit his second job . . .

When they reached home, as the children ran inside Annette stood under the front tree to hear the leaves swish.

It was no longer the rattling machine that sputtered a chicken almost on her lap; this time Annette controlled it with her foot. Her heel went down.

ANNETTE ESTIMÉ

275

Clonk! The machine pierced the belt. *Clonk, clonk*—all the women around her. She was grateful not to have the smell of raw chickens rise to her throat on the subway ride home, when she could close her eyes and let her mind go off to the wide trees back home, to the children throwing stones at mangoes. Her three little ones back there with Man Lolo. All she could do for them was work. Put money aside and work. To bring Jojo over first, then one day the two youngest while they were still of school age. Her hands fondled the brown paper bag on her lap. She'd collected plastic straps, empty rolls of masking tape, and from the street a wide-mouthed jar. Toussaint said she'd get over it like everyone else. He hoped it would be soon. The box under her bed was full of things she said someone could use back home.

Another Christmas passed and summer came. On Saturday, Annette in a red dress and white pumps rested the back of a chair against the front tree to think of Jojo, her fourth child, arriving in two weeks. The chair was turned away from the building with barred windows, not to see a woman's head bobbing like a parrot behind the poles. Annette had seen a job for Jojo on television. He could fling newspapers before people's doors while riding a bicycle. That would have been a good job for him, but New York houses didn't have yards as nice as those. Only rich people's children, who don't need the money, can do these jobs, she said to herself. Her eyes drifted toward three men before the corner brownstone drinking out of paper bags, the irises of their eyes floating in pools of white. She thought of the cot Ti-Michel was going to drive them to buy. When open, it would be difficult to move in the apartment, but closed, it could fit snugly behind Roro's folding bed. She needed a house. If she'd had one, even things with Toussaint would have been different. If they'd had more rooms or a yard where they could have lain and made love, there was nothing she would want to go back for.

"Eh! You think you're in a yard." Ti-Michel's voice came from the street as he parked away from her tree.

"Right, but no dust in my face." Her smile spread.

"How's he today?" Ti-Michel nodded to the door.

"The usual. He's not the same."

"The same when you first got here or the man you remembered back home?"

"I don't know."

"It's night and day he's worked, *wi.*"

"We're all working."

"He's brought four of you here."

"After Jojo it's just two more."

"He hardly knows them."

"He knows we can't leave them there."

"Ay, Annette . . . when this thing hits you, Annette . . . I've been back. Toussaint hasn't. Think if you were here on your own, one paycheck wouldn't get you far. It's because there are five of you now. . . ."

"Once I've bought the house, we'll have one room just for Toussaint and me."

"Well. . . . Is he coming to the store?"

"Go get him. He'll come."

The wind passed through the thin foliage above her; from the hydrant water ran like a spring. A pigeon sat on the tuft of green grass that had sprung between the cracks in the sidewalk. Annette looked at it. The bird, its wings ruffled by the breeze, stared back. Where did it come from? Which seas did it cross before landing under a tree and nest between the cracks of a Brooklyn sidewalk? She wondered.

"Annette!" Ti-Michel's voice startled her. "Annette!"

She sprang to her feet, slammed the gate aside, ran. Ti-Michel stood against Toussaint's back, holding him up by the armpits.

"Some water, quick!" he shouted.

Annette filled a glass at the tap, poured sugar from the box, stirred quickly. She could not see Toussaint's face, but it must be as clammy as her hands. She stood before him, held his chin up, made him take long swallows.

"You gave me a scare," she said, looking into his eyes.

"It's nothing. I just felt weak."

"You better lie down," she said.

Toussaint's condition did not improve. Each time Annette came home that week, he was asleep. When he seemed rested, he complained of weak knees. "If I had some *arawout* or some *akasan*," he wished.

Annette told a woman at work how Toussaint was losing weight and that it wasn't like him to be without an appetite.

"How can you explain to a doctor here what hurts you? There's a Haitian doctor on Eighth Avenue. Go to him. But you'll have to pay."

Annette didn't care about the money as long as Toussaint got better. Together they sat opposite the doctor. Toussaint nudged her, smiled before he began to speak. How he complained to the doctor, pains here, pains there, weakness in his legs, but even after putting his ear to Toussaint's chest, the doctor found nothing. So Toussaint said, "Doctor . . . don't you understand? The pain is here, *en bas ké'm*, right under the heart." He diagnosed fatigue.

The day of Jojo's arrival, Annette was polishing her nails red, singing to herself.

"You're happy today," Toussaint said.

Annette continued to sing, "*Sé'm penyen'm byen, pa penyen'm ti trés.*" Sister, comb my hair well, don't plait it.

"Why do you want Jojo here?"

"Jojo will go to school."

"You're crazy, woman. Jojo is weak. Who's going to cook for him here? And who will stay with Man Lolo, just the two little ones?"

Annette could not restrain herself. "Why don't you go stay with Man Lolo and let Jojo come here?"

Toussaint looked down in shame. The pain under his heart and that weakness in his legs, the backache, were getting to his head.

"Maybe he should go home," Loulouse suggested, "the sun may set him right."

"The sun may set him right," Annette repeated, slowly, pensively. "A glass of *akasan* each morning to give him strength." She turned to him. "Okay, Papa, go, go back. Once I've bought the house, I'll send for you and the two little ones."

The Elixir

LESLIE NIA LEWIS

 "This superb cocktail of spirulina, kelp, Irish moss, raw honey, bee pollen, and natural vanilla extract tones and rejuvenates, repairs and invigorates to maintain optimal energy levels and maximum health."

"Black people do not understand customer service."

Kenya suppressed a giggle.

"No, I'm serious," Michael insisted. "We really don't."

The cook sailed past them, dealing out plates of joll of rice like a hand of cards, but she did not glance at them once. The young brother at the cash register alternately rang up customers and stared off into space.

The restaurant was busy. Young men and women perched on stools and leaned over the juice bar. Duets and trios around the small folding tables murmured, rustled community newspapers, and sipped herbal tea. The walls glowed with murals of Billie Holiday and Nefertiti, Malcolm and

LESLIE NIA LEWIS grew up in Chicago's suburbs and attended Howard University and N.Y.U. She wrote and performed with the LatiNegro Theatre Collective in Washington, D.C. She is the author of the plays *Miss Marie's Last One*, *Sandra and Sashi*, and *The Universe Is Safe*. In 1991–92, Leslie was a screenwriting intern for Touchstone Pictures. She now lives and works in Los Angeles.

Marley, but the bright gray fluorescent lights made the primary colors pall.

The diners politely applauded as the final notes of "Zimbabwe" arced high in the air and vanished; then the keyboard player and the saxophonist swung into "Afro Blue."

Kenya and Michael still stood hungry at the counter. The cook's back faced them, and her hands drew cabalistic signs in the steam over stir-fried greens.

"Excuse us, could we have a menu?"

"They're at the register."

"Excuse us, brother, could we have a menu?"

By that time two stools had been vacated and they could sit down, laughing and shaking their heads.

"Sometimes I will go into a Black-owned store and the brother (or sister) will look at me like they want to kick my ass or something. No 'Hello, how are you, can I help you, thanks for dropping by.' They look at me like, 'I got mine.' And I'm just trying to give homey some business."

A menu dropped on the counter. Its laminated cover announced, *Our service may be slower, but we prepare your meal individually with loving care.*

Kenya and Michael cracked up.

"So how are you doing this evening?" Kenya called to the cook. The cook did a double take, then finally made eye contact.

"You all ready to order?"

"Yeah, two chili tofu dogs. Nice place you got here. How's business?"

"Could be better."

"Food looks good."

"It's nice and spicy. Not like that bland stuff over at the Golden Temple."

"What's the Golden Temple?"

"Bland." She turned her back, refocusing her energies on the hot plates.

"I like their juicer," said Kenya, nodding at their large vintage Champion. "I've got a little electric one. I'm always making carrot juice."

"Have you ever tried carrot juice with a little celery in it and just a piece of apple? Talk about good? That stuff is serious."

"Oh, yeah, it's the apple that does the trick. Love it," said a brother in a kufi seated at the corner of the counter.

"You should try it with ginger," Kenya said to him.

"Carrot juice with ginger? That sounds good."

"Hey, brother, what's going on tonight? Are they going to keep playing music, or is it a poetry reading?"

"No, it's a seminar. Talking about the Vita Elixir Colonic and Natural Tonic."

"Are you selling it?"

"I'm not, but you can talk to that brother in the bow tie. I just want to get some more. I was in here the other day, and they gave me a sample, talking about how it cleans out your system and purifies your skin. I'm skeptic, but shoot, it was free so I took it home and used it for three days just like the instructions said. Man, on the third day I woke up with a buzz. My head felt all light and clear, my skin was glowing, and I had this sweet taste in my mouth. I jumped up, put on my shorts, and ran all the way from Marina del Rey to Malibu."

The hum of conversation faded. A small clean-shaven man in a suit and bow tie had stepped up to the microphone.

"Good evening."

"Good evening," the audience replied.

"Nice to see you all here tonight. My name is Jamal Mohammed, and I would like to thank the Ibis Nature House and owner Fareeda Wilson for inviting me here to talk about the Vita Elixir Colonic and Natural Tonic.

"The Vita Elixir Colonic and Natural Tonic is a powder. As you can see, it is jade green. Green, the color of life. The color of chlorophyll, packaged in a form to be readily assimilated by your body to refresh, replenish, rebuild, reenergize, and beautify."

A silver platter glittered in his hands. It was covered with dozens of little paper cups filled with emerald foam.

"Mixed with water, soy milk, or juice, the Vita Elixir is one of the most potent combinations of vitamins, minerals, amino acids, and trace elements known to woman or man. Vitamin A, the full range of Vitamin B, vitamins C, D, and E, iron, calcium, magnesium, potassium . . ."

He circulated the room, and his listeners took the little paper cups and drank, licking their lips.

". . . selenium, zinc, iodine, silica . . ."

The fluorescent lights faded to pale gold, and all the colors in the room began to pulse and hum. The deep blue in the brother's kente-cloth kufi, the yellow dress of the painted Nefertiti, and Michael's hand, veined and translucent like an autumn leaf cradling the cup of green foam—they all glowed. Jamal Mohammed was suddenly beside Kenya, and she took a second cup. The second cup of Elixir did not make Michael more beautiful to her. That would not have been possible. But it gave her the audacity to say so.

The saxophonist was playing "Trinidad" with one hand; the other cradled the ripe waist of a woman as round and golden as a cantaloupe. The keyboard player was hand-dancing with the brother in the kufi.

"The sea drinks up the sun and the last dreg of day, sit with me and see the moonrise. . . ."

A tiny woman, her 'fro shot through with silver spirals, floated in the embrace of a lion-locked brother.

"Moonrise . . ."

Two sisters spun on the axis of salsa only they could hear.

"Bring the constellations, well-loved toys worn with play, sit with me and see the moonrise. . . ."

A tall man with vertical scars on each cheek was delicately feeding the cook forkfuls of her own spinach pie and staring into eyes as brown as her freshly brewed peppermint tea. And when Kenya leaned into Michael's kiss, the face of her watch shattered and the hands stopped.

"Moonrise . . ."

The young brother of the cash register and a long, lanky young girl with waist-length braids slow-dragged behind the juice bar. They giggled and nuzzled as he blindly reached for the checks. There was six dollars in quarters and dimes where Kenya and Michael had been. They danced through the door, out to Crenshaw Boulevard, into the night.

She was swimming in a warm black sea when a whirlpool suddenly sucked her up and thrust her into the light. A dune of something crunchy was rustling under her back and arms. Michael's face loomed above her, framed in gold and green. Kenya sat up abruptly and their mouths collided, the hundredth time in several hours. She turned and saw two winos on a bench watching them as intently as TV. Kenya and Michael sat in the dry leaves under a magnolia tree in Leimert Park.

In an embarrassed silence, they picked twigs from each other's hair and shook magnolia petals from their clothes.

"Are you all right?" asked Kenya.

"Yeah, I think so," muttered Michael, helping her to her feet. They walked slowly, arm in arm, trying to find words to confirm or deny the night before.

Crossing Martin Luther King Boulevard, they approached a crowd in front of a corner store. Men in suits and women in elaborate Sunday hats clutched handbags and Bibles like machetes. The less religious, in tank tops and shorts, and kids in Cross Color T-shirts stared at the corner store like their eyes could set it on fire. An ambulance roared up. Over the siren from a half block away, a woman could be heard wailing, "Cheryl! *Che-ryl!*"

"Here comes her mother—"

Three men in pale blue pushing a stretcher hurried inside the store. They came out minutes later carrying a body swathed in white.

A woman screamed, "That Korean lady shot Cheryl!"

Now police cars spun around the corner, parking on diagonals. Dozens of policemen leaped out, frantically pushing through the crowd.

"Just in time—before we burn these motherfuckers to the ground!"

Now police were pulling out truncheons. Men and women were screaming into the sky, and blue bodies were hurtling past or into them. Michael and Kenya clutched hands, dodging deftly aimed shoulder and elbow blows. Bruised and dazed, they broke out of the growing circle of rage. Careful not to walk too quickly, they did not look back.

A very special BUSINESS OPPORTUNITY for health-conscious Brothers and Sisters. Share the goodness of VITA ELIXIR COLONIC AND NATURAL TONIC with your community and reap financial rewards! Call J. Mohammed for details at (213) . . .

"Usually we have quite a crowd here on Tuesday nights, but I guess the rain has kept them away."

Kenya and Michael were the only participants in that week's sales seminar at the Mohammed home. Jamal Mohammed, just as formally dressed as he'd been at the Nature House, perched on the edge of an easy chair. His wife Fatima, with her smooth black skin, luminous eyes, and sloping, pregnant belly, looked like a little eggplant. She glided in and out, serving cinnamon tea spiked with Elixir. It produced a sensation of alert calm.

"So why do you want to sell the Vita Elixir Colonic and Natural Tonic?"

Kenya and Michael glanced at each other. "Money."

Jamal Mohammed beamed at them. "Well, that's a good reason."

"You mentioned base pay plus commission," said Michael. "That's how much per hour?"

"And I've got another good reason for you. There is no satisfaction compared to the satisfaction of selling Black folks something they truly need." Jamal Mohammed's eyes blazed at them. "You will not be pushing swine or cigarettes; you won't be selling malt liquor or bad meat. What you'll have to offer is cleansing, healing, life-giving—"

"Jamal is always telling me," said Fatima, "that what we're really selling is love."

"What we're really selling is love," said Kenya.

"What a coincidence, baby. I can't give you anything but love," said Ike.

"Come on, Ike, just a couple of cans. You can resell them."

Ike gestured around his domain, the Quick Stop. "Look, people come in here for gum, for candy, for wine, and for beer, but don't nobody want to drink that funny green stuff. Sorry, Kenya. Here, have a button on the house."

The button carried the somber face of a young girl and the words RE-MEMBER CHERYL—AND BUY BLACK! Kenya pinned it to her T-shirt, put on her shades, and headed back into the heat.

At Rasheed's Islamic Books, she pushed open a swinging door and stepped into cool sandalwood-scented dimness. Three men at a counter looked up from a chess game and glared at her disapprovingly. A gaunt man in a skullcap spoke up.

"Sister, your legs are uncovered."

Kenya looked down at her shorts. "Yes, I know."

"I'm afraid you're going to have to step outside." Out on the sidewalk, the man in the skullcap continued graciously, "Now, how can I help you?"

"Brother, I would like to introduce you to a new health care and health enhancement product, manufactured and marketed by an African American entrepreneur here in our own community, that provides optimal energy levels and maximum fitness and ensures—"

"What is it, my sister?"

"The Vita Elixir Colonic and Natural Tonic."

"That's Jamal Mohammed's tonic?"

"Yes, it is."

"Can't help you, sister."

"Please, wait. Have you ever tried the tonic?"

"No, and I don't want to."

"If you've never tried—"

"We allowed ex-Brother Mohammed to serve his narcotic at the fund-raising dinner for our Boy's School Number Four. In effect, we unknowingly and unwillingly submitted to being guinea pigs in an experiment. There was only a limited amount of his drug available, so I allowed others who were more foolish or less prudent than myself to try it. What I witnessed was the loosening, the *loss* of inhibitions. People doing provocative, sensuous dancing, engaging in shameless fondling and caressing, and conducting lewd banter. My second wife tore off her veil and did a handstand on top of a table. No, sister. There is no way that poison, that hallucinogen, that *corruption* will cross the threshold of my store. *Salaam aleikum.*"

The door slammed, jingling bells and blowing sandalwood in Kenya's face.

She was achingly hungry but didn't even have money for a sandwich at the Nature House, so she trudged home, pulling the shopping cart of elixir behind her.

Michael was lying next to the air conditioner and in front of the TV when she opened the door.

"How's it going?"

"Hot and heavy, walking in the sun and dragging these boxes. You gonna help me this afternoon?"

"I'm kind of tired, Kenya."

She stalked into the kitchen and came out with a box of graham crackers and a jar of peanut butter.

"He's talking about giving us more money."

"I don't think I want any of his money."

She looked hard at him, then sat down beside him on the couch. "Michael, what's up?"

"I don't want to sell that stuff anymore. That's all."

"That's all? You get a chance to do something positive for your community, get paid for it, and you don't want to help?"

"Kenya, what makes you think this is so positive?"

"Look how it makes people act, makes people feel! All the shooting and dying could stop. Jamal wants to recruit some Crips and Bloods to help with sales—"

"And they could sell it to the LAPD."

"Maybe. This is just a start—"

"Just a start? How come he's starting with *us*?! Kenya, do you even know who this man is? How do you know he's not with the FBI or the CIA? My friends are saying this is another plot to emasculate the Black man."

His hand flipped quickly from channel to channel; *click* bud *click* coors *click* guns n roses.

"Emasculate?! We could save lives by stopping the violence, and you call that emasculating somebody? And what is Jamal? *He's* not an African American man?"

"How should I know? What about the white boys? Let Jamal push his elixir to *them*, and to the murderous Koreans. Damn, that shopkeeper shot that girl in cold blood!"

Kenya's throat tightened and tears filled her eyes. "We can make it stop."

At Great Western Stadium, the Lakers trotted on court to a standing ovation.

"I will not emasculate my community," said Michael.

The Day of Solidarity in Memory of Cheryl Hardaway had a much larger turnout than had been anticipated or hoped for, ominously noted Sherm Buckey of Channel 4. A number of diverse groups had collaborated in the hasty organization of the march. Some groups like the Afro-Asiatic Nation had been adamant about it being a Black thang, but Calvary AME and One Thousand and One Black Professionals were less dogmatic and welcomed MPP (Madres Por la Paz) and QPJ (Que la Placa se Jode).

There was a secret path winding through the marchers that only the most observant, a plainclothes cop or a Fruit of Islam brother, would have noticed. Among the solemn, disgusted, eager, hungry, and outraged faces in the crowd, every so often, at ten to twenty paces, there would be one face radiating joy.

Some kids took up the chant of the city's most notorious rapsters. Law enforcement knuckles, ashen white or dark gray, clutched their sticks even tighter.

"Fuck tha *po*-lees—Fuck tha *po*-lees!"

One man was not chanting but singing soulfully "Cisco Kid." Another man looked at him incredulously, then sucked his teeth in distaste. A woman crooned "Buffalo Soldier." An older couple had actually started to Lindy hop, to the great annoyance of their fellow marchers.

The trail of happy souls led directly to Jamal Mohammed. Kenya was back on Slauson hawking cans of dry elixir without much success, but Jamal had actually mixed a batch and was offering little paper cups to the curious and the thirsty.

A megaphone addressed the crowd. "All right, y'all. *Listen up*. We got company. Simi Valley Boys Club heading south on Crenshaw—"

"Fuck the *po*-lees—"

"—just dying to break heads and kick ass—"

"I can see them from here," someone muttered. Still a few blocks away, a broad blue wave approached with the glitter of sun shining off Plexiglas face shields.

"We are not marching to Martin Luther King," said the megaphone. "We are taking a detour on Vernon—"

But the march surged on, and the megaphone was reduced to begging and pleading until it was drowned out by the chant.

Helicopters swung overhead watching two waves meet, one blue, the other a bristling patchwork. Jamal Mohammed worked the crowd with growing desperation. He tried to steady his box of paper cups, but he kept getting wedged between people, and then the crowd would break and a stampede would almost knock him over. No one could hear him over the thunder of propellers and voices. He smelled tear gas. The crowd parted again, and he faced a wall of blue.

He looked through Plexiglas into a mirror. The cop was dark-skinned, short, powerfully built. Jamal Mohammed was so close he could see sweat running down the bridge of the man's nose. Hand on holster, the cop stared wide-eyed into the box.

Far behind him, Jamal heard someone scream, *"Remember Cheryl!"* The crowd rocked forward again, toppling Jamal. Plexiglas, blue bullet-proof vest, and blue pants were sloshed with green.

A young woman saw the enormous red flower bloom on Jamal Mohammed's chest, but she didn't hear the shot. The blast deafened her for hours afterward.

The blackened skeleton of a Boys supermarket on Vermont loomed behind a chain-link fence. Red-eyed and ravaged, Kenya drove on without a glance. It was the first night after the lifting of curfew. Every few blocks, the gutted remains of stores or shopping centers jutted into the dark. The streets were still empty except for the National Guard. Looking like GI Joe action figures, they converged on street corners, striking poses and aiming rifles at the Chevette as it rode by.

At the hospital, she found a well-lit parking space and carried a large arrangement of flowers across the lot to the entrance.

The receptionist said Jamal Mohammed could receive visitors briefly this evening. It was requested that she make no statements to any reporter in the building on his case.

Tonight the hall outside Jamal's room was empty. Kenya knocked gently on the door, waited a moment, then stepped inside.

Jamal Mohammed sat up in bed, gleaming tubes trailing from his nose and arms to an IV pole. His head rested in Fatima's arms. The two of them watched a man hunched over in a chair. The man looked up, and Kenya wondered if he was Jamal's twin. He noisily blew his nose, then sipped from a paper cup.

"I've always liked my job. The uniform. That 'aww shit' look people get when I pull them over. Everybody getting out of my way when I come down the street. And if somebody made me use my gun, that was their problem. I didn't get all upset—I never had to see the therapist—" The man's head dropped, and his shoulders shook silently. "Until now. . . . You all are the only people I've been able to talk to about it. Doesn't make any sense."

He got to his feet.

"Mr. Mohammed, Mrs. Mohammed, I'm . . . I'm sorry. . . . Thank you for listening to me. . . . Thanks for the drink. Someone's been selling this stuff down at the division—"

"Write down your address and we'll have it delivered to your home," rasped Jamal.

The man wiped his eyes with the back of his hand. "God bless you. I hope you get every penny of that twenty-one million—" and he disappeared through the swinging door.

"We're suing the LAPD," said Fatima, smiling serenely.

Kenya has a small single on Dracena on the second floor. Her neighbors are Filipino, so the sight of drying seaweed doesn't amaze them, but this is the first time they've seen it this country, hanging from the balcony of a Black woman's apartment.

By day she goes out to fight the traffic on her way to an office job, but in the evening the Filipino family see her silhouette through shades and hear the metallic clink of spoons, colanders, pressure cooker lids, and thermometers. Exotic and familiar odors drift from her window, and the Filipina grandmother sniffs, intrigued.

Late at night she goes out again, carrying crates and boxes to load into her Chevette. Passing headlights illuminate gleaming mason jars filled with green.

Nzinga's Treasure

DEVORAH MAJOR

 The air eased out of her in a whine. No one paid her any mind anymore. She was identified generically by the bags that sat heavy and swollen near her ankles, swinging from the end of her long brittle arms: "bag lady," "homeless," "street person," and, by women of similar age but far more substantial finances, a "poor poor unfortunate, dear me." She had become less than ordinary, a shadow hung over a garbage pail, perched in a doorway, slumped on the backseat of an all-night bus. People called her whatever was convenient at the moment, seeming to think that because she chose not to offer a name, she had none. Sometimes she was Sadie, other times Moms, others Bitch or Ol' Lady, whatever was convenient and suited the caller's mood. Social workers who roamed the streets in search of easier cases came to believe, because she shied away from their persistent inquisitions, that she lacked sense and knowing, that whatever feelings her water-soft body had were long since frozen in the slime and frost of street living. She seemed sordid to them, rotten, smelling of dead skin, feces, and death.

DEVORAH MAJOR is a poet, and a fiction and essay writer. *Callaloo*, *Left Curve*, *Zyzyvva*, *Adam of Ifé*, *California Childhoods* and *Pushcart XII* are among the numerous periodicals and anthologies which have featured her work. She has a book of poetry, *Traveling Women* (Jukebox Press), with Opal Palmer Adisa.

So no one saw her, as she carefully wrapped it in the sky-blue jacket she had found on a bus seat just the other night. It was, she thought, an appropriate shade of blue, kind of milky and smudged with chocolate candy, sticky and still smelling of a sweet soap. No one paid any attention as she pushed aside the protectors she held in those bags. The ones that had managed to save her from rape or dismemberment, those that somehow saw her through, providing just enough food in her belly to go on another day, those that kept her legs strong and many of her teeth intact. She carefully parted the spirits who guided her away from desperate young men who, when drugged, found substance in creating a blood-filled waste of others. She asked for understanding from the spirits who made her invisible when the streets were cleared of refuse, including her friends, who were swept into waiting hospital rooms to be shaved, deloused, and given jars of antibiotics, which did nothing but cause stomach cramps and diarrhea but couldn't cure the real illnesses. There's no way to cure being an extra in the wrong place, an expendable, an unneeded, an eyesore seeming to have impossible dreams, like a quiet clean room, perhaps a soft bed, a table on which to place an altar—little little dreams. No, no one saw her apologizing to each item, disposing of some, pushing others down, until there was room for the fresh blue present, the wonder of it all.

She placed it, with a forgiving tenderness, in the middle of the largest bag, double reinforced for the season's shoppers and embossed with golden letters from the area's finest store. Then, sensing it was not quite safe, she covered it with layers of her other gems. Ready to travel, she stood up, straightened her back with an almost military stance, and spit three times into the gutter, spewing out a gray sludge mixed with red and black blood. Then she began her trek.

Charlie, one of the city's few regular people who actually looked at and remembered her, offered a morning paper from his stand, which she usually took wordlessly, barely nodding acknowledgment. This morning, though, she turned it down, stopping and measuring his breadth. "Come on," she rasped. "Need you to witness me." Charlie was old and lived almost as many hours on the streets as she did. Used to the ways of "those people," he tried to defer,

"Can't leave the stand, y'know, Sadie."

"Name ain't Sadie." She spat in disappointment and disgust and walked on.

As she passed a downtown elementary school, a group of children hanging from the wire corded fence began to call out hoots and whistles to her, snickering and pointing their short smooth fingers. She turned swift and sharp and stared the loudest in the eye.

"I was a queen before this. You are nothing but trash." They wilted as she turned elegantly and walked away and then began to whisper about "I told you, she's crazy!" and "Y' better watch out 'cause she's probably a witch that'll grab you one a these days." Then they moved away from the fence, relieved when the end of recess bell rang, and crowded, without having to be called twice, around the skirts of their teacher.

The old woman strode on, her bags hanging at each side, barely scraping the ground. The sun, although only halfway up the horizon, was already round and hot. The woman began to pour sweat, which left streaks that resembled ritual scarification across her cheeks and brow. Her hands cracked and cramped around the bags' handles. She paused, readjusted them, and moved forward. Sister Donnetta joined her, Bible in hand, sweeping a long skirt in back of her and raising her voice to sing, walking a few feet in back of the old woman.

Four Fingers threw his matted dreadlocks out of his eyes and stretched, in between the stanzas of the corner ode he was rapping, one of an endless stream of poems that shot out images in jolts of pain, pestilence, and desire, invading the minds of fine-suited workers who offered him money, unasked, hoping a quarter here and nickel there would quiet his ranting and allow them their private ignorance. Seeing the two women he changed his rhythm, making the group a trio as he chanted soft lines of a new poem full of the bitterness of last night's wine and the clarity of the stars that had blanketed his reveries.

Joseph was smiling, having gotten both a new cigarette and dollar before breakfast with almost no insult or derision, and while still having a drop of night train seeping through his veins. "Poor white trash," Sister Donnetta always called him, telling him to be white and fall from grace is for sure to be hounded by the devil. He tolerated her abuses because her angel voice comforted him when he too wondered what paths had led him here, forgetting for a moment his choices of gutters and alcohol over the mundane loading and unloading of crates that made up most of his former life.

"Where you three going? Something up?"

The old woman coughed, put down her bags, rubbed her hands, and smiled. "Found me a present for the mayor. Want to thank her for her fine accommodations. Got her a little something keep her feet warm at night. Come on, Joe, you got dues to pay. Bear witness, bear witness."

And he, too, joined the line, falling in step, rocking back and forth between the cadence of Four Fingers's chanting and Sister Donnetta's hum.

One by one, more people joined the line: junkie Phillips and his Chinese girlfriend, slow and deliberate; the three Bills, ragged and evil, debating on why they were marching to city hall; Silly Girl, still traveling in galaxies while dragging her jean-skirted, sandal-footed, slumped skeleton down dark alleys looking for flowers that never bloomed. Finally they were a group of thirty-six, if you counted the baby in Shirley's stomach, which nobody, including her, did. Motley and smelling of the city, they stopped at the foot of the city hall steps waiting for "it" to begin.

The old woman dusted off a stair with much ceremony and carefully placed her bags down. Then she climbed two steps and began to speak.

"You all know that when royalty come to visit we supposed to come with gifts. Now some bring gold, and that's good, and some bring diamonds, and that's good too. Some bring cloth they have their subjects weave, fulla pictures and blood, and, why, that's all right too. But I know I come from a warrior people, and my voices, they told me I needed a special gift and told me where to find it. Something straight from the Master."

Sister Donnetta immediately started to clapping and saying, "Amen, let's hear it." Four Fingers stood unusually still, looking for some vision, for a moment confused, and the three Bills started feeling disgusted because it didn't look like an extra meal was coming from the journey. The old woman continued,

"Now I want you all to be real quiet because I brought the mayor just what she needs, a gift from a queen to a queen. Sister Donnetta, sing us a song."

Voice cracking, Donnetta had begun "Amazing Grace" when the old woman held up her hand imperiously, correcting her. "Sister Donnetta, the song is 'Mary, Don't You Weep,'" and Donnetta, without missing a phrase, began again. As Sister Donnetta sang, the old woman carefully emptied her bag until she pulled out the soft blue package. Seeing a younger, well-dressed woman in a smart navy suit with a small hat perched on the side of her head, she blocked her path and began the presentation. "Madam mayor, may I offer a small treasure from my kingdom—" The woman pulled away but found herself surrounded by the entourage, who wanted to see what had brought them there. The younger woman decided it was indeed the better part of valor to listen to the short speech it was sure to be and then hurry inside. This was, after all, the price one paid for living in one of the world's finest cities. Gently and with, she was sure, no sign of the terror that was growing in her belly and making her tongue a desert, she smiled. "I think you have me confused with somebody else."

"No, Mrs. Mayor, I would know you anywhere. This is your kingdom, as I have mine, and I want to present you with the fruit of your labors, the reward for your justice, and the finest gift I could find, from my kingdom to yours. A small thing really, a simple bed warmer."

"Tell it, sister!" Four Fingers shouted, not sure what was inside the jacket, but enjoying watching the scream about to pierce through the young woman's lungs, seeing it growing between her wire-stiff breasts and get caught in the dryness of her throat.

The old woman spat again, three times, the last wad, laced with blood, falling across the young woman's shoe. Unable to move, the young woman stood trembling, sweat squeezing from the upper lip of her pinched mouth, and unwillingly took the cloth bundle in limp hands, receiving it for a moment before she caught herself and let it slide onto the stairs.

The jacket opened up and sent rolling a newborn baby boy, its dead eyes pulled open, its tiny fingers still coated with the cream of a timely birth, a torn cord dangling from its belly. Fragile and grotesque, it lay on the stairs as the suited woman finally was able to scream, dropping her handbag, which Joseph quickly retrieved and emptied. She stood shrieking without taking breaths, glued to the city hall steps, until nearby police came and helped her indoors.

The old woman's following faded away, becoming once again invisible nonentities in a world of plenty. Having delivered her bounty, the old woman picked up her bags and wound toward the church where she knew she could find an afternoon meal. Today, she believed, it would be fish. Her mouth watered in expectation. As usual, no one paid her any mind. No one ever did willingly see her. That's why she never told them who she really was, because no one ever really wanted to know.

Yellow Rooms

RICHELLE A. MCCLAIN

"Care for a cocktail before dinner?" the aproned waitress asked, placing the laminated menus in front of them.

"I'll have a Rolling Rock with—" Soma started.

"And a martini, very dry," Emmett interjected. His chin shimmered with each syllable.

It was an omen. Grandpa Pierce had a cleft in the same place, and before he died he summoned her to his bedside and reminded her once again that she was going to make some lucky guy very happy. She studied Emmett's indentation from across the table. At one time it might have been a dimple, the kind that endeared him to girls, arresting them in mid-sentence during their flirtatious pursuits. But the years' turbulence had wrought havoc on the face and altered the youthful beauty mark into a common gaping blemish. Still, it possessed a certain seductive charm.

It was indeed a sign, like Noah's radiant rainbow or the wet fleece Gideon found at dawn. Like the five pieces of junk mail she received postmarked from New York the day the American Stock Exchange offered her the job. Signs had long been a source of insight for her. In fact, she relied

RICHELLE A. MCCLAIN lives in Brooklyn, New York. She holds a Bachelor of Music degree from Wesleyan College and has studied fiction writing at the Frederick Douglass Creative Arts Center. Ms. McClain is currently a Marketing Manager at *The New York Times*.

on them, treating them as a matter of course, as routine as gleaning tidbits from the *Wall Street Journal* or trading gossip with her co-workers. Ever since she was eleven and wanted more than anything the redskates in the window of Miller's department store. Two weeks before her birthday, she'd spied the very pair under a large maple at the corner of the playground beneath a pile of leaves. Left by some neglectful classmate, no doubt, although surely none of *her* friends. The temptation to take them for herself was almost overwhelming, but the bright metal wheels were instead presented to the principal, who in due time traced down their rightful owner. Nonetheless Soma recognized the challenge and bargained that, by doing the right thing, she would be rewarded. And sure enough, the biggest package next to the birthday cake held her prize. Yes, this man might be just what she was looking for.

The copper sun bore down on her face, softening the taut, anxious lines. For their first date, he'd selected a charming restaurant on the edge of the West Village known for its barbecue.

"This roof view is spectacular," she whispered, in awe of the shadows cast on the skyline by the retreating sun. She leaned back in her chair, permitting the last rays to lavish their warmth on her neck and exposed shoulders.

"It's one of those secret spots that only we indigenous New Yorkers know about. The commissioner once treated me to lunch here, and it's been my regular hangout ever since."

The waitress brought the drinks. "To you and tonight," he toasted. They raised their glasses to the tune of "My Foolish Heart" playing softly in the background.

"You remind me of the women in Morocco. I traveled all over the continent in my early thirties—the Ivory Coast, Zimbabwe, Kenya," he added, as if in an aside. "Of course, Morocco was my favorite. Lived there for three years."

She pulled a piece of bread from the small loaf in the middle of the table and spread half a pat of butter on it while he rambled on about his travels. A smile curled her lips involuntarily, prompted not by his attempts to impress her but by the dull white sideburns. In earlier years, guys her age left her cold. She gravitated toward the mature men with gray accents and deep green pockets. Now she laughed openly because her choices relegated her to those who sported not only graying temples but white crowns and napes, chests, silver groins even. She wondered about his. Only time would tell.

"Ready to order?" the waitress asked.

"Yes. We'll start with a bottle of wine," he began.

"So where'd you find this Emmett?" Marcy asked, traces of her South Carolina accent spilling over the syllables. She lay sprawled on her side across the bed in her guest—soon to become baby—room, propped up on one elbow. The television droned in the background. The news anchor signed off with his two-minute human interest segment, and with her available hand Marcy zapped through the channels with the remote. Soma sat on the rocking chair searching through a blue canvas bag, then moved to the bed and dumped the contents onto the rumpled sheets.

"Damn, I must have left them at home." Soma sighed, sorting through the varied assortment of loose coins, pens, bills, and old receipts. Marcy, her old college roommate, had invited her to spend the weekend at Marcy's New Jersey home while Soma's own midtown Manhattan apartment was repainted.

"Left what?"

"My silver earrings. Got anything to go with this outfit?"

"Try the top middle drawer." Marcy pointed. "And stop avoiding the question."

Soma slid open the bureau drawer, pulling out a carved wooden box. "At the museum. You know—those afternoon concerts they sponsor in the sculpture garden during the summer. We met during the intermission. He called and asked me out." She neglected to tell Marcy that he'd phoned just yesterday. And ever since, feverish with adolescent exhilaration, she'd anticipated the unfolding of this evening.

"Hm," said Marcy thoughtfully. "You gave him your number? Must have been a real charmer."

"Look. His subjects and verbs agreed. He didn't carry a beeper. And he's not married . . . as far as I know. Besides, he's a jazz fiend. How about these?" She held up a pair of gold hoops to her ears.

"No. You need something more dramatic. Try the turquoise and silver ones I picked up last summer in Taos—they should be in there somewhere." Marcy sat up, crossed her legs futilely, and then stretched them out, using her arms to support her from behind. "But does he have a *job*, Soma?" she asked pointedly.

"Look, I didn't give him the third degree."

"Twenty years ago you would have asked the man his name, rank, and serial number."

"Exactly. Twenty years ago I was twenty-one. I weighed thirty pounds less and had a waistline. Twenty years ago I wasn't a horny, middle-aged . . ." Her voice trailed off.

"Ah. Soma Pierce. Never thought I'd live to see the day. I remember when they were lined up waiting to get a chance with Miss Soma Pierce. Lord, what I wouldn't have given for some of the men you threw away. And you—you didn't pay them no nevermind—and always had some trumped-up excuse. Reggie talked too much shit. Lawrence spent more time with his mama than he did with you. BK's clothes looked like they came from the Salvation Army. And remember Trent?" She mimicked Soma's voice. " 'Trent is too fine to be any good.' Personally, I would have checked that one out."

"Okay! Okay! But at least I didn't waste my time with some of the trifling stuff you used to drag through Two-seventeen." They both laughed. Two-seventeen was the room they shared their two years together in Merrill Hall.

"Didn't do *too* bad, if I may say so myself." She blew a kiss to the framed picture on the bureau of a balding man with a mustache. "Sometimes it's worth kissing all those toads." Roy, Marcy's husband of fifteen years, had just last week celebrated his promotion to Senior VP at a prominent pharmaceutical firm. "I mean, like, whatever happened to that little investment analyst who couldn't take his eyes off you at that gallery reception last fall? I ran into him last week on the corner of Fifty-ninth and Lex. He asked about you. Didn't you two go out?"

Soma nodded.

"So?"

"Don't remind me."

"Go ahead, tell. What atrocity did this one commit?"

Soma hesitated. "He took me to a Szechuan restaurant, asked for a fork, and then at the end of the meal used his fingers to push the last morsels of fried rice on it. Okay?" Even now, Soma shuddered, the moment still embarrassingly fresh.

"There. See? I mean . . . okay, so the guy needs to work on his table manners, but that doesn't mean you can't work *with* him. Honey, I hate to tell you this, but you ain't going to find your black knight nowhere but from nine to five . . . as in P.M. to A.M. . . . . in your dreams."

Marcy was getting on her last nerve, and she'd already volunteered more than she cared. Soma removed the earrings from the velvet-lined case, clasped them on, and looked at herself in the full-length mirror behind the door, her eyes drawn abruptly to her stomach. She sucked it in. Held her

breath for several seconds. The sleeveless turquoise tunic covered a multitude of sins. She wore it over ribbed leggings. Thank God for Spandex.
The combination was pleasing: elegant yet casual. Still, she felt uncomfortably bloated.

"No dessert tonight." She sighed barely audibly, patting her abdomen
like a newly pregnant mother might.

These admonishments were useless, though. Her round belly bulged not
with child but with the decay of spoiled passion. It bore the vapor issued
from punctured dreams. She carried the emptiness well, holding the vacu-
ous mass close to her. Not even Marcy suspected she'd been celibate for
over two years. Soma wished again for the days when she was young and
men plentiful. If only the goods had been apportioned more evenly over
the course of her life.

"Eat dessert and work out tomorrow. Tonight, just relax and enjoy
yourself. Wish I could join you. Roy's got this bridge thing we have to go
to, but with any luck we'll be home before midnight. *If* you decide to come
back tonight, call us from the train station and we'll pick you up." Marcy
paused. "And give the guy a break, okay?"

"Bridge?" Soma commented sarcastically, still standing in front of the
mirror. She fussed with her freshly washed hair, rearranging the few no-
ticeably gray strands.

"Stop picking. You look fabulous."

Soma hoped so. She wanted him to notice.

He did . . . staring at her now, between smacking his lips and providing a
commentary on the fate of South Africa. "You're lovely."

"Thank you." Soma lifted the wineglass to her lips. The Chianti was a
good choice, although he'd neglected to ask her preference before ordering.
A small annoyance, one she could overlook. She sank the meaty rib into
her teeth just as the sun slipped into the Hudson. By northeastern standards, the barbecue wasn't half bad. And so far neither was the company.

Soma's eyes—huge expressive ones that mirrored her every thought—
studied the creases on his face, running from the corner of each nostril to
his mouth, forming a fleshy parenthesis. Were the punctuation to have
clarified him in any way, "pretentious" might have been the qualifier. The
brackets deepened when the waitress interrupted his remarks to pour more
wine. After she replenished the glasses, he dismissed her with a wave of his
hand.

Soma caught herself being too critical again. Maybe Marcy was right.

He reached for the oversized napkin in his lap, flapped it twice, and dabbed the corners of his mouth. Yes, she was definitely nitpicking. He now launched into a discussion on the value of continued economic sanctions, having finished sizing up the fate of the ANC.

Still, despite his sophistication and politically astute observations, Emmett was missing . . . Soma couldn't put her finger on it. Sex appeal? He wasn't particularly attractive, but looks were no longer a priority for her. That dream died long ago. She preferred to call it confidence. Not the arrogance some men wear as armor, but assurance that oozes from the body like a fragrance. A confidence so embedded that a man needn't be beautiful, or schooled, or talented . . . he didn't have to open his mouth to dazzle. Men like this were as relaxed being themselves as they were in letting you be yours.

The waitress brought the dessert menu and recited the specials. Emmett declined for both of them, requesting coffee and the check.

"Let's go for a walk. I need to work some of this off," he explained, patting his stomach. "I know a great place with the best cheesecake in New York. We'll stop there for dessert."

Soma saw the bill. It came to $73 and change. He reached in his pocket and laid down four twenties.

"Ready?" he asked. "Let's get out of here."

They strolled the bustling street. By the time they left the restaurant, dusk had settled over the city in the way evening is born in New York summers—barely glimpsed. The metamorphosis of day was less discernible than the altered attitudes. Loosened ties and faces. Night lights softened the hard edge of the streets. The swift pace never slowed, but the rhythms blurred.

"Ever been married?" he asked.

"No . . . and you?"

"Once. Seven and a half years." He grabbed her hand. The night was steamy, the air sticky, and the grudging breeze that dared pass over her was a delectable treat, cooling the thin moist film covering her body. His palm was crusty and wet. Soma held as loosely as she held her body. They followed the aroma of roasted peanuts to the corner vendor and shared a sack. She stopped to examine the birds of paradise at the Korean grocer and commented on the fresh mangoes and papayas. He pulled her away and pointed toward the street musician playing steel drums. They walked at a quickened, lazy stride while browsing at the boutiques.

She listened impatiently for the telling comment that might foreshadow their destiny. Treasured words, recalled years later during a candlelight dinner. Or a simple phrase repeated next week in the lunchroom, preceded by, "You know what he had the nerve to say?" In Soma's experience there was always that definitive moment when one unwittingly knew the outcome.

These men with their savvy lines and practiced hands hadn't a clue as to what turned a woman on. Darryl, her only college sweetheart, thought it was his lean brown physique and Number 24 jersey that had won her heart. But it was really the "What do you want?" said while she looked in the mirror, brushing her hair.

"My sister thinks I should go with braids, but my hairdresser wants to experiment with one of those asymmetric cuts. What do you think?"

Darryl answered simply, "What do you want?" And right there in front of the bureau, her bared breasts brazenly erect, she'd cupped his large hands over them and said, "I love you." They'd lasted seventeen blissful months together.

Emmett stopped at an antiques store and peered inside at a porcelain doll. "Used to collect those," he said, "but I recently sold them, along with all my books—those I didn't give my daughter."

"Your daughter? You have a daughter? How old is she?"

"I don't know. Twenty-three, twenty-four. She's still in school—a real bitch."

"Excuse me?"

"Yeah, my daughter. I love her and all, but she's still a bitch."

"And your son—is he a bastard?" she challenged as they crossed the avenue against the red light. He parted his lips to speak but grabbed her instead, wrenching her from the path of an irate cabdriver, zigzagging across the street.

They stopped at a table of dusty books lined up in neat rows. "Won't find 'em in the stores this cheap," the vendor said. "What're you looking for? See here, I got it all: dance, finance, and hot romance. Half the bookstore price."

Emmett picked up a book of cartoon illustrations. "No other kids, thank God. Just my daughter. She's enough."

"What's her name?"

"Lena. She's studying design. Textiles. Lena the bitch."

The comment jolted Soma. Up to now the evening had been passable, if not somewhat enjoyable. She would concede the affected posturing and the four drinks he guzzled before coffee. But she could never expect to pursue a relationship with someone who called his daughter a bitch. What label would he assign *her*? Soma fingered the pages of some how-to paperback blindly, the disappointment bearing down on her so hard that she shrugged her shoulders when Emmett asked if she was ready to continue their stroll.

They walked silently down the next block, the evening having died for Soma somewhere between 5th and 6th streets.

He seemed oblivious to her silence and started jabbering about one of her favorite female pianists, a thirty-five-year jazz legacy. "Her new release is bad. Have you heard it?"

"Not yet. Isn't she playing at Charlie's tonight?" Soma asked in a perfunctory tone, gazing at her watch.

"Yeah. Wanna catch the next set?"

Soma hesitated, her earlier good mood rebounding. "Sure. But isn't it about to start soon?"

He nodded.

"Then we'd better hurry."

"Are you always in such a rush?"

"No, I just don't like walking into places late."

They pushed their way through the standing-room-only crowd, cutting a path to the bar. Soma leaned against the brass railing. The first set was almost over. Emmett stood behind her, scouting the room. She stood very still, mesmerized by the music. The old woman's unsteady voice cracked on the higher notes, but her fingers, still remarkably agile, danced across the keys. The bartender handed them their drinks just as the musicians went on break. Emmett spotted a couple of familiar faces.

"I'll be right back," he offered apologetically, then fought his way across the club, his drink steering the course.

She followed him with her eyes to two men, both huddled over the table. They looked as if they'd been there awhile. Old cronies, she thought. Men with bulging guts and creased faces, just like him. The three turned in unison to appraise her, their cheeks ballooning into wide grins of approval. Emmett continued talking, as if sharing an intimate confidence. And they kept grinning, proud to be privy to the secret. She tried not to think about the details of their conversation as seconds later they burst into laughter, their loud voices carrying across the room. Soma clutched her drink.

Twenty minutes later he was still at their table. Her glass drained, she slid off her seat and headed for the ladies' room. She looked at her watch as she passed the pay phones and realized she still had time to catch the 11:35. If only Marcy were home. She dropped in a quarter and let it ring fifteen times. Hung up and tried again, this time waiting only nine rings before slamming it down. She sulked by the booth a few minutes, reading the directions for placing collect calls, and picked up the phone again when the music started. Still no answer. By the time she reached her stool, he, too, had returned.

"Want another drink?" he asked, lifting her empty glass.

"No, thank you. I've had enough," she replied, her voice seething with the irritation women exude when they find themselves compromised without quite knowing what they have relinquished and how.

"Well, then, what about buying me one?" She whirled around on the stool, scrutinizing him to make sure she heard correctly. She had. He examined her closely also, a sardonic grin spreading. She felt tested. And in the second before her answer she knew she hated him and how much she had despised him all her life. They fought the battle silently, casting insults with their eyes; she remembering his cheap gifts and stingy promises; and him berating her for her bourgeois ways. Soma smirked as she flagged the bartender. He'd won the round but lost the prize. Not that she minded picking up the tab, of course, but that he asked. He'd asked her to join him at the bar and to pay the tab, all in one night.

"Do you always ask your dates to pick up the bill *after* you invite them out?" she finally sniped.

"This is the nineties, I thought you women were into that sort of thing." Soma sucked in her breath and glared.

"Another round?" the waiter asked, placing fresh napkins before them. Soma nodded, then turned on the bar stool, her back toward Emmett. The old woman sang hauntingly, her words filling every pore in the room. Soma closed her eyes, lost in the woman's voice.

So she jumped in reflex when Emmett's hands touched her shoulders, his thumbs kneading her neck—slowly, in tempo to the ballad. Her first impulse was to spin around and slap him, crash her purse over his head, dump the wine in his lap, and kick him, in quick succession. But she hesitated a split second too long, negating the impetus—and the justification for these acts. She remained instead perfectly still, frozen in stature, as if she hadn't noticed, emphasizing his inability to move her. The hands were remarkably soothing, surprising her with their tenderness. Had it not been for his loathsome behavior, she would have welcomed the long overdue touch. In fact, after a few moments she did, tilting her head and shoulders just barely to position his probing fingers where the sun had stroked her earlier. He continued for a long while, well into the next tune, watching her through the mirror behind the bar. Their eyes met briefly, though she still didn't speak. But the tab didn't seem to matter so much now. As long as she continued to feel this way, she didn't mind paying.

By the third tune they decided to leave and she accepted an invitation to his apartment.

The taxi stopped in front of a dilapidated building on Central Park West. She became skeptical when the armed doorman in blue uniform, looking more like a security guard, buzzed them through the second glass door. But with these New York apartments, you could never tell. Many a luxurious suite was fenced in by a treacherous lobby. When they reached the steel-plated elevators, though, the acrid odor of urine filled Soma's nostrils, and when she entered the stale hallway, she suspected she'd made a mistake.

He opened the door and walked in, leaving her standing in the doorway as he turned on the dim ceiling light. Soma flinched when she saw the one dismal room. Her eyes quickly scanned what was little more than a cubicle, attempting to latch on to something engaging, some object worthy of her attention, anything that might mask her visible distress and quell the rising flurry in her stomach.

"Are you just going to stand there?" he observed flatly. He turned to face her and flung his jacket on the bed. On the faded smoke-smudged wall hung a framed print of a man playing a horn.

"Interesting," she commented, walking closer to study it, wishing with each step that she had never come to this desolate room. Mortified that she was there. She feigned engrossment with the work, tracing the horn's profile with her fingers, buying herself time for composure. "Where did you get this?"

"Hell, I don't know," he said, dismissing her question as she had already dismissed him. The casket of a room, a dirty beige, was nonetheless tidy. A chifferobe stood in the corner, almost as high as the ceiling itself. And beside it a shorter one with a portable TV and hot plate on top. The TV had antennas so large they seemed to stretch, to grope even beyond the room, as if in a desperate attempt to tune in to something live. The bed, a simple double mattress covered by a yellow chenille spread, took up over three quarters of the room. The bed was made. Soma sat in the one chair, next to the bed, in front of the half-opened, screenless window. She turned and looked into the courtyard, hoping for a slight breeze that might redeem the room and the night . . . salvaging her pride . . . but only heard a neighbor clanging pots. A white woman across the way, two floors up, slammed the window shut and yanked closed her red curtains when she caught Soma staring. Soma counted the number of windows with lights. Three. Three out of dozens, hundreds, maybe. She couldn't imagine a room such as this, infinitely replicated throughout the building. She sat very still, afraid that if she moved the hot, stagnant air would rub off on her.

Emmett piddled around, moving things with no place to go, apologizing with his body for her discomfort. "This isn't what I'm used to. It's just temporary." He paused. "Why am I apologizing? Do I need to?" he demanded.

Soma felt herself caught. Caught between the contempt in his voice and her reluctance to be compromised—ensnared by the torment she recognized in his desperate eyes and her own guilt, which he could surely see sprawled across her face.

"No." She sighed, shaking her head more vigorously than she'd intended. "There's no reason to apologize."

He lifts her hands, pulling her to him, unaware she fled her body when she entered the room, leaving only an empty carcass. A malleable one, nonetheless, that shudders when kissed. He pushes back the hair that has fallen into her eyes, damp from the humidity. Then pulls her to the bed and plasters her mouth with wet kisses. She returns them, pressing her lips tightly to his to avoid his slobber. His hands quickly find her breasts and he kisses them through her shirt. She wonders whether he will leave a stain on her silk tunic. His fingers reach for her belt, but he can't unfasten it. He needs her to help. She resents having to.

Her eyes close. Perhaps if she is still enough. If she concentrates hard she can make the room disappear. She looks at the lusterless spiral of light on the ceiling. It too is yellow, like the dingy carpet that hasn't been cleaned in years.

Now he peels off her top and unsnaps the bra, beginning the ritual of seduction, an ancient but familiar chant. He tells her how he will make her feel. She winces at the crude rhapsody. The dead yellow air has finally covered her, and she now surrenders to the room. She has decided. She will not see him again. The words "pussy" and "lick" decided his fate. He stares at her eyes and she looks deeply into his. There she sees the flicker of life that threatens to die leaving more waxed droppings to harden, like everything else in the room. She tries to shake off the yellow, while listening to him beg. He struggles to seduce her with words. She hears only tin cups. He whispers impatiently, "I love you." At that declaration she returns to her body.

"Stop it! Don't say stupid things!" But in the few moments she returns to the carcass, she notices the wetness between her thighs and a small stir almost forgotten. The sensation startles her.

"Do you have any protection?" she asks.

He nods.

"Then let me change."

He offers a robe. She asks for the bathroom.

He points to the door. "Down the hall, second room on the left."

Numbly she stumbles toward the bathroom with its blue tile and strong white light. She stops in the hallway briefly and touches the barred windows overlooking Central Park before continuing. It's fresher than his room, she thinks, and breathes deeply, the first voluntary breath since she arrived. She flushes the toilet and watches the water spiral down the basin, observes herself in the dingy mirror, and puzzles over her face: Is it the same one she woke up with this morning? Are they the same eyes she painted just this evening? She wonders what her little investment analyst is doing tonight and fingers the turquoise stones in Marcy's earrings. She regrets having ridiculed her for going to a bridge party. They must be home by now, tucked in the comfort of their bedroom. She pulls his kimono from the plastic cleaning bag and slowly wraps it around her body. It feels smooth and cool against her skin.

She walks back to the stuffy room. The boom box is tuned to the jazz station. He has stripped and pats beside him her place on the bed. His slovenly kisses smother her mouth, and she retreats. She feels the cool tip of his tongue on her breast, leaving it slightly chilled, the nipple erect. The stubble of his evening shadow scratches her as his head moves to her belly, and she wonders why she worried earlier that he might notice the small mound of fat there. His kisses travel lower, and she, anxious that she has lost the capacity to be stirred, pushes forward. His kisses leave no burning trail, no seared flesh. But eventually she responds to the repetitious sensation, although the pleasure has not yet reached her head. Her body says yes. Her mind, though, is still yellow.

She watches now and counts the seconds till he enters her. She holds her breath. He holds his penis, out of breath, before plunging it into her. He begins to move. She moves with him. He doesn't realize he's fucking a carcass. She focuses on the yellow light coiled around them, ignoring the fly buzzing over her head.

GARRETT McDOWELL

Stones tilting
at kaleidoscopic angles,
shattering colors.

—Richard Ford, "City Glass"

1

The automatic doors swing shut as Milton skips down the post office steps and turns right, striding in the drizzling rain past shadows along the marble wall. He steps around a puddle and a man's hand jiggling change in a Styrofoam cup. Farther on he hears muffled talk and quickens his step.

"Don't be pushing me, sombitch!"

"You better go on, man."

"Humph! I don't have to be here. Even over 'cross the street I'm gon make more'n you."

"I don't give a damn, just move."

At the end of the wall Milton turns from a woman's voice—"Some change, sir?"—and waits at the corner for the light. His eyes narrow in the glare of headlights glancing off the wet asphalt and he watches the rain streak the beams of passing cars. He looks up across the street at the cloud-like mass of Union Station. Just as he once told Joanna, it's like a huge

GARRETT McDOWELL was born in Oklahoma City and raised in Los Angeles; he has traveled a tangled path abroad and across the country to finally arrive at living and writing in Washington, D.C., where his short fiction won an award in the 10th Annual Larry Neal Writers' Competition. He is a founding member of the Writers' Workshop of the African American Writers Guild and continues to be an active participant.

stone city beast, beheaded at the shoulders, but still sitting there towering as if it hadn't noticed.

Milton, gazing from the great vaulted roof down the front of the structure, suddenly sees a figure, a man, running from the tunnel and crossing the plaza to the street. The man stops at the curb and looks around, squeezing a shoulder bag under his arm. Then he dashes into the busy intersection, waving off with his free arm the onrushing cars and blaring horns, emerging on the other side where a bus is parked and loading passengers. It's the 96 bus that Milton wants to catch, if only the light will change. Caught without an umbrella, he's anxious to get home before the hard rain starts again.

Well, I'm not going to get run down trying to catch a bus, he thinks. The light turns green and he's stepping off the curb when a faint breeze moves and he feels a tugging at his sleeve.

"Please, sir," she says.

Milton tenses but turns to look at her. He can hardly see more than the eyes, they are so large and focused on his face. Even the taut lines of her cheeks point to the eyes, and the rain escaping the tangle of her matted hair runs into them. Her coat, drenched despite the shined-on dirt, hangs open showing a cutaway T-shirt above her pants and the bare shapeless waist that frames her navel. Damn, she probably turns tricks with this, he thinks.

"I can see you're a good man, sir. Please. A little money to help me feed my kids."

And this is her line, Milton thinks, and with his finger he pushes his glasses back to his brow. But he heard a Spanish accent in her voice and looks more closely at her face. Beneath smudged oiliness and dirt her skin is dark. A black Puerto Rican, he thinks, maybe in her early forties—except something about how she stands or wipes water from her temples makes him think she's younger than she looks. Then looking into her eyes again he shudders, finding that he's thinking of Joanna.

"Please, sir," she says. Now she is very close, with her breast touching his elbow. And he smells the sharp stale odor of her wetness like fingers up his nose. He hurriedly takes a fist of change from his pocket and puts it in her hand. Then with a grimace twisting on his face he rushes to catch his bus, loping across the splashy street and dodging in front of the headlights just as the bus starts from the corner. The bus hisses to a halt, and in the swath of windshield wipers the driver's face glares down at him. He jumps the wide stream running in the gutter and makes the curb. When he steps on, the folding doors close and the bus lurches forward.

"Naw, man. Naw, I'm not sellin nothin."

Three young toughs had the man pushed against the white tile wall.

"You a lie, mothafucka! I just saw you stoppin a dude."

"Naw. He was askin *me.* He was askin was I sellin. Naw, man."

Their voices were tense and loud, but smothered in the permeating noise of crowds beyond the passageway they occupied. The young men were contesting an arena of tables and chairs, with people sitting down or milling in the aisles, that sprawled through the underground expanse like city blocks in a bustling section of town. Here was the lowest ring of the Union Station mall, and where these men were thrown together, despite the people occasionally passing, was perhaps its quietest place. It was a short rear passageway shut off from blocks of tables by a section of wall on one side and an up escalator on the other. This escalator, though little used, was a way out through the cavernous opening of the lower ceiling to the upper rings, whose stylish balconies were visible from below. Across that sky of space, great lighted globes, like heavenly bodies suspended on metal rods, marked the threshold. And people above, pausing from the gleam of their fashionable shops and restaurants, occasionally looked down. Here, below, fast food counters of all kinds lined the outer walls—pizzas, burgers, sushi, fruit drinks, everything. And every counter had its lighted signs, like one announcing BANDOLERO SPECIALS, free sombreros with orders of triple tacos. Here in the arena, the mood reflected glitter and neon lights that bounced off the white tile walls with raw-color renderings of fruits and flowers and into the consciousness of people and their talk.

"The fucka's lyin. I been watchin him for twenty minutes checkin people out up and down the aisle."

"You tryin to cut in on our space, ain't you, sonofabitch."

"Naw, man. I didn't know. I didn't even know this was somebody's space."

"Don't give us that shit! Everybody knows that *here,* it's *us.*"

"Tell us who you with, mothafucka."

"Man, I'm not with anybody. Look, man, I just got in town, just got off the Amtrak from New York and came down here. I didn't mean no harm, didn't mean to cut in on nobody. I'm just in town to see my cousin."

"What's your cousin's name?"

"Pensacola. Pensacola Brown."

"What kind of fuckin name is that?"

"He's makin this shit up as he goes along."

"Naw, I'm not lyin, man. He lives on Tenth Street, Northeast."

"Come on, what kind of action you pushin, sonofabitch?" With his question he grabbed for the man's large shoulder bag.

"Hey, don't mess with my bag, man." Wrapping his arm around his bag, the man pulled back.

"Yeah, he's got somethin in there."

"Yeah, let's take this shithead out!"

"Look, man, I'm just down from New York and I don't want no trouble—"

Two of the men grabbed his arms and he started to struggle, until the third man raised the waist of his sweatshirt enough to show his piece. The three began forcing him out along the main aisle. On the left side the large archway opened onto blocks of people tending their fast food and chatter. On the right, beyond two opposite flights of spiral stairs, the main blocks of tables, thick with people, stretched out nearly the vast extent of the floor. And dividing the blocks, defined by planted partitions and white tile columns, the aisles were alive like busy side streets.

Now in the open, the man tried to draw attention.

"Naw, man, leave me alone!" He was shouting and trying to twist his arms from the two men's grip. But the third man, close behind, smashed his fist against the man's kidney.

"Don't try to loud-talk us, mothafucka. Straighten up!"

The man bent sideways in pain but tried to straighten himself. And in the din of people intent on their private amusements the men got only fleeting notice. Even people near them in the aisle passed without pausing a step.

Passing the down escalator and the schedule monitors overhead, the men now moved through the arena's broadway. In front of the color-lighted movie arcade of the Union Station 9 the varieties of life in the place projected a carnival air. A thick line of patrons waited to watch one of nine screened fantasies inside, while out front, beneath an array of glittering circles and one expansive sparkling chandelier, everywhere someone was watching the fantasies pass in people's faces. Everywhere someone was waiting for a familiar face, as if here, eventually, whomever you had in mind would come. And here was an arena for generations—couples pushing baby carts, roaming singles eager to connect, a few disheveled middle-aged souls whose homes might have been the frayed clothes on their backs, and brash young teens on every corner playing their laughing games and rituals. In faces young and old the eyes said this was a classroom of choice.

The men now approached the long west corridor leading on one end to the next level up by escalator and, on the other, to the Metrorail through automatic doors.

"Brooks, we got this fucka," one of them said. "You go and bring around the van."

The third man stepped from behind and grabbed the man's arm and Brooks walked ahead to the escalators. As he got there, for an instant he stopped short. When he stepped on, two policemen stepped off. Once past them he turned and signaled to his friends.

"Aw, shit, there's the heat!"

The man felt them ease their grip on his arms and took his chance.

"Hey, man! I ain't bothering you, leave me alone!"

The officers looked up and started toward them.

"What's going on here?"

The man pulled himself free and took off toward the Metro doors. He heard a policeman yell but didn't look to see if the officer was chasing him or one of the others. At full stride he slammed through the automatic doors. On the Metro side he quickly decided his chances were better on the street than on the train, so he turned up the Metro escalator, pushing by passengers, taking stairs by twos and threes. An elderly woman in his path looked back and stepped aside, just missing the sweep of his arm. He had run out across the plaza to Massachusetts Avenue before he wiped the light rain from his face and let himself look back. He was near the bus stops now and decided to take a bus, any bus. The only one around was pulling toward the stop diagonally across the intersection. He dodged through the oncoming traffic and waited to board behind a woman and her little girl. He took another look toward the Union Station tunnel to make sure no one followed.

Once he had stepped on and put change in the fare box he took a deep breath. He started to sit on a side seat in front but caught his nose and frowned at the shabby old man sitting there with his bearded chin on his chest.

"Damn, grandpaw!" he said, and turning away he walked to a seat in back.

3

At the corner of Florida Avenue and Seventh near the bus stop, a mild wind played in the paper debris around a lonely two-story building whose bricks were faded and chipped with weathering. Its doors and windows, mouths for tales it contained, were boarded up from galleries of addicts, vandalizing youths, and homeless squatters. Scraps of paper brushed the pavement and, skittering under the metal stairs in front, ran circles in a corner.

In the pattern of shadows from a streetlight shining through the iron-work of the stairs, an old man moved, disturbing newspapers he had arranged to cover his sleep. He opened his eyes and became aware of the glob of mucus hanging from his nose, which he wiped away with the back of his hand, then wiped his hand on a page of his covering. Twisting around to get comfortable again, he caught sight of two men standing at the bus stop. "Ice cream," he mouthed to himself in a raspy voice, and burst out laughing as he moved unsteadily out of his shelter and started toward them.

"Ice-cream cone. Heh-heh-heh."

"Aw, hell. Here comes Bobo," one of them said.

The old man went on talking, both to them and to himself.

"They think they already know, but it ain't so easy. Heh-heh. I did too. Thought I knew. Everybody think they know a killin when they see one. But you get fooled sometimes, heh-heh-heh. A vanilla ice-cream cone—and it melted all over my face. . . . But all I could see was that big black forty-five. And that thing wouldn't have hurt worth a damn!"

The old man bent over in a fit of laughing and coughing. Another man and a woman came to wait at the stop and eyed him warily.

"Go on now, Bobo," the first man said. "Just let that old tale rest awhile, that stuff you dream up. Nobody wants to keep hearing all that." He took some change from his pocket and handed it to him.

"Go on now and get yourself some ice cream."

The old man took the change, but his eyes got big and he didn't move.

"Naw. Naw, I got to tell you! I finally got it figured out. See, it didn't come from somethin big—wasn't just that ice-cream cone. It had to start before that. Must have come from somethin small. Heh-heh-heh, some small thing. And I figured out it must have been . . . when I first kissed my boss's ass. Heh-heh. That was first blood!"

"Now, Bobo, you want to respect this lady here."

"Kissed his ass! Kissed his ass! Everybody takes a smack once in a while. Yeah! And the first time I laughed at the bastard's stupid joke, the juice was leavin me. Ha! Sprung a leak and that was that!"

"Bobo, just go, will you?"

"Huh? You think you can't get killed? Kissin your boss's ass and can't get blown away? You think that? Yeah? I was set too! Me and the wife." He was waving his arms now and trying to get his feet to do a jig.

"Had it all set up—the house, the cars, the stocks, all them things. Had so many things, so many things that . . . I couldn't see killin sittin right in my face—and that goddamn ice cream . . ." The old man's gestures had swung him around, but he kept talking, as if the building heard his words.

"If she just hadn't woke me up . . . I could still be sleepin—right now, sleepin. . . . But that's what she did, and I opened my eyes and white was everywhere, glistenin, shinin. I'd never seen a face so white before, dead white, right there in our bedroom, and the biggest piece I'd ever seen, pointin, wavin. He had some of them things under his arm, but that grin was on his face, and *Git out of bed,* he was sayin to me, *but leave her there,* he said. Unh-uh! Naw! I just couldn't do that, just couldn't do it." The old man was shaking his head, swinging one arm behind to protect his wife and holding up the other to ward off the man's attack.

" 'Man, just take the money and whatever you want and leave us be— just leave us be, leave us be. . . .' " The old man had sunk to his knees, and tears mixed with the grime on his face and wet his scraggly gray beard.

"But naw. He had this grin on his face and the tip of his tongue out one side of his mouth. *Aw, you a brave fucker, ain'tcha*—that's what he said. . . . He called me brave. And he put down them things and went and sat on the chair in front of my wife's dressin table, and *Now you come over here,* he said, and when I didn't the muzzle of his piece, with barely a sound, shot sparks, and I saw where the bullet tore cotton in the mattress. And when I looked again and saw how wild his eyes were, like he was high on somethin strong, I got up. 'Man, we've got some money in the house. I'll show you. Take it all, and just leave us—' and sparks spat out again and hummed past my ear and shattered the picture on the wall be-hind me, and *Git your ass over here or I'm gonna quit missin!* And when I came up to him all I could see was that big forty-five, and he grabbed my pajama front and pulled me to my knees between his legs, and in the mirror I could see the vase of roses I'd brought my wife the day before and her crouchin in the bed with her hands up to her face and horror in her eyes. And he had this forty-five in my face and was zippin down his fly, and he says to her, *It's all right, missy. Your man do good here, you don't need to worry none. It's all right, missy,* he's sayin, and with his hand he's pullin my head onto him, and I'm tryin to—tryin not to vomit, tryin to imagine, to pretend . . . a vanilla ice-cream cone. . . ."

The old man was doubled over on the sidewalk, sobbing and wheezing air through his congested passages. Slowly he turned back to the bus stop. But the bus had come and the people were gone. He gathered himself up and after a moment was talking again to the building, or to whatever elements would listen.

"And it melted all over my face. Heh-heh-heh. And it melted—and he made me . . . I had to . . . swallow it. . . ."

He was now hunched over on the metal steps, his arms holding tightly to himself, trying to squeeze from his threadbare coat whatever warmth he could.

". . . forty-five wouldn't have hurt worth a damn. . . . Naw. . . . It don't come from somethin big . . . it's somethin small. . . ."

The old man dozed in a fitful sleep but soon was awakened by the chill of rain on his neck. It had started to come down hard and he saw water running under the steps of his shelter. He started down the street to find a dry doorway but changed his mind when the 96 bus pulled up. He was fumbling in his pocket for some change as he stepped on, out of the downpour.

4

Milton chuckles, relieved to catch his bus.

"Thanks for waiting," he says.

The driver glances at him. "All right, sir," she says, "but you don't want to be running in front of the bus like that."

There's that word again, *sir*, Milton thinks. He's still not used to it. Of course the woman by the wall had used the term for her own purposes. But people increasingly say *sir* to him—as if he looks older than he feels. Sure, there's more gray on his face and less hair on his head. Maybe that, with his glasses, has people seeing him as an older professional who's due a certain deference. People might mean well, but hearing himself called *sir* always makes him cringe.

Milton had given that woman his change and now has none for the fare, so he fumbles for the folded bills in his coat pocket. Then he ticks his tongue, annoyed with himself that the smallest he has is a five, and that's more than he's willing to put in the fare box. The driver, eyeing him, sees his plight and they exchange wry smiles. I'll take a taxi after all, Milton thinks. It's another reason he and Joanna need another car, though they make too little to afford one anytime soon.

"Just let me off at the next stop," he says, and turns back toward the folding doors.

As the bus slows for the stop it occurs to him to check with other passengers.

"Anybody got five bills?" he shouts toward the back.

The few scattered passengers just stare at him—the woman sitting across from the driver's seat, who seems to be keeping the driver company; the young mother with her hair in cornrows, sitting halfway back beside her baby daughter; the teen-aged couple farther back on the opposite side, too preoccupied with each other to take much notice; and two young men in the back, one on a rear side seat with a blank look on his face, the man Milton had seen running for the bus, and the other in the last rear seat on the left, bobbing his head to his Walkman music. On the side seat in front across from the woman, an old man sits squat and wide with his dirt-stiff coat pulled loosely around him. Milton notices his scraggly gray beard is blotched with crusted saliva and food. The old man's eyes are closed and his chin is resting on his chest. He breathes heavily as in a stupor, looking and smelling like a rotten stump.

Milton turns again toward the folding doors and starts to get off, when the man in the rear side seat speaks up.

"Hey, man. Yeah, I got it."

"Ah, great!" Milton says. And with a nod from the driver, he walks back to the man as the bus starts up again, getting out his five-dollar bill.

The man is rummaging through the large shoulder bag on the seat beside him. He holds out his hand and Milton gives him the five as he looks for the change. Then he motions with his head.

"Sit down a minute."

Milton sits across the aisle on the seat opposite him. He smiles, wondering if the NEW YORK across the man's designer sweatshirt says anything about where he's from. The man is maybe twenty-two, about the age of Milton's nephew, and looks big enough to have played football as his nephew had. His hair is cut in the fade style popular with young men nowadays, with a clump of hair at the neckline like the tuft, the *coleta*, of a matador. Milton suddenly remembers a bullfight he witnessed at about this man's age. He and some friends were down from UCLA on a Sunday afternoon in a Tijuana bull ring and he sat transfixed with tears in his eyes as the matador was gored bloody by the bull and was carried off by his helpers, but fought with them to take the cape and face the horns again, and made even more daring passes, acting with such abandon as to be possessed, compelled to make that single moment with the bull, that survival or death in the arena, the value of his life.

At the sound of the little girl's voice, Milton looks around and sees the mother laughing and sitting down between her daughter's straddled legs. The little girl has pleaded, "Come on, Mommy, now you sit in my lap." And now she happily spreads her short arms as far as she can across the back of her big new baby.

When Milton turns back, the man is holding out to him a wrinkled Metrobus pass.

"Take this and show it to the driver," he says.

"What?"

"Show this to the driver and then I'll give you four bucks."

Milton hesitates, then takes the card and looks at it. This guy wants the dollar I'd pay the Metro, he thinks. He has no problem with that except he isn't sure the driver will buy it.

Milton chuckles. "Look, I wouldn't mind but I don't know whether you can transfer these things."

The man says, "Just take it and show it to the driver."

"No, the driver's looking in her mirror at us. Better just let me have the five bills." And Milton holds out the man's pass card.

The man insists. "Just show the damn card to—"

The bus goes sharply around a corner, and before the man can grab it, his bag falls heavily off the seat and spills onto the floor.

"Goddamn it! Fuck!" The man squats down, trying to keep his balance and get his stuff back in the bag. Milton gets up to help but the man waves him off. Apart from a cloth-wrapped bundle sticking partly out of the bag and a few coins and ballpoints, most of what spilled is assorted papers, like batches of receipts. The man doesn't look like a student, and Milton has noticed his gold watch and the gold on most of his fingers. Milton wonders how the man gets his money, but decides he can't really know and it doesn't matter anyway. The man picks up the last coins and tosses them into the bag. He sits back down with a huff.

Milton looks at him and smiles. "Here, take your card and give me the five bills and we're straight."

"Man, just show the driver the card. Show her the card!"

Milton begins to see this isn't going to work at all. "Okay, here's your card. Just give me back my five."

"Naw, I'm not takin the card. Go on, show it to the driver. I'm not takin back the card." The man turns away with the five-dollar bill in his fist and settles in his seat as if this is the end of the matter. Reflections from the passing traffic make his face a dull, irregular neon light.

Milton looks at him and blinks. Then he lets out a voiceless laugh and looks around in a gesture of disbelief. He sees the driver's face, visible but impassive in the rearview mirror, and the other passengers have gone quiet, pretending not to hear what's going on. The woman has stopped playing with her daughter and has sat beside her again. But the shabby old man has raised his head, and his dark hollow eyes, with a look of tense remembering, are fixed on Milton's.

Turning back to the man, Milton chuckles and tilts his head to the side for emphasis.

"Man, are you just going to keep my five-dollar bill?" He says it to show the man, as well as himself, how ridiculous the situation has become.

The man doesn't look at him. "Yeah, I'm keepin this. I need it to get home."

The words send silence through the bus, so that even the sounds of the grinding engine and the rattles and bumps of cutting through the rainy street go mute. The quiet almost covers the sound from the fellow in the rear corner seat, who has taken off his earphones and sharply sucks in air as if the man's remark has burned his ears.

The smile wilts on Milton's face and begins to wrinkle into an awful realization. The atmosphere thickens, as if the man's sucking in air has pulled in the elements from outside and they hang heavy like a hand pressed on the body. A presence is moving in the space, perhaps some spirit truth whose habit is to choose any moment, including the ridiculous, to reveal itself. Milton is almost sorry he asked the question, because the answer removes all ambiguity. His mind floods with awareness that moves like an urge: This man wants my death—as if I'm now so old that children take my money and dismiss me on a whim . . . to kill me to *myself* . . . and kill me to my wife! Because Joanna will *know*. Like that woman by the wall, she's got deep eyes and she'll see, and I'll have no face to show her. I see her face sagging at the sight of me and feel her shoulder shrugging from my touch, and when I lie beside her shriveled upon her naked leg, too weak even to reach into the willing nurture of her body, she wearily turns from me onto her side and, even before my eyes are closed, snaps off the light. Can this man know the void he's forced us to, where it could lead? Does he care? Maybe he wants his own death too. Or maybe in that bag he's got a knife, a gun, and feels immune. A dread sweeps through Milton's head, unformed in words or thoughts, and his mind whirls like a molten rush of instinct.

With a lurch of the bus Milton finds he is standing over the man, balanced with one knee pressed against the seat and the other hard against the man's leg. He has the eerie helpless feeling of a spectator observing from above, as from a grandstand seat. And he's amazed that despite the rage that shakes his body his face is calm. But his voice is almost visible in the air.

"Here, take your card."

The man glances up at him and takes the card, then looks away.

"Now, you give me my five-dollar bill."

The man jerks back to face him—and hesitates. The bull moves his eyes from the *muleta* twitching in his face to the eyes of the matador, thinking which way to toss his deadly head. Perhaps the man sees playing in Milton's eyes the colors of streetlights flashing beyond the rain-streaked windows; perhaps he distinguishes in that kaleidoscopic universe, beyond what even Milton is aware, the glinting point of the matador's sword that would thrust into his future. And with a small jump of his head he blinks, shifting from another realm, and loosens, like the opening of a rose, his clenched fist.

At the next stop when Milton steps off the bus, the old man stumbles after him. The old man's eyes, now glittering dark pools, stay fixed on Milton. For a moment Milton stops, looking sideways at him through the drizzle. Then, pushing the crumpled five into the old man's hand, he turns and walks on.

Oda Rainbow

J. R. McKIE

She opened her eyes and thought, Hawaii. Instead, Oda was lying in her bed at home. She'd fallen asleep again on the telephone. (The forlorn receiver lay next to her, buzzing on and off like an all-night car alarm.)

"Umph, I reckon I went to sleep on somebody."

She hung up the phone and lay still, pondering the rays of light (morning?) blasting through her curtains. Her bed felt good, warm, cozy, embryonic. But her stomach urged her to action, crying out for a portion of breakfast grits and coffee. I'm hungry, she thought, but kinda tired, too.

Using most of her strength, she pushed herself up to a sitting position and rested her back against the headboard. Her teeth smiled at her from a water glass on the end table. "Naw. I don't need y'all for grits and coffee. I'll put y'all in later."

Then, grunting with effort, she threw the covers back and urged her legs off the side of the old bed. "Lord have mercy, it sho' is hard to get up." Barely standing, she felt somewhat dizzy. But her spirits were high,

J. R. McKIE's work has appeared in a number of literary journals. His fiction combines funky verisimilitude with poetic lyricism. He was raised in St. Louis, Missouri, he graduated from the University of Missouri in Columbia, and he now teaches at LaGuardia College and New York University.

and after a momentary pause, she straightened her nightgown and ambled (for the 6,374,341st time) down the hall toward her kitchen.

Ri-iiing! "Oooo, Lord!" she gasped, holding the wall for support. "Who is that?" In a few difficult steps, she was at the telephone on her kitchen wall. "Hello?"

A voice came to her from a seeming far distance: "Hi, Grandma! What you doin'?"

And then, suddenly, "Mama? That you? Get off the phone, Leticia! Mama?"

"Yes," answered Oda, "it's me."

"Hi."

"Well, hello. Where are you?"

"At the house," said Cora.

"We goin' shoppin', Grandma. Downtown!"

"Leticia, I told you to hang up."

"What you want her to hang up for? I might go downtown myself."

"See? That's exactly why I'm tellin' her to get off the phone."

"Why?" asked Oda.

" 'Cause she got it all wrong. We not even goin' downtown; we goin' to the mall."

"The maw?"

"The mall, Mama. The shopping mall, out in the county."

"Well . . . whatever it is."

"You want to come, Grandma?"

"Leticia! . . ."

"Naw, sweetheart. I ain't particular 'bout . . . I just ain't like your mother."

"Meanin' what?" said Cora.

"You know what I'm talkin' 'bout."

"Mama, white folks shop everywhere."

"Not downtown, they don't."

"Yes, they do, too. They all movin' back to the city now, buyin' condos."

"Kon-doze?"

"Big apartments, Mama. Never mind. Anyway, what you goin' downtown for?"

"Yeah, where you goin', Grandma?"

"Hang up, Leticia."

" 'Cause. I need me some money out the bank."

Cora's eyes shot to the ceiling. "Mama, please don't take any more money out the bank."

"It's mine, ain't it?"

"I know it's yours." Cora's voice was tense, strident: "That's not the point."

"Yes it is, too, the point."

"Mama. . . ."

"That's all right, now. You just listen to me—"

"All right, Mama, never mind. We have to go."

"Well, you just go 'head on, then. And stay outa my money affairs." And Oda hung up. Hard.

Her kitchen was done in red and white, but the years had coated everything with stratified layers of time and use, so the colors now appeared dull and matte. Yet to Oda everything was crimson electric, heat-white, and wildly abuzz. The cabinets and table hummed and wavered like dense, permanent mirages, constantly re-creating, yet old like Oda herself.

"Grits," she whispered, "and some coffee. Too bad Art Linkladder and them kids ain't on the radio no more. (Are they?) And Lucy, neither. Jack Benny and Rod-chester, too. Liberachee. Groucho Marx. Ain't nothin' good on."

Oda sat heavily at the wooden kitchen table by the window and sniffed the warm smells from her grits and coffee. Just before, she had used her largest spoon to scrape breakfast from the pot's charred bottom. Like always, she had burned the grits, but no one else was there, so in reality they weren't burned at all. They were, as always, good.

"No butter, Oda. I mean it." Leaning casually against a cabinet, Abe Silverstein peered authoritatively over the cut-off rims of his bifocals. His white lab coat was immaculate, his clothes tailored and distinctive.

"Dr. Sillstine, you don't have to worry 'bout that. I don't even want no butter."

"Good," he said. And thus satisfied, Dr. Silverstein, Oda's physician for many years, instantly disappeared and presumably returned to his swank, calm offices. (Some would maintain, if asked, that he'd never left.)

Previous to all of this, Oda had turned from the wall phone (still vibrating from the abrupt termination of Cora's call); veered to the cabinet; removed the grits, coffee, pot, and bowl; scrubbed a few of the encrusted, stacked-up dishes in her sink; and prepared her perennial breakfast.

Throughout, she felt flip-flopped, somehow immersed in a backward logic, her present move slipping impossibly into a staggered past and, of course, vice versa.

Suddenly, too loudly, the insistent rapping of someone's knuckles on her front door startled Oda, interrupting her disorientation. Who is it? she wondered, perturbed also at the interruption of her favorite meal.

The knock sounded again, and this time Oda attempted a rise to answer. But she quickly thought better of the notion and said to herself, "Naw. I'm eatin'."

Then followed a whole succession of bangings, raps, and pounding keys against the front door. Oda was by now thoroughly riled, and so she managed to rise from her table and head quite rapidly down the long hall toward the front of her house.

Passing the bathroom, she was halted by the sight of the open door. And inside, Mr. Cox (Oda's husband) languished easily in a tub of hot water. His head—oddly adorned with Oda's ornate, feline eyeglasses—was tilted back. Beneath the thick lenses his eyes were closed, and his arms floated out in front of him. He seemed totally at peace, eternally preserved.

"I told you not to put on my glasses," said Oda, "and close the door if you gon' be in there nekid like that." Then, slamming the door, she screamed toward the front, "Who is it!"

"It's me," a muffled voice answered. "Open this door, girl."

"Me? Who is me?"

"Oda, open the door, child. It's Pauline."

"Pauline?" Oda's voice was somewhere between tentativeness and high irritation.

"Yes, girl. I got somethin' for you."

Arriving at last at the door, Oda required several moments to negotiate the heavy, high security lock she'd had installed.

"Hurry up, girl. What you doin'?"

As Oda opened the door, a whirlwind of perfume and rustling paper bags—swirling all about a large, bowlegged woman—swept past her.

"I thought you wasn't home at first."

"If you thought that, you woulda left."

"I was gettin' ready to," said Pauline, waddling up the stairs. "And put your teeth in, girl. You got company."

"Shuh . . . you ain't no company."

"Well, if you gon' be evil today—"

"Listen, Pauline, I was eatin' my breakfast, and I'm hungry. And you start to knockin' hard on my door makin' all kindsa noise and not sayin' who you was."

"I told you it was me."

"Well, you didn't talk loud enough."

"What's wrong with you, girl?"

Oda's face took on a pained expression. "I get tired a goin' up and down these steps. And I got to go out later as it is."

But Pauline was no longer listening. Instead, she strode confidently into the living room, deliberately and slowly taking in the scope of Oda's life. "Girl, why don't you get somebody up here to clean up?"

"If you want to use the bathroom, Pauline, you can't."

"Ain't nobody said nothin' about no—wait a minute. How come I can't use it?"

"Never mind," said Oda. "I got to go to the kitchen."

"Wait a minute, child. You ain't talkin' 'bout Mr. Cox again . . ."

"I'm cookin' Pauline."

". . . 'cause that man is dead, Oda. He gone."

At that, without further word, Oda spun around and disappeared down the hall toward her kitchen.

Immediately, like a TV detective, Pauline perused the room, mentally noting the location of every object and its possible implications.

As for Oda, she once again passed the bathroom; and as she did, the full-blown sounds of church, in service, lapped at her ears and spirit.

"I'll be back there in a minute!" Pauline called toward the kitchen. "They left some mail for you at my house."

Suddenly, almost impossibly, Oda stood once again at the entrance to the living room. "Ain't nobody left no mail for me at your house."

Pauline was taken aback by Oda's quick reappearance (caught, so to speak), but she managed to say, "Then how come I got these letters with me, then? And this here look like a check."

"You got 'em out my mailbox, that's how come they with you."

Pauline was silent, stunned this time by Oda's quick, accurate assessment.

"And let me tell you another thing," Oda continued, "nobody don't have to tell me when Mr. Cox died." And again, she was off down the hall.

"Well, I was just tryin' to do you a favor." Like a penitent child, Pauline's voice followed Oda down the hall, begging to be heeded and believed. And yet, even as she lied, Pauline again turned to the living room and began her search: flipping pillows, peering beneath lamps, leafing quickly through scattered books and magazines, searching along windowsills and under furniture. But she could find no trace this time of a cloistered, hidden bill. (Last week she'd found a long-forgotten twenty, pinned inside a lampshade.)

Just then, quietly and slowly, the hallway door from Oda's basement creaked open just enough to admit a slight, short figure dressed in green. Oda stood facing away, staring off through the kitchen window in the general direction of Sears.

The visitor paused a moment, noticing the shape of Oda's back and the smooth, graceful bend of her elbow. He saw in the old woman a beauty and humor that caused him to laugh softly.

Oda spun quickly around—"Who is that?" But she needed her glasses to see (the ones Mr. Cox had on in the tub).

"Are you ready?" said the visitor.

Her voice was tremulous: "Ready? Ready for what?"

"Pasadena, the Rose Bowl."

Funny, but after an immediate wave of startlement, Oda felt a warm and complete rapport with her strange and unexpected visitor, a sense from the cells and atoms of her body that he meant no harm. And so her voice was the voice of curiosity, amazement, not fear: "The Rose Bowl?"

"Girl, who you talkin' to?" Pauline made her way down the hallway and stopped two feet from the man in green.

Oda started to answer, but the visitor brought a gnarled finger to his lips and shushed her response. A pause, and then: "Nobody," said Oda. "You want some coffee?"

Standing (uncomprehended) right next to Pauline, the visitor began a series of movements, something like a weird dance, and then laughed uproariously, pointing all the time at Pauline. Against her halfhearted desire not to, Oda felt tickled, and visibly succumbed to an irresistible lightness and humor. It was funny.

But Pauline was perplexed and thus peered intently at Oda. "Is somethin' wrong, girl?"

"With what? I just asked if you want some coffee."

"Well . . . what is it, instant?"

"It's free," said Oda, turning serious. "You want some or not?"

"Fine." Pauline stared but tried not to.

"What you lookin' at, Pauline?"

"Nothin'. You just seem to be actin' strange, that's all."

Oda drank her coffee, making no move to prepare a cup for Pauline.

"Really, Oda, how come the bathroom door is closed?"

Again, the visitor stopped Oda. He silently (and clearly) told her not to repeat that Mr. Cox was in the bathroom and that now church service was also being held there. It was strange, but somehow Oda and the visitor were friends, bound by a new irony, the sole initiates of a dyadic Religion of Laughter. And in the grip of their secret ecstasy, the spirit-happy visitor bugged. He fell to the floor, pointing at Pauline and falling out, "Ask her . . . ask her about the money."

"What you lookin' at, Oda?" asked Pauline, glancing quizzically about her but seeing nothing in the direction of Oda's gaze.

"Pauline," said Oda, "why don't you just ask me for some money?" The visitor and Oda both laughed.

"Money?"

"Yeah, you know . . . money." More laughter.

"Girl, what are you talkin' about?"

"I'm talkin' about how you tore up my front room just now lookin' for my money."

"Wh . . ." Pauline slipped and stumbled for an explanation, "I didn't tear up nothin'. Besides that, if—uh, if I want somethin', I know how to just ask for it."

Right at Pauline's feet, the visitor rolled over and over, pounding the floor, holding his stomach, and kicking his legs in laughter.

Then—irrepressibly and against her will—short, strong guffaws tore between Oda's cupped hands, and finally she succumbed (like the visitor) to a complete and total bug-out on the floor.

Pauline was livid. "Well, I don't know what's so damn funny! It's your own fault, anyway." Her hands were on her hips now, her feet spread apart, her head twisting tortuously from side to side. "You got too much money for you own damn good. You don't even know where it's at around the house. That proves it's too much, right there. Quit laughin'! You ain't nothin' but senile, heffer!"

And thus, Oda's last glimpse of Pauline: from the rear, waddling rapidly away, totally insulted, bowling herself furiously down the hall toward the front door.

Oda's favorite dress was from Bergdorf Goodman. But she had long ago lost the matching belt, and now she played it with a makeshift hookup of half-braided wrapping yarn and safety pins; nevertheless, she still had the contrasting scarf, and this—as far as Oda was concerned—would offset any gaucheries inherent in the raw, untailored belt.

As she dressed for downtown, Oda would fall back, without warning, into her earlier laughing fit, and then her preparations would slow. Fine, though; she enjoyed laughing at Pauline's ignorant expense.

There was, however, serious effort involved in making sure all her documents and keys were in place. Let's see—front door key, senior citizen's bus pass, bankbook (have to take that), handkerchief, breath mints, keys (already got that), checkbook (need that, too), passport . . . what else?

At last it was time to catch the bus downtown.

Outside, the sky was gray, what many would call a bad day. Oda, though, felt a kinship with the weather. The humidity in the air was good. The muted colors and muffled sounds were pleasing and easy to hear. Cars, moving slowly past her on the street, left behind soft *whoosh*ing whispers from their tires. These tickled Oda's ears and nearly made her legs jam closed in pleasure.

And so her steps, though slow to watch, were fun-filled and exciting. Her world that day was large, amplified, blasted past the usual. As she walked, she reminisced in brief flashes, reliving one moment and then suddenly another, each image strangely compressed, yet complete, occupying time in a shared all-at-once way. These memories, these replay visions, should have bled into one another—but they didn't. Crazily, many things happened at once, but they all happened.

"Watch out!" shouted Mr. Davis from across the street. His sudden warning, when it reached Oda, brought her to an immediate, startled halt.

Quickly, she darted her eyes in all directions to spot the alarm, but when Mr. Davis doubled over and grabbed a tree for support, she knew that once again she'd fallen for his geriatric immaturity.

Oda turned toward him and shook a slender, brown finger. "You think that's funny, mister?"

Davis laughed. "What's wrong? Somebody after you?"

"You ole jackass," she muttered. But privately, to herself, she smiled. Old Davis'd got her again.

At the corner she peered westward, straining to make out the approaching shape of her bus. Oda had trouble seeing things far off and often mistook even large objects to be something else. But, being Oda, she considered her sight to be good. And just as she'd thought, her eyes had correctly spotted the B-48 local downtown. It approached slowly, moving in and out of view as it slalomed its laborious way along Page Boulevard until finally, like a leaning leviathan, it veered toward Oda at the curb.

Then, stopping directly in front of her soft, squinting eyes, it hissed gently, dipped in her direction, and pulled back its folding, blue-and-white doors.

Moments later, Oda was jolted from the odd, prescribed feeling she got from the plastic-molded, ergonomic seats.

"Ma'am!" called the fortyish driver toward her. "May I see your pass?"

Oda's lips stretched tightly around her face. "I showed you my pass."

"No, you didn't." The driver seemed definite, immutable.

"Well. . . ." Oda began fumbling through her purse.

Instantly, the other passengers became impatient, irritable. Much sighing and shifting of rear ends accompanied Oda's noisy, uneasy search; yet the driver remained inert, his hand resting solidly on the hi-tech electronic coin box to his right. Moments grew dense.

"Come on, man. Let's go," said someone near the front.

"Tell *her* that," spit the driver, jerking his head in Oda's direction.

"I'll pay the fare," offered a well-dressed woman. "I have to get to work."

"Naw, you ain't gon' pay it, neither," said Oda. "I rides the bus for free. I got a pass." And she returned earnestly to her hunt for the senior citizen's pass.

Everyone turned away and made a fresh attempt at waiting, but the driver then began tapping on the coin box.

"You can hit on that thang all you want," said Oda, "but I'm ridin' this bus. Here, here it is." She took hold of the wrinkled pass and held it up.

The driver glanced back, then paused. "I can't see it from there."

In a quick, snappy motion, Oda returned the pass to her purse and settled resolutely in her seat. "Well, you better get to walkin' back here—or drivin', one."

"We can sit here all day as far as I'm concerned," said the driver. Then he leaned back and folded his arms across his chest.

"Sho' can," said Oda, turning away and instantly losing herself through the tinted, panoramic window.

A winding, dusty road wound past shacks of weathered planks flanked by rotted, brittle farm tools. Suddenly, everything went white. The shacks became leaning trapezoids against a spread of whiteness. White-sprinkled forests all around. A snow sight.

And then—as suddenly again—it was hot. Someone sang from behind Oda. It was a childhood song, barely beneath recall, a refrain about a child and a tree.

From nowhere, a large, screaming crow flew straight for Oda's head—"Go to town! Go to town!"

Just before that, the sky had taken on an orange tint, then shifted rapidly from purple to gold to green.

And all along, the wagon—which switched from time to time to a taxi and then back again—moved onward with the help of strange people whom Oda didn't quite know. But like heaving canal horses, they pulled at taut ropes stretching from the sides of the wagon, moving it along a magical path.

Throughout, a distinct breeze blew, bearing with it diverse, subtle fragrances that changed arrhythmically, marking in turn continuous shifts in temperature—hot, tropical rushes to crisp fall-like gusts. Voices (new, yet known) rolled around her head; they sang sometimes and spoke, too, in whispers and then in quick, sharp shouts. "Oda!" they called. "Cotton candy. Your sisters. Come on!"

"Come on!" yelled a scowling passenger. "She got the thing. Why she got to walk up there with it?"

" 'Cause I got to see it," the driver barked.

"Well, then, carry your motherfuckin' ass back there and look at it!" shouted a stocky, serious kid. Standing up, he started toward the front of the bus.

"What are you doin'?" cried the driver, urgency and apprehension in his voice.

"I'll drive this motherfucker myself."

A chorus of support sounded.

"Yeah, that's right."

"Right on, let's go!"

"Damn skippy! Get this shit movin'."

Slowly, then, because he had to, the driver pulled the bus from the curb and lumbered into the wet, lazy stream of eastward, downtown traffic.

Oda enjoyed the trip. The rolling, hydraulic progress of the bus lulled her into a comfortable rest, her open eyes playing among shadows and contours hidden from others. Lingering images clustered for her at each corner and posed playfully along spiritual stretches of city street. Springing vividly and full-blown before her, these holoscenes depicted a fluid, phantasmagoric medley from Oda's life.

There, at Vandeventer and Sarah Avenues, she had trudged wearily through each day of the Depression to get cheese and peanut butter. Later, she had walked that same stretch, her load finally lightened by what they called a postwar boom.

At Franklin Avenue, rows of pawnshops and dangerous honky-tonks jumped noisily alive; but then, Oda quickly remembered they'd actually long since disappeared, yielding in time to pastel angular-looking buildings with brand-new old-fashioned streetlights in front. As the bus stopped to take on passengers, she noticed large red letters above a modern, well-lit storefront:

GASLIGHT CONDOMINIUMS

"Last stop!" called the driver. He turned and looked pointedly at Oda. "Everybody off."

Suddenly, Oda realized she was all the way downtown. That was fast, she thought. We here already?

On the street, she looked around, searching to gain her bearings. But what she gained instead was a singular realization: inexplicably, and against all odds, Cora had been right!

In small, scattered groups—and singly as well—clean-looking white folks (the kind Oda had seen in Europe) had invaded the Midwest. Were these the same crackers who had run panic-stricken to the suburbs when a few colored people had somehow bought some houses on the North Side?

They wore sculpted hairstyles now, mostly short but full on top and pompadourish. Everybody had on big leather coats, opulent shearlings, and sundry prestigious wraps. The men seemed to love wing-tipped shoes, but a lot of the women wore sneakers and little ankle socks over pantyhose.

The bank was a vaulted, landmark masterpiece. Inside, frescoes adorned the domed skylight: cherubs surrounded a pale, Rubenesque woman in a loosely fitting robe. Her free, rosy breasts rode prominently (yet modestly) before her, while chubby, naked cherubs entreated a muscular, god-type guy with a beard as he casually reclined upon a floating cloud chaise.

Yet, in all her life, Oda had never lifted her eyes to see this wonder. She was always all business at the bank.

Easily remembering the procedure for cashing checks, she moved in her usual direction, only to stop abruptly upon seeing three men ahead of her nod conspiratorially and reach into their coats. Right away, Oda could tell by their movements and rigid, tense postures that they meant to rob the bank.

What if they took all her money? How could she make the trip home flat broke? And who would pay her back for what the robbers took? No way. That's what happened to the banks in the Depression. When your money was gone, it was gone.

Oda didn't quite understand what she did next, but she did it. Walking toward the men in her usual manner, she took a place behind them in line and asked, "What y'all think ya doin'?"

The robbers looked stupidly at each other, then turned, all together, back to Oda. "Ma'am?" one of them stammered.

"You heard me. I said, 'What y'all gon' do in here?'"

Again, the three men searched one another and turned together toward Oda. "We're just conducting some bank business, lady. That's all."

Then, turning away, they laughed among themselves and said something about Oda she couldn't quite hear.

"Mister!" she called in a shrill, loud voice to a bank guard nearby. "Mister!"

"What are you doin', lady?" One of the robbers. Stocky. Mean-looking. Lumberjack cap.

By then, a rough-hewn guard was approaching. "What's the matter here?"

"Nothin'," said another of the three. "I think this lady's a little confused, that's all."

"You the one," said Oda. And then, looking steadfastly at the men before her, "Ask 'em what they talkin' about."

A pause followed; the guard's mind raced.

"Ask 'em what they got in them coats," said Oda.

By then, many eyes bore upon the tight knot of Oda, the guard, and the three men. No one spoke.

"Hey," said a short, pleasant-looking guy (Oda figured him for the smartest of the three), "this is gettin' crazy."

"Maybe you should all just rest your hands on your heads," said the guard, his own hand easing quietly onto his pistol. "Step away, lady."

But Oda didn't move. Instead, she stood still and watched as several other guards—and a bald-headed executive with a flower in his jacket—ran toward them. The guards pulled large pistols from their patent-leather holsters. Wide-eyed and out of breath, they all arrived at the same time.

"What'sa matter!" they shouted.

"What's goin' on?"

And then, as the bank posse slid to a halt several feet from the group, the bald-headed executive looked quizzically at one of the three robbers (the short, smart one), "Jerry . . . that you?"

"Stu! Tell these guys to take it easy, for chrissake!"

"He the ringleader," said Oda.

The executive took a jerky, deliberate look at the situation: the armed-and-ready guards, the three men touching their heads, and Oda. "Bill," he said tersely to the first guard, "what the hell's goin' on?"

Bill stiffened—"Sir?" His look was wary and confused.

"Stu," said the smart one, the leader, "could you tell 'em to put those guns away? Their hands are shakin'."

"Put 'em away," said Stu. "Put 'em away—it's all right." Nervously, the three men brought their hands down. Then Stu turned again to the first guard and spoke in a rising, anxious tone, "Bill?"

"You know these gentlemen, Mr. Rash?"

Stuart J. Rash III, president of First National Bank, waved his hand dismissively at the guard; then he turned imploringly toward Gerald A. Laclede, Jr., one of his largest depositors. "I'm sorry, Jerry."

The short man smiled easily now, wiping his hair back and slowly exhaling, "Hey, Stu." He grinned. "I've heard of a hard sell before, but this. . . ."

Rash crossed quickly to Jerry's side, smoothing his jacket, glancing quickly at the guard.

"It's okay, Stu." Jerry looked toward the guard. "This guy's just doin' his job."

"I apologize, Mr. Rash," said the guard, "and to you sir. You see, this lady—"

But Oda was gone. Impervious to the commotion in her wake, she had proceeded to the next available teller: a powdery, bleached trainee perched securely behind a bulletproof plastic window. "What was that all about?" the teller asked.

"Those men was robbin' the bank," said Oda, "and I called the *po*-lice on 'em."

Meanwhile, the chastened guard returned to his post as Mr. Rash gently ushered the other men toward his office.

"Forget it," said Jerry. "We needed a laugh, right guys?"

A ragged chorus of mixed chuckles and half-grunts sounded.

"All in a day's work," said the lumberjack.

"Stu, meet my head honcho, here. He's put up more condos for me than Carter's made liver pills."

The two men shook hands. "Nice to meet ya," said the president. "Jerry, why didn't you tell me you were comin'? You don't have to get in line."

"I didn't want to bother you with this. It's just a small check."

"Nonsense," said Mr. Rash. "Come on, I'll take care of it myself."

To Oda, their fading conversation was a low, indiscernible drone, background to the real world—the one in which she now took her money, turned, and left the bank.

On the street outside, she felt wonderful. Sunlight blasted the sides of buildings with a wild, white-golden light. Stark street shadows lurked among randomly buzzing, primary colors. Traffic—which had frightened Oda ever since a car plowed into her some-odd years ago—now sang to her vibrantly like a snaking, a cappella chorus. Even the noxious exhaust she breathed touched off lifetimes of sensory recall. She knew these goings-on; they were nice and familiar, strongly comfortable.

Later, walking along Bayard Avenue to her house, she felt once again that strange reversal of sequence. For her, it was in essence a cognitive dizziness, a déjà-vu blanket smothering each sensation with an eerie recognition. These were supranatural, redundant events. Experience without surprise.

Inside again, the familiar smells of her house and the orchestrated creaks and moans of her stairs sang a welcome to her return. She took them slowly, leaning against the wall three times for support on the way up. But near the top, where the stairs curved to the left, her ears caught the low tones of a hushed conversation. Someone was in the house.

"Who is it!" shouted Oda. "Who up there?"

Her answer was a quick silence, followed by a hurried shuffling of feet. And then a familiar voice: "Oda, I'm in the kitchen."

Wary and unsure, Oda nevertheless started toward the back. "Who is you?"

An unlikely sight greeted her. At the table, full of leisurely smiles, was the earlier visitor in green. "About time you got back, woman."

Oda glanced toward the hallway door. "Did I leave the door open?"

"Some doors stay open," he said, "no matter what you do."

"What you talkin' about?" she asked. Then she smiled. "What you want up here, anyway?"

"Actually," said the visitor, stretching, "I was thinking about a nap."

"A nap?"

"Aren't you tired from that trip downtown?"

And then, all at once, Oda felt the weight of a week's effort. "Yes," she admitted, "I am. I'm very tired."

"It's settled, then. Let's take us a nap."

"Oh," she said, "you tired, too?"

"I feel what you feel. If you're tired, so am I."

"Well, I guess you better take one too, then. You can lay down in Mr. Cox's room."

"I like your room better," the visitor said.

Oda laughed, grabbing her stomach and rolling her head back on her shoulders. "My room? Never mind, now."

"What's wrong?" asked the visitor.

"That's all right. I don't need that kinda company."

"What kind?"

"The kind you talkin' about."

"How do you know?"

" 'Cause I don't, that's how."

"Well, I'm not sleepin' in his room. You made it into a museum."

"Well, stay up, then," said Oda, but as she started down the hall, she paused.

The visitor spoke softly: "The beer mug from Munich is still on the dresser, so is the half-empty Prince Albert can, that dingy lamp is still in the corner, and every last double-breasted suit and chest-warmer tie is hangin' in the closet. . . . Besides, if you don't let me lay down with you, Oda, I'll have to go back where I came from."

The basement?

"Please," he whispered, "let's take a nap."

Somewhere inside, Oda knew what he meant, so she simply took a slow, deep breath and turned again toward her room. "Come on, then," she said, "you can come in."

Together they circled the open-ended room, entering off the front side. Her bed was to the right (antique, rich, dark). Facing it was a fifty-five vanity: A large, round mirror—flanked by three-drawer sets on each side—hovered majestically above two shallow shelves. Perfume, curlers, clips, lipstick, Polident, change, a penknife, and a tiny framed picture lay piled and scattered upon these shelves.

"Nice room," said the visitor. "I like it."

"It is nice, ain't it?" said Oda. "Uh-oh, I need to change the sheets."

"Come on, then," he said, "let's change 'em."

Moments later they were flapping a crisp, white sheet above the bed, bringing it delicately to rest—like a parachute—on the old four-poster. They laughed and giggled and took turns yanking the covers from each other in a giddy, gentle tug-of-war.

Afterward, while the visitor watched, Oda fluffed the pillows, first toss-ing them roughly in the air, then catching and twirling them like huge pizza doughs, and finally launching them high again toward the reaches of her cracked, sagging ceiling.

At last, Oda and the visitor stood almost still, heaving from the exertion of their games and laughter, looking at each other across the freshly made bed.

"Well," said the visitor, "in I go."

Like kids at a pajama party, they both leaped into the air and hit the bed, bouncing. A glee, a pure happiness surrounded them, and for a moment they lay quietly, feeling the ordered mechanics of their own breathing; the regular, strong course of blood through their veins and arteries; the millions upon millions of chemical-electric transactions firing simultaneously among the junctions and circuits within their bodies.

Then slowly, like a radiating warmth, Oda sensed serious desire welling within her. Autonomically, her labia began to twitch. Her silver pubic hairs were electrified, standing almost on end and crackling. "Ooo, Lord!" she cried softly.

"Really," sighed the visitor. And then he moaned in a low, long voice. His eyes were closed tightly; his fingers fluttered wildly, like a spastic piano player gone off. His knees jumped, as though triggered by an invisible, random current.

And finally, in slow degrees, their hands inched toward one another, each small movement bursting with sensual excess; each thought, each mental impulse, a caress. Life as foreplay.

At last they touched, and the sensation sent them both reeling inward. And then, like a flash, the visitor was straddling Oda, his huge, purplish penis arching toward her, bouncing rhythmically up and down, suspending from its snakish tip a clear, shiny liquid.

Oda seized his *thangamajig* greedily with her hands, lips, and dentures. It swelled even more, stretching and expanding her jaws, and for a moment she could barely contain it. But at last she and the visitor harmonized, and the warm, salty flesh filled her perfectly. Her body succumbed to wave after wave of ecstasy. Her voice hummed uncontrollably. She thought she might die.

But just as her pleasure rushed toward an abyss, the visitor withdrew himself and, reaching under her thigh, gently nudged her onto her stomach. And then, without missing a beat, he slid fully into her from the rear.

She was spaced. They flew out the window and rode—orgasmically coupled—above the rooftops of the city. Breezes licked their naked bodies as they rolled over and over, flipped head over heels and spun round and round like seed pods spiraling through the spring air. Together they made sounds unknown to most humans: preverbal utterings, direct-meaning vibrations tied to nature and creation. They spoke in original communion, a syntax beyond thought and name.

Riding madly upon this impossible passion, they exploded together . . . and descended finally into a soft, quiet, undulating denouement, the visitor resting perfectly upon Oda's back, each breathing in perfect rise and fall with the other. The world was furiously quiet. They slept.

Oda awoke from another world. A muted yet definite wash of daylight splashed across her bedspread, and with it the sudden shock of having overslept. "Ooo, Lord!"

Instantly, without pain or stiffness, she rose from the bed and stepped nimbly toward the bathroom. "What time is it?"

The bathroom light turned on the radio, and "Seventy-six Trombones" blared off one pink-and-black tiled wall onto the other. Oda washed quickly (skipping one or two steps because of time) and tore into the kitchen for coffee. "Naw," she decided, "too late."

She dressed unconsciously, grabbing whatever appeared, and put her hand against the window pane to test the temperature. It was warm. Warmest day of the year. "I'm late," she panted. "This is awful."

Once on the sidewalk, she took short, quick steps—grunting audibly with each—and then looked in all directions to see that no one heard her.

The day seemed oddly sluggish, too subdued to be morning; nevertheless, Oda made her way instinctively for the bus stop. The route was ingrained in her being: one-half block to the corner, three blocks to Kings Highway, and then wait there for the K-16.

She was in luck. Only blocks away, it dodged in and out of traffic, swaying to one side each time the driver switched direction. Still, time seemed incubated, gestating, dormant. Oda grew painfully anxious, and her patience eroded more with each nonpassing moment. "Foots," she muttered, "come on!"

At last the doors opened, but the sight before her froze Oda mid-step; this wasn't the driver. Not the one she'd seen every day since God-knew-when. This one was new, strange.

"Gettin' on, lady?" he asked.

"Yes, I'm gettin' on," she snapped, climbing easily up the rubberized steps to come face-to-face with the unknown driver.

He pulled brusquely off, causing her balance to shift, but Oda caught herself and held on while she rummaged her purse for the fare. After a few moments she found the fifteen cents in change and dropped it into the steeplelike, four-paned coinbox. Automatically the driver reached over and released a trap bottom, precipitating Oda's money into a busy mechanism—whirring and clicking noisily as it totaled these last coins with earlier fares.

Perilously, Oda made her way to her usual seat, grabbing the support posts whenever she could to counter the groaning accelerations of the aging bus. But her steps were absent, hesitant. For she could see that the passengers, like the driver, were unfamiliar. These were not the faces she normally saw as she made her daily way to the city's affluent outskirts to wash clothes and clean house.

Uneasily, she settled into her seat and glanced nervously about. Her brown, veiny hands gripped the handle in front of her tightly. Her brow was deeply furrowed and she breathed quickly, in shallow, short takes. Since she never wore a watch, she asked a nearby white man, "Pardon me, what time is it?"

"Seven-thirty," he answered.

That was about right; it should be seven-thirty. "Thank you." Oda settled back, but still she wondered, *Who are these people?*

The winding, eclectic journey to the county normally took about forty-five minutes. At a certain point, the bus would transgress an unmarked—yet apparent—demarcation and leave the black community, immigrating so to speak to the scented, cleaner-than-white reaches of the midwestern nouveaux riches. Through her window, Oda could see the not-so-subtle changes: The streets were smoother, wider, brighter, and yet the overall impression was dim. Things, though more opulent, became less clear, more murky and veiled.

Immediately, Oda rose and bounced her way toward the driver. "Excuse me, is it about eight o'clock, mister?"

The driver, this time, was courteous. "Yes, ma'am," he answered, glancing expertly at his pocket watch as he negotiated a tricky turn near Washington University, "eight-oh-two, to be exact."

"Well, then why is it so dark?"

"It's gettin' dark earlier now."

"It sho' is." Oda turned away and teetered (physically and mentally) back toward her seat, lowering herself slowly, almost against her own will, into the straw-stuffed padding once again.

Then, in an odd, unusual way, the driver suddenly steered the bus to the curb; and after the normal amount of hissing and gentle jerking, the front doors unfolded and a short man in a green outfit ascended. Not bothering to deposit any fare—and unmolested for doing so by the driver —he headed straight for Oda. With each step, she warmed to his approach. He was the visitor from the basement.

Halfway down the aisle he broadened his face in a gigantic grin and even winked. "Well, imagine that," he laughed. "What you doin' out here?"

Oda found their meeting and his question equally odd. "I'm goin' to work." She flashed suddenly on the wild "courtin' " they'd done—whenever it was. "What you doin' here?"

"Catchin' the wrong bus," he said, glancing mischievously toward Oda, "same as you."

Then suddenly—crashing upon her like cold North Sea swells—it hit home. Of course she didn't know the driver. Or the passengers. It was nighttime! She had awakened in the evening and then almost broken her neck to run and catch a morning bus. Suddenly, though, another, crazier realization seized her (it nearly stopped her heart): this had all happened already, fifteen years ago.

For a minute Oda was scared; then the visitor spoke softly: "You want to go to the Rose Bowl now?"

A subtle relief eased over her. "There you go again about the Rose Bowl."

"Let's go," he said. "You ain't been there in a while."

"I ain't been to Paris in a while, neither."

The visitor peered beyond the windshield, beyond the horizon. "You can always go to Paris," he said.

And then, on cue, the bus turned off its normal route and inexplicably pulled into the Rose Bowl parking lot in Pasadena, California.

The sun there was bright, midday California style. "Ladies and gentlemen," the driver/tour guide intoned to his assembled audience of passengers, "this is the world-famous Rose Bowl, home of the Southern California Trojans. Why don't you all follow me inside?"

From the top row of seats, the bright red rose petal resting at midfield still loomed large. "Some place, ain't it?" said the visitor.

"Yeah. It's nice," said Oda, "but I don't watch football. What else do they have here. Parades?"

Like Sammy Davis, Jr., the visitor opened his mouth and screamed silent laughter. Several times, he bobbed his head up and down, clutching his stomach all the while. "Naw. Naw. The parade ain't in here." And then he laughed all over again. "It's on television!"

Oda looked at the visitor, leaning her head away from him in mock apprehension. "You silly, ain't you?"

But the visitor was too tickled to answer.

"I want a hot dog," said Oda.

"Where you get your last name from?" asked the visitor.

Below, they could see scattered groups of other passengers milling among the brightly colored stadium seats. The driver still lectured to an audience of one just in back of the end zone.

"It's a lotta Indians in my family."

"What's the Indian word for rainbow?"

"Me," she said. "Oda Rainbow. Look at that." She pointed toward the end zone. "That man still talkin'."

"That's his job."

"Well, I want him to take me somewhere for somethin' to eat."

"Where?"

"Anywhere."

For a moment, the visitor simply looked off. Then, "I know . . . let's go to the beach."

"What beach you talkin' about, man?"

Moving along the highway a short time later, the passengers all seemed content, chatting amiably among themselves and turning every now and then to glance back at Oda and her visitor.

"What they keep lookin' back here for?" she asked.

"They know who you are," he said. "They want to see you."

Oda waved her hand in front of her in a shooing motion. "Y'all tend to y'all's business. Turn around."

Embarrassed, the others turned to face the front of the bus. "They gon' have to get off if they keep botherin' me," said Oda.

The bus continued along a panoramic, whining its way along the coast. Suddenly, Oda could see the ocean. It sprawled before them many feet below, bordered inland by a golden, narrow beach. "That's it!" said the visitor.

As the bus descended the winding road to the bottom of the cliff, Oda's ears popped and her heart thumped numbly in her chest. Her breaths were shallow and quick. Her hands trembled, each unable to still the other in its grip.

Seemingly in sync with the accelerated pace of Oda's body, the bus picked up speed. Faster and faster it rolled, until finally it seemed beyond any possibility of control. Surely, it seemed, the descent to the beach would end dramatically in fire and wreckage. But somehow, as they reached the climax of their spiraling dive, the bus slowed. The driver turned the wheel deftly, sliding it through his palms with ease and confidence, guiding them at last to rest along a two-lane highway facing the Pacific Ocean.

"Everybody off," said the driver. "West Malibu Beach."

Like kids at recess, the passengers charged from the bus and ran in a howling mob across the highway, falling finally and euphorically upon the warm, deserted beach.

The visitor and Oda were soon behind. "Where's the snacks at?" asked Oda. "And I'm thirsty, too."

"Ow!" a passenger suddenly screamed from down the beach. Others shouted, too, and some cursed out loud.

"I stepped on somethin' sharp!"

"Holy shit! Looka dis!" A weathered-looking worker-type dangled a plastic bag from a stick. Inside, purplish blood marinated what was unmistakably a severed human body part.

Then, looking hard at the ground, everyone noticed what all had missed at first: used condoms, scads of second-and-third-hand syringes, blood samples, unfathomed body tissues, sanitary napkins, tires, a doll's head, shards of glass, and plastic—plastic bags, plastic containers, plastic objects, wrappers, sheets, pieces, fragments (assorted, assembled, and asunder) of all kinds of plastic—everywhere.

And then, suddenly, a roar emerged from the far end of the beach. And behind it—rolling beneath a cloud of sand, dust, and debris—a crowd of people ran straight toward the passengers.

Frozen at first, Oda sensed within the next instant a profound venom, a pure, solipsistic malevolence that festered from the droning, gaining mob.

"Get back on the bus!" screamed the visitor. But as they all turned to run, the driver waved from his lofty seat inside, smiled . . . and drove slowly off.

The shocked, stranded riders could now plainly hear hateful shouts spewing from the bum-rushing rabble.

"Kill 'em!"

"Get the fucks! Kill all of 'em!"

"Yank out their guts! De-ball the cunts!"

"Rape every fuckin' bitch you see!"

"Fuck 'em up! Fuck 'em up!"

The passengers turned to run, but the highway behind them suddenly teemed with frothing, newly sprung mobs. They were caught on the beach.

Then, too quickly to be real, the hordes were upon them. Six passengers at once went down beneath vicious thuds and dull, fleshy smacks.

"No! Please!" cried a woman. But a relentless, slick-haired tough stomped her face and abdomen again and again with steel-toed boots.

A sick smell filled the air: erupting blood, exposed bones and organs, voided feces and urine.

Finally, waves of maddened humans converged on Oda and the visitor. She shut her eyes tightly and prayed inside for something good, something saving to happen. Then, feeling an insistent but gentle nudge in her side, she turned instinctively to catch a final glimpse of her friend.

"Oda," he said quietly, "go home."

She heard the clicked, familiar sound of a key in her front door. Then . . . quick, energetic bumps traced the rise of her stairs and sounded urgently, without hesitation, down her hallway. Running now, the footsteps pivoted into the dining room, nimbly sidestepping strewn magazines and scattered, unopened mail. Gingerly, happily, they echoed past the bathroom. Finally —like glory itself—Oda's granddaughter burst into the room.

"Hi, Grandma! What's up?"

Touching

TERRY L. MCMILLAN

 I suspected someone was there in that *very* same spot before me, but I didn't let the thought grow in my mind or rot there, till I saw her swinging on your side like a shoulder-strap purse early this morning. And this was after I had already let you touch me all over with your long brown hands and break down my resistance, so that you left me feeling like the earth had been pulled from under my feet.

First, I see your lean long legs coming toward me on that crooked gray sidewalk, the silver specks glaring in my eyes like dancing stars. But I was not blinded, even when you dragged them in that elegant yet pompous kinda way of yours. And you watched me coming from at least half a block away, and those size 13s didn't seem to lift up off the cement as high as they did the other night when we walked down this *very* same street together.

I know it was me who called you up the other night to say hello, but it was *you* who invited me to come down and walk your dog with you.

TERRY L. MCMILLAN's first novel, *Mama*, received a National Book Award by the Before Columbus Foundation. Her second novel, *Disappearing Acts*, was published in 1989. She has also edited and compiled an anthology of contemporary African-American fiction, entitled *Breaking Ice*, published in 1990. *Waiting to Exhale* was published by Viking in 1992. Her latest novel, *A Day Late and a Dollar Short*, will appear shortly from Viking.

Sounded innocent enough to me, but all along I'm sure you knew that I wanted to finally find out how warm it was under your shirt, behind your zipper, and if your hands were as gentle and strong as they looked. I was really hoping we could skip the walk altogether 'cause I just wanted to fall down on you slowly and get to your insides. Walk the dog another time. But since you could've misconstrued my motives as being unladylike, I bounced on down the street to your apartment in my white jogging outfit, trying to look as alluring as I possibly could, but without looking too eager.

I even dabbed gold oil behind my ears, under each breast, and on the tips of my elbows so as to lure you closer to me in case you couldn't make up your mind. The truth of the matter is that I was nervous, because I knew we weren't gonna just chitchat tonight like we'd done before. I went out of my way in five minutes flat to brush my teeth twice, put on fresh coats of red lipstick, wash under my arms, Q-tip my ears and navel ('cause I didn't know just how far you might go), and wash my most intimate areas and sprinkle a little jasmine oil there too.

Even though it was almost ninety degrees, we walked fifteen blocks and the dog didn't let go of anything. You didn't seem to mind or notice. You handed me the leash, and even though I can't stand to see a grown man with a little cutesy-wutesy dog, I wasn't hostile as I tugged at it as we continued to walk through the thick night air. For the most part, I like dogs.

When our feet dropped from the curb, and I jumped and screamed because a fallen leaf looked like a dead mouse, I let go of the leash and grabbed your hand. You squeezed it back, though you had to drag me to chase after your dog, who had taken off down the sidewalk, running up to the tree's bark and just panting. When we finally caught him, we were both out of breath. I regretted wearing that sweaty jogging suit.

"You scared of a little mouse?" you asked.

"Yes, they give me the heebie-jeebies. My stomach turns over and I want to jump on top of chairs and stuff just to get away from them."

Then you told me about the time you busted one on your kitchen counter eating your ravioli right out of the can and how you wounded it with a broomstick and then tried to flush it down the toilet, but it wouldn't flush. I laughed loud and hard, but I wanted to make you laugh, too.

So I told you about the time I was on my way out of my house to take a sauna when I accidentally saw a giant roach cavorting on my kitchen counter. I whacked it with my right hand just hard enough to cripple it. (I am scared of mice but I hate roaches.) I didn't want it to die immediately because I had just spent $9.95 on some Roach-Pruf which I had ordered through the newspaper and wanted to see if it really worked. So, I sprinkled about a quarter teaspoon on his head as he was about to struggle to find a crack or crevice somewhere. He kept on trying so I kept on sprinkling more Pruf on his antennae. After five minutes of this, he was getting on my nerves 'cause I still had my coat on, my purse and gym bag thrown over my shoulders, and since my kitchen was designed strictly with dwarfs and children in mind, I was burning up. It was then that I decided to burn him up too. First I lit myself a cigarette, and with the same match burned off his antennae, but the sucker still kept trying to get to one corner of the counter. I got real mad because my Pruf was obviously not working and I just went ahead and burnt him up quickly and totally for not dying the way he was supposed to.

You thought this was terribly funny and cracked up. I liked hearing you laugh, but I didn't know if you thought this was indicative of my personality: torture and murder and everything.

We continued to walk a few more blocks, making small talk, and the dog continued running up to tree trunks, kicking up his little white legs, and finally squirting out wetness, but that was about it.

By this time, I was sweating and picturing your head nestled between my breasts. I like feeling a man's head there, and it had been so long since any man even made me feel like dreaming out loud that I didn't even hear you when you asked me if I liked the Temptations and had I ever been to a puppet show. I didn't understand the connection until we walked inside your apartment.

Today, though, you watched me come toward you like this was a tug-of-war but the rope was invisible. The gravity was so dense it pulled us face-to-face, and when I finally reached you I could smell your breath at the end of the rope. You were uneasy and sorta turned in a half turn toward me as I brushed past both of you. You loosely smiled back at me, squinting behind those tinted glasses, and I smiled back at both of you 'cause I don't have a grudge with this girl; wasn't *her* I spent the night with.

"What are *you* doing up so early?" you asked. I didn't really think it was any of your business since you didn't call last night to see how late I was up. Besides, it was almost ten o'clock in the morning.

"I've already had my coffee, done my laundry, and now I'm trying to get to the plant store to buy some dirt so I can transplant my fern and rubber tree before the block party this afternoon."

"Oh, I'm sorry. Marie, this is Carolyn," you said, waving your hands between us like a magician.

We both nodded like ladies, fully understanding your uneasiness.

"Why don't you have the Chinese people do your laundry?" you asked.

"Because I like to know that my clothes are clean; I like to fold them up nice and neat like I want them. And besides, I like to put things together that belong together."

You just nodded your head like a fool. For a moment you looked puzzled, like someone had dropped you off in the middle of nowhere. You didn't seem to mind either that the girl was standing there watching your poise alter and sway. Me neither. But I had to move away from you 'cause I could really smell your body scent now and it was starting to stick to my skin, gravitating around me, until it got all up into my nostrils and then hit my brain, swelled up my whole head right there on the spot. This was embarrassing, so I tried to play it off by pulling my scarlet scarf down closer toward my eyebrows. But you already knew what had happened.

I make my feet move away from you as if I am trying to catch a bus I see approaching. I take my hands and wipe away the burnt-red lipstick from my mouth and cheeks at the mere thought of letting you press yours against them. Was trying to forget how handsome you were altogether. Fine. Too fine. Didn't listen to my mama. "Never look at a man that's prettier than you, 'cause he's gonna act that way." I was trying to think about dirt. The leaves of my plants. But I never have been attracted to pretty men, I thought, trying to miss the cracks in the sidewalk after stubbing my toe. You were different. Spoke correct English. Made puppets move and talk. Wrote your own grant proposals. Drank herbal tea and didn't smoke cigarettes. You crossed your legs and arms when you talked, and leaned your wide shoulders back in your chair so your behind slid to the edge. Made me think you thought about the words before letting them roll off your tongue. I admired you for contemplating things before you made them happen.

You yelled at me after I was almost halfway down the block. "Are you selling anything at the block party?"

I had already told you the other day I was making zucchini cake, but I repeated it again. "Zucchini cake!" and waved goodbye, trying to keep that stupid grin on my face though I knew you wouldn't be able to see my expression from a distance.

I liked the attention you were giving me in spite of the girl. I thought it meant something. I was even hoping as I trucked into the plant store and got stuck by a cactus that you would call me later on to explain that she was just a friend of your cousin or your sister. I was hoping you would tell me that your back hurt or something so I could come down with my almond oil and rub it for you. Beat it, dig my fingertips into your shoulder blades and the canals along your spine until you gave in. Or maybe you would tell me you broke your glasses and couldn't see. I would come down and read out loud to you: comic books or the Bible.

Now I'm out here on this sidewalk with a bag of black dirt in my hands in the heat walking past your house, forcing myself not to stare up at those dingy white shutters of yours so I twist my neck in the opposite direction, looking ridiculous and completely conspicuous. I thought for sure I was gonna be your one-and-only-down-the-street sweetheart, 'cause I carried myself like a lady, not like some dog in heat.

I really had no intention of transplanting anything today. I just told you that because it sounded clean. I was more concerned about whether this girl touched you last night the way I had. Probably not, because only I can touch you the way I touch you. But as you were standing there on that sidewalk, I kept seeing still shots of us flashing across my eyes: twisting inside each other's arms like worms and caterpillars; you kissing me like you'd been getting paid for it all these years and this was your last pay-check; and my head getting lost all over your body. I could still hear your faint cries echoing in my head right there on the concrete. Saw my tongue moistening your chest and your hands rubbing all across and around my back like I was made of silk. I *was* silk and you knew it. You smelled so damn good. And you never stopped me when my head fell off the bed. You came after it. You never said anything when I screamed and called out your name, just took your time with me and kept pulling me inside your arms, inside the cave of your chest, and would not let me go. And when I woke up, you were the dream I thought I had.

And yet, there you were out on that sidewalk in the heat with another girl chained to your arm, walking past my house without a care in the world. This shit burns me up.

I mean, look. You didn't have to make me laugh out loud, tickle me, and change the Band-Aid on my cut thumb, or sniff my hair and tell me it smelled like a cool forest. You didn't have to tell me it didn't matter that my breasts were small, and I was relieved to hear that, 'cause my mama always told me a man should be more interested in how you fill his life and not how you fill your bra.

I mean, who told you to show me the puppets you'd made of James Brown and Diana Ross and the Jackson Five? Who told you to burn jasmine candles and make me listen to twelve old Temptations albums after telling me your favorite song of all was "Ain't Too Proud to Beg"? You didn't have to climb up on a bar stool and drag out your scrapbook and give me the privilege of seeing four generations of your family. Showing me your picture as a little nappy-headed boy. What made you think I wanted to see you as a child when I'd really only known you as a man for three weeks? But no, you watched me turn my key in my front door for two whole months while you walked that little mutt before you allowed yourself to say more than "hello" and "good morning."

I never did get around to explaining myself, did I? I mean, I think I told you I was a special education teacher. I think I told you that once in a while I write poems. Even wrote one for you but I'm glad I didn't give it to you. Your ego probably would've popped out of your chest. But maybe I should've told you about the nights when my head pumps blood, and about the dreams I have of being loved just so. How I have always wanted to give a man more than symphony inside and outside the bedroom. But it is so hard. Look at this.

You just should not have wrapped your arms and shoulders around me like I was your firstborn child. You should not have shown me tenderness and passion. Was this just lust? I mean, I wasn't asleep when you kept on touching and rubbing my face like I was crystal and you were afraid I would break. I pretended because I didn't want you to rupture this cocoon I was inside of. So I just let you touch; never wanted you to stop touching me.

Three hours ago I transplanted my plant anyway. I baked three zucchini cakes that cost me almost thirty dollars, but after this morning I cannot picture myself sitting out on those cement steps in the heat trying to sell a piece of cake to total strangers. My roommate said she didn't mind. And I'm not going to sit in this hot house all day and be miserable.

"Wanna meet me for brunch?" I ask a girlfriend. She has no money. "I'll pay, just meet me, girl, okay?" She understands I'm not really hungry but will eat anything just to take up inside space and get me away from this street.

The block was starting to fill up with makeshift vendors displaying junk they'd pulled out of attics and closets and basements so they wouldn't have to drag them to the Salvation Army. I could already smell barbecue and popcorn and hear the deejay testing his speakers for the highest quality of sound he could expect to get from outside. It was very hot and the sun was beating down on the pavement, making the heat penetrate through your shoes.

I'm wearing my tightest blue jeans and think I look especially good this afternoon on my way to the train station. I work hard to look good. Not for you or the general public, but for me. Here you come again, strutting toward me with that sissy little dog tagging alongside your big feet, but this time there's nothing on your arm but soft black hair and a rolled-up red plaid shirtsleeve. I can see orchards of black hair peeking out at me from your chest, and though my knees want to buckle, I dig my heels deeply into the leather so as to make myself stand up straight like a dancer. You smile at me before we meet face-to-face and then do one of your about-face turns. Start walking beside me without even being invited.

"Hello," I say, as I make sure I don't lose the pace of my stride I worked so hard on establishing when I first noticed you.

"My goodness, you *do* look pretty today. Pink and purple are definitely your colors."

I smile because I know I look good and even though I can hardly breathe from holding my stomach in to look its absolute flattest, I don't want you staring at anything on my body too tough because you've seen far too much of it already. I take that back. I want you to be mesmerized by this sight so that you remember what everything looked and felt like underneath this denim because you won't be anywhere near that close again: daytime or nighttime. I move closer to the curb.

"Where you going today?" you ask, showing some real interest. And since I want you to think I'm a very busy woman and that this little episode has not fazed me in the least, I say, "I'm having brunch with a friend." I really wanted to tell you it wasn't any of your damn business, but no, I'm not only polite, but honest.

We walked six hard hot blocks and when we finally reached the subway steps, you bent down like you were about to kiss me, and I stared at your smooth brown lips puckering up as if you had a cold sore on them, and turned my head. You kissed that girl this morning.

"Can I call you later, then?" you asked.

"If the spirit moves you," I said, and disappeared underground.

By the time I got home it was almost ten o'clock and the street was still full of teenagers roller-skating, skateboarding, and dancing to the loud disco music blasting from both ends of the block. Kids were running around and through a full-spraying fire hydrant in high shrills of excitement, while grown-ups sat on the stoops sipping beers and drinks from Styrofoam cups. My roommate was sitting on our stoop and I joined her. Though it was hard to see, I found myself looking for your tall body over all the smaller ones. When I didn't see you immediately, this disturbed me because I could see your lights on and I knew you couldn't be sitting up in that muggy apartment with all this noise and activity going on down here.

When I saw you leaning against a wrought-iron fence across the street, there was a different girl stuck deep into your side. You spotted me through the thick crowd of teenagers and I heard you call out my name, but I ignored you. I was too proud to let myself feel sad or jealous or anything stupid like that.

My roommate told me she sold exactly three pieces of my zucchini cake because folks were afraid to buy it. Thought it might be green inside. I didn't care about the loss.

I felt spry and spunky, so I kicked off my pink pumps and marched down the steps and walked straight into the fanning water of the fire hydrant along with the kids. The hard mist felt cool and soothing as it fell against my skin. My entire body was tingling as if I had just had a massage. And even though I could feel your eyes following me, I didn't turn to acknowledge them. I sat back down on the steps, wiped the water from my forehead, the hot pink lipstick from my lips, ate a piece of my delicious zucchini cake, and popped the lid on an ice-cold beer. The foam flowed over the top of the bottle and down my fingers. I shook off the excess and leaned back against the cement steps so it would scratch my back when I rocked from side to side and popped my fingers to the beat.

Innocens Comes to Cotton

TOM MITCHELSON

*"Come on, baby. Time to hit the base and make us some money.
Payday's the best day to do business, you know."*

*"There's a blizzard out there, Zeke, if you haven't noticed. And
like I told you from the start, what we do is not just about money.
. . . I shoulda known you'd never come to understand that."*

*"Yeah, right, Gussie. Look, I understand as best I can, but I'm
sorry: I'm in this with you for more than just some warped ideals.
The money is what keeps me keepin' on, girl. Besides, it's starting to
get a bit risky, you dig? The APs is gettin' suspicious, asking questions
about my dealings with you."*

"But you haven't said anything, have you? . . . Have you?"

"Not yet."

"What do you mean, not yet?"

"Just that. Silence comes easier when pockets are full."

"You insensitive bastard—"

TOM MITCHELSON, the Director of the New Renaissance Writers Guild, is a poet, fiction
writer and writer of radio drama. His poetry has appeared in numerous anthologies, and, as
a performance poet, he has been featured as either co- or lead vocalist of several jazz-poetry
groups, including his own New Dawn Ensemble. The short story "Innocens Comes to Cotton"
is an excerpt from a larger collection, entitled *Untold Lies . . . as Love Tales.* He dedicates
this, his first publication of fiction, to the memory of DorisJean Austin.

"Best lighten up on the name-callin', Gussie. Especially that bastard stuff. . . . Now, as I was sayin', how about hittin' the base? I already made arrangements. We got us four easy markers."

"Can't you see I'm not in the mood, Zeke? They can wait until tomorrow, I'm sure. Or at least till the storm breaks."

"Humph. . . . Well, if that's the case, then suppose we try makin' our waitin' around worthwhile?"

"Good Lord. Everything my cousin tells me about you is true, Zeke; you ain't worth spit!"

"How about seein' if anything else she tells you about me is true? Here. . . . Think this C-note is good for a tiny whiff of what all those cats be dyin' to taste? One-fifty? A yard-seventy-five?"

"Let me explain this to you one last time, Ezekiel Jones: It ain't about money and it surely ain't about you and me like that. . . . Jesus, you make me sick sometimes!. . . . Damn. . . . All right. . . . Give me five minutes to get ready. Then we'll head out for the base before you make me hurt you. Hurt you bad."

 In Little Rock around 1966, if you were Black or felt the need to be, and a social gathering of sweat and impropriety was what you sought on your Friday, Saturday, or Sunday nights on the town, then Grizzly's was the place. Unmissably red on the outside and mustardy yellow and flat black on the inside, it was a huge renovated barn located less than ten miles past the city line on a lonely state road and named for its owner, a burly, goateed, Kodiak-sized man. If Grizzly had a real name, folks either didn't know it or didn't care to share it with those who did not, and the nickname "Bear" was used only by the chosen few who were told they could do so.

Grizzly's was a BYOBB joint, and if you don't know what that means, you didn't need to be there back then, and if the joint's still standing, you don't need to be there now. The only things served from behind the bar were setups and keg beer for the party makers and a taste of .45 caliber revolver or pump-action shotgun for the troublemakers. Hungry? Well, best take that short trip to the all-night rib joint down the road apiece, 'cause Grizzly's kitchen didn't serve no food except to feed the Bear himself.

Social climbing was laughably unheard of there, and peacock posturing only got you so far. And if some of that cool jazz or pop rock was needed to get you in the mood, well, again, you were in the wrong place. Might as well have been a sign hung out front of Grizzly's saying "Gutbucket to no-holds-barred rhythm and blues only. No pretensions allowed." Grizzly's was Little Milton and Johnnie Taylor. Bobby "Blue" Bland, Otis Redding, Sam Cooke, and B. B. King. Etta James and Jackie Wilson. James Brown pleading in front of Bobby Byrd and his Famous Flames. A mess of slow-burn stewing, deep-fry crackling, 'fess-up testifying blues, with the tight melodics and street-corner harmonies of conk-headed do-wop groups, fronted by falsettoed or hard-edged lead singers crooning their way out of New York, Philly, D.C., Chicago, and Detroit, stirred in.

Grizzly's music reflected his patrons and the man himself: pseudo-nothing.

The Temptations lamented, *"You've taken away my reason for livin'/ And you won't even tell me why."*

Johnnie Taylor responded matter of factly, *"I got to love somebody's baby/'cause somebody, somebody, somebody's lovin' mine."*

Lament and vindication. A simple solution and quite all right for that night or any night in Grizzly's Den.

There was no long courtship between us. After my first visit, no matter where my hanging out began, I always wound up there. It was the music and its congregation that held me close, the hot-tongued sway of it in my ear that kept me coming back. I had always prayed at love's altar in the impassioned, silky, heart-wrenching lyric of a Smokey Robinson or a Little Anthony. Memorized and employed more than my share of a bended-knee line or two, secretly recognizing that romantic, that poet hidden in me. But gutbucket was more than just going to a different church of the same denomination across town. It was a whole 'nother religion, a more earthy expression of the same passion. And so it was with Grizzly's for me: a new way of being, a new people showing me how. Me, a repressed worshiper amongst a holy-rolling blues multitude, baring my lame soul in their midst, shouting my newfound *Halle-blue-jah!* at the top of my lungs.

But being a joyously testifying novitiate in that den of iniquity was not without its drawbacks.

Johnnie Mae Merriweather was a regular at Grizzly's, who rode life hard like it was a snorting, bucking bull trying to toss her off before trampling her to death, a life full of two-fisted drinkin', fightin', and fornicatin' in any order she chose. And while she might have gotten thrown off that bull a time or two from the looks of her, she never got trampled.

Word had it she packed a straight razor down in her drawers. Always.

And with the blood-curdling, black-brown scar that screamed its jagged, meaty statement from behind her left ear, down her cheek, and on to the middle of her chubby chin, well, you'd feel safer asking Grizzly about his real name than asking Johnnie Mae about the origins of her scar or whether or not that straight razor was really where folks said it was.

She was myth, Johnnie Mae. Myth that grew as her legend got told and retold, distorted and exaggerated, larger than life and certainly much larger than the woman herself. But unless you peek behind it, myth gets accepted and even enjoyed for what it is.

And so it was. . . .

Now, as large as Grizzly's was, you'd never think it could get jam-packed. But with a live show that night featuring blues legend John Lee Hooker, en route to Memphis on the chitlin circuit and just stopping by to pay respects to his old friend Bear, it was tight as jobs and money on the dance floor, even at the edges. I recall standing off to the side, not able to dance another further, mopping myself down with a damp handkerchief, when . . . with a rough tapping-slapping on my shoulder, her raspy voice came from behind.

"Hey, sweet thing. How's about rubbin' bellies wid ole Johnnie Mae?"

It was more order than request.

Turning, I couldn't keep the frown from jumping across my face. We had never been introduced, but hell, everybody knew Johnnie Mae Merriweather. "Not right now, baby. I'm a little tired and sweaty. Maybe later," I replied as nonchalantly as I could. Just the thought of holding her close was more violence than I could stand, and the gnawed-on, greasy turkey drumstick she waved in the air didn't encourage me none.

"I done seen you dancin' wid everybody else in heah. What's wrong wid me? . . . Don't you know who I am, dahlin'?"

"Yeah, sure, Johnnie Mae. I know who you are," I answered warily.

"Then you should also know I'm not good with rejection. And you sweatin' ain't hardly no problem. The way I sees it, wasn't good if you ain't sweated some. Matter 'fact, why don't we just skip the dancin' and hit the backseat of my Chevy for some sho'nuf hot-sweat, buck-nekked belly rubbin', 'cause that's what I really got on my mind right about now anyhow?"

The face of too many dreams deferred, long-festering and forgotten, loomed before me. Even in the dark, her teeth looked ripsawed. The scar, the myth, and the look in her eyes, a look at once both wild and cruel, a look I was sure could not be induced by mere alcohol or lust but a lunatic something lurking inside her, waited impatiently for my answer.

What had Zeke Jones said to me on my first trip downtown not too many months ago, after saving me from indoctrination at the hands of one of the many gold-toothed, silver-tongued, shiver-hipped women of the off-limits 42nd Street Bar and Grill? "You'd better ride the ponies a bit," he'd said, "before you try ridin' the horses." I'd only ridden one pony since then. My first and only pony, as a matter of fact, and a relatively tame one at that. And even if I was ready for the horses, I couldn't see myself riding, mounting, or even being left alone in the barn for too long with this one anytime soon.

Nevertheless, she took me by the hand and turned toward the door. Hers were laborer's hands, coarse and strong. Hard and tight-gripping. I couldn't get loose.

"I ain't goin' nowhere with you," I protested, dragging my feet, trying to break free. But she just yanked and scolded at me like I was a stubborn pup refusing to walk alongside its master.

"Yes, you is, and you's gonna love it when you gets there, sweetmeat." She grunted between tugs. "Gar-un-teed. I been called the Gateway to Paradise, or ain't you heard? So stop showin' out before I gets upset and has to give you a good thrashin' right here in public."

Johnnie Mae was not tall, but solid and strong as most men from years of working the cotton and soybean fields near her hometown of Conway, I'd been told. Solid, strong, and stubborn, and not used to asking for any damned thing more than once. Not even sex, and hers was intense and more than enough for one or two good men. Or so it was said by those who had gone with her and survived, and not ashamed to admit going in the first place.

"Well, well, well," came a deep, familiar voice from the shadows near the door. "And where are you dragging this tenderfoot off to, Johnnie? Wherever it is, I do say he don't look too happy about it. . . . Is you happy, young blood?"

It was Zeke Jones. Again. Damn, if he bailed me out of this one, I'd have to build him a shrine.

I was shaking my head no as Johnnie Mae spat out, "You need to be mindin' your own, Jones, and let us on by."

"Wait, Johnnie," said Zeke, his voice gently mocking. "I'm actually tryin' to do you a favor here. Save you from some major frustration, girl. Now it's my understanding that this here kid ain't even been unwrapped yet, if you get my meaning. And if you do him anywhere near like I knows you can do, not only will you be mighty disappointed, but the boy might be ruint for life. I mean, you ain't exactly known for tenderness, patience, and mercy in bed, Johnnie Mae. Hell, woman, you might just cut him 'cause he can't keep up. Tell you what. If you so ready to shake that ole tail-feather a taste, why not shake it with me instead? We kinda did all right the last time, as I recollect."

"Don't flatter yourself, Jones. I don't recall writin' no letters to Mama when we was through. 'Sides, I'm a-lookin' for some new blood to drink tonight, and this looks like it." She gave me a big sly wink to go with her lecherous grin, threw down the leg bone, and with her free hand grabbed me roughly down below. "In fact, I think he's jes' 'bout ready. He-ah, feel for yo'self."

"Girl, you just got that boy's heart pumpin' so hard, both his heads be confused about now, that's all. Probably more scared than excited. Let's make a deal. Suppose I give you twenty dollars to turn him a-loose?"

"Why you so interested in this here fella, Zeke? It ain't natural. You ain't gone funny on me now, have you? I mean, he ain't your secret thang, is he?"

"Now, Johnnie, you knows me much better than that." Zeke chuckled, reaching for her. "Let's just say I hate to see your good stuff go to waste and leave it at that. So . . . how 'bout it? You, me, and twenty bucks sounds kinda good from where I stand."

She studied me slowly up and down, front and back, all the while humming darkly to herself. Finally, with a pronounced tug of her scarred chin, a half-closed eye still fixed on me, she said, "Make it twenty dollars and another ten for a coupla jars of shine, an' I'll call it did."

"How about twenty-five straight up?"

"Thirty or it's the back of my Chevy for ol' Peach-fuzz here."

"All right, all right, thirty. . . . Damn. Well, son," he said, turning to me, "you heard the woman. Pay up so we can get this thing over with."

"Why don't I just go sit down?" I huffed, pulling my jewels loose at last. "It won't cost me a cent to do that."

In one easy motion, Johnnie Mae threw up the front of her dress and her hand disappeared down between her legs. I saw the top of the fabled straight razor catch a ray of green neon from somewhere up above. Legend had it that if she pulled it, she meant to use it. Bluffing and woofing was over at that point; begging and pleading fell on deaf ears.

"Don't be so sure about the cost of tryin to sit, Babyface. I'ma startin' to feel a wee bit ornery right about now," she hissed, "and some strong johnson and good shine is about the onliest things gonna make it right. Look at the money as ransom for refusin' to deliver me my propers. I'm sure that pretty face of yourn is worth the price, don't you think?"

I gave Zeke the last of my money, wished them both a good night, then eased outside behind the club and, leaning against a wall, puked until my shaking stopped and my shame became bearable.

Was this how my new church took up collection?

Now, as a rule, it rarely snows in Arkansas, and when it does, it's never more than an inch or two. So the blizzard that came through that next payday caught everyone by surprise.

I had the day off and slept till noon despite the eagle's flying. Around 1300 hours, I put on long johns, thermal socks, lined pants and boots, and a wool shirt and hat, zipped up my hooded parka, and headed out across a vast tundra stretched between my barrack and the mailroom. The wind was a swift-moving, angry banshee, effortlessly tossing endless drifts. I looked down for footprints I could follow but, looking behind me and barely seeing tracks I'd just made, gave up and forged ahead, cursing and following my instincts through the knee-deep whiteness.

None too soon, through driving sheets of frigid snow and swirling, frosty mist, the mailroom, its huge American flag flapping and snapping above, came into view. Just a few more feet, then across the road—

"*Beep, beep, beep!*" The sleek car slid to within inches of me, causing me to jump in fright before falling backward onto a mound of powdered drift.

"Hey!" a male voice screamed from behind a hastily rolled-down window. "You lookin' to die, fool? Can't you see where you be walkin'?"

Zeke Jones behind the wheel. A female passenger by his side. "Oh, no. Look, baby. It's the rookie," he said to his companion. "Pierre, what are you doin' out here? Only Eskimos and poor desperate folk out walkin' in this storm. Wanna ride? . . . Come on, come on, we got plenty-a room and plenty-a heat. Come on." He reached back and opened the rear door of the black Coupe de Ville. The heat escaping from inside blew a thick, steamy cloud across the field.

"Hurry up, man. You lettin' Joe Chilly up in here!"

I was in in a wink, surrounded by warmth, plush red leather, and heavily perfumed air.

"Goin' to let that bird shit on you, eh, man?"

"Yeah." I sniffled, the frost on me melting and gathering into pools on my face.

"No sweat," Zeke rumbled. "We can swing back around, right, baby?" he said to his companion. "We got time."

She didn't say a word.

"Pierre, this here is Gussie B, the Black Stallion of Arkansas. Gussie, this here is Pierre. Mike Pierre."

She turned halfway in the large front seat, offering a hand soft as spring rain.

"My pleasure, Mike," she said huskily. "Oh, you poor thing! Your hands are freezing. Let me warm them a bit," she offered, taking both my hands in hers. "Don't you have gloves?" she asked, massaging them.

"No. I kinda lost 'em a week or so ago. Don't know where. Sure need them today, though, right?"

"For true. And where might you be from, Pierre, if you don't mind my asking? Certainly not from down here, not from the sound of you." She released my hands from hers.

"No. I'm from Philadelphia, as a matter of fact," I lied, reaching into my pocket, fumbling for something to wipe the water now streaming down my face, never taking my eyes off her. "Is it really that easy to tell?"

"Easy enough," she said with a faint smile, passing me a scented lavender handkerchief from her lap. "Here. Use this."

We pulled up in front of the mailroom.

"Go on, Pierre," said Zeke. "We'll wait for you. No sense fighting this weather just to cash that tiny ducat you gettin'."

"Thanks," I said, more than grateful. I had expected to be making my own way to the paymaster's office to cash my check. And besides, if I didn't see more of the so-fine-she'll-bring-tears-to-your-eyes woman Zeke Jones was with, life would have no meaning. Oh, yeah. Made you glad to be a man. Skin smooth and rich like fresh wet mud. Full lips and high cheeks rouged just so. A thick, majestic mane the color of midnight, and eyes just as black and deep and wondrous. . . .

"Me and Gussie B are headed for the bowling alley for some burgers and beer. Wanna tag along?" Zeke asked when I got back into the Caddy, check in hand.

"Sure," I responded quickly as she shot him a glance. I was going anywhere Gussie B was going. "We're hittin' the paymaster's first though, right?"

"Yeah, sure. Whatever you say, kiddo. . . . Pierre here met Johnnie Mae last weekend, Gussie. Ain't that right, Pierre?" Zeke said with a smirk and a short laugh as he watched me in the rearview mirror.

The angel Gussie B turned to me, pouting at my blushing face. "She didn't hurt you or anything, did she, Pierre?" she asked, full of dread and concern. "She's nothing but trouble, that one. I don't know what any man sees in her, crude heifer. And that goes for you too, Zeke Jones. I know you be messin' around with that maniac. Huh!" She snorted. "They didn't pull that scam on you, did they, Pierre? You know, that 'Give me some money or some sex or you die' routine? Did they?" I guess my expression said it all, and with that she faced forward, pressing back into her seat, shaking her head from side to side. "Give the man back his money, Zeke," she said angrily. "How much does this con artist owe you, hon?" she asked, glaring at him.

"Come on, baby," he protested. "I was gonna give him back his money, honest. As a matter of fact, here," he said, pulling a thick wallet from inside his coat and handing it back to me. "And take an extra twenty just so there's no hard feelings. Okay, Pierre? Seriously. Take it."

After I cashed my check, we glided eerily through the blinding storm in a charged silence. What they had discussed while I was in the paymaster's, I'll never know.

The bowling alley was warm and relatively empty. Zeke ordered our food as Gussie B slipped out of her fur coat and sashayed off to the rest room flaunting matching black ski pants, an oversized sweater, and hip boots. All heads, male and female, turned to watch the stallion go by.

Our table was soon filled with plates of food and pitchers of beer. Zeke dug in with a vengeance and I was about to do the same when Gussie B returned.

"Well, I'm glad that *someone* has the manners to wait for the lady to be seated before they begin eating." Her voice jabbed at Zeke, who could only throw up his hands and grin sheepishly. "Anyway . . . Pierre." She sighed, settling in, "where'd that name of yours come from? You got some *voulez-vous* in you somewhere?"

"I suppose. I'm not really sure."

"Humph." She snorted. "Probably some of that Creole or Haitian. You need to know these things. And Zeke," she scolded, "I told you about loading up on those grease-burgers, lover. Keep it up and you're gonna look like a blimp before you know it. You ain't a kid no more like Pierre here, and you haven't exercised a lick since I've known you." She quickly cocked her head at me. "He can probably burn that stuff off without even thinking about it. Probably good at it, too." She stopped abruptly then, apologizing. "Excuse me, Pierre. I know all you GIs consider yourselves *men*, but what the hell, I figure you for no more than what, eighteen, nineteen? You can tell me, baby. It's all right."

"Eighteen," I said softly.

"Oh, how sweet! You're blushing!" she cooed, patting my hands. "But like I said, it's all right."

She started in on her salad and iced tea.

Zeke scanned the room between mouthfuls of wolfed-down food and guzzled beer, wiping his mouth with the back of his hand.

"Baby, *please use a napkin!* I declare. I don't know why I put up with you," Gussie B complained. "In Philly, Pierre, did you attend public or private school?" she asked as she wiped Zeke's face with a napkin.

"Private. Catholic."

"Is that right?" she replied, suddenly enthusiastic.

"Uh-huh."

"And what was your favorite subject?"

"English. I liked reading. Writing, too."

"I knew it! I could just tell. I went to a private school down here. St. Ignatius. And got two years of college under my belt before I was asked to leave for—uh, indiscretions, so to speak. Kind of . . . influencing grades." She smiled broadly at this remark. "I always say I'll go back one of these days, but in the meantime I'm a self-employed businesswoman. I deal in commodities on the market and foreclosures of outstanding debt, so to speak. But I have this creative side that I'm trying to nurture at the same time."

Zeke snickered.

"Pay him no mind, Pierre. He's an uninspired, disillusioned slug, jealous of anything creative, ain't that right, punkin?" she chided softly, grabbing his thick, tightening face. "So much fear of the unknown in that big yummy body. Oh, come on. Smile for me, sugar. When you get red like that, it means you're gettin' upset. . . . You know how I like to tease."

I realized then how little I knew about Zeke Jones. He had bailed me out of some tight spots a couple of times, a guardian angel of sorts, though always for a price. Until now, he had always seemed to be disdainful and recklessly fearless, controlling whatever and whoever was around him. But this Gussie B had him muzzled and in check.

"You know, Pierre," she went on, "when folks flee from Little Rock, and they do flee, they head for one of two places: St. Louis or Los Angeles. Got to the point where LA stands for Little Arkansas. These Arkies go out there for a month or two, come back here, and tell whomever, 'Oh, yes, *dah-lin'*, I'm from LA,' pinkie in the air, sippin' champagne instead of moonshine. I say to them, 'Why, *dah-lin'*, didn't you just graduate from Central High, right here in Little Rock? No? Coulda swore that was you

I saw in the yearbook. No?' Negroes! Too, too funny." She paused to push a glistening black olive between her lips. "Anyway, I went on out to both places to see for myself. St. Louis first. My old girlfriends were doing the same thing out there that they were doing here, and with the same kinds of lowlife people. So I started hanging out on some local college campuses while they were busy or at work. Even snuck into a few college classes. I love literature, you know. Especially that old stuff. Eventually, I hooked up with a professor of Renaissance literature at a school just across the river in Illinois. An older man." She sipped some tea, clearing her throat. "White man. . . . I tolerate him because he serves a purpose. And reserved, generous. Not at all demanding. But most important for his mind: creative and analytic. He still sends me a plane ticket once, maybe twice a month, though I don't oblige him as much lately. But his expectations are so far removed from the rest of them. There's no Gussie B, Brick Shithouse, no Black Stallion unless I choose to be that. I'm totally different up there with him."

The wind yowled an out-of-control harmony as a snow-covered quartet entered, stomping their feet free of snow, knocking it off each other's parkas and blowing on their hands before choosing their seats.

"All I needed, Pierre, was all anybody ever needs. An honest chance to try to be who you are."

"Excuse me, highbrows," Zeke cut in. "I think I see some people at that table over there I need to talk to. Be right back."

"What about Los Angeles?" I asked as Zeke left. I wanted her to continue the tale she seemed to enjoy telling. To me alone. For whatever reason. "What was that like?"

She resumed slowly, gazing intently at Zeke and the newcomers he had joined. But soon her voice picked up its natural cadence and timbre as her story continued. "The whole idea of moving away is to do better. Better than where you came from. Wouldn't you agree, Pierre?"

"Yes," I answered patly, but not really sure. I mean, where had I ever been?

"I say, why make the move if it's only from one quagmire to another? Sunshine and warm weather don't mean a thing if you're bogged in a life that's shit. My friends out there called me siditty, but hey, I wasn't stuck-up; they were the ones who ran out there thinking that that alone was gonna change them. But they were either content with or resigned to who they had become over the years, or maybe just scared, like Zeke." She put the tea to her lips, then changed her mind, glancing over at Zeke at the other table. "And so, Pierre, I met an instructor out at UCLA. Young guy.

Black. Into filmmaking. Knows all about it, every phase of it. Sharp as a whip. Good mind. A vibrant, passionate lover. We'd hang out at those pretentious LA soirees. Said he liked to take me because whenever somebody started talking that iambic-pentameter talk, I could run it right back at them. In Black. And with gusto!" She laughed heartily, as if we were the only ones in the room.

"Pierre," she said in a near whisper, looking around conspiratorially, "I'm going to share something with you that might shock you, okay?"

"Sure," I said, so anxious to please.

"Well. Are you familiar with the Italian poet Dante?"

"Dante Alighieri, best known for his allegorical narrative poem *The Divine Comedy*, written in the thirteen hundreds? That Dante?" I blurted proudly.

"One and the same." Gussie B nodded slowly. "And do you remember what *The Divine Comedy* is about?"

"Let me see. . . . As I recall, it has to do with a journey down through Hell, up a mountain to Purgatory, and finally into the presence of God in Paradise."

I was absolutely beaming, silently giving heartfelt, humble thanks to sweet Brother Anselm, my minuscule, balding English literature instructor in my senior year of high school.

"Very good, Pierre! I knew you wouldn't disappoint. Well, in Canto Three of the Inferno, Dante and his guide, the poet Virgil, come to the gate of Hell. Now, for an A-plus on the quiz, Pierre, can you tell me the inscription on the gate?"

"Of course. That's easy. ALL HOPE ABANDON, YE WHO ENTER HERE."

"Superb, Pierre! Just superb!" She squealed with excitement. "Well"—she sighed deeply—"I was sitting in on one of the old Professor's classes one afternoon, listening to him lecturing brilliantly on that third canto, actually able to see Dante and Virgil standing before the Infernal Gate and preparing to enter with great trepidation but an equally great resolve, in spite of those words of warning above them. And I knew right then that I had to use that inscription, somehow make it my own. So that very night I went back to St. Louis, shaved my coochie nice and clean, and had one of my girlfriends tattoo those foreboding words above and around it in bright red letters! Can there be a better and more personal irony than that, Pierre?" She howled incredulously. "Juxtaposing my gates of Paradise and the gates of Hell and making them one?

"I've always said my stuff is the entrance to either a great satiation or a great frustration. Heaven or Hell. And if"—she seemed to recite—"we can get beyond the confinements of lust, conquer that incapability to feel, that unwillingness to acknowledge love when it's offered, bliss will surround us, because lust is but a small part of making love. . . . Don't you agree? But then again, Pierre," she whispered as I nodded dumbly, pulling me close, "it's only when I'm with some special someone that I'll shave down there. Oil it up real good so the words stand out like drops of blood on my bare sweets. . . . Not everyone gets to stand before my Gate, Pierre. And of those who do, very few understand its meaning like you do now. So who knows"—she grinned, sitting back slowly, licking those lips—"maybe one day I'll shave it for you."

The moment was ended abruptly by Zeke standing over our table. "Gussie, honey, those boys over there have some money for me back at their barracks. Why don't we go collect?"

"Is it really worth the effort, Zeke?" she asked, looking them over.

"I reckon four hundred dollars makes it worth the effort, wouldn't you say, little darlin'? Especially in this weather."

"I suppose. . . . Well, let's get going, then. Nice talking to you, Pierre," she said as she stood up. "I know I'll be seeing you around." She kissed my forehead and smiled. "Oh, my! You're blushing again, you sweet dear."

"Listen, Pierre," Zeke half whispered as she turned to put on her coat, "don't put too much stock in that Dante story. I been knowin' Gussie goin' on three years, and I ain't seen whatever it is she's talkin' about yet." With that, he pawed me heavily on both shoulders and moved off to catch up with Gussie B, who was already sprinting through the snow to the car with four ruddy-faced GIs. I wished I made it five.

Two, maybe three weeks passed before I ventured back to Grizzly's. The thought of running into Johnnie Mae Merriweather was the main reason, even though I had some sort of explanation of our encounter. But still, after careful consideration, I laid low at the Ambassador, an intimate supper club near the heart of the city, thick nightly with the smug air of pseudo-sophisticated hipness and practiced nonchalance. Jukeboxed music segued easily from lightly bleached, textured jazz to soulful yet not too naughty rhythm and blues, and its cuisine was both tasty and tastefully overpriced.

Casually clad in muted tweed, satiny suede, or soft-as-warm-butter leather jackets, turtle-necked males posed and primped at the crowded bar, vying for attention with classic-striped or paisley-tied, wing-tipped, three-piece-suited competition. Between sips on hip ice-clinking cocktails or tongue-parching wine, they endured each other's forced conversations and deft exchanges of meaningless business cards, absently tugging on tight-tamped pipefuls of *tabac du jour,* all the while eyeing a most willing prey: nervous first-timers or femme fatales, sprinkled or huddled throughout the room, ladder-climbing seekers of status, women demurely awaiting their turn at gracing those hard-to-get bar stools or, perhaps, that one chance at strutting their stuff, controlled yet seductive, out on the softly lit dance floor. Or best of all, an invitation to partake in an ingratiating meal served at one of the tiny, secluded, candlelit tables.

Fashionably complemented in velvety dresses and sensible pumps or just-the-right-length skirts and loafers, they were for the most part college girls or college types or workers blessed with steady jobs, titillated by and on the prowl for those one-way tickets up the ladder or out of town, the professionals and servicemen to be found lurking in the shallow depths of the Ambassador.

Though outwardly blasé, all these players were an aggressive, heavy-breathing mix of ascenders and condescenders, locked in a slave-old game of color and class. And teenage or not, by being a prep boy from up north and well versed in the pretentious airs of urban Black bourgeoisie, I could fit right in.

Restless boredom soon became greater than my apprehension of Johnnie Mae Merriweather, however, and a rush of familiarity filled me as I walked through the doors of Grizzly's once again. Muddy Waters moaned sweetly in the night, bodies clung and swayed as one on the dance floor, Bear towered behind the bar. Just as I had left it. I stopped to get a setup.

"Hey, kid." He grunted. "See you made it back. Most folks don't stay gone that long 'lessen they dead, moved away, or owe me money."

I never knew he paid me any mind.

"Good thing, though. Some of these old broads in here been askin' about you. Sez you got—"

"—a tight ass and loose cash!" laughed a too-familiar, raspy voice from behind, grabbing my buttocks tightly as she spoke.

"Get your hands off me, woman," I barked at Johnnie Mae, turning to face her. "Enough is enough!"

"Sounds like he means it, girl," chuckled Bear in mock seriousness. "Maybe the kid done grown up since we seen him last."

"He's just sayin' that 'cause you're here, Bear."

"I wouldn't care if nobody was standing here," I shot back. "I said *quit!*" removing her hand as I looked into her ratty grin.

"You know, boy, I got a good mind to—"

"You don't have a mind, Johnnie Mae. Good or otherwise."

"Now, now, children," Bear interceded. "Why don't you go play somewhere else before the mean ole Bear gotta put a bullet hole in one of you, hmmm?"

"You right, Bear," Johnnie Mae growled, backing off into the crowd. "You right." Pointing a menacing finger at me in retreat, she muttered, "But don't think this is over 'tween you and me, boy. No, suh!"

"Don't mind her, kid," said Bear, going back to washing glasses and holding them up for inspection in the light as if nothing had happened. "She just needs somebody to love her, and I guess she figures you might could understand that. Maybe oblige her some. Shit, son. Everybody gots needs. . . . What you say? Long as it ain't you?" He laughed and shook. "Well, here's your setup anyhow. Go on with your buddies and enjoy yourself—after you gives me my three dollars and fifty cents, that is."

That night there was live entertainment. A dark, thin, scraggly-bearded fellow who called himself a "blues poet, head bishop M-fourteen of the Holy Ghost Fallout Shelter," one Gylan Kain. Backed only by a piano, upright bass, and congas, he espoused that:

"*Life ain't nothin' but a river,*
movin' through an empty hand,
I said life ain't nothin' but a river,
just movin' through an empty hand,
well, you can hold on if you wanna,
but Lord, when the truth hits the fan . . .

I remember him preaching and teaching that:

"*Ain't nobody gonna love me if I don't love myself . . .*
who's gonna take that weight if I ain't?
who's gonna lift me if I don't?
who's gonna deliver me if I won't?
who's gonna write my name, I say
who's gonna call my name in the echo of the rain?"

To each of his rapid-fire calls, the congregation responded raucously, "Ain't nobody!"

By the time his public confession was shared, Bear's church was his for the taking:

"Inside the vessels of too many women,
I've hid from myself far too many times,
when I lacked the courage to be alone.
You see, I cannot afford to spend another day
as a co-operator in a conspiracy against myself . . .
I just wanna be a man . . .
just wanna be the man that I am and nothing else,
just me, just God. . . ."

His sermon, in the midst of its swelling acceptance, ended on this note:

" 'Cause you see, there's only two kind of people in this world, now ain't that right? Huh? Somebody who can love and somebody who can receive that love . . . and when those two people can exist in the same person . . . I mean when you both love and receive that love, then, my friend, you are truly blessed and the kingdom of heaven is yours. . . . May the words from my lips find acceptance in thy sight, and the sight of all things holy, whether present or gone before us, as we continue our journey on into the night, grappling with this river we call life, a mighty river that flows around and through us all, this holy gathering, right here . . . in Bear's Den . . . my, my, my . . . *what it is?*"

It was after midnight when I finally took a break from dancing and drinking and testifying, Johnnie Mae Merriweather far removed from my thoughts. I stepped outside into the chilly winter breeze to cool off.

"Psst! Hey! Pierre!" A woman's voice wafted across the dirt parking lot. "Pierre! Over here, silly."

I followed her sound through the darkness to her silhouette, still not knowing who she was.

"Wanna see the inscription from canto three of Dante's Inferno?" she asked.

"What are you doing out here?" I asked Gussie B as I approached her. She sat sideways in the driver's seat of the Cadillac, feet on the ground.

"Just listening to the sinners," she said, opening the rear door, motioning for me to sit. "Come on. Take a load off." She offered me her silver flask. "Tie one on. . . . Bear doesn't like me to show my face in his place," she went on tipsily, "because his tiny-tit woman thinks I'm tryin' to steal him away. Shit, if I wanted that big old Negro, it'd be done. . . . And what are *you* doin' back out here? Catharsis for your wounded manhood? Ooops!" She giggled into her mouth. "That was a slip, Pierre, a slip."

"I don't mind. Besides, I'm not even sure I know what that means. But no, I like coming here. I gotta party somewhere, and this beats the hell out of the Ambassador."

"You got that right," she agreed as I took a long pull on the flask.

"What did you think of the blues poet?" I asked as I tried catching my breath, snatched away by the cognac, smacking my lips.

"Loved every word, Pierre. Every word. 'Can't love nobody till you love yourself.' So true. But you knew that, right? . . . Yo, stop hoggin' the cognac, Jack." She giggled again, slapping my knee. "I like you, Pierre. You're cute and smart, open to ideas. I like that in a man. . . . Hey, let's go get some more drinky-poo, whaddaya say?" She turned the empty flask upside down.

"Fine with me. But where? I mean, it's after midnight already."

She shook her head slowly from side to side. "Tsk, tsk, tsk. Did I just say you were smart? Here. Get on up front with me, Pierre."

She pulled off, tires kicking up loose gravel. "You ever drink shine, baby?"

"No," I replied as we sped off into the darkness, the unlit road whizzing by under our headlights. I had no idea where we were or where we were headed, but with Gussie's free hand roaming merrily between my thighs, why concern myself?

She pulled off the road to a red-lit house trailer in the middle of a thicket and told me to wait in the car. She wasn't gone long, returning with a jelly jar filled with a clear liquid. "Now here's your true welcome to the South!" she toasted.

Before she could warn me, I took a swig like I had with the cognac. Every inch of me grew hot immediately, and my head swam somewhere between spinning toplike and nausea.

"Oooh, I meant to tell you, take little sips." She laughed. "But I guess you know that now. If you start feeling sick, *please* open the window quickly."

I settled into a manageable inebriation, however, and shortly we arrived at what looked like a shack of sorts.

"We're here, lover," Gussie B announced with a flair. "All ashore for ice-cold beer and hot sex! Last one's buying!"

I groped along, trying to get reaccustomed to walking, shivering in the cold as I remembered the overcoat I'd left behind at Grizzly's. Gussie, meanwhile, dashed up two steps and into the unlocked shanty, turning on a lamp inside.

"Beer's in the fridge. On ice, too," she was saying as I finally made it inside. "There's more cognac on the counter if you've had enough shine. I'll be back in a flash." She blew a kiss and disappeared into the back.

There was another lamp in the dingy front room, but it didn't work. Roaches crawled boldly all over the rotted sink and sideboard. I passed on the cognac and gingerly took a beer out of the ancient icebox. I stood while drinking it, afraid to sit in any of the three dilapidated stuffed chairs, which seemed alive with crawling things. Just in time, Gussie called, dripping sweetness, "Pierre, honey, could you bring your Gussie a cold one . . . *and a hot one?*"

The light in the back room went out.

My Gussie? Visions of Dante, gates of Hades, devils and angels pranced in my head. Flushed and erect, I knew this was gonna be worth much more than any topcoat.

"Over here." She beckoned softly from the shadows. I moved closer, placing my beer on a nightstand as I took her by the waist. "Wait," she whispered, "not so fast, Pierre." She turned on the lamp; Johnnie Mae Merriweather stood grinning before me, razor in hand.

"I told you it wasn't over 'tween you and me, boy!"

I grabbed both her wrists, screaming for Gussie B as me and Johnnie Mae danced around the room. She laughed hysterically, not trying to break free, but rather enjoyed watching my eyes bulge in horror and the veins stand up in my neck. We sort of ring-around-the-rosied faster and faster until my clammy hands lost their grip on her. I flew through a closed, screened window, crashing with a thud onto the frozen turf outdoors. Gathering myself, then running and shrieking toward the front of the house, I prayed that, *a:* the Cadillac was open and, *b:* the keys were in the ignition. Only *a* applied. I locked all the doors once inside and lay down on the rear floor, cowering and whimpering. Shit! I cried silently, pounding the floor with my fists. Shit, shit, shit! You're gonna die out here in only God knows where, and all because you pissed off some deranged bitch you don't even know! My tears and sobs flowed freely and I didn't try to stop them. They probably won't even find your body, stupid. Shit!

Suddenly, there was a determined thudding at the window. "*Pierre!* Hey, Pierre! Open up, honey! It's me, Gussie! *Pierre, open up, goddammit, it's cold out here!*" I popped my head up to see Gussie B grinning her wide grin. "Open up this fuckin' car, baby, and let me in. I'm serious!"

I wiped the snot and tears off my face and carefully opened the door. "Where is she?" I asked as Gussie clambered in on top of me.

"Where is who, silly?" she asked, licking my nasty face, covering it with kisses.

"Wait, no, wait," I said shakily, holding her off, looking around in a panic. "Johnnie Mae. Johnnie Mae Merriweather. You didn't see her? She's here! She's here! She tried to kill me . . . and you set me up!"

"She's not here, Pierre, sweetie. You just thought you saw her. . . . Set you up? I wouldn't hurt you. Come on back inside and I'll explain."

"No! I'm not goin' in there. Johnnie Mae is in there!"

"Pierre, now calm down and stop this foolishness. No one is going to hurt you. Trust me." She sat me upright. "Come."

She led me to the back room, its light still on. The hole in the window had a blanket shoved into it. "Sit on the bed, honey," she said. "I want to show you something." Patting the bed, she repeated, "Sit."

She took a large cardboard box from a closet and plopped it down beside me. From it she took out a short-cropped wig, some soft, flesh-colored, latex likenesses of Johnnie Mae Merriweather, complete with grotesque scar, a few blocks of clay, and some makeup pencils. "Howja like to see ole Johnnie Mae up close, sweetmeat?" she cackled, the voice of Johnnie Mae filling the room.

"You see, Pierre," she said in her normal voice, pulling me back down onto the bed, "Johnnie is just a lot of makeup and imagination. My young guy out in Los Angeles taught me about this makeover stuff, and I just took it a step further. Johnnie only comes out at night and makes love as best she knows how in the dark. It's hard to pick up the imperfections of a masked face. A face you don't want to see in the first place. The rough hands are gloves with a sandpaper finish. Some of my teeth I blacken out; I put sharpened caps on others. I even bought this shack and the Chevy for her, lived another life through her. My life. In need, but afraid. In control, but in need. But now she's got to go away. And I've got to go too." She took my hands in hers, saying slowly, "I've been killing GIs from the base, Pierre. The base here, and in Texas and Louisiana, too."

I gulped hard. "What?"

"For a few years now," she continued evenly. "Killed so many white boys, I've lost count. GIs who thought I was just another fantasy-fulfilling, nigger hooker. White boys like the ones who forced me and my mama at gunpoint that night. On the road behind the base. We never saw their faces, but I can still remember their smell: only whites smell like that. . . ."

"Wait," I interceded, but she waved me off.

"Mama begged for them to spare me, cried that she would pleasure all four of them, right there on the road if need be, just spare me, and all she got was a gun butt upside her head for her troubles. And then they took us, whooping and cheering like it was a football game. Some sport. Something to be rooted for . . . holding that gun on us as they took their turns. And when they had enough, they drove off, throwing pocket change at us, still braying and howling. Mama died not many weeks after, and sometimes . . . sometimes I wish I had died along with her.

"I been killing them ever since that first one I pushed out my womb, the one that came because of that night. Had it just so I *could* kill it. Pushed it out of me and took it down to the river. Held it under . . . held it under, then released it, saluting as it drifted out of sight downstream."

"Stop, Gussie," I said firmly, not willing to just let her go on. "What about going to the police or the base commander or—?"

"What for, Pierre? To tell them four white boys just like them took what they felt was part of their birthright? That they violated the honor of some negligible pieces of Black ass? No, no, no, Pierre. It wasn't worth the time or humiliation.

"The most vivid thing I remember is their cold skin slapping against mine. The pounding. The tearing. I became so numb with fear and shame that I didn't even feel them after a while."

"Why are you telling me this, Gussie? You hardly know me, and I—"

"Confession. Good for the soul. . . . It's true, you know."

"But I'm just a stranger, not a confessor."

"Everything precious and dear to us lies outside the realm of importance to them," she continued, ignoring my comment, "and my virginity may as well have been the dirt it bled onto that night. It took years for me to come to this, being able to feel comfortable in my solution. Once we start, I block them out again, not feeling or hearing, not even smelling them, just focusing on the task ahead. At some point during the act, or later, when they roll off me and fall asleep, I rub a poison into their skin. How they love the feel of my velvet gloves skimming up and down their backs, Pierre, not knowing that my fingers are drenched with their demise. Besides, the sensation gets them to finish quicker. I even put some more on the inside of their clothes if I can, just to make sure they get enough. In a day or two they feel an intense fire growing in their bellies that gets to be so painful they pray for death to come. And, very soon, their feeble prayers are answered. They discover Paradise has a cost more dear than mere pocket change.

"I trusted Zeke with my secret, let him supply me with eager, panting victims who more than liked what they saw. Panting and more than eager to pay for their not-so-secret fantasies to come true. But Zeke didn't appreciate the significance of what either of us were doing, nor did he appreciate my resolve. Only thought in terms of dollars and cents, that one: *his cut.* Could not see the connection between the life of the spirit and the life of the flesh and the importance of that connection and, as a result, was not able to revel with me in the sweet taste of revenge served cold. And I needed for him, as a man, to be able to do that. So you see, all things said, by his lacking vision and compassion, he became no better than the victims themselves. That's part of why I'm telling you, Pierre. You're no stranger. I know you can understand why I've done what I've done and not pass judgment. It feels good to just tell it without being judged. You question me only to be sure that I'm sure. Unfortunately, it's too late for much more than that and I've got to move on. I'll be leaving in the morning for destinations best not mentioned. . . . But before I do, my bright-eyed Innocens," she said coyly, reaching for the moonshine and sipping gingerly, "how about you and me in a nice cushy hotel for the rest of the night? I promise you'll live to tell about it."

The corpse of Zeke Jones was found sometime that same night in a far corner of Grizzly's parking lot. His throat had been cut from ear to ear. No weapon was found, but it was thought to be a very sharp knife or straight razor. Further, there was no sign of struggle. The ensuing investigation turned up nothing but speculation, and both Johnnie Mae Merriweather and Gussie B became wisps of smoke, grabbed at but never there, not really, then gone and vanished.

That night in the hotel, lying in bed, waiting for Gussie B to come out of the bathroom and join me, my head ached with too many questions. Was Paradise worth waiting for? After all, it was just a metaphor. An enticing one, but a metaphor just the same. And if Paradise overwhelmed me, would it still be considered such? By me? By her? Lovemaking and lust were still not sharply defined for me. And in the face of Death? . . .

Lust won out when she came to me. I ventured hesitantly beyond her Gothic-inscribed gate, its warning a shimmering bright red against the oiled brownness of her, and when love was asked for, clearly, consciously, I was able to both give and receive it.

And after Paradise, I did not fear sleep but chose not to. Just in case.

As we rested, Gussie asked if I had read anything of Jean Toomer's, a Black writer during the Harlem Renaissance of the 1920s. I had to admit that, in spite of (or maybe because of) my wonderful northern prep school education, I had never encountered any Black writers nor had I ever heard of this Harlem Renaissance. We used passion to soothe the hurt of my ignorance and to release the anger of our omission. Later, as we rested once more, she told me of her favorite book by Toomer, a book entitled *Cane*, a compilation of stories and poems, and how one story in particular, "Karintha," had struck her. She quoted:

> "Karintha is a woman. Men do not know that the soul of
> her was a growing thing ripened too soon. They will all
> bring their money; they will die not having found it out. . . .
> Karintha at twenty, carrying beauty, perfect as dusk when the
> sun goes down. Karintha. . . .
> Her skin is like dusk on the eastern horizon,
> O cant you see it, O cant you see it
> Her skin is like dusk on the eastern horizon
> . . . When the sun goes down.
> Goes down. . . .

"She and I share so many things. But I'll let you read it so you can see for yourself."

Out went the lights; this was no time to think. . . .

Much later, I lay panting on my back. Eventually, I tried making a connection between Gussie and the fictional Karintha. But, "Do you remember Precious?" Gussie interrupted. "Yes, your precious Precious. Your first woman."

Stunned, I turned my head in her direction. "How do you know that? You know her? I mean, you've spoken to her?"

"Of course. Kinfolk, no matter how distant, do talk from time to time. She'd got so disillusioned when Zeke wouldn't marry her. And while I admired her for sticking to her guns about sharing her precious gift for her wedding night, we both knew Zeke never intended to get hitched. Way too many women told her as much. So she agreed to live out my first-time fantasy, since it had been ruined for me already and it was getting mighty late for her. Said we deserved as much. . . . We picked you out at that party because I remembered you, the virgin from the Forty-Deuce, spread-eagled against the wall, your back facing death and yet your last wish in this life was for consummation."

The blankets and sheets on our bed twisted tightly as I jerked onto my side to face Gussie in the chilly darkness.

INNOCENS COMES TO COTTON

"Oh, my God! You were there? At the party? And the Forty-Deuce?"

Outside, harsh winds howled just as they had when we were making love.

"I was there. And before you ask, you got picked because you still looked—well, as innocent as Precious was. As innocent as I had imagined, had hoped *he* would be for me . . . and after she felt it with you, that feeling, that safe-to-share, tender, loved feeling, I wanted to feel it for myself. Johnnie Mae was my test. And you passed. Do you follow?"

"Because I refused her? . . . I suppose. But Precious. . . . Will I see her again?"

"It's best that you don't. Besides, it's impolite to talk about one woman when you're with another. Especially when they're cousins."

And one last thing Gussie told me.

"My mama used to call growing up and understanding the ways of grown folk 'comin' to cotton.' Do you truly understand the depth of rape, Pierre? The justness of taking your raper's life in return?"

"I never considered it before tonight. Before you."

"And what is it you understand now, Pierre?"

"I acknowledge how precious is the health of the spirit and the health of the flesh and the connection between the two . . ."

"Yes . . ."

". . . and how, either in sickness or in health, you must be able to love yourself, be able to call your name. . . ."

"And what else? Come on, you're on the right track."

"Rape is a violation of both spirit and flesh, a violation that can never be repaid . . ."

"Yes!"

". . . not even by taking the violater's life."

Gussie fell silent.

"Gussie, you have to let this go. Leave it behind. The men you've killed are guilty of their fantasies, nothing more. They had nothing to do with the death of your mother or the death of your spirit. I'm young and maybe naive. Rape and death were abstracts to me before I came here. But I do know that an eye for an eye doesn't hold water if the receiver of the vengeance is blind or not given a chance to see what the vengeance is for. Their deaths serve no purpose. They become hollow metaphors, symbols only you can appreciate, symbols who won't bring consolation, can't bring healing. After you are able to love yourself, Gussie, don't you think it's important for somebody to love you? Life over death?"

Her silence spoke more than our words. She sighed wearily. "Innocens, seems like you're not the only one come to cotton. No, I believe you've brought me to cotton too. Now let's get some sleep."

I went home on leave for two weeks. When I got back to the base, the military and local police came around to ask me questions. Did I know a Johnnie Mae Merriweather, a Gustavia Beatrice Holloway, or her procurer, the late Airman Basic Thomas Ezekiel Jones? Had I known he was the alleged illegitimate son of a white congressman in New Orleans? What about a woman known only as Precious? Did I know her? I said I had made the acquaintance of all four but was not especially close to any of them, and this was the first I was hearing of Airman Jones's death. Had I heard about white GIs mysteriously dying on bases in at least three neighboring states? No, I replied, I had not. Any idea where the three aforementioned women might have disappeared to? No, I had none.

"Pierre," Gussie whispered to me as I lay behind her in bed on that last night together, "I'm gonna slide you inside of me and then I don't want for us to move. Just lie still for as long as we can. . . . Mmmm, goood. . . . Now still, Pierre. Just hold me for a while. Yeah, like that. . . . I can't remember the last time I've just been held and whispered to. The Professor couldn't and the movie man wouldn't. Sometimes—ooooooh—sometimes that's all a woman wants, all she needs. Most men—mmm—don't understand that, and most who do would rather not—yeah, yeah, yeah—so let's call this our coh-h-h-hm-pro-mise po-si-tion. Oooh, shit, Pierre! You can be inside me and I can get my hug at the same time—mmm, mmm, mmm!—and it feels—oooh, yes . . . tsk, tsk, tsk—it feels just fine."

Firstborn

D. S. MODUPE

I'm not a person who remembers names. In fact, at a party once, three years into my marriage, to my mortification when making introductions, I blocked my wife's name. My friends have all learned to suffer this frailty and recently have taken great pleasure in my having several times forgotten my own name— that is, my reconstructed self, my African name. And yet, a name I haven't heard in over forty years rings in my ears now as sharply and familiarly as the chimes announcing 9 P.M. on the opposite, exposed-brick wall. MISSY, I write, putting pen to paper after a writer's block of seven years, and there is a tingle of expectancy. Missy, catalyst to my rebirth! This seems somehow so appropriate, like an African-fabled lesson I grasp at the level of intuition but fear I cannot yet put into words.

My immediate family—my mother, my four-year-old baby brother, and I —had just recently arrived in Harlem, a place I return to frequently now,

DANJUMA SINUE MODUPE (a.k.a. Henry L. Evans) has published fiction in college and literary magazines, such as *Amistad III* and *Balaam's Ass*, in the international anthology *Persia: An International Review*, as well as the popular *Essence* magazine. His latest work, *Afrocentrically Grounded*, is to be included in a multicultural writing textbook. Modupe received a Master of Fine Arts degree from Columbia University, and he teaches writing for the Academic Skills Department at Hunter College.

to attend Black arts and political functions, eat soul food, and buy African clothes. Though our street was 138th Street, I spent school-day afternoons at Brownie's, the sitter's, on 140th Street. My brother and I wound up there on most weekends, too. The Harlem street, the corner fruit stand under whose bright green awning we kids sheltered from the rain, the "nickel-a-pickle" candy store, the row of five-story houses, the stoops upon which we children played—these casualties of progress are now gone. The oasis of a playground, which lay beyond the forbidding two-way traffic of Lenox Avenue, crossed only in the company of some responsible adolescent or adult, remains, dense with renovations and vibrant with colorful community murals. On occasion, Wendel, the super's adolescent son, volunteered to escort us kids—when he was not tinkering with his chemistry set or sneaking around the corner to a Lenox Avenue storefront, where between the spaces of the large painted symbols on the windows I would peek in to see him among men wearing long white dresses and little crocheted caps and women wearing even longer dresses and white scarves over their heads. The scene reminded me then of how Grandma Allie had insisted we boys wear "Grannie sack" smocks and had braided our hair until with the help of the menfolks we rebelled with the starting of school. It was one thing to dress kids like that on the farm, the menfolks said, but another to send them boys like that to school. The men I saw through the storefront window spoke funny words, and always some person up front was yelling angrily at the audience about white and black people. The I-talian boys across the street from Brownie's would fight if you called them white, said they were black, a word I was not allowed to use. It was like a cussword, but Missy used it freely. She didn't believe those I-talian boys, said the black people that looked like them I-talian kids didn't have *two* white parents. I sort of sensed this was true.

Missy and I were both seven years old that early summer. But she was two grades ahead of me—one because I had been put back for having come up from the South, and another because she had already been skipped. But I was soon to gain back my grade the following year when I transferred to the all-Black school up on Sugar Hill.

Missy was "wild," most grown-ups said, and her mother didn't go to church. Instead, she practiced something that had to do with "roots." But I knew, as my uncle said, Grandma Allie "fooled around with them roots," and it seemed like everybody around for miles at one time or another had appeared on the horizon walking or poking along in a buggy or spinning up dust clouds in their fast cars as they came down our winding dirt road past the cemetery, the cow pasture, the wooded area of pines, then were announced by a front-yard flurry of blackbirds in the plumb, apple, and lotus trees, then finally strolled up onto our porch for the "workings" of them roots. And yet Grandma Allie went to church *every* Sunday *and* got the spirit, spoke in tongues.

When Missy showed up on our stoop, Brownie never called us kids inside, as did some mothers, who hung out of their windows and monitored street life with a sagacity and moral aptitude that rivaled the attention paid to their "dreamed" numbers. "She's just a child, like any other child," Brownie would argue to the women in the building, including my aunt Minnie, who, with her husband Bennie and my cousin Marie, lived "temporarily" in the top floor front three-bedroom apartment with two other families, each saving for a "home." If memory hasn't deceivingly slipped into hindsight, I had already learned—intuited, actually—not to notice Missy too much. Sometimes when I had jumped the most stoop steps or won at skellies, or made my yoyo sleep the longest, I would look over and find Missy staring. My skin felt prickly, and yet underneath I glowed.

Skinny, ashy legs, limbs quick with a movement I can describe now as a want of freedom that twirled her short, colorful skirts, and the glimpse of white cotton drawers seen and unseen back then return suddenly, and I pause from the writing, sit up at the desk, sigh, and sip my lukewarm coffee. There is a longing—for some "Missy quality" apprehended but still not at the level of consciousness. Usually, I'm good at faces, but Missy's features remain a blur. Her hair was plaited in short tight braids, the prominent black eyebrows shiny against a velvety skin almost as black. Nothing memorable about her eyes, only they could narrow and pin you down like a won thumb wrestle. I remember her smell, clean, a scrubbed-child smell. She had this habit of biting down on the corner of her lip and staring off into the distance, and then . . .

The chipped slate steps were hot to the touch every afternoon, those last days of school. But on either side of the top step, gray marble pillars set in blocks supported a shading concrete overhang. Between the blocks and the building was a balustrade, forming an area we called wells. Cool places not much help in hide-and-seek, they formed cul-de-sacs. Through the apartment building glass doors, at the end of a long tiled hall, the older kids hung out in a much cooler place under the stairwell. They smoked cigarettes and allowed us smaller kids in only by invitation.

For whatever reason, the two of us, Missy and I, wound up on the stoop, alone, that afternoon. I sat realizing a prayer had been answered I hadn't even known I'd said.

"Where you from, again?" Missy was saying.

"I done told you I don't know how many times."

"Well, say it again. I like the way you say it—all singsong and smooth like."

With anyone else I would have been fighting mad, but Missy really liked my accent. She could imitate it perfectly.

"Nort Calina," I said, and I remember Missy's flashy infectious smile that made me homesick for the warm starry nights on our back porch laid out with pallets for us kids, and all around me late into the night the eruption giggles and laughter until my sides ached.

Missy and I watched the street life and talked and talked and talked. Then we were slapping and bumping each other, laughing as the *I*-talian kids across the street, all six of them, stripped to their underwear and darted in and out of the water spray of the dump truck as it whined and groaned its way down the block. Under our laughter, though, was a heaviness, an envy and a regret that made us avoid each other's eyes. At one point in the conversation, Missy said matter-of-factly, as she stretched her forearm out alongside mine, "You're as black as me."

We had moved from the steps to the secrecy and cool of one of the stoop's wells. I stretched my arm the length of hers, coming into a startled, queasy recognition.

"Yes," I said.

Grown-ups didn't care much about being tattletales. In fact, in those days, if you sneezed on the steps after school, by the time you walked those few blocks home, your mother would be waiting with a handkerchief.

When the woman had come up on us, unheard and unseen, Missy had me pinned down against her in a headlock, her legs wrapped around mine to keep me from getting leverage by pushing off the wall. Before capitulating, I was suffering the indignity and pain as long as I could. "Give? You give?" she screamed.

"Get up off of that girl," the woman exclaimed. And she was reaching for me, jerking me by the arm. Looking up into a yellow-brown face with a small scattering of cheek moles, I saw a pinched mouth as pink as my favorite doll's, secreted away and waiting for me in the bureau drawer of the attic back home in North Carolina. I resisted, frightened and confused.

"Where's your mother, boy?" the woman demanded, shaking me. "And you, you little hussy."

Missy had sat up, and the way she looked into the woman's eyes so questioningly seemed for a moment to make the woman falter. I didn't want to tell the woman anything, but I didn't want to be spanked in front of Missy, either.

"You wait right here, you hear me? Don't either of you budge, not one inch!"

Through the glass doors I watched the woman, listened to the click of her high heels fading down the hall until she reached the two doors past the stairs. The one on the right was Brownie's. When I turned to Missy, she was gone.

"Too big for your britches, boy," Brownie said.

"But I didn't *do* nothing."

"Then why you running from me?"

In the South, with anywhere from two to two dozen cousins of all ages around, there was always someone who had done something to get a switching. I felt I had been getting them all along too but realized I hadn't, hadn't even been slapped. I had always been "sickly" and "bright" and, like Grandma Allie, "saw things." I was certain to be a minister, everybody said. But I didn't think Brownie knew all this. Although I was terrified, my running was more a function of just not knowing how to stand still for a beating. I was on the corner, attracting attention. God didn't like ugly, and I was surely acting ugly. I felt if I could just draw this out, the truth would somehow materialize. But there were all these people standing around now, and Brownie, big and square and black, and breathing scarily deep, her brow wrinkled, catching the beads of sweat, was still clutching the cut-off broom handle.

Mr. Lionel, the corner fruit-stand man, had actually left his cash register, stood just outside his door. Like my never-seen father, he too was called a "Geechee." He was between me and any attempt at turning the corner, and although he had complimented my mother on how mannerly and well-behaved her southern children were, I was sure he was out of his store with the express purpose of grabbing me. Terror swept me again, and I almost sprinted. Instead, I merely shifted from one foot to the other, clutching myself. I had to go something terrible. Then, to my amazement, Brownie had turned and was walking away. I wanted to melt into the ground. After a while, quick-stepping, I followed her.

As always, the apartment was surprisingly cool and occupied familiarly with gospel music, like back home. Brownie was standing over the ironing board. Behind her one of the two windows that looked out on the backyard, from which we children dropped kitchen matches to explode on the concrete, was sucking the thin curtains onto the fire escape. The Chesterfield hanging from her lips was half ash, but it never dropped to the clothes. The broom handle was nowhere in sight.

"Shut the door, boy, and go on in there and use the bathroom."

I stood my ground.

"Didn't you hear me, boy?"

"I don't have to go," I said softly.

"What?"

"Said I don't have to go."

Brownie looked up, stared at me a moment.

"Mr. Big Britches," she said. "Well, you're going to stay in those wet pants until your mama comes."

I closed the door.

"And don't go sitting your stinking butt on any of my furniture." She looked down at my pants again. "In the hall?"

I managed a nod.

She sighed.

I shifted away from the door when she passed, mop in hand. "A big boy like you!" she added.

Mary and Carol-Anne were taking a dance class at the Y (they had my brother with them, took him everywhere), so the sounds coming from the rear of the apartment meant that Bill was up. But that didn't matter, at least in terms of my catching it. It did somehow seem to mean that I couldn't watch Bill shave, then comb his hair. Always before he put on his mailman's uniform, he would stand before the bathroom mirror in his BVDs and with each front-to-back stroke of the comb run a hand over the jet-black straight hair with the waves up front.

I was sitting in the window praying for a breeze when Brownie came in with the mop. She cut me that Be still! look, which meant, Don't go out onto the fire escape, don't go get any books off the shelf, and don't go bothering Bill, don't go doing *nothing!* When my mother arrived—the woman I was just getting to know, whom I still called by her first name, and who still awed me with her fair-skinned and long straight-haired beauty, Brownie didn't mention a thing about that afternoon. No one ever found out. The next time I spent the night at Brownie's, when my mother was around the corner at the Savoy (she was always being asked out somewhere, sometimes with us kids), Brownie did something funny—gave me my bath with Carol-Anne.

No one after that had to tell me to leave Missy alone. She sensed my coolness quickly, gradually stopped hanging around on our stoop, and didn't walk with me and the guys anymore on the way home from school. Then, the week between school letting out and my being sent south for the summer, Wendel took a group of us kids over to the playground one day. Off in a far corner, a bunch of older girls were jumping rope. Among them was Missy. It wasn't long before I spied her coming across the playground. The way she was biting down on her lip, I thought she was going to give me a good tongue-lashing or sock me one, and when she didn't, I reached for the hope that she might even apologize for leaving me to face Brownie alone and we could maybe be friends again. I knew now that I wanted to be her friend.

When she reached the monkey bars, she jerked me by the hand so hard that I almost fell, then pulled me over to the back, shading wall of the recreation center. She let go my hand and it remained for a moment suspended, filled with the imprint of hers. She was looking at me queerly, like you look at a stranger, someone you want to but aren't quite sure you can trust.

"I just wanted you to know," she said, "my name."

I stared at her, confused, somehow both relieved and disappointed.

"I already know your name," I said.

"My real name," she said. "It isn't Missy." Then she said it, and told me what it meant.

I felt somehow betrayed, but felt, too, the revelation sink into place somewhere deep inside me like a *click*. Before I could respond, she had turned and was running back across the playground to her friends.

I put down my pencil, the fourth from a bunch of freshly sharpened ones with crisp clean erasers taken from a cup on the desk. First drafts I always do in longhand. I get up to go into the kitchen, just as the chimes begin to strike for a new day. In the dark hall, the wall display of African art objects and masks reminds me of something, but I lose it as I step into the white glare of kitchen light. Waiting for the water to boil, I go to the kitchen window, pull back the left curtain. Lamplight pools on the glistening wet street below, illumines a sheet of fine, gentle rain. Before my divorce, before my psychic change, I was in love with the Upper West Side, particularly its brownstone floor-through apartments, in one of which I now reside. The empty, bright-lighted street that I now look down upon appears hard, foreign, and alien—softened and rendered hospitable only by the rain. I make a mental note to call my mother and ask for the photograph taken of me and my brother that summer, the one of us sitting on the running board of my uncle's, my namesake's, '47 Chevrolet, the summer I returned to find Missy had moved. The story written, I want to see myself, as if to reaffirm something I only half believe I will recognize in myself in the photograph. The kettle whistles, and I go to the stove and pour the water for the coffee.

Sitting in the study again, I look at the title of the story, MISSY, written in large block print at the top of the yellow legal pad. At the bottom of the pad I begin to doodle. It is not long before I am somewhere distant, just below the line of wakefulness. Suddenly, I am remembering the two outstretched arms, mine perhaps even darker than Missy's. The face that appears before me, Missy's and not Missy's, is a carved ebony mask. Like a blind man sensing with his fingers, I touch the almond eyes, the nose, the chin, then hear her voice. It sends me back above the line, and I am awake. I sit for a weary moment, trying to remember Missy's face, but it is no use. I rise finally, sighing, ready for bed. I take a few steps toward the light switch by the door, only to return to the desk and pick up the pencil and pad. I put a line through the story's title and write MOSI, which I recall Missy having told me means firstborn.

Excerpt from Beyond the Limbo Silence

ELIZABETH NUNEZ

 It was in 1956 that the Americans saved our family. Just a few weeks before our rescue I had hardly known they existed. Not that there weren't Americans in the world. I knew they lived in a place called THE STATES. Wanna go to THE STATES? Just came back from THE STATES. Yeah, man, I have family in THE STATES. I thought it was a stupid name to call a country: THE STATES. I once looked for it on the map. We had geography in elementary school, but the only countries we studied, of course, were England and Western Europe—sometimes Australia or New Zealand, rarely the Windward and Leeward Islands or the Caribbean. I knew where the Americas were: North America and Central America, but not THE STATES. I concluded it must be New York, since sometimes it would be used interchangeably with THE STATES. *Just came back from* THE STATES. *Man, that New York ent playing, it cold, man.*

I had seen some Americans in Trinidad. They had built a military naval

---

ELIZABETH NUNEZ is the author of two novels: *When Rocks Dance* (Putnam, 1986, and Ballantine, 1992) and *Bruised Hibiscus* (Amistad, 1994). Dr. Nunez is a professor of English and chairperson of the department of Literature, Languages and Philosophy at Medgar Evers College, the City University of New York. She is director of the National Black Writers Conference sponsored by the National Endowment for the Humanities. Born in Trinidad, Dr. Nunez now makes her home on Long Island, New York.

base in Chaguaramas on the northwestern seacoast not far from Port-of-Spain. My uncles told me they remembered the time when they used to ride their bicycles from Diego Martin to Tetron Bay, but it was difficult for me to imagine any Trinidadian lying on the beaches in Chaguaramas. For that place was as foreign and distant to me as THE STATES, though it was just a few short miles from where I lived. Sometimes I saw the Americans when they came to Port-of-Spain to shop. Yankees, we called them as children, laughing at their clothes that no self-respecting Trinidadian would wear. Bright-colored pants, sometimes sun yellow or shocking pink. They had no shame. Pants cut off at the knees like overgrown schoolboys. We laughed at their hairy legs. No shame. Even the eleven-year-old boys in my class begged their mothers for long pants. It was a mark of maturity. And the shirts they wore! They loved flowers. The bigger the better. Splashes of hibiscus, or coconut fronds, bougainvillea or upside-down flamboyant. Whatever flower they thought we grew in the tropics. The English loved flowers on their clothes too, but they were much more sensible: tiny rosebuds, lilacs, a sprig of silver bells. It was all part of their grand plan, the burden they bore to cultivate and civilize the wild and untamed.

Then there was always the inevitable camera swinging on the necks of the Americans. We posed for them, laughing, wondering why they got so upset when we refused their money. "What for?" we would ask. And even if we were tempted, how could we explain to mothers who knew everything that someone wanted to pay us just for standing there, arms around each other, acting the fool? On Jouvay, the first morning of our two-day Carnival when people wore their silliest costumes, we dressed up like them. Big men and women did the same. We put on the most outlandish colors we could find, clashing them against each other. Blinding lime green with sunset orange. Bleeding red with seawater blue. Cameras swinging. We laughed at ourselves talking Yankee talk with slurring r's and vowels that whizzed down our nasal passages.

They had a fairy-tale quality about them, Americans. Loads of money, big cars, huge mansions, hardly any children; I never saw an American child before I was twenty. Unreal people. The stuff of calypsos and the make-believe world of Carnival. Kitchener teased us about them: *Rum and Coca-Cola—Waiting for the Yankee dollar.* Sparrow warned: *Jean, Tina Rosita, and Clementina,/Round the corner posing/bet your life is something they selling/If you catch them broken/You can get it all for nothin/Don't make a shout/Yankees gone and Sparrow take over now.*

They came in black and white, the Yankees, but I thought them all the same. Americans. Yankees. As different from us as the English. Distinguished from them only by their accents and the fact that the English wore cultivated flowers on their clothes, straw hats with ribbons or more flowers, white gloves in the middle of the day. But the Americans became real enough for me that June of 1956 when my schoolmates began to get sick.

June in Trinidad can be a month of contradictions. The two seasons meet then, the dry swirling parched dry dust across burnt brown grass, snapping twigs off half-dead trees; the wet grumbling thunder around noontime, sending slivers of liquid silver rain gleaming in the sun. The devil and his wife fighting for a hambone, children chanted. Such it was that June. The sun and the rain. The dry and the wet. We were accustomed to getting colds then in that mixed-up weather. "It made you stronger for August when the hurricanes came," my grandmother used to say. "Do battle with the germ in June and you'll master it in July." So at first it was not strange that the children in my town were sick in June—the burning fevers in the morning, the cold shivers by afternoon. The pains in the limbs were different. We couldn't explain them. A different type of cold this year, the older people said.

My grandmother told my mother to give me senna-pod tea to drink every three days and to bathe me in shining-bush-tea water. Almost all liquid brews in Trinidad were called tea. Children drank cocoa tea in the morning, adults had coffee tea at night; we all drank black tea in between. We took orange-peel tea for stomachaches and senna-pod tea to cleanse our insides. I hated the taste of senna-pod tea, not to mention the embarrassment of what it did to me, especially on a school day when everyone knew from my frequent trips to the lavatory that I had been forced to drink it. My mother put milk and sugar in it so it would taste like black tea, but that never masked the bitterness. When the sickness came that June of 1956 schoolchildren all over Port-of-Spain were going to the lavatory and there were many accidents.

For my shining-bush-tea baths, my grandmother sent a small bag of herbs that had been blessed, she said. We knew she did not mean blessed by the priest, and although my mother was a rigidly religious Roman Catholic, she dipped that bag once a day in my bathwater. I asked her one night if the obeah man had blessed it. She slapped me. After my bath she made me say the rosary with her. She said the first part of the Hail Mary, I said the second part: Holymarymotherofgodprayforussinnersnowandatthehourofourdeathamen. I never heard the words. Just the music. The rise and fall of the voice. The cadence of the lines. Sometimes my mind drifted but I always felt the beat, and at her blessedisthefruitofthywombjesus I would respond, Holymarymotherofgod. . . . Sometimes I thought of what we had done before the rosary. My mother would light a candle at the foot of the bathtub, dip the bag of herbs three times in the shining-bush-tea water and make the sign of the cross. I wondered if the obeah man and our parish priest met at the street corner.

One night my mother broke her silence during the ritual of the bathwater. "I don't really believe any of this, you know, Sara, but we can't take any chances. This sickness is so different."

But she believed. And just a few years later I would catch her with her obeah woman. Three operations in England and still there was only me. Then, desperate to give birth to another child, she had the obeah woman burn roots for her.

My friend, Nancy, was the first one to die in my school. She leaned over to me one day in class and whispered that her legs hurt her so bad she could hardly move them.

"Where?" I asked. "Which part?"

"The bones," she said. "Right in the very center."

They had hurt her before but not in the very center. I offered to tell the teacher but she shook her head vigorously. "It will pass," she said.

It had passed before.

Her fever flared up after the noontime rain. We had found shelter under sprawling leafy branches of the tamarind tree that shaded one corner of the schoolyard. It was still lunch recess, and while we had that freedom nothing could send us back to those hot stuffy classrooms—not even rain. By accident I touched Nancy's face. I wanted to point something out to her, and my hand brushed her cheeks. Her skin felt like burning coals. One second later she slumped to the ground. She could not move. The headmaster picked her up in his arms and took her home in his car. She died the next day. We began to fear this June cold that gave fevers in the afternoon and pained the legs.

The Sunday after Nancy's death my father took me to the movies. It was an unusual treat. My father, who only seemed to notice my existence peripherally when we sat together at mealtimes, or when my mother complained about something I'd done, or when I gave him those innumerable plastic ashtrays for his birthday, suddenly seemed to notice that I existed the day that Nancy died. There were a lot of questions.

"Did you and Nancy share your juice at lunchtime?"

Yes, we always did, drinking from the same bottle. We were friends forever. For eternity, we had sworn.

"Did you share your sandwich with her?"

Yes, we did. She took a bite of mine, I took a bite of hers, and so on.

excerpt from BEYOND THE LIMBO SILENCE

That's how we ate our sandwiches. We were friends, sworn to eternity.

Yet I didn't give my father any of these answers that traveled through my mind. "No," I answered to all his questions, not knowing why, but grieving so for Nancy that I wanted to be fiercely loyal to her. I wouldn't tell of the things we did together. They were her secrets and mine. My father was satisfied.

I cried my heart out all that day for Nancy, as much because she was dead as because I wouldn't see her the next day and we wouldn't be able to share our deep, dark secrets, the deepest and darkest of them about the silent, painful, mysterious transformations that were taking place under our nightgowns at night without our consent and against our wishes.

My father took me to the movies to console me in my grief. I was hardly consoled. I still thought of Nancy and her pain. The sudden and persistent aches in her legs. This too must be part of the transformation, we had thought, when she first told me of the pain in her legs. A numb, dullish feeling, she said. The soreness around the nipples, the flesh that was pushing upward, the funny sensations between the thighs. The bleeding. The legs had to be next. It was only natural. I was envious. She would be taller. Her bones were stretching before mine. We didn't think it would hurt as much as it hurt her. I didn't think she would die.

I thought of her for long hours at a stretch. Of our folly. Of my envy. If only I had told our teacher. Not that day—it was too late then—but on the days before when I wished that like her my pains would come. Her bleeding had come before mine and now her legs. If only I had told someone, I could have helped her.

In the movie theatre my guilt grew. I felt the numbness begin in my toes. A dull pain. It rose up my legs. My knees felt weak. The Von Trapp family had escaped Vienna and were now singing in America. My father leaned over to me and whispered, "Only in America. You could be a millionaire overnight."

The hills are alive with the sound of music.

He whispered again. "But not if they were Negroes."

I barely heard what he said, but in the flicker of light that crossed the screen I glimpsed his face. The anger there—raw and savage—sank deep into my memory. It was the same anger I saw years afterward when he did not answer my question about the lynching of his father's brother. Now I thought only of how much angrier he would become if I told him I wanted to go home.

My legs now felt like sandbags. They hung heavily from my knees. Then the pain began. In the very center of my bones. I tugged my father's sleeves.

"My legs," I whispered.

He looked down on me.

"They hurt."

He brushed his hand across my cheek. "No fever," he said.

"But they hurt. I can't move."

He touched my knees.

"I can't move them," I said.

"Let's go." He grabbed my hand.

"I can't move."

He stood up. The people behind us grumbled.

"Could you wait until the end of the movie?" he asked.

I shook my head. "I can't move," I repeated.

He picked me up in his arms.

That night the Americans came to help us. I can only guess how my father persuaded them to come to our house. My father was working then for the Ministry of Labor. His job was to settle wage disputes and to stipulate working conditions for Trinidadians employed by foreign companies. It was my father's responsibility to see that our people were treated fairly. Ironically, his orders from the government at about that time made it appear as if the opposite were true. He was the one assigned to inform the Americans that they could no longer pay wages to Trinidadians in U.S. dollars. Trinidadians were discovering that with the rate of currency exchange they could make a teacher's salary cleaning toilets on the American base. They began to pour into Chaguaramas in droves. The Americans found this amusing until my father stopped them. Workers could no longer be paid directly by the Americans. Wages had to be given to the Trinidadian government, which would in turn pay the workers based on the country's standards for fair wages.

The Americans were furious. An unheard-of demand, they said. Taking money away from people. It was the first step to socialism. Communism to follow. Private enterprise, open competition, capitalism, monopolies: these had worked for them. How else would they get the best workers for the base? What did it matter if some mother was finding it difficult to explain to her son that he needed to study math? The dollar was all that counted. And who needed math to clean a toilet bowl?

They blamed the British for their experiment in allowing a transitional government of local people. Independence was not guaranteed. The British were still the colonial rulers in Trinidad. What did they have to say? But

excerpt from BEYOND THE LIMBO SILENCE

the British were licking their wounds from the war, and the allure of days without nights—the sun never setting on lands they ruled—was beginning to wear thin. Let the Americans save the world.

I remembered the gifts that started arriving at our house from the Americans that year. Boxes of chocolates, cigarettes, chewing gum. My father returned them the next day but the gifts kept coming. Each time more numerous, more expensive. Radios, cameras, watches. My father returned them all. The gifts became more tempting. A washing machine that caused such arguments between my parents when my father gave it back that my mother did not speak to him for a week. Then a bicycle and a pair of roller skates that sent me into a screaming frenzy when they were all returned. But that night of my sickness I saw the captain of the naval base hand my father a small box of chocolates and witnessed the humiliating smile of gratitude that crossed my father's face as he accepted it. The shock of that moment thawed my legs. The joints in my knees loosened. The cold resolute chill that had taken hold of me in the cinema when I willed myself to feel Nancy's pain dissipated. It seemed unfair. For a box of chocolates. The wide grin on my father's face. The dullness in his eyes. Captain McNeil slapping him hard on his back, flicking the ashes of his cigar on my mother's polished floor. I rushed to my father and grabbed the box of chocolates. I tugged hard. He held it firm. We struggled again. The tears poured down my cheeks. He gathered me in his wide arms and pressed my head against his chest. I heard the pounding of his heart. It beat fast and furious. He whispered in my ear. "It's all right, Sara. All right. You'll be well now. You won't be sick. We'll all be fine."

I wanted to say I was sorry—his broken voice shamed me for my actions—but at that moment the American captain put the needle in my arm and I screamed instead.

We were like thieves in the night, my family. Captain McNeil with his parcel of syringes filled with Salk vaccine. My father accepting the box of chocolates. All my cousins, the children of my father's brothers and sisters, lined up one by one, accepting the American protection.

Polio raged through my town that year. June, July, August. The lucky ones died, the less fortunate were fed into iron machines, the courageous accepted their twisted limbs and kept on going. September. The English colonists brought the vaccine to our town, but by then it was almost too late for the children who lived on our block. By Christmas, about ten of them had disappeared.

September is the saddest time of the year to leave Trinidad. Like April of the country I would soon journey to, it ushered in new life from the destruction of the old. Out of the hurricane-whipped foliage rotted into the damp earth, it burst out fresh-dressed greenery: new growths of delicate lime green and dazzling emerald shimmering against the bold olive of trees that survived the hurricanes; coconut palms shaking hurricane waters from the spaces in their fronds, *poui* and immortelle disentangling themselves from the smothering grip of dead vines. Mango trees flowered, tiny white buds folded between new green leaves. The flamboyant spread out its thick brown arms and sprouted flames of fire, red and yellow, from its branches.

On the Sunday before I left Trinidad, already feeling nostalgia for the landscape I would not see for years, my father drove me through the mountains north of Port-of-Spain to Maracas Bay on the other side. He wanted to say his goodbyes to me. Give me his last words of advice on the price of gifts.

Along the road he reminded me that this too, the freshly paved road we traveled, was a gift from the Americans to the Trinidad colonial government. "They built it after the war," he said, spitting out the word *war* between clenched teeth as he always did, as if merely voicing it threatened to release an anger in him he had chosen to stifle. His older brother George, obsessed by a sense of obligation to his mother country, deluding himself perhaps into believing that as a British subject he was a British person, had enlisted in that war. Sometimes my father would boast about how his brother had learned to fly the British bomber planes in six months. "Just imagine," he would say in wonder, "one day before that he'd never even been in the insides of a regular plane." Then at other times my father would grow morose and speak bitterly of the war that took his brother's life and the lives of the best of the young men in the colonies and gave nothing back.

But not so the Americans, he would tell me. They knew how to repay debts. By then I knew more about the Americans than I did as a child and America had already begun to lose its fairy-tale quality. . . . A military air base in Walter Field stretching across central Trinidad. The farmers just rolled their belongings into bundles and left their lands when the British told them to move. Then a naval base in Chaguaramas. The fishermen simply had to find new waters and there would be no more family picnics on Sundays on the beach at Tetron Bay. All for fifty battered American destroyers when the mother country was afraid Germany would become their father country. And no one asked us anything! my father would shout. Now I was barely listening to him, smelling the wind full of the sea, fishy

excerpt from BEYOND THE LIMBO SILENCE

and salty. Now my mind spun circles. Could I live without this in Wisconsin? Prairie lands whose borders touched only land and more land thousands of miles away from the sea?

I pressed my face against the car window greedy for the forests of fat-trunked trees, the clutter of leaves and vines on their tops sifting the sun, the sudden surprise of precipices that plunged with dizzying speed from the edge of the road as we curled around the tight bends up the mountain to the sea on the other side. "For ninety-nine years," my father was saying to me. I shut off his words with the roar of the white surf crashing onto the huge rocks below us. I didn't want to feel his anger, not then, not when I was etching in my mind for Wisconsin white frothy mists hugging mountain peaks, sparkling jewels reflected in the sun. "Even the Americans knew that they had taken too much," my father said, and then mercifully like me he grew quiet, silenced by the beauty of the landscape around us.

I knew the rest of what he would have said. Even the Americans realized that the best seaports in Trinidad, Sunday picnic beaches, acres of cocoa fields and farmlands, and anything else they wanted on the other islands were too much payment for fifty old destroyers when no one asked the people if they minded paying. And for ninety-nine years. It was too much. But when our car skated down the last stretch of road from the mountaintop and the bay appeared shimmering blue against a sunlit sky, its edges skirted with cotton-white surf and then ivory brown sand, I was ready to forget. The road the Americans had built, giving Maracas Bay to us—though only to those of us in the middle class who had cars—eased the resentment of ninety-nine years. I was ready to filter out my father's words, his anger about discarded fuel and debris snaking down from the huge military ships in Chaguaramas, soiling our waters in Carenage Bay. Fishermen's sons, naked and brown like the earth, splashing in oil-drenched waters, wondering later about the eczemas that grew on their legs, pussy and ugly.

On the beach my father peeled my eyes off the sunlit sea. He wanted to warn me, as he had said before when we left Port-of-Spain, about the cost of gifts. I wanted to turn away from him, keeping my etching intact for Wisconsin, but he held my shoulders firmly and looked deeply in my eyes. He had something important to tell me, he said. Eric Williams had come back from America and he had learned a lot from him.

"When you get to that college in America," he said, "I want you to be careful. Don't let America fool you with its righteous words. Freedom, independence, the right to choose, justice. These are for them alone. They are sentimental. They cry and weep at the movies—make-believe—but don't think real life moves them. Be careful, Sara. To them, you owe them everything. They owe you nothing. Your scholarship? They have paid for your silence and your friendship."

He spoke in generalities and I fought to understand him, abandoning the sea. "Not every smile is a smile," he said. "And you lie with your face and keep your heart."

The sun blazed down on my back and burned the sand, and then I remembered and too late tried to erase the image of the other burning my father was pressing me to recall. "Not every smile is a smile." I knew it was his own smiles to Captain McNeil he wanted me to understand. My back grew hotter and I placed my hand on the back of my neck and felt my perspiration hot and steamy as the water that rolled off the toolshed my father had burned, the toolshed full of Captain McNeil's gifts. He wanted me to remember that fire. To understand his smiles after he had accepted the Salk vaccine from Captain McNeil, to know why he accepted the other gifts that came after that, each one perversely less expensive than the other, each one larger and more cumbersome: a bottle of perfume for my mother, then a stack of towels, a carton of beans, bags of flour; cuff links for my father, then a case of beer, cans of soda, fertilizer for our lawn, chewing gum. Afterward my father would store them quietly in the tool-shed, and his mood would darken and he would drift like a shadow through the house.

Each day I saw him grow more and more sullen and he fell deeper and deeper into a silence that even my mother could not break. Then another American came to our island, Paul Robeson. Captain McNeil invited my father to a concert Robeson was giving on Christmas Eve on the base. It was the only invitation my father ever accepted. Later, when he returned, he set the toolshed on fire.

Our neighbors grieved for us: Who would do such a heartless thing on Christmas Eve? My mother, uncanny, hiding our secret, fanned their sympathies. "All our Christmas gifts had been stored there," she said.

Her lie allowed catharsis. It permitted us to admit, while concealing the horrible truth, that my father had stored the gifts from the Americans there. It released the humiliation we had endured, the guilt we had not acknowledged even to ourselves when we accepted our vaccine in silence and watched helplessly as polio ravaged the children of our neighbors. What price had my father paid for my life? The fire consumed the need to know, to give voice to the question. It eradicated from my memory, or so I thought at eleven years of age, the significance of my father's silent acceptance of the Americans' gifts. Yet it left in its ashes suspicions that never died.

excerpt from BEYOND THE LIMBO SILENCE

Now sitting in the sun on the beach at Maracas Bay, my father was to fuse forever the memory of that fire with the beauty of the landscape I didn't want to forget.

"Just be careful what you accept from them, that's all. Just be careful what you take."

I would wonder later, why, in spite of what he knew, he'd let me go to America.

My mother also had her special goodbyes to me before I left for Wisconsin. No more advice on how I could be transformed into a swan. No hair straighteners, food to make curves where I was all angles, clothes that would never make me look like her. I was leaving Trinidad, taking with me the embarrassment of her failure. There was also no need to warn me of the price of gifts from the Americans. The fire had released her guilt and she had chosen to forget. Now the Americans were angels. Yet something about the physical appearance of the American who brought the gift of my scholarship troubled her and she wanted to protect me. There should have been no reason to distrust Father Jones. He looked like us. Not that he resembled my family directly, but that he could have been any one of the hundreds of Trinidadians who walked up and down Frederick Street in Port-of-Spain. He was about five feet seven. His skin was a fresh, ruddy brown color like the rain-washed sides of a clay mountain. His hair, short and nappy, was cut close to his head. He had a sturdy nose bridge with a matter-of-fact nose meant for breathing: open nostrils to draw in the air, attractive on a man of his complexion, high cheekbones, and an expressive, generous mouth. He talked with his hands. Our instinct was to trust him. In one respect only did his physical features dramatically differ from ours. It was a feature that dominated his face, that, in spite of the similarity of the rest of his body to people on my island, filled us with an uneasiness that fought against our natural inclination to accept him as one of us. It was the color of his eyes—the clearest blue, like the early morning sky, normal on the abnormal albino but disconcerting on a man of color.

Perhaps that was what troubled my mother most about Father Jones, though she did not identify it so. Her final goodbyes to me the night before I left were as enigmatic as my father's. She gave me a medal of Saint Jude, the patron saint of impossible causes, and a bag of herbs to put away and never use. "Never," she warned, pressing it into the palm of my hand and folding my fingers over it. "Never, unless you have to, and you'll know when that is." Father Jones, she said, was like us and not like us. More like Captain McNeil than like us. Yet, in the long run, she'd trust him first.

But I should remember that, colored or white, Americans were the same. When push came to shove, they would band together. Still, if she were me and she got into any trouble while she was in America, she'd ask the colored people for help first. She'd trust them first, but only after she'd prayed to Saint Jude and put the bag of herbs in her bathwater.

LINDSAY PATTERSON

I see this sign emblazoned on a plate-glass window near 14th Street and Third Avenue: SALESMEN WANTED FOR QUALITY PRODUCT. I walk in and a receptionist sends me to talk to a little hawk-nosed Mongoloid with blondish hair. The deal is to peddle dollar neckties for three ninety-eight. "Pure silk." He rants and raves. I shrink visibly at this deception. He deplores my lack of aggression. But more than that, my "indolence."

"All niggers are lazy," he sneers.

"All chinks are dishonest!" I shout.

His face falls, and tears overflow his watery blue eyes.

"No one has ever accused me of being dishonest before!" he snivels.

I feel shame and hurt, yet I cannot help but plunge the knife in deeper.

"What an ugly little freak you are," I say.

He quickly regains his composure and spews out a barrage of racial epithets. I go to the stationery store next door and bomb my last quarter

LINDSAY PATTERSON, a native of Bastrop, Louisiana, has written extensively on black film, theater and social issues. His published books include *Black Theater: A 20th Century Collection of the Works of Its Best Playwrights*, *Black Film and Film-Makers*, and *A Rock Against the Wind: Black Love Poems*. He is currently working on *Freedom's Plaza*, a novel; and *The Unfinished Society*, a collection of his articles, essays and criticisms, and *Black Playwrights on Their Plays, Playwrighting and Theater*.

on a Magic Marker. In black I scrawl a huge X ACROSS QUALITY PRODUCT on his plate-glass window. The receptionist screams "dirty nigger!" I thumb my nose, make a vulgar sign with my forefinger, and walk quickly away. But I do not get far before remorse sweeps me like the north wind. My urge is to rush back and eradicate his misery, but I do not yet have the necessary Equipment. I find myself on Bowery near Spring. Someone yells, and I turn to see a face vaguely familiar.

"Heard you been away," he says.

"Yes," I answer. "I've been on a long, long journey."

"Where'd ya go?"

"I think it was somewhere south," I answer, pointing south on Spring.

But before he can set the trap I sprint away, only to be stopped farther down Bowery by a protestation. For one awful moment I envision that it is me standing in the middle of a concrete island with arms enfolded around a mangy, sore-ridden body. Except for his matted blond hair he could be me in distress.

"Someone please come and love me," he chants in laughter.

I start to him. I want to put my arms around him and hug him like my father never did, but the stench is too much. I turn at the next corner and lie against a doorway, racked with frustration. For the first time since I can remember I am frightened at what the Revolution is going to do to these miserable creatures if I cannot help them. I bang my head against a doorway until it is past hurt and quite numb. If only I had the Equipment.

Two doors down I see a sodden drunk steaming in his own confusion. I rush to him and confront him. "Are you my father?" He seems genuinely pleased and grins at me with rotting teeth. I hold my breath as I clean out his two front pockets. He swings at me with feeble hands. "Father," I say to him, "it is for the Revolution." He grunts some profanities but is too weak to do more than that. "Thank you, father," I call over my shoulder. "You have saved the enemies of humanity." Around the next corner I settle in a bar.

But four beers and two whiskeys fail to eradicate the awesomeness of the Revolution from my mind. Two more whiskeys and I begin to feel woozy. My stomach churns. I haven't eaten for two, maybe three days. The thoughts of the Revolution are wearing me thin. In some ways I will be happy when it is over. I try to get up from the bar, but the strain of preparation weighs heavily on my shoulders. I lay my head on the bar. It is cool and refreshing. But the bartender has other ideas.

"Get the hell out!" he brays.

"I won't save you when the Revolution comes," I shout as I struggle to the door.

"What the hell's the matter with niggers nowadays?" He addresses the bar.

There is depraved laughter. I am now more determined than ever to obtain the Equipment. But first I must have another drink to steady my weariness. I settle in another bar. Two stools over is a jowled, powdered-face fag. I order a shot of brandy. My hands shake as I bring the glass up to my lips. A calmness sweeps over me as the pungent liquid spreads joyously throughout my body.

"Feeling better now?" says Powdered Face. I nod my head. He quickly moves over and settles a hand on my thigh. It is warm and caressing. He offers me a joint. It is too strong and I choke. He rubs and taps my back until annoyance scowls my face.

"I'm Ron," he tells me quickly. "Who are you?"

"Pete," I lie.

"Pete. What's a nice boy like you doing in a place like this?"

I gesture with my hands in helplessness. I do not want to let on who I am.

"You?" is all I can safely muster.

"I find the people in here real people," Ron says. "Not phonies like those pretentious bastards uptown."

"You're perfectly right," I say. "Nothing but pretentious bastards uptown."

"You're not like any colored boy," he says, smiling. He tightens the grip on my thigh. "You're intelligent . . . and good-looking. I don't have to tell you that you're good-looking. You should know that."

I wondered when the Revolution would come. The anxiety was beginning to get me down. A rumbling is beginning near my bowels, but before I can react properly it splashes Ron squarely in the face.

"Black bitch! Black bitch!" he shrills, as I near the door.

Unaccountably, I find myself in Washington Square Park. It is late afternoon. I stretch out on a bench and doze until a cop bangs my buttocks with his nightstick. It is twilight and Ron comes swirling by. He lets out a savage scream.

"Don't come sniggling to me when the Revolution comes," I scream back. "I'll let them take your ass!"

But I knew I wouldn't, for I suddenly feel this overwhelming remorse for all God's creatures, which is what impels me to go and fetch the Equipment. But before I do I must go to my room in Harlem and shake some of this weariness from my body.

At the subway booth an Asante warrior smiles recognition about the Revolution. At 96th Street two white couples come aboard, and as the subway groans and creaks its way toward 110th Street they lock themselves in each other's arms. Across from them slouches a Watusi elder muttering revolutionary songs. I try to reassure everyone that they have nothing to worry about. But the white men draw their women into strangulation holds. In a rage I rip off the Watusi's armaments to expose all that the Revolution would.

The train jerks to a stop at 125th Street. I wander off. It is a hot, seductive night in Harlem. Strange odors press against my nostrils, both disturbing and exciting. I walk up Lenox and turn east at 128th Street. Big buxom women sit fanning. I want to go and sink my head into their heaving breasts, more for protection than comfort. A tall, thin girl stops me at the corner of Fifth Avenue.

"Got some time?" she asks.

"No, and you haven't either," I say. "The Revolution is due any minute now. There's no time left. You'd better go and get yourself prepared."

"You crazy nigger," is all she can say.

I shrug my shoulders and continue my stride toward Madison, where I have a cubicle. On the stoop sits the trollop who lives in the one next to mine. She giggles.

"Don't it look good to ya?" she asks.

"Why do you ask?"

"You lookin'. It must look good to ya."

"I guess it does," I say, but she senses my indifference.

"Don't look at nothin' that don't look good," she volunteers.

"If it's there for the public," I say, "why not?"

"I knowed a man who looked once too often," she says.

"Does that include public property?" I ask.

"Git your black ass upstairs and stop botherin' me," she says, standing up and twitching her bony hips.

"As you wish," I say.

"As you wish, hell!" She snorts. "You sound like some gotdam white man. As you wi-i-sh! She-e-i-t!"

I trudge up to my cubicle and plop wearily on my bunk and sleep until lumbering footsteps in the trollop's cubicle awaken me. Only the flimsiest of partitions separates her orgiastic stench from me. I listen in amusement at the violence of the act. It is over quickly, but the customer wants more. A struggle ensues. He is easily the victor. Her viraginous cries send me into a fit of depression. Her whimpering leaves me immobile long into the night. A deathly stillness pervades the air. The rotting of flesh titillates my nostrils, but the thought of death carries me into spasms of despair. I am beginning to have doubts about the Revolution. I jump up and hasten to the nearest bar. After three whiskeys I begin to sing songs to myself. Two Masai warriors come in and begin to talk indirectly about the Revolution. But I can no longer bear the thought of all those people dying. I walk until the flat dull rhythm of a jukebox entices me into another bar. There are several customers undulating to the music. One is stripped bare, her big boobs flapping like paper in the wind as she gyrates to the music and shouts "Freedom!"

But I am rapidly becoming disillusioned about the Revolution. Even in vulgarity it has taken root. I flee to Marcus Garvey Park and lie on a bench. My head swirls with dark thoughts. I can see into the past: Miss Liberty. Ships. Troops. Tropical nights. Fields of bloodless victims. It is time for me to secure the Equipment. But I must choose carefully, for I am now against bloodshed, a bloody Revolution.

I make my way surreptitiously to the dungeon where the arsenal is and give the password. I plead for a bloodless Revolution, but the Grand Master agrees only to give it some thought. Meanwhile, I load a shopping bag with the Equipment. I go to a vantage point and lie in wait for my victums.

The little hawk-nosed Mongoloid with blondish hair comes swirling by. I step out of the shadows. He is surprised to see me. Again, he shouts racial epithets. I take a dart from my bag and let it go into his chest. He is stunned for a moment. The prick in his skin begins to swell into a dark bubble. It bursts and his chest slowly begins to turn purple, then black. Within a few minutes his whole body has turned black. He starts to howl as his blondish hair bristles for a moment, then turns kinky. I feel relief. The Revolution has begun smoothly.

"You black bastard!" shouts a policeman. "What are you doing lying here this time of night? Get on!"

I must have fallen asleep. I jump up quickly and search for my Equipment. It is nowhere in sight.

"Where is it? What have you done with it?" I demand of the policeman.

"I got it and you're not going to get it back," he says, with a silly smirk on his face.

But I knew he was lying. I could not have been so careless as to have left it out in the open. I rush back to my cubicle and search it from top to bottom. It is not there. What if it has fallen into the wrong hands? I had been warned about that. Maybe the arsenal has been discovered and the Revolution foiled. I stumble out of my cubicle and make my way up to the roof to see if there are any signs of resistance to the Revolution, or betrayal. It is not yet dawn and the darkness reveals nothing unusual. But the rotting of flesh is overpowering and the street below seems cool and restful and I need badly to sleep. I climb over a small rise of bricks, and as I glide down toward the street I can feel the cool, uncontaminated air rushing through my nostrils, wiping out the stench of a lifetime.

Raoul's Silver Song

KALAMU YA SALAAM

 Raoul stood on the wooden patio balcony enjoying the twilight's slow departure. With the patient concentration of a piano tuner unhurriedly working in an empty ballroom, Raoul watched the evening shadow creep up the pastel cream-colored concrete wall as the sunlight gradually dimmed and the crisscrossing sunbeam shafts merged into the darkest green of the shadow-shrouded banana tree trunk.

With each slow breath, through nostrils that barely moved when he inhaled, Raoul caught the bouquet of courtyard odors: frying sausage from somebody's pan, shrimp in the alley from last night, and the sweet subtle fragrance of watermelon waffling upward from the Johnsons just below him, sitting out eating the pink-fleshed fruit and chatting about their grandchildren.

But more than what he saw or what he smelled, Raoul liked what he heard, the sounds of a New Orleans evening in the Treme area muted by the wood of old buildings, sounds mingling like the melodic strains of a

KALAMU YA SALAAM is "an African American man trying to live up to my fullest potential—to do my best to contribute to the empowerment of my people and to the betterment and beautification of the whole world." He is the author of numerous published poems and short stories, and the author of the recent book *What Is Life: Reclaiming the Black Blues Self.*

brass band improvising, different elements going to the fore and then re-ceding: a rancorous car horn blown at two kids chasing a ball into the street, the high squeal of the car's brakes a cacophonous counterpoint to the car's blasting horn; Mabel singing to herself while she cooked, today her natural alto stuck on "Amazing Grace" sung in C; the Johnsons listen-ing to their favorite Louis Jordan recordings; someone's radio on loudly (the person was probably sitting on the front steps with a beige touch-tone Princess telephone perched on the doorsill, talking to a friend who was probably doing the same in her neighborhood), the station was WWOZ and the fifties R&B show had not too long ago come on; water and sewage moving through the plumbing—thick, heavy iron pipes which were com-mon decades ago—that ran up the outside of the building next to the stairwell; a television barely heard, Raoul couldn't tell what show it was or where it was coming from, but he could tell it was television because every 35 or 40 seconds a burst of forced laughter erupted instantly and died down quickly; a long soft watermelon burp from below; and the low eruption from his own bowels as Raoul passed gas. What he liked about all these sounds is that no one sound was supreme; neither noise nor music was so loud or lasted so long that it dominated the soundscape. This was a good band.

Although the catalogue of sensual stimulants was long and varied, Raoul felt relaxed here. He savored the ballad tempo of day's exit in this little courtyard. The atmosphere was soothing; it invited reflection, medi-tation, catnapping, snoozing, quiet cigarette smoking, thinking things through, forgetting, reading letters over and over, a good long novel, mem-orizing a short poem. Everything. Nothing. Raoul liked this.

Raoul's hand rested lightly on the heavy wood railing, a railing pitted by the bombardments of time, a railing no longer smooth as it was when initially, proudly, installed by the Heberts, a neighborhood family of laugh-ing carpenters (a father, Harold, two sons, Francis and Eric, and a cousin, Daniel, whom everyone called Two-Step). Whatever paint had once graced the railing was long since gone. Now the wood was colored by the pigments of natural aging: rain-borne atmospheric dirt and rodent excrement, bird droppings, and tiny insect slime; the bleaching of the merciless semi-tropic Crescent City summer sun; the seasoning of sweat and other body fluids; sundry dyes from a plethora of spilled drinks composed of every imaginable concoction of alcohol, juices, and flavorings used to disguise the sharp taste of the alcohol; colorings from an exhaustively long line of liniments, po-tions, and medications (for example, a three-quarters-full bottle of some chalky white substance of dubious medicinal value which had been pitched in real anger at the genitals of the third in a long series of tenants by a live-in lover on the way out—the bottle broke on the railing when the tenant successfully sidestepped the not-unanticipated missile); the indelible blotches left by blood from a terrible accident with a knife which left a little hand permanently scarred; soot streaks from a holiday-inspired out-door barbecue that should never have been lit there in the first place; not to mention the many burns from snuffed cigarettes and the 159 icepick holes assiduously bored into the wood by someone who was bored out of his skull one day waiting for a certain individual who never came. None of this would have surprised Raoul. Like the patina of most elderly humans we meet whose skintones reflect a full life, this railing had a long survival story. Raoul liked graceful survivors: people and things that held up well, didn't cry or carp about life's severities, but rather simply persisted in being what they were.

Raoul lived alone. He chose his lifestyle. He—

Someone was knocking at his door. He stood motionless. The knock came a second time. Raoul thought about not answering the door. A third knock, louder. With the unhurried motion of a man who has enjoyed a long life and feels no pressure to accomplish anything else, Raoul moved slowly from the balcony into the front room and to the front door.

When Raoul opened the door a young girl stood there.

They looked at each other. She couldn't have been more than seventeen or eighteen.

"Raoul Martinez?"

"Good evening."

"Excuse me. Good evening. Are you Mr. Raoul Martinez?"

"Who wants to know?"

"My name is Mavis Scott."

"And?"

"And I'm—uh, looking for Raoul Martinez."

"What for?"

"Music lessons."

"I don't give music lessons."

She stood there.

"I said I don't give music lessons."

"I know all your music."

"What music?"

Mavis unhitched her large leather bag from her shoulder, lowered it gently to the floor, knelt beside it, and quickly retrieved her flute case. She placed the case on top of the bag, opened it, and assembled the flute, blew air through the silver cylinder to warm it, stood quickly, and began "The Silver Song."

"Well. Uh-huh. I still don't do lessons."

Without hesitation Mavis started into "Ra-Owl."

"Where you learn that from?"

"A record."

"I ain't got no record."

"*June Johnson—The Copenhagen Connection.*"

"That was . . . how you got holt to that?"

"I like your music."

"How you found me? How you know I was here?"

"I like your music."

"I like a lot of stuff. That don't mean I know everything."

"But if you really like something, you learn about it."

"Mavis . . ."

"Mavis Scott."

"All right. Come back tomorrow. Four-thirty."

"You'll teach me?"

"No, I'll think about it. I'll tell you my answer tomorrow."

"You want me to call before I come?"

"Can't call."

"Oh, they have phones at school."

"Can't call *me*. There ain't no phone here."

"Oh."

"Good evening, Miss Mavis Scott. I'll see you tomorrow."

"Come on in."

When Mavis walked into Raoul's room, she felt she was falling into a past she had never seen but a past she wanted desperately to know about.

Raoul walked away from her. He opened a half-closed door and disappeared into the adjoining room.

An old armoire and an old piano dominated the room where Mavis stood. She looked for a television, but there was none. She looked for anything that would give clues to Raoul's personality, but there was nothing else personal in the room. The balcony doors were open to the courtyard, and the window on the street side was closed and tightly shuttered.

Raoul reentered the room, a trumpet in his hand.

Mavis looked at the piano. Raoul assumed she could play some piano. If she couldn't at least play some chords it would be a waste of his time to try and teach her anything.

"Okay, hit some chords."

He pointed toward the piano with his horn.

"Go 'head, girl. You say you wanna learn. This your first lesson."

She sat at the stool, her hands just above the keys. She wanted to cry, unable to think of anything that seemed appropriate to play.

"Mavis. Blues. B flat, watch me. Uh. Uh. Uh-uh-uh-uh."

Mavis rested her fingers lightly on the keys and tried to think of blues chords, some notes, blues songs even. Every song she thought of she rejected because it was not the song he wanted. She didn't know what he was going to play, but whatever he was going to play she knew it wasn't what she was trying to recall. With great effort she lifted her hands. It felt like some invisible force was trying to hold her hands down. Her hands dangled above the keys, coiled tightly, a leopard waiting to pounce, but no prey passed her way.

Mavis bit her lip. Her nostrils itched and burned slightly. Tears formed on the inside edges of her left eye. He had already counted it out. Would it be too corny to play "C. C. Rider"? That was too simple. So was "St. James Infirmary" or even "Goin' Down Slow." But what key? B. Yes, he had said B.

Whenever Mavis was under pressure to perform, her subconscious would flood her mind with so many possibilities that the hardest part of the creative process was not the thinking of something to play but rather deciding on which *one*.

Once she had sat in at Jay-Jay's place . . .

"Girl, you don't know no blues? You don't know no blues, how I'm gonna teach you to play jazz?"

Raoul walked out the room.

Mavis cried quietly to herself. When Raoul returned with a piece of paper in his hand he pretended he didn't see her tears. Mavis quickly wiped her eyes with her forearm. Raoul set the sheet of music on the piano stand. It was just a series of chords. No melody. No time signature. No bass lines. Just chords.

Raoul snapped out a slow walking tempo.

"Uh. Uh. Uh. Uh."

Mavis smiled when she heard Raoul's trumpet. This was "Ra-Sing." She hadn't recognized the changes written out on paper, but she knew the song. By the time they were at the tune's bridge, Mavis was very comfortable with the chords. If she were playing flute there was much more she could have done, but on the piano all she could do was feed chords.

Suddenly he gave it to her.

Mavis was ready. She did a break and filled the hesitation with three deftly timed, chiming block chords. Then started a phrase that consisted of four chords which resolved on the next chord in the progression. At the bridge she dropped the tempo completely and strung out a set of altered chords which she had thought of two years ago while listening to the record over and over. Mavis was ready.

"Go on, go on, girl."

"I could play it better on flute. I don't have much piano chops."

"Okay. Do it."

Mavis picked up her flute case from beside the piano stool, assembled her flute, held it to her lips, and waited for Raoul's count.

Raoul closed his eyes. The only count was an almost imperceptible nodding of his head. But Mavis saw; she saw and was ready. He would see. She was ready.

They played "Ra-Sing." At the bridge he dropped out and Mavis confidently flew.

"Play it pretty, baby, play the pretty way you talk."

They played the song through twice.

"Yea. Now that's better. Where you from, girl?"

"Right here."

"Yea, huh."

"Yes." She smiled, resting her hands and her flute in her lap, allowing her head to tilt a bit to one side. "Same place you from. We both coming from the same place."

"Yeah," he said with a slightly mocking we'll-see-about-that tone. "Let's take it from the git go. Watch me, now."

They chased each other, playing a fleet "Ra-Owl." He laughed at her swirling trills.

"Don't put no dress on this man now."

"No, just a pretty shirt," and she did it again.

It was uncanny the way this young girl played something like June did. At the bridge June had always hung back, quarter-noting just behind the beat. She was playing it like June played it. They ended together, Mavis voiced below Raoul.

"Solid." He smiled. There was nothing like playing. Raoul thought about playing with June. Mavis was still laughing. "Ya know, June always used to say"—Raoul altered his voice to imitate June's famous growl—"mannn, ya don't *play* music. You *serious* music."

Mavis stopped laughing. She didn't stop smiling. She looked at Raoul.

"Girl, music is more than just a love, it's a passion and that's the way you got to play. It's got to be like you can't help yourself."

"You mean you got to give yourself to it."

"No, baby. I mean you got to get everything you need to live *from* it. Fish need water. Birds need air. You got to need music. Ya know, you got to need it bad, so bad that when you don't play, you can't live."

There was still so much Mavis did not know about herself, especially about what she needed to feel fully alive.

Raoul wasn't looking at her. He started to play. His horn was at his lips. He fingered the valves quickly. His cheeks puffed out. He almost started but didn't. Raoul thought of something. Mavis didn't know what he was thinking but she could tell he was thinking of something.

Raoul didn't know why he thought so suddenly of Martin Luther King getting shot in the neck, except that *really living* was the only thing worth dying for. Living the way you wanted, doing what you wanted to do, that's all that was worth dying for. Raoul played "The Silver Song." Mavis joined him.

They had played forty-six and one half choruses when Raoul just stopped suddenly. He put his horn down. Stood up. Walked out the room. The lesson was over. It was almost night. Mavis packed her flute quietly and sat for a minute looking at Raoul's horn. She fingered the top of her flute case like it was a piano; she was fingering the changes to Raoul's "Silver Song."

She played the piano well, so well that her piano teacher encouraged her to become a piano major. He said she had the passion to play like he had never seen in a student in a long time. When Antonio Luzzio said that, Mavis wondered what did he know about her passions. All he could teach her was technique, she remembered thinking, when Mr. Luzzio spoke softly about piano and her passion. Later, Antonio Luzzio said to her one day when she was playing Chopin for him, "Your hands love the piano and the keys love them back. I will teach you the technique so you can forget the technique."

Now, studying with Raoul, Mavis blushed to herself. She never thought she would be so thankful for what Mr. Luzzio had taught her. He had taught her to play correctly, so now there was nothing between her and the music. She could hear the changes and hit the right chords. She could also alter the changes and create new chords that were harmonically correct. "Thank you, Mr. Luzzio," Mavis said to herself.

Raoul finally came back into the room. He was getting his soft leather cap out of the almost antique armoire. She had seen cedar robes before, with the long dressing mirrors and the strong but pleasant wood smell.

"I can't come tomorrow," she said as she watched him methodically place the black cap on his head. The cap looked expensive. Mavis did not know that the cap was from Norway, nor did she know it was a gift Raoul cherished.

Her saying she couldn't come tomorrow reminded him to tell her she couldn't come on Friday; she didn't need to know why.

"Neither next day, either. Look here, for next time, work us out a 'rangement for 'A-Train' in slow to mid tempo. You better mute me too."

"Why?"

"Why? 'Cause I said so."

"No, not the lesson, I understand that. I mean why I can't come on Friday."

"I done already tolt you, 'cause I said so."

"Okay, Raoul," God, she hoped she had said his name casually enough, "because you said so."

He didn't answer. He left the room. The lesson was over.

They were playing Monk—rather, Raoul was playing Monk and she was struggling to find something to play. Everything she thought to play was so obviously not what should be played.

"Why is Monk's music so hard to play?"

"It ain't hard to play. It's hard to fake!"

Mavis chuckled almost inaudibly, agreeing with Raoul's pithy summary. Raoul played a half chorus and stopped.

"Monk made you play or else sound like you couldn't play."

Silence.

"Like the hardest thing about Monk is rhythm, and that's the hardest thing in life, to find your own rhythm."

"But when you playing with others you can't just play your own rhythm."

"The trick, baby, is to know when to solo, when to ensemble, when to comp, and when to lay out. That's life. That's music. Sometimes you take the lead with a solo, sometimes you play your part right 'longside everybody, sometimes you're in the background accompanying what's going on, sometimes you don't play. Dig?"

"But how do you ensemble when everybody else is playing a way you don't want to play?"

Raoul turned to the piano and played the head of "Evidence" again. He picked up his horn and played variations on the theme. He got up off the piano stool and kept playing, motioning for Mavis to sit at the piano. Mavis put her flute on top the piano, sat, and comped the changes. He stopped. She stopped.

"When you can't play, lay out." He played some more. She joined him. She started to go on. She stopped.

"Some fools think shedding is about perfection, ya know, that 'practice makes perfect' bullshit, but that ain't where it's at. Shedding is for learning what *not* to play, learning what doesn't work and learning not to do that. I mean your woodshed ought to be fulla all your mistakes. Practice making mistakes. Playing makes perfect. Shedding is all about making mistakes, baby." He started again. He stopped. She started to play something. It didn't work. She stopped.

"When you *can* play what you *can't* play now, then you can play." Raoul started again. Before she could start, he stopped. "Ya know, it ain't about you. Monk was about Monk. But when you play Monk, you got to be you playing *Monk*. When you play *your* stuff, then it's about you." Raoul played "Evidence" again. Mavis comped. Raoul soloed. He altered the changes. Mavis followed, laughing. Raoul's logic was so clear. He returned to the head. They ended together with a flourish, she had the sustain pedal down, and the piano's resonance undergirded the mirth of their entwined laughters.

"Mavis. Blues. B flat. Use the flute. Uh. Uh. Uh-uh-uh-uh." And they were flying. She had a variation of "Killer Joe" that was smoking and matched perfectly what he was doing. Soon she found that she was leading the song. At the bridge she stomped her foot loudly on the floor, indicating a stop-time. She ripped off four measures and threw it at him. He was pleased with her self-confidence and began trading fours with her. She started flutter-tonguing and screaming false notes. He wah-wah muted the horn with his hand. She hummed into her horn. He picked up a metal ashtray and got right nasty.

This was something like that night in Jay-Jay's when she had sat in, but it was better because it was just happening and she was not having to prove anything. Mavis remembered something she had played that night, it was something she had heard Rahsaan do on a record and she had copied it. When she did it that night, the crowd loved it. When it was her turn, she did that same thing.

Raoul stopped.

"Nah, why you played that? That shit don't fit. It ain't you, is it?"

"What do you mean it's not me."

"Who you heard do that?"

She started to deny that she had heard anyone do that. They were having so much fun playing. It had felt so good to be playing on an equal basis with him.

"Rahsaan."

"Who?"

"Rahsaan Roland Kirk on the album—"

"Rahsaan can play Rahsaan. You play you, and when you ready to play Rahsaan then you be you playing Rahsaan, but don't be taking Rahsaan shit trying to make it yo' shit. You don't know what all that man went through to get that sound. You don't know what he was thinking. And I don't want to know what you thought he was thinking or feeling. I wants to hear what you thinking and what you feeling, even when you playing his shit. Play me some Mavis Scott. I wants to hear Rahsaan, I'll put a record on."

"I just—I just thought it would fit there."

"Imitation don't never fit in jazz. Don't care how much some people might think they like it. Jazz is for real, and if you ain't being for real, you ain't playing jazz."

Raoul walked out the room. Lesson was over.

Just as Mavis was about to leave, her flute packed and her feelings shredded like a tomcat's favorite scratching pole, Raoul returned into the room with a picture in his hand. He held it out to her.

Mavis looked at it quickly.

"That's me and June in Copenhagen."

"Um-hmm." Mavis barely held the metal frame a few seconds before gently returning Raoul's most treasured photograph.

"I thought you might like to see it, you know, you knowing all about me and June and such."

Raoul had no way of knowing that Mavis saw his picture every day. How could he know that Mavis had her own copy, sent to her mother by June, who was her second cousin? Raoul knew everything but he didn't know this. He thought Mavis was hurt because of what he had said to her; why else didn't she look at the photograph, which he had seldom shown to anyone?

"Thanks." They stood uncomfortable in the silence like musicians listening to the playback of a sad take late in a recording session that has not gone well—even though they had tried their best, the outcome did not sound too good. Maybe the best thing was just to pack it up and try again on another day.

After knocking twice and getting no reply, Mavis tried the doorknob. The door was unlocked. She let herself in, moved quickly to the piano, and set up to shed—it was no longer like basic lessons; now they spent most of the time practicing together.

The way they played together was almost like they were equals—well, not really equals, because Mavis was only a beginner, but they played together like colleagues, musical colleagues. No, it was more than that, their communion felt to her like more than band mates who only played periodic gigs together and seldom saw each other beyond that. Well, although it was true these sessions were the only time they saw each other, still it was more than just sessions.

The way they would break out laughing simultaneously after playing a good exchange or after hitting an unplanned ending abruptly but precisely in tune with each other, that was like friends. That's what it felt like, good friends.

After all, Raoul didn't play in public anymore. Absolutely refused. So, in a sense, Mavis was Raoul's only peer. "Don't nobody want to hear no old man playing no more."

"You ain't old."

"You too young to know what old is."

But there was also something else simmering between them, something just beneath the surface. At least, Mavis wanted there to be something else. Well, at least, sometimes she wanted there to be something else. She wasn't sure if he wanted there to be something else. He had never even so much as touched her. Well, he had touched her shoulder once and had nudged her with his hip to catch a beat or something, but his bare hand had never touched her skin.

Where was he?

Mavis played her flute for a minute or so, waited. Raoul did not appear.

Another Raoul-less minute passed slowly.

"Raoul?"

Nothing.

Mavis looked at the bedroom door, or rather looked at the door she supposed led to Raoul's bedroom. She had never gone any farther into Raoul's apartment than the front room, where they shedded, or quickly dashing in and out of the little bathroom on a couple of occasions.

Should she go inside the bedroom?

She went to the door.

Should she knock?

The door was already ajar.

"Raoul," she called out.

Nothing.

She touched the door.

Should she push the door open?

She opened the door.

Raoul lay sleeping on his bed, naked to his waist. Or maybe he was totally naked and only exposed to his waist; a spread covered the lower half of his body. Mavis could not tell if he had any other clothes on.

She trembled.

Should she?

She started to call his name.

Should she wake him?

Or, should she . . . ?

She undressed quietly, quickly. Maybe if she just climbed into his bed. The window was open. A breeze blew through. Maybe he wasn't really asleep. Maybe he was waiting to see what Mavis was going to do. What was she going to do?

Mavis felt the wind dashing slyly between her legs, mocking her quandary, challenging her to move from the spot where she stood glued in confused frustration.

The wind blew again. She felt a chill *there*.

The curtain moved.

Mavis turned her head to look at the curtain. Is this what Lot's wife felt like, unable to go and unable to stay? Mavis's head hurt. Why was she even thinking about the Bible, and where did Lot's wife come from?

Something moved.

Raoul had moved, turned halfway over toward her.

No.

Raoul snored. It was a soft snore, but a snore. Would he wake up before she could get out of the room?

Carefully, slowly, Mavis bent to retrieve her clothing, which lay in a shameful little pile beside her. This man was older than her father. Almost old enough to be her grandfather. Mavis did not understand the attraction or the repulsion, but she felt both, and, after initially acting on the former, was now being swayed by the latter.

The curtain moved again.

Mavis held her breath.

God, this was stupid.

With clothes in hand, Mavis stood trying to figure what was the better choice, try to dress quickly and silently in here, or slip naked back into the front room and dress in there. Suppose Raoul woke up while she was dressing? Suppose when she moved to go into the front room the floor squeaked or the door squealed and Raoul saw her naked?

How could she explain this to Raoul?

Raoul moved again, rolled away from the door.

Mavis dashed quickly into the front room. It took her so long to get dressed. Her hand trembled terribly.

Once dressed, she picked up her flute—the metal felt so cold—and stood silently in the middle of the floor. What now?

Eventually, she decided to leave.

At the front door she wondered whether Raoul was all right.

Mavis opened the door and closed it softly behind her and started to walk away. But suppose he was sick? He hadn't looked sick or anything. He looked all right. But maybe he'd had a heart attack. But she was sure he had been breathing normally. At least she hoped he had. Mavis didn't remember his snoring because she herself had not been breathing normally. If something was wrong and she left him like that? She couldn't do that.

Mavis went back into the apartment. Everything sounded okay.

Mavis walked across the room. She didn't hear anything that sounded wrong.

Mavis stood in the bedroom door. Raoul slept soundly, except he had turned toward the door and lay fully exposed. Mavis saw him facing her nude. She trembled anew. Finally she left.

"Hey, girl, what happened to you yesterday? I fell asleep about two and didn't get up till six. Did you come and think I wasn't home or something?"

"No. No. I didn't—couldn't come yesterday. I just came by today to pay you what I owe you because I won't be able to come anymore." Why had she lied? She wanted to call it back but didn't.

"You don't owe me nothing. I just want to hear you whenever you start playing, if you do like you say you gon' do and if you keep playing like you been playing."

"Yes, when I really start playing I'll let you know, and if you play, you have to let me know."

"I won't, but then, one never knows, do one?"

"No, for sure, one never knows until one does."

"Yeah, you right, girl. Until one *does*, one *don't*."

Mavis stood up. "Raoul, thanks for your help." Her hand was sticking out toward him. He took her hand into the warmth of both of his and held it. He looked her in the eye.

"Mavis, you pass it on whatever it is you think you learned funny, girl."

"For sure. Always learn. Always teach. And always know when you suppose to be learning and when you suppose to be teaching."

He was still holding her hand. "Lady, you got it." He slowly returned her hand to her.

Everything felt so final, like this was graduation and even if they saw each other again, it would be different. Maybe that's what calling her "lady" meant.

"Do you still, I mean, are you still tied up on Fridays?"

"What made you ask that?"

She walked toward the door away from him, "Oh, youth, I guess."

"You'll get over it."

"Yes, well . . ."

"Goodbye sweet lady, play what you must, but always be ser—"

". . . always be serious about the music."

Raoul kissed her on her nose. She turned quickly, nearly stumbling as she ran hurriedly down the stairs onto the waiting sidewalk below. She heard a radio. She heard a TV. She heard some kids playing. Cars passing. Somebody arguing about something. A riverboat whistle blowing on the river. The St. Claude bus pulling away three blocks away. And, quietly above it all, Mavis heard Raoul's "Silver Song." At first she thought the sound was in her head. Then she looked up.

Raoul was sitting by his front room window, playing with his horn stuck out the window, playing for the whole neighborhood to hear.

A Real Man

ESMERALDA SANTIAGO

 If she opens her eyes, Raúl Julia will disappear. Graciela ignores the siren wailing down the street and pushes her face into the pillow. He leads her, hand in hand, down a golden stretch of beach. She's dressed in white, her face veiled. He lifts her fingers to his lips, kisses the tips, opens her palm close to his sleepy eyes, as if reading her fortune. With his long tapered finger, he presses the soft mound under her thumb and writes his name on the pink flesh of her palm. He whispers her name: *Graciela*.

The siren wails closer, blasts into the room, fades down the street. A familiar voice comes from a hard dark place at her feet. Her brother lies in shadows at the bottom of steep granite steps littered with garbage, empty beer cans, broken bottles. He lifts his hand and, in a muffled voice, begs her to pull him out. Behind her, a bolero crooner promises undying devotion. She sways along a street festooned with flowers. A gentle breeze shakes petals off their stems, and she smells gardenias. But the putrid stench of stale beer, garbage, and dried feces comes up from where José Juan has slumped into the darkness.

ESMERALDA SANTIAGO's short stories and personal essays about Puerto Rican women in the United States have been published in the *Christian Science Monitor*, *The New York Times*, and *Sojourner*. Her memoir about growing up in Puerto Rico and New York appeared in 1994.

She wakes up with the scent in her nostrils and nausea so strong she runs to hang her head over the toilet. She heaves, and a cold sweat spreads from the soles of her feet to the crown of her head, soaking her nylon nightgown. She spends the rest of the night shivering under three blankets, even though outside the temperature is in the 70s.

She's up at first light, tunes her radio to the Spanish station, tiptoes around it, as if the announcers will give her the bad news she fears in their mellifluous voices. The pink foam curlers in her hair hang every which way, with no memory of the neat rows she rolled up the night before. She tightens the ones at the front of her head and steams up the bathroom before stepping into the shower, where she hums a love song as she rubs lather under her breasts and along the curve of her round hips. The tips of her fingers soap the curly mound between her legs, but she stops short of the soft, bald flesh below it.

A stillness hangs over Fulton Street, its litter bunched at the edges where buildings rise up to a yellow mist that presses down hot and heavy, slowing people, cars, trains, and buses to a dreamy pace. As she goes by Leon's Insurance and Travel Agency, Graciela lifts her eyes to meet those of Raúl Julia under a grove of coconut trees. A warm breeze rises from the ground, remains trapped inside her skirt. She quickens her pace to the subway.

All morning, as she works, there's a peculiar tremor inside her skin, like internal goose bumps. Every so often she has to stop the rhythm of her work to rub briskly along her arms, behind her neck. Bent over her sewing machine, she stitches silk sleeves on blouses she can't afford to buy for herself. She attaches the cuff to the sleeve with double needles, turns it over and stitches the French seam, then picks up another and does the same thing, over and over again. For a week she's been stitching pink silk. Last week it was turquoise, but next week the line will look like a lawn, when the cutters send in a batch of green blouses.

For lunch, she heats soup in the microwave Mr. Greenblatt installed in the small room that serves as the workers' cafeteria. Someone slides a cassette of El Puma's latest love songs in the portable player. The women listen to it as they eat their sandwiches, heated leftovers, and canned meals.

"Now that's a real man," Manuela sighs as El Puma reaches for a high note that sends shivers down Graciela's spine and flashes the memory of Raúl Julia's droopy eyes, begging for love. The face transforms into that of José Juan, his eyes heavy, begging for money with which to get a drink.

"Bah!" Feliza spits out. "They're all alike. Whispering boleros in your ear just to get what they want. Then they dump you for the next fool willing to listen to their sweet talk."

"It's like they get together to figure out how to ruin a woman's life," Sandra mumbles through her sandwich.

"But there must be some good ones out there," Manuela protests. She's new to factory work and hasn't learned that, according to the veterans, men are infidels. The women spend their entire coffee and lunch breaks discussing the inadequacies of the men they're stuck with. Not one woman in the factories Graciela has worked the past sixteen years has ever admitted to being happily married. Most of them tell the same story of seduction, a short honeymoon, sudden abandonment.

"They're leeches," Feliza says. "They suck everything they can out of you, then leave you dry."

Manuela's face hardens. Graciela remembers being that young once, that innocent, full of romantic notions about men. Years ago, her brothers' friends would ask her out but she always refused, afraid to end up like these women, abandoned and burdened with children they can barely support.

"You're lucky," the women on the line tell her, "you don't have to depend on any man. They say they love you, but all they do is take advantage." A bitter longing settles in Graciela's chest. The pain of her *compañeras* is real, has served as a living reminder. Be careful, they tell her. Don't be fooled by sweet words and empty promises. But once, just once, Graciela wants to feel a man's hand on her breast and a lover's warm breath against her hair.

The phone call comes just before her afternoon coffee break. She presses the telephone hard against her ear, shuts her eyes, and concentrates on the English words streaming into her brain. Hospital. emergency room. Critical.

"*Sí*. Yes, okay. I come soon."

She cradles the phone and wriggles her fingers to loosen the stiffness. Fear palpitates under her breast, makes her ears ring. She draws in gulps of air, right hand on her chest, eyes closed. The women on the line send timid glances in her direction. Graciela dries her damp hands on her skirt and steps out of Mr. Greenblatt's office. He bounds toward her from the pattern table.

"Is everything all right?" She knows he's really asking if she'll finish her shift.

She looks down, as if the English words she needs were etched in Mr. Greenblatt's loafers. "Is my brother. In hospital."

"I see. Yeah. *Lo siento*. Get your card and I'll sign you out early."

He speaks too fast. His beard makes it impossible to see his lips. She stares at the worn seam on his cuffs, rubs her sweating palms against her hips.

"I no understand. . . ."

He makes a motion with his hands, like sticking fingers into honey. "*El cardo*. For *ponchar*."

"Ah, *sí. Ponchar*." Her face hot, she retrieves her time card from its slot by the clock and punches out. Mr. Greenblatt scribbles his initials next to the blue numbers.

"*Buena suerte*," he says, and waves off. She may not have a job if she stays out too long.

At her work station, she turns off her machine and slides her scissors into a blue quilted case. She dusts stray threads away from the needles and blows into the bobbin case, releasing fine silk fibers that dance up, then float slowly to the ground.

Mr. Greenblatt watches her through his glass wall. His phone rings, and he leans on his swivel chair to rest his feet on the windowsill. As soon as he turns his back, the women on the line slow the pace of their work. Consuelo, who works the Merrow next to Graciela, looks up at her through dusty glasses.

"Is there anything we can do for you?"

"*No, gracias*. It's just . . . my brother is in the emergency room at King's County."

"We will pray for him then." Some of the women bow their heads, others smirk. Leave it to Consuelo to bring God into every little thing. Consuelo lays her hand on Graciela's shoulder, and the younger woman squeezes it, grateful.

"Pray that he doesn't die until I get there," Graciela murmurs.

As she walks to the door, the women on either side of the line reach their hands out to touch hers, propelling her forward.

"*¡Valiente, niña!*" calls a woman whose own courage has been tested several times by her crack-addicted sons. Graciela's face admits a sad smile, and they shake their heads in sympathy for her inevitable sorrow, while some mumble that maybe now the bum will finally leave her alone.

It's July in New York. The garment district is swathed in a gray, muggy cloud, the air inside it hot and gritty. Car horns blare, trucks rumble past too fast for the crowded street. A cabdriver whizzes by, almost knocking Graciela off her feet.

Men push carts laden with plastic-bagged ready-to-wear, stare and hiss at her, mumble compliments under their breath. There was a time when she was flattered by these attentions, but now she knows they will whistle at any woman who looks better than the homeless sprawled in doorways and air vents.

Her heels *click-clack* down the steps to the subway. The station is cool. She has just missed a train, and the back stream chills her, makes the trembling inside her skin worse. She looks down the long platform for the lights of the next train, but the tunnel is dark, dotted here and there with feeble white bulbs.

Graciela has been called to a brother in an emergency room three times in five years. The fear that she may be too late is as familiar as the grimy subway station with its torn posters, its graffiti, its dripping tiled ceiling. She wants José Juan to last long enough for her to see him alive one last time. She hasn't seen him in two years, and she needs to touch him again, to hold his hand while it's still warm, not stiff, like her two younger brothers, who were corpses by the time she got to them.

She paces the station. When Carlitos and Rafael died, she sent their bodies to Puerto Rico. It was so expensive that she didn't have enough money left to go to the funeral. If José Juan dies, she'll have to do the same thing. She shakes her head to loosen the heaviness inside. It doesn't seem fair that just as she's saved enough money for her own trip back, she has to spend it on a dead brother.

At the far end of the platform, a young man with earphone wires dangling into an unseen tape player sings salsa under his breath. It's a song Ruben Blades performed in *Sábado Gigante*, the Spanish station's Saturday variety show.

The way he sways to the music, the way he taps his fingers against his jeans, reminds Graciela of Carlos Fidel, her youngest brother. Five years ago, Graciela received a call at work, a different job from the one she now has. Carlitos had taken some bad stuff. She didn't even know he was on drugs. Ever since he died, she stares at the young Puerto Rican men she sees on subways and street corners, sitting on stoops, hanging out in front of the bodegas. Are they on drugs? How can anybody tell?

A sour, angry taste curls the edges of her tongue. "*¡Títere!*" she mumbles, as if calling him a hood would transform him into something else.

The young man looks around, scans the black subway tunnel, pulls the earplug out to catch the distant thunder of an approaching train. They're alone on the narrow platform, so close she can make out the sparse fuzz on his upper lip. His back stiffens, and he stares into her, his macho hips thrust out, the hands in his pockets bulging the zipper of his trousers. She backs toward the barred token booth, inside which a large woman clinks coins. He saunters to the far end of the platform, hands in pockets, pulling tight the seam between his buttocks.

The train rumbles in, screeches to a stop. Graciela sits in a corner, hands folded over her purse. Across the aisle she catches her reflection in the filthy window. Her brown eyes are small, widely spaced. Both her eyes and her lips turn down at the corners, which makes her look disgusted. She's thirty-two, but her hair is gray and coarse. She had it dyed once. It cost so much she decided the difference in the way she looked wasn't worth the money. She pats it down, tames the frizzy halo away from her eyes. She was pretty when she lived by the sea in Puerto Rico, when she ran barefoot along a sandy beach, the ocean warming her toes. When José Juan sent her a one-way ticket to Brooklyn, she was still pretty. *"¡Qué linda eres!"* he told her when he saw her coming down the jetway, her long hair braided into a crown at the top of her head.

It was over a pretty woman that her second brother was killed in a dark bar in Flatbush. Another man stabbed him through the heart when Rafael tried to defend a woman he was beating up. Graciela didn't know her, or the man who killed Rafael. She was called to the emergency room of King's County Hospital to identify a puffy, mauled face that looked like her brother. He was the one who came with her to Brooklyn, the one who told her on the plane high over the Atlantic that as long as he was her brother no man would dare so much as look at his little sister the wrong way, "so don't you go making eyes at any strangers. It's bad for their health."

The train lurches with a shriek. Its metal doors clang open, and Graciela steps off. She rushes down the stairs and runs the two blocks to the large doors above which a red sign flashes EMERGENCY ROOM. Maybe José Juan is still alive. Maybe she can see what he looks like after two years.

The receptionist wears a name tag that identifies her as M. Herrera.

"¿Habla español?" Graciela tries to keep hope out of her voice.

"No. I'm sorry." M. Herrera looks truly sorry, then turns away.

A nurse leads her to a cloth partition. José Juan's head droops against white sheets. His sunken eyes are rimmed in red, his lips are puffy, blue. Thick gray stubble covers what was once a handsome face. Graciela chokes back a sob. She's too late. She touches his hand, rough, callused, the fingernails chipped into sharp edges. It's still warm.

José Juan lolls his head up and with great effort opens his eyes. Enormous tears fill the orbs and overflow onto his leathery cheeks.

"Graciela!"

He reaches for her, but the effort gets him only a few inches off the sheet draped up to his bony chest. He cries, and his nose runs, and Graciela finds a tissue with which to wipe him, to clean the tears and the snot and the look of sorrow and approaching death.

"Don't cry. It's me. I'll take care of you." She pushes back the thin strands of white hair matted against his forehead. Deep grooves filled with soot run from temple to temple. His ears are large, delicate, covered with dark fuzzy down. They lie flat against his scalp, innocent, intricate decorations.

José Juan is wheeled to the detox ward where he will join other men like him—poor, old before their time, livers corroded by alcohol. It is a long room, its floor shiny as ice, the beds close together, the bodies on them like ghosts. A gallery of wasted lovers and husbands, fathers, brothers and sons. Graciela tucks the sheets around José Juan, clumps the foam inside the pillow to hold his head up.

"¡Sinvergüenza!" she hisses at his closed face.

He was the first one to come to New York. The one whose letters to the barrio in Salinas were full of praise for the American way. He picked Rafael and her up at the airport, his breath stale against her cheek, apologized that the place he'd found for them was not up to his usual standards but it was the best he could do.

"¡Embustero!"

They lived in a five-story walk-up in New Lots, above sleeping drunks and the open doors of rooms where women wore faded flowered shifts that were too tight and too thin for the winter cold breezing through the unheated rooms. José Juan worked odd jobs at factories and restaurants. When he didn't work, he drank. Summer evenings he sat on the stoop of their building with other drunks, sharing bottles of cheap wine. She'd come back from work in the garment factories of Manhattan to find José Juan sprawled on the stairs, his arms crossed in front of him, a bottle of wine in a dirty paper bag clutched to his chest.

"¡Desgraciado!"

As soon as she could afford it, Graciela got her own apartment. But José Juan regularly showed up at her door, his clothes smelly, his pockets empty, his lips full of excuses, swearing he'd never do this to her again. She nursed him back, gave him money, helped him find work at the factories where she worked. But after a few weeks, he'd disappear again. She dreaded coming home and finding him slumped in her hallway, smelling of cheap wine and urine.

The last time she saw him sober, she gave him money and told him to get out of her house and never come back, that she was tired of being a mother to a grown man. His eyes were full of reproach, but he turned on his heel and disappeared into the streets. Two months later, she moved and didn't leave a forwarding address.

"*¡Hijo de la gran puta!*" She curses into his ear, into the bitter sweaty musk that rises from between the covers. "*¡Maldito seas!*"

"I'm afraid you have to leave." The nurse is gentle, quiet, a large woman who moves on tiptoe, checks the bags of solution dripping into her patients' arms, folds a blanket over a heaving chest, wipes sweat off beaded foreheads.

Graciela stares at her, not understanding, ashamed that the nurse may have heard her damn her dying brother to hell.

"There's nothing you can do for him now. We'll take care of him." The nurse smiles at her, looks in the direction of the lit sign that says EXIT.

Graciela steadies herself against the bed rail, cool on her hot fingers, solid. "*Gracias.*"

"We'll call you if his condition changes." The nurse pats her shoulder, and Graciela fights the urge to fall into her arms.

"*Sí.* Thank you. Goodbye."

She takes a breath, stumbles, regains her step, then walks away, her hips swaying, her heels tapping a female rhythm on the tiled floor.

She races into the dusk. Every doorway is the entrance to a cave from which she may never come out, every alley an endless tunnel. She walks quickly, alert to movement and sound, avoiding the eyes of passersby. When the subway comes, she sits by the conductor's booth, her hands crossed over her black vinyl purse.

It will take every penny she's saved to send José Juan to Puerto Rico. Money she's been putting away for her first trip back since she came to New York. "Only for a visit," she tells herself, "to see my parents." Every week she sends half her salary to them, and they spend it to modernize their house and pay their medical bills. They write that all their neighbors are jealous of their good fortune, their devoted daughter who respects and supports her parents. They hope someday she will return to care for them in their old age, like a good daughter should.

But she can't imagine going back to Barrio La Cumbre with nothing to show for her years in New York. She'd like to bring enough money to buy a *parcela* in the mountains. She'd like to learn to drive and get a car that will take her to the parts of Puerto Rico shown in documentaries. The hot springs in Coamo. The rain forest. Luquillo Beach. The phosphorescent bay. She'd like to wear flowing white dresses and ride bareback along a shore flanked with coconut palms. And she'd like to dance under a full moon by the ocean, her head cradled in the shoulder of a man who smells like Brut.

When the train pulls into her station, Graciela waits to be the last passenger off. When she comes up to the street, she steps quickly across the intersection, walks past a drugstore, a pizza parlor, and a lawyer's office, then looks in every direction before inserting her key into the hall door of her building. Once she's up the stairs, she breathes, the clutch on her handbag eases, and she lets herself into the studio apartment with kitchenette that's her home.

Everything inside is tidy. White ruffled curtains hide the street at the front of the apartment, and the gray windows of the building in back. A lace cloth covers the Formica dining table, where, this morning, she left a place setting for dinner. From the refrigerator she takes leftover rice and beans, which she reheats in her Corning Ware pots. While the food warms, she showers and changes into her nightgown and slippers, then sits down to eat, a small color television set tuned to the Spanish channel, where the first of the night's soap operas is about to begin.

It is her favorite, *Chains of Love*, about a beautiful young girl who marries into a rich family and is tormented by her mother and sister-in-law, while her father-in-law tries to seduce her.

The phone rings during a commercial for McDonald's.

"Hello?"

"Mrs. Graciela Ortiz?" In the background she hears the beeps of a hospital paging system.

It takes all her strength to put the receiver down. By her bedside is an altar for St. Lazarus ringed with votive candles in red glass cups. His arms are outstretched, eyes up to heaven. She kneels before him and crosses herself. The only prayers she knows are the "Our Father" and "Ave Maria." She recites them more from habit than with hope for comfort. The words are meaningless, but the dead deserve a prayer.

Pictures of her brothers surround the saint, amid magazine cutouts of the Condado, Old San Juan, John Kennedy, and the governor of Puerto Rico. There's a picture of Raúl Julia in the role of a Nicaraguan priest called Romero. It's the only picture of him she's ever been able to get, and she cut it out of the newspaper and bought a special frame for it so it wouldn't tear. Carlitos's picture has curled at the edges, and she untacks it from the wall and rubs it flat against her palms. Rafael's picture is under a piece of glass she salvaged from a broken window. She looks through its scratched surface at the handsome young man smiling back at her. Everyone loved Rafael's smile. He had the whitest teeth.

José Juan's photograph rests near the straw given her the last time she went to church, on Palm Sunday ten years ago. He wears a white suit and shoes. His hands grasp the rail of the Circle Line boat that tours around Manhattan Island. Behind him rises the city, hard-edged and gray, its buildings in sharp focus, José Juan's face a blur under his panama hat. She strokes it with her index finger and makes the sign of the cross over it.

Her knees creak when she gets up, and the weight of her body settles into the familiar hollow of her bed, where she lies on her back, hugging herself. Tears track down her temples, dampen her gray hair. Through the half-open windows, the roar of the city sounds like a stifled moan. The altar candles flicker dancing ghosts on the ceiling, and through her tears the shapes sparkle, making the shadows beyond them darker. She's alone. Even her dead have returned to Puerto Rico. When she dies, there will be no one left to send her home.

Dawn breaks gray and hot. Graciela's eyes are swollen, her cheeks blotchy with dried tears. As soon as she's showered and dressed, she walks down the street to Gonzales Funeral Service. Around her, people rush to be first at the subway, first on line at the coffee shop, first inside the elevator. She moves in slow motion, as if the thick air were water and she a clumsy swimmer barely staying afloat.

The Gonzales Funeral Service smells like candle wax and disinfectant. Mr. Gonzales is solemn in his dark suit, but as he leads her into his office, she notices he walks with the telltale bounce of the streets. After Mr. Gonzales prepares him, there will be just enough money left for José Juan's airfare to Puerto Rico.

She withdraws all her money from the bank. On her way back to the funeral home, her purse clutched against her side, the odor of fresh brewed coffee reminds her she hasn't had breakfast, and she steps into Pito's Bodega and Delicatessen for a fried egg sandwich and *café con leche*. The radio is tuned to the Spanish station, where Yolandita Monge sings of tragic love and betrayal.

Graciela stands at the counter by the store window, chewing slowly, and sips the strong coffee with a faint sucking sound. Across the street, next to Gonzales Funeral Service, the owner of Leon's Insurance and Travel Agency rolls up the steel doors that protect his storefront. The poster of Raúl Julia in front of a grove of coconut palms invites people to come see the Puerto Rico he knows. He wears a white shirt open at the neck and white pants rolled up to his calves. His hands are bunched in his pockets. He smiles seductively, his half-closed eyelids promising passionate kisses.

On the radio, the announcer swoons over Yolandita Monge's lovely voice and begins reading the news from Puerto Rico. The price of coffee is up. Rice is up. Unemployment stands at 22 percent. A man is wanted for murder in connection with the bludgeoning of his wife and teenage nephew.

For all his drunkenness, José Juan was never violent, unlike the men Graciela's co-workers talk about. To hear them, every man is a wife beater, a loud drunk, good for nothing. They're not at all like the men on *telenovelas*, who look like Raúl Julia and always talk of love. José Juan spoke softly, never beat anyone, and, when he was not drunk, looked as handsome as a movie star.

She crushes her half-finished sandwich into the paper plate and napkin, shoves everything into the Styrofoam cup, and dumps it all in the trash can under the counter. Raúl Julia beckons to her, while inside the basement of the funeral home next door, other Puerto Rican men are embalmed so they can go home.

She fingers the stack of bills in her purse. There's just enough to send José Juan home. But how much would be left if he were buried in Brooklyn?

She hoists her purse under her arm and pushes the door of the bodega. Brassy salsa music follows her outside, but the palm trees behind Raúl Julia sway to the strains of a bolero. She crosses the street, listening to his voice singing words of love into her ear.

Four and Twenty

NAN SAVILLE

There was this part from a book that I read to him about a woman, a country singer, who left a man she was married to because she just couldn't stay with him any longer. She went to the circus one day with her daughter, Celestine or something like that, and saw a man with flames shooting out of his head. A spark caught, and all of a sudden she was on fire for him. She sent her daughter home to the family and they ran away together. The family never heard from the singer again. I thought hearing that story would put him in mind of a woman leaving a man, like maybe a woman like me and a man like him. Well, I don't think it came to him, not right away, that I was telling him goodbye because he had a second helping of chicken, and did it to me after he threw the red and white cartons in the trash, and then he went to sleep. I thought it might come to him later that I could go the way the woman in the story did, not because of someone whose head was on fire but because I just couldn't take it anymore and was looking to leave.

Maybe it was because of Zorita that it finally got to be too much. Somehow, things were almost all right up till the night we did it in her

NAN SAVILLE lives in Greenwich Village, where she has taught freshman composition at her alma mater, New York University, for over fifteen years. She is currently the director of N.Y.U.'s Collegiate Science and Technology Entry Program.

apartment and she came home just after we finished and made that comment about some filthy bitch's come on her satin sheets and told him to get out. He told her, "Baby, I love you, this ain't what it look like." I knew he had been doing her for the blow she got from her man for him, but I accepted that because he had said being with her was more like a job or something, and some more talk about currency and rates of exchange that I couldn't quite understand, not being so smart like he was. He said besides all that she was too freaking old and stuff, but he had called her by his word for me and told her he loved her just as if he were talking to me. And then he told me to shut up, to stop trying to make things worse, that I didn't understand about a man and his shit.

My grandmother's sister had an outside man once; well, anyway, what I mean is that she was his outside woman. He didn't tell her until after he had had her a few times that he was married. He was tall and did odd jobs for people—this was down south way before Tia moved up here—he was good with his hands, she said. He talked soft to her and made good money and was going to leave his wife, after the holiday at first and then when her sickness passed. He just didn't have no more feeling for her like that, although she wasn't a bad woman. Tia would sit on the porch step and look for him in the evening. She was pretty then, almost. He would come up the back way in his work clothes and bring her a little something—stockings or some blue flowers that she would put in a jar. And he would push the screen door open and take her again and again while the moon made its way up the sky. Lots of holidays came and went and his Gertrude's condition healed well before the time they were seen riding together in that new carriage he had bought her. She sat next to him holding on to his arm with those little birdlike, fluttering fingers of hers, with her hair pulled back neat and hidden under a shiny straw hat, not loose like Tia's hair that only saw the inside of a hat on Sunday mornings maybe.

Maybe that's why Tia baked him a special pie, a blueberry one, his favorite kind. She got up extra early to pick the berries herself from a special place she used to go to with my grandmother when they were girls. She bought white sugar from the sundry later that same morning and used a hammer and the brown bag they'd packed it in to break a large drinking glass into fine little bitty dustlike pieces. She added a lot of butter to the flour for the crust; that was the secret of the flaky kind she was known for. She let the blueberries simmer for a while in a cup of vanilla water with two and a half cups of sugar and pulverized glass. Into this she measured a tablespoon of rosewater and a bit of cornstarch to make plenty of thick, sweet juice. It smelled wicked and sweet—like *she* was, he said, eating almost half of it with a little ice cream she had made before he walked up from town. He would leave his Gertrude soon, for though she had made him a good enough wife, she just didn't make him feel like this. He kissed her hard like he did those times when he said he couldn't live without her. His eyes teared when he told her how bad he wanted her right then, but he was starting to feel a bout of indigestion coming on, so he would go home and let it pass. Back in town, he put two bits on number 1059 and complained of a bit of tightness and wind, saying he seemed to taste just a trace of blood when he was able to belch. That little taste grew heavier as evening gave way to night, and he did leave his Gertrude before the next sun. Tia stopped making blueberry pie forever.

Maybe I didn't understand about a man and his shit, but I knew something about love, and I was sure that my Jimmy wasn't about to leave Zorita and that her hold on him was only partly tied to her old man's blow. I found my things in the darkness of Jimmy's apartment, got dressed, and went outside to wait for the bus. I thought about how soft he almost looked, sleeping sprawled out on top of the covers, but there was nothing soft about Jimmy. He was like a bullet when he was awake. He tore into everything and blew it apart.

The bus moved like it was tired and my exact change joined everybody else's as the BX-19 continued down the street. I never went back. At least that was my plan. And I almost didn't go back either, not for a long time. I was feeling pretty good that my plan had gone so fine. By the time Jimmy realized what I had been telling him, it would be over. I'd be gone and he would not be able to disagree or try to over-talk me because I would already be away from him. The sky seemed electric blue, like it does sometimes when it's real cold out and the haze that normally clouds its face lifts or moves to some other part of town for a while, and evening turned the buildings into blackened silhouettes against its color. Maybe Jimmy had understood after all; maybe it wouldn't be so hard for him to let me go. He had said he didn't need anybody or anything, for that matter. He wanted me as much as he wanted a little blow now and again, but that wasn't like anything he couldn't cut loose. Too much trouble to need something. Rather do without.

Through the trying-to-be-tinted window, I caught glimpses of the cookie-cutter lives being lived inside the gingerbread houses along the streets. From the bus, it looked so simple, too far away to hear the anger and hurt in their voices or see the fear glaring from their eyes. Maybe these people were no different from me and Jimmy, but the neat little porches

FOUR AND TWENTY

and trees that sheltered them made their lives look like fairy-tale stuff. No stairs to climb when the elevators weren't working, which was most of the time. No smell of the aftermath of someone's good time in the hall 'cause too much liquor and/or dope had him feeling too good to give a fuck where he was pissing or sticking his thing. Not that you needed to have a thing for this kind of pleasure. High times loved everybody, and you could party for as long as life and something to get off on lasted, which was never long enough. I would go back to cosmetology school. I had what you'd call a flair. Someday I'd work in one of those big and elegant midtown places with a lot of mirrors with chrome around them and ten or so chairs with real vinyl seat covers and a steady clientele.

I heard the phone ringing in my apartment and I tried to run up the last few steps to the fifth floor, knowing full well I didn't have that much breath left. I always took my keys out of my bag before getting off the bus in case I had to fight my way out of something. I couldn't find the keyholes for the last two locks; the light in the hall always made more noise than it gave light, but finally I was inside, having long missed the phone. I thought it sounded like Jimmy's ring, all sharp and jagged. It wasn't always like that, though; at first the phone sort of purred when he called, but that was way before I told him how much I loved him and before Zorita became his connection. That was when he still lived uptown. Sometimes, he would take me up to the roof where he kept his birds, to feed them and do a joint. He knew every one of those birds by name, Jorge being his favorite because of the scar under his right eye, and he told me I was his baby and we did it standing up, right inside their pen, and the birds scattered, leaving feathers everywhere. They wouldn't fly away though, because he had clipped their wings—he said you had to be real careful—so they would stay right there out of harm's way where he would always be able to bring them food. I used to wonder how they had smelled in the fire that burned them in their cages like so many matchsticks and gutted the whole top floor of the building. He really loved those birds. It hurt him so to lose them. Nobody ever boarded up the windows or figured out what started the fire. Jimmy left Manhattan after that.

The phone cut through my thoughts, making me jump. It was Jimmy, wondering why in the fucking hell I had left when it was just starting to get good. I told him I loved him, but I had to get away because it wasn't the same anymore and just didn't feel right and there was nobody else, but I wouldn't be coming back because I had to get away and couldn't stay with him anymore. He said he didn't understand, and so I said it to him again and then again, but in the middle of the last time I said it to him, he hung up, saying I didn't understand. And I thought, well, maybe I didn't, but I knew I couldn't go back there.

There were dishes left over from a few nights before that I would have to wash before I could have a cup of tea. A roach on top of the refrigerator watched me in perfect stillness but for one antenna which, as if surprised to see me, he lifted in the air. Without thinking, I smashed him flat with my hand and rinsed him down the sink. I lit the fire under the kettle and washed the knives, forks, and glasses first before starting the plates and more greasy stuff. A sudden clap of thunder burst from the heavy metal front door, and I knew Jimmy was outside. I started to tell him no way, but I knew nothing would keep him on that side of the door. I asked him to please baby don't be mad at me, and he said to open the fucking door and stop acting like a cunt and some other foul talk. I don't know why I thought about the people who lived across the hall from me, they had certainly had plenty to say to each other coming in or going out in the wee hours, but somehow I started to feel sort of embarrassed, so I opened the locks and let him in.

It was as if something, some force, blasted the door in. I half expected to see it fly off the hinges, but I didn't have time to notice because Jimmy had me by the throat, pushing me into the kitchen where he used his other hand to pull my head by my hair into the soapy, warm water in the sink. I heard myself screaming *no, no, no* over and over and then *please Jimmy*, but he held my neck so hard, and I think he was crying too. He said I was his and he couldn't let me go, and he picked up the carving knife that I had just washed from the drainboard and he looked at it and he kissed me while I screamed. Then he started talking to me real slowly and clear. I felt a thin line of fire slide across my neck and then kind of a seesaw pressure back and forth. My fingers ripped open when I tried to grab the blade to make him stop and I saw blood all over his face. His eyes were big, the black parts opened up so wide they could have swallowed me, and his lips were moving and talking real soft. They said if he couldn't have me he wasn't going to leave me for someone else to hurt; that if someone else hurt me it would be his fault because a man is supposed to protect his woman and he was protecting me forever. Each time he pushed and pulled the knife, he kept saying, "This is because I love you, baby; you are mine, and I don't want nobody else to hurt you." I wasn't moving anymore. I wanted him to think that I was dead, that I was safe. I was as still as I could be; my body felt like it was jerking, but I stopped it somehow. I looked deeper into the black of his eyes. I didn't see any kind of light.

FOUR AND TWENTY

The next thing I remember was whiteness all around and the taste of shoe polish. Somebody had heard me screaming and had actually called the cops. A lot of faces I had never seen before kept leaning over me, some seemed to touch me and others just looked, leaning over from the side of the bed—nurses, attendants in green, cops in regular clothes with pictures of themselves sealed in plastic and clamped on their shirts. All of them said the same thing about holding Jimmy, me pressing charges, and keeping a sick maniac from messing up another pretty girl. None of them had Jimmy's spark or his rhythm. None of them understood that Jimmy loved me and wanted me for himself. When the tubes and machines had been taken away, I found a voice that was finally able to tear loose from my mouth and tell them that nobody had ever loved me like Jimmy had. They said I was as crazy as he was and some foolishness about me liking it and going back for more. Still, I would not let them make me charge him. They counseled and advised; they preached; they finally offered what they said was "psychotherapeutic intervention"; he would not go to jail.

I wanted him. The counselor was an older woman. She said there was no guarantee that I'd survive my next encounter with Jimmy. She told me I was battered and talked about abuse and how so many women don't know that it doesn't have to be that way. She said love was different from pain and people who love you shouldn't make you hurt—you can "learn to give and accept caring in a positive, nurturing way." She used words like "unacceptable" and talked about liking yourself. She pinned me between her eyes and tried to push herself inside my head. She wanted so much for me, but all I could think about was Jimmy. Usually, she was very steady and cool, but now her hands shook. I looked at the thin, pinkish snake that crawled through the black wires around my neck, and I knew that no matter what happened, I would always belong to Jimmy.

Most of the stitches finally were out and, despite the counselor's seeming wish to keep me in for observation till I "responded" to her treatment too, they let me go. She wanted me to come back once a week to see her, but I doubted that I would; even though for all intents and purposes I had no one else to talk to, I just never really trusted head-shrink types; what do they really care?

Besides, deep inside, I knew what I had to do. I called Jimmy first thing when I got home and arranged to meet him on Thursday. The linoleum on the floor in the kitchen was badly stained, and the dishes that weren't broken had to be washed again. I still had to be careful scrubbing and carrying things so that my neck would not come loose. Mostly, I tried to make things like they were before. I went to the store and made food; I took a long walk, all the way to the market downtown that sold wonderful fresh fruit, even though much of it was out of season. Next door to a funeral parlor, I found a place that sold fresh coffee beans, the fragrance completely overwhelming the flowers that people sent to their dear departed and, if not actually waking the dead, giving the living cause to wonder about it. I wandered into a church, following the scent of the frankincense that drifted through the large wooden door and lured me inside, where it blended with the musty smell of ages upon ages of unanswered prayers. Kneeling in the darkness, I added mine and hoped to hear the story about that city in the Bible that was destroyed because no one could find enough people there who had any good in them, and that one man who was spared and told to go, but whose wife chose to look back. I used to wonder why she had done that, what she had looked back to see, especially if things were so bad there. Maybe she figured that what she was leaving behind was no worse than what was to come and so she just turned to salt. I stood, crossed myself, and walked out. I would do the only thing I could. I would choose between bad and bad; I could not pick salt.

Jimmy was on my mind all the time. At night, I could feel his breath and the weight of his lips on my face. He kissed me and I said for him to stop, Jimmy, but he kissed me again. On Thursday I fixed my hair a new way and tied it with a scarf. I walked almost all the way to the back before I found a seat on the BX-19. I rested my purse on a little box holding what you'd call sort of a peace offering for Jimmy as the bus rattled up the street, jostling people standing and sitting inside. The engine droned a heavy chant interrupted by horns and sirens as we rushed through the fierce rhythms of the street. Through it all, I could almost hear the counselor, her unyielding voice repeating "unacceptable." I knew she would never understand, but this was something I just had to do. Sometimes, you don't have words to even make a thing into a thought, but it is inside you so much that it is you after a while, and that's how it was with this.

Jimmy looked at me as if he had seen a ghost. His face was tight and his eyes were shiny and hard, and he said how he was disappointed in me, how he had thought I was different and had more stuff going for me than that. He asked me why I had bothered to come all the way up there since we were supposed to be through. I put my things on the little metal table just inside the door and told him I had been doing a lot of thinking and I needed to see him; even if it was for just one last time, I needed to see him. I told him that maybe I shouldn't have left like I did. He said I was "damn right, fucking A" and none of this shit should have happened in the first place with the cops all into his business, and he smashed his hand against the wall behind my head and stood there as little flakes of plaster drifted to the floor. Then he hit the wall again, like for emphasis or something. I told him I was sorry and I wanted things to be like they were before, even if just for a little while. He said he hadn't done anything to deserve somebody like me or to be treated like that, but then he looked at me almost sweet and said that maybe he was crazy or something, but he still wanted me, and he told me to take off my clothes and he threw the cushions from the couch and pulled out the mattress with the sheets all twisted up and knotted in the middle of it. I straightened out the sheets and smoothed them out over the mattress while he pulled his shirt over his head and took out a little vial of white powder and dipped some of it into a little spoon. He asked if I wanted a toot and I shook my head, no, Jimmy, as he sniffed it up his nose and then again. He rubbed his teeth with his thumb and unfastened my bra and pushed me almost playfully onto the sheets, sitting over me with one hand rested between my breasts. I almost shuddered when he touched where he cut me and told me, "Baby, you are mine; you are wearing my ring." I let him kiss me; his lips burned where they touched. I stretched out beneath him and looked into his eyes. I touched his hair and told him that I had hoped he would still want me.

I held my breath when he moved his hand down my body and opened my legs and asked me over and over, Did you miss me, baby? while he slid in and out of me. I told him yes, Jimmy, yes, and he sucked my lips and pushed harder and harder inside me and began to breathe in little snorts and said for me to do it, baby, and he told me it was good pussy, baby, and he began repeating whose pussy was it, at first like sort of a chant and then like a demand, and when I said to him, "Yours, Jimmy," he shook a little and clenched his teeth and hollered something like yes, baby! while he came real hard inside me. He flopped down over me and blew air slowly into my ear until he began to snore. I held one side of the mattress and eased myself out from under him part by part and unknotted one of the sheets again, throwing it lightly over Jimmy's back and feet. I watched him sleeping for a long time.

I found a clean fork and took a slightly scratched plastic plate from the cupboard. Then I opened the package that I had wrapped so carefully that morning before leaving home. Sitting on the side of the bed, I told him I had brought him a little surprise to show my love for him if he wanted it. He told me I was still his woman and that though he would probably be sorry for it later, he would take me back if I could stop playing stupid games. He sat up and rested the box on his thighs. He looked sort of surprised, sort of pleased with himself when he lifted the top and saw the brown flaky crust with a little pure sugar that sparkled like glass and seemed to say *eat me* sprinkled on top. Refusing the plate, he paused the fork in midair over the box and asked if I wouldn't like some too, and I told him, no, Jimmy I had already had my dessert, and this time I kissed him in real soft little circles all over his face. He said it was something else when he tasted it and asked me where did I buy it, and I told him with pride that I didn't, that the recipe had been in my family for years. Then he told me I was something else, and I promised to be his until the end of time as he licked his fingers and helped himself to more of my blueberry pie.

FATIMA SHAIK

Everything goes by the corner of St. Bernard and Broad in New Orleans. There are four bus stops where the drivers call out to anyone waiting, "What time you got?" or "Want to cross go get me a snow cone? Ambrosia."

From the record shop, from the big cars at stoplights, and from the black-painted glass-windowed barroom blares the same music—for inspiration to dance, to make love, or to kill somebody with a shotgun and nobody hearing.

On these corners are children going to and from school and playing hooky behind the gas station. The seafood store, the drugstore, and the bakery are set in a triangle and are ever expanding.

Everything in life happens in this neighborhood at one time or another, as does everybody.

FATIMA SHAIK is the author of a collection of novellas, *The Mayor of New Orleans: Just Talking Jazz*. Her work is included in the anthologies *African American Fiction* and *Breaking Ice*. Her stories and essays have also appeared in *Tribes, Callaloo, The Southern Review*, and *The Review of Contemporary Fiction*. She recently completed two children's books, *On Mardi Gras Day* and *The Jazz of Our Street*.

Cynthia Delahoussey walks these corners and her hips flow in multiple rhythms. They take their upbeat from her center of motion and they hit the downbeat at her perimeter.

"That girl is New Orleans," people watch her and say. She has the city's loping pulse in her step and her gravity is centered low, like the street eases down into the pavement. She is cheaply, coolly dressed, as everyone with sense saves their money for important things like a gallon can of oysters or po-boy sandwiches enough to feed the family.

Cynthia's whole life, attitude, and moral persuasion are apparent in her smile, her uncontrollable hair, her extra insulation of flesh, and her pathways, which are the same day after day in these streets and the few others surrounding. "That girl is New Orleans." People smile and shake their heads at their familiarity to her and their common goodness and bounty.

To be "New Orleans" is their highest compliment. It means "You are our hope, tradition, and family." A man called "New Orleans" is in his prime, even if that prime is eighty years old. "New Orleans" on an older woman is a sister ever facile with the white handkerchief in her bosom to wipe a brow, or a tear, or to whip out for a second line after a funeral. God is with the man or woman who is New Orleans all of the time.

Cynthia is young, healthy, and blessed as New Orleans. Could there ever be a better combination? "No," the men emphasize to her frequently and fan themselves when her backside rocks in its daily parade. "No, no, no." Sometimes they hold their crotches and swoon with feigned pain.

But today is hot, a record temperature with no rain and 100 percent humidity, so the men don't move much to appreciate Cynthia. They only give her sleepy looks and wave.

Cynthia pushes one big arm up in greeting to them, standing in a doorway wearing white undershirts and eating snow cones. The juice runs red and green or purple from their fingertips to their wrists and crusts the fringes of their heavy mustaches.

"Hey, Mardi Gras," she says to a man on the street who always is dressed too brightly in the middle of the week.

"Where y'at, Fairgrounds." She acknowledges the daily horse gambler.

"Oo-ee, Miss Jelly Roll," Cynthia drones to a fat little girl approaching puberty, like everyone takes the responsibility to remind her. Only the men still remind her older sister with the same words in a different tone.

When Cynthia waves, an artificial snow of talcum descends from the undersides of her sweat-greased upper arm. She powders up following her afternoon bath like a fried beignet douses itself in a plate of sugar. Before she left the house, Cynthia made a trail of powder on the rough wooden floors.

"Mawmaw"—she passed her young child to Elise—"keep Nanette till I come back."

Her mother did exactly as Cynthia knew she would do. She took the sleeping girl and soothed a palm over her head.

"Where you think you going?" Her mama watched the back of Cynthia's dress go out the door, "Don't you wear slips no more?"

The screen latch *click* was her answer.

Cynthia knows, this day as she steps off the curb and passes her hand in the air with greetings as the rain of her talcum temporarily obscures her view. She knows the place and makes the choice to feel with her feet for the wide crack in the neutral ground, the grass median that separates the traffic in opposite directions from heading into itself and disassembling into heaps of the metal, glass, rubber, bones, and skin in which people transport themselves from one location to the other.

She knows that something is missing, and right now that is her man. It is her job to place him. Every day after work, Desmond goes to Smithy's Restaurant and Bar to get a beer just like the others in the neighborhood. So she trots over to spend the hours there before dinner. She sometimes asks herself if she were not at Smithy's would he come home looking for her? "No, no," goes a little voice inside her head. But she doesn't let herself in on the answer.

She knows Desmond loves her. Ever since they were children, they were a match. Weren't his first words to her one morning after attending confession, "Baby, your calves so big make me lose my absolution."

That was the beginning of a beautiful relationship. She knew because everyone told her. They looked like brother and sister, they said. The children would be beautiful.

Cynthia didn't know how to make a baby even at fourteen. But she trusted Desmond to the details. Men were offering her compliments as long as she could remember. Doing it meant only giving in her to her ripe pride. So it was easy.

Nanette was born on time and unexpectedly, a hot rainstorm conjured from a summer sweat, conceived in the auto repair shop where Desmond worked at night. He and Cynthia made love, fortified by the masculine smell of gasoline, in a small space near the hollow cars.

It was their secret coupling shared in whispers to the open air of the streets, the auto shop yard surrounded on two sides by empty lots and the backs of houses on two others. Cynthia knew that she and Desmond had entered a world that contained a complicated, private, and well-known society.

In every house in this Seventh Ward neighborhood of single shotguns and doubles, on every block where children in herds gathered and happily ran the sidewalks, in every time from the biblical to the end of human existence with one exception, people were doing it like she and her man.

They had slept until morning washed the stars invisible and the neighborhood dogs' lonely howls brightened with the companionship of roosters and the chase of garbage-can lids thrown by men singing.

And love from that time on became as complex as the people on earth, sky and stars working together while acting in apparent disharmony. It was something she could not yet control or fully understand.

But Cynthia traveled to womanhood with the same fervor of chosen destiny as when she made her vow to the church on her day of confirmation. Almost giddy while the organ played and the priest gave her a slap on the face, she knew this was right.

Nanette was her mother's first answer and her father's last mistake.

Or so Cynthia thought. But Desmond at Smithy's showed outside inclinations. It must have been because Stella put in front of him the temptation of herself.

Stella worked waiting tables, the last unmarried girl in the neighborhood. She was still thin and, some rumored, virginal. Cynthia had watched Desmond's eyes watch Stella, the near occasion of passion.

Desmond's desire was outside religion, beyond the sanctimony of marriage, an old New Orleans passion that Cynthia did not want to know in this generation was stretching the couple of them. How many old people did she know that live harmoniously or at least obviously in sin: the husband, the wife, the mistress; the wife, the husband, the boyfriend?

That was New Orleans tradition as well, the triangles and squares and all kinds of configurations that the old ladies on porches whispered about, full of knowing.

Cynthia protested when she was young, "Not this one. Not when I have a man. My man is going stay just for me."

And they shook their heads with the same resignation that let their mothers become concubines and then landowners in the previous generations, and let women earlier dress daughters in French silk and learn English manners for men who could free their children, the same women who saw their boys repeat the recklessness of their fathers rather than their mothers' courage. So the old ladies knew more about Cynthia than she could for a long time. They went back to their rosaries. Fait accompli. They nodded heads with each other, and looked at Cynthia with sadness and sympathy, and encouraged her to school with the nuns for a few more years of innocence.

But now she was a wife and a mother and could not suffice if not for control at least within illusion.

As Cynthia reaches the wooden swinging door of Smithy's someone grabs it from the other side. She trips over the frame and catches her heels on the worn plywood under the linoleum.

"My baby." Desmond half laughs and pats the chair for her to sit down next to him. He snuggles his face in her hair, kisses the wide, quickly chilled back of her neck, and stretches his arm over her shoulders to shelter her from the air-conditioning.

"Stella," he calls, "two beers over here."

Cynthia pries the sandals off her feet with opposite toes. The straps make marks on the skin. Her feet are flat and wide with a briny waterline where they go from pink to tawny. Like her hips, calves, and thick hair, her feet are not easily tamed.

Stella, by contrast, is narrow and quick, pretty, and still needy in a way that men and even Cynthia can see. She watches her husband's eyes study the waitress as she brings the beer.

He is still looking as Cynthia offers a toast. Instead, their glasses miss, making a half orbit around each other. And a spill from Cynthia's beer flies out, falling first on the table and dripping down to the floor. It soaks into the black-and-white pattern underfoot, through the rotten plywood covering rottener tongue-in-groove plank and joint, and her drink rains under the shack into the ancient mud like so many beers, tears, toilets, and floods before.

Stella took off early and walked the long way home where the people seeing her would have nothing to say. Esplanade Avenue was constructed for urbanity rather than camaraderie, like the homes on smaller streets behind it. So there was no care or obligation to exchange greetings between the dark young woman passing before plots with massive iron gates and, behind them, the aged spinsters raised on white wooden porches.

Stella took freedom in this disconcerting path. Following the shade of oak trees held captive by new sidewalks, she escaped the summer heat and basked in the silence.

The sun was setting to a dampness from the lake. It smelled clean like fresh shrimp and salty like a day laborer. It spread the moss dangling above Stella like a girl's curly hair, swelling with the evening.

Neatly symmetrical in a close-fitting blouse and skirt, the petite Stella contradicted the loose creation around her. Her mules clicked against the rolling pavement and slapped against her heels, hard little bits of skin that her soft green eyes did not see.

When Stella turned off Esplanade, she rushed home with little electric steps. With distaste that she was seen walking at all, she added a switch to make herself noticeable.

She didn't have money for a car. Her bills were too much. She owed for her mother's funeral and her sister's doctor enough to take one day a week of her salary for the next two years. That's if she was able to keep on working.

Smithy's got slim pickings of the drinking crowd these days. Like mutual assistance clubs all over New Orleans that changed in one generation to bars and to dives in the next, the regular clientele was dying off and the new one sank pretty low. It used to be a place where all the neighborhood bricklayers and plasterers stopped on their walk home or came in a boisterous clutter, jumping out of the beds of painting trucks when the driver jerked to a stop. These men carried their shoulders loosely behind their high chests, generously offering the room bright, wide faces as they entered.

In a place the size of a big living room, three generations had gathered. Those beginning to work, those now burdened under, and those who worked mainly for tradition. Stella's old neighbor once existed in a drunken stumble as she walked home from grammar school. "God bless you, my baby," he said, as he wet her in a hug salty with perspiration. Then he faced in the direction of his home to eat, sleep, and join the men the next day.

Today, mainly drinkers stayed in Smithy's, skinny men who wished their lives were as interesting as the soap operas they watched, lingering from noon past dinnertime. They came one by one, in and out, some in a fog, clutching a scotch to straighten them up. Sometimes they conversed with others who smelled sweetly only for their own sake. They had cute words to say to Stella, like she was different from them and had a weaker kind of understanding. Some working men still arrived, but they were like insurance men and new politicians. Wearing suits bought off Canal Street, they loosened their ties when they reached the table, pretending that was a part of their sitting. Then they all talked in comparisons, pointing out the things that they claimed were "the best."

excerpt from BAYOU ROAD STREET

"The ones who come in want to sit all the time, and none of them want to pay," said Smithy, who was hardly even considered a white man because of his long neighborhood duration. He now told Stella he didn't think he could last in business much longer, but she could stay as long as he. Anyone could see business was bad with this new crowd of men. Their women, for the most part, never came in. Afraid of what they would be called for drinking alone in public, they embraced their houses, growing increasingly indifferent with age.

But Stella appeared interesting to all of them because she presented herself so. The people thought all kinds of things about her. They said she was smart because she was quick-witted and sexy because she dressed in clothes that fit. Lately, they hinted that she had Desmond now. Actually, she never did.

It was because Stella and Desmond shared occasions that everyone knew. Drugstore love, high school attention, is not something New Orleans forgets, not the kind of people who name their boys Tristan and their girls Evangeline. In their history, Stella should have gotten him long ago. But Stella's mother, Landee, in those years was not a romantic. She made sure Stella was not much around.

Desmond, as a boy, played at the corner of Stella's house where his friend Robert lived and fixed bicycles after school. For company, Stella would go down the block, sit on the steps, and watch.

Desmond's pleasure was picking up tales as he rode around the neighborhood on his bike and then acting them out on the corner for everyone's entertainment. Stella heard that Willamena was so pregnant her wedding dress was short in the front, that Mrs. Dowald's son switched like a girl, and that Rupe Pete had heavy bags of money hidden under his house that the boys were going to dig up after he died.

Stella's first cigarette was from Desmond. But he promised it to her only if she'd kiss him. The other kids shut their eyes at his orders, even though Robert was allowed to peek under his arm. Desmond stood directly in front of Stella with one hand behind his back and the other dangling the cigarette. He closed his eyes and pushed his head forward. Stella saw a big bull face, yellow and flat, coming at her. She had slammed the door and was inside the house already when she discovered the cigarette, fragments of tobacco and white paper sticking to her moist palm.

But like children and some adults do with the space in their heads before they have learned to think, they spread a story all over. Stella, they said, was hot like her mother in love. She had as good as kissed Desmond in public by their telling, and she felt ashamed to be their joke. Desmond, for his part, would not defend her. He acted proud. If this was the feeling between men and women, Stella decided, it was not comfortable.

"No daughter of mine is going to be carrying on with that dimwit town crier," Stella's mother greeted her after school at the door. "I'm trying to educate you, raise you out of this southern tedium." She had been drinking. When Landee had too much, her vocabulary went up so far Stella could hardly understand it. Her voice changed too. Her accent came from some-place else. Landee began sniffling and let loose, from her squeezed eyes, big alligator tears. Stella's chest burned. She hated the scene. So she decided it would be simpler, since it wasn't that much fun anyway, to just stay inside after school until she could travel away.

So while the group around Robert's step grew to add more members who carried on a daily repetition of limited knowledge and news, with enough fantasy to make a world that was an acceptable place to grow up, Stella created her world from silence and solitude. As her choice, it began quite satisfactorily and later served her better when the friends she once had, like Desmond, found other favorites, like Cynthia.

Just like the days demand a patter of activity, life itself became easier for Stella by rote. Still, there was much to remember. Her sister, Ida, had to be checked after she washed herself. Somebody had to teach her to cook. Even though Ida was older than Stella, their mother reminded Stella that Ida's slow mind kept her from doing things on her own. Ida appreciated Stella's attention. Stella inspected her like a pot or a floor.

Hardly anyone came to the funeral when their mother died. People told one another they were not invited. But they lined the streets as the hearse passed from St. Bernard to Galvez, to London, and on to Mount Olivet Cemetery. Some people crossed themselves, mostly ladies on porches, their dresses carelessly bunched high over their round bellies, their aprons and slips dripping about the same length past their dress skirts.

Many schoolmates of hers pointed. She stared at them while Ida waved. It was like a parade for Ida, her chance to be the queen. The windows of the hearse were smoke gray. So it didn't much matter what she did. No one could see through the glass.

The afterlife was a good place to be, Stella thought, as long as her mother was dead. "Death is only the front gate to a new beginning," the priest said. At least, Landee got to be somewhere else.

Stella was seventeen, so there wasn't much different for her to do. There is no place in New Orleans for teenage girls who don't get pregnant or debut. So she was able to finish her junior year in high school and, in the summer, get a job at Smithy's. She stayed on in the fall, because the money was good and it kept her from having to spend all day with Ida. Her sister kept up an unconscious but vocal litany of soap operas, plans for Stella's meals, and experiences from their past.

But these days, Stella even had aggravation away from home. Desmond was coming around Smithy's and acting like he knew her. And Cynthia trailed him and eyed Stella too. She finished her long walk that let out a little of her bother over this. But a dead ache arose in her knees.

Her house appeared as she approached it like a worn hat with a new band. Flowers and rosebushes circled the bottom, taking attention from the brown peeling paint. Confused blossoms opened colorfully all in between each other's stalks and stems. Ida planted orange sunflowers among pink roses, daisies, sweet peas, and zinnias like she had first mixed them up in a bowl. With Stella not around, Ida turned her attention all day to her garden, and each morning it called her anew into life.

Stella climbed up the steps with her palms on her thighs, a motion to give herself strength and balance across the boards that were leaning. She looked over the front yard to the neighborhood before going through the pane-glass door. The children of her schoolmates lingered on several porches. Televisions roared out into the street. People who were couples when she was a child shouted to each other from the front room to the back. Fat-armed women went through their doors carrying the same weight as their grandmothers. It was a problem that Stella did not know how to attain.

Inside her house, in the bedroom, she looked at herself in the mirror. The face belonged to someone who was both younger and older, nobody that Stella knew. A copper-colored woman with tight green eyes stared at her through dark penciled circles. Orange-pink powder covered drawn, sallow cheeks. It was so thick that if you touched the face in a caress, it would come off in your hand. The lips were smudged from a once-painted *oh*, an *oh* like a sigh.

Stella picked up the comb on her dresser. It was 6 P.M. and time to put up her hair before dinner. Ida would be waiting on her side of the shotgun house with food already on the table for them both. For her only company, Ida would have a conversation full of remembered surprises.

Stella rubbed the top of her head, stirring it hard like she could bring new ideas to the surface. She sought the center of her scalp and passed her hand from front to back, then traced with the comb in the opposite direction. She made the crucifix with her second sweep from one ear to the other. Then she scraped the plastic teeth across her head, dividing and pinning her crowning glory into neat little squares.

Evening stopped for a few minutes to consider the city of New Orleans. The breeze grew breathless with this thought. Where at first it wanted to offer pouring rain to make everything fresh and new, it waited for a moment to figure out if this was possible. The houses with their rotten wood and fat green gardens would just soak up the water like it was nothing. So thirsty, they would never know what they consumed. The evening felt that its rain was useless, not wanted, only needed. It wondered if there wasn't a better, more appreciative place to go.

The front-room lights were coming on in the houses. Men and children gathered, waiting for food to appear. A ruckus of routine: children growing, men abiding their mannerisms. Women move quietly near the stove, thinking and blending.

In sleeveless determination, they re-create the important dinner tradition. Even for them, it is a condition of religious and instinctual awe. Females stand in the kitchen stirring their family creations, semantics or substance.

The world revolves. But, they say, the sun goes down.

Eye-Hand Coordination

NTOZAKE SHANGE

 Eye-hand coordination is what takes so long. Just look, not watch, the figure. Let my hand move along the same lines as my eyes. Let my hand go where my eyes go. At this rate I may be finished drawing this young man, maybe, next year; when twin full moons hang outside my window. This is not the most ethical of experiments. I don't have any idea who this young man is. I am indulging in anonymous sexual stimulation. Does that make me as venal as that stoop-shouldered Greek deli deliveryman I stood behind at the Rite-Aid counter? His face couldn't have been more than two inches away from some sleek girlie magazine centerfold. Made me wonder if this was one of those scratch-and-smell bonuses I'd heard about at an anti-porn meeting not too long ago. Here's this grown man with his face up inside this centerfold. From where I was standing, all that was visible were two ankle-height boots with very very high come-fuck-me heels fitting into both of his hands, like in the circus when acrobats balance flying women in their hands. Then two equally parallel legs creep from his rather stubby fingers

---

NTOZAKE SHANGE is a renowned playwright (*for colored girls who have considered suicide / when the rainbow is enuf*), poet (*Nappy Edges* and *The Love Space Demands*), and novelist (*Betsey Brown* and *Sassafrass, Cypress & Indigo*). Her most recent book is *i live in music: poems by Ntozake Shange, paintings by Romare Bearden* (Stewart, Tabori & Chang, 1994). She lives in Philadelphia with her family.

to his forehead, so he looks to me like a fellow growing tawny calves and suede boots from his skull.

He must have felt my eyes disclaiming his behavior as the activity of a healthy adult. He dropped the magazine, featuring the legs that belonged, it turns out, to a smiling white woman, holding her backside open where the staple was. He jumped back, looked up at me, smiled. With aplomb, I say, "Sir, you've dropped your magazine." He replies, "Oh?" I point directly to the stapled anus. "There." Blushing, the deli man brushes his hand across his mouth, mumbles, "I'm finished."

Eye-hand coordination. Eye-hand coordination, that's what makes a certain kind of painter. This guy is definitely not going to be a painter. He's still looking at his magazine, now underfoot. But his fingers are in his mouth. Why'd he drop the poor girl on the floor of a convenience store? That's not something I would do to a body I'd taken pleasure in, albeit minimal anonymous pleasure. Can you imagine me flinging a brown body of well-defined muscle and mass in front of the milkshake machines at the Wawa? No.

As a matter of fact, exactly the opposite happened to me, or looking to the future happens to me.

My eye-hand coordination is improving, coming along nicely. At least I feel good as I experience myself. I wanta draw me a Jesus look like Mr. Olympia, a Malcolm X any woman would wanta grab close, like Zapata or Atahualpa. But this is America, and outside Detroit, Christ is an effete white man, Malcolm X is dead and beyond sex anyway. Zapata defeated. Atahualpa confined to myth and language barriers. Such is the state of the world today, *querida*. Heroes whose bodies cannot support the vitality of their ideas, least not my idea of their ideas.

What are you going to do, Lili? How to fix this situation where the mind battles the flesh, leaves us lacking the strength to sustain joy, protect hope and desire?

Dilemma. Everything I see is too much. Too thick. Lines seep into textured mass but lack form. I lose perspective. Really, even stick figures cuckold me. Maybe I am restricted to building havens of torn tree limbs and scavenged tree trunks. From the shadows of arcs suspended over the space of any shotgun shack, I'll follow the shadows of figures 'neath double moons. I can't even jerk myself along that much. Only Marron knows the solace and rigor of bare branches to be a mystical sanctuary. I'll have to seek my salvation somewhere in my body, some music.

There's this place, a spot, on the mid–West Side where I used to meet a fella who stayed with me off and on. Well, I used to see him. I stopped going out with him because he had this terrible habit of wearing my shirts to meet me. Now I am virtually sure he wasn't a cross-dresser or something, someone who just adores putting on women's clothes. I think he was one of those men who was working on himself. You know: the man of his times not afraid of his female side, his softness and all that. I'm not against any of that, but I'm not sure men's consciousness-raising groups in the forest with animal skins and drums is the path to their female side. Plus, I resented him. His name was Alex. For that matter, I can find no good reason for him to constantly show up in my clothes. It's amusing before making love, I guess, to exchange things: roles, scents. Yet I can't help thinking about his actually not investing his own money, the time it took to find these particular garments, that—well, that look like me.

Maybe Alex imagined wrapping me around and about him when he slipped those wiry arms in my sleeves. The wildest thing I can conjure up is that when he put my pants on that was some simulation of fucking. I don't know. I just got aggravated when he'd casually appear with none of my hips or bust and look perfectly adorable. Alex could probably have walked all over Manhattan naked if it wasn't against the law. And come to meet me, too. Oh, whatta husky cherub he was: eyes so deep I could wake all up in them; lanky, wiry brown, taut like wound hemp. Maybe he wasn't such a bad idea after all. He could've worn my shirts so he'd be closer to me. Now, that could be interesting, a fellow with a fetish for me. Maybe Alex didn't actually have anything to wear. Hummh.

Anyway, I met him at this place that had one of the greatest R&B jukeboxes of all time. From Chuck Jackson to Johnnie Taylor, B. B. King, the Orlons, the Cadillacs, even the Five Satins. For fifty cents I could enter any rollicking summer of my life, any New Year's Eve, every teenage dream, and take Alex with me. I probably was too hard on him, expecting familiarity with a past I didn't share or refer to, unless some ditty by Ruby and the Romantics or Mary Wells grabbed me up.

I can't exactly say what Alex did with a lot of the time he had on his hands. He was gone a lot, on the road a lot with this rock band or that avant-garde group. He wasn't a musician; I was boycotting musicians at that time, but I couldn't quite find my way out of "the industry," you know what I mean? So Alex did lights, sound, road management, that sort of thing. Thank goodness I am not a groupie, never was. But I don't feel in charge of what I'm doing now. I am not able to move this pencil off my paper, nice heavy-grained paper I searched for yesterday, knowing I would come here today to draw this man I don't know and then take all that I drew from and of him home with me again.

What baffles me is that this is the same table I would sit at to wait for Alex, always-in-my-wardrobe Alex, yet there's none of him around me. All I manage to do day after day is to go look at art—Julian Schnabel, Brice Marden, Jennifer Bartlett, "The Nigger Drawings," and I end up here looking for him. How, you say, can I obsessively seek out a man of whom I have no knowledge? I know the nape of his neck from ten feet; how his braids fall over his shoulder blades; the angle of his chin when he laughs; the curve of the delts and the arrogance of his posture; his ease among friends. I just look at him. I watch and my hands do the rest. I keep coming back on some ritual of expiation. I've burned no candles, strewn no flowers, asked no questions. And this is a place to ask some questions. Lemme tell ya, if there's some dirt to be had, dug up, or fabricated, we are in heaven. From the bathroom to the bar is a nest of intrigue, seductive badinage, and income-appropriate drug trade. Remarkable insights offered from all quarters. That's not including the men's room. I have some friends—rather, acquaintances—who pass through. Nadia, who must be one of the most beautiful women in the world: deep copper like wildflower honey, a laugh like a million snuggles, the libido of a great Dane in heat. She was a professional backup singer: Frankie Calle, Lou Rawls, John Cougar Mellencamp. She had all the looks, the voice, and the coke. A couple of high-living Guadeloupeans gave the place a twinge of sophistication. Otherwise, it was straight-up industry profilin' or procurin': of pussy or cocaine, whatever made you happy. Name that tune, baby.

It's not that no one paid me no mind. I sent any number of evil "Don't sit your ass down here" looks at men who were gracious, good-looking, well-nourished; I always pay attention to that. All I wanted was to draw this man with the braids who sat just beyond an arch that separated the serious diners from the middling drug-booty cruisin' set. He always had a full meal. I found something exciting in that: What he wanted to eat. The muscles he used when he raised his fork to his mouth and set it down. How he pulled brown bread with raisins apart and spread real butter. I am telling you this from inference. I can't see his face. Never tried to. What would be the point? I come every day. I sit right here and wait. He comes every day and sits right there. I draw as much of him as his time allows, before he's surrounded by these women who've made an art of themselves. When the curls and busts start to hover, I pick up my things and take the local train home. That way it takes longer to leave him.

I don't like wanting anything too much, that's just my way. In a fit of independence one evening, I think Little Willie John was singing something, I bounced off to the ladies' room with my friend Nadia. We must have stood outside those two itsy-bitsy stalls all of a half hour before these girls couldn't anybody hardly see, if it wasn't for all them eyelashes and bags coming ahead of them, came falling right down in front of us. We could have laughed, I guess, but we were getting ready to powder our noses too. I swear I've spent as much care and energy examining Nadia's nose for traces of white powder as I spent seeing to myself. I had lived with a junkie once who was adamant that being a junkie didn't mean one had to look like a junkie straight off.

Well, Nadia and I got right lit up. I forgot about my other obsession. I even told Nadia there was a guy right outside who'd give Teddy Pendergrass or Reggie Jackson a run for they money outside this very door. But we didn't budge. Stayed up in that mirror like goddamned Snow White's step-mama. Oh, Jesus. Talk about some *peligrosa* foolishness.

Somehow Nadia and I managed to stumble and giggle our way back to the café itself. She was in amazing suede shorts that made me reconsider the significance of thighs. No matter, we came screeching and hooting 'bout stuff that was nobody's business into the rush of the late supper crowd (as opposed to the early morning crowd, which was a boisterous collection of educated hoodlums). We hushed abruptly. That's how folks were looking at us, like we should hush. We did.

I looked up by the arch to fine dining and he was gone. He was gone. I heard the Chantels weeping "He's gone, my baby left me." But I don't know who this guy is. Nadia thinks I made him up. He exists in my mind, she says. I'm having a panic attack. I go to my notebooks. There he is. There he is again. He's real. I've got him right here. I look up. Heads of Sly Stone–looking muthafuckas get in my way. Jerricurled Luther van Dross types block my view. Boyz, early in the scene, put they nasty-lookin' sweat-shirt-hooded heads in my way. I don't know what he looks like. I mean, only I know what he looks like. He's disappeared. I can't breathe. I can't find him. I push the cognac Nadia's brought me aside. I decide to search for him. He could not have left. He means too much to me. He cannot be gone.

Trying to get niggahs busy chatting up a girl to get out of my way is almost a lost cause. I think their feet grow in my direction when I'm not looking for them but somebody else. Trip, bitch! their feet proclaim. I keep looking in men's faces. Other men I don't know. I don't know his face, either. I should walk backwards, looking for his braids. I know his braids, black twists they are really, not braids at all. They come down his back like black string cheese. I know this. I should go backwards. He would never have left me. I take him home every night. I take him home with me.

And I can't find him.
And I don't know how to ask for him.
I don't know his face, though I feel it.
I don't know his name, though I breathe it.

I sleep under a six-foot incarnation of his braids in bronze. This is not funny. I'm not in control of this. I can't stop myself from laughing. I need to find this guy I don't know. Yeah. Everybody does, they say, "I don't know his name, but I'll recognize him."

"Right."

"Baby, you sure you not talkin' 'bout me? Look close, now."

Why everybody look so seedy? Everything so stink and nasty? The place deserted, still fulla those no-count sycophants. What else to do but find the music. Go directly to the jukebox, Liliane. Find a melody, Lili. Go get you some music. I brush by smells of bourbon, musk, weed, and sweat. Any other time I'd at least check out a silhouette, but not now. I get to the jukebox, temporary Promised Land. Thank you, Jesus. Lemme see. Lemme see. Lemme see. Yes, the Shirelles, "Blue Holiday"; Barrett Strong, "I Apologize"; and Willie Colon, "The Hustler." For me. I dedicate all this to myself. Nadia is rubbing up behind me like she's 'bout to pee on herself. "What in the hell do you want, Nadia? He disappeared. He's outa here. And you, you s'posed to know every goddamned thing. And you don't know who I could be talkin' 'bout."

"Now, hold your horses, Miz whatchamacallit. . . . All I said was I couldn't place nobody quite how you explained. Sound like Gabriel and his horn on a Concorde jet or something."

"I don't make fun of you like that," I stammered. Well, what difference did it make? I've got my drawings, got my bronze braids, and I ain't got my feelings hurt.

That's not quite true. I'd grown dependent on this set of shoulders. That's not like me: to give up so much to a man's guardianship. I'd worked with fire and peculiar mixes of metals to fashion myself a canopy in his image. I was bashful, demure even, when I pictured myself before him. And we know I don't know who he is. Well, the crux of it is that I wanted a technologically proficient Third World man to enter the twenty-first century with me. From the back that's what he was. That's what he is. How do I know this? I know, I know a Barbarian when I see one. I know I'll know the King of Kings, when it's that time. I know this boy ain't the Apocalypse, but—you can't hear it? Oh, God, whenever I see the line from his elbow to his earlobe, Carla Thomas jumps all over my ass, talkin' bout "Gee Whiz." Is this the real nature of pornography? Have I lost my mind and any sense of integrity a feminist has to have to be taken seriously? There's a possibility that no one can tell. He's not like a tattoo or scarification, I mean.

Can you tell by looking?

"Non."

"Nadia, shut up. He could take you to his house and bring you back in six weeks and you wouldn't know."

I'm going to down a magnum of Perrier & Jouet in my black satin teddy and the lace panties with the open crotch. I'm gonna stay home and draw drawings of the drawings of him that I've got. I'm not going to come out of my house until there are some hip black people in outer space. I'm gonna play me some Ruth Brown records, eat hominy grits with brown oyster sauce, and do all the things I been told make a woman feel like a woman should. Yes, I am.

I'm going to the telephone that's not a direct line to the coke man, so I can see if this guy who sorta likes me is busy. This is so crazy. I know I gotta do some reality work here. Call a man you know, Lili. Don't go all the way on out there, darling. Call Alex, see if he wants to wear some of your clothes while you walk round naked. All right, don't call Alex. Be a class A lunatic and sleep 'neath them metallic dreadlocks hanging over your bed. Nothing kinky there, huh? I am trying to let my tears fall in my snifter like Courvoisier got the best of me. I want to ask Nadia to take me to the ladies' room again for a quick toot or two. I want to stand on my own two feet, but I've grown to depend on him being there. I liked what his beauty brought out of me, eye-hand coordination and all. I'm thinking maybe the rush from the enigma he is is sufficient. That'll get me through, you know.

Right on cue, some sideman plays the Isley Brothers, "Love the One You're With." I feel my survivor kick in and take a deep breath. She lets me run my tongue over my lips. Chastises me for gritting my teeth. Helps me tilt my chin with insouciance. Now, we ready? she asks.

When I raise my eyes and feel all that defiance burning behind my lashes, I'm struck dumb.

He's walking toward me.

He's smiling at me.

His braids fall over his chest too. I'd never allowed for that.

I'd never imagined seeing him face-to-face.

I'd never meant to ask his name.

I'm losing my breath, he's lifting me off the ground.

He's whispering my name. "Liliane, Lili, Lili."

I know I don't know this man.

I steal upon him in the late afternoon in a studio musicians' hangout.

Nobody, only Nadia, knows me here.

I never said anything to him.

"Lili." He takes my mouth in his and I lose any semblance of anatomical realities. How, how, how could such a man know me already? I am staring, an imbecile, *une idiote joyeuse*. I'm managing to smile. I can't help myself.

I am touching the rafters of my dreams when all of a sudden the Isley Brothers' sideman's selection "Shout" blares all round me in a twirling swish of me in his arms in this den of colored iniquity that was clearly Eden.

"Liliane, right?"

I should think so, I say to myself, trying to steady myself from a true swoonin' faint.

"Yeah, *sí*. Liliane."

"The artist?"

"Yeah, most of the time, yeah."

"I haven't seen you since you let all those blackbirds free out some tower you built in Port-au-Prince a couple of years ago."

"You mean the birds with messages from the first free Africans in the New World?"

"Well, baby, they weren't the first free ones—"

"The first ones freed by their own armed struggle."

"Right. . . . I gave you a message to put on one of them. Don't you remember?"

I am feeling my face get red, so red I'm going to explode. I can't say anything. I am talking to the man I've been taking home with me every night, a man I don't know. He says he's been in one of my projects. And how he has, every sinew, contraction, and gesture. Yes.

"Liliane, are you all right? Can I get you something?"

I still can't say anything. I just shout for a colored joy; a gritty pelvis-born glee rises up outa my throat and I haveta smile to let it out.

"Oh, pick me up and kiss me again. Then we can talk all night long."

EYE-HAND COORDINATION

"You sure?" he says with a twinkle in his eyes would make a guy with eyes in the back of his head jealous.

"Oh, yes," I say.

"You know what my message on the free flyin' birds said?"

"No, of course not. They went out in the sky around the world, tied up our dreams and desires, to be found like anything else that's precious."

"My message said—now I wrote it out by hand, now—my message said, 'I want to see this woman again without machetes and barbed wire so close.' "

"C'mon, now."

"Seriously, I thought about that a lot. You sending them birds anywhere they wanted to fly with whatever wishes anybody brought you. I never thought I'd run into you again, though."

"I've been . . . could you put—here, here—your left hand by my cheek? Yeah. Humm. I've been trying to draw this."

"What?"

"This feeling, your hand from this angle: there."

"Lili, I'm not sure I'm gettin' all this. Go slower."

"No, you don't want me to go slower. I'll get too confused. Just let me tell you the truth."

"Well, okay, but everything's all right."

"No. No. Everything is not all right. I've been drawing you. Every day from right over there. Eye-hand coordination I was working on. I practiced getting you just right. I sleep underneath braids, huge bronze braids like yours, I made from drawings of you I took home every day. And I never said hello to you or asked how you were feeling."

I'm every shade of purple now. I am crying. He lifts my chin. I do not look at him. I cannot.

"What's wrong with that? You're an artist, right?"

"Yes. I was perfecting eye-hand cordination."

"Fine. That's good."

"Well, probably it is, but I think my friend Anna-Maria is right. She says feeling you with my eyes helped my hands draw you with my heart."

"Anna-Maria sounds on the mark to me."

I feel his forearm 'tween my waist and my rib cage, lava, a house-music triple-threat bass mix.

"Yeah. Now all you gotta do is kiss me again. Then tell me your name, so, I know how to say, Please do it again . . ."

"Thayer."

"Thay—"

I want to have a decent conversation, but his tongue is all up, back in my mouth, so all I can do is remember drawing with my heart. My hands are swept up in muscles; Aretha's wail is coaxing me off my feet.

"I ain't never, no, no. Loved a man the way that I love you."

But that's me, Lili, sayin, "Kiss me once again, Thayer. Don't you never say we're through. 'Cause I ain't never loved a man the way that I've drawn you."

MARTIN SIMMONS

"Shit."

Zik cursed the snow that stung the back of his neck as he bent low, squinting at the keyhole in the meager light from the streetlamp. Sweating with exertion in the near-zero-degree darkness, he stabbed at the hole with the bright aluminum key he held between frozen fingers, which, in his drunkenness, seemed too long to be his own. The wind and the snow screamed that he needed to be inside; his bladder and his roiling stomach howled *now*! He wanted to pound on the stupid goddamn door.

"Shhh, shhh," he told himself in a stage whisper, preposterously putting the stiff index finger of his empty left hand to his lips. "Shhh, shhh." Silence was of the utmost importance. So what if she were actually awake and listening to him struggling feverishly on the other side of the door; she would feign sleep if he didn't make it impossible. Jesus, he hated that sneaky shit. But at four-thirty in the morning, his stomach a-bubble, the

MARTIN SIMMONS has taught fiction and nonfiction writing and literature classes at a number of schools and art organizations, including Bronx Community College, NYU, the College of New Rochelle, and the Frederick Douglass Creative Arts Center. He is a former member of the Harlem Writer's Guild and a co-founder of New Renaissance Writers, and has been published in *Blacks on Paper*, *Blackstage*, *Essence* magazine, *MBM* magazine, *New York Newsday*, and numerous other publications. Mr. Simmons lives in New York with his wife and two children. He is working on a novel, *Blood at the Root*, and a screenplay.

last thing he needed was another argument; he'd kill any woman stupid enough to get in his face tonight!

"Shhh, shhh, shhh," he told the key congenially when it finally found its nest. He slowly turned the key in the lock; his lanky six-foot-one body recoiled with each magnified click of metal on metal.

Now the bottom lock. He damned the society that required multiple locks and keys for security, the neighborhood that demanded them, but this key went home immediately and now he was slowly rotating the frozen metal knob. Anticipating and cursing each squeak, he nudged the door open. Why hadn't he gotten around to buying the small can of 3-in-1 oil or WD 40 that would make his almost nightly sneak-ins less nerve-racking? Because he never thought about it until four in the morning, he answered himself sardonically. And since childhood he had wondered whether it was better, while creeping in or out, to open a squeaky door very quickly or very slowly. Quickly, probably—the same number of squeaks but compressed in time. He kept his mind intentionally on these recondite questions and away from the urgent earthy demands of his gut as he squeezed through the door and began to inch it shut behind him.

He was going to be sick. He shoved the door the final distance and it closed with a heedless bang. But by now he was hurtling toward the bathroom in the dark, fighting to control the rising gorge spewing up out of his stomach. The corner of a kitchen chair caught him in the groin and sobered him immediately, if only temporarily, as he went to one knee, holding himself and whimpering fierce damnations. He grabbed the chair in silent rage, wanting mightily to break it in two, wanting to rip off a fat wooden leg and rush it into the bedroom to smash her ribs. His rage helped to ease the pain, bringing back his more imperative bodily needs. He used the chair as a brace to get to his feet; he hobbled hurriedly toward the toilet.

Once there, he didn't know whether to sit on the bowl or bend over it. His stomach was in total rebellion. He vomited. It came in a hot acid rush, most of it into the blue toilet water, but some of it splashed on the marbleized pink plastic seat. Meanwhile, he ripped his pants open, pulled his hip-length jacket up over his hips, thought to clean the flecks of vomit off the toilet seat before sitting down, but ran out of time. He sat on the seat and put his head in the hot-pink sink next to the toilet.

He thought he'd never been so sick in his life, but laughed even in this sickness: wasn't that what he supposed last night, or was it the night before?

Tonight was different, though. He wouldn't have drunk so much if it wasn't for George. That motherfucker really pissed him off bad, saying that shit.

He want me to find something. I'll find my foot up his ass!

Zik was running water into the sink, trying to wash down the watery vomit he had put in it, when another wave of nausea washed over him. *I know I've never felt like this before* was his last thought before he found himself with his cheek on the cold tile of the bathroom floor. It took him only a second to understand that he had blacked out, and another second to realize he must have only been out for a second. And another second to realize he was going to throw up again. As he scrabbled around bare-assed, clutching for the toilet seat, clutching for the flush handle, and putting his head over the water in which he beheld his own shit, he wanted most of all to be dead. Dead and away from all of this. He vomited and flushed at the same time and, exhausted, watched as the blue-brown water swirled and noisily drained, floating up with some remaining fragments of his foul excretions. He flushed again, and then a third time. The water, now barely tinted blue, was finally free of any evidence of him.

He was shivering and clammy with sweat, but now feeling well enough to realize just how cold the bathroom was. He got to his feet and began to get himself together. He wondered if Charlene was listening to him, and he wondered what she was thinking.

Charlene lay on her stomach in the bed, her chin on a forearm that smelled of the Avon cologne she had dabbed on it, and in the deep cleft between her breasts, at 8:30 P.M. the previous evening. She listened to the sounds from the bathroom and wished that Zik would die. That he would choke on his own vomit; that he would get stabbed to death in that hangout of his, or stagger into the street and be hit by a careening truck, or fall out in the snow and freeze his black ass to death. Just please die and be forever gone. Tragically gone.

She mused bitterly about identifying Zik's body at the morgue. The man down there would roll him out. He'd be in one of them long file-cabinet-drawer things, under a white sheet, unable to wink or smile; cold and harmless. Yes. She would take a taxicab downtown and identify his body. She would make all the arrangements for his funeral by herself. Wear her new black dress! She still hadn't worn that black dress she'd bought for George's party. That dress was hot, maybe too revealing for a funeral, people be too busy looking at her chest! They wouldn't pay any mind to Zik. Old dead Zik. But she always did look good in black; people always said black went good with her cinnamon skin. She had looked forward to that party, but that bastard George had called himself to uninvite his own brother. Said it wasn't a party. Said it was a reception and was only for his colleagues. Charlene knew George was lying, and when she gave Zik the message, she could tell he knew George was lying too. That was the last time Zik had spoken to George, far as she knew. Dirty emef; whole no-good family a bunch of dirty emefs. She wouldn't even tell them he was dead; the funeral would be her own business. It would be a nice funeral, too. Her friends would be there. Who else? Who else would be at his funeral anyway? Those bums he hung out with? Those dummies he worked with? Hell, no. No drunks, furniture movers, or proper stuck-up Matthews brothers would even know he was dead. She rather sit in the church alone. Would they let her bury him in a church? Well, not bury him in the church, she realized, giggling into the darkness.

She heard the toilet flush and knew it would take at least ten more minutes for Zik to clean himself up and come to bed.

She would bury him in that blue suit she had made him buy. He looked real good in that suit, when she could get him to wear it someplace. Well, he'd wear it to his funeral and she wouldn't have to listen to his mouth either.

She'd mourn him alone in whatever holy and peaceful place they laid his body out. Truly she would mourn him. She would mourn for them both. A church would be best. Her friends would be there. She'd wear a black dress—but not *that* black dress—and a cute little black hat with a veil, a long veil. She would lift the veil only once, to kiss him at the end of the ceremony. They'd say, "See, she really loved him. He treated her like a dog, but she saw him through to the end." Kiss his sweet lips. They'd be cold, but she'd bend like a lady and kiss his sweet lips sweetly, like Mrs. King did way back then. But she wouldn't cry. She wouldn't cry anymore for Zik. Or for herself and Zik. That's over. That bastard had seen enough tears from her. He said he was coming home early tonight. He *promised*. Again. Liar. She'd mourn all the dried-out and wasted food she had cooked, all the freshly washed linen and perfumed nightgowns just for him, all the funny-serious-private conversations they'd had only in her mind, all the places they had never seen, all the rooms they'd never made love in, all the liquor he drank in that filthy bar, all the sickness he had at night, all the hangovers, all the fights, the curses, the tears, the lies. Everything.

She could hear nothing from the bathroom now but the sound of running water. She drew her nylon nightgown up over her hips and arranged herself so that he would have to come into contact with her warm flesh when he lay down. She drew the blankets up to her eyes so she wouldn't blink if he decided to turn on the bright overhead light for some reason.

She would mourn the beginning, that clear sunny day when they met. Him with the glittering brown eyes, the half smile, and the lying mouth. That afternoon she stood talking to Carol and he passed and glanced Charlene's way and stopped and came back and interrupted Carol in the middle of whatever she was gossiping about to blurt out, goggling all the while at Charlene, that he was lost. He looked so tall and good that day; she'd noticed him half a block away. She knew he wasn't lost. She would mourn ever having been found by him, ever having been shown, thank the good Lord, that she didn't need Ernest and Ernest's fists to be loved. She would mourn that first sweet afternoon when she opened to Zik and he was shy and softlike, and he caressed her and whispered to her and gentled her like a virgin. That afternoon when she opened to him, opened totally so there never had been, never could be a love like theirs; it was good, as good as all the books and magazines said it could be. Better, because it had never been so good before. And it stayed good for months. Everything was good until . . .

She would mourn the bitterness of knowing that he had gotten tired of her, or bored with her, or something. If he would only tell her what was wrong! He never said anything. She would mourn his lying silences, his lying absences, his lying presences. She would mourn him if he were dead, but no more than she mourned him now. No more than now; he was finished in the bathroom. She pulled her legs together and her nightgown down. No more than now; he was entering the bedroom, naked, clothes in hand. She pulled the covers up totally over her nose and eyes. No more than now; he still smelled of vomit and alcohol and that barroom. Carelessly, like one asleep, she curled into the fetal position. No more than now; he was tipping around the bed trying not to allow her to acknowledge that she was awake. She could not mourn him more than she mourned him now, this liar, this thief, this bastard. This bastard who was lying down next to her, careful not to touch her. She could not mourn him any more than she did at this moment as he turned his back to her and pushed himself to the very edge of the bed away from her. This bastard, who carefully, gingerly pulled the covers over himself. This bastard; she would mourn him if he fell out in the snow if he got hit by a truck if he got shot in that bar. If he decided one night not to come home, she would mourn for him. She would mourn for herself, but no more than she mourned now, as she stared, eyes wide, at the darkness inside the blanket and hated herself for needing him so badly. No more than now, as she listened to him sigh. No more than now as she waited for his drunken snore so she could wipe away the fat tears that rolled down her face.

The alarm.

He didn't reach to turn it off.

Fuck it.

He dropped a leg off the bed and touched the floor with the bottom of his dark brown foot. Slid it around but found nothing but grit and dust.

The alarm clock wound down.

Now he could hear her in the kitchen: her feet shuffling across the floor, her silver bangles jangling, the frequent yawns and sighs, the occasional singing along with the inanities from her favorite radio station, and the deliberate banging of skillets to make sure he awakened.

Bitch.

Minutes later, head on the pillow, foot on the floor, he was riding back off to sleep.

She yelled from the kitchen, "Zik?"

He sat up abruptly, and immediately the thumping pain was in his head, a tribute to the cheap bourbon and watered beer of the night before. Every morning he woke up to the reality of his reality. He brought his hand to his face to hold his eyeballs in their sockets and to wipe the sleep out of his eyes. His hand smelled like vomit. His breath smelled of alcohol and vomit. His mouth tasted like shit.

"You up on the wrong side of the bed again?"

A half smile tarried in her eyes and at the corners of her lips; she had neither forgotten the night before nor forgiven him, but it was spilt milk. The morning light always brought her the hope of a better relationship. Yesterday he had awakened in a good mood; a touch, a smile, a cheerful "Morning" could be the beginning.

He turned one bleary and malevolent eye on her. To that eye, her good humor was derision. She slouched in the doorway wearing his slippers, his raggedy-ass bathrobe over her red nightgown.

She's just waiting for me to say something. I was suppose to come in early last night. Meant to. Ain't my fault I forgot.

Charlene spoke again. "I guess you want your slippers?"

He remembered their first Christmas together when he somehow managed to scrape together $87.81 to buy her the dress she wanted. She gave him a pair of Sears slippers that didn't fit.

excerpt from BLOOD AT THE ROOT

"You keep them."

He rose from the bed and sidestepped past her and scuffed toward the bathroom at the end of the dark corridor, stepping over the framed photograph of the two of them that he knocked off the wall almost every night when he lurched out of the bathroom. Most mornings he picked it up and rehung it almost as an act of penance. It had now been on the floor for three days.

Hope gone, Charlene followed Zik to the bathroom door.

"If you'd get some sleep. If you'd come home at a decent time. What time'd you get in last night. Or this morning?"

"Late."

"I know late. You out again with that negro from southeast?"

"Yeah, I was out again with that negro from southeast."

"Well, I'm telling—"

He closed the bathroom door in her face, farted intentionally and loudly to cover her response.

But heard most of it anyway.

"—gonna come in here at three in the morning, I won't let you in! I'll change the locks! Don't come back in here at all, you can't treat me right! This's my house!"

He brushed his teeth and tongue thoroughly before climbing into the tub and beginning a long, very hot shower.

Occasionally she would come to the bathroom door to make a point about his staying out, his work habits, his friends, her indignation, her wretchedness, her disgust, her inability to take this stuff much longer.

He tried not to hear her, but, in fact she was merely echoing thoughts that had been resonating in his head for months. The interminable cacophony of her complaints had only recently been penetrated by the drumbeat reality that this situation was not going to change. It couldn't get worse, and neither of them had the ability to make it better. They were both miserable for the same reason: he wasn't what they wanted him to be.

He knew he'd never be what she wanted and could never be what he wanted, whatever and wherever that was, as long as they were together. And it was this dead self that required her companionship in this grave of their existence. He had problems with the woman he found at home at night. Warm and waiting; angry, but only because her passion was thwarted; striking out at him because he had deprived her of his company. That woman would very easily become tender, loving. Her hopes and dreams would wash over him and render him sentimental and agreeable. Render him pliant and willing to "give it another try." He preferred the woman she was on these mornings. He could live with her when she was like she was right now, angry and snarling. This twenty-five-year-old Medusa of the morning hardened his heart, his soul, and made it possible for him to ride to work and face the insentient stone men who would order his existence until the weekend, until five o'clock, until he had enough to drink.

George don't know nothin about it. Find my fist down his throat.

Clutching the soap so tightly that his fingers made deep ridges in it, Zik angrily soaped himself again.

Last night soon after leaving work and arriving at Tekay's bar, before he finished his second drink in fact, he had realized it was his mother's birthday. Congratulating himself for remembering in time, and full of good intentions, he went to see his mom. He hadn't seen her in a couple of months, or spoken to her in a few weeks.

He heard voices and laughter when he got to his mother's door. Zik understood that tonight of all nights she was bound to have other guests, particularly her sons, but he was nevertheless leery of just who might be visiting. The laughter made it seem that Michael, who was always laughing uproariously at the many jokes he told, might be inside; he hoped George wasn't also there.

A scowl creased George's face as soon as he opened the door and saw Zik, and he released the doorknob immediately, so that the heavy metal door began to swing shut before Zik could come inside. Zik caught the door and caught himself before he could react with anger. He resolved not to let his oldest brother's perpetual indignation faze him.

"Hi, George, what's up?"

"Yeah."

Inside, Curtis and Michael, seated at the yellow Formica-topped dinette table with their mother, greeted Zik more warmly, and he shook their hands as he passed them to kiss his mother. He noted the three open gift boxes on the floor beside her chair, the bottle of champagne and the cake inscribed HAPPY BIRTHDAY in front of her, and the saucers sprinkled with crumbs and the half-filled glasses on the table. He wondered if he should keep the small card he had bought her in his pocket; it obviously couldn't compare to the gifts his brothers had brought. George immediately reclaimed the fourth and last chair at the table.

"Hi, son, came by to wish your old mom happy birthday?"

"Sure did."

"Lord, I couldn't ask for a better birthday than this. Got all my children together for once."

excerpt from BLOOD AT THE ROOT

Zik bent to kiss her, she inclined her cheek slightly and reached up with a hand as if to touch his face, but her arm was held stiffly away from his body and the hand never made contact. He would have been surprised if it had. Toward him, her youngest child, she was especially stingy with her affection. He wondered why for many years, but when he learned that during his mother's seven-hour labor with him, his father was packing and leaving this apartment, this woman and these sons, he decided he knew.

"Happy birthday, Mama."

"Thank you, Zik. You want to sit down?"

"No, thanks, Mama."

"You want some of this champagne George brought me?"

"No, Ma, champagne gives me a headache."

Zik pushed the gifts out of his way and kneeled on the floor, facing his mother solicitously.

"This is good champagne."

Zik half turned toward George. "If you bought it, I know it's peachy-keen, George, but all champagne gives me a headache."

"This stuff isn't that good," Michael kidded.

"Be good, Michael," Mama said, seeming to admonish her second son. But Zik heard it as "Be good, Zik." Everyone in the room knew that he and George were always at each other's throats, and Zik knew, as they all did, though only he was willing to admit it, that Mama favored George far above everyone else.

"That little chair is in the back room, Zik; why don't you get it and come have a piece of this cake?"

"No, I don't think so, Mama. I just came by for a minute to see you on your birthday. You doing okay?"

"Making it, just making it."

"Why don't you sit down like she asked you?" George's voice, demanding compliance. Zik ignored it.

"You've been feeling all right?"

"What do you care how she feels?" George rumbled. "Since when do you care?"

"Come on, George," Michael said.

"Can I talk to my mother?" Zik asked.

"Talk, talk. That's all you know, talk. Talk is pretty cheap, though."

"Can I talk to my mother?"

"That's all you can do, isn't it? You don't spend any time with her, you won't even sit down. I see you didn't bring her a present, did you? No, no, of course not. Talk is all you've got."

"What did I do to you? What is your problem?"

"He's been in this champagne," Michael told Zik by way of explanation. "Can't y'all just chill?"

George and Zik ignored Michael. They ignored the growing look of distress on their mother's face. They ignored Curtis as he sat up, his huge body tightening and dangerous, his deep-set eyes moving first to one, then to the other, and then to his mother, whose own body was beginning to slump.

George spoke again. "What, you think they're gonna miss you at the bar you spend your time in?"

"No, George. They are not gonna miss me at that bar. I didn't bring Mama a present 'cause I didn't have the money to buy her a present; she knows that. She knows I'll get her a present as soon as I can. And as for spending time with her, I don't mind; it's spending time with you that makes me sick."

"Makes you sick? You lousy no-count drunk, got the nerve to come in here poor-mouthing, talking about somebody makes you sick? I'll slap you down."

"Well, come on, then! Come on!" Zik shouted as he got to his feet. "You ain't man enough to take me. Never have been."

George stood also.

Curtis's voice boomed as he rose quickly out of his seat, the flimsy, too-small chair he had been sitting in falling backward to the floor with a bang. "That's about enough! You two might not care what you do to Ma, but I do. That's enough!"

George continued to glare at Zik, but his words were now said almost under his breath. "Talk about somebody being a man. Lousy bum."

"One of you is leaving right now," Curtis continued.

No one had disputed Curtis in years. He was always silent and brooding, and he was larger than any of them, as large as any man they knew. They all suspected he wasn't as dangerous as he seemed, but neither they nor anyone else who came into contact with him ever wanted to find out for sure.

"I'm leaving anyway," Zik responded. He bent and kissed his mother again. "I'll talk to you soon, okay?"

George shouted, "You need to leave. Go out there and find your manhood!"

"Don't nobody got to leave," Mama said, but to Zik's ears her words were perfunctory at best.

"Somebody has to, Mama," Curtis assured her softly. "These two will

excerpt from BLOOD AT THE ROOT

never get along, and this kind of thing doesn't do your pressure any good."

So Zik left, all the good feelings he'd arrived with replaced with anger and confusion and George's final words, "find your manhood." It was always he who left first, always he who seemed to have the least reason to stay because it was he who least aspired to amuse, protect, or support his mother, and he whose company his mother seemed best able to do without.

Still, even now, as he let the hot water of the shower flood his mouth and dribble down his face, he wished she would have taken his side last night; they all knew George had started it.

Last night he had left his mother's apartment, the very apartment he had grown up in, hurried straightaway to Tekay's, and begun to imbibe a quantity of alcohol sufficient to make him sick. Again. As if he needed another reason.

After showering and carefully shaving, Zik sat across from Charlene at the kitchen table in his underwear, eating fried eggs she had deliberately overcooked. She almost looked good. As always, she'd made use of his time in the bathroom to change into her bra, slip, and stockings; to comb her hair back and pin it; and to put on her makeup. As always, he knew she knew how much he liked to see her getting dressed, and this was another way she sought to deny and punish him.

She was keeping time to the music from the radio with a bouncing leg. Her abundant bosom jiggled slightly, whetting his appetite for her. They shared an awareness of this too.

His head had half cleared, his hunger was half slaked, his eyes were wide open. She did look good. She was smiling and humming and chewing deliciously; not for him, he decided, but for herself and maybe for some joker somewhere else, probably some chump at her job. Some lawyer who liked to give her work to do so he could bend over her desk, look down her blouse or something.

He sat watching her long burgundy-tipped fingers as she picked up her teacup, her plump red lips as she bit into dry toast, her throat and chest as she swallowed and breathed. And he felt the heat rising in him, equal parts anger and desire.

"What the fuck are you so happy about?" He regretted saying it even as it left his mouth.

"Why you have to be like that? Was I doing anything to you?" She got up from the table and turned her back to him.

"Sorry."

"You hate me so much I can't even smile around you no more?"

"I said sorry."

"Well, do you?" She turned back to him. Her tears, which always came too quickly for him to trust, now spilled down her cheeks. "Do you?"

"You know I don't hate you."

She began bawling, tears flying and streaming; she coughed and choked on a bit of toast and ran out of the kitchen. He found himself up from the table, running behind her, wondering what the hell now. Feeling like the lowest kind of dog.

When he got to the bedroom she had already thrown herself across the bed and was sobbing into the sheets.

I didn't say anything that bad. What's her problem? How'd I get in this mess?

He sat next to her on the bed and placed his hand on her back, touching her for the first time in days. He smoothed the furrows out of the satiny black slip, soothed the warm flesh it contained.

"I'm sorry. I don't know what gets into me sometimes."

Punctuated by sobs and muffled by the blanket, her voice is that of a little girl. "I know you don't like me anymore."

It is a voice that always cuts deep. He pleads earnestly. "Please don't say that. It's not true."

"It is true."

"No, it isn't."

"It is; you never—"

"I never what?"

No response.

"I never what?"

"You never say anything nice or do anything nice anymore."

She curled into the fetal position facing away from him, her satiny ass touching his naked thigh.

"Anything like what?" he asked, understanding immediately where this was going, and noting the time, eight past eight, on the clock.

"Anything."

The pressure and heat on his thigh increased. And he knew that was all it was, all she wanted. He could stand up, get dressed, and walk out now. Go to work, get sloppy drunk with Chang at Tekay's Bar, come in tomorrow morning at 4 A.M., but she would still be here and she would still want the same thing.

Besides, he was also in need. In need of more than pussy, to be sure; in need of much more than she was capable of giving him anymore; in need of so much more than he could even express to himself. His emptiness was a landscape so vast that its horizon was unknowable. He was sinking,

excerpt from BLOOD AT THE ROOT

463

sinking fast, and she was like a mote in the Pacific. And yet to the drowning man, anything that floats holds hope.

He curled up next to her and began stroking her thigh, belly, breast. She pushed backward against him, hard. And he found himself responding, eagerly responding. Thinking that it wasn't difficult to love this woman. To press against her like this. To kiss the back of her smooth brown neck. To lick and explore an ear. . . .

She turned to him, reaching between his legs, pulling and stroking his penis through his cotton briefs, verifying its hardness, his desire. She opened her mouth and he filled it with his tongue. She murmured and pushed herself under him. Lifted her hips as he reached under the slip and pulled at her panties. Simultaneously, he opened his eyes and she spoke, and it seemed to him that when she spoke she was looking not at him but at the clock.

"Put it in."

And as he pulled off his drawers, and she sat up to pull her slip up and over her head and to kick off her panties, he knew he had been trapped into this. Trapped by the radiating heat of her vagina, the jiggling at the breakfast table, the alarm that had awakened him. There was no stopping, no escaping, no not putting it in. He could retreat only insularly, insidiously, only by withholding his inner self from her. He was now sickened by the breasts which stood aggressively full and naked when she took her bra off, sickened by the self-satisfied look on her face. Disgusted by his own penis, which rose hard and traitorously to answer her look in the affirmative. Sickened unto death by his own weakness, as she reclined and he rolled over onto her, and as she immediately pulled him into her.

Cursing himself and Charlene, he went at it with the angry determination to fuck her eyeballs out, and also to deny her the pleasure of satisfying him. In this he failed. Her vagina had always been a place of madness for him. His resistance collapsed in seconds, and within two minutes he was gasping, unable to catch his breath. She bucked belligerently beneath him. He pushed against the soft skin of her shoulders.

"I—I—ah—ahhgh—"

"C'mon, c'mon, c'mon," she told him, "it's all right, it is, it's all right, c'mon. I love you so much, too much. It's all right. . . ."

Her eyes were wide open. Pulling him. Every inch of her body sucked at him, pulled him into her. *Pulled.* And oh, Jesus, he wanted to be inside her. Completely inside her; safe and warm always. Not twenty-three and miserable and hating her, but a know-nothing, be-nothing do-nothing baby again.

He collapsed onto her. She embraced him very tightly, shuddered twice briefly, then pushed at him. He toppled off to the right and saw the clock, 8:17. She turned toward him, leaned up on an elbow. Abundant brown breasts touching the sheets. Bunched sweaty hair between thick thighs. She grinned down at him. And it was his nightmare. Every interaction was a battle, and he felt as though he were the constant loser.

RONALD STROTHERS

Some men think women should stay in their place.
And some know where that place is.

"Man, you ain't nothin' but a dawg. I saw you wit' that lady last night. I bet she wudn't even yo' wife."

"If she was a lady, you know she wudn't my wife," Neck Bone assured.

Maybe in business and education and politics and life Neck Bone was the original Mr. Nobody, but in the 3C Garage he was the Man. In that private fantasia where screwdrivers and ratchets took precedence over stocks and bonds, lying had nothing to do with ethics; it was a barometer of manhood. Honor was given in direct proportion to how well one lied. And Neck Bone received a lot of honor. He bragged relentlessly about how fine his lady was, but Big Money told him that if she had to rely on her looks to eat, she had seen her last meal. When Neck Bone wasn't exalting his lady's pulchritudinous attributes, he was berating women in general.

"Ya see, you gotta always watch a woman. Take my ole lady—"

"Naw, thass all right, you keep 'er," Gutbucket interrupted, as every-

RONALD STROTHERS, a former journalist and currently a freelance fiction writer, received the 1990 George Jones Award for English Literature, and his story "Pass the Beans," appeared in the 1976 anthology *Sweet Lucy*. He is the author of the collection *Memories of Never*, and the one-man play *Fly in the Buttermilk*, which he performs. Mr. Strothers, an alumnus of North Carolina A&T, Bloomfield College, and Drew University, teaches English at Bloomfield College in New Jersey.

body in the lounge laughed, knowing that would add fuel to the fire Neck Bone was starting.

"Aw, you wish you could get sump'n that sweet," Neck Bone fired back. "Like I was sayin', you gotta keep a eye on a woman. Like my ole lady, she know she got mo' man than she ever dreamed of, yet an' still I got to keep the hawkeye on 'er. Thass the way a woman is. She'll change her mind in a second wit'out thankin'."

"You got a point there," Invisible confirmed. "Last Sat'day, Bonnie was houndin' me 'bout she wanted to go dancin'. Then soon's I said I'd take 'er down to the Cave, she changes her mind just like that. They just don't thank."

"Aw, that ain't had nuttin' ta do wit' thankin'," Gutbucket corrected. "Frail as you is an' wit' all them poles in that place, she prob'ly was afraid she'd get confused an' lean on you an' try to walk out wit' the pole."

"Regardless," Neck Bone continued, "you just cain't let a woman make up her own mind. She got to be led. Now that ain't puttin' a woman down, they just cain't make decisions for theyself."

"Thass right," Big Money added. "I know they sho' don't know nothin' 'bout money an' bidness. An' don't let 'em see a credit card. They'll run you over faster'n Neck Bone will gettin' to some collard greens."

"Thass for real," Neck Bone continued. "It's just in they blood. Thass why the man got to be the boss. Take, for a example, socializin'. A man can go out an' do the town all by hisself, but a woman got to have three girlfriends wit' 'er just to go to the corner. Thass 'cause one woman by herself cain't make a decision."

SchoolBook had been to college for seven years but didn't graduate. For all his intelligence and knowledge of world affairs, he wound up at the garage.

"Actually," he began authoritatively, "the herd syndrome you're alluding to is vital to the emotional stability of women because of the discrimination they encounter living in a patriarchal society."

"I know," Neck Bone agreed, not understanding a word SchoolBook said, "I was just gettin' ready to say that. My mama tol' me all about discrimination when I was a kid. An' she was always tellin' me 'bout how pastryawful society is. Thass why we marched wit' Martin Luther King in the March on Washington back in 1942."

"Man, what'chu talkin' 'bout, the March on Washington was in 1963," Gutbucket responded indignantly. Neck Bone set him straight.

"Ya see, thass where everybody got fooled. That was the second march, but ain't nobody know it. Dr. King first marched on Washington in 1942 but there wudn't enough people for anybody to know about it. It was just him an' fifteen of us from Georgia. An' lemme tell ya sump'n else ain't nobody know: We went up there by bicycle."

Everybody broke up. "Neck Bone, I think you been suckin' on too many o' them bones." Invisible laughed.

"Yeah, man," Big Money added, "first of all, Dr. King was only thirteen years old in 1942, an' plus, you know ain't nobody rode no bicycle all the way from Georgia to D.C.!"

"See, thass why y'all don't know nuttin'," Neck Bone countered, holding his ground and growing bolder with each word. "Um tryin' to learn y'all sump'n an' you don't believe it. I oughta know, I was right there. Back in those days, livin' in the South was a real chromatic experience. An' Dr. King was so chromatized by livin' down there, he decided to march to Augusta, the state capital, an'—"

"Wait a minute now," Big Money interjected. "Whuss wrong wit'chu, Neck Bone? Everybody know Atlanta the capital o' Georgia."

"Yeah, it is now, but it didn't used to be. See, the United States used to be a part o' England, an' the King o' England made one o' those thangs called a dee-cree, where he dee-creed that the capital was gon' be Atlanta. But his secretary made a typo—that mean mistake—an' typed Augusta. An' do you not know, it wudn't till 1963 that it was officially changed to Atlanta. Thass one o' the thangs Dr. King went to D.C. for but ain't nobody know it."

"You tell 'em, Neck Bone," Invisible urged.

"Anyway," Neck Bone went on, "by the time we got to Augusta, one o' the womens said since we had come that far, we might as well go on up to Washington. See, I tol' ya a woman gon' change her mind every time. So we went on up to D.C., marchin' for our eekle rights. But it didn't catch on till 1963. See, y'all don't know nuttin' 'bout history."

"Neck Bone," Big Money marveled, "if you got paid by the lie, you'd have to carry yo' money home on a freight train."

"Well, I'm glad you straightened us out," SchoolBook acquiesced sarcastically. "But getting back to the plight of women. What makes you think women aren't autonomous?"

"See, you young bloods just don't lissen. Ain't nobody said nuttin' 'bout no tonamus. All I said was it's against the laws o' nature for a woman to stand on her own, 'cause like I tol' you, she just cain't make up her mind an' gotta blow everythang all outta pr'potion. Take two men, if they have a problem, they beat each other up till somebody fall out. Everythang settled just like that. But wit' two women, they gotta go through all this gettin' in touch wit' they feelings, an' openin' up the lines o' communication an' all that kinda nonsense. The only thang the men wanna open up is each other's skulls. Bip-bip and it's all over."

"That's precisely the point," SchoolBook challenged. "Perhaps if men adopted a less Neanderthal attitude regarding the resolution of discrepancies, real solutions to the problems plaguing men and women could be found."

"Now, whuss a plague got to do wit' anythang? See, them schools done messed up yo' mind. We up here discussin' mens an' womens an' here you come talkin' 'bout some plague. I thank them schools done fried yo' brains wit'out usin' a skillet."

"Well, all I know is we too easy on 'em," Invisible said. "We lets 'em get away wit' too much."

"Sho do," Gutbucket agreed. "I gave my ole lady sixty-five dollars to go to the beauty parlor last week. I don't know what I musta been thankin' 'bout."

"Me neither, cause it don't look like she spent no more'n a dollar an' a quarter," Big Money cracked. "Now don't you feel shame?"

"He should feel shame," Neck Bone added. "Any man give a woman mo' than fifty at one time deserve to be shame."

SchoolBook was amazed. "You know, you have a remarkable inability to understand the sophistication of the female psyche—"

"I understand they a buncha psychos," Neck Bone scoffed.

"Listen," SchoolBook continued. "Women are sensitive to subtle things, and if a man wants to have a meaningful relationship with a woman, he should attune himself to those things. Horatio, you and Zachary would particularly benefit from doing so."

The only people who called Neck Bone Horatio or Big Money Zachary were their mothers. But for SchoolBook, everything had to be formal. Dignified.

"SchoolBook," Neck Bone objected, embarrassed, "you just pitiful. You use all them fifty-dollar words an' they ain't nuttin' but counterfeit. What'chu know 'bout womens? I saw yo' so-called girlfriend, 'bout big as a twig on a diet. You a schoolbook an' she a pencil. Why don't'chu come back an' say sump'n when you get a real woman."

"Yeah, man," Big Money echoed, "you know all the words 'cept the right one. This all you gotta say to a woman." He pulled a $20 bill partially out of his pocket and pointed.

Sid, the manager, then walked in and distributed the checks. "Looka there on the top o' yo' check." Neck Bone motioned to SchoolBook. "Why you thank this called the 3C Garage?"

"I don't know," SchoolBook answered.

"I know you don't. None o' y'all do, but I found out the other day. It stand for 'cash, connections, an' common sense.' Now, who you thank got those three thangs?"

"Go'haid, Neck Bone," Gutbucket seconded, "tell it like it is."

"Always do," Neck Bone boasted. "Thass what run the world—cash, connections, an' common sense. An' mens is the only ones thass got 'em. All you gotta do is look round this garage. See how everythang work like clockwork? Look at all this new equipment, thass the cash. Look at the cars we fix, some o' the biggest companies around. Thass the connections. An' look at us, the best mechanics in town. Thass the common sense they had to hire us."

SchoolBook gave in. "Well, sir, I defer to your expertise." He got up. "Gentlemen, as always, it's been most enlightening. Now if you'll excuse me, I'll take my leave."

He left the lounge, but before leaving the garage he stopped in Sid's office for a reimbursement check.

"Excuse me, Sid, do you have my twenty-five for that filter I paid for the other day?"

"Oh, yeah, I'm glad you asked. I meant to give it to you when I passed out the paychecks." Sid took an envelope out of a stack he had in a tray on his desk. "Here you go, sorry about that. Make sure it's right."

The amount was correct. But before SchoolBook put the check in his pocket, his eye caught something. "Sid, how come this check is different from our regular checks?"

"What do you mean?"

"How come it's signed differently?"

"Oh, that's just because it's a different account. The mechanics get paid out of a special account. That check there is a regular 3C check. Is something wrong?"

SchoolBook looked at the check for a couple of seconds and just smiled. Then he looked out of Sid's office and saw Neck Bone and the rest leaving the garage. He laughed quietly as he stared at them.

"No, Sid, everthing's just fine."

He looked at the check again, smiled, and left Sid's office, marveling at his newfound information: Charlotte Charmaine Collier.

PATRICE E. WAGNER

When Henry closed his eyes and let go of his soul, there was a sudden brief flutter of activity as his gulls and butterflies, habitually still, responded to the shift in energy in the small cavern less than one mile from the hub of the world financial district and cultural center. His goat, Oneida, along with the cats, Shale and Slate, did what they always did when Henry closed his eyes. They rubbed against him and licked him intermittently until he opened them.

Which is why, when Zipporah found Henry six days later, nearly eight hours passed before she realized that Henry, as she had known him, would never again respond to her voice.

Henry's sanctuary was Zipporah's oasis after a long night of work. She came, always, just before the sunrise. The only reason she ever looked at the newspaper was to make sure she took her last customer one hour before the sun rose. That gave her twenty minutes to make him feel he was the most important man in the world, ten minutes to sit and forget about him, and thirty minutes to scurry across the highway that looped the city and slip down to Henry's hovel at the edge of the water.

PATRICE E. WAGNER is a teacher, writer, and activist. She was born and raised on the south side of Chicago, and holds degrees from the University of Pennsylvania and Columbia University. She lives in Harlem with her son, Ayinde.

As was their custom, they never greeted formally and she never disturbed his current activity. Henry had taught her, first and foremost, to find the rhythm that was her own, independent of who or what was going on around her. It might be minutes or even hours before they spoke or acknowledged each other's presence.

So on the Tuesday morning she entered the cave and found him sleeping, she nibbled on some of the acorns Henry had shelled and sipped on cold tea from boiled river water and spicebush leaves that sat in the pot on the rocks. When Henry did not stir, she lay down to rest on the pile of rags that Henry had prepared just for her, his only visitor and the only person besides his grandmother who had been able to love Henry for who he was.

She fell into a deep sleep, and when she opened her eyes the sun had fallen behind the city across the river. She sat up with a start. She did not like to have to climb the rocks and push through the bushes to the street after dark because sometimes thieves and derelicts lurked in that part of the city. The cave was pitch black and she fumbled around for the matches and candles that Henry kept on the makeshift table. She hated to awaken him but she had no choice. He would have to walk her to the street. She lit the candle. Her eyes stung and watered as the shadows and figures came into focus. Henry had not moved. Shale and Slate were licking him and Oneida was rubbing. She moved closer to him.

"Henry," she whispered softly. She didn't want to startle him, and most of the time he was not sleep anyway so she never had to speak loudly or even repeat his name, but this time he did not budge.

She walked over to him, kneeling with some difficulty, and put her hand to his face, repeating his name. His face was warm, but something in the slight upturn of the lips almost hidden by the mantle of hair that twisted, gnarled, and aged his thirty-three years made her hand feel for a pulse that was not there. She put her head to his chest. Nothing. She felt his neck. Nothing.

Shale and Slate pushed her hands aside as she probed his body for signs of life. She had always had a visceral reaction to death. Dead roaches in her apartment and dead birds on the street forced her to recoil visibly and physically. Dead dogs and cats on the highway sent chills through her. But before she knew it, she had stretched her body the length of Henry's, stroking and rubbing him with her free arm. She could not shake the feeling that Henry had finally achieved hibernation. The blank, waxen mask of death had not settled on his face. There were no signs of pain or remorse. He seemed to be in a deep restful sleep, his lips turned slightly at the corners into the small smile, Zipporah believed, of satisfaction that comes when a person has accomplished his task and found his place. That Henry had found such a space on an island where a swarming mass of humanity lived landlocked lives, a place in Manhattan where one could live whole and die in harmony, a natural space where nature in most of her forms was non-existent, was, indeed, a minor miracle. It was Henry's greatest victory and achievement.

It was what Zipporah wanted to tell Sarah and Big Henry when she faced them in the doorway of their small walkup on West 143rd Street between Seventh and Eighth avenues later that evening. She wanted to tell them that, except for a short difficult period at the beginning, their son, Henry, in searching for life in its most natural form, had found a peace and satisfaction that eluded most men in suits with pockets of green paper and plastic who came to her every night seeking escape, pleasure, love, and belonging. She planned to start by telling them about the smile that curled Henry's lips and then she was going to describe his sanctuary, the haven and oasis only Henry could have found in the middle of Manhattan.

Though she had recited her story over and over again in her mind, when Big Henry opened the door and looked at her as if he had never seen her before, she stood speechless, looking into the face that would have been Henry's had he lived to be sixty-five, shaved, and gained a hundred pounds.

"What is it, Zipporah?" Sarah had moved next to a silent, glowering Big Henry.

"Your son has passed. His body is in a cave on the river at West Street," was all she could manage as she turned and headed down the steps, but just before she did, she turned to them. They had not moved from the doorway. "I will miss him terribly." She ran down the steps and out of the building, leaving Sarah and Henry to mourn the passing of their only child and son, Henry Graves Washington, Jr.

Sarah inhaled sharply, shuffled to the other side of the room, and sat down heavily on the sofa. Big Henry just stood there, watching Zipporah's back as she disappeared down the steps. Their first thought and prayer, unspoken but shared, was that they had never unconsciously, in their pain and confusion, wished for the death of the child whose life they had so fervently hoped and prayed for.

They did not know they shared this prayer because it had been so many years since they had shared anything, let alone a feeling of intimacy or a secret. When Big Henry turned to face Sarah, he sought solace and answers but he could not form the words to speak to her because it had been years since he had sought either. Sarah looked in his eyes, but she could not speak because her guilt and her pain kept all the answers and the comfort locked inside.

She was Henry's mother and, as such, she believed she was ultimately responsible for all Henry was or was not. It was why she rarely discussed Henry's life or his actions. To do so would bring her own life and actions into question. The longest conversation she ever had about Henry was with her sister, who tried in vain to get Sarah to see that, although she had given birth to Henry, his destiny had nothing to do with her.

Sarah refused to believe her and, although she never told Big Henry, she believed deep within her soul that Henry's life and Henry's pain, Henry's emptiness and Henry's death, were her fault. Every night from the week after he was born, when she realized what she had done, to the day she died, she asked God's forgiveness.

Henry Jr. was born to Sarah and Henry after too many years of marriage and before the era of Lamaze and staged breathing techniques. By August 6, 1945, Sarah had been in labor for two days, and her body was limp with exhaustion. She was totally absolved of the power to hold on or in, so when the doctor told her it was not time to push yet she had lost all will and control. So it was that the second Henry Graves Washington burst into the world at the exact moment that Little Boy exploded over Hiroshima.

It was a fact that Sarah, who rarely if ever read the paper or listened to the radio, would probably have never known had not Big Henry, who because of his flat feet and heart murmur could not go to Europe, read every account of everything that happened, made it a part of his birth announcement. Henry junior was his redemption for not going. He passed out cigars to celebrate "their bomb and mine" or "their little boy and my little boy."

But by the time little Henry was six months old, Big Henry had stopped bragging. His son was so different from the bouncing baby boy fantasies they had cherished for the ten years of their marriage before he was born. His movements were late and seldom. He was almost nine months old before he sat up and close to two before he walked. When Henry died, Sarah could recall and count on one hand every single time she had seen Henry smile, and she never heard him laugh out loud.

Though they had expected brain damage they were assured by numerous doctors and tests that Henry was simply progressing at his own rate and that his intelligence was at least average, if not above. Once brain damage, which would have been easier to accept, was eliminated, Sarah had no choice but to accept the will of a God who manifested her wrath and, through Henry, thrust into life at a moment when millions died.

Big Henry, though, blamed Henry's life and consequently his death on Sarah's mother, whom he felt in his heart to be a witch who had cursed his son because she felt Big Henry was not good enough for her daughter. He had tried to refuse when she offered to come and take care of Henry when he was two months old and Sarah had to go back to her job at the insurance company or lose it. But Sarah said the only person she felt comfortable leaving little Henry with was her mother. Although Big Henry never told his wife, he always believed that it was Sarah's mother, the old woman called Nanati, who put strange ideas in his son's head that kept him from talking and acting like normal children and made his son want to leave home, act like an animal, and live in a cave.

Henry spent all day with her, from the time he was two months old until he went to school, and then every afternoon and evening, from the time he started school until the time his grandmother went home to die.

Nanati's physical body had begun to wane long before she left her beloved island to come to the fake island her only daughter called home to care for her only grandchild. She spend most of her waking time in a massive maroon floral chair that dominated the small living room. She never talked baby talk to Henry or treated him as a child. She never shushed his incessant prattle or told him to wait until she finished doing something before he could ask a question or speak. She never gave cursory answers to his many questions, and she always thought deeply and long before she answered, no matter how seemingly insignificant the subject.

One day in the December of his sixth year Henry walked in from school in tears, wanting to know why the birds had to live outside in the cold in the wintertime with nothing to eat.

Nanati instructed him to take off his coat, to dry his tears, and to sit, which Henry did immediately. Nanati looked at him for a long time with eyes that were covered with a gray-blue film. Almost everyone thought she was blind. Henry waited patiently. He knew she would answer when the answer came to her.

"The seasons change and the birds and animals change with them," she said. "Most things in nature move with nature so when it is warm and there is lots of food, they eat and get nice and fat, and when winter comes and there is not much food around, their bodies live on the food that is stored. Everything slows down and they don't need as much food in the winter. Mr. Wellburn's dog Poncho grows a thicker coat in the winter to keep warm, and he gets rid of it in the spring. Bears hibernate; they go to sleep when everything dies and do not wake up until everything begins to grow and live again. Don't you cry for them; they know how to get along in the cold."

"How do they know?"

"They just know. They are born knowing."

"But who teaches them?"

"God teaches them."

"Why doesn't God teach us things like that?"

"She did but we forgot. Don't cry for the birds, cry for us."

Henry sat and thought about what she said. It must be a wonderful thing to be able to do.

"Could I learn what they know?"

"Of course."

He climbed onto her lap and pressed his face against hers, his arms around her neck, whispering softly, though they were the only two in the house, "I want to live like the animals live." She hugged him tightly and kissed his neck, though she did not say a word.

He was a child with a driving ambition. He quizzed Nanati constantly on animals and their habits and patterns, and she taught him everything she remembered from the island where she grew up. She told him about people who could read minds and heal and who could live in the woods or the mountains for days and days without food, of people who could communicate with animals and galaxies. She taught him about the importance of being still, of knowing what was important from what was not important.

Henry read everything he could about the habits of animals and was constantly amazed by their brilliance. He would stare for hours at a pigeon or a cockroach as if he could learn through osmosis. He begged to go to the park to watch the squirrels and the birds.

He had no interest in anything else, not sports or girls or television. He was obsessed with animals. He begged constantly to go to the zoo or to the aquarium. It was not when he refused, adamantly, the trips to baseball games and playgrounds, to amusement parks and museums, that Sarah began to worry. It was when, sitting motionless for over an hour at age seven, he told her he was being the snake at the zoo, that Sarah began to worry.

At Abraham Lincoln High School, Henry excelled in biology, failing everything else. His favorite place was down by the river. He would walk to the western edge of the city and go under a tunnel with big wet puddles of water that never dried. He'd cross a part of the highway that led to the grassy patch that led to huge rocks and the riverbank.

At first he just sat on the grass; then he began to sit closer and closer to the water, first on the rocks and then down with his feet in the murky, stagnant water that supported just the hardiest and most resilient life forms. It was the only place Henry felt he could breathe. His favorite spot was a wide rounded rock that was almost the height of a stool. From here Henry would sit and watch the rats.

The first time he saw them, he thought his heart would stop. There seemed to be thousands of them, but he knew there could not have been that many. They scrambled over each other, scurrying back and forth, in and out. Dim memories of stories of hordes of rats that attacked people and ate them came to his mind but caused him no fear. He sat motionless for hours. Except for the occasional blink of an eyelash, he might have been stone. Sometimes he would close his eyes, practicing how long he could sit with his eyes closed.

They came out like that about three times a week. Every evening as dusk fell over the city some of them would come from beneath the rocks, scurrying around for sustenance. They'd dash up over the rocks past Henry to the garbage cans. But when all of them came out, Henry could not shake the feeling that some type of unified consciousness was taking place among them.

One day one of them walked up to Henry's foot and sniffed at it. Henry did not flinch or budge. The rat, long and gray, sniffed Henry's side and smelled all around him. Henry began to hum slowly, a song that his Nanati used to sing to him. He hummed over and over again, very low. The rat climbed on him, stuck his nose in the bottom half of Henry's face, sniffed him, and jumped down into the pack. Every time Henry came out, that rat or one that looked like him would run up to Henry and sniff him as if in greeting. Henry began to talk to them, telling them things he told no one because, at home and at school, Henry would talk to no one unless they spoke to him first. He would go to school and then go to sit by the river until it was dark.

When Sarah asked him where he had been, he would make things up like playing basketball or wrestling, something strenuous so when they asked him why he was sitting so still he would say he was tired, and most of the time they would leave him alone.

The growing sinking feeling that his only child was mad elicited only anger from Big Henry, who preferred to believe that Henry was acting strange on purpose. How could there be anything wrong with him? There was clearly nothing wrong with his father or Sarah. That witch mother of Sarah's had spoiled him and made him weird. Maybe he would join the army when he finished school; that would make a man out of him.

Sarah was optimistic about Henry's future. All he needed was a nice girl to bring him out and take care of him. He was after all, a decent boy, well brought up, even if he was quiet. Thus, Sarah, who had always considered herself open-minded, unlike her husband, was stunned, when in getting some things ready for the laundry, she found a love note to Zipporah Peters in Henry's pants pocket.

Zipporah was the oldest of five in the Peters family, who had lived on the corner as long as the Washingtons had lived in the middle of the block. Zipporah had been the tiniest thing as a child. When all the other children grew up, Zipporah never really got tall. Four feet ten inches was as far as she made it. She grew out instead of up. If she had been taller she would have been called statuesque, but as it was, she was a plump girl who would be fat by the time she hit twenty-five.

It never seemed to bother her, though. While her classmates envied and tried to emulate the pale, rail-thin girls in the fashion magazines, while they walked around hunched over trying to hide their burgeoning womanhood, Zipporah reveled in her weight and her femaleness. She walked, shoulders flung back, arms swinging, breasts unrestrained and bouncing every which way, buttocks jiggling, completely heedless of the stares of the young boys and the old men. She was a frisky thirteen without a trace of self-consciousness, who, despite her mother's insistence, refused to wear a bra or a girdle to restrain her flesh. Her ruin had been prophesied by Sarah and the other good women on the block.

It was not Zipporah's body, however, that caught Henry's attention. It was the lips that looked like she was wearing lipstick even when she wasn't; they were the color of red cherries, the kind Henry loved, the hard dark ones, almost black. One day while she was standing near the park she caught Henry, who was on his way to the river, staring at her mouth. She asked him how much he was willing to pay and if he had anywhere to go. Henry, who had been lost in his thoughts, said "down by the river," which is how they ended up on the rocks that jutted out from under the bridge until midnight. Henry told Zipporah that his parents thought he was crazy because he did not belong in the place that he lived, and Zipporah told him how her parents had thrown her out of the house for loving a man in her bedroom.

"Do you think I am bad?" she asked Henry.

"No. Do you think I am crazy?"

"Of course not. People end up places where they shouldn't be all the time. Why, just the other day I got off at the wrong train stop, talk about lost."

Henry told her about his efforts to achieve the skills the human race had lost and about his quest for the sea, and she assured him that those were as worthy goals as any she had ever heard.

Henry asked Zipporah to marry him but she refused, telling him it would not be good for her career. He did not tell this to his mother when she confronted him with the note.

"What is this, Henry?" Sarah had waited until Big Henry was out of the house. She held out the note, which had little hearts and *I love you*'s written all over it.

Henry was embarrassed and stared down at the linoleum.

"You can't be in love with her," Sarah said, as if reassuring herself. He had never demonstrated a hint of a sense of humor, but this must be his feeble idea of a joke.

"Why not?" Henry asked, genuinely puzzled.

"What do you mean, why not?" Sarah believed that Henry was a little strange but she knew he was not stupid. Everybody else on the block knew what Mr. Peters's oldest daughter did for a living. He could not be that naive. She had never talked to him about sex but she assumed that Big Henry must have or that he had read something in school or talked with —well, maybe overheard other boys talking.

"I don't know what you mean," he murmured softly. He did not care what Zipporah did. He loved her. He did not want to talk to his mother about Zipporah.

Sarah could feel her body getting hot. She wanted to slap Henry for making her say it, but she had not hit him since he was small and there was no point in starting at eighteen. "Why do you act so dense sometimes? That's why people think there is something wrong with you. How can you be in love with a girl who has no respect for herself, who sells her body to men for money?" She could not bring herself to say *prostitute* but she was thinking *tramp* and *whore*.

Henry's eyes followed the mustard pattern as it skipped from block to block. "She has to make money," he whispered. "She has to eat. . . ." His voice trailed off. Sarah had to strain to hear him. "Besides, she doesn't love any of them," he added, with a slight touch of defiance in his voice, something Sarah had never heard. "And she never kisses them in the mouth."

Sarah's eyes widened. She could not believe she was having this conversation. She found it even harder to believe that she had given birth to this person. "Your father will kill you if he ever finds out." She turned and walked into her bedroom, leaving Henry looking down at the linoleum.

Henry decided to make sure his father never did. He knew it was time for him to follow his calling. He went into his room and packed a small bag, trying to think of all the things he would need. He didn't want to look homeless; the outdoors was his home. He was going to become who he was.

Had it not been for Zipporah, Henry would have perished when he first left home. When she saw that she could not dissuade him and warned him of the treachery of life on the streets, she took him under her wing and set out to teach him all she had learned. Henry was a willing and eager student, and within three weeks he knew where to go and where not to go, how to find decent food and clean water, how to keep himself reasonably clean, and how to protect himself from vultures and parasites.

His only fear was of being stared at, but that quickly vanished because no one ever really did. People who accidentally caught his eye quickly looked away. And he realized that he minded less being looked at than he minded being pitied. His was a life he had chosen.

He learned how to take deep breaths and to preserve his energy. He learned what he could eat and what he could not. He knew where all the free food and clothing giveaways were. He could not believe the things that people discarded. He acquired a cashmere coat from the Armory on the East Side. On Wednesday and Thursday he ate lots of raw produce, and on Friday he ate raw fresh fish. On weekends before the crowds and the joggers and the pet walkers he ate fresh dandelion and sorrel salad with wild mushrooms from the park. He never begged because he did not have to; he had all the things he needed.

For weeks on end he did not converse with another human being. He felt a closer kinship with things not human. He knew he was no better or different from a dog or a cat.

When he learned he could live, he made his way to the river. He walked down the long flight of steps next to the highway and the tall shallow cavern of the underpass to the slip of grass next to the river. He stretched out his arms and breathed deeply. The sky was blue and clear, the temperature perfect. He pushed his way through waist-high weeds to the rocks at the river's edge and sat breathing the slightly rancid smell. He walked along the edge of the water where he could trail his foot in it. Soon the land began to climb and the drop was four feet, then six feet, then twelve feet. Henry grabbed a thick root and dropped back down to the water's edge. He was able to walk along a narrow shelf. He would have missed the cave entirely if he hadn't tripped on a wet rock and nearly fallen in it, a natural cave in the side of the earth that couldn't be seen unless you were right in front. Henry had to stoop slightly to get inside.

The walls were rock, the floor dirt, and brush nearly covered the entrance. Henry stood in it with tears running down his face. He knew it was going to be a special day when he awakened that morning with a squirrel sitting on his chest. He scrambled up the grass to gather his few belongings.

He began to make a home for himself, pulling large branches and bushes down so that nobody could see it. He made a bed from pieces of wood and branches and leaves that he covered with a blanket from the Christmas giveaway. He found a rock where Zipporah would come and sit at the end of a long night and watch the sun come up. More and more she would come down here and sleep during the day. She never got much rest before. Sometimes she would bring Henry something he hadn't eaten in a long time. She never gave him any money and Henry never thought to ask. He did not, for the most part, want things that money bought. Once he stole some seeds from the five-and-dime, and another time he could not resist a craving for a double-fudge chocolate brownie, but it made him sick.

It was during Henry's interminable walks that he collected his animals. Shale and Slate were sitting on a window ledge on a first-floor apartment on 79th Street and Fifth Avenue across from the park. Henry stood and looked deeply into their eyes for ten minutes. Shale jumped into his arms and Slate followed. Oneida, his goat, had been left for dead behind a bush in the park, a sacrifice gone awry. Henry heard her whimpering on the verge of death, bleeding profusely. He nursed her back to health.

Henry picked up two cocoons, thinking they were pinecones, and was shocked to discover they were in fact butterflies. By the end of the summer in Henry's house there were squirrels, butterflies, caterpillars, cats, gulls, and pigeons, which he ate without abashment, and Oneida, the baby goat.

Zipporah came by one day when all the butterflies were in cocoon with dark elongated balls looking very much like turds lying all over the cave. They would have bothered her except she had seen them when they metamorphosed and Henry's cave became a bevy of all shapes and colors.

Henry learned from his menagerie all the things he ever needed to know. From Shale and Slate he learned stealth and centeredness.

Henry watched the leaves across the river turn and began to contemplate the winter. He had stocked up on blankets and coats from the church. He had collected firewood and stored food. He had been practicing hibernation for weeks. Not only did he believe it to be his only hope of surviving the winter, but he believed it was possible.

He chose the November new moon to enter his state of rest, his vow and hope that he would not stir until the warmth of spring quickened his blood.

The day after Zipporah came to his apartment, Big Henry went in search of his son. He combed the parks and lots that bordered the city. He found places he would never have believed existed. He found himself distracted by animals and places he never imagined, but he did not find his son.

He searched all day on the weekends, and on weekdays after work he sat until long after night had fallen with a big flashlight; unafraid, he scoured the rocky, desolate shore of the city. He would sit for long periods, watching the falling sun and the scurrying animals, feeling the moist air on his skin. Breathing deeply, he pulled the smell of the river into his body and brain, and sometimes he forgot the years of frustrated dreams and why he was there in the first place. He wandered, following an instinct that evaded logic or reason. The smallest and most inconsequential things caught his attention. He ended up in places totally different from where he had planned to go.

It was almost by accident that he stumbled upon Henry's cave. He was walking along the rocks when he saw a movement to his right. He turned and saw nothing except a wall of rock, but he knew something else was there. He climbed up the bank and walked instinctively to an opening that was invisible to the eye from every angle unless you were right up on it. Big Henry hesitated at the entrance. He wanted to knock or ring a bell but since he could not, he said hello, somewhere between a shout and a whisper, and waited for a response that did not come, even though he waited expectantly and patiently for more than ten minutes.

He stood insulated between damp, cool rocks, unable to see or to move in or out, feeling the light and the air change. His immobilization was not due to fear or indecision, to anger or pain or shame. He was surprised to realize he felt none of those things; they were emotions he had recently let go. He did not move; he wanted to savor and remember himself and that moment because he knew that once he moved, in either direction, everything would change irrevocably. He asked for guidance and protection from a God he did not know and stepped slowly into the cave.

His eyes were pulled immediately to the body that lay on the pallet and he knew it was his son, even though the face was not even vaguely familiar. He was not sure how long he stood there staring. As the days had passed, he had prepared himself for a body withered by death and time. Perhaps it was the river air or the fall temperature, but the body before him had not deteriorated in any way. It could easily have been the body of a man at rest. Big Henry felt himself an intruder in a place he did not belong. He felt as he had often felt when Henry was an infant, fearful that excess movement or sound would awaken him from a deep and peaceful sleep.

His eyes scanned the space in which his son had lived and died but kept returning to his son's face. He knew his son had found a home and a life in this place. It was in the air and on his face. He did not touch anything or move anything and finally he turned to leave.

Sarah sat silent and immobile in the maroon chair when Henry returned. The first thing she saw was the change in his face.

"Where is my son?"

"He is at rest. Trust me."

Sarah did and never asked again.

ORLANDO WARREN

 After the funeral was over, after everyone had left, after the condolences, after all the amenities—fried chicken, potato salad, and enough spirits to float a small vessel—she stepped out into the fading September sun, and I tagged along, not knowing what else to do.

The funeral was for my brother, Evan. He would have been twenty-nine in several days—plans were made for a party—then suddenly he was gone. And the woman, who at eighteen was only a child, who hadn't spoken in three days, who stood huddled like a mummy during and after the ceremony, at whose side I now walked, was his wife, Kallie.

I did not know her and had spoken to her only once, long distance, after their wedding. I'd been away at school; it was finals, so I couldn't leave. But Evan (who was ten years my senior), had often written me of her, so she wasn't a complete stranger. Evan had been a professor of English, and she was his favorite student. From his letters I knew, probably, even before he, that he loved her. Once he even expressed the hope that I might find someone like her to love.

ORLANDO WARREN was born in the Bedford Stuyvesant section of Brooklyn, New York. He is a high school dropout who considers Homer, Dante, Kafka, Wright, Hurston, and Baldwin his teachers. He recently graduated from the College of New Rochelle, with a B.A. in English.

Evan was my only brother and my only kinsman; now there was only this girl dressed for mourning. A girl who pulled me into her steps, into her silence, a girl who hadn't acknowledged my presence, yet needed me as much as I needed her.

We walked for hours, no place in particular, walked till the sun was lost in the stars and kept moving through the autumn chill that had severed the trees of their leaves and the street of its noise. The only sounds other than an occasional passing car were in faint echoes of our steps turning over and over, reaching one corner, then the next, till finally, and without trying, we were in front of her door.

There she waited, staring inside the window, as if for some sign of a life that didn't exist; but there was only the darkness, the emptiness that was felt from where she stood. Then she leaned against a fence, and I watched her as if it were for the first time.

Kallie was dark, so dark that from a short distance she seemed almost featureless, like one of those African carvings; and as one neared, one saw skin that was as smooth as marble and as soft and scented as ripened fruit, filled with the mappings of her ancestors: the African nose and mouth, eyes black as berries, large as almonds, and hair which usually fell woolenly across her shoulders now tied in an ebony scarf made from the same cotton material as her dress, a dress that covered but couldn't conceal the lines of life lingering within it.

And she was tall, and as fluid as water, and like water her limbs stretched and pooled. I could imagine my brother diving and disappearing in her darkening expanse.

They had been like flowers, whose earlier than usual spring now lay buried under an even earlier frost. And it wasn't fair. So brief was their love—my eyes began to fill with tears—was it because they cheated or was it the wind whipping through the street? Turning, she saw me; then, screaming as if a knife had been plunged into her heart, she ran inside and locked the door. I banged, calling her name, but she didn't answer. And I was a little afraid to bang and call any louder because it was her grief and she had a right to spend it as she pleased. But I was even more afraid of what she might do if I stopped.

Then the lock clicked back and I went inside. She hadn't turned on the lights, but I could see her seated in front of a window; it framed her like an ebony silhouette, and as I approached, partly to see how she was, partly to prove she was real, I knew for the first time beauty could exist as sorrow.

A hand extended, but the darkness was so immense that for a moment it just hung there, as if waiting for the rest of itself to form. Then the hand found mine, but it wasn't hers. Then she shrieked, and was suddenly standing. Then the roughness of the hand I held receded into the softness of her own, and the rest of her followed. The night was long; in it we were warm and happy and we didn't know why and we didn't care.

We stood, looking out the window; we stood there for hours; we stood there like children, counting the stars till they all flickered and gathered into one enormous sun.

Crawdaddy

DENNIS A. WILLIAMS

 "Good morning, Crawdaddy."

"Fox! That you?" Quincy surprised himself with his own voice. He had been ready to chat awhile with whoever it was—that's why he settled into the seat before lifting the receiver—but he was genuinely happy to hear her.

"Who else but your conscience would be bothering you this time of night? What are you doing up?"

"Now when have you known me to go to bed early? What time is it, anyway?" He squinted at the clock on the bookshelf but couldn't make it out in the dark.

"When you don't have a date. It's quarter to three. Who is she?"

"Nikki Giovanni. We're covering the revolution in class next week. So what is it, midnight out there? You must be back to drinkin coffee."

"I don't know about out there, but it's quarter to three here in Jersey, and I'm on a natural high."

"You're back east? Oh, shit, when'd you get in? How long you gonna be around? *Talk* to me, girl." As he spoke, raising his voice, he realized it

DENNIS A. WILLIAMS is the author of the novel *Crossover* (Summit Books, 1992), and co-author (with John A. Williams) of the biography *If I Stop I'll Die: The Comedy and Tragedy of Richard Pryor* (Thunder's Mouth Press, 1991). A former writer and editor for *Newsweek* magazine, he teaches writing at Cornell University in Ithaca, New York.

was worse than he'd thought. Over the years he had perfected a soothing Barry White monotone that covered every contingency, both caller and company. Dropping the mask now, he knew, had less to do with Fontelle than with Max. He just didn't give a shit anymore. He grabbed the pack and lit up. That he could do in the dark.

"I heard that," she said. "You still tryin to kill yourself?"

"Fuck you."

"You wish."

"I'll live. So?"

"Well," she said, "I got in a few hours ago, and I'm here to stay, I guess."

"What happened to the institute and artistic freedom? What happened to what's-his-name?"

"Why something gotta happen? I can't come home if I want? Maybe I just wanna look at the sky from a different direction for a while."

"Hey, yo. Uh-uh. This is me, remember? What's up?"

"I don't know, Quince. Everything and nothing."

He hadn't expected her to fold that easily. He'd heard it before, but she usually managed to stay aloft for a few more rounds.

"Sounds like trouble," he said.

"Not really. But I need to talk to you, okay? Not right now. I just wanted you to know I was back."

"You got it."

"You got the number out here?"

"Please. I got 'em all."

"I know. That's your problem."

"Fuck you. Again."

"My dear, I thought you'd gotten over that obsession."

"Who told you that lie?"

Silence. He'd misjudged her altitude.

"Hey, you there?" he asked.

"Soon," she said. "You know how dead it is in Jersey."

The last part was a feeble rally.

"Okay," he said, automatically shifting into low as he leaned over the phone. "Soon."

"Night, Crawdaddy."

He eased the receiver into place and held it there for a moment with both hands, feeling a tingle ease down through his body. Then he lit another from the smoldering butt and closed his eyes with the intake. *Call soon, or . . . ?* Still throwing him curves after—what, six years? More.

Seemed like forever. Definitely more of a diversion than he'd bargained for.

But a diversion nonetheless. Stabbing out in the dark, he kept hitting filters from earlier in the evening and knew he'd exceeded his limit. Fuck it. He peeled himself from the fake leather chair, like ripping a Band-Aid from his naked behind, and stood. Time to get back. Past time, if he cared. His hesitation, though, was not all about the business at hand. He cherished these moments. The light from the streetlamp, when it was working, arched upward to illuminate the slimmest corner of his curtainless room. Any fool who dared to haunt Morningside at this hour might wonder about the goings-on within, and as often as possible Quincy tried to substantiate any potential fantasies. But even—especially—on off nights, he liked moving around naked through his one-room kingdom, plucking just the right record from a shelf or even a book that he might hold, unseeing, standing or sitting at the cluttered desk table, hearing the real or imagined voices, replaying or forecasting intimacies that, despite all his efforts, were truer when he was alone.

Maybe she was asleep.

He could lie still with one leg and one arm draped over her, holding on as much as holding her, and watch their ghosts till the sun rose. He had always done that, even when it was all good. In the dark he could see them, over and over again. Cooking Chinese food in the tiny kitchenette. Watching the good stuff on channel 13 when they begged for money. Watching the anchor puppets mouth her words while she critiqued their delivery. Him grading papers. Her reading the paper. And fucking every which way, any time, for any reason or for no reason. Her ghost was always clearer than any of the others, her presence in the apartment more pervasive. When she was there, in fact, he never saw the others, but she used to turn up when he was with somebody else. That had been awhile. Would she still be there when she was gone?

"That your friend from California?"

He almost wished there'd been an edge to her voice, but that wasn't her style. And she knew better. The phone calls, the nights he insisted on being alone, were intended to create the illusion that she did not hold a monopoly.

"Yeah, she just got back for a while."

"Are you going to see her?"

"Of course," he said, surprised that she'd asked. Maybe there'd be a fight after all.

"Good." She was entirely awake and beginning to dimple. "You can tell her all about me."

"What would you have me tell her?"

"About this," she said and reached out to where he was already rising to meet her.

She drew him in quickly; they were both ready. And she talked, more than usual, deep, dirty talk that propelled them into special-occasion contortions. At the moment he felt himself bracing his feet against the wall; he slipped into double exposure. The ghosts were right there with them; it was the night, more than three years ago, when they bent his old bed frame, which was why his mattress remained on the floor. The night—only the second time he had laid eyes on her—when he knew she would be staying.

He was cruising down Broadway, about to swing east across the walk, and he caught her behind flash by out of the corner of his eye. It wasn't doing much, just easing around the corner and so moving in the same direction about ten yards ahead before he made his turn. It had kind of a lazy country sway to it—out of place even in an area full of non-natives, where most attempted a version of the typical uptown hustle or somehow called attention to themselves (like Fontelle's, which he had discovered near that very spot). It was nice enough, by itself not worth much more than a few steps' worth of hard looking. But she carried all of herself that way, and that's why he slowed down to identify the species. Too tight to be called sassy, not bold enough to be regal. Casually precious. Fully formed and content, for the moment, to be out of step. A first-year grad student, he decided as he fell into her wake. Maybe from a black college, definitely from some all-black, non-ghetto environment. Someplace she'd be known as medium brown, which meant a little on the dark side, and her restrained voluptuousness would count as both character and charm. He tried to figure whether, if he talked to her, she would straight-up ig him or offer some chilly, slightly-too-proper putdown. It would be one or the other, neither particularly interesting, and he wasn't sure he wanted to talk to her anyway yet, so he watched her on down a ways.

When she paused at the bookstore, he knew what play to run. He hadn't done that since his freshman year when, using a technique he'd developed at Harvard Square, he cornered a slight, exotic-Jewish sensitive type in the poetry section. The hit was good for a couple of transition weekends before they both moved on. He had known he didn't want to get sidetracked in a white thing anyway (was that the Sly or Huey period?), and she turned out later to be gay—and a pretty good poet, actually—so it was cool all around. In a way, he was a freshman again, a month into Teachers College, back in the fishbowl after a treacherous year out on the open seas, a year which had convinced Fontelle, who had cut him adrift in the first place, that he was some kind of pussy pirate.

He could never see it that way himself and wasn't intent on plunder when he reached out ahead of her to open the bookstore door. It was not an anonymous gesture; he gave it enough personality—yes, this is for *you*—to invite a pleasant acknowledgment, which might have been enough to send him on his way. Nothing doing, we wanted to be a hinkty bitch today, so he recommitted to the mission. Checking her direction, he looped around and took up a position by the magazines, blocking the aisle she'd be coming through, so she'd have to say Excuse me, or Kiss my ass, or something to prove she had a voice. Instead, it was a testy (but surprisingly resonant) Do you mind? He stepped forward without looking up and noted her destination. He gave her almost ten minutes before he followed. Luckily, he wanted to check out *Mumbo Jumbo* as a funky example of literature as history and so didn't feel entirely depraved. He found her in political science, working the shelves like a researcher, trying to locate information, not just a book. He liked that and stood at the end of the aisle, openly admiring her diligence. The moment he forgot he was stalking—he should have been scheming a way to force a conversation—she turned as if expecting him and spread a dimpled front-porch smile. That was enough, too much, and by the time she made her choice he had fled with Ishmael Reed and some funny hoodoo vibes.

A few weeks later, depressed by Nixon's victory and a half-semester's teachings that contradicted most of what he knew about children and schools, he went down to check out Roy Ayers at Mikell's on the Upper West Side, where Fine Young Negroes with Good Jobs had begun to cluster in increasing numbers during his time in the city, bumping up against the older intellectual crowd. Between sets, he noticed a honey-hued newcomer at the bar, black-stockinged legs snaking out of a tight short skirt. I got your four more years, Tricky. Maybe it won't be so bad after all. He slid into a convenient vacancy beside her, signaled David for another Dewar's, and asked if he could get her something. She looked doll-eyed at him and back to her half-full wineglass, considered her options like a child choosing a toy, and finally (before the impatient but considerate bartender moved away) nodded yes. She turned toward Quincy and thanked him. As he responded, preparing to build his case for repayment, he noticed her eyes shift away, behind him.

"Do you mind?"

Quincy took a step back from the bar, yielding the space to its rightful owner, Miss Lazybutt herself.

"I think my friend would like another vodka tonic," the first said, both to the bartender, delivering her wine, and to Quincy.

"Of course," he said, surrounded.

"Max, will you watch my drink—uh, drinks? I'll be back."

Quincy breathed deeply and watched the skirt call attention to itself, bopping away from the bar. Tag team. He paid for the three drinks. Put his wallet back calmly. Sipped his scotch. Watched Number Two settle into her seat and study her vodka. Ignoring him, as he thought the first time, but then, he hadn't said anything yet. And he was less sure than before if he cared to. Her friend's skirt sure was working.

"You're welcome," he said at last, on general principle.

"Thank you." She spoke over her shoulder. He didn't need this. "So how was it?"

"A little draggy," he mumbled, surveying the crowd. "They sounded like I feel."

"No, not the band. I mean the book. *Mumbo Jumbo*."

"Damn, you've got good eyes," he said and, looking at them as they now measured him, decided he meant it.

"I'm in journalism. I notice things. I tried to read him before but it was too freaky for me."

Yeah, but not for your friend, I bet. He stole a glance toward the ladies' room. "Well, then, don't bother. It's more of the same. But better. What else do you notice?"

"Are you in English?"

"No. I was. I teach high school. Taking a break to get my master's."

"You don't look like a high school teacher."

"Oh, yeah? What do I look like?"

She repositioned herself to take all of him in. The smile that had startled him in the aisle of the bookstore made a quick appearance, but he knew it was less for him than for the guessing game. She crossed one leg smoothly over the other and held it. Her skirt, not as short as her friend's, crawled up her medium-brown thigh. A delicate hand with clear-polished nails rested there a moment and rose to the side of her head, drawing his eyes back to hers. It was a steady gaze, not playful or even challenging. Neutral, like a camera.

"A writer," she said.

He blinked. Drank some scotch. She was waiting.

"Why would you say that?"

"The way you held the book. The way you look at things and see something else."

"Like what?"

"Like me."

"Max, was it?"

"Maxine Love." She held out her hand.

"Quincy Crawford." He took it.

The glass and a half of wine remained on the bar when they retreated from the noise of the second set. He needed to hear her better because she wanted information, not conversation, and he felt compelled to give it. It had been more than a year since he had spoken to anyone but Fontelle about the stories, longer since he'd mentioned the more expansive dreams lost forever in the hunt for experiences to justify them. She absorbed all he said, without judgment, and added little about herself except the certainty that she would become a White House correspondent. And she spoke, for the record, about the election and politics in general, and the way they were covered, and about education and literature. All the things he knew her friend would not have talked about, and that he hadn't known he wanted to.

The conversation continued, without the slightest overt sign of flirtation, right up to the moment in his room when she took the book he'd been reading aloud, Morrison's *The Bluest Eye*, from his hand and unbuttoned his shirt and kissed his nipple. And he tasted the medium brown of her shoulder and the peek-a-boo thigh. And he wondered for the first time where everybody had gone, the ghosts of others like her eel-hipped friend who always came out to greet a new playmate. When he fell into her she spoke again. Her precise pronunciations melted to a near-demonic whisper that asked no questions but told him what she was going to do to him, and for him, conjuring up a ready-made vision of some jointly ambitious future, and the more she said the deeper he drove to find the source of the spell that banished all others and held him fast. The bed frame groaned; he thought it was him. She wrapped him up like a baby and cushioned the impact when the mattress dropped. She cried out, he cried, and she held his face with both hands an inch from hers.

"Tell me what you see," she demanded.

He had never been able to, had never really known what kind of answer she wanted. But the question, continually implied by her presence, haunted him. It—she—reminded him that he ought to be seeing something. That his life should have a focus. When she left for Cleveland after J school, she took the question with her, leaving him aimless and confused. And the apartment filled again with ethereal, unseeing strangers (including the slinky he'd come to know as her roommate). When she returned more than a year later, he thought she could help once again to sharpen his vision. Now he could see all too clearly that the question could not also be the answer. Though neither her presence nor his desire had faded, his attention had. Good as they were together—she was telling him so right now (and then) hypnotically, in the low tones that carried the authority of a special report—they were too often out of phase. She was intent on taking him somewhere—like now—that he didn't want to go, but did. Outwardly, he seemed to retain a separation, but he knew she was winning; all he could see was her. He was convinced the moment of disengagement was at hand.

But he couldn't move. Not because, when they finished, he was exhausted and stuck inside her, but because the collapse of time, the unprecedented merging of past and present, shadow and form, paralyzed him.

"Tell her that," she said, engulfing him in flesh and spirit.

"You're dangerous," he said.

"No, I'm not. I can't hurt you, Quince. This is the worst thing that can happen, me being here with you, making you feel good. That's not so bad, is it?"

It was the same promotion as before, as always. *It's all right. I'll stay with you. We'll be happy together.* She did. They were. He was never sure if he loved her, though he had chosen to believe he did. With her, he could do everything he wanted to do except, sometimes, be alone.

"Is it?" she repeated.

"No," he confessed.

He extricated himself and rolled onto his back. She rolled with him, placed her head on his chest, reached a hand to the side of his face, and slid a thigh across his groin. Surrounded.

"Why don't you tell your friend that you're going to be a father?"

Her bright eyes beamed into his, requiring, as always, a response. The goddamn red light never went off.

"Don't play that, Max," he said, and cut to the ceiling, where he wouldn't find her. "That's serious shit."

"I'm not playing."

He came back to her eyes and found no hint of a punch line. His left arm cleared a space, and he rolled off the mattress.

"What the fuck are you talking about?" he demanded from his knees.

She turned to face him, not laughing but pleased, like a girl who'd tricked the teacher. The dimples she seemed to control at will creased her cheeks. Her relaxed Afro drooped sexily on her forehead.

"I'm going to have a baby," she said, with the kind of dramatic reading that made her cringe on newscasts.

He stood, spun, and stalked across the room to the desk, where he swiped at his pack and matches.

"*Whose* baby?"

She started giggling, and he knew the question was lame; this was part of the script, like the frenzied father in the delivery room. He tried to light up but had a handful of cigarettes and no matches. Like rubbing two sticks together. She laughed some more. He was being cute.

"Whose do you think?" she said too happily, and kind of rose up to invite him back to her side.

He was there in two strides and slapped her in the mouth with a handful of tobacco. She screamed.

"This ain't no *show*, Max!" he yelled, standing astride her on the mattress. "What the *fuck* do you think you're doing? You're *pregnant!*" He slapped her again. She spat out bits of tobacco and paper. "How you gonna get pregnant?"

Quicker than he could see, she planted a foot in his chest and pushed him hard into the wall. A framed Alvin Ailey poster bounced on its wire, danced off its hook, and crashed to the floor.

"How the hell do you *think* I got pregnant?" she snarled. "You *fucked* me and made a baby. I *thought* you'd be happy."

"*Happy?*"

"Don't you touch me!"

"Little late for that, don't you think?" he asked, and almost started laughing himself. "You want me to be happy? You tell me I'm gonna be a father, *you're* gonna be a mother—we're supposed to have a baby, and you want me to be happy?"

"It was an accident," she said, "but I'm not sorry. I found out yesterday. I wanted a good time to tell you. I know it's right."

"Right?" he howled. And he did laugh. "You know what *I* was waiting for? I was waiting for a good time to tell you to get the fuck *out of here!* There ain't no right for us, you stupid bitch. Nobody asked you to come in here and take over my life, tell me who I'm supposed to be. Think you know *every* goddamn thing, but you don't know shit about me, and now you wanna produce a fucking Mother's Day special. *Fuck* that shit!"

". . . should've known, I should've known," she was chanting. "Goddamn you, Quincy, goddamn you to fucking hell, you weak son of a bitch. You can't take it, can you? You're just like all the rest of those sorry motherfuckers. I *am* stupid, 'cause I thought you were special. Always talking about your kids and your father."

"Hey—"

"Thought you knew what it was about, thought you had what it takes, thought you wanted something, but you just want the pussy, don't you?"

"Don't you talk about—"

"You don't even *know!* You just wanna fuck. Fuck *this*, nigger." She threw a pillow in his face. "It's about love. It's about going someplace. I thought you could see that. I thought you *knew!*"

"*I* know. I know more than you think. I know that kids are real. I know what it's like not to have a father, not to be wanted. I know this isn't some goddamn fantasy, and it's *not* gonna happen."

"That's what you think. Talk about too late, well, listen up, *Crawdaddy*—isn't that what she calls you?—you're gonna be a sure-nuff daddy now 'cause I'm having this baby whether you like it or not."

His skin crawled, but he collected himself, crouching on the mattress and leaning back against the wall. "No, I don't think so. I get to vote on this, and I *will not* have my seed floating around like some kinda milkweed pod."

"Shit . . ."

"No, listen, 'cause I'm serious about this. You don't know, see, so let's—I'm sorry I hit you; you know I never—let's just talk about this. It's no good, Max. I mean, I don't even think we should be together, and you can't do this alone."

"You already voted, Quincy. You don't want any part of this, fine. But don't you even think about telling me what I can't do." She began to lift from the bed.

He pitched forward and grabbed her arm. "Max, I'm tellin you—"

"Get the fuck *off* me!" She broke down as she tried to pull free. "You want me out, I'm going," she cried, and then, in his face: "I'll send you a picture."

"*No*, goddammit!"

Her arm came loose, and she took a step away. His leg lashed out, and his shin smacked her stomach. She hit the wooden floor sprawled. He felt the rumble, but the sound was drowned out by one of those piercing Melba Moore screams that plummeted into a growl.

"You *bastard!*"

He stopped, let her voice work him, and stared at her writhing form in the light that floated from the ceiling. He was excited and didn't move when she turned over in slow motion, reached out for the wine bottle on the floor, and brought it back to smash against his knee. A rush of cool air, a sprinkle of red drops, and tiny fireworks of glass preceded the pain.

He seized her wrist and bent it away from him, pulling her toward him, locked a hand on her breast, watched her face cry, gasp, and moan. She continued to struggle. He brought the arm still holding half the bottle down across his knee and heard the bottle fall. The sweat on their skin loosened his grasp. When she began to fall away, he kicked her and felt his toes caress her ass. Her feet flailed at him. He stepped in between them, took hold of her legs like a divining rod, and, squeezing hard to control them and to feel their strength, he dragged her across the floor.

He had to let go with one hand to unlock the door, and she scrambled away. He tackled her from behind. Lifting from where they fell, he pressed her more tightly than ever, strangling whatever life there was in her smooth stomach and helplessly nibbling her satin back with his panting mouth. There was no yield. He turned her just as she parted his slippery hands, and she fell stumbling into the hallway. Not daring to look at her, for fear he would follow her across the threshold and kill them both in a desperate embrace, he turned, gathered her clothes, dropped them softly onto her, and shut the door.

The darkness dizzied him. He hobbled deeper into it. In the middle of his room, at the point where he could see everything, he paused and focused carefully. She was gone, all of her, three years of her, leaving only distant crying, like a baby's, which drew him to the window. In the strengthening light he could see the blood trickling down his leg, and the sight brought back the pain. Pain like salt, sharp and tasty. A groaning hunger dropped him into his chair. He wrapped a hand around his stiff penis and gazed across the park to the east, toward his son.

Excerpt from Mothersill and the Foxes

JOHN A. WILLIAMS

The parties at Marj and Marilyn's were legendary around the office. They were whispered about and invitations to them sought. For they—Marj and Marilyn—walked a line between being crazy and not giving a damn and were considered to be swingers. Mothersill guessed their parties were also famous outside the office. He'd gone to one and had not recognized most of the people.

This time there would be a known quality besides the two hostesses: Annabelle. He wondered how many other black people would be there; not many, he guessed. There hadn't been any the last time, white girls and white guys trying to outwait and outwit each other, with Marj and Marilyn overseeing it all.

Ready to leave his apartment, Mothersill paused at the door, strangely depressed by the evening before him. As he was examining his feelings, the phone rang. He remained motionless. Who? he wondered, and then, Why? He left before it stopped ringing.

Marj Garrity and Marilyn Press shared a large apartment in the East

JOHN A. WILLIAMS is the author of eleven published novels and nine nonfiction books. He has also edited or co-edited nine collections of writings. Williams is Paul Robeson Professor Emeritus of Rutgers University.

Seventies close by FDR Drive. The Irish and East Europeans still bossed the turf, so Mothersill cabbed to the place, hoping that when he left he wouldn't have to wait long on one of the neighborhood corners and have to tackle one of the Irish or Hungarian gangs. He passed muster with the elevator operator and was lifted upstairs where, on the opening of the doors, he heard music and voices filling the hallway. He didn't think anyone inside would hear either a knock or a doorbell, so he opened the door and the noise battered at him like a gust of wind.

The instant before he closed the door he saw them, Marj, Marilyn, and Annabelle, holding three separate little courts, surrounded by guys who were sweating a lot and grinning a little. The few girls who'd come with some of the guys were standing in a corner, talking and smiling to each other, a little bravely, Mothersill thought, guessing that each was determined to lay so much body on her man that he'd never look at another type like Marj, Marilyn, or Annabelle; or not give him any at all, to punish him for even being so close to such whorey stuff. Mothersill smiled as he closed the door. The fact was that Marj, Marilyn, and Annabelle only complemented the less aggressive types who haunted the corners at parties. Between the aggressive and recessive babes they gave away so much, in New York at least, that Mothersill hadn't yet figured out how any self-respecting, honest-to-goodness, Times Square–type whore, heart of gold or not, ass of brass or not, could make a quarter.

He stood, back against the door, detailing the scene set out before him. Annabelle had the largest crowd, sitting, crouching, or standing before her. He had an exploded vision of thousands of Elizabethan sailors, whipped out of England's jails and onto ships deviously owned by Burleigh, Cecil, and Elizabeth, landing in Africa, cock-crazed and cunt-conscious, quickly dispatching, by blunderbuss, arquebus, and musket, puzzled and angry black men. Above the music or maybe in it, a muted high-register note on a trumpet, crying children, and then wailing women, overflowing with the instinct of their sex that death, capture, and slavery was not all that sailed into the channel with these ships. Mothersill thought of the sailors, despised in their own lands where pussy, all of it, from the basest member of the servant class on up, belonged to the moneyed, the powerful, for *droit de seigneur* still waited upon the Revolution to pretend to die. Now they were free, these sailors, league upon league away from home, and these black people were despised as the basest chemical in the alchemy of capitalism, still a fetus. There were no restraints; commanders approved, for fornication drew off energy, gave reward to the loveless seamen, and made them leave off for a time the punking of cabin boys not already assigned to do

excerpt from MOTHERSILL AND THE FOXES

the bidding of the ship commanders. A freedom to fuck at will, with only the conscience of a stiffened penis to attend, and with all the blessings of those who remained back in Merrie Olde England. For a moment Mothersill envied the sailors that freedom and wished that black men had had it for a time as well. That, however, might've produced another kind of black man, one who, like the whites gathered before Annabelle, would be more restrained by time than by law, and afflicted with the disease of remembering free-time fucking, and sweating with that remembrance, for things weren't at all what they used to be.

"Odell!" Annabelle called, waving cheerfully over the heads of her supplicants. The eyes turned toward him, the only black man there, seared him, and he felt their combined surprise, instinctive hate at his coming to collect his own. Annabelle, he knew, was aware of this as she moved through them toward him.

His first words were, "Let's get the hell outa here."

But she blithely ignored them and led him to her group and tried to introduce him, and Mothersill got the message: right there, all about him, were white men, a number of them ready and willing to service her even more eagerly than Marj or Marilyn; for the thing of which they accused black men was theirs in origin, flipped. Perhaps Marj and Marilyn knew it and, behind a twisted avant-garde liberalism at that very moment slipping through the crooked streets of the Village, utilized her as bait, the yellow-tailed fly on the swishing, curling line. Annabelle placed before him this challenge of time, race, and sex and by her manner demanded that he best it. Show how much man was left in the black shell. Mothersill glanced at Marj and Marilyn, both big girls, classically American, the Russian Pale and Irish bogs bred out of them: *Dionaeae muscipulae.* There was that look about them, shared, radiating. Did he see relief in their eyes that he had come to match off with Annabelle, or did he only imagine it?

The good jazz music made Mothersill feel at home. He was not, after all, the only black soul there, excluding Annabelle; various black quartets, quintets, and sextets played to him, and he conjured visions of musicians crouching over chord changes, smoothing out fifths and ninths, getting back to an old thing, but on a higher level; roots coming green aboveground.

"C'mon," he said to Annabelle. People were dancing around them although it was not music you danced to; the dancing was an excuse to press body to body. Although he'd never danced with her, he knew she could dance. It was like high school back in Hough, when the white kids backed off the floor to admire the coloreds because they could *really* dance. They found one of the interior beats and moved to it, conscious of the eyes on them, and Annabelle grinned and whispered, "Work, Odell!"

Does one make love the way he or she dances? Mothersill wondered, and was that why the women looked at him? The reason why guys drilled their eyeballs into Annabelle's smoothly rotating behind?

On the slow pieces he felt buttocks and breasts passing briefly over his body as he pressed close to Annabelle. Once he felt a hand pressing possessively but fleetingly against his behind, and when he turned Marj Garrity winked at him.

Annabelle whispered, "These guys are sure wearing my buns out. Can't keep their hands off them."

"This is no place to be making it, Annabelle. Too many crazies."

"I know, but I have to stay a little while longer."

"That's cool, but not too long."

She said, "Believe it, baby."

After a pause she said, "What'd you do Monday, go into the field?"

"Monday? Oh, I went home."

"Mmm."

"I did."

"I called you."

"Well, I went out for a few minutes, and the rest of the time I just didn't answer the phone."

"So you say, buster."

Mothersill ground his pelvis into hers. "Did you call Monday night?" He'd returned from New Jersey by then and knew she hadn't.

"No."

"Why not? You were in a big hurry to talk during the day."

"I told you I had to take care of some business with Bert."

"Yeah."

"Business is business, baby. Let's sit down and watch."

"Yeah, see how they move."

Mothersill grunted as they squatted on a large, empty floor cushion. He said, "The way you were carryin' on when I got here, I thought you were the main attraction." He grinned. "I guess I changed that, huh?"

"Never mind. You're the main attraction for Marj. She talks about you all the time. I think she has something she wants to give you."

"You know I don't mess around the office."

"No," she said. "Just me and all those mothers you diddle out in the field."

"Who, me?"

excerpt from MOTHERSILL AND THE FOXES

The bantering and another drink relaxed Mothersill. It was going to be all right. Annabelle was not going to go through all the phony changes, the coy advances and retreats, just because there was a room full of paddy boys. Some black women did. But now it was only a matter of catching a discreet wind to his apartment.

"No, no," Annabelle said, good-naturedly waving off a young man they'd seen bouncing and jumping over the floor with a variety of unwilling partners. On one of the slow pieces Mothersill had been startled to hear him breathing heavily as he danced; staring at him, he'd seen his eyes glazed as if about to have a heart attack. The man shrugged and moved on to the next woman.

Annabelle frowned. "Strange guy. I wonder where they found him. I don't understand Marj and Marilyn. This isn't what I'd call swingin'."

Mothersill caught sight of a woman he'd been introduced to in the first flurry of greetings when he entered. She smiled briefly at him, her eyes lingering momentarily, a palpable sadness in them. He hadn't looked at her closely then. He smiled back brightly, trying to say Don't be sad. She neither smoked nor drank and this too made him curious. Ellie was her name.

"Stuffy in here," Annabelle said.

"Let's get some air, then."

"Not yet, Odell."

"No, no. I mean just down in front for a moment or two."

"Be right back," she said, as they rose and headed for the door. She was speaking to no one in particular. In the hallway Mothersill walked determinedly to a mop closet he'd passed on his way to the party.

"Odell," she whispered, but not pulling back. Then, "Oh-ho," as he pulled her inside and closed the door. Their nostrils were filled with the odor of rough soaps and damp cloths, of dust and dirt barely caressed with water. Without a wasted motion Mothersill pulled up her dress and pushed down her pants.

"Odell!" But spoken softly, as if in admiration of his daring. He heard her shoes scuffling on the floor, enabling her to widen her legs, which'd already begun to tremble. Mothersill crouched lower and felt his own legs tweak with the strain; under and up, rising slowly on the balls of her feet as she now raised one leg, a ballet movement felt rather than seen. His breath came in bursts and she clung to his neck, whimpering.

"Awwah," he said. The bottom of her pelvis was rotating on his straining groin. "Annabelle," he whispered in amazement. "Ease up, *ease up!*"

But Annabelle, like most women, sensing she was close to bringing him down before he took her off, began rotating more furiously, twirling.

"Tell Momma how good it is. Like it like this?" Twirling all the time. Mothersill turned his head into a damp mop and bit it.

"Wait up," he said, trying to hold off.

But she put a super twirl on him and felt him snap up with trying to hold back. Ready herself, her head rocking a can of cleaner on the shelf, she hissed, "Now!"

Mothersill clutched and raised her, aiming her, as it were, in the darkness, all strength, all god for the moment; then, mortal and weak again, he set her down and they leaned against each other panting, their faces draped under the mops and cloths.

Outside the closet they brushed off and reentered the apartment. Tired, they eased past the thinning crowd into Annabelle's room, where they lay on the floor and went to sleep.

Two hours later Mothersill woke with a start, puzzling over Annabelle's absence. The music was now low, hanging in corners. He heard it clearly, for although he heard soft voices and even softer laughter, he thought most of the people were now gone. Annabelle, shoeless, came into the room and sat down beside him.

"Odell, let's go now, right now." She reached for his hand. "C'mere." Mothersill removed his shoes. They passed through the empty living room, still heavy with smoke. The voices were nearer now. From one of the bedrooms a cold blue light merged with the blackness of the apartment.

"Lick it, lick it." Mothersill recognized Marj's voice. "Ketchup, ketchup, red like blood, but sweet, oh, do lick it."

A sigh of pleasure told Mothersill the ketchup was being licked. He did not have to look, and yet he did; words create pictures; pictures often make words unnecessary. There were things he didn't know or wish to know; maybe they were too far away for him to take the time. But this was just around the corner. He felt Annabelle pushing him to the edge of the door. Marilyn spoke coyly, challengingly: "Strawberry jam is better than ketchup. Jam, anyone?"

There'd be no thrills, nothing comical once he looked around the door. He'd be like the kid at once horrified and attracted to Frankenstein films; like the young man thinking *ugh!* while reading de Sade but envying him too. If what was in that room upset Annabelle, he knew it would upset him also. But, Mothersill thought, I ought to *know* about these people I live and work with. And he looked.

excerpt from MOTHERSILL AND THE FOXES

He saw five figures, whose whiteness was heightened by the blue glow of the lamp. None were facing him; they were a frieze brought to life, complete with small sounds, of sudden sibilant utterances, "Greeks or Romans Busy at Orgy"; they moved slowly upon the entablature of bedroom floor, prolonging their pleasures.

Mothersill drew back from them, the high, vinegarish odor of ketchup, and they tiptoed back to Annabelle's room. Quickly they drew on their shoes. She pulled on a short coat and they went out, not speaking until they were in Mothersill's apartment.

After her first half glass of bourbon, Annabelle shook her head and said, "Goddamn, I didn't know they were into that. I mean"—she fluttered her eyelashes at Mothersill—"I dig a little lick-a-my-split myself from time to time, but I don't need any ketchup or strawberry jam on it for me to like it. I bet they put that damn jam on the breakfast table tomorrow morning, too. Those chicks are somethin' else, and I'm getting my hat next week because they're bound to turn up someone even more screwed up than they are." She started to laugh. "Odell, good thing I'm around, otherwise you'd have been down there making that ketchup and strawberry jam scene, the eyes Marj's got for you. Maybe she'd be taking it off you! Damn. Going through all that just to get some new kind of laid. Whoooeee!"

Mothersill had disdained his usual stiff scotch, preferring instead half a tumbler of pure gin. Gin made him do crazy things, foolhardy deeds; he became all id when he drank it, bacchic, superhuman. He drank it on those rare occasions when some untoward event unsettled him. He had listened to Annabelle's mutterings and now he spoke.

"Listen, Annabelle."

"Yassss, Poppa?"

"You think those people gonna get into peanut butter too?"

She was gone in the morning. Mothersill rolled over for his morning taste and clutched emptiness, but his hangover drove him back to sleep, and it seemed he'd been out hours and the doorbell'd been ringing all that time, insistently, in dots and long-time leaning dashes. He staggered to the system. "Hey," he mumbled.

"Odell, Odell! Let me in, quick, quick!" Although her voice sounded tinny and fuzzy over the intercom, he recognized the near panic in it. He pressed the buzzer and staggered to the bathroom to splash cold water on his face, and then into the kitchen to get the coffee on, his mind racing, or trying to, around the reasons for her return. Ole cool Annabelle vanished from your bed to be seen neat and well poised on the job the next day; it was as if the closeness of the night did not, could not, carry over into broad daylight. He was back at the door by the time Annabelle got upstairs. She brushed past him, heading for the kitchen and the bourbon. She drank from the bottle, long gulps that filled her cheeks before flooding down her throat. Mothersill wondered what all this had to do with him, but he could not avoid asking, "All right, baby, what is it?"

"Marj and Marilyn. They're dead, cut from their throats to their vaginas, lying in six inches of blood, ketchup, and jam—" She broke off and ran for the bathroom. Mothersill heard her vomiting.

I'm having a nightmare. The gin did it. I'm still asleep. I'm dreaming all this shit. It hasn't happened. No way it could've happened. When I wake up it'll all be gone and, man, will I be relieved.

But he heard the water running and the coffee smell filled the apartment, and then he moved to the bathroom and watched Annabelle washing. "What'd you do, Annabelle?" She gurgled emptily over the toilet bowl, shaking her head and finally saying, "Nothing. I ran out."

This happens to people you read about in the *News*, Mothersill thought. "You didn't call the cops?"

She shook her head again and gulped water into her mouth with her hand.

Why didn't they stop looking for kicks and look for kids instead?

"They'll be looking for you," he said. "You're a roommate. They'll look for you first."

She stopped drinking.

"C'mon, have some coffee; then we have to call them." Mothersill drank gin with his coffee. Dizzy, dizzy broads, bathed in blue, nude, a standing streak of light, the knife standing in the jar of jam, the breasts smeared with it, the falling hair shrouding the profiles, the bent taut muscles, the languidly widened legs, the glinting eyes reflecting some inner triumph, perhaps the deflection of seed. Mothersill got another gin.

"Maybe it'd be better if you just went to the cops," he said.

"Will you come with me?"

No, hell, no, Mothersill wanted to shout. No. I want nothing to do with it. Annabelle's question echoed around and around in his head like a distant, barely heard scream. She was afraid of more than the cops. Fucking would not be fun for a while. She'd look for the psycho behind every man's eyeballs from now on. Now, *now,* she realized that not every nut needed ketchup, strawberry jam, or even peanut butter. But she knew him and trusted him, like the children, in a way. He stroked her neck, sighed, and

excerpt from MOTHERSILL AND THE FOXES

agreed to go with her. Then she broke down, trembling, crying; the delayed reaction had set in.

They rode in the police car from the Nineteenth Precinct Station where they'd cabbed to report the murders. Mothersill held Annabelle, pressing hard when her shudders came, and stared at the backs of the heads of the cop and the detective in the front seat. Two other cars were with them, one in front, one in back, both cruising through lights, their flashers and sirens on.

Almost noon, Mothersill thought, the gin slithering through his stomach, up to his throat, and back down. On a normal Sunday morning he'd just be sitting down to breakfast, the mound of Sunday papers at his elbow, his building almost silent, at peace with himself. But here he was, hung over, from time to time patting the woman beside him, rather automatically, as one pats a baby who stirs under hand. And two cops in the front seat. A bad dream, a nightmare.

When they arrived at Annabelle's building there were already police cars there jamming the street, and people huddled together, whispering, looking up and down, judging the size of the crime by the numbers of policemen present. "You okay?" Mothersill asked Annabelle, helping her out.

"No," she said thickly, looking at the entrance fearfully.

"Mrs. Johnson?" The small man waved his finger in the general direction of the brim of his hat. He looked at Annabelle without expression, then glanced quizzically, briefly, at Mothersill. "I'm Detective Elson. You'll make it all right."

He took Annabelle's arm and led her inside, Mothersill and the horde of uniformed and plainclothes cops following.

"Goes my afternoon at the stadium," Elson said in a low voice. "Conerly'll have to do without me."

"There's always next Sunday, Teddy," someone said behind them.

"Yeah, but maybe there'll be another one of these."

The elevator hummed to a stop and Annabelle led the way out, looking around for Mothersill and clutching his sleeve. She had to let go to get her key; then her hand trembled as she sought the keyhole. Mothersill took the key and, after a few seconds' jiggling, opened the door.

No one moved. Annabelle was standing in the way. "I'm not going back in there," she said, shaking her head for emphasis and reaching for Mothersill again.

Elson spoke calmly. "It'll be all right, Mrs. Johnson. You and Mr. Mothersill just step right inside. That's all we'll ask you to do."

She looked at Mothersill for assurance. He put his arm around her waist. "Just inside," he muttered. He felt the cops bunching up to move forward behind them. "Just a second," he said to them, barely turning his head.

"C'mon, baby. Just inside," Mothersill said again, squinting at the sunlight which revealed the detritus of the party in the living room. She moved inside and pressed against the wall. "That's my room on the right side of the hallway," she said, pointing. "The first left is Marj's. They're in there. The next left is Marilyn's."

Detective Elson said, "Okay. You just wait here with Mr. Mothersill while we have a look." At the door to Marj's room they bunched, backed up, and then flowed in. Mothersill heard a low whistle and there was silence. Elson's voice carried out to them. "Quite an orgy. Everything but the toast and hamburger buns. Jesus. Fuckin' kids, beatniks, what they won't do for kicks."

A smaller group of men passed Mothersill and Annabelle, followed the sound of the murmur of voices, and vanished into Marj's room. Voices rose again.

"Hey, Tom-O, shoot up this mess, will you, so it can get cleaned up? Arnie, dust every fuckin' thing you can lay your hands on. Doc, I know you'll give me your best time on the report." Elson's voice became louder as he left the room and approached them. "Bet they came from good families." He looked at Annabelle. "Right, Mrs. Johnson?"

"I guess," she said quietly.

"You coulda been in there too," he said.

"No," Annabelle said primly. "I don't go for things like that."

Elson looked at Mothersill. "You wanna see them?"

"No." Now that they were dead, it was all right to look at them nude, Mothersill thought.

"Okay," Elson said. "You're both gonna have to come with me until we get some reports in. Shouldn't take long. No charges, we'd just like your help."

Four hours later, after alternately dozing and looking out of the chief of detective's window at the view of Center Street, the reports were ready. The coroner's report listed time of death at between three and four. The

night elevator man said Mothersill and Annabelle left at two. "He remembered," Elson said with a crooked smile, "because he wondered what two
colored people were doing leaving at that time. I guess he didn't know you
lived there, Mrs. Johnson."

"Guess not," she said.

"Good thing for the both of you," he said.

"All right, where does that leave us?" Mothersill asked.

As if he hadn't heard, Detective Elson went on. "Two young men left
about forty minutes after you, and a single man about three. Your descriptions match the elevator operator's." He placed the reports on the desk.
"That leaves you, for now, material witnesses. You're free, but we'll be
around to talk to you at your office tomorrow. Mrs. Johnson—uh, will
you be staying with Mr. Mothersill for a while now?"

"No."

Mothersill stared at her in relief, the detective in surprise.

"I'm going back to my husband."

"Oh," the detective said. "Good idea." He arched an eyebrow at Mothersill. "Better give us the address." As he was taking it down he said, "Let
me tell you something: that really could've been you, too, Mrs. Johnson.
It's your own business, but I've been on the force twenty-two years, and
I've never known you people to do this kind of thing. Stick with your own
kind. That's advice, nothing else. You know the rules about leaving town;
they're in all the movies. I'll see you at the office tomorrow. Better get some
sleep now."

After putting Annabelle on a train for Mount Vernon, Mothersill went
home where, waking and sleeping, he tried to recall the faces of the men
at the party, one that would reveal in its features the guilt of the murderer.
Once he started, thinking about Ellie, who'd come walking sadly across his
mind; she could have been one of the victims. He sat back. No, too shy.
But who really knew what one was unless chosen to share?

When his sleep finally came and carried him restlessly into the next
morning, the questions began again and the news stories broke. Mothersill
took out his baseball bat and placed it near the door, waiting for the inevitable arrival of Annabelle's husband, Big Mariney. But he never came.

Weeks later, after round upon round of questioning, in the office, at
home, and in Elson's headquarters, a composite picture of the murderer
was published. It was the man who'd wanted to dance with Annabelle.
There were periodic reports that progress was being made in the search for
him, and it was true that people were picked up, accompanied by headlines,

only later to be released for lack of evidence unattended by a single line of copy anywhere.

Meanwhile, vestigial, like the appendix or the coccyx, Mothersill's penis hung limply, serving only as a spout through which the vessel was emptied. It rose to no occasion, was enticed by no movement or thought. And when he dreamed of "The Sower," he dreamed the grain sack was empty.

excerpt from MOTHERSILL AND THE FOXES

Betrayal

LESLIE WOODARD

 I betrayed him. That's what the prosecutor said. He stood up, looked right at me, took a sniff and made that face people make when they want everyone to know they smell something bad, walked over to the jury, leaned his elbows on the railing like he was going to talk to some friends. Then he whipped round real fast, pointed his finger at me, and screamed so loud this old lady in the jury jumped. "She betrayed him!"

I didn't betray him. I killed him. There's a difference.

At least I thought there was when we started this. But when I hear it all laid out, starting from when I first met Byron, I'm not sure. Byron, I should've known better. What the hell kind of name is Byron? I can still see him, with his little blond head, his glasses, and all those books. He used to watch me all the time with this funny smile. It would've been creepy if he hadn't been such a geeky little kid. One day right before my fortieth birthday, I'm sitting on the steps by myself, like usual having a soda, smoking my cigarette, and I see him coming. He comes all the way across the

LESLIE WOODARD retired from the Dance Theater of Harlem after ten years of performance and returned to school at Columbia University's School of General Studies. She graduated Phi Beta Kappa in May 1994 with a B.A. in Literature/Writing. She currently attends New York University's graduate writing program.

campus to talk to me. All I could think was "Lord have mercy! What can this li'l white boy want?" He wasn't in any of my classes. Anyway, he comes over, puts his hand out, says, "Hello, I'm Byron, like the poet. Byron Adams." Well, I fell out. But he pays it no mind, puts all the books down, starts going through them, till he finds the one with Lord Byron. Then he holds it up like Show and Tell and says, "See, just like him." It was so strange. He knew I knew who Byron was; hell, I teach English, least I used to. And he knew I was not going to be impressed by any college kid knowing who Byron was. But that wasn't the point.

That prosecutor is pointing at me and shouting again. He's speaking so formally, the way I talked to my classes. I can't hear him, but I can see his Adam's apple going up and down and all his teeth are showing. When Byron bit pizza all his teeth showed.

I ate pizza with him because after that first day he'd turn up all kinds of places. So we ate pizza, we drank coffee, and he'd talk about anything, for as long as I'd listen. And you know something. He was the sweetest, most charming creature I ever met. Once he said, "You never tell me anything." I argued with him, told him I did so tell him stuff. But he said, "No. You never tell me anything about you." So I evaded. I told him I was basically very dull and he wouldn't be interested and it was inappropriate for a professor to discuss certain things with students and any other inane excuse I could think of. And he got this look on his face that, I swear to you, no one eighteen years old should be allowed to have. And he said, "You should be careful standing behind all those walls. They could fall on you." Well, it wasn't what I expected him to say but it wasn't like I hadn't heard similar before. So I said, "What do you know about walls falling on people?" He said, "A lot," and I believed him. I knew he did. But for some reason it never occurred to me to ask how he knew.

We started seeing each other often after that. We'd have coffee, I'd read over his papers. He liked old movies, so sometimes we'd go down to the Thalia, see Bette Davis. Oh, God, he loved Bette Davis! After the movie was over we'd be leaving and he'd open the door for me with this big theatrical gesture. It was stupid but it made me laugh. I laughed so much with him.

I haven't laughed in a very long time. I'd like to laugh at that prosecutor. He storms back and forth screaming like the troll that lived under the bridge. He doesn't want me to get across without paying my toll, but I won't pay it to him. I'd have paid it to Byron. But he would never have asked.

Byron came to my apartment once, kind of by accident. We were supposed to be going to the movies but he didn't show up. I was so disappointed. I waited outside the theater longer than I have ever waited for any man in my life. Late that night my buzzer rang. It made my cat jump. I wasn't going to answer it at first, but I did. It was him. He sounded upset, even through the intercom. When he came upstairs, he just kept saying how sorry he was, how terribly, terribly sorry. When I think back about it, he wasn't apologizing to me, not for not showing up. I mean he was. He was sorry about that. But he was terribly sorry about something else. But I didn't get it.

A couple of days later he shows up at my house again, with *Little Foxes* and yellow roses. I can't tell you how long it had been since somebody brought me roses. They were just gorgeous, every one of them opened up. And he told me how pretty I looked. I knew I looked like shit, but it felt so good to have somebody who was willing to lie to me. So I say to him, playing, "Byron Adams, are you planning to make love to me?" And he looks at me so serious and he says, "No. I am making love to you." That one threw me right on my ass. I had to sit down. He looks at me so perplexed and he says, "If you aren't making love, you're losing it." I lost it.

Anyway, we sat and watched the movie. I ordered Chinese, sat in my big old chair, dug my toes into the carpet, and we talked. We talked about stuff I couldn't tell anybody 'cause the words would never come out of my mouth. But they came to him. I told him about being a little girl, about being a big girl, and how frighteningly similar they were. I told him about being lonely, ugly, scared; about being happy, ecstatic; about the stupidest stuff. And this boy, this little blond boy, understood it all. Isn't it amazing how one-sided things can be? How one person can understand everything while the other one understands nothing at all? He left around midnight. Nothing happened. It didn't feel like anything ought to have. How could it? Me and an eighteen-year-old boy. I'd learned to be content with my own company long ago. After all, there was a reason I never commented on sex in the nineties. I had no information on which to base an opinion, and it didn't bother me particularly. But then I watched him, I listened to him, and it was like he was wearing a cape made out of spiders' webs, so sensitive he felt my emotions before I did. And I wanted to get as close to that as I could. So when he got up, put on his jacket, said what a wonderful time he'd had, kissed my cheek, and left, I was hurt.

Strange, I never thought of myself as a selfish person until now. Somebody ought to teach an economics course on the intrinsic value of love, no matter what form it takes. Most people, including myself, deal with it like it's something on a menu that you can order up "your way," but it isn't. You have to take it the way it's served. But once I set my mouth for love, well done, nothing else would do.

One afternoon, one rainy afternoon, I was supposed to meet him at the theater to see *Dark Victory*. I didn't have any classes to teach, he didn't have any to attend, so we planned to meet for the early show but I was late, forty-five minutes late. A student came to see me over some grade she didn't think she deserved; the subway wouldn't come. So when I finally arrived and he wasn't outside I wasn't surprised. I didn't expect him to wait in the rain. But I knew how much he liked the movie so I figured he might have gone in anyway. So I buy a ticket from this bubble-gum-popping girl at the booth and run in. There's almost no one in the theater, but I hear these kind of wet noises over on the side. I glance over and I can just make out a man's gray head, lolling back and forth on his neck like he's having some kind of seizure. I start into the aisle to see if he's okay. I get about halfway there and I see this blond head in his lap. I know this blond head. For a minute I'm just frozen. I don't feel like I walked in on someone. I feel like I've been walked in on, like I'm the one caught, exposed. I don't stay long enough to see the gray one hand over the money. I heard about that during the trial. It wouldn't have made any difference anyway. I was too busy being betrayed.

I don't remember deciding to leave. I remember my legs were leaving and they took me with them. I looked like one of those characters in bad movies that you couldn't feel compassion for if you tried. I ran into the lobby and it felt like everyone stared at me: the popcorn man, the usher, that damn bubble-gum girl. I knew when I left they would all start saying, "Why did she run out? What's wrong with her?" They would go into the theater to look. Then they would see and they would all laugh.

I think I started crying before I got home, but I didn't cry officially until I got in the shower, so the water would keep my eyes from swelling. I wanted to be beautiful when I called him a slut, asked him if he knew he could get Aids from giving a blow job, and threw him out of my home and my life forever. I thought he used me, even though I couldn't imagine for what. But it didn't go like that when he came.

But it isn't like that prosecutor says either. He says I planned it, that I lured him to my apartment intending to kill him. Yes, I can hear you now and you're wrong! I wonder if that means you were right before when I couldn't hear you. They say your mind does that, you know, screens out things you can't bear to hear. Oh, I don't know about that, but I know I didn't plan it.

Byron just appeared at my door dripping wet, smiling like a sun shower. I let him in. He stopped by because he said he thought I might have been kept late. He rented *Baby Jane* on the way, bought a bottle of soda, he knew I didn't drink, and some microwave popcorn. I asked him if he'd stayed for the movie. He said, "Yeah, it was great but I missed you." So I said, "You had to watch it by yourself?" And he said, "Oh, no. I met this man going in. Nice guy." It never occurred to him that he needed to lie, that I needed him to lie. He took off his blue slicker, said, "Fix the popcorn. I'm starving and I can't wait to see this movie." So I went in the kitchen and fixed the popcorn. He was leaning on the counter, watching me with that same little smile. I handed him the bowl and he said, "I adore you." He adored me. So I took a butcher knife and planted it in his chest.

How could I not have known he was gay? I can't say he ever did anything to deliberately make me believe otherwise. No. I didn't see it because I needed him to be straight more than I needed him, more than I needed his affection. I always considered myself so open, so tolerant of the way people choose to lead their lives. But when it came down to a choice between me and my needs and a beautiful boy who loved me, I chose me and my needs. I guess I'd been choosing them all along. That's why I sat there and listened to the man who said he was Byron's lover talk about all the sweet, silly things you know about someone you care for. How he wanted steamed milk for his coffee every morning; how he chased after their dog, shouting, "Don't you run from me!" when the dog stole his slipper and ran away wagging its tail; how they laughed together on the good days, consoled each other on the bad; and how no matter how long he'd been asleep, if his lover came to bed after him, Byron would wake up and kiss him good night. I didn't even know his favorite color or his middle name. I didn't know till I heard it in court that Byron was gay. His lover cried, said how sorry it had made him that Byron had had to provide a service for older men since he was sixteen, so he could live after his parents threw him out. He felt sorrow. I had felt . . . betrayed.

One thing they didn't say in court was why he chose me. I know why. He chose me for the same reasons everyone chooses a friend to love. Because we're drawn to people we think will understand, people we think we can trust.

Funny. I can hear quite clearly now, and now I think the prosecutor is right. I did betray him. Not because I killed him, but because I thought his love was less precious when I found out he was gay. And he thought I loved him the way he loved me.

In every corner of the world, on every subject under the sun, Penguin represents quality and variety—the very best in publishing today.

For complete information about books available from Penguin—including Puffins, Penguin Classics, and Arkana—and how to order them, write to us at the appropriate address below. Please note that for copyright reasons the selection of books varies from country to country.

In the United Kingdom: Please write to *Dept. JC, Penguin Books Ltd, FREEPOST, West Drayton, Middlesex UB7 0BR.*

If you have any difficulty in obtaining a title,.please send your order with the correct money, plus ten percent for postage and packaging, to *P.O. Box No. 11, West Drayton, Middlesex UB7 0BR*

In the United States: Please write to *Consumer Sales, Penguin USA, P.O. Box 999, Dept. 17109, Bergenfield, New Jersey 07621-0120.* VISA and MasterCard holders call 1-800-253-6476 to order all Penguin titles

In Canada: Please write to *Penguin Books Canada Ltd, 10 Alcorn Avenue, Suite 300, Toronto, Ontario M4V 3B2*

In Australia: Please write to *Penguin Books Australia Ltd, P.O. Box 257, Ringwood, Victoria 3134*

In New Zealand: Please write to *Penguin Books (NZ) Ltd, Private Bag 102902, North Shore Mail Centre, Auckland 10*

In India: Please write to *Penguin Books India Pvt Ltd, 706 Eros Apartments, 56 Nehru Place, New Delhi 110 019*

In the Netherlands: Please write to *Penguin Books Netherlands bv, Postbus 3507, NL-1001 AH Amsterdam*

In Germany: Please write to *Penguin Books Deutschland GmbH, Metzlerstrasse 26, 60594 Frankfurt am Main*

In Spain: Please write to *Penguin Books S. A., Bravo Murillo 19, 1° B, 28015 Madrid*

In Italy: Please write to *Penguin Italia s.r.l., Via Felice Casati 20, I-20124 Milano*

In France: Please write to *Penguin France S. A., 17 rue Lejeune, F-31000 Toulouse*

In Japan: Please write to *Penguin Books Japan, Ishikiribashi Building, 2-5-4, Suido, Bunkyo-ku, Tokyo 112*

In Greece: Please write to *Penguin Hellas Ltd, Dimocritou 3, GR-106 71 Athens*

In South Africa: Please write to *Longman Penguin Southern Africa (Pty) Ltd, Private Bag X08, Bertsham 2013*